Evelyn Hood was born
currently lives on the Cly
An ex-journalist, she has
several years, turning her talents to plays, short stories, children's books and the novels that have earned her widespread acclaim and an ever-increasing readership.

Praise for Evelyn Hood

'Immaculate in her historical detail'
The Herald

'Quite simply, I couldn't put it down. A rich and rewarding read'
Emma Blair

'Evelyn Hood has been called Scotland's Catherine Cookson. Unfair. She has her own distinctive voice'
Scots Magazine

'An intriguing plot and a range of complex characters and lives . . . offers an extraordinary woman's perspective on history in a plain, satisfactory style'
Scottish Field

'Highly entertaining'
Manchester Evening News

'Bold and compassionate'
Liverpool Daily Post

'An extremely good read'
Historical Novels Review

Also by Evelyn Hood

The Silken Thread
A Matter of Mischief
The Damask Days
This Time Next Year
A Handful of Happiness
A Stranger to the Town
McAdam's Women
Pebbles on the Beach
Another Day
The Dancing Stone
Time and Again
A Procession of One
The Shimmer of the Herring
Looking After Your Own
A Sparkle of Salt
Knowing Me
A Certain Freedom
Birds in the Spring

EVELYN HOOD OMNIBUS

Voices From the Sea

Staying On

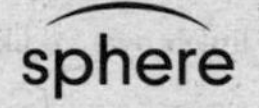

SPHERE

This omnibus edition first published in Great Britain by
Sphere in 2009

Previously published separately:
Voices From the Sea first published in Great Britain in 2006
by Time Warner Books
This paperback edition published in 2007 by Sphere

Staying On first published in Great Britain in 2001
by Little, Brown and Company.
This paperback edition published in 2002
by Time Warner Paperbacks

A CIP catalogue record for this book
is available from the British Library.

ISBN 978-0-7515-4149-6

Printed and bound in Great Britain by
Mackays of Chatham Ltd, Chatham, Kent

Sphere
An imprint of
Little, Brown Book Group
100 Victoria Embankment
London EC4Y 0DY

An Hachette UK Company
www.hachette.co.uk

www.littlebrown.co.uk

Voices From the Sea

This book is for Ruth, Nigel and Robert –
former neighbours, and friends for always.

Acknowledgements

Although this book is set in the beautiful Moray Firth village of Portsoy, the characters and their actions all come from my imagination.

Only three historical facts have been echoed in the book. Fordyce graveyard is indeed the resting place of one of Mary Queen of Scots' ladies-in-waiting, the famous 'four Marys', the story of the *Grace-Ellen* is based on the tragedy of the Portsoy fishing vessel *Annie*, lost in January 1887 (*Banffshire Journal, 25th January, 1887*) and Duncan Geddes's plans for the marble quarry were borrowed from similar plans by the real lessees of the quarry, Messrs. McDonald, London, (*Banffshire Reporter, Friday, October 13th, 1876*) which never came to fruition.

My thanks to the following people for their invaluable assistance in researching for the book – Moira Stewart, Portsoy Librarian; Christine Urquhart of Fordyce; John Watson, who patiently explained the workings of a nineteenth century marble quarry; Finlay Pirie, who gave me permission to use his research material; Jean Forsyth; Betty Welsh; Irene McKay and Tom Burnett-Stewart, the owner of the Portsoy marble and craft shop.

My thanks also go to the Past Portsoy website at http://www.pastportsoy.co.uk

Evelyn Hood

Glossary

Hoosie – A small house, such as a fisherman's cottage
Hoose – A larger house
Whiley – A short while
Quine – A term of affection for a girl or woman
Loon – A term for affection for a boy or man
Fit – What

1

Portsoy, August 1865

Most of the villages strung along the Moray Firth coastline were built to a neat plan, with their sturdy stone-built houses in orderly rows, their windowless gable walls facing the sea in order to withstand the winter storms. But in Portsoy the houses were at all angles, as though the builders had simply set them up wherever they happened to find a piece of spare land.

Walking down towards the harbour after tramping round the surrounding villages, selling fish from door to door, Eppie wondered, as she often did, whether the village was rushing eagerly towards the sea, or clambering uphill, panic-stricken and desperate to get away from the rocks not far offshore, waiting with their sharp black wave-lashed fangs bared in the hope of one day being able to swallow up the entire village.

The first time she had voiced these thoughts aloud, Murdo had laughed the easy deep laugh that seemed to come from the very centre of him and made his sea-green eyes crinkle and his mouth stretch almost from one side of his brown face to the other. When Murdo laughed everyone within hearing could not resist breaking into broad smiles. It was his glowing zest for life that had made Eppie fall in love with him. He had teased her, telling her that only a lassie from Fordyce could think up such an idea.

'It's a' that education they fed you wi' instead o' porridge and good herrin',' he had teased, 'and dinnae try tae deny it, you that comes from a family o' school-teachers. Education makes the brain work too hard.' And when she had tried to protest, 'It's hooses an' rocks ye're talking o', lass, no' livin' creatures. Hooses dinnae run and rocks dinnae eat folk!'

Even though the conversation had been more than eight years earlier, she remembered it vividly. The two of them, newly-weds and still joyful at having found one another, had been walking hand in hand on the grassy hill near to the marble quarry at the time. When Eppie, determined to explain, started to point out the way the sharp rocks protruding from the green, spray-flecked water below looked just like teeth, he had tickled her until she squealed for mercy, then tumbled the two of them on to the springy grass and kissed her squeals into a happy, submissive silence.

She didn't even realise that she was smiling at the memory of it until an elderly fisherman passing by her as she went through the town square squinted at her beneath thick grey eyebrows and remarked, 'Ye're fairly content wi' yer ain company, m'quine.'

Eppie blushed. 'It's just – it's been a good day for the fish,' she stumbled to explain, but he had already gone on his way, his own face wreathed in a smile.

It had indeed been a good day; the creel on her back was almost empty though her shoulders were tender where the straps had been rubbing them for hours. Eppie tried to ease the creel into a different position as she left the square and began to walk down North High Street towards the harbour.

She had been right on that day after all – the rocks did eat folk. They had eaten her Murdo a scant two years after he had laughed at her fancies. As the boat he and his father crewed on struggled back to harbour one dark and stormy night, weighed down in the water by the fish filling the holds, the rocks lurking beneath the surface had torn a great hole in the hull. They had scooped her precious man out as easily as the women baiting the hooks for line fishing scooped the mussels from their shells, and had chewed his bones and flesh so thoroughly that no matter how much she had screamed and wept and begged the next day, the grim-faced men who had found what remained of Murdo on the beach refused to let her see him.

'It's yersel', Eppie. Have ye had a good journey?' Barbary McGeoch, calling from her open cottage door, shattered the bitter memory. Eppie smiled at her friend, grateful for the interruption.

'Aye, well enough. No' much fish left.'

'I'll take a hauf-dizzen if ye've got them.' Going by local custom Barbary's name would normally have been shortened to Babs, or Babbie, but her father, who had crossed and re-crossed the world's seas and oceans in his youth, had insisted on naming his only daughter after the wild and beautiful Barbary coast, and had never allowed anyone to alter it. Barbary, tall and straight-backed, with smooth olive skin, long black hair and high-cheekbones, suited the name; although Portsoy born and bred, there was an exotic look about her.

'Have ye no' got a' the fish ye need?' Eppie asked now. Barbary's husband Tolly was a fisherman and the young woman, as well as being a friend and neighbour, was one of the two gutters in Eppie's crew at the farlins. Fishing families always had a barrel of salted fish available.

'Aye, but there's no' much left an' some friends are comin' over from Sandend for their dinner the night.' Barbary gave the neighbouring town its local pronunciation of 'San'ine.' 'They like a dish o' herrin' and they've got terrible bellies tae fill. The way they eat ye'd think they never had a meal except when they come tae us. I'll fetch the money.' She disappeared, to return swiftly with a dish in one hand and a small child tucked beneath her other arm. As Eppie transferred the fish from creel to plate the afternoon sun made the silver scales glitter and the baby immediately removed his fingers from his mouth in order to reach out towards the new pretty playthings.

'Na na, my wee loon, we'll no' have that.' Barbary deftly swung her body round so that the herring was beyond wee George's reach. 'He'd have a' six o' them in his mouth afore I could stop him if he got the chance. He's teethin', so everythin' he can get hold of gets pushed intae his mouth.' She kissed the thwarted child, who had started to grizzle. 'Ye'll like it better when it's cooked,' she assured him.

'He's comin' on,' Eppie said as the other girl put the dish down on a table just inside the door and dipped a hand into her pocket.

Barbary's dark eyes shone with maternal pride. 'Aye, they grow fast, do they no'?'

'They do.' It was all Eppie could do to keep from snatching the child into arms that ached to hold a solid squirming little body again. Her Charlotte was seven years old now, but every time Eppie saw a mother with her children her heart ached for her own bairn.

'Come an' eat wi' us the night, ye'd be more than

welcome,' Barbary said warmly, but Eppie shook her head.

'I've got work tae do in the hoosie.' Part of her would have welcomed the company, for there was little pleasure in eating alone, but on the other hand she knew that being with a family would only make her feel all the more lonely when she returned to her own cottage afterwards.

When she left Barbary another dozen or so steps brought her to the small cottage where she lived. As the door closed behind her, shutting out the noise and bustle of the street, the silence seemed louder than anything she had heard all day.

The coals in the range were still glowing, and the hob was hot. Slowly, wearily, she set a shallow iron pan in place and dropped a knob of butter into it. While it melted, she took the two remaining herring from the creel, splitting and gutting them with practised ease. Then she dipped them in oatmeal from an earthenware crock and dropped them into the butter which immediately began to sizzle. While the herring cooked she sliced the potatoes she had boiled that morning.

Once the meal was eaten she cleaned pan, plate and cutlery before going to bed. It was still daylight, but the boats would start coming home early in the morning, which meant that she and the other fisher lassies would have to be at the farlins before dawn.

There was little comfort in going to bed. Eppie had always been used to sleeping close to others. Once she was old enough to leave the cradle in her parents' room she had shared a bed with her elder sister Marion, and after her wedding she had slept soundly in Murdo's strong, warm arms, or lain awake, thinking of him, on the nights when he was at sea. On the terrible night of his death she had huddled in a chair until, unable to bear the wild keening of Mag, her mother-in-law, she had slipped into bed with the older woman, holding her close and trying to soothe her, when all the time her own heart was breaking. And every night after that she had slept with Mag, trying to ease the terrible nightmares that tormented the woman during the dark, silent hours.

Mag had never recovered from the shock of losing both her husband and her son on the same night. A strong, active woman all her life, she had taken to sitting in a chair by the fire all day, scarcely speaking, leaving the housework and cooking and shopping to Eppie. The only person who could coax a smile to her grey face was wee Charlotte, then two years old. When she was with the little girl Mag was more like her old self, which was fortunate because it meant that Eppie could leave her daughter in Mag's care while she worked long hours at the farlins.

When the barrels of herring were covered and stacked and the other fisher lassies were free to go back to their homes and families, Eppie then started on her second job – tramping inland with a full creel on her back, selling herring from door to door. Every penny she could earn was needed to keep herself, her mother-in-law and her daughter fed and housed and clothed.

She would return home at the end of the day to find Mag singing to Charlotte, or telling her a story, or playing a game with the little one while the housework and cooking awaited Eppie. The only work the elder woman stirred herself to do was to keep the fire going so that Charlotte was warm, and to set out the cold midday meal that Eppie had prepared for them both before setting out with her creel. Bone-weary, Eppie would cook an evening meal, put Charlotte to bed, then spend the evening cleaning and washing and darning.

At least in those days the house was occupied. Charlotte, too young to be touched by tragedy, bustled about the place like a tiny whirlwind, playing with her rag dolls and chattering and laughing. Neighbours called frequently to keep Mag company, and as often as not, one or another of them would bring a little soup or a few scones to add to the midday meal. But when, eighteen months after Murdo drowned, Mag was laid to rest beside her husband and their son, Charlotte had to go to Fordyce so that Eppie's parents could look after her. And then, for the first time in her life, Eppie was alone.

Being on her own in the cottage carried no physical fears for her. Nothing that might happen to her could ever be as bad as losing Murdo, and in any case, this was Portsoy, where the folk were decent and law abiding, and neighbour looked out for neighbour. But she had never realised until she experienced it that being truly alone was like falling into a deep black void, with not a glimmer of light in it, and no hope of ever reaching the bottom. Every night in bed she curled up into a ball, shut her eyes tight and said her prayers, then filled her mind with pictures of Charlotte, sleeping soundly in her little bed in Fordyce, with her long, silken lashes brushing her round, rosy cheeks and her hands tucked beneath her dimpled chin.

She thought of Charlotte awake, laughing and talkative and always busy at something, be it standing on a stool, swathed in a pinny as she helped her grandmother to bake, or sitting at the table, drawing a picture with the tip of her tongue poking out between her lips and her hazel eyes squinting in concentration.

Tonight, though, she had something to look forward

to, for tomorrow was Saturday. As the fishermen kept the Sabbath, their boats never went out on Saturday nights, which meant that once she had finished work Eppie was free to walk to Fordyce. She would get there in time to play with Charlotte and put her to bed, then in the morning after the family attended church she would have the rest of the day with her daughter. She wouldn't have to leave until the evening.

She held on to that thought, clutching it to her like one of the lucky charms the gypsy women sold from door to door in the summer, until, finally, she slept.

A quick knock at the door brought Eppie out of a dream that she knew was happy, but had flown the instant her eyes opened. 'Time tae get up, quine!' Will Lomond, the cooper who employed the fisher lassies, shouted, and even before she had time to respond with, 'Aye, Will, I'm wakened,' she heard his boots clattering on down the brae towards the harbour, and his fist hammering on another door.

She lay for a moment, trying to recapture the dream – trying with such determination that fragments of it floated back up from the depths of her subconscious. Murdo had been in it, alive and well, and they had been walking on the shore together, with Charlotte, a wee bairn again, riding high on his shoulders with her two fists buried in his thick fair hair. They had been talking together, but the words refused to come back, though the happiness of the dream ran through her like a golden river, giving her the strength to get out of bed and pull on her clothes.

It was still dark outside, and the air was cold against her bare arms. She had forgotten to steep oats for porridge the night before, so she hacked a thick slice of bread from the loaf and spread it with butter and the last of her mother's home-made raspberry jam, then poured out a mug of strong, black tea from the pot that had been stewing on the stove all night. The jam tasted of summer and sunshine, and the almost-perfumed flavour of the fruit painted a picture of her parent's back garden where, in season, the raspberry bushes were weighed down with large, soft berries that melted in the mouth.

Before going out she pulled on an extra skirt and a sturdy fisherman's jersey. She had been knitting it for Murdo when he died, and although he had never worn it, she felt, each time she put it on, as though he were holding her close. As she hauled on her thick-soled boots she could hear the women passing by on their way to the farlins, their voices hushed in the chill morning air.

Eppie tied her long, stiff oilskin apron around her waist before hurrying out to join the steady stream of women on their way to work.

When selling fish, her first call on a Saturday was always at the three-storey house owned by Alexander Geddes. Jean Gilbert, his housekeeper, had been a friend of Mag's, and Eppie could usually be sure of a cup of tea, a home-made pancake, and a chance to sit down for ten minutes before starting the walk up through town, stopping at doors along the way, then out into the surrounding countryside.

Today, Jean's usual smiling calm had a faint edge to it. 'Come away in, lass,' she instructed as soon as she opened the door. 'The tea's ready and waitin' for ye.'

'D'ye no' want tae look at the fish first?'

'And why should I bother my head wi' that? I know they'll be fine. I can trust ye. Just put a dizzen o' them in the pantry,' Jean said from the range where she was pouring tea into two thick cups, 'then sit yersel' down. I've somethin' important tae say tae ye.'

Eppie always felt a sense of awe when she went into the Geddes pantry, the same awe she felt in church. The cool room with its stone flags and scrubbed shelving was almost as large as her kitchen, the main room in her cottage. One long shelf held crocks filled with flour, rice, currants, raisins, lentils, barley and goodness' knew what else, while another shelf held cheeses. Hams and cuts of beef had a shelf of their own, as did jars and bottles of preserved fruit, home-made jams and jellies and pickles and chutneys. The cupboards below held an amazing collection of cooking utensils including stewing pans, saucepans, frying pans and baking tins.

She selected a dozen of the best fish from her creel, laid them carefully on the marble slab awaiting them and then covered them with a white earthenware lid before tiptoeing back into the kitchen.

'There's the money, m'quine,' Jean was sitting at the table, sipping at her tea. 'Sit yersel' down now and listen tae what I've tae tell ye.' She cast a glance over her shoulder, as though making sure that the door leading to the rest of the house was firmly closed, then leaned forwards lowering her voice. 'I've decided it's time for me tae stop workin' here.'

'Leave here? Why?' Eppie was dismayed; since Mag's death she had come to look on Jean as the nearest she had to family in Portsoy.

'Och, it's a' these stairs – my poor auld knees are tired of carryin' me up and down them day in and day out. Look at them . . .' Jean got up from her stool and hoisted her skirt up to her thighs, displaying puffy ankles, calves lumpy with varicose veins, and knees that were clearly swollen far beyond their normal size.

'They look awful' sore!'

'They are, lass, they are. I doubt,' Jean said, shaking her skirts into place and lowering herself carefully back on to her chair, 'if I could manage anither winter in this hoose.'

'But where will you go?' Even as she asked the question, Eppie recalled that Jean had a married daughter who lived not far along the coast.

'Tae Lizzie's in San'ine',' the older woman confirmed. 'Now that her eldest's got a good position as kitchen maid in a big hoose in Aberdeen there's room for me. And I can earn my keep by helpin' oot with the younger bairns.'

'Mr Geddes'll be sorry tae lose ye.' Eppie knew that Jean had started working as a kitchen maid for the present owner's parents when she was twelve years old, left when she got married, and returned as housekeeper after she was widowed. By then, Alexander Geddes, the only son of the house, had married and inherited his father's business interests.

'I've no' told him yet,' Jean said now. 'I wanted tae speak tae ye first. Eppie, lass, I want ye tae apply for the position.'

'Me?' Eppie sat bolt upright suddenly and tea almost slopped over the rim of the cup in her hands.

'Aye, you. Why no'?'

'What would I ken about bein' a hoosekeeper? I'm a fisher lassie, an' a fishwife.'

'Ye look after a hoosie, dae ye no'? And ye keep it spotless. Ye can cook an' bake, I know that from when I used tae veesit wi' poor Mag.'

'There's a difference between seein' tae a wee cottage and lookin' after a place this size!' Eppie waved a hand at the ceiling to indicate the two floors above. 'And cookin' for gentry's nothin' like cookin' for mysel'!'

'I've got some very good recipe books ye can have, and there's two lassies that come tae help with the hoose-work. An' if I stay on here for another few weeks after it's decided you could come in every day tae work alongside me and get tae know the way o' the hoose. That's why I've no' said anythin' tae the master as yet. I wanted tae talk it over wi' you first an' make certain ye're willin'.'

'That's another thing – it's no' just Mr Geddes that'll make the decision. What about his mither?' Eppie had heard often enough from the other fisher lassies that old Mrs Geddes, who had moved back into the house to be with her son when his wife died, was a strong-willed woman.

'If I can get him tae go along wi' the idea o' hirin' you in my place then she'll have tae go along wi' it tae. She doesnae always get her own way, and he's no' a man that takes kindly tae domestic worries. He'll want the matter settled and the new hoosekeeper in place as soon as it can be done.' Jean leaned forwards, her eyes fixed on Eppie's. 'Listen tae me, lass. If you worked here ye'd get bed and board as well as a decent-enough wage. Ye wouldnae have tae find rent for the cottage, an' lookin' after this hoose'd be easier than the hard work ye're at now.'

There was no denying that. Eppie was a packer, and working at the farlins for long hours in all weathers, filling the big barrels with layer upon layer of herring, was sore on the back. Constant immersion in cold brine meant that her hands were red and swollen, the skin chapped by cold working conditions and salty brine, and scarred by cuts from sharp fish bones. In some cases, helping to lift barrels full of fish and pickle had caused internal damage to fisher lassies, resulting in difficult childbirth and early ageing.

Jean was watching her closely. 'Ye'll soon have tae follow the boats doon tae England, will ye no'?'

'Aye, that's right.' The herring were beginning to swim south and already the catches brought in by the local boats were shrinking. In another few weeks the autumn season would show its face and the fleet would start preparing for the day when it would set sail for the English ports. The gutters and packers would have to follow them. It was hard enough having to go for a whole week without seeing Charlotte; every year Eppie had come to hate being away from her child for up to two months.

'If ye take the post o' hoosekeeper here ye'd no' have tae go south,' Jean pointed out. 'Give it a try, lassie. Let me tell the master that I've found someone tae take my place. Ye'll no' regret it, I'm sure o' that.'

Eppie drained her tea and got to her feet, scooping up the money for the fish, which had been put out, as always, on the table by her cup.

'I'll have tae be on my way. But I'll think about it, and let ye know my answer on Monday,' she promised.

2

Eppie loved the walk from Portsoy to Fordyce. Although she had almost three miles to cover it was a pleasant journey, and she enjoyed the peace and quiet as well as the freedom of walking without the weight of a creel on her back.

Leaving Portsoy behind, she strode out along the road leading to the town of Cullen, then took a right turn that led her between fields where flocks of sheep grazed. Ahead of her the fields sloped up towards Durn Hill, a great rounded mound where, her father had told her when she was a little girl, there had once been an ancient Celtic settlement protected by a series of ditches to deter invaders. The narrow road took a turn to the left and began to climb, passing a stand of tall trees, their leaves beginning to show the first yellow and red tints of autumn, before levelling out. Again, there were fields to either side, with several small farmsteads to be seen in the distance. Ahead, she could see the wooded slopes of another hill – Fordyce Hill.

Striding along, breathing in deep lungfuls of the country air, she reached the triangular field known as the Feein'

Market, where the local farmers and those looking for farm work came together twice a year to strike work contracts. Tinkers used another triangular area of rough ground on the opposite side of the road as a makeshift camp when they came to the area to sell their wares.

To Eppie's relief, the camp area was empty of the tarpaulin and cloth shelters that the tinker folk could set up in no time; she had never had any problems with these people and was always happy to deal with the women when they came to her door to sell their goods, but at the same time she was uneasy whenever she passed along that road while a clan was in residence. The women and children tended to disappear silently and swiftly into their makeshift homes when she or any other stranger approached, while the men watched warily, and their lean dogs curled their tails between their legs and flattened their ears back, narrowing their eyes at her. Her father, who maintained that all folk were equal and nobody should fear anyone else, always passed the camp with a cheery word and a friendly wave of his walking stick, but to Eppie there was something alien and vaguely menacing about the dark-skinned people when they were gathered together in groups.

Almost as soon as the Feein' Market and the tinkers' ground fell away behind her she was in Fordyce itself, passing the Free Kirk schoolhouse with the one-roomed school behind it, then the church itself and on down the sloping street to where the small castle stood in the middle of the village. From there it was only a minute's walk to the lane where her parents' cottage stood.

Charlotte, as always, was waiting at the garden gate. 'Mother!' she cried as soon as Eppie came into view. She came rushing out of the gate, her golden brown curls flying about her round little face. 'Mother!'

Laughing, Eppie dropped the basket she carried and held her arms open. Charlotte flew into them and as Eppie hugged her daughter she saw that her own mother, alerted by Charlotte's excited screams, had come out to the gate and was waiting there, beaming.

Eppie was home.

'You should apply for the position,' Marion McNaught told her sister in her usual decisive way. 'It's a sight better than working on the farlins and selling fish door to door.'

'But what if Mr Geddes doesn't consider me good enough to be his housekeeper?' Eppie had become almost bilingual since marrying Murdo and moving to his village – in Portsoy she spoke as the other fisher lassies did, but when she was home in Fordyce she reverted to the more formal speech her family used.

'Of course you're good enough – more than good enough. You're the daughter of a schoolteacher and the sister of a schoolteacher, aren't you? You've been educated in Fordyce – that alone should be sufficient to make the man's mind up.'

'But in Portsoy I'm a fisher lassie and a fishwife,' Eppie protested.

'Is that what they call folk that smell of fish?' Charlotte asked. She was sitting at her mother's feet, playing with the little doll that Eppie had brought for her. 'You always smell of fish, Mother.'

'Everybody in Portsoy,' Marion told her little niece, her nose wrinkling, 'smells of fish.'

'And some of the folk in Fordyce smell of chalk,' Peter McNaught put in, smiling at his younger daughter in an effort to take the sting out of Marion's hectoring tone. 'Charlotte, most of the folk in Portsoy earn their living by catching fish, just as your father did, God rest his soul, or by cleaning them and selling them as your mother does. It's only natural that they should always carry the scent of the sea about them.'

Grateful for his intervention, Eppie returned his smile, then said defensively to her sister, 'Nobody down in Portsoy knows or cares about what I did afore I married Murdo.'

'"Before",' Marion corrected her without thinking, and then, as Eppie flushed and bit her lip, 'I can write a recommendation for you if you like.' Marion taught at the village's infant school, while her father taught at Fordyce Academy.

'That'll no' – not – be necessary,' Eppie said hurriedly. On occasion, especially when she was tired, she found it difficult to make the transition from her Portsoy voice to her Fordyce voice. 'Jean Gilbert's recommendation'll be good enough. What do you think I should do, Mother?'

Annie McNaught was sitting in her rocking chair by the window, listening to the conversation but keeping her own counsel. Annie tended to leave the talking to her husband and her elder daughter, both well read and with strong opinions of their own. But when she did choose to speak she was worth listening to, as Eppie knew. Now she said, 'I think you should listen to this Jean Gilbert, lass. If she thinks you good enough to fill the position, then you must be. There's nothing wrong wi' being in service.'

'I'm not saying that there is anything wrong with being a servant, Mother,' Marion protested. 'I know fine well that you were in service yourself, but you didn't have Eppie's education. She should have been a teacher, like Father and me. She's got the brains for it.'

'But not the will,' Eppie decided that it was time to speak up on her own behalf. 'I'm grateful to all of you for your advice, but I'll wait till I get back to Portsoy tomorrow before I make up my mind. In the meantime, I'm off to take a walk round the garden.'

'I'm coming too,' Charlotte said at once. A placid, contented child, she was happy enough during the week with her grandparents and Marion, but when Eppie was there the little girl stayed close to her side all the time. 'I'm going to call her Peggy,' she said as the two of them went into the walled garden at the side of the cottage. She held up the doll, made from a clothes peg and dressed from scraps of material stitched into a frock. Eppie had drawn smiling features on the peg's round top and glued on some yellow wool to give the illusion of hair. A tiny bonnet was tied over the little head. 'She's a very pretty lady and she lives in a castle.'

'Like the one in Fordyce?' Fordyce Castle was a tiny fairy-tale building nestling in the centre of the village. Mary Beaton, one of Queen Mary Stuart's four ladies-in-waiting, had married an Ogilvie of Boyne and lived in the castle. She was buried in the local graveyard.

'Much, much bigger,' Charlotte said. 'A castle like King Arthur's, with knights and horses in it and a big table. We got told about that at school. Lady Peggy has a big white horse with silver reins and a golden saddle, and she rides all over the castle grounds on it.' She skipped off down the garden between the fruit bushes, clicking her tongue to simulate the sound of horses' hooves and dancing the little peg doll up and down, as though she were rising and falling on a saddle.

'She's doing fine, lass.' Peter fell into step with his daughter. 'She's enjoying the school and she's a clever bairn.'

'Like Marion.' Eppie, the younger by three years, had always lived in her sister's shadow.

'Och, you're just as clever as your sister.'

'That's why I pack herring, then sell it door to door,' Eppie said drily.

'What sort of talk is that?' Peter took his daughter by the shoulders and turned her to face him. 'We both know that you could have been teaching alongside Marion in the infant school if you'd wanted to. And what stopped you?'

'I met Murdo.'

'Exactly. You put your heart before your head and there's nothing wrong with that,' Peter said firmly. Then, closing one eye in a huge wink and lowering his voice until only Eppie could hear the words, 'You take after me, for I did the same thing myself. When I fell slave to a bonny face and a sweet smile my father was raging because the lass I wanted was a servant and they had me marked down for marriage to another teacher, or mebbe even a gentleman's daughter. But I went ahead and married your mother, and I've never regretted it, just the way you'll never regret choosing your Murdo, God rest him.'

They had reached the end of the garden, where the three bee skeps stood close by a wall of rose-coloured bricks. Bees flew in and out of the entrances and a low contented buzz could be heard from inside each skep. One or two bees came to investigate the visitors, and when they landed on Eppie's hands she made no move to brush them off. If startled, the tiny creatures might sting, and that would be a tragedy, for Eppie had learned almost before she could walk that honeybees had a barbed sting that stayed in the wound, and once bereft of its sting the bee then died. Peter, like his father before him, had always had skeps, and even as a small child Eppie had learned to work with them. Bees held no fears for her.

She watched the bees crawl over her hands and then, curiosity satisfied once they had flown away, she asked 'How are they doing?'

'It's been a good summer and they've worked hard. Now they're beginning to settle down for the winter. Your mother'll have a few jars of honey and some beeswax for you to take back with you,' her father said. And then, rubbing his hands together in eager anticipation, 'Now then, it's time to go indoors, for even at this distance I can smell that herring you brought sizzling away in the pan, and it's fair making my mouth water.'

As always, Eppie's visit to Fordyce passed too quickly. She and Charlotte always shared a bed, and she lay awake most of the night, listening to her daughter's slow soft breathing and making the most of the child's nearness.

On Sunday morning the family, all members of the Church of Scotland, attended morning service in the sturdy little church where her parents and she herself had been married, and where she and Marion and Charlotte had been christened, then as evening approached it was time to return to Portsoy and what she looked on as her other life.

As always, the parting from Charlotte was heart-breaking, and the walk back to the fishing village had none of the pleasure she had known the day before.

When she came back from selling fish on the following Wednesday, Eppie fetched the hipbath kept in the lean-to at the side of the cottage and filled it with water that had been heating on top of the range all day. She sank into its comfort with a sigh of relief, and would have stayed there contentedly until the water cooled if she had had the time.

Instead, she reached for the small stiff-bristled brush and the cake of washing soap laid out on an adjacent chair and scrubbed herself all over, taking special care to run the bristles of the brush right under her fingernails until the tender skin began to tingle.

Then she washed her long brown hair, rinsing it again and again in an attempt to rid herself of the smell of herring that clung to all the fishermen and fisher lassies. Charlotte sometimes referred to her 'Fish Mam', and although it was meant as an endearment, the name, coupled with Marion's barbed remarks, embarrassed Eppie.

When she had dried herself, and dried her hair as best she could with the towel, she pinned it up before putting on her best clothes. Finally, she opened the cottage door and took a long, deep breath to calm her nerves before setting off for the Geddes house. It was located at the harbour, a handsome three-storey building on the corner of Low Road and Shorehead. The house faced on to Low Road, with two narrow flights of stairs set flush against the house wall, running up from the street to meet on a landing before the main door, which was on the first floor. A door set in the Shorehead side of the building led to the kitchen and servant's quarters on the ground floor.

'Ye look grand, m'quine,' Jean said as she opened the kitchen door.

'Ye think so?'

'That I do. The master'll see for himsel' that you're a clean, decent quine. And mind,' Jean said as she opened the door leading to the rest of the house, 'that he's the one ye want tae please, and nob'dy else.'

Eppie had never been further than the kitchen; venturing beyond it and up into the area where the family lived was like travelling into a hitherto unknown land.

She followed Jean along a flagged passage with doors to either side, then up a flight of stone steps to a wide hallway where the doors were polished, panelled and decorated with fine brass handles. Large paintings hung on the walls between each door. To Eppie, who had never been in such an imposing house before, it looked like a palace.

'The ground floor's got the kitchen an' pantry, an' a store room an' my own wee room,' the older woman explained as she bustled along. 'Up here's the room where they eat their meals, an' the big parlour, an' the master's library an' a wee room that Mrs Geddes uses as her own parlour. The four bedrooms are on the next floor. Now then . . .' She paused before one of the doors and turned to face Eppie. 'Are ye ready tae meet yer new master, lass?'

'I-I don't know if I'll be suitable . . .'

'Of course ye will. He's no' an ogre, even though he's no' what ye'd cry a man wi' a keen sense o' humour. No' that he's got much tae laugh about, poor soul.' Jean lowered her voice to a whisper, though Eppie was doubtful that anything louder than a shout could penetrate the solid panels of the door before her. 'And I've given ye a bonny reference,' she added briskly, 'so that should go a long way tae makin' him look on ye wi' favour.' And without further ado, she tapped on the door.

Butterflies began to flutter so hard in Eppie's stomach that she clutched her waist with both hands. She thought of turning and fleeing back down the stairs and out of the kitchen door, but almost at once a man's voice barked out a command and Jean opened the door and stepped into the room beyond.

'Eppie Watt's here, sir, tae apply for the post of hoose-keeper,' she said, and then, opening the door wider, 'Come on in, then, lass, an' let Mr Geddes take a look at ye.'

Everyone in Portsoy knew who Alexander Geddes was, for the man was involved in several of the local industries. Eppie knew that he was part owner of the fishing boat that Tolly McGeoch crewed on as well as the small marble quarry to the south of the harbour. She had heard that he also had an interest in the salmon bothy, where salmon caught locally was prepared and packed. He shipped goods in and out of Portsoy, and she had seen him often enough striding about the place or riding through the streets on his horse. But she had never been as close to him as she was now, or been the subject of his piercing gaze.

'So – Mrs Watt.' He had been seated on the far side of a large desk, but now, to her surprise, he rose to his feet, for all the world as though she was gentry like himself.

'Sir.' Not quite sure what she should do, Eppie dipped a hasty curtsey.

'Jean tells me that you've got experience of housework.'

'Just in my mother's house, and then my own. Not in a big place like this, sir,' Eppie kept her gaze fixed on the desk. It was as large as her kitchen table, with piles of paper stacked neatly on its polished surface. One pile was held in place by a large lump of polished marble, the light from the window striking green glints in its glossy surface.

'I'm sure one house is much like another. Mebbe this one's larger than those you've known, but it's got furniture to polish and floors to wash and stairs to sweep like most other homes. You'll have daily help with the heavier work, of course. And you know about how to do laundry, and cooking and baking?'

'She kens a' these duties, Mr Geddes,' Jean said firmly. He was still on his feet, and now a few steps carried him around the desk to the long window that looked out over the harbour. He stood gazing out for a moment, framed by the graceful sweeps of the heavy curtains which were caught back with cords. Eppie glanced at Jean, who smiled and nodded encouragingly. While she waited for Alexander Geddes to resume the interview she glanced round the room. It was easy to see why the room was known as the library, for three of its walls were hidden by shelves of books, from the floor to the high ceiling. The fourth wall held a handsome wooden fireplace flanked by two dark brown leather armchairs, and two portraits. One, directly above the fireplace, was of a very beautiful dark-haired, green-eyed young woman, her soft rosy lips slightly parted as though about to curve into an amused smile. The other, slightly smaller portrait was set to one side of the fireplace, and was of an older woman with dark brown hair drawn smoothly back from an oval, serious face.

'I understand that you are a widow, Mrs Watt, and that you work at the moment as a fisher lassie.' Alexander Geddes had turned away from the window to face into the room, hands clasped behind his back. With the light behind him, Eppie could see little of his features; all she could make out was that he was quite tall, and lean-built.

'Aye, sir, I'm a packer, and when we're done at the farlins I take my creel round the doors an' sell fish tae the housewives.'

'A fishwife as well as a fisher lassie? You must work long hours.'

'Needs must, sir.'

'I suppose they do. At least it proves that you're hardy, and not afraid of work. Since you come from Fordyce I take it that you've had a good education? The place is well known for its fine school and academy.'

'My father teaches at the academy.' Pride in the

declaration helped Eppie to lift her head and look squarely at the dark outline against the windowpanes. 'And my sister teaches too, at the infant school.'

'Indeed? But you chose to turn to the sea for your living.'

'I chose marriage, sir.'

'And as I understand it, you were widowed young. That,' he said, his voice suddenly bleak, 'happens all too often. Jean tells me that you have a child.'

'A daughter who lives in Fordyce with my parents. She's content there,' Eppie said swiftly, suddenly worried in case he thought that she expected him to take Charlotte in as well.

'How old is she?'

'Seven years, sir.'

'The same age as my own daughter. I asked about your child, Mrs Watt, because I would not want a housekeeper with no experience of children. I have a son too, but he's a good few years older than his sister. I don't suppose you would object to working in a house where young folk live?'

'Of course not, sir!' Eppie was shocked at the very thought.

'In that case . . .' Geddes was saying when the door, which Jean had closed, opened and a querulous voice said, 'Alexander, I really must speak to you about – who's this?'

Eppie turned so sharply that she almost stumbled. Her first impression of the woman confronting her was of a pair of piercing eyes as blue as a summer sky, but with none of its warmth. Cold and hard, they were set in a strong, lined face with a long, straight nose and a thin mouth. The newcomer had a head of snowy white hair; once, she must have been breathtakingly beautiful but now, in the winter of her life, she was striking. Eppie had glimpsed her in the village, looking out of the window of the small carriage she used to travel even short distances.

'Who are you?' the newcomer wanted to know, though the tone of her voice was really asking, 'And what do you think you are doing here?'

'Mother, this is Mrs Watt, come to discuss the post of housekeeper. As you know, Jean has decided to move to Sandend . . .'

'I know that very well, and I have been setting my mind to finding another . . .' the terrifying blue eyes raked Eppie from the top of her head to the toes of her boots, then travelled back again '. . . *suitable* housekeeper,' Mrs Geddes finished.

'I believe that I may have found one,' Geddes said calmly, while Eppie wanted nothing more than to sink through the thick carpet beneath her feet and fall right out of sight.

'What households has she worked in before?'

'Mrs Watt works at the moment as a fisher lassie and a fishwife.'

'I could have told you that, for the room reeks of fish,' Mrs Geddes snapped, and Eppie took a step back, one hand flying to her mouth. She felt as though she had just been slapped hard.

'I was not aware of it – and even if it is so, almost every soul living in Portsoy and along the entire Moray Firth smells of fish, since catching, preparing, selling and cooking fish is the main industry in these parts,' Alexander Geddes said calmly. 'It is honourable work and there is a lot to be said for anyone involved in it. You can't deny, Mother, that you enjoy eating fish as much as the next person.'

The woman's already thin lips tightened even more, and Eppie saw a splash of crimson appear on each high cheekbone.

'If you insist on interviewing prospective servants – though I believe that you have better things to do with your time than that – then I should be present in order to advise you. Hiring servants is not a man's work.'

Alexander Geddes began to move, and as he passed Eppie he ceased to be a shadowy outline and she saw that his hair was thick and dark, greying at the temples. His eyes were dark and heavy-lidded, while he had his mother's long nose and straight mouth.

'Perhaps, Jean,' he reached the door and opened it, 'you could take Mrs Watt to the kitchen and offer her some tea. I'll be with you shortly.'

3

'Now then, ye might as well start learnin' where things are,' Jean said when they were back in the kitchen, 'so we'll just start with a fresh pot o' tea. The tea caddy's on that shelf, and there's the pot. There's oatcakes in that tin and butter on yer left hand as ye go intae the pantry. I'll put the plates out.'

'There's no sense in me learnin' where everything' is, since I'll no' be gettin' the position.' Eppie's hands shook as she lifted the caddy down, and there were tears behind her eyes and in the tremor of her voice.

'Fit makes ye think that, m'quine?'

'Och, Jean, Mrs Geddes would never have me in the hoose. You heard her – I'm no' good enough an' I smell of f-fish.' Eppie scrubbed at her eyes with her free hand and sniffed loudly.

'Ach, that old woman doesnae like anyb'dy. It's nothin' against you,' Jean said airily. 'She's vexed because the master didnae ask her tae see ye along wi' him – or instead o' him. An' he didnae ask her because he kens fine that she'd scare ye off. The final word'll rest wi' him – and he listens tae me, does Mr Geddes, for he kens I've got a good head on my shoulders.'

'I wish she didnae bide here!'

'So does Mr Geddes, I'm thinkin',' Jean said drily. 'Oatcakes – and butter.'

'I'm gettin' them.' Eppie put the tin of oatcakes on the table and then located the butter.

'Ye just have tae be polite tae the woman and get on wi' yer own work,' Jean said, buttering oatcakes. Eppie, used to making every scrap of food go a long way, watched in astonishment as the rich yellow butter was spread thickly. 'She invited hersel' here when young Mrs Geddes died and the maister was left wi' two bairns tae raise, one o' them newborn. I could have managed fine wi' the help o' a sensible lassie tae nurse wee Lydia, but Mrs Geddes was inside the hoose before me or the maister got time tae sort ourselves oot. An' she's had her feet well lodged under his table for the seven years since, lookin' after her son and his bairns, by her way o' it.' Jean poured some tea into her cup and studied it. 'Ye make a good strong cup o' tea, lassie,' she said approvingly, then went on as she filled both cups. 'If the truth be known, she's stayin' here tae make certain that the man doesnae get the opportunity tae make another bad marriage.'

'A bad marriage?'

'Eat up, lassie.' Jean buttered another oatcake for herself. 'An unfortunate marriage, I should have said, for there was nothin' wrong wi' both the lassies he married, other than bad fortune. The maister's her only child and his first wife was the daughter o' a friend o' his parents – that was Duncan's mither. She brought a dowry with her, enough tae let Mr Geddes expand his business interests. Then she died, and for a good few years he was too busy tae consider marryin' again. Then one day he met up wi' a young lady visitin' the place wi' her faither, who'd a share in the marble quarry here. Mr Geddes fell head o'er heels for her, and afore his mither realised what was happenin' he'd followed her back tae Glasgow an' asked her tae be his wife. Mrs Geddes never took tae the poor lass, though she was a lovely lady and she made the man very happy. Then did she no' pass away when wee Lydia was born. It was awfu' sad—'

She broke off abruptly as the door opened and Alexander Geddes came in.

'You're still here, Mrs Watt.'

'Aye, sir.' Eppie scrambled to her feet, almost knocking her cup over in her agitation. 'I was just about tae leave, sir.'

'Take your time. You thought, Jean, that Mrs Watt could come in every day for a month to work with you and get to know her duties?'

'Aye, sir. I'd no' leave ye without makin' sure that ye're a' bein' well cared for.'

He smiled at the housekeeper – a warm smile that lit up his dark eyes. 'I know you'd never leave us in need, Jean,' he said, and then, to Eppie, 'So perhaps you could start next Monday, and arrange to move in once Jean feels that you are ready to take over as housekeeper?'

'But what about—?' Eppie began, then as Jean's booted foot sent pain flaring through her ankle, she said meekly, 'Aye, sir. Thank you, sir.'

'I'll miss ye,' Barbary said as she helped Eppie to clean out the cottage and make it ready for its new tenants.

'I'm only goin' as far as the harbour.'

'You're goin' further than that.' Barbary, who had been

scrubbing the floor, sat back on her heels and used her strong, rounded forearm to sweep a lock of thick black hair from her face. 'You're goin' up in the world. You'll be livin' in a big hoosie.'

'In a room next tae the kitchen, just.'

'Even so – who'd have thought when we were workin' thegither at the farlins that you were goin' tae be livin' in the same hoose as the man that's got a share in the *Grace-Ellen*?' Barbary said, referring to the vessel her husband sailed on. 'An' he's got an interest in the cooperage that employs us tae gut and pack the herrin' too. I'm tellin' ye, Eppie Watt – ye've gone up in the world!'

'It won't make any difference tae me – or tae you,' Eppie said, suddenly worried in case she lost her closest friend. 'We can still see each other, can we no'?'

'Aye, but you'll have tae come tae my wee cottage, for I'd no' feel right in that big place.' Barbary plunged the scrubbing brush back into the pail of soapy water, spattering her apron.

A hand seemed to catch at Eppie's stomach and squeeze it painfully. 'Ye don't think I'm makin' a mistake, do ye, Barbary?'

'I do not.' The other girl was working so vigorously that the water sprayed from her brush with each sweep forward and back. 'Ye deserve a better life, and it's hard work ye've been doin' for the past few years, slavin' at the farlins and then walkin' for miles wi' a heavy creel on yer back. You're doin' the right thing, m'quine!'

At first Eppie doubted her friend's faith in the move from the farlins and her tiny cottage to Alexander Geddes's big house. Despite the fact that three other people lived there – she had not yet seen Duncan, her employer's son, since he was boarding in Aberdeen, where he attended school

– the house was unnervingly quiet. Although she had often felt lonely in her little cottage she had always heard boots and horses' hooves and wagon wheels clattering and rumbling along the narrow cobbled street just outside her windows. The farlins too, were noisy, with the fisher lassies talking and singing, seagulls screaming, the coopers hammering at their barrels and the voices of the fishermen, buyers and spectators all about the place. But even the noise from the nearby harbour failed to penetrate the Geddes house's thick walls, and its occupants were silent most of the time – Mr Geddes working at the big desk in the library when he was not out and about on business, and his mother in her own small parlour, or prowling about silently in order to spy on the servants.

Even seven-year-old Lydia made little noise, spending most of her time in her own room or with her governess in her grandmother's parlour, which was used as a schoolroom in the mornings. Eppie, used to her Charlotte's constant chatter, found the little girl's adult behaviour quite worrying. It wasn't natural in a child of that age.

Throughout her first week in the house she lived in constant terror of doing or saying something wrong, or of breaking one of the lovely, delicate glass and china ornaments. 'It's Mrs Geddes,' she told Jean nervously. 'She moves about the hoose so quietly that I never hear her comin', and then I get such a fright when she speaks, or when I turn round an' see her standin' there, starin' at me. Can I no' work in the kitchen just now an' leave the rest o' the house tae you?'

'An' fit use wid that be? When I'm gone tae San'ine tae bide wi' my faim'ly you'll be in charge o' the whole hoose. I know ye'll have Sarah an' Chrissie comin' in tae dae the heavy work, but you'll be responsible for where they go an' what they do. Ye cannae hide in the kitchen an' leave them tae run aboot upstairs on their own, especially Chrissie. She's a grand strong worker, and nob'dy can scrub stairs or polish furniture like her, but ye darenae leave her on her ain, for she gets so carried away wi' what she's doin' that she's apt tae send one o' those wee ornaments flyin' aboot the room.'

'Mebbe I'm no' the right one for this position . . .'

'Aye, ye are, an' I've already told the maister that, so ye cannae let me down now,' Jean said calmly. 'Ye'll be fine. Just treat Mrs Geddes wi' respect – she likes that – an' give yersel' time tae settle in.'

As the days passed and Eppie became more accustomed to the big house her nervousness eased, just as Jean had predicted. Mrs Geddes still frightened her, but she learned to hide her nerves behind a calm face and quiet voice, and the woman began to accept her, albeit grudgingly.

'Though I don't know how I'll be when Jean leaves and I'm on my own,' Eppie told her parents and Marion on her next visit to Fordyce.

'You'll be fine,' her father said comfortingly, 'you've got a good sensible head on your shoulders.' While her mother added, 'An' ye're a grand cook, so they'll no' hae any worries on that score.'

'You're just as good as they are,' Marion added almost fiercely. 'They're fortunate to have you working for them. Keep telling yourself that.'

It was easy for Marion to say that, Eppie thought ruefully. Her elder sister had always had a good opinion of herself, and neighbours had been known to say in amusement when Marion was little more than a toddler that she behaved as though God had created the world just for her benefit. It sometimes seemed to Eppie that Marion had enough confidence for both sisters, while she herself had almost none.

But a month later, when Jean had gone off to live with her family in Sandend and Eppie had moved into the small room next to the Geddes kitchen, she was surprised at how well she was settling in.

Each time Eppie visited Fordyce, Charlotte insisted on hearing all about Lydia's nursery. 'Tell me again,' she begged whenever she could get her mother's attention. 'Tell me about that girl and her toys.' And then her hazel eyes and neat little mouth rounded into three almost-perfect Os as Eppie described the big dappled rocking horse with its bright-red harness studded with tinkling bells, the enormous dolls' house with every room furnished in perfect detail, and the shelf of dolls and teddy bears. Charlotte's favourite doll, formerly Prudence, was now known as Lydia.

'Now tell me about her clothes.'

'We'll keep that for after church tomorrow,' Eppie said, but Charlotte was already bouncing with impatience.

'Now, now!' she insisted, and when Eppie had described the tallboy filled with vests and petticoats and stockings and drawers, and the wardrobe holding handmade dresses and skirts and blouses, she said, 'That girl must go to a lot of parties.'

'No, she doesn't,' Eppie said in surprise. It was something she had not thought of before. 'In fact, she doesn't go out much at all unless she's in her grandmother's carriage.'

'Why doesn't she go out every day?'

It was a question that Eppie was beginning to ask herself. 'Mrs Geddes says she's too delicate to go out,' she said, and then, as Charlotte's brow furrowed, 'that means that she isn't very strong and she has to be careful in case she catches a chill from the cold wind, or gets her feet wet.'

'De-li-cate,' Charlotte said thoughtfully. 'Write it down.'

Words fascinated her, and since starting school she had taken to carrying a bundle of paper and a stubby little pencil in the pocket of her smock. Now she laid them on the table and watched as her mother wrote down the word 'delicate'.

'Now me.' She took the pencil and copied the letters one by one, the tip of her pink tongue protruding from one corner of her mouth and her eyes narrowed in concentration. 'De-li-cate,' she said with satisfaction, stuffing the papers back into her pocket. 'I'm not delicate, am I?'

'No, you're not, you're a very healthy lass, and I'm glad of that.'

'Does Lydia go to school in the carriage?'

'She doesn't go to school at all. A teacher comes in every day to do lessons with her.'

'A teacher like Aunt Marion?'

Delighted by her niece's natural enthusiasm for learning, Marion had taken to giving Charlotte extra lessons at home. It troubled Eppie, who wondered at times if the little girl was being worked too hard, but dependent as she was on her parents and sister to look after Charlotte on her behalf, she could say little. When she did mention her concerns to her father he told her soothingly that Charlotte enjoyed the sessions with her aunt, and that he would not allow Marion's zeal to give the child more work than she could cope with.

'Yes,' she said now. 'A teacher like Aunt Marion.'

'But if she doesn't go to the school, and she doesn't go out to play, how can she see her friends?' Charlotte persisted.

'She doesn't have many friends,' Eppie admitted. 'I think Mrs Geddes takes her to houses sometimes where there are little girls to play with.'

'I could be her friend. You could take me back to Portsoy with you, and I could play with her. I'd like fine to see that rocking horse with the bells that ring when it's rocking, and the bonnie hoosie that her dolls live in.'

'One day, mebbe,' Eppie said, knowing full well that old Mrs Geddes would be horrified at the very idea of her precious grand-daughter having anything to do with the housekeeper's child.

As she set off for Portsoy the next day Charlotte's 'How can she see her friends?' rang in her head. It had seemed to Eppie from the very beginning that Lydia Geddes was a lonely little girl. Missing Charlotte as she did, Eppie would have liked to take Lydia for walks, or down to the water's edge to show her the wonders of the seashore with its shells and pebbles and rock pools. But when she suggested such an outing to Helen Geddes the woman was shocked.

'My grand-daughter is not a strong child and I will not have her exposed to the bad elements that float in the air.'

'But the sea air's good for bairns, surely?'

'For bairns from the cottages, may be, but not for the likes of Lydia. We'll have no more talk of her going out with you, if you please,' she said sharply. 'Perhaps you should bear in mind that you're employed here as the housekeeper and nothing more than that. There's plenty of work indoors to keep you occupied, and Lydia's welfare is none of your business.'

There was such a difference between Charlotte and Lydia, Eppie thought as she walked along the road between Fordyce and Portsoy. Charlotte was brown from the summer sun, and her cheeks were rosy, whereas Lydia's oval face was milk-pale and her beautiful green eyes and black hair, inherited, Jean had said, from her mother, made her skin seem even whiter. Her only outings were when she went with her grandmother in the carriage to visit Mrs Geddes's friends, but she seemed content to spend the rest of her life either at lessons in her grandmother's little parlour, or playing in her room. Although it was clear from the way Alexander Geddes looked at his daughter that he adored her, her upbringing was left to her grandmother, who spoiled her and indulged her every whim.

It was Eppie who had to bear the brunt of the little girl's spoiling. Following Mrs Geddes's example, Lydia never put anything away when she had finished with it. On the few occasions when she returned from an outing her hat, coat and gloves were left discarded on the floor, and her bedroom was littered with toys every day. To tell the truth, Eppie quite enjoyed tidying the child's room, for it gave her the opportunity to handle silks and satins and muslins and velvet, as well as toys she had never even known existed before – pretty dolls with real, silky hair, and delicate china faces – along with miniature furniture from the dolls' house, perfect in every way.

Unfortunately, Lydia knew where everything should go, even though she herself did not see the need to put it there. No matter how careful Eppie was, she could never get it right. 'Not there,' Lydia would snap if she happened to come into the room when Eppie was settling a doll into a doll-sized chair, or carefully putting a piece of furniture back into the large, exquisite house that stood on its own table to ensure that it was just the right height for Lydia to play with. 'It goes there, can't you see?' And she would snatch whatever it was from Eppie's hand and put it in its rightful place, sighing loudly or tutting over the housekeeper's stupidity.

'It would be better if you just put them in the right place when you finished with them,' Eppie suggested one day, her tone deliberately mild. To her astonishment the child turned to gaze at her with cold green eyes and said, 'Why should I, when my father pays you to keep the house tidy?'

'If my own wee lassie had said that to me,' Eppie said in the kitchen later that day, 'I would have put her over my knee.'

'That's the trouble,' Chrissie grunted. 'That bairn's never been taught right from wrong.'

'It's the way rich folk do things,' Sarah chimed in. It was Tuesday, and the two women had come to help with the ironing and floor scrubbing. 'Why should she lift a finger when we're paid tae dae everythin' for her? But ye're right, Eppie – if one o' my bairns spoke tae me like that I'd warm her arse for her.'

'It's that Mrs Geddes,' Chrissie nodded. 'She's ruinin' the lassie, and Mr Geddes is that caught up wi' makin' money that he never notices it. No' that it matters a' that much, for Lydia'll be bonny enough tae find hersel' a rich husband when the time comes, and he'll supply enough servants tae run aboot after her for the rest o' her days.' She drained the last of the strong tea and laid the mug on the table. 'Well, I suppose we'd best get back tae work.'

Lydia had her sweet moments too. Sometimes when she had nothing else to do she would seek Eppie out, following her around the house or sitting at the kitchen table while Eppie baked or darned or prepared the next meal, talking about the lessons she had been doing earlier that day, or about her brother.

'He'll be home for Christmas and Ne'erday,' she said, her eyes shining at the thought. 'I've got a calendar on the wall in my bedroom and I'm putting a big cross on it every night before I go to bed. Duncan will be here in . . .' she paused, her face screwed up in intense concentration, her pursed mouth moving silently as she calculated '. . . ten weeks. Seven days a week equals seventy days. Seventy days isn't as long as ten weeks, is it?'

'It doesn't sound as long,' Eppie agreed tactfully.

'Do you know my brother Duncan?'

'No, I don't.'

'He's very nice and kind. He laughs a lot and he plays games with me.' Lydia's normally sulky little face glowed with hero-worship. 'He's the best brother in the whole world and I wish he could stay here all the time. I like it when he's here.'

'Do you not have any wee friends who could visit you when your brother's not here?'

Lydia's dark curls bounced as she shook her head. 'There's nobody for me to play with,' she said, adding as Eppie thought of the many children running around Portsoy, 'nobody good enough. I sometimes play with two girls I meet when I visit grandmother's friend Mrs Bailey, but I don't like them very much. They're nasty to me when grandmother's not looking. My brother Duncan's nearly grown up and he has to work very hard at school. His school's in Aberdeen. Have you ever been there?'

'No, never.'

'Duncan says he'll take me there when I'm older.'

Difficult though she could be, the child's loneliness made Eppie's heart ache, especially when she visited Fordyce and saw Charlotte playing with the friends she had made since going to school. But there was little she could do for Lydia, apart from welcoming the child any time she chose to seek Eppie out. She did, once, let Lydia help her with the baking, but unfortunately Helen Geddes chose that day to make one of her rare visits to the kitchen, and when she discovered her grand-daughter happily rolling out a round of dough at the table, her face tightened with rage.

'Lydia, what do you think you're doing?'

'Making a tart for Father's tea.' The little girl folded the dough over and attacked it with the roller. 'Look, Grandma, look what I can do!'

'Put that down at once and come here,' Helen ordered, and when the child obeyed, 'Look at you – you've got flour all over your face, and in your hair!'

'It'll brush out, Mrs Geddes,' Eppie hurried to assure her, but was ignored.

'On your pretty velvet dress too. And me expecting visitors! What'll they think when they see my grand-daughter looking like a child from the gutter?'

'I'll put her to rights . . .' Eppie began, then fell silent as the woman turned to survey her with eyes as blue and as hard as sapphires.

'You,' said Helen Geddes, 'have done enough damage. I will see to my grand-daughter myself, and I will certainly speak to her father about this disgraceful episode. Come along, Lydia.' She held out her hand, then drew it back sharply as Lydia went to clutch it. 'Walk in front of me, I don't want flour all over my clothes, thank you. I am expecting two visitors in one hour's time,' she added icily to Eppie as she followed the little girl out. 'See that tea is ready to be served in my parlour as soon as they arrive. And make sure that you have a clean apron on when you open the door to them.'

Then she and Lydia were gone, and Eppie was on her

own, struggling to hold back her tears. She was convinced that she would be dismissed before the day was out, and even though nothing was said she went about in fear for a whole week before realising that either Mrs Geddes had kept silent, or her son had decided to take no action. Eppie doubted, given the outrage in the woman's eyes and voice as she swept Lydia from the kitchen, that she had been able to hold her tongue, but she found it even more difficult to believe that Mr Geddes had let the matter pass without comment.

Just when she had begun to believe that she was safe from any further reprisals he came into the dining room one morning as she was clearing the plates from the table.

'I'm sorry, Mr Geddes,' she stammered as she looked up and saw him standing in the doorway, 'I thought you'd finished in here . . .'

'I have. Eppie, I hope you're settling in here.'

'I am, sir, I like it very much. I'm just not sure . . .,' she suddenly faltered, recalling his mother's rage when she found Lydia in the kitchen, covered with flour '. . . if I'm suitable.'

'You're very suitable. At any rate, you suit me, and if you have any worries I hope that you will bring them to me so that they can be dealt with.'

'I will, sir. Thank you, sir,' she said, and escaped to the kitchen, realising that she was fortunate to be working for such a kind and decent man.

4

Even though she was in the kitchen two floors down, Eppie heard Lydia's high-pitched squeal, followed by the thud of feet rushing down the stairs from the nursery.

Startled, thinking at first that something had frightened the child, or that she was hurt, Eppie rushed along the flagged passage and up the flight of stairs to the hall. She had just arrived when Lydia reached the final step, screaming, 'Duncan! Duncan's here!' and dashed to open the front door.

Eppie stopped short, one hand clutching at her thudding heart, as Alexander Geddes and his mother appeared, he from the library and she from her parlour. By that time Lydia had lifted the latch and rushed out, heedless of her grandmother's cry of, 'Lydia, you'll catch a chill, get back in here at once!'

'Duncan!' the child screamed again, and Eppie saw her launch herself off the doorstep, arms spread out as though she were flying. For a terrifying moment it seemed that she was doomed to fall to the pavement with a bone-shattering crash, but instead, a tall figure came striding up the steps and into the hall, Lydia's arms wound tightly around his neck and her stockinged legs wrapped about his waist.

'Lydia Geddes!' Helen screeched, reaching out to tug her grand-daughter's skirt over her legs. 'You're making an exhibition of yourself! Duncan, set her down this moment!'

Laughing, the newcomer did as he was told, rumpling his half-sister's hair as he straightened. 'It's grand to get such a warm welcome home,' he said, and then, leaning forwards to kiss Helen's proffered cheek, 'How are you, Grandmother?'

'All the better for seeing you.' For once, her face was wreathed in smiles. 'Did you have a good journey from Aberdeen?'

'Well enough. Father, how are you?'

'In fine form, as you can see. Welcome home, Duncan.' Alexander Geddes shook his son by the hand. 'There's a fire burning in the parlour and your room's ready for you. You'll be eager for some food, I've no doubt?'

'Laddies of his age are always eager for food,' Helen said warmly, and her grandson's ready laugh rang out again.

'I'm starving. I've not had a proper meal since I was last here. Let me just get my boxes upstairs.'

'And while you're doing that I'll ask Eppie to bring the food from the kitchen.' Alexander was turning to go along the hall when Eppie said timidly from the shadows, 'I'm here, sir. I'll see tae it at once.'

Suddenly the house was filled for the first time with sound and movement. As Eppie made tea and heated broth and arranged plates and cups on the big tray, she could hear Duncan Geddes running upstairs and then back down again almost immediately. Lydia was chattering as she never had before and her father and grandmother also sounded unusually animated. It was as though the young man's arrival had wakened the house from a deep sleep.

She was ladling the steaming broth into a large bowl when Lydia burst into the kitchen, followed, to Eppie's surprise and embarrassment, by her brother.

'This is Duncan,' the little girl announced importantly. 'This is Eppie, Duncan. She works here.'

'How do you do, Mrs . . . ?' Duncan Geddes, with his dark hair and long straight nose, was very like his father apart from two distinctions; his eyes, heavy-lidded like his father's, were a warm brown, and his smile, as he held out a large hand, was surprisingly quick and warm.

'Just Eppie,' Lydia insisted.

'It's Eppie Watt, but Eppie's fine, sir.' She wiped her hand on her apron and, blushing, put it into his for a brief moment.

'Then Eppie it shall be.'

'Duncan's going to be a physician,' Lydia said proudly.

'I don't know about that. I doubt if I'm clever enough.'

'Father says you are, and he should know. So you will be,' Lydia insisted, but her brother was brushing past her to take the tray from Eppie.

'I'll see to that. Open the door, Lydia,' he ordered, and they set off in procession, Lydia skipping ahead while Eppie brought up the rear.

Both of the Geddes womenfolk seemed to Eppie to blossom during Duncan's brief visit home. Lydia bloomed like a sunflower, stretching and growing almost overnight to welcome the sun's warmth, while her grandmother was more like a rose with its tightly packed petals relaxing, while at the same time remaining formal. There was a change in Alexander Geddes too; Eppie, quietly going about her duties, noticed the warmth in the man's dark eyes as he watched his son, thinking himself unobserved. And yet when he and Duncan spoke to each other there was always a stiff formality between them. It was as if they were both afraid to show their true feelings.

It was a great pity, Eppie thought, that they should be so careful with each other; she put it down to the way the gentry behaved, and, having been raised in a home where affection was a natural way of life, she pitied both the father and son, but particularly Duncan, who was at his happiest when alone with his young half-sister. Only with her, it seemed, could he be himself, letting his natural, warm affection take over. Eppie hoped that one day, when he was grown to manhood, he would find a young woman who would understand and return his need for affection.

When his father and grandmother were out of the house, or busy with their own pursuits, Duncan took to coming into the kitchen where he sat watching Eppie about her work, asking her about herself and her family, telling her about his school life, and eating anything that was to hand. He had a healthy appetite, and no amount of eating between meals prevented him from clearing his plate at every opportunity.

One day he wandered into the library when she was dusting. Alexander Geddes was a man who liked order in his life, and so his large desk was always tidy and the many books he possessed stood in ordered rows on their shelves. 'The master cannae abide tae have his things moved out o' their proper places,' Jean had told Eppie, 'and if anythin' goes missin' you'll be held responsible, even if it wasnae you tae blame at all. The only answer is tae always attend tae his possessions yersel'.'

Today, the desk was empty but for a neat pile of papers

and the marble paperweight standing, as always, near the right-hand corner. Eppie dusted beneath the papers and then replaced them just as she had found them. Then she picked up the paperweight and gave it a good rub. It fitted her hand easily, its cool smoothness comforting against her palm. Before setting it back down she turned to the window and marvelled at the way the light made the green marble glow. She stared into it, seeing black whorls and flecks deep within, and marvelling at the beauty of it. Then she almost dropped it as Duncan said from the doorway, 'It's a miracle of nature, is it not?'

He came forwards and took it from her, then used his free hand to draw her closer to the window. 'D'ye see how the colours seem to move as you turn it about?'

She nodded, fascinated. 'It's like the sea on a summer's day, with the big green waves comin' in.'

'Well described. Imagine such beauty,' the youth said, 'hidden from sight in ordinary rock, waiting to be released by the quarrymen.'

'What makes it look like that?'

'It takes millions of years.'

'Millions?' she asked, and he laughed at the way astonishment made her voice rise to a squeak.

'More years than your brain, or mine, or anyone else's can even begin to imagine. I've read a lot about it; it's made up of calcium carbonate – that's the bones of tiny sea creatures that lived millions of years ago. It takes layers and layers of those wee skeletons. Then over those millions of years, volcanoes that used to be all over the earth heated them, and they were under tremendous pressure from the movement of the mountains. That's another thing that's hard to believe – that mountains can move, but they do, very slowly. That's how we get coal and diamonds and emeralds – and marble. We're blessed to have all that beauty at our feet, just waiting to be released.' He ran a finger lovingly over the surface. 'It's real name's serpentine – that's a form of marble. Look . . .' He laid the marble down and pulled open one of the desk drawers. From it he took a small stone that he placed in her hand. 'That's what marble looks like before it's released from the rock and treated.'

'But it's just like any other stone you'd find on the beach. How do you know there's marble in there?'

Duncan laughed, delighted by her interest. 'The quarrymen know all right. They can read the rocks.' He put the stone back into the drawer, then caught at her hand. 'Come with me.'

She had no option but to follow him along the hall to the family parlour, blushing to think of how rough her fingers must feel against his. 'This came from our own quarry,' he said proudly, indicating the room's fine mantelpiece. 'Well, it's not entirely ours. The Ramsays in Glasgow have leased the right to quarry the area from the Earl of Seafield – you'll know that he owns all this area – and my father has shares in it and works it for the Ramsays. So that nearly makes it ours.'

'This is from Portsoy?' She had always admired the mantelpiece, which, like the paperweight, was a translucent green, marked with black and white streaks and patterns.

'Indeed it is. And there are two mantelpieces in the Palace of Versailles, shipped all the way there from our Portsoy quarry. The palace I'm talking about is in—'

'France,' Eppie said without thinking, and then, seeing surprise in his expressive brown eyes, 'My father's a school teacher,' she said, and watched the quick colour rise to his cheeks. He hadn't thought that a mere housekeeper would know such a thing, she thought with a mixture of amusement and resentment.

'Oh – I see. Have you ever been to the marble quarry?'

'No, never.'

'I could take you there if you like.'

'I'd like it fine, but what would your father say?'

'I doubt if he would mind, but we could go when he's elsewhere on business if you like. And when my grandmother's out,' he added, one eye closing in a swift, amused wink. 'Tomorrow afternoon. I know that they're both going to be away from the house then.'

'I'm not sure that I should, Master Duncan.'

'Nonsense, there's no harm to it. We'll go tomorrow.'

'Go where?' Lydia asked from the doorway.

'I'm taking Eppie to see the marble quarry and you must keep your mouth shut tight and not tell on us.'

'Can I come?'

'Mrs Geddes wouldn't want me to take you out in this cold weather,' Eppie began, but the little girl stamped her foot.

'If you're going then so am I! And if you leave me behind I shall tell Father and Grandmother!'

'You're a little minx,' Duncan said, a mock scowl on his face and laughter in his voice.

'You'll take me too? Oh, please, Duncan! I'm never allowed to go anywhere interesting!'

'I don't see why you shouldn't come too. Nobody will ever know,' Duncan went on as Eppie began to protest. 'I'll tell the men at the quarry to keep quiet about it, and we needn't be away for long. But one word out of place, madam,' he added to Lydia, 'and I shall pick you up and swim out to the black rocks and leave you there for the fishes to eat.'

And Lydia squealed with laughter and promised that she would never ever tell a living soul about their adventure.

A brisk wind blew in from the sea on the following day, and on the horizon the heavy grey clouds seemed to be bearing down on the tossing, white-capped waves.

'Can we not wait until the weather's better?' Eppie asked nervously as Duncan and Lydia arrived in her kitchen only moments after the front door had closed behind Helen's straight, narrow back.

'It's not raining, and I'm going back to school tomorrow,' Duncan reminded her, while Lydia chimed in with, 'You promised!'

'You must wear your warmest clothes then.'

'I will, I will! Come on,' Lydia grabbed Eppie's hand and rushed her upstairs. 'Let's get ready and go before they come back!'

As they left the streets and began to climb to the headland Lydia skipped ahead, revelling in the pleasure of being able to run without being told to behave like a young lady.

'How did Mr Geddes come tae be in charge of the quarry?' Eppie asked Duncan as they followed the child.

'Through Lydia's mother, Celia Ramsay. Her portrait hangs over the fireplace in the library.'

Eppie had often looked at the portrait when she was cleaning the library. The woman in it, little more than a girl, was dark and vivacious, and very beautiful.

'My stepmother,' Duncan was saying, 'came from Glasgow. Her father owned several quarries and was a shareholder here – that's how she met my father; her own father came here on business and brought her with him. When they married, Mr Ramsay asked Father to look after the Ramsay interests here. When he died he left his share in the quarry to my father. Eventually, it'll be Lydia's.'

He eyed the small figure bustling along ahead of them, now jumping from one clump of grass to another, and sighed. 'Lydia's the fortunate one – I love the quarry, but my grandfather on my mother's side was a physician and I'm told that my mother had set her heart on me following him into the profession.'

'Physicians are highly regarded,' Eppie said.

'I know they are, but I've no interest in being highly regarded, and it's hard to be good at something if your heart's not in it.' Then he stopped and lifted his head to the wind, which was getting stronger as they climbed. 'Listen – can you hear it?'

She listened intently and caught an irregular chinking sound. 'It's like a lot of bells that are ringing flat.'

'That's the men splitting the rock. You can't use explosives to get to marble because it's too fragile,' Duncan said, jamming his hat down on his head more firmly lest the wind take it. 'We've arrived. Lydia, come back here.'

A moment later the small quarry lay beneath them, with men dotted here and there on its slope, working on the rock face. A few were gathered round a large slab of rock on the beach below.

'How do we get down?' Eppie asked nervously, and Duncan nodded at a pathway running down the side of the quarry.

'We use that.' He grasped Lydia's hand. 'It's easy as long as you take it slowly.'

By the time the three of them had scrambled down to the beach they were breathless and almost too hot in their warm clothing. The quarrymen, intent on their work, threw swift glances at the newcomers, and some nodded to Duncan before turning back to their work.

'They're shaping the marble, probably for a mantelpiece,' Duncan explained as Eppie studied the pulley-operated machinery the men were working with. 'They use a template with the shape cut out of it, and a mixture of slurry and rough sand. By hauling on the pulley they can pull the template back and forth to wear the marble down into the shape they need. They have to keep washing the sand out and replacing it.'

Eppie was so intent on watching the men work and listening to Duncan's explanations that she became quite oblivious to the cold until Lydia, who had wandered off along the beach in search of pebbles, returned to tug at her sleeve.

'Can we go home now? I want to go home!'

Eppie glanced down at the little girl and saw to her horror that Lydia's eyes were watering and her face chalk-white, apart from her nose, which was like a little red button. Her hands were bare, and blue with cold. When Eppie pulled her own glove off and caught at one of the child's hands it was as cold as ice.

'Where are your gloves?'

'There, s-somewhere.' Lydia indicated the beach behind them. 'I took them off to pick up some nice stones and I c-can't find them. I w-want to go home!' Her teeth were chattering and the words were stuttered out.

Eppie pushed her own gloves on to the little hands and then called to Duncan, who turned at once, his eyes darkening as he saw the little girl's ashen face. 'Come on,' he scooped his half-sister into his arms and settled her on his shoulders. 'I didn't realise we'd been here for so long. Can you link your arms about my neck, Lydia? That's the lass. Off we go.'

Eppie followed him up the path, her heart in her mouth. It wasn't fear of the climb or knowing that behind them a steep slope fell to the stony beach that frightened her, but the realisation that they had spent longer than they should have at the quarry, and now they would be fortunate if they got back to the house before Mrs Geddes.

At the top of the hill Duncan swung Lydia from his shoulders and then gathered her into his arms as though she were a baby, and set off at a run, Eppie panting along by his side.

'I'll take her straight up to her room,' he said as they sped along, 'and you bring some hot water to warm her. She'll be fine, you'll see.'

By the time they had reached the house Lydia was beginning to enjoy the journey and laughing at the way Eppie's gloves flapped at the end of her short arms.

'There, home and dry,' Duncan said as Eppie opened the back door and stood back to let him in. 'Now then, young lady, it's upstairs with you—'

He stopped so abruptly that Eppie, turning after closing the door against the cold grey day, almost walked into him. Peering round his arm, she saw Helen Geddes, still in her outdoor clothes, standing at the inner door.

'So you're back at last,' the woman said. 'And where have the three of you been?'

'I promised not to tell,' Lydia piped up, while at the same time her brother said, 'Just out for a breath of fresh air.'

'On a day like this? You took the bairn out into that cold wind when you both know very well that she's got a delicate chest? And what's that she's got on her hands?' Helen swept forwards and snatched the gloves off. 'My goodness, lassie, your hands are like ice. And so's your wee face! Give her to me at once!'

She dragged her grand-daughter from Duncan's grasp. Lydia, sensing trouble, burst into tears, throwing her arms around Helen's neck and burying her cold face into her while Helen ignored Duncan, concentrating instead on Eppie's stricken face.

'I blame you for this,' she said, and then, raising her voice to drown out Lydia's sobs and Duncan's attempt to speak, 'You're paid to look after this bairn, not drag her out on a bitter day like today. You'll suffer for this – make no mistake about it!'

5

It had never been Alexander Geddes's intention, or his wish, that his mother move into his house after the death of his wife, Celia. Indeed, he had been too stunned at the time by the shocking unexpectedness of his loss to think clearly about anything.

Celia had been well throughout her pregnancy, and unlike Alexander's first wife, a timid young woman with a chronic fear of pain, she had looked forward to the birth of her first chid with eager anticipation. He would never, as long as he lived, forget his last sight of her; propped against a mound of pillows, her dark hair spilling over her shoulders, her cheeks flushed and her eyes bright with excitement.

'It won't be long, my love,' she had said as the midwife shooed him towards the bedroom door. 'And just think – when we next meet, Duncan will have a brother or sister of his very own!'

On the way downstairs Alexander had passed the doctor, who slapped him on the shoulder and said jocularly, 'Sit yourself down and have a tumbler of whisky, man. She's a healthy young woman and I warrant she'll not keep you waiting long.'

Six hours later, some time after the sound of a newborn child's mewling had drifted down the stairs to where Alexander paced in the hall, he was finally allowed into the bedroom. This time, despite the whimpers of the child in the cradle, there was a terrible sense of stillness about the room. As before, Celia lay back against her pillows, but now she was silent, her lovely green eyes hidden by blue-shaded lids, her mouth with a slight downturn at the corners as though she had died blaming herself for the sudden haemorrhage that had taken her from him.

'No rhyme nor reason to it . . . did all we could, Geddes, but . . .' the doctor's words fluttered like intrusive birds about Alexander's head as he took his young wife's hand in his. It was still warm, but limp and unresponsive, and no matter how hard he tried to will her back to him her eyes remained closed, the dark lashes smudged against snow-white skin.

'God's will, man, and there's little any of us can do against that,' the doctor said, and then, in an attempt to give some comfort to the man who finally turned to look at him, his own eyes dead in a bone-white face, 'The bairn's well, though. Ye've got a bonny wee daughter, Geddes.'

He nodded at the midwife, who stepped forwards and waited beside Alexander. At first he paid her no heed, for all he wanted to do was to stay with Celia, holding her cooling hand, until death found the kindness to take him as it had taken her.

When the bundle in the woman's arms let out an angry yell he turned, frowning at the interruption. The nurse had drawn the blanket back from the baby's face and Alexander stared down at the tiny red features and flailing fists, so wrapped in his own misery that at first he was not sure why the little creature was there at all. Then his daughter's screwed-up face suddenly smoothed itself out and she opened her eyes, her mother's beautiful green eyes, and looked directly at him.

And in that moment Alexander Geddes knew that his Celia had not deserted him entirely; she had left this little part of her to comfort him and give him reason to continue with his own life.

When Faith, Alexander's first wife and the mother of Duncan, died of pneumonia Jean Gilbert had taken over the running of the house and care of Duncan, then seven years old – the age Lydia was now. Alexander and Jean were so used by then to each other's ways that the arrangement suited them both.

When he married Celia she and Jean got on well together, and when fate decreed that he become a widower for the second time Alexander – and Jean herself – had taken it for granted that she would continue to look after the house, and the baby as well, with some help from a wet nurse.

But Helen Geddes had no intention of leaving her son to his own devices for a second time. An ambitious and possessive woman, she had chosen for her own partner a man some ten years older than herself, a fisherman who owned his boat. With his young wife's active encouragement and assistance Duncan Geddes had invested in another boat, and then a third. The proceeds from the boats' catches soon enabled him to stay on land while his crews risked their lives, and when he died of a heart attack it was in his own comfortable house and in the knowledge that he had left his widow and young son well provided for.

Helen had then turned her attention to Alexander himself. Like his father, he was willing to work hard, and with his mother's encouragement he began to invest money earned from the fishing boats. Before he reached his mid-twenties he had shares in the rope works, limestone quarries and the salmon bothy, as well as the three boats he had inherited from his father. Realising that he might well turn his mind to thoughts of marriage, Helen had chosen a suitable wife for him, the daughter of a doctor who lived in Roseneath, a nearby town. Alexander, who had been raised to do as his mother wished, had married Faith and used the dowry she had brought with her to buy some property in the area. One of the houses, by the harbour, became home for him and his bride, while the other properties were rented out.

Alexander was more interested in business than in relationships, and although there was no passion or fire in his marriage, he was content enough, and delighted when Faith presented him with a son and heir named after Alexander's father. The boy, they agreed within days of his arrival, would receive the best education money could buy, and would become a physician.

To his mother's relief, Alexander showed no interest in marrying again after Faith died. He had his son, and Jean Gilbert looked after them well. Helen decided that she need have no fear of having to share her son with another woman, and was therefore taken by surprise when Alexander, in his thirties, fell passionately in love, for the first time in his life, with Celia Ramsay.

When James Ramsay came to Portsoy to inspect the quarry the wealthier residents in the area, excited at having strangers in their midst, set themselves out to entertain the man, who had brought with him his wife, son and daughter. Alexander and his mother were invited to a social evening held in the Ramsays' honour, and it took only one smile from Celia and one glance from her sparkling green eyes, to tell Alexander that at last, he had found his soulmate.

By the time the Ramsay family were due to return to Glasgow Alexander had managed to win Celia's heart. His sharp-eyed mother had noticed what was going on, but felt, when the visitors left, that the danger was over. She had no idea that Alexander and Celia were writing to each other, and that the young woman's letters made him hunger for her so much that he soon found a reason to go off to Glasgow on business. By the time he returned, with a spring in his step and a glow in his eyes, he and Celia were engaged to be married.

Helen was furious, although she made a good job of hiding it. Alexander had made up his mind and there was little she could do about it. A few months later he and Celia were man and wife. From Helen's point of view, the only saving grace about the entire business was that she would not lose her son and grandson entirely. Celia was more than happy to move to Portsoy and Alexander was given the task of making sure that his new father-in-law's investment in the marble quarry brought good financial results.

Alexander Geddes had never been so happy or so fulfilled. For the first time in his life he knew what it was to love and to be loved. The house that had simply been somewhere to live until Celia came to it as his wife now overflowed with light and happiness, and his only comfort when he had to be out and about on business was the pleasure of returning to it, and to Celia.

One short year later she was dead and as soon as she had been laid to rest Helen announced that she was going to move into her son's house.

'There's no need,' Alexander had protested.

'There's every need. How can you look after a tiny

bairn yourself – and then there's Duncan, coming home from school for the holidays. We must put your children first, Alexander.'

'Jean's going to look after them – after all of us.'

'Jean's a housekeeper, not one of the family. You need family about you at a time like this,' Helen said. 'And where's the sense in me living at one end of the town and you at the other, in this big place? I'll sell the house I've been living in, and you can be comfortable in the knowledge that I'm here for you and your children.'

Alexander had never been able to win an argument with his mother, and at that moment, so soon after Celia's death, he was too dispirited to try. So Helen moved in and took over the running of the house and its inhabitants. The little happiness left to Alexander came from Lydia, growing up to be the image of her mother, and Duncan, who was doing well at school. Alexander had never lost sight of his determination to see his son become a successful physician, and each year brought the prospect a little nearer.

A year after Celia's death her father was killed in an explosion at one of the stone quarries he part-owned. To Alexander's surprise and Helen's delight, the man left his share in the Portsoy marble quarry to his son-in-law with the proviso that it would pass to Lydia. The main share in that particular quarry belonged to Celia's brother, Edward Ramsay, who was content to leave the running of it to Alexander.

At least having the quarry to think of as well as all his other business interests kept Alexander's mind occupied, although Celia was never far from his thoughts. He had been dismayed at Jean Gilbert's decision to give up her duties as housekeeper, but the young woman she had found as her replacement was eminently suitable. Lydia was thriving and Duncan doing well at school, and Alexander's only problem, he well knew, though he would never admit it even to himself, was his mother.

Riding home at the end of a busy day, his face chilled by the cold wind blowing in from the sea, he wished, guiltily, that he could be returning to a house where it was just him and his children, with Eppie Watt presiding over the kitchen and looking after the three of them.

As he neared the harbour opening his son stepped forwards, and Alexander drew his sturdy horse to a halt.

'Duncan? What's amiss?'

'I wanted to speak with you before you got to the house.' The boy came to stand by Alexander's stirrup, one hand smoothing the horse's neck. 'Grandmother's vexed with Eppie, but it was my idea entirely.'

Alexander sighed; more family problems! 'What was your idea?'

'To take Eppie and Lydia to the marble quarry.'

'Dear God, there's not been an accident, has there? Lydia . . . !'

'Nothing like that. It's just that we meant to be back at the house before Grandmother, since she doesn't like Lydia to go out in the cold. But she was well happed-up, Father. It's just that . . .' the boy bit his lip. 'We stayed longer than we meant to and Lydia got cold, and when we reached the house Grandmother was waiting for us. Now she blames Eppie, the way she always does. But it was my fault. I wanted you to know before you spoke to Grandmother—'

Alexander held up a hand. 'All right, I'll deal with it.'

'You'll not let her turn Eppie out of the house, will you?'

'No, I'll not do that. Run on, now,' Alexander said sharply, seeing that his son's face was almost blue with cold. The boy must have been waiting for him for some time. 'Get indoors, out of this wind.'

His heart was heavy as he rode to the stables not far from the house. He had had a busy day and all he wanted was a good hot meal and some peace in which to enjoy it. But it seemed that he was going to be denied even that simple pleasure. 'You're fortunate,' he murmured as he dismounted and stroked the horse's velvety nose, 'to be staying in this nice quiet stable.'

Leaving the animal with the stable hand, he walked the short distance to the house, wishing as he went that he had had the strength and the sense to stop his mother from moving in after Celia's death. But he had never in his life been able to deny her, and even though he was a man now, and a successful man at that, the child he had once been, the child nurtured and trained by Helen Geddes, was still locked into the core of his being, rendering him powerless to defy her. It was a wonder to Alexander that women were thought of as the weaker sex, when mothers had such terrifying power over their children.

Normally he entered his home by the front door, but this evening he walked round to the side and found Eppie working in the kitchen. She whipped round when the door opened, ladle in hand.

'Mr Geddes . . .' Her eyes were wide in a pale face and Alexander, who well knew how his mother's tongue could sting like the lash of a whip, found himself feeling sorry for the poor young woman.

'I met Duncan on my way home.' He put his hat and gloves on the table and began to unbutton his coat, relishing the kitchen's warmth. 'I understand he took you and Lydia to the marble quarry this afternoon.'

'It was my fault, sir. He saw me admiring the bonny marble stone on your desk and offered to let me see the quarry for myself. I thought it would be a nice outing for Lydia, but we stayed overlong and she got awful cold . . .'

He went over to stand by her at the range, holding his hands out to the heat. 'Where is Lydia?'

'In her room. I gave her a hot drink, and she's fine and warm now . . .'

'Then no harm's been done. Did you enjoy the quarry, Eppie?'

'It was very interesting, sir,' she faltered, taken aback.

'I think so too. It's a cold day, as you said. I'm looking forward to a good hot dinner when it's ready.'

'I can have it on the table in ten minutes, Mr Geddes.'

'I'm glad to hear it,' Alexander said, picking up his outdoor clothes.

As he had expected, his mother appeared at the door of her small parlour as soon as she heard his step in the upper hall. 'Alexander, I have something serious to discuss with you. In spite of my orders, Eppie took wee Lydia out today, and to that marble quarry, of all places!'

'I understand that it was Duncan's idea.'

'You've spoken to him?'

'We met in the town. He wanted to give his sister a treat before leaving for Aberdeen.'

'Even so, Eppie should have known better than to let him take Lydia out on a day like this. She knows fine that the bairn has a delicate chest. She was blue with the cold when they got back!'

'Mother, every child living in Aberdeenshire has to get used to cold weather. Cosseting Lydia might do her more harm than good, and in any case,' Alexander went on firmly as his mother opened her mouth to protest, 'Duncan had my permission to take his sister out.'

Her face went red. 'You knew about this? And you didn't tell me?'

'I didn't see the need to tell you. It was an arrangement between me, my son and my daughter. Now if you'll excuse me, I'm going upstairs to wash before dinner's on the table.'

Mounting the stairs, he wished passionately that Celia had lived. If she were only here she would have known right from wrong; as it was, he had had to tell a lie to his mother, and the knowledge of it sat uncomfortably in his mind, for he was an honest man.

He took time to look in on his daughter before going back downstairs. She was sitting on the floor playing with her dolls, looking bright-eyed and cheerful. 'Duncan took me and Eppie to the quarry,' she said as soon as he entered. 'I got stones there – look!'

She picked up the box at her side, and Alexander peered in at the collection of pebbles and agreed that they were very bonny.

'It must have been very cold at the quarry today,' he remarked, and she gave a shiver at the memory of it.

'It was freezing cold, and Duncan said my nose was all red.'

'But you're warm now?' He put the back of one hand to her soft cheek as she nodded. He would have liked to pick her up and hold her close in his arms, but he had never been cuddled as a child and now he felt awkward with the strong affection he felt for his own children.

That, he thought as he went back downstairs, was something else that Celia might have helped him with if she had lived.

If only she had lived!

6

Lydia survived the outing to the quarry with no ill effects, much to her grandmother's secret annoyance, but in March, despite being zealously protected from the bitter winds, she took a fever and lay in her bed, flushed and irritable, with both Eppie and Helen fussing over her and Alexander returning home at intervals during the day to find out how she was.

The doctor advised bland food and plenty of liquids, and Eppie, returning from a visit to Fordyce with several jars of her parents' honey, proceeded to administer some to the little girl in hot milk, and as a spread on tiny little doll-sized scones specially baked for Lydia.

The child summoned up a smile at sight of the scones, but eyed the pale golden spread with some misgiving. 'What's that?'

'Honey. Have you never tasted it before?'

'No.' Lydia's flushed face screwed itself into an expression that said that she had no desire to taste it at all.

'It's very good for sore throats. It will ease the pain,' Eppie coaxed, and eventually Lydia consented to lick a little of the honey from a scone. She liked it, and although the scones, small as they were, annoyed her throat, she ended up licking the honey from most of them, then taking a little from a tiny silver spoon that Eppie had found in a kitchen drawer. 'A special little spoon for a special little girl,' she flattered as she popped honey into Lydia's mouth.

That night the little girl managed to drink a cup of warm milk with honey stirred into it, and in the morning, she declared that her throat felt a little easier.

Eppie sweetened her breakfast porridge with more honey and as she fed it to Lydia she told her about the bees that lived in their skeps in her parents' garden, and how they made honey, and about how a bee that had found a good crop of flowers could tell its companions about it by performing a special dance.

'But they're nasty and they sting people,' Lydia objected. 'They stung me once, on my hand.' She held out a small hand. 'Right there, on my middle finger. And it *hurt*!'

'What were you doing when you got stung?'

'Picking flowers in the garden.'

'And the poor little bee must have been inside one of the flowers, trying to gather pollen to make honey to feed the other bees in its hive. It must have got a terrible fright when a big hand suddenly picked it up. It was only trying to tell you not to hurt it. They don't want to sting you,' Eppie went on as Lydia's face puckered up into the threat of tears at the memory, 'because once a bee stings, it dies.'

'Does it?' Lydia's eyes rounded in astonishment. 'Has a bee ever stung you?'

'No, but that's because my father taught me when I was smaller than you to treat them gently, and not to get frightened when they settled on me. They just want to know if you're a flower, and they fly away soon enough if you just let them alone. Some folk say that you can talk to the bees,' she went on.

'Do they talk back to you?'

'No, but they listen, and they're very good at keeping secrets. Sometimes if you have a very special secret that you mustn't tell to anyone, or if you're unhappy about something and you can't talk about it, you can tell the bees instead.'

'Have you ever told anything to the bees?'

'Lots of times,' Eppie said. The bees had been the first to know when she fell in love with Murdo, and when he asked her to marry him. They were the first to know that she was carrying Charlotte, and they were witness to her tears and her despair after the sea took Murdo from her. 'Lots of times,' she said again. 'It helps to talk to the bees.'

'When I'm better, will you take me to see the bees in your father's garden?'

'I don't think your own father would allow that. My parents live quite far away.' Eppie knew that Mrs Geddes would not be pleased at the idea of her grand-daughter visiting the housekeeper's family.

'I don't mind walking – or we could go in my grand-mother's carriage.'

'Wait until you're better before we think of anything like that,' Eppie said evasively, and Lydia put a hand to her throat and swallowed carefully.

'I think I'm getting better already,' she said cheerfully.

'Father,' she wheedled that evening when Alexander went upstairs to say goodnight to her, 'can we have bees in our garden?'

'We can't avoid having bees in the garden during the summer. Do you not remember the time one stung your hand?'

'But that was because I frightened it. They won't sting you if you talk to them,' his daughter explained earnestly. Alarm shot through him, but close inspection showed that the feverish flush of the past few days was less hectic than before and the brightness in her eyes owed more to enthusiasm than sickness.

'You want to talk to bees?' he was asking cautiously when his mother came into the room.

'Ach, this is just some nonsense Eppie's filled the bairn's head with! Would you believe that she wants to go to Fordyce when she's better, to visit the woman's family?'

'To see the bees,' Lydia corrected her. 'Eppie's father has bee skeps in his garden and her mother makes beeswax that she uses to polish the furniture, and honey too. Eppie gave me some of the honey and now my throat feels much better. Can I go and see the bees, Father?'

'Of course not,' Helen said sharply, before her son had the chance to reply.

'Then can I get a bee skep of my own in our garden? Please, Father?'

'I've already said no, Alexander, so don't go telling her otherwise!'

But in her enthusiasm Lydia was so like her mother that Alexander Geddes shut his mother's voice out, and smiled down at his small daughter.

'Let me think about it,' he said, and she lay back on her pillow, satisfied.

'You're just confusing the bairn,' Helen nagged at him as the two of them left Lydia, already half-asleep, and made their way back downstairs. 'I'm going to have to speak to Eppie, for she's got no right to go filling the child's head with such nonsense. And as for taking her to Fordyce – that's just sheer impertinence!'

'Leave Eppie to me. She's a good housekeeper and I'm

sure her intentions are always good. It seems that the honey she gave Lydia has helped her to feel better,' he went on, ignoring his mother's loud sniff. 'In any case, the wee one'll soon forget this nonsense about having bees of her own.'

But Lydia, whose busy little brain normally danced from one thought to another, never lingering for long, had been enchanted by the housekeeper's talk of bees who loved flowers and danced and listened to folk and made honey to eat, and beeswax to keep furniture gleaming. Once she was up and about again she began to pester her father until at last he sought out Eppie, finding her polishing the big dining table.

For a moment he stood in the doorway, unnoticed. There was something soothing about watching a woman go about her domestic duties, he thought. Eppie's sleeves were rolled up to above her elbows, and her rounded arm moved swiftly and firmly to and fro as she swept the cloth over the glossy table. The frill on her white cloth cap bounced in time to the hymn she was singing beneath her breath. Every part of her body moved to the rhythm of her work, he noticed, then was suddenly embarrassed at watching her unawares.

He cleared his throat and she immediately swung around, her face, flushed from her work, reddening even more. 'Do you want to be in here, sir? I can come back later . . .'

'No, Eppie, not at all. I wanted to talk to you.' He went to the table, looking down at it to see his face, and hers, reflected in its rich tawny surface. 'That polish you're using – would it be beeswax?'

'Aye, sir, from my father's bees. It's the best thing for furniture.'

'There's a pleasant smell to it,' Alexander acknowledged. 'My daughter tells me that your father keeps bees in his garden.'

'Yes, sir.'

'And she also claims that the honey they make has eased her sore throat considerably.'

'It's very good for painful throats, and for the chest too, if it's constricted.'

'She wants me to set up a skep in our garden, but I admit to being apprehensive about that. I wouldn't want to see her or her grandmother suffering from bee stings.'

'They wouldn't be, sir, not if the skep was put right at the back, where the bees would be undisturbed. There are some nice flowering bushes there,' Eppie said enthusiastically, 'that the bees would like fine.'

'And where would I get a skep, or the bees to occupy it, come to that?'

'My father could help you there. The young queens swarm in the summer in search of a home of their own, and that's when the beekeepers have to find somewhere for them to live.'

'Hmmm.' He pulled at his lower lip, frowning, then said, 'And you know how to look after these bees and keep them under control?'

'Aye, sir. I always helped my father with the bees, even when I was younger than Lydia is now.'

'In that case,' said Alexander Geddes in the full knowledge that as well as pleasing his daughter, the decision would infuriate his mother, 'I believe that it would be in order for you to ask your father if he could let us have some bees when the time is right.'

After all, he thought when the housekeeper had returned to her kitchen and he was alone, pleasing

Lydia was far more important than keeping his mother contented.

When Duncan came home for summer Lydia was able to lead him proudly to the far end of the garden to show him the bee skep, with some of its inmates flying around and hurrying in and out of the entrance.

'They make good honey,' she told him importantly, 'and they talk to each other by dancing.'

'Not by buzzing, then?'

'I suppose they can buzz to each other too,' Lydia said seriously. 'If you go close enough to the skep you can hear them all buzzing because that's the way they keep the skep aired, by using their wings like ladies with their fans. But we mustn't go near the skep unless Eppie's with us because she knows the bees and they know her. You can talk to them too. You can even ask them to do things for you, if they're really important things that you want very much.'

'And do they grant your wishes?' her brother teased her, amused by the little girl's air of self-importance.

'No, that's what fairies do, and magic folk. Bees aren't magic. You can talk to them and they just listen. They just . . . help folk sometimes. And the best part is that they don't tell anyone what you've said, so you can tell them anything at all, even the things you shouldn't even be thinking. They're my very best friends.'

Lydia had taken to sitting on an old tree-stump within sight of the skep but at a safe distance, with one of her dolls in her arms, talking to the bees in a low monotone. Eppie, gathering in vegetables for dinner or pegging out washing on the clothes line, did so on pleasant, warm days to the sound of the little girl's voice droning on for up to half an hour at a time. She never went near enough to hear what Lydia was saying though, for she knew from her own personal experience how important it was to know that only the bees heard what was being said.

Lydia had been stung once since the skep was brought from Fordyce. A bee had landed on her wrist, and before Eppie could do or say anything the child had brushed it away automatically, then let out a shrill scream and clutched at her wrist.

Eppie caught her up and ran with her into the kitchen, where she snatched the pantry door key from its lock then sat the little girl on a chair and pressed the head of the key against the red area. 'Hold that for me,' she instructed as the tiny dark sting appeared at the surface of the skin, 'and push it down hard.' Lydia, curiosity beginning to win over pain and fright, did as she was told, and by the time Eppie had fetched tweezers and drawn the sting, the patient was becoming interested in the operation.

'Now then . . .' Eppie fetched an onion and cut off a generous slice, which she rubbed gently over Lydia's arm. 'That'll take the pain away.'

It did, but not before the pungent smell of the vegetable had set Eppie to sniffing and blinking her tear-filled eyes. Lydia laughed at the sight, then as Eppie removed the onion and said, 'There, has it stopped hurting yet?' the child's mouth suddenly turned down at the corners and her own eyes filled with fresh tears.

'What is it, my wee quine? It is still hurting?' Eppie asked anxiously, and the girl shook her dark curly head.

'No,' she sobbed. 'I'm not c-crying for me, I'm crying for the poor wee b-bee. I k-killed it and I didn't mean to!'

It was fortunate that Mrs Geddes was out of the house at the time, but as soon as she returned Lydia was anxious to spill out the story of her latest adventure and proudly display the tiny red mark on her arm. The woman wasted no time in seeking out Eppie and giving her a tongue-lashing that ended with, 'And what my son is going to say when he hears of this latest mishap I dare not think. But I do know that he will wish that he had listened to me when I advised him to hire an older and more responsible person as his housekeeper!'

Eppie could only agree, and when she heard Alexander Geddes's firm tread on the passageway outside the kitchen door that night her heart started to thump faster. As soon as he came in she started to stammer out an apology, but he held up one hand to stop her.

'I have heard my mother's opinion, and my daughter's story of what happened today, and now I would like to hear yours,' he said, and stood listening without interruption, his dark eyes steady on hers, until she had come to a breathless stop.

'A cut onion, you say?'

'Aye, sir. Or vinegar, or mebbe bicarbonate of soda in a little water. The important thing is to get the sting out first. But I should never have let Lydia get too close to the bees . . .'

'We have to learn all through life, and Lydia tells me that if she had done as you told her and stayed calm when one of the creatures decided to alight on her, she would not have been stung. In fact, she is quite eager to be given another chance, so that she can behave properly next time. No harm was done, and her pleasure in having the bee skep outweighs her chance of being stung again. The matter is closed,' he said, and left the kitchen.

As had happened over Ne'erday, the house seemed to come alive when Duncan returned for his summer holiday. His doting grandmother made no objection when he took Lydia down to the harbour to watch the boats come in, each one followed by a fluttering banner of screeching seagulls.

They saw the silver scales flashing in the sunlight as the herring were brought ashore, listened as the quayside auctioneers sold the catches to waiting merchants and watched the fisher lassies slit, clean and pack the fish so quickly that it was impossible to make out each moment of their deft hands. They squatted over rock pools to study the tiny crabs scuttling about their business, and peered into the lobster pots, where great sharp-edged claws snapped and clashed in panic and baffled frustration inside skilfully woven prisons.

Duncan also took his young half-sister to the hills beyond the village, where they gathered flowers and played games and rolled down grassy hills. Lydia came home from each of their outings pink-cheeked and glowing with excitement. Her appetite improved noticeably, and so did her temper, for Duncan would not allow the tantrums that Eppie often had to tolerate.

There were also some occasions when he went out on his own, refusing to take the little girl with him. When she discovered that no amount of pleading or coaxing would sway him, she would draw her breath in sharply and bottle it up in her lungs until her face turned first red, then purple; or she would throw herself down and scream at the top of her voice, going rigid and drumming her heels on the floor. But each time she tried one of the ploys that generally brought her whatever it was that she wanted, her brother merely looked at her with dislike and said, 'You're much too old to behave like a baby, Lydia. You look ridiculous.' And then he would turn on his heel and leave her to her tantrum.

At first, Eppie suspected that Duncan's long outings

were to do with a young lass. He was almost sixteen years of age, and a good-looking youth – the fisher lassies were always quick to flirt with him when he went to the harbour to watch them at work – and she was sure that plenty of girls would be more than happy to be his sweetheart. Then she realised that he never wore his good clothes when he went out, and that when he came to the kitchen in search of something to eat between meals, and stayed to talk to her as she worked about the kitchen, that almost all of his conversation was about the marble quarry. Without even realising it she was learning a lot about the process of mining the beautiful patterned marble from the dull rocks near the harbour.

When he realised that she shared his fascination, Duncan loaned her some of the books he had in his room, and even helped her to chose a little marble pendant for Charlotte from one of the local shops – a chip of ruby-red marble set in a silver frame. It cost more money than Eppie could afford, but her daughter's birthday was approaching, and she wanted to buy something special to mark the event.

'Did she like it?' he asked when she returned from her weekly visit to Fordyce, and grinned with pleasure when she described Charlotte's delight.

'She says that she'll wear it all her life.'

'Even if she grows up to marry a rich man who can give her gemstones every day of the week, she'll never have anything bonnier that her Portsoy marble,' he said.

'You know, Duncan, I've never met anyone who likes stones as you do. Most folk are only interested in marble and the like after it's all been quarried and turned into something nice, like a vase or a mantelshelf or a bit of jewellery, but it seems to me that you like it best before it gets to that.'

He was sitting at the kitchen table, eating scraps of dough that she had trimmed from an apple pie in the making. 'It's the thought of it changing slowly, then lying all those hundreds of years within the stone, waiting to be discovered,' he said enthusiastically. 'It's like those stories Lydia likes, about the princess sleeping for a hundred years, waiting for her prince to come and find her. Marble has to wait a lot longer than that.'

'I can't for the life of me see those big dusty quarrymen as princes, and you're sure to get a bellyache if you eat much more of that raw dough, laddie.'

'Not me,' Duncan said cheerfully. 'I never get a bellyache.' Then as they heard the door from upstairs bang against the wall and Lydia come hurrying down the stairs, newly released from her lessons and anxious to seek out her brother, he swept the last of the dough from the table, popped it into his mouth and stood up, ready to catch her as she came rushing into the kitchen and threw herself at him.

7

As the time came near for him to return to Aberdeen and his studies, Duncan grew quieter and spent more time out on his own, or in his room. Eppie worried about him, wondering if he was sickening for something, but his appetite remained as hearty as ever. It was only his mind that seemed to be out of sorts.

A week before her grandson was due to leave Portsoy, Helen Geddes went to her bed early, complaining of a headache.

'I'll have a cup of hot milk in my room at nine o'clock, Eppie,' she ordered as she left the dinner table. 'Mebbe an early night will ease the pain.' Eppie delivered the drink as the grandfather clock in the hall was chiming the hour, then looked in on Lydia, who was sleeping soundly. She was passing the study door on her way back to her kitchen when she heard Duncan say passionately from behind the library door, 'It's my future, Father – not yours to use as you wish!'

'I am your father!' Alexander Geddes snapped in reply. 'And it is my duty to set your feet on the right road!'

'There's no need for that, since I've found my own

road. It would be wrong of you to try to force me in another direction against my will, surely you can see that?' Duncan's voice was almost as deep as his father's now.

'And surely you can see that it's a son's duty to heed his father? I followed in my own father's footsteps—'

'Then let me follow in yours!' Duncan said. 'Is that too much to ask?'

'I didn't have the brains to do otherwise, but you do. You can make something of yourself, boy, can you not see that?'

'I have every intention of making something of myself, you may have no concerns as to that. But I will do it in my way, not yours.'

There was a pause, and Eppie found herself imagining the two of them facing each other across the big desk, faces flushed, neither willing to give way. Then her employer's voice came again, almost pleading this time. 'It was your mother's wish, boy. Would you deny her?'

'Over a matter as important this, aye, I would – to her face if she were here.'

'You dare to say such a thing about your own mother?' Alexander Geddes barked out the words, and Eppie's heart began to beat faster.

'Perhaps if she was here in this room with us, she would listen to what I'm trying to say to you, and perhaps she would understand that I must follow my own inclination. What sort of a physician will I be if my heart's not in the work?'

'A disciplined one, benefiting from the need to deny your own needs for the sake of the poor sick folk you'll be helping. I'll hear no more,' Alexander said as the boy began to argue. 'I have work to do and you'd better go to your room now and think long and hard on what I've said to you, for I won't change my mind!'

'I think best out in the night air,' Duncan snapped back, his voice getting louder as he headed for the door. Eppie fled, and only just managed to get herself on the other side of the door opening on to the kitchen stairs before he emerged.

It was fortunate that the young man didn't choose to leave the house by the back door, as he often did, for he would have run into her before she had time to scurry to the kitchen. As it was, he left by the front door, closing it just as his father called him back. Standing at the top of the back stairs, clutching the door handle, she heard her employer's hiss of anger and frustration, then the study door closing again.

Then, and only then, did she dare move quietly, as guilty as a thief in the night, to the safety of her kitchen.

As far as Eppie could tell, no more was said about the quarrel she had overheard between father and son, although there was a strain between them. They spoke to each other as little as possible, and when they had to it was in brief, formal sentences. She was certain that neither of them had mentioned their disagreement to Helen, for the woman was her usual self, continuing to make a fuss of her grandson as though nothing amiss had happened. Had she known the truth, she would almost certainly have taken one side or the other and thus managed to fan the flames of the disagreement between father and son. Eppie wondered which of them Helen Geddes would have supported – the grandson she adored and spoiled as much as he allowed her to spoil him, or the son who had been taught to do as she wished.

Duncan divided his time between Lydia and his solitary walks, but rarely came to the kitchen. At first, Eppie's guilt at eavesdropping on her employer and his son made her suspect that Duncan knew what she had done, but then she decided that the lad had a lot on his mind and was in no mood to chatter and laugh as he usually did when he spent time with her. Throwing swift glances at him as she served at table she saw that when he was not talking to his half-sister or his grandmother his face, usually open to the world, was closed and his eyes darkened by inner thoughts. He was deeply unhappy, and she longed to be able to comfort and help him, but she could not say a word.

His father too, was quiet and spent more time than usual, certainly more time than he had since Duncan's arrival, away from the house. At night he sat in the library long after the rest of the household had retired. Eppie, lying in her bed below stairs, would hear the library door open and the tread of his feet along the hall long after the grandfather clock had struck midnight.

It hurt her to see father and son estranged like that, and when she next went to Fordyce she confided in her father when the two of them were alone in the back garden. 'Duncan's going back to Aberdeen in a few days' time, and it wouldn't be right for the two of them to part on bad terms. I'm sure they both want to make it up – I can tell by the way Mr Geddes looks at the lad that he wants to make his peace – but it seems to me that making up their differences would mean that one or other of them would have to give in, and neither wants to do that.'

'It's a sore thing when father and son fall out, right enough, but it happens. We're so used to guiding our sons and daughters when they're small that sometimes we don't notice they're close to becoming adults themselves. We still want to do what's best for them. And all too often, what's best is what we want, not what they want. That's when the tempers start to rise.'

'You never tried to push me and Marion into doing something against our wills, not even when I said I wanted to marry Murdo,' Eppie said, and then, as he suddenly became interested in picking a dead leaf from a nearby bush, understanding dawned. 'Father, were you and Mother against it?'

'Never against it, for Murdo was a decent hard-working loon, and God rest his soul, he'd still be a good husband and father if the Lord had seen fit to spare him . . .'

'But marrying a fisherman was never what you wanted for me, was it?'

Peter McNaught stooped and pulled off a sprig of mint, rolling it between his palms and then breathing in its sharp aroma before he said, 'You'd have made a fine teacher, Eppie. I always knew it, and I never made a secret of it. But you had to choose your own way in life, lass, and besides . . .' he turned and gave his younger daughter the slightly mischievous grin that always made him look years younger than he was '. . . our Marion was so against the idea of you giving up the classroom that she said more than enough for the three of us at the time. You'd enough opposition from her without your mother and I chiming in as well. In any case, I know you, Eppie – opposition just strengthens your mind. If we'd all gone on at you, you'd have proposed marriage to every eligible fisherman on the Moray coast just to spite us.'

'I only wanted the one and I'll never regret marrying him, even though we only had a short time together.'

'How can anyone regret it, lassie, when the two of you brought Charlotte into our lives?'

'I'm not sure that Mr Geddes is as wise as you are. And even if he did agree to let Duncan go his own way, old Mrs Geddes might well be against it. Duncan's own mother was daughter to a physician, and seemingly she'd her heart set on him following his grandfather.'

'Poor laddie, to have to carry such responsibility on his shoulders. Still, it'll work itself out,' Peter assured his daughter. 'Life always does, though sometimes it takes a few strange turns along the way.'

As the date of Duncan's departure approached he spent more time away from the house. When he was in his father's presence, the two of them continued to be formally polite to each other, and it seemed to Eppie that they were not going to make up their differences before the boy left for Aberdeen.

Unfortunately, Duncan's grandmother had also become aware of the tension, and her sharp mind must have worked out what was amiss, for one day Eppie overheard the woman telling Duncan how proud she would be of him when he was a fine successful physician, with his own grand house and a bonny carriage for his wife to ride in.

'I've not given much thought to taking a wife, Grandmother,' the boy said with a laugh in his voice.

'Not yet, of course, for you'll have years of study to get through first. But when you're finished with all that . . .'

'Grandmother, I don't see myself as a physician. It's my father's idea entirely,' Duncan said in a rush of words, 'not my wish at all. Could you not . . .'

'You'll make a grand physician,' Helen said swiftly, raising her own voice to drown his out. 'And I'll be proud of you, so proud of you.'

'Yes, Grandmother,' he said, and the resigned, hopeless way he said it wrenched at Eppie's heart.

During the week before he left she was kept busy

washing and ironing all his clothes, and making sure that everything was ready. She baked too, making extra supplies of his favourite pancakes and scones so that he could take them with him to Aberdeen. She would have happily packed his box for him, but he refused her help.

'I like to do it for myself, then I know where everything is,' he insisted.

The day before he was due to leave she took the last armful of carefully ironed and folded linen to his room and put it on his bed. The trunk he was packing stood in one corner, and one of the shirts he wore while at home had been thrown casually across a chair. She picked it up and went to hang it in his large wardrobe. Opening the door, she stared in surprise at the interior, where all the shirts she had prepared for Aberdeen still hung, cheek by jowl with his jackets and trousers and waistcoats.

Puzzled, Eppie went to the chest of drawers only find that it too was still full of the clothes prepared for Duncan's return to school; then she moved over to the trunk in the corner of the room. She raised the lid and was staring down at the pile of books and the few neatly packed clothes inside when Duncan asked from the doorway, 'What are you doing?'

She jumped, feeling the heat rush to her face as she turned to face him. 'I – I was putting the ironing away when I saw that your good school clothes are still in the wardrobe. And in the chest of drawers too.' Then, as he said nothing, she opened the lid of the trunk. 'You've packed old clothes in here – clothes you don't need at school.'

He closed the door and came into the room. 'You've no right to go snooping through my possessions!' His voice was low and tight with anger, and his normally friendly face had darkened. His brows were drawn together and in that moment Eppie saw him as he would look when fully grown to manhood. He was the image of his father and, like his father, would not suffer fools gladly.

Her mouth had gone dry, and when she swallowed in an attempt to relieve it, the gulping sound she made was ridiculously loud. 'You're right, I shouldn't have looked in the trunk,' she said, almost in a whisper. 'But I did, and the harm's done now. Why are you packing the wrong clothes?'

'That's my business.' He opened the door and moved to one side of it in a clear, unspoken command for her to leave the room. But when she started to obey he closed the door before she had time to walk round the narrow bed.

'You'll not speak to my father, or my grandmother, of what you've seen.'

It was meant as an order, she knew that, but halfway through the sentence his voice wavered, and it ended up as a question – almost a plea.

'Duncan, I work for your father. I can't keep secrets from him, you must see that.'

'You might if you knew why it had to be a secret. Sit down, Eppie – please,' he added as he closed the door.

As she sank on to the edge of the bed he drew up the only chair in the room, a wooden kitchen chair that stood against the table he used as a desk for studying, and placed it so that when he sat down they were facing each other, their knees almost touching.

'You must know that my father and I have been having our differences this summer. He wants me to be a physician like my grandfather, but I've no heart for it. I want to work in the marble quarry and learn to manage it and make it prosper. There are many improvements in quarrying now,' he rushed on, his eyes beginning to glow. 'Improvements that would help us to get more benefit from the quarry without having to increase manpower. And less dangerous ways too – if he would just let me go to college to learn about these things I could do so much! But he can't see past doing what my mother wanted. I was only a baby in swaddling clothes when they planned my whole future, Eppie. Surely that can't be fair!'

'He's your father,' she tried to argue. 'He has the right.'

'He might have sired me, but that doesn't mean that he owns me. I'm a person, Eppie – flesh and blood and with a brain in my noddle.' He thumped a frustrated fist against his temple. 'Don't *I* have any rights?' Then as she stared at him, trying to find the right words, 'Look at you – your father's a schoolteacher, isn't he? And your sister too. Didn't he want the same for you?'

'Aye, but . . .'

'But you married a fisherman. I mind you telling me about it. Did your father try to stop you?'

'No, he didn't.'

'Then you're fortunate, Eppie Watt, and I wish to God I had a father like yours. But even if I had,' Duncan said, his voice bitter again, 'even if he were willing to let me have some say in my future, my grandmother would talk him out of it. She doesn't mind living in this fine house and spending the money the quarry and his other businesses bring in, but she'd not want to see me working the marble myself. No matter how hard I might study geology and engineering, she'd still see it as demeaning work for her grandson! And he'd listen to her, for he always does. And that's another thing, Eppie. I don't want to be hag-ridden the way he is.'

'Duncan!'

'Don't make that face at me – it's the truth and you know it. He's been raised to think that he has a duty toward her and he can't break free of it, much as he'd like to. She spoiled me when I was a bairn, but I was fortunate to be a boy, so I was sent off to school where I had the spoiling knocked out of me. Now she's doing the same to Lydia. The poor quine's going to grow up fit for nothing but marriage to a man soft enough to let her have her own way for the rest of her life. Well,' he ended savagely, getting up and pacing about the room, 'not me. I'm going to break free, Eppie.'

'What d'ye mean?'

'I'm going to Glasgow, to Lydia's uncle.'

'Does he know this? Is he plotting with you behind your own father's back?'

'He knows nothing – it was all my own idea. Mr Ramsay owns several quarries, and I'm hoping that he'll agree to take me on so that I can earn my way and learn how to be a quarryman. I'm not asking to be sent to college or the university – I can learn just as well, mebbe a sight better, by working my way up.'

'You're running away?'

'I suppose I am.'

'But how will you get to Glasgow?'

'I'll leave from Aberdeen. I've got some money, mebbe enough to get me there. And I've got a good Scots tongue in my head – I'll find ways and means. I've packed all my school books so that I can sell them to raise money if I need to, and all my books on quarrying and geology too, though I'd never sell *them*.'

'Lydia's uncle might send you back to Aberdeen.'

'I'll take my chance,' Duncan said grimly. 'If he does, I'll just run away again. Mebbe to sea the next time – I could work my passage to the Americas; they have a lot of quarries there and I could learn as well there as in Scotland, mebbe better. But you have to hold your tongue, Eppie, at least until I get well away.'

'If your father ever found out that I knew, and said nothing, I'd be put out of the house.'

'How could he find out? I swear to you that I'll never tell him. We must trust each other, Eppie – God knows I've nobody else to trust!'

'He'll go out of his mind with worry when he discovers that you've not gone back to the school. And your grandmother too . . .'

'I'll write to him as soon as I get to Glasgow, I promise. Just let me get away without them knowing,' he begged.

There was a long silence, during which Eppie's mind circled wildly, seeking a way out of the dilemma she had been forced into. Duncan had returned to his chair and now he watched her closely, his brown eyes anxious.

'If you promise to write to your father as soon as you reach Glasgow . . .' she said at last, and he jumped to his feet, plucking her from the bed and into a hug that almost bruised her ribs.

'Thank you, Eppie, and bless you!' he said, and planted a hearty kiss on her cheek.

When she returned to her kitchen five minutes later it was with a heavy heart. Mr Geddes trusted her. She could not let Duncan down, but the knowledge that she had betrayed his father's trust was a burden she could scarcely cope with.

8

The only person Eppie could spill out her worries to was Barbary. She took time, the next day, to visit her friend while she was shopping.

'There's one thing for certain – ye cannae tell on the loon,' her friend said decisively. 'I've seen him around the farlins, and he's a pleasant lad, with no badness in him. Tae tell ye the truth, Eppie, if I'd a grandmother like that old Mrs Geddes, I'd want tae run away mysel'. And his father's a cold man too.'

'Mr Geddes is a good, kind employer,' Eppie hurried to defend him, 'it's just that he's too busy tae think much about his children.'

'He should, instead of leavin' it tae that mother of his,' Barbary said firmly. 'They're only given tae us for a wee while, then they grow up and go off – just as that lad is. We need tae make the most o' them while we have them.'

'Aye,' Eppie agreed, glancing down at three-month-old Martha, who was slumbering in her arms. The back door was open and George sat just outside, happily sorting out buttons from a large tin box.

Sunlight splashed through the doorway and window, lighting up a great fistful of large, bright-red paper poppies jammed into a jug and placed on the broad stone sill. Every spring the travelling folk came round the area selling clothes pegs, lucky heather and paper poppies; Eppie's mother had always bought some to brighten the house after the long, dark winter, and she had done the same when she'd had her own home. She had also bought poppies during her first spring in the Geddes house, and had arranged them carefully in a pretty vase and put them in the family parlour – only to have them ridiculed and then thrown out by Helen Geddes.

Suddenly she felt homesick for the small cottage where she had lived with Murdo and his mother and little Charlotte.

On the day of his departure Duncan came to the kitchen to say goodbye to Eppie.

'Are you still determined?' she asked, low-voiced.

'I've never been more determined. I'm standing on the threshold of the rest of my life, and I'm happy, Eppie.' He looked happy – surprisingly happy for someone returning to school. When she pointed this out he grinned at her before putting on a mock-sad face.

'What would I do without you?'

'What will your father and Lydia do without you?' she parried, and for a moment the amusement was gone and his sadness was genuine.

'I'll be home again – next year, probably, once the fuss has died down. In the meantime, have a last look at me as a young gentleman. The next time you see me I'll be a working man.' The grin returned, and he circled slowly around, arms held out so that she could admire his fashionably short twill jacket and slightly flared trousers, which were becoming more popular than the formal fashion for narrow trousers strapped beneath the feet. A blue cravat was tucked into the collar of his pale grey shirt.

A lump suddenly formed in Eppie's throat and her eyes stung. She hadn't known this lad for long but she was already fond of him. 'I made this for you, for the journey.' She held out a packet and then, as he took it, she dipped into her apron's deep pocket. 'And take this as well.'

He opened the purse, looked inside, then shook his head and tried to hand it back to her. 'No, Eppie. I told you that I had some money saved. I'll not take your earnings.'

'Aye you will.'

'You've got a wee lass to think of,' he insisted.

'She doesn't have to go without. Take it, Duncan, then I'll not have to lie awake imagining you sleeping under a hedge because you've not got the price of a bed for the night.'

He hesitated, then stowed the purse away in his pocket. 'You'll get it back,' he promised, 'with more to keep it company.' Then, holding his hand out, 'Wish me good fortune, Eppie.'

'You know I'll always wish you that. Goodbye, Duncan.' She gave him her hand and to her astonishment and embarrassment he lifted it to his lips.

'What's your wee girl's name?' he asked as he released her fingers.

'Charlotte.'

'Charlotte.' He savoured the name, rolling it around his mouth. 'A bonny name – and she's fortunate to have you for a mother,' he said, and then he was gone, and

Eppie was left to scrub back the tears that threatened to overflow.

The house was like a mausoleum without Duncan in it. Lydia wept inconsolably for two days and her grandmother was even more irritable and waspish than usual. Alexander Geddes spent most of his time out on business, and when he was at home he was more likely to be found in his study than anywhere else.

For her part, Eppie kept to her kitchen as much as possible, waiting for the storm that she knew would erupt when her employer discovered that his son was not, as he thought, back at his studies in Aberdeen.

It took some time, for Geddes went off to Edinburgh on business for the best part of two weeks, and it was not until he returned and began to deal with the post that had gathered during his absence that he discovered that Duncan had absconded.

The first Eppie knew of it was a full-throated roar of 'Mother!' from above. She was baking at the time, and she jumped and dropped the roller on to the newly floured board. A puff of white flour rose up to cover her blouse while the roller itself hit the ball of dough she had been flattening and ran along the table before dropping off over the edge. Eppie clapped her hands to her face, then hurried noiselessly from the kitchen and into the corridor. She stood, trembling, at the foot of the stairs leading to the doorway to the upper hall; there was no need to go any further for Alexander Geddes's voice was loud enough to be heard all over the house.

'Mother!' he roared again, and Eppie calculated that he was standing just outside the library door, which was not far from the kitchen stairs.

'I'm coming!' Helen screeched in return, then her voice

grew louder as she came down the stairs from her room. 'God save us Alexander, do you have to make such a noise? Is the house on fire?'

'Have you heard from Duncan?'

'Not since he went back to school, but I wasn't expecting to hear from him. He's never been one to write letters, even to his grandmother . . .' Helen started to complain.

'Well, he's written to me, and you'll not believe where he is!'

'In Aberdeen, surely.'

Alexander made a sound that was half-bark, half-laugh. 'You think so?' he began, then Lydia's piping voice suddenly cut in.

'What's wrong? Has something happened to Duncan?' she demanded to know, while in the background Eppie could just make out a questioning murmur from the little girl's governess.

'There's nothing wrong with Duncan,' Alexander Geddes said curtly. 'Miss Galbraith, kindly take Lydia back to her lessons. Mother—'

The door to the small sitting room closed, and a moment later, the door of the study also closed. Now there was nothing to hear – not even the murmur of voices.

Eppie returned to her work, her hands shaking.

That afternoon Alexander Geddes packed the bag he had only just unpacked, and went off on another business trip.

During his stay in Edinburgh his mother had insisted on having the entire house scrubbed, polished and cleaned from top to bottom; Eppie, with help from Sarah and Chrissie, was kept hard at work from the time she rose early in the morning until she collapsed thankfully into her bed late at night.

On several occasions she had had difficulty in preventing Sarah and Chrissie from throwing their aprons off and walking out. 'Who does that old woman think she is?' Chrissie had asked furiously. 'My mither minds when Helen Geddes went tae the school wi' her and lived in a wee hoosie just the same as everybody else. Tae hear the airs and graces she puts on ye'd think she'd been born tae money, when the truth is that she's no' any better nor me!'

'I'd as soon go and work in the rope factory,' Sarah agreed. 'At least we'd be among our own sort, and we'd no' have tae put up with the cheek that woman gives us.'

'It'll not be for long,' Eppie had pleaded, and although they grumbled they had stayed by her side until the work was done. Even when the two women had returned, thankfully, to devoting just one day a week to the Geddes house, Eppie was forever having to stop what she was doing to dust a picture frame or sweep up a few cinders from a hearth at Mrs Geddes's bidding. She would have given anything to walk out of the place herself, but instead she nipped her lower lip between her teeth in order to control her rising anger and meekly did as she was told, praying as she did that Mr Geddes would come home soon.

When he did get back his arrival was unannounced and unexpected. Eppie was shaking the dust out of the mats at the back door and revelling in the mellow sunshine; when she went back into the dim passageway the sun still dazzled her eyes and she could see nothing. As a result, she jumped when a voice said, 'Good morning, Eppie.'

'Who . . . ?' She blinked, and as her eyes became

accustomed to the interior she saw her employer standing before her. 'Ye're back, Mr Geddes.'

'Aye, it would seem so,' he agreed with tired irony. 'Unless I'm a ghost. Is my mother in?'

'She's gone into the town, sir.'

'And my daughter?'

'Miss Galbraith has the toothache, so Mrs Geddes took Lydia with her, since it's such a pleasant day.'

'Good. I've been travelling all night and I'd appreciate the chance to rest. And have a wash,' he added. His face was drawn and lined and his clothing dusty. 'Can you bring some hot water to my room? No . . .' he went into the kitchen '. . . just pour it into a jug and I'll take it up myself.'

She hurried to obey. 'You'll be hungry – I'll set some food out in the dining room.'

'Don't bother yourself, I'll have it in here. Some broth, and cheese and bread would do. But first, a wash and a change of clothes.' He was still carrying the bag he had taken with him, and now he picked up the ewer of hot water with his free hand and went out.

The food was ready when he returned. 'I'll just go and tidy the parlour,' Eppie said, but he stopped her as she was about to hurry out.

'Sit down and keep me company.'

'I'd best get on, sir. Mrs Geddes . . .'

'Mrs Geddes doesn't pay your wages, and I'm in the mood for company.' He tore a thick slice of bread apart and dipped it into the broth, then stuffed it in his mouth. 'Have some tea,' he mumbled through it.

She sipped at the tea as he ate hungrily. When he had emptied the soup bowl he spread two slices of bread with butter, then sandwiched a wedge of cheese between them while Eppie poured his tea.

'I've missed your cooking,' he said, leaning back in his chair with a contented sigh. 'Tell me, how are those bees of yours?'

'Settlin' in well, sir. You've a good garden for bees.'

'I look forward to enjoying their honey. Are you happy here, Eppie?'

The question was unexpected, and she stammered slightly as she said, 'Aye, s-sir.'

'It must be hard for you to be away from your child. A daughter, isn't it?'

'Charlotte.'

'Much the same age as my own daughter, I believe. You should bring her to play with Lydia,' he went on as she nodded.

'I don't think Mrs Geddes would approve, sir.'

'I suppose she wouldn't,' he agreed, a flicker of annoyance crossing his face. 'Tell me, Eppie, do you worry about your daughter when you're not with her?'

'I think of her, sir, but I've no need to worry for I know she's in safe hands.'

Alexander Geddes picked up the mug she had set before him and took a deep draught of hot tea. 'Ah yes, with your family in Fordyce,' he said. 'Did you not tell me that your father is a school teacher?'

'Yes, sir, and my sister too.'

He raised an eyebrow. 'Did you have no wish to go into the same profession yourself?'

'I'm not as clever as my sister, and in any case, I wanted to marry.'

'And now, like me, you're alone. Fondness for other folk can be a curse at times,' he said, 'especially when they take our hearts and then leave us too soon. It must be a blessing to go through life without knowing that loss.'

For a moment, Eppie thought of Marion, who had never loved and never lost and who lived her life on her own terms. For a moment, she almost agreed with the man sitting opposite, then she heard herself saying, 'It's not a blessing I'd have wanted, sir. If I'd not met Murdo Watt my Charlotte would never have been born, and I'd not deny her life, or deny myself the blessing of knowing her.'

For a moment he stared at her, startled, then said bitterly, 'You may find out for yourself one day that children can bring sorrows as well as blessings.'

'I may, sir, but that's a chance that I must take.'

He paused, eyeing her closely as though wondering if she could be trusted, then he leaned forwards and was about to speak when they heard the front door open and the sound of Lydia's feet racing along the hall floor overhead.

'Damn!' Alexander Geddes said beneath his breath, then went to meet his family.

Helen Geddes usually insisted on putting her granddaughter to bed at night, but that night it fell to Eppie. Lydia, unsettled by the faint but unmistakable air of tension that hung around the house, took some time to settle, insisting that she could not sleep without a certain doll, then changing her mind as soon as Eppie brought it to her and wanting another doll instead. Then she demanded a story, but rejected all the books lined up on the shelf in her room. Finally, in desperation, Eppie discarded the books and started on a story that she made up as she went along. Lydia, who had been bouncing around the bed and showing no signs of going to sleep, began to listen, wide-eyed, and then as the tale wound on, with more and more characters coming into it, her lids began to droop. Not long after that she was fast asleep and Eppie was free at last to hurry downstairs to serve the evening meal, which had been left to simmer on the kitchen range.

As she went quietly down the stairs she could hear voices from the study, where Alexander Geddes and his mother were closeted. Helen Geddes's sharp voice came to her as she reached the final step. 'But you should have brought him back here, where he belongs!'

Alexander's voice was low, his reply little more than a mumble, and his mother snapped, 'Nonsense, man! When my uncle ran away to London to become a soldier my grandfather went after him on horseback and made him walk every step of the way home at his stirrup. That cured him of running away, I can tell you! It's not as if the quarry has anything to do with him – Lydia's the one who will benefit from it.'

Again, the reply was too low for Eppie to catch it.

'You're too soft on that lad, always have been.'

For the first time, Alexander Geddes raised his voice. 'And you, Mother, have ruined him.'

'*I'm* not the one who's allowing him to do as he wishes instead of getting on with his studies. I've a good mind to go to Glasgow myself to fetch him back.'

'You'll do no such thing!' Alexander's voice was like the crack of a whip, and Eppie, creeping silently past the door, shivered at the cold anger in it. 'He's made his mind up and I'll have no more to do with him.'

'But he's your son!'

'If he wants to come back to beg my forgiveness he will have it, but the move must come from him. And I'll not have you interfering, Mother, so take heed of what I'm telling you!'

The last thing that Eppie heard before she hurried

through the door leading to her own part of the house, was Helen's gasp of outrage. And when she served supper to the two of them in the dining room half an hour later they sat at either end of the table, backs ramrod straight, never once looking at each other or speaking to each other.

When they had left the room, Helen Geddes going her own bedroom and her son to the library, Eppie cleared the table, tutting over the scarcely touched food, then set it again, this time in readiness for the morning meal.

She left a covered bowl of oatmeal steeping in the kitchen, made sure that all was in readiness for the morning, then went upstairs to tap timidly on the library door.

'Aye, what is it?'

She slipped into the room, staying close by the door. 'Is there anythin' else I can bring you, Mr Geddes?'

He was sitting at his desk, a decanter and glass by his hand. 'No, nothing. Go to bed, Eppie.'

'Aye, sir,' she said, and retreated.

9

Portsoy, February 1870

Someone was thumping on the side door with a fist, or possibly, given the noise, a lump of wood. Eppie, drowsing in her chair by the fire, awoke with a start. Her knitting wires had slipped from her hands to her lap, and as she hurried to the door they fell to the floor, trailing blue wool.

A man she knew as one of the coopers stood outside, rain plastering his hair to his skull while the wind that had been gathering strength all day tugged at the hem of his jacket.

'Is Mr Geddes at home?'

'Aye, but I think he's gone to his bed.'

'Then he'll have tae get out of it quick, for he's needed at the harbour.'

'What's wrong?' But she knew already, for she could hear the slap of swift feet on the pavement. Looking beyond the caller she could see dark shapes hurrying by, all heading towards the harbour. It could only mean one thing.

'One of the boats . . . ?'

All afternoon the weather had grown worse. Most of the boats had returned early from the fishing grounds;

any stragglers would have to cope not only with the rising seas and the darkness as they approached the harbour, but also the hungry rocks, hidden beneath the tossing waves.

'It's no' a wreck – at least, no' as far as we can tell. It's the *Grace-Ellen*,' the man said. 'The other boats are safe in harbour but she's no' come in yet. Ye'd best tell Mr Geddes, since it's one o' his vessels.'

He turned and disappeared into the darkness, and Eppie, now wide awake, and chilled by more than the cold damp air that had swirled into the house, closed the door and hurried upstairs. The *Grace-Ellen*, missing. The boat that Barbary's husband, Tolly McGeoch, crewed on. Missing . . .

She glanced into the library and finding it empty, carried on upstairs to the bedrooms, where she tapped gently on Alexander Geddes's door, not wanting to waken Lydia or her grandmother.

The door opened almost immediately. She could tell by the tousled state of her employer's dark hair that he had been in bed, but he was wearing a shirt and trousers and pushing one arm into his jacket sleeve. 'I heard the noise of the folk outside.' Most of the houses in a fishing community turned windowless walls to the sea for added protection against the worst of the weather, but the Geddes house had two windows facing the harbour; the lower one belonged to the library, the upper window to his bedroom. 'What's amiss?' he wanted to know now, thrusting his arm into the other sleeve of his jacket.

'The *Grace-Ellen*, sir. She's not come in yet and it seems that nobody knows where she is. You're wanted down at the harbour.'

He was shrugging the jacket into place over his shoulders when his mother's door opened and she came on to the landing, her slender figure clothed from top to toe in a woollen robe and her hair hidden beneath a white cap. 'What's happening?' Her eyes were puffy with sleep.

'One of the fishing boats has failed to come home.'

'And what can you do about it at this time of night?' Then, alarm sharpening her voice, Helen Geddes said, 'You're not going out on one of the wee boats to look for them in this weather, are you? Alexander, I forbid it!'

'Nobody's going out on the water, Mother. From what Eppie says the vessel could be anywhere. It doesn't seem as if she's foundered just outside the harbour walls. But I must find out what's going on. Get back to your bed, Mother; there's nothing you can do.'

'If you'd any sense, you'd go back to your own bed.'

Alexander was already on his way down the stairs. 'Not while there's a boat out there mebbe needing help.' He threw the words back over his shoulder in an exasperated whisper. 'Go back to bed before you wake Lydia!'

Muttering to herself, the woman did as she was advised while her son, followed by Eppie, continued on down the stairs and then down the back stairs to the side door.

'You might as well go to your own bed, Eppie,' he said as he lifted the latch. 'There's nothing you can do either.' The wind swirled in as he opened the door, bringing with it a smattering of rain. Eppie's apron immediately blew up over her face and when she had pulled it down the door frame held nothing but black night.

For the second time she pushed the sturdy timber door shut against the elements. The kitchen was safe and warm, but its comfort only made her more aware of the missing boat and its crew, somewhere out on the storm-tossed waves. Her mind raced over the dangers facing them. Perhaps a heavy sea had broached them while the hatch covers were off, and the weight of tons of water crashing into the very centre of the vessel had caused it to go down like a stone. Perhaps the wind had torn the big red dipping lugsail away; without it, she knew, they could be drifting, helpless. Or the mast may have snapped off . . . Or they had been blown by the gale on to a submerged rock and holed. There were so many dangers . . .

The fishing boats were built to cope with all that the sea and the weather could do to them and the crews were all experienced, but even so, every time men up and down the coast, or even all over the world, raised sail and took their boats to sea they were gambling with their very lives. Every fisherman's wife knew that, but they also knew that their menfolk knew no other way of earning a living, and so the gamble had to be made, time after time.

Eppie thought of Barbary, and decided that she could not stay indoors, safe and sound while Tolly McGeoch and the others aboard the *Grace-Ellen* were missing. She fetched her warm cloak and pulled it closely about her shoulders, pulling the hood over her head before letting herself out into the wild night.

She went first to the cottage; as she had half-expected, there was nobody there. The door had not been latched properly and now it swung creakingly with every gust of wind. Eppie secured it before hurrying down to the harbour.

It was thronged with folk; women and men huddled in segregated groups, many of the women carrying infants and with older children, half asleep and bewildered, catching the air of fear from their elders but not knowing why they were afraid, clinging to their wet skirts. Men and women alike spoke, if they spoke at all, in low murmurs, their heads close together to give the gale less chance to snatch the words from their lips and carry them in unheard fragments into the dark. In the light from the oil lamps that many of the men carried their sombre faces looked waxy and almost unreal. Rain lanced down, falling faster and heavier than it had been when Eppie first arrived from the Geddes house.

Normally most of these men would still have been out on the water, their nets overboard and filling with the 'silver darlings' – the herring that swam in huge shoals in the calm beneath churning, foaming waves. But the advent of the storm had caused the fishermen to bring their nets in before they were full in order to raise sail and hasten back to the shelter of their harbours.

It would be a poor catch, and the farlins would only be half-full, if that, when morning's light finally arrived. As she searched for Barbary, Eppie could hear above the keening of the wind the boats in harbour grating against each other. Falling rain gleamed like silver and gold threads in the lamplight, which gave glimpses of swaying masts and made the men's wet oilskin coats and hats gleam like the scales of the fish they sought year in and year out.

'What happened?' Eppie thrust herself into one of the huddled groups of women.

'It's the *Grace-Ellen*,' someone told her. 'She's never come in.' While another added, 'The *Homefarin'* was fishin' alongside her when they had tae bring in the nets. My man's wi' her. He says that when the first squall came up they lost sight o' the *Grace-Ellen*, but they'd seen her ahead o' them before that, and thought she was well on her way home. But when they got here there was no sign o' her. They've gone back oot tae look for her,' she added, her face tight with the terror she felt for her own man's safety.

'Barbary McGeoch – has anyone seen her?'

'She's here somewhere, I saw her a wee while since,' someone said vaguely.

Eppie struggled on, with the wind continually trying to pull the hood from her head. It took some time to find Barbary, who was standing against a warehouse wall, the rain streaming over her black hair and down her face. Her two oldest children, five-year-old George, who had been a babe in arms when Eppie first went to work for Alexander Geddes, and Martha, close to her fourth birthday, clung to her legs while the baby, Thomas, whimpered in her arms.

'Barbary?' Eppie touched her friend's arm; it felt as cold as marble. There was no response. 'Barbary!' she said again, raising her voice, and this time the other woman turned to look at her.

'His boat's no' come in yet, Eppie.' Her voice was flat.

'I know. It'll come soon. Barbary, you cannae stay out in this weather. The bairns are cold, and wet. We'll take them home, eh?'

'Aye, m'quine, you take your bairns home, awa' frae this place.' Agnes McBrayne, an elderly woman who lived opposite Barbary's cottage with her widowed daughter and grandchildren, stepped forwards from the huddle of shadowy figures close by. 'You go wi' Eppie, and get the wee ones intae shelter.'

'I have tae be here when Tolly comes back,' Barbary said in the same flat, toneless voice. 'He'll be lookin' for me as the boat comes intae the harbour.'

Agnes and Eppie looked at each other helplessly, worried for Barbary, the three children, and the bairn she was expecting in the summer. 'He'd no' want ye tae make the bairns ill, though,' Agnes persisted, while Eppie held out her arms.

'Give the wee one tae me, Barbary, he's too heavy for you. We'll take the three of them home. They can wait there for their daddy.'

For a moment it seemed that Barbary was going to cling on to the baby, then her grip on him relaxed and Eppie was able to take him.

'I cannae leave till the boat gets back,' Barbary insisted.

'Then I'll stay wi' ye and we'll let Eppie take the bairns home,' Agnes suggested. 'Go on, Eppie, an' we'll follow ye in a wee while. Eh, Barbary?'

'As soon as Tolly comes intae harbour,' the woman agreed as Eppie, clutching Thomas close in an effort to warm him with the heat of her body, persuaded the other two to let go of their mother and go with her.

When they reached the cottage and she lit the lamp in the kitchen she saw that all three of the children were blue with cold. As usual in every cottage, the kettle was steaming gently on the range, and Eppie, working as fast as she could, stripped and bathed them before drying them vigorously with a rough towel.

Mute with exhaustion and bewilderment, they submitted without protest, and after dressing them in dry clothes she sat the two oldest down beside the warmth of the range and laid the baby in his crib so that she could heat up a pan of milk. Breaking bread into bowls, she poured the warmed milk over it, then added generous spoonfuls of sugar.

One by one the children fell asleep before they had finished eating; George, determined to stay awake until his mam and da came home, held out the longest before suddenly collapsing into his half-empty bowl. If Eppie had not been there to lift his face clear and wipe the milk from it, he might have drowned. She tucked George and Martha into the truckle bed that, by day, was pushed under the wall bed. Then she heated more water and washed the bowls they had used.

Barbary and Agnes were still not back from the harbour. Eppie longed to go back out into the night again to look for them, but the children could not be left on their own, so after emptying the basin she sat down to wait as patiently as she could. The wind moaned around the house walls and the rain beat against the windows. The fire spat and crackled now and again in response to rainwater seeking entrance by way of the chimney, and once or twice one of the children coughed or whimpered or thrashed restlessly for a moment, though thankfully without wakening.

Another hour crawled by before Barbary arrived home, leaning heavily on Agnes's arm.

'There's no news comin' tonight, an' if the *Homefarin'* gets back afore the mornin' someone'll come tae tell Barbary,' the older woman said. 'So I've persuaded her tae come home tae her bairns.'

Barbary checked all three of her children carefully, as though finding it hare to believe that they were safe, then she sat down by the fire, staring vacantly into its red glow, oblivious to the water dripping from her clothes and her hair and her chin to form a puddle on the floor. She looked, Eppie thought with an inward shiver, as though she herself had been drowned and returned from the sea.

She was deaf to suggestions that she might be more comfortable if she were to change into dry clothing, and finally Eppie and Agnes had to strip, dry and dress her. She lifted her arms when told to, submitting to being turned this way and that and to having her damp hair brushed out and tied back with a piece of string, without a murmur. At one point, looking into her friend's face, Eppie realised that Barbary's beautiful dark eyes, with their unusual upward tilt at the outer corners, were looking at her without seeing her. It was as though Barbary's mind and her body had come adrift from each other. Her body was in Portsoy, being tended to by her friends, but her mind was far away.

Eppie, having lost her own man to the deep, knew well enough that inside her head Barbary was searching for Tolly, calling across the water to him in the hope that she could unite in his struggle against whatever was keeping him from reaching the shore, and home, and her empty, hungry arms.

She refused to lie down on her bed, so they settled her back in the chair. Agnes made tea, and they wrapped Barbary's long slender fingers around the cup and coaxed her through the process of lifting it to her lips and taking little sips of the hot, sweet liquid.

By then, half the night had gone by. 'I'll have to go,' Eppie murmured. 'Mr Geddes'll be expectin' me tae have the breakfast ready in the mornin'.' She looked hopefully at Agnes. 'Could you . . . ?'

'I'll sit wi' her till the mornin', for I'm no' needed at hame. Ye'd mebbe knock on the door an' tell my Lizzie where I am, m'quine.'

'I will, and I'll be back as soon as I can in the morning,' Eppie promised, then went out into the night.

The wind had abated and the rain too, had eased off. She could hear voices from the harbour, and as she reached the side door to the Geddes house she could see that there were still folk crowded there, staring out into the darkness. There was nothing they could do, but as happened when tragedy hit any community that depended on the sea they needed to keep vigil until, one way or another, the crisis was over.

She went into the house quietly, wondering if her

employer was still at the harbour with the others, or had come home before her. Perhaps he was looking for her to make food, or tea. But he was in the kitchen, sitting at the table, a glass in his hand and a bottle close by.

'Mr Geddes! I was just seein' tae Barbary McGeoch. Her man's on the *Grace-Ellen*. I didnae realise you were lookin' for me. Can I make ye some tea?'

'I'd not mind some, as strong as you want to make it.' He looked bone-weary. 'It's a terrible thing, Eppie, when a boat goes missing – but you'd know that yourself.'

'Aye, sir.' She busied herself with the kettle. 'Is there any news?'

'None – and I doubt if there will be any until daylight. The *Homefaring* won't be back before then. We can only pray to God that they've found the other vessel.'

When the tea was put before him he drank it down swiftly although it was scalding hot. Then he emptied his glass before getting up from the table.

'I'm going back out. You get to your bed, Eppie,' he said, picking up his coat, which was still wet.

By the morning the storm had blown itself out and the sea drifted, quiet and innocent, beneath blue skies. The *Homefaring* returned with nothing to report. There had been no sighting or sign of the *Grace-Ellen*, not even a piece of driftwood. As the day dragged on, hopes that she had been crippled and taken shelter elsewhere along the coast began to fade.

It was not until the afternoon that the mystery of what had happened to the *Grace-Ellen* and her crew became clear. Word ran along the coast, eventually reaching Portsoy, that a cargo ship putting into Aberdeen that morning had reported a collision some thirty miles off Kinnaird Head on the previous night. No other boat had been sighted in the vicinity before the collision, and after it, thinking that they heard voices crying out in the darkness, the captain of the cargo boat had ordered it to be put about. But after remaining in the area for some time without receiving any replies to their shouts and whistles, they had continued on their way.

A swift check up and down the coast showed that the only boat missing was the *Grace-Ellen*, which had been fishing in the area earlier. It could only be assumed that the collision with the larger vessel had caused such damage to the fishing boat that it sank within minutes, giving the crew of eight little time to save themselves.

A collection was raised for the bereaved families, and Alexander Geddes pledged to pay them a small pension and to seek a Board of Trade inquiry into the worst disaster that Portsoy had ever known.

In the days and weeks after Tolly and his fellow crewmen were lost, Barbary retreated into a world of her own. She was still able to care for her children and to work at the farlins, but she had become a mere shadow of her former self, her once-glossy black hair lank and her dark eyes lifeless.

Agnes, the elderly neighbour who had brought her home on the night Tolly went missing, did all she could to help the young mother look after the children, and Eppie went to the cottage as often as she could. They both believed that eventually Barbary must accept what had happened, if only for the sake of her children, but time went on with no sign of this happening.

It seemed that bereavement had dealt Barbary McGeoch a blow so hard that somewhere inside her head, or her heart, of perhaps the very soul of her, she was injured beyond healing.

10

The basket on Eppie's arm had grown steadily heavier during her long walk. She paused at the square, taking a moment to set it down and ease her stiff shoulders.

'Aye, Eppie,' a woman passing by greeted her. And then, nodding at the laden basket, 'Ye'll have been visitin' hame?'

'My mither seems tae think that nobody can make jam or scones like herself, and my faither's certain that his bees make better honey than my own.'

'Well, they're Fordyce folk.' The woman's voice sharpened slightly while her smile tightened. 'Fordyce folk are always of the opinion that anythin' they do's better than anyone else.'

Eppie, used to such remarks about her home village, held her tongue and picked the basket up again before setting off down North High Street on the last leg of her journey.

Passing the double flight of steps that led up to the front door of the Geddes house, then rounding the corner into Shorehead, she reached the entrance to the kitchen quarters and was thankful when she was finally able to set her heavy basket on the table. She started to unpack it and then paused, head to one side as she heard a noise from overhead.

It came again – a high-pitched screech. Eppie's spirits, which had begun to rise at the thought of a cup of tea and a rest in the comfortable chair by the range, sank as she realised that once again, Lydia and her grandmother were at loggerheads.

She went out into the passageway and up the stairs leading to the upper hall. Now she could hear Lydia shouting from behind her bedroom door, which was slightly ajar, 'It's not fair, you hate to see me enjoying myself!'

'You are a selfish, spoiled girl and you can enjoy yourself when you have earned the right!' Helen Geddes's voice was clear and cold.

'I am not spoiled! You're so old that you've forgotten what it's like to be young like me,' Lydia retorted, and Eppie, realising that the two of them must be separated before things got out of hand, began to mount the next flight of stairs. 'That's why you're so mean to me,' she heard Lydia shout as she hurried upwards, 'it's because you hate being an old woman who—'

There was a sudden sound, as though someone had clapped their hands together loudly, and Lydia's voice was cut off in mid-sentence. Eppie, realising that there was no time for niceties, pushed the door wide open.

Lydia stood by the window, one hand to her face, while her grandmother stood in the middle of the room. The two figures were immobile, and as Eppie looked from one to the other, she saw the same look of shock mirrored in the girl's green eyes and the older woman's clear blue eyes. Then, as they became aware of Eppie standing in the doorway, Lydia's face crumpled and her eyes flooded with tears.

'She hit me!'

'I chastised you,' Helen Geddes snapped, 'because you were being disobedient, and you know very well that you deserved to be punished!'

'You hit me!' Lydia said again, her voice beginning to rise toward hysteria.

Eppie took a step forwards, frantically trying to think of a way to calm them both without drawing the older woman's sharp-tongued fury down on her own head. Then she spun round as Alexander Geddes's voice thundered, almost into her ear, 'What is going on here?'

Eppie immediately stepped aside, while Lydia's sobs redoubled at the sight of her father.

'She hit me!' she roared.

'I chastised her,' Helen Geddes repeated, the two bright red spots already over her cheekbones deepening. 'She was being impertinent, Alexander, and I will not have it. You don't want to see your daughter behaving like a common village girl, do you?'

'She slapped my face and it hurts,' Lydia threw herself at her father and wept into his chest. 'I was only dancing and she came in and hit me!'

'Dancing, you call it? She was crashing around the room, making a terrible noise.' Helen put a hand to her forehead. 'I was about to lie down because I have a headache. Is a little consideration too much to request?'

'I was only dancing! Father—'

'Be quiet, Lydia.' Alexander's voice was low, but firm enough to make both of his womenfolk fall silent for the moment. 'How can I find out the truth of this – this unseemly brawl if the two of you keep screeching at me?'

'The truth?' His mother almost choked the words out.

'You dare to doubt what I'm telling you?' Then, pointing at Eppie, 'And must we discuss our private family affairs in front of the servant?'

'For pity's sake!' he suddenly burst out, making them all jump. 'Can a man not even get peace in his own home now? Eppie, take Lydia down to the kitchen and bathe her face. Then, Lydia, you can return to your room and wait until I come to speak with you. Mother, we will continue this conversation in the library, if you please.'

There was no denying that Lydia's face had been slapped, and slapped quite hard. Her left cheek glowed fiery red, and finger marks could be seen clearly against the smooth skin. At first she refused to be attended to, insisting that her father should see the damage first, but when Eppie pointed out that he had already seen her, and that without swift treatment she might end up with swelling or even bruising, she gave in.

'It's not fair,' she stormed as Eppie sat her down on a stool and began to bathe her face with water and vinegar. 'I was only dancing to the music on my music box when Grandmother came in and started shouting at me to stop it at once.'

'And did you?'

'Why should I? I like dancing, you know that I do.'

'So you answered her back instead.'

'She deserved it,' Lydia said obstinately. 'She knows I like dancing, and she never lets me do anything now. She hates me!'

'Of course she doesn't hate you.'

'She does – she *does*,' the girl insisted. 'I can't please her no matter what I do!'

'Lydia, she's your grandmother and she loves you.'

'She used to love me. She used to give me sweets and

brush my hair and tell me stories and take me visiting with her, but now she only finds fault with me. She hates me and I hate her!'

'But she's your grandmother,' Eppie said again, and the girl twisted round, almost getting the vinegar-and-water sponge in her mouth.

'That doesn't mean that she can treat me cruelly, and I still have to be polite. I don't like her because she doesn't like me and she's mean to me, you know she is. At least I've got a reason,' she said, her eyes dark with hurt and anger.

When her face had been dried she slipped from the stool and went to examine her cheek in the wall mirror. 'Does it look all right?' she asked anxiously.

'Of course it does. You'd not know that anything had happened. Where are you going?' Eppie asked as the girl headed for the door.

'I'm going to tell the bees.'

'Your father told you to wait for him in your room – and that's where you're going, young lady,' Eppie said as the girl opened her mouth to argue. 'You don't want to make him any angrier that he is already, do you? You can talk to the bees later,' she added as Lydia's shoulder's slumped.

At the door, the girl turned. 'I wish Duncan would come home,' she said, her voice suddenly very young and forlorn. 'I miss him, Eppie.'

'I know you do, m'quine.' Without thinking, Eppie opened her arms – then held her breath. Sometimes, unused to affection, Lydia rejected her when she tried to hug her. But at other times, her need overcame her reticence. And this, to Eppie's relief, was one of those occasions. She came across the room and let her tense body relax into the housekeeper's arms.

'Do you think he'll come back soon?' she asked, her face buried in Eppie's shoulder.

'Only Duncan knows the answer to that question.'

'I pray every night that he'll come back,' Lydia confessed, 'but I sometimes wonder if I'll ever see him again in my whole life. Ever.'

'I'm sure you will. You're his wee sister, and he'd never desert you.'

She had said the wrong thing. Lydia immediately pulled herself free. Her eyes were filled with tears and her face flushed with the effort of holding them back. The pale imprint of her grandmother's hand stood out against the red.

'But he has,' she cried. 'He already has!' Then she turned and deliberately swept her arm across a corner of the table as she rushed to the door. Before going through it she turned and shouted, 'I don't pray for Grandmother any more!' Then with a whisk of her skirts she was gone.

Fortunately the only object that had been within her reach was a small, empty pot. It crashed noisily to the floor while its lid flew off and came to rest beneath the dresser.

Eppie rescued it, and the pot, and put them away, her heart aching for Lydia. She had now been housekeeper to Alexander Geddes for almost five years, and during recent years she had watched the once-close relationship between his mother and his daughter deteriorate steadily. When Lydia was small, her grandmother had treated her like a little doll, spoiling and indulging her, but as the girl grew older and began to form her own character Helen Geddes proved to be incapable of realising that her once-loved grand-daughter could not be an obedient, loving child for ever. She had begun to demand

Lydia's love, with no thought of earning it, and even used it as a form of punishment. On more than one occasion Eppie had had to watch helplessly, unable to intercede, as Lydia's attempts to hug her grandmother were spurned because of some small, often imagined, piece of bad behaviour.

'Why should I let you kiss me when you refused to play dominoes with me last Wednesday?' she would say in a hurt tone. 'You wanted to go and watch your precious bees instead of spending time with me. Why should I hug you now, just because you want me to?'

Lydia, hurt and confused, made to feel guilty over something she couldn't recall doing, had begun to withdraw from the woman for fear of yet another rebuff while, for her part, Helen interpreted the withdrawal as yet another indication of her grand-daughter's lack of respect and affection.

Comparing Lydia with her Charlotte, and Mrs Geddes with her own parents, Eppie had come to realise that she and her daughter were blessed. Annie and Peter McNaught had had the wisdom to give Charlotte room to grow and develop. She was able to speak her mind without fear when she felt the need, and even Marion, with her inclination to dominate, had had the sense to recognise that Charlotte was moving towards womanhood, and to guide, rather than dictate.

But Lydia had nobody to consider her needs. Alexander Geddes, wrapped up in his various business interests, was completely unaware of what was happening, and much as Eppie would have liked to warn him, she was a mere servant and so it was impossible for her to do so.

She had done her best to show affection towards the child; at first, when Eppie hugged her Lydia froze and tried to struggle free, but there were times when, knowing how hurt the girl felt, Eppie clung on, even though it was like hugging a stone pillar. And eventually, Lydia's rigid body would relax slightly, though she never returned the hug. Sometimes she tore herself free, but Eppie kept on trying for she could not bear to think of Lydia growing up to be as cold and uncaring towards others as her grandmother was.

At least once a month she made a point of walking to Sandend to visit Jean Gilbert, now enjoying a well-earned rest with her family. Apart from the fact that she enjoyed Jean's company, the former housekeeper was the only person she could talk to about the Geddes family, in the knowledge that not a word spoken between them would go any further. Only the week before, she had spoken of her growing concern for Lydia.

'I've always had a feelin' that somethin' of the sort might happen,' Jean confessed. 'Lydia was the bonniest wee bairn ye could ever imagine, the image o' her mither. It was easy tae spoil her, specially since the poor lass never had a mither o' her own. Mrs Geddes doted on her, but there were times when I wondered what the old lady would do once Lydia began tae find her own mind. That's when spoilin' starts tae turn, jist like curdled milk. Mebbe ye'll have tae take your courage in both hands and tell Mr Geddes what's goin' on, since he cannae seem tae see it for himsel'.'

'How can I say such things about his own mother tae his face? If Duncan was still comin' home for the holidays I'm sure he'd see what's happenin' and do something about it, but . . .' Eppie threw her hands out helplessly '. . . nob'dy seems tae care about him, either.'

'That's what happens when folk are rattlin' about in a big hoose. When ye live in wee places like this . . .' Jean indicated her own humble but comfortable surroundings '. . . ye're so close tae each other that if one sneezes the other wipes his nose. Ye have tae learn tae get on thegether. But wi' the Geddes's, ye've got him sittin' alone in his library an' his mother in her wee parlour – and the bairn on her own too, most of the time, in that nursery o' hers. All blood kin, yet they never seem tae spend time in each other's company. They might as well be complete strangers. If ye ask me, that woman was behind the door when the good lord was dolin' out kindness and understandin'. She used tae sweep about Portsoy with her nose in the air, with never a word or even a nod tae folk she grew up with. The only person she really cares about is hersel'. It's a wonder her eyes werenae put intae her head the wrong way round so's they could look in instead o' out.'

Alexander Geddes dined alone that night. Lydia, as was the custom, had eaten earlier and retired for the night, while Helen Geddes had decided to have her dinner in her room, on a tray. When Eppie took it in the woman was sitting reading her Bible. Without deigning to lift her eyes, she had said, 'Set it out on the table by the window. I'll ring the bell when I want you to collect it.'

When Eppie went to clear the table in the dining room she was surprised to see that her employer was still sitting at the head of the table, staring down at his empty plate.

'I'm sorry, sir, I thought you had finished.' She hesitated at the door not sure whether to go in or back out. Normally he retired to the library after his meal and had a glass of brandy while working at his desk.

'I am finished, if you want to clear the dishes away. I don't suppose you drink brandy, Eppie?'

'No, sir, I don't.'

'Have you ever tasted it?'

'No, sir. I'd a wee sip of ale given to me once by my father, but I didn't like it at all. I'm happy enough with tea.'

'Then perhaps you would be good enough to make some tea and bring it here.'

'Of course, sir,' she said, puzzled. In all her time as housekeeper to the man, she had rarely seen him drink tea after his dinner.

When she returned to the room with teapot, milk jug, sugar bowl and cup and saucer on a tray, he was still seated at the head of the table, but he must have visited the library during her absence, for the brandy decanter normally kept there was now on the dining table, and the fingers of one hand curved lightly round a full glass of the spirit.

'Your tea, sir.'

'No, Eppie, it's your tea. Sit down and pour yourself a cup.' He indicated a chair close to his own, adding when she began to protest, 'I want to talk to you about this afternoon.'

It felt strange to be sitting at the handsome table, looking down at her own reflection in the surface she polished regularly. It was even more strange to be pouring tea and sipping it carefully from one of the fine cups reserved for the Geddes family and the few guests who had come to the house in the five years she had worked there. And it was unnerving to be sitting, dressed in her usual blouse, skirt and apron, so close to her employer. At least, she thought, taking a sip of tea in an attempt to calm herself, her apron was clean on.

'About this afternoon,' Geddes was saying. 'What's your account of it?'

'I don't know much more than you do yourself, sir. I had just come back from Fordyce when I heard the voices upstairs. I went up to Lydia's room to see what was amiss, and you came in just after that.'

'My daughter's face looked quite sore.'

'It's fine, sir. The bathing took the heat out of it.'

He leaned forwards, holding her gaze with his own so intently that much as she would have liked to look away, she could not. 'These – disagreements – between my daughter and my mother are happening more regularly, are they not?'

'I wouldn't know about that, sir,' Eppie pleaded. He had been absent when most of the sudden rows erupted, and she had no wish to make things worse by telling him the truth.

'But I would,' he said firmly. 'Just because I'm not here it doesn't mean that I'm unaware of what's happening under my own roof.' Then, as she stared at him, puzzled, 'My mother makes sure of that, by reporting every happening and misdemeanour – be it real or imagined,' he added, 'that takes place. So you'll not be telling tales, if that's what you're thinking. They've already been told.'

He took a sip from his glass, set it down, and then got to his feet and paced to the window, then back again. 'The question is, what am I to do about it?'

'I wouldn't know, sir.'

'Your daughter's much the same age as mine, I believe.'

'Twelve years old, sir. Lydia's the elder by three months.'

'Then you understand girls of that age.'

'I don't know about that, since my parents have brought up my daughter. I've been working all her life.'

'Yes, of course; I'd forgotten. It must have been hard for you, being away from her during her growing years.'

'I know that she's been well cared for, and she's happy. And I see her every week.'

'Even so – does your daughter have tempers like mine does?'

'Not that I know of, sir.'

'And why would that be? Eppie,' he said, a slightly impatient note coming into his voice as she hesitated, 'I am trying to make sense of the ridiculous scene I came home to this afternoon. If I can't understand it then I can't cure it. I have had my mother's story, and my daughter's, and all the two of them do is blame each other. You are the only person who can tell me the truth, and perhaps advise me on this matter.'

'But I'm only your housekeeper, Mr—'

'For pity's sake, woman, will you stop trying to hide behind excuses and help me? D'you think I haven't noticed that there's something far wrong between my mother and Lydia? D'you think that I am not concerned for both of them – for all three of us? I swear that if I don't get this business settled once and for all I will send Lydia to a boarding school and then set off to see the world on one of the ships that come into our harbour to take cargo aboard!'

There was a short silence, during which she stared up at him, astonished; then he gave an abrupt bark of laughter and sat down again. 'Poor Eppie, your face speaks volumes. I'm sorry if I've startled or offended you, but you must see that I can't go on like this – none of us can. I need advice from a friend, and I would appreciate it if you could bring yourself to talk freely to me. I promise that not a word you say will be repeated, nor will it be held against you in the future. Now, drink your tea before it gets cold, and then explain to me exactly what is going on in this house.'

11

'We'll start with Lydia,' Alexander Geddes said when Eppie, having finished her tea and refilled the cup at his urging, still found herself tongue-tied. 'You surely have some idea of what's in her mind, from watching your own daughter. It's difficult, trying to raise children without the benefit of a woman's assistance. I have tried to do the right thing, but it seems that I've gone wrong – first with my son,' he added in a harsh, bitter aside, 'and now with Lydia.' He sat down behind his desk and asked quietly, 'Why have I gone wrong, Eppie?'

'You haven't, sir, you mustn't think that,' she said, upset by the despair in his dark eyes. 'It's just – well, she's mebbe a wee bit spoiled . . .'

Far from being offended, he nodded slowly, considering her words. 'I've often wondered if trying to make up for her not having a mother's love meant that I indulged her too much. But I care for her, Eppie, with all my heart. It's difficult not to spoil such a sweet, bonny lassie. At least, she used to be sweet . . .'

'She still is, sir, but – it's not you,' Eppie burst out, throwing caution to the wind. The man had said that he wanted the truth, and if giving it to him was the only way to escape from the embarrassment of sitting at his grand table in her working clothes, drinking tea out of a china cup so delicate and fragile that she was frightened out of her wits in case she set it down too hard on its fluted saucer and broke it, then the truth he would have.

'It's Mrs Geddes, sir. She spoiled Lydia far more than you ever did, and that's understandable since she was such a lovely wee thing. But she's growing up, sir. She'll soon be a young woman. Mrs Geddes says she's become difficult and rebellious, but I don't believe that. I think she just has a mind of her own now, and that's only to be expected with bairns as they grow older. Mrs Geddes wants to keep Lydia the way she was, and because that's not possible she blames the lassie for growing up. And then Lydia blames her for not understanding and – that's what it's all about, Mr Geddes.'

She stopped, exhausted by the unexpected torrent of words and horrified by her own impertinence. When she set the cup back on its saucer they rattled against each other, sending a faint, melodic chime into the silent room. Then she folded her hands tightly together in her lap and waited for her employer's reaction.

She had counted a full ten ticks of the clock on the mantelshelf before he said, 'I see. Thank you for telling me the truth, Eppie.'

'I'm not saying that it's the truth, sir. It's just the way I see it.'

'And you put it clearly. I appreciate that.' He got to his feet, picking up his glass and the brandy decanter. 'I have work to do,' he said, and went out of the room. When she carried the tray to the kitchen, the china chiming softly because she was still shaking, the library door was closed.

* * *

It was the hardest thing Alexander Geddes had ever had to do in his entire life. As a businessman he had developed a thick skin when it came to dismissing bad employees, or dealing with surly behaviour – he had even been cursed to his face. Once he had managed to give a good account of himself when attacked by a particularly resentful former employee. He had dealt with everything that came his way and in the process he had earned the name of being a fair, but strict man who would brook no idleness or dishonesty from anyone, including himself.

But he had never before had to tell his own mother that she was no longer welcome under his roof.

It took him two days to work up the courage to face her, and two wakeful nights, during which he rehearsed speech after speech. He had decided, by the third day, that his best method would be to turn the situation to her own advantage. Lydia was growing older, he explained to her when he finally faced her in the small parlour that she had made her own, and she was beginning to test the patience of the adults who looked after her. This natural phenomenon was something that he would have to handle himself, but, he said earnestly, it was not fair on his mother, who had reached a time in her life when she was entitled to – indeed, had earned – a life of peace and quiet. It was for this reason, he explained, that he had decided to buy a house in the town where Helen could live in comfort, with her every need attended to by a good, respectable housekeeper of her own.

'I, of course, will pay the woman's wages,' he went on while Helen Geddes sat bolt upright opposite, her blue eyes impaling him in a way that reminded him of a tray of butterflies, each pinned down securely, that he had once seen in the home of an acquaintance. He had not enjoyed the sight, and he liked it even less now that he felt that he had become one of the poor insects.

'So,' he finished, 'what do you think to my proposal, Mother?'

'I'm surprised that you bother to ask my opinion, Alexander.' Her hands gripped the arms of her chair so tightly that her knuckles looked as though there were no skin over the white bone. 'It seems to me that you've already made up your mind. The only surprise to me is that you have found the time to tell me of your plan instead of just bundling me into a carriage and rushing me off to whatever cottage you might deem suitable for me. Or, indeed, to the workhouse. That's where most old folk go when they've outlived their usefulness and they're no longer wanted by the children they gave their lives to raise.'

'There's no question of the workhouse, or of you not being wanted . . .'

'Indeed? You surprise me. Are you or are you not telling me that you no longer wish me to live under your roof?'

'I am saying that I know that you have found Lydia difficult of late, and you would surely be happier if you had a place of your own.'

'I would be happier if you would learn to control your daughter, Alexander, and teach her to treat her grandmother with civility. I have devoted the last twelve years,' Helen Geddes said passionately, 'to looking after your motherless children, and how do the three of you repay me? Duncan runs off without a word and you just let him go, when you should have done as I told you and made him walk every step of the way back to Aberdeen to continue his studies.'

'I told you, Mother—'

'I have given Lydia the love that her own mother, God

rest her soul, was unable to give her, and when she thanks me by sulking and storming and behaving like a – a spoiled brat, you find fault with me, instead of giving her the whipping she deserves. Mark my words, Alexander,' her eyes blazed into his and her voice lashed him like a whip, 'you've already lost Duncan, and you will soon regret that you did not take a stronger line with Lydia.'

He drew in a deep breath to steady himself before saying, 'I would ask you to remember, Mother, that they are my children and not yours. I have the final word on the way they are raised, and I will most certainly not subject my daughter to a whipping or to any other punishment. If anyone has spoiled her or indulged her, it's you.'

'How dare you accuse me of such a thing!'

'I am just as much to blame. I believed that you could give my daughter the womanly love that a man can't understand. But I should not have allowed you to make such a pet of the child.'

'To think,' Helen almost choked in her fury, 'that I gave up a comfortable home in order to look after you and your two young children . . .'

'There was no need of that, for Jean Gilbert was perfectly willing to help me care for them.'

'Jean Gilbert was only the housekeeper. I will not have my flesh and blood raised by a mere servant!'

'Jean had already raised a family of her own, and they have all given a good account of themselves. Eppie has a daughter of Lydia's age. Both women have had experience of caring for children.'

'And I have not? Did I not raise you on my own after your father died?'

'Yes, you did,' he conceded, remembering his cold, lonely upbringing.

'There is a difference,' Helen Geddes swept on, 'between being raised by someone from the lower classes and being raised by your own blood kin. Housekeepers cannot prepare Lydia for the life she will lead. As you and I both know, Alexander, discipline plays a large part in the lives that people of our station lead, and as far as Lydia is concerned that discipline is sorely lacking. I don't consider Eppie Watt to be a suitable housekeeper and I never have. She does not know her place.'

'I disagree. She is fond of Lydia and I believe that the child has grown to trust her.'

'That,' his mother said, 'is all the more reason why you must replace her with someone more – aware of her position in your household. Because Lydia has never known what it is to have a mother she has a regrettable tendency to attach herself to every woman she meets. As a result, she is easily drawn to the wrong sort of woman. It is a great pity, Alexander, that both your wives died young, before they could fulfil their duties towards your children. That's probably what went wrong with Duncan too . . .'

'That is quite enough!' Alexander, unable to bear her taunts any longer, jumped to his feet and glared down at her. 'I will not listen to such nonsense. Now that we have settled the matter, I would be grateful if you could find a new home for yourself, Mother. Or, if you wish, I will find one for you.'

She started to speak, but he glanced at the pretty little clock on the chest of drawers then said swiftly, 'Now I must go down to the harbour; a boat is coming in shortly to unload some goods and I want to make sure that everything goes well.'

As he strode the short distance to the harbour, he drew in deep lungfuls of air in an attempt to calm himself.

The first step had been taken and now, having heard what his mother had to say, he was all the more determined to remove her from his house. He was well aware that the fight had only just begun, but it was a fight that he would win, he promised himself grimly, nodding to a group of fishermen mending their nets. He *would* win it, even if it meant leaving his mother where she was and moving himself, Lydia and Eppie to a new home.

The next few weeks were a trial to the entire household. Helen Geddes made life almost impossible for Eppie, and she treated Lydia with a distant frostiness that confused and troubled the girl. The few friends she had, women of her own age and temperament, visited her more often than usual, and each time Alexander happened to meet one or other of them on their way in or out of her little parlour they stared at him coldly. One or two hesitated, clearly on the verge of taking him to task for his cruel treatment towards his own mother, his flesh and blood, but each time he steeled himself to meet their eyes with his own steady gaze, and had watched their resolve crumble into a sharp lift of the head or a slight, but audible, sniff as they walked by him.

Helen herself, whenever she found the opportunity to be alone with him, tried sulking, arguing, and even reverted on one occasion to weeping pathetically and accusing him of deliberate cruelty to a woman too old and feeble to defend herself. But for the first time in his life, her son stood firm.

'Mother, I am sure that once you are settled in your own home you will agree that this move is best for all of us. Lydia will no longer annoy you as she has been doing for some time, and I will of course visit you regularly. So will Lydia, I will see to that. You will always be welcome in my home – as a guest,' he added firmly. 'Now – shall I start to look for a suitable house?'

'I would prefer to do that myself, rather than end up in one of the fisher cottages, cheek by jowl with my neighbours and with no peace or privacy,' she said huffily, and rather than protest that he would not dream of sending her to a cottage, he merely smiled, bowed, and left the room.

When she eventually found a house that she deemed suitable, he was taken aback by her choice – a villa on the outskirts of the town. Like his own home, the house consisted of three floors. A large kitchen, a laundry room and a servant's bedroom, as well as a pantry, scullery and coal cellar made up the ground floor, while the well-appointed dining room and drawing room were on the next floor, together with the main bedroom, which had its own dressing room. Three more bedrooms were on the top floor.

'It's a large place for one person, is it not?' he said when he went to inspect it.

'I am used to large rooms. I would feel that I were suffocating in anything smaller.' Helen surveyed her son through narrowed eyes. She and her friends were all agreed that if she must be ousted from the place she had come to look on as her own, she should make the move as heavy on Alexander's purse as possible. 'If I must leave your house I am surely entitled to my comfort. But if this house is too much for your purse, then no doubt one of my dear friends would be willing to take me in . . .'

'That will not be necessary, Mother. I am perfectly willing to buy this house if it's what you want.'

'As you can see, one servant would not be able to keep

this place as it should be, as well as attending to my own personal needs. I shall require at least two.'

'Very well,' Alexander agreed, while pounds, shillings and pence started running through his brain. Business had been somewhat sluggish of late and until the Board of Trade met to investigate the loss of the *Grace-Ellen* he was also paying out small pensions to the families of the men who had drowned when the fishing vessel went down. The fine family house that his mother insisted on, and the staff he would have to pay to run it, would eat into his savings. But it would be worth it to resolve the matter.

'And I shall need a gardener, and an assistant gardener,' Helen added, nodding out of the dining room window at the pleasant flower garden in front of the house. There was also a large kitchen garden at the rear – Alexander noted that he must find a cook who knew how to make the most of homegrown vegetables. That, at least, would save a little money every week.

'Of course. I will visit the lawyer this very afternoon and make an offer for the house.' I am sure that you will be very comfortable in it – and very happy.' Alexander turned to face his mother and saw, with guilty pleasure, the frustration in her cold blue eyes.

He had never been a gambling man, but now he felt that he had ventured on one of the greatest gambles of his life, and had won. He had won his freedom, and his beloved daughter's future, and although it was going to cost him dear, it would be worth every penny.

'Mrs Geddes is goin' tae live in a hoose of her own,' Eppie said, and then, as Barbary said nothing, 'A fine place, by all accounts. It'll certainly make life easier for me once she's gone. And mebbe for Lydia too. Her grandmother was always nippin' at her and complainin' about her bein' sulky or difficult. What growin' lass isnae difficult at times? I mind my own mother despairin' of me . . .'

She could hear her own voice going on and on in an attempt to connect with her friend, but when she turned from the sink, where she had been washing clothes, Barbary was still sitting by the range, the baby in her lap, staring vacantly at the steam dribbling from the kettle's spout.

Eppie put the clothes through the big mangle that stood in a wooden lean-to Tolly had built at the back door when he first brought his bride to the house, and then took them outside to the clothes line. George and Martha were playing in the backyard; when she spoke to them, they both looked up at her, George with his mother's dark eyes and Martha with her father's clear blue gaze. Their little faces were solemn, as though they carried the weight of the world on their small shoulders.

And so they did, Eppie thought as she pegged the clothes on to the line. She could see by the way they watched Barbary, the way one or other of them tended to put a small hand on top of hers as she sat dreaming, that their mother's depression had seeped into their own minds.

Barbary was rising to her feet as Eppie returned to the kitchen. 'He's sleepin',' she said. 'I'll put him tae his bed.'

'And I'll pour away this tea, for it's cold, and put in some hot.' Eppie emptied the untouched cup into the sink and refilled it, knowing that it too would probably be left to cool.

When she had laid the baby in his cot, Barbary put both hands to the small of her back and stretched in an attempt to relieve the pain of stiff muscles. Her once-rounded body was thin and her seven-month pregnancy showed as a huge bulge protruding between her hipbones.

'I have tae go now, but I've left some soup, and some stew, enough for all of you. Mind and take your own share. You've the new bairn tae think of,' Eppie urged.

Barbary gave her a sweet, absent-minded smile. 'I'm no' hungry these days.'

'Ye have tae keep yer strength up,' Eppie pleaded, and then, as the other woman drifted over to the window, where she stood watching her children, 'They need you, Barbary. Never forget that.'

'Everyone needs someone. I need Tolly,' Barbary said, and looked at her friend with eyes suddenly awash with tears.

Once he had settled his mother into her new home Alexander Geddes made up his mind to pay more attention to his daughter. She was growing fast and it was time, he realised, that he took more of an interest in her life and her well being.

First of all he turned his attention to her schooling and was horrified to find that it consisted of little more than the basic elementary education that he himself recalled mastering when he was about seven years old. When he questioned her carefully about the books he had bought through the years and which were lined up on a shelf in her room, he realised that Lydia had not opened any of them other than, perhaps, to look at the pictures. He suggested one evening that she might like to read to him, but the ruse turned out to be a disaster. After stumbling slowly through half a page, Lydia burst into tears, threw the book down on the floor, accused him of laughing at her, and ran to her room.

Her father, distraught, hurried to the kitchen to beg Eppie to soothe her, It was not an easy task.

'Why can't he leave me alone?' Lydia wailed, casting herself down on the bedroom floor and banging her fists on the carpet. 'He's never wanted me to r-read to him before, so why must he d-do it now?'

'I'm sure that he just thought that it would be pleasant to be read to. You have such a pretty voice . . .'

'But he chose a book that was too h-hard! He looked at me as if I was daft just b-because I couldn't understand some of the words!'

'Does Miss Galbraith ever ask you to read to her?'

'Of course not. It's her fault,' Lydia said, suddenly realising that she had found a scapegoat. 'She never asks me to r-read so how do I know if I can do it?'

'I'm sure your father feels very sorry that he upset you when he didn't mean to. Come along, Lydia, there's no need to behave like a baby. You're twelve years old now. Sit up and let me dry your eyes, then you can wash your face and get into bed while I fetch you some hot milk and a biscuit. Then I'll read to you, if you like,' Eppie suggested. 'My daughter Charlotte likes to be read to before she goes to sleep.'

'Does she?'

'Oh yes.' It had been years since she had been allowed to read to Charlotte, who had insisted on doing all her own reading as soon as she had learned a sufficient number of words, but Eppie kept that information to herself.

A suspicious green eye peered up at her from beneath a tumble of black hair. 'You won't make me read to you instead, will you?'

'Of course not. Choose a book while I'm away,' Eppie said, and went back to the kitchen.

Her employer met her in the downstairs hall. 'How is she?'

'She'll be all right. I'm going to take her some hot milk and a biscuit. Mr Geddes, what book did you ask Lydia to read to you?'

He held it out to her. 'Surely she should have been able to read that?'

Eppie glanced at it, and nodded. Charlotte had long since left that sort of story behind. When she looked up at her employer, his face was grim.

'I must go out early tomorrow,' he said, 'but perhaps you would ask Miss Galbraith to wait behind after lessons? Tell her that I will be sure to come back as soon as I can. I can see that I shall have to have a word with her.'

12

'But Mrs Geddes was satisfied with my work,' Miss Galbraith protested.

Alexander Geddes took the brightly coloured book from his desk and held it out to her. 'I asked my daughter to read this to me last night and she could scarcely pronounce any word of more than four letters. I don't consider that satisfying, given. that she is twelve years old.'

'Mrs Geddes—'

'Mrs Geddes does not pay your salary, Miss Galbraith. I do, and I am not satisfied with the standard of my daughter's education.'

'I understood that she was to be taught the ways in which a young lady is expected to behave.'

'I'm not even sure that she has succeeded in that respect,' Alexander said drily, thinking of Lydia's temper tantrum on the previous evening.

Bright crimson flared over the governess's cheekbones. 'You may not recall this, Mr Geddes, but it was your mother who interviewed me for this position, and your mother who watched over my work. She was content with me, and if you are not, then clearly we have come to a parting of ways.'

'Clearly,' he agreed, 'we have. I will pay your salary for the rest of this week, but I think it best that we look on today as your last visit.'

When the woman had gone, he gathered up the work he found in the schoolroom and took it to the principal of the girls' school in Durn Street, who happened to be an acquaintance. The man frowned as he looked through the small pile of lesson books and exercise books.

'How old did you say your girl is?'

'Just turned twelve. I was thinking of enrolling her in your school in the autumn.'

'She's got a way to go before she's ready to join a class of her own age. I'd advise you to find yourself a good governess to bring her up to the proper level first.'

Alexander sighed. 'Do you happen to know of a suitable woman?' he asked wearily.

Miss Hastie, an elderly woman who had previously taught at the girls' school in Portsoy, came with excellent references. When Alexander explained that he wanted to see his daughter's education brought up to the standard accepted by the school, the woman bobbed her head in a series of swift movements that reminded him of a bird pecking through grass in search of insects.

'I quite understand, Mr Geddes.'

'But at the same time,' he added, 'Lydia needs to be treated with understanding. She never knew her mother, and was more or less raised by her grandmother, who recently moved into her own house. My daughter has been somewhat upset by the changes in this household, and you may find her a little difficult until she gets used to you.'

'I lost my own mother when I was very young,' Miss Hastie told him, 'but I was fortunate in that an aunt took me in. A God-fearing woman who understood that education is the greatest gift a girl can have. I can assure you that your daughter is in safe hands.'

It took some time for Eppie to realise that with Helen Geddes out of the house, she could get on with her work without fear of being criticised and lectured. For the first time she began to feel like the mistress of her own kitchen – and a very pleasant sensation it was too.

At her employer's insistence she began to take her evening meal with him and his daughter. 'But what will folk say if they hear about it?' she asked, dismayed, when he first suggested it. 'Servants don't sit at the same table as their masters.'

'You've been with us for almost five years now, Eppie, and to my mind, you've become more than a mere servant. In any case, it will be good for Lydia. Now that my mother has her own home, you are the only woman in my daughter's daily life. You will eat with us every evening,' he said firmly, and she had no option but to obey.

Lydia found it harder than anyone to accept that her grandmother was no longer dictating her every move. If anything, she became more difficult, as though testing her father and the housekeeper, challenging them to lose their tempers with her. It was hard on both of them, but since Alexander was out of the house for most of each day, the burden tended to land on Eppie. She bit back her exasperation and managed to develop a system based on allowing the girl to win the small battles while Eppie herself doggedly held out for victory in the larger issues.

With her employer's permission, she began to take

Lydia with her when she went to the shops, or down to the harbour. Although the girl affected disinterest, standing back from the people Eppie stopped to talk to and sighing loudly to indicate how tedious she found everything, she sometimes forgot herself and allowed a look of interest to creep through.

'I don't know if you realise,' Eppie said one day as they walked back to the house after one of their shopping expeditions, 'that with your grandmother gone, you're mistress of the house now.'

'Me? But what about you?'

'I'm the housekeeper.' When she was with Lydia, Eppie made a point of reverting to the way she and her family spoke at home. 'You're the lady of the house. That means that you need to learn about things like what food to buy, and what meals to order. So you have to learn all about your father's favourite foods. And at the same time, you'll be learning how to run your own hoose – house – when you're a grown married woman.'

'I'm not sure that I want to marry,' Lydia sniffed.

'You will if you meet the right man. But there's plenty of time for that,' Eppie went on briskly, 'and a lot to learn. I can teach you how to plan menus for each day. Every morning before Miss Hastie arrives we will discuss the meals for the following day, and then after your lessons we can go to the shops together. You need to learn how to choose fresh vegetables, and the best fish and meat.'

From then on each morning she and Lydia gravely pored over the recipe books that Jean Gilbert had accumulated during her time as housekeeper, and in the afternoons the two of them went round the shops. The shopkeepers and people they met in the streets started to know the girl, and to greet her civilly. She nodded, and occasionally smiled, but being unused to speaking to strangers, she was reluctant to say too much.

Her shyness concerned Eppie. She didn't want Lydia to grow up with no friends and no experience of dealing with folk outside her own home. She was summoning the courage to speak to Alexander Geddes about her concerns when he asked her, for the second time, to bring a pot of tea to the dining room after they had finished the evening meal.

'I called in on my mother this morning, Eppie, and she tells me that my daughter has not yet visited her.'

'I suggested it to her the other day, but she paid no heed to me.'

'Perhaps you need to do more than suggest it.'

'If you don't mind me sayin', sir, it's not my place to make her do anything she doesn't want to do.'

He raised an eyebrow at her. 'My mother seems to think that the blame lies with you – that you are discouraging Lydia from visiting.'

Eppie felt colour rush to her face, and the hand holding the teacup began to tremble so much that she had to lower the cup to its saucer, the tea untested. 'I'd never do such a thing, Mr Geddes! How could Mrs Geddes think that of me? I've asked Lydia every day if she should not walk up to see her grandmother but she's refused every—'

He held up a hand to stop the agitated flow of words. 'I know my daughter, and I never for a moment thought that you were responsible for her dereliction of duty. Do you know why she won't visit my mother?' he asked, and then, as she remained silent, staring down at the cup and saucer on the table, 'You're right, that is an unfair question. The matter is between Lydia and myself. Tomorrow morning I will order her to visit her grandmother, and you will accompany her. And that,' he emptied his glass and poured a little more brandy into it, 'will be an end to the matter.'

'And if she refuses, sir?'

His face and tone hardened. 'Then perhaps I will have to assume that my mother was right all along, and Lydia needs to be taught a lesson about the need for courtesy towards her family.'

'Mr Geddes, Lydia's only a child as yet. You can't expect her to—'

'A child fast approaching womanhood and old enough to know how to conduct herself.'

'I'm not so sure about that,' Eppie said, and could have bitten her tongue out as soon as she had spoken as he set his glass down and stared at her.

'Indeed? And why would that be?'

She had let her foolish tongue lead her into a difficult situation and now, she knew, she had to justify her impertinence towards this man who paid her wages and owned the roof over her head and the food she put into her mouth. She drew in a deep breath and said, her voice trembling slightly, 'Lydia has little confidence in herself, Mr Geddes.'

'It's my mother's opinion, and mine at times, that she has over much confidence in herself.'

'That's just a pretence that she wears like a cloak to cover up her uncertainty. She's spent most of her life inside this house. She's never had the chance to meet other children because she's never gone to school – and that's because Mrs Geddes kept her home for fear of her catching some disease or other. I take her to the shops with me now, and I can see how shy she is when she's with folk she doesn't know. She needs to learn to be comfortable among strangers. I was thinking, sir,' she rushed on, raising an idea that she had wanted to discuss with him for some time, 'Lydia enjoys dancing and I often hear her in her room, playing that wee music box of hers.'

'Really?' he asked in surprise, and then began to say something else before biting his lip and staring down at his glass again. His fingers reached out to grip it so tightly that she saw his knuckles whiten, and feared that the glass might crack under their pressure. Then at last he said, 'Her mother was very fond of music, and of dancing.'

'Then that may be where the bairn gets her sense of movement. I've seen her dance, and she's very graceful. So I was wondering – if you don't mind me being so outspoken . . .'

His brows began to draw together over his straight, longish nose. 'My dear woman, I would have hoped that by now you would know that I'm not an ogre. Whatever you want to say to me, get on with it.'

'There's a man in the High Street who runs a wee dancing class, and I was wondering if you'd consider letting Lydia have proper lessons.'

'Dancing lessons? Would that be – seemly?'

'Oh yes, sir, I've been asking around and some of the young gentlemen and ladies from the big houses around the town go there. You'll probably know their fathers, sir.'

'I may. I can't say that I've ever discussed dancing lessons with any of my business colleagues though.'

'It would help her to meet up with folk of her own age – and her own class too,' Eppie hastened to add. 'She's growing up and she needs to learn the art of conversation. It's not something that I can teach her.'

He deliberated for a long moment, then shrugged his shoulders. 'Very well then, perhaps you should suggest this notion of yours to my daughter and see what she makes of it.'

'If you don't mind me saying, Mr Geddes, I believe that it would be better coming from you. You're her father,' Eppie pleaded on as his frown reappeared. 'She'd be pleased if she thought it was your idea, and she'd mebbe consider it seriously.'

'You really think that she would care for it?'

'I think she would.'

'Then I shall strike a bargain with my daughter. I will send her to this dancing class if she will visit her grandmother on one afternoon a week. If she agrees, you will take her there to make sure that she keeps her word.'

'Very well, Mr Geddes.' Eppie picked up her cup and saucer and as she prepared to leave the room she added with quiet dignity, 'But I'm confident that if your daughter agrees to anything, she will keep her word.'

Alexander had hoped that now that they were free of his mother's presence he and his daughter might become more at ease with each other, but to his disappointment Lydia had continued to be moody and temperamental.

It was not easy, therefore, to bring up the subject of dance lessons, but after two days of deliberation and false starts, he decided to plunge in and get it over with.

'I heard someone in the street the other day, talking about a dancing master who's set up in High Street,' he said when he and his daughter were at breakfast together. 'Would you like to take classes with him?'

'Me?' Lydia had been staring down at her plate, making circles in her porridge with her spoon and then watching them fill with milk to form a pattern. 'Why should I want to learn to dance?'

'Lassies like to dance, do they not?'

Lydia eyed him warily, suspecting a trap of some sort.

Alexander cleared his throat. 'Your mother enjoyed dancing, very much. She was good at it – very graceful on her feet. And that trouble between you and your grandmother not long before she moved to her own house – was that not because of you dancing in your room?'

Her face reddened and she ducked her head down and concentrated on the porridge again. She loved music and she loved dancing, and she desperately wanted to take the lessons her father now offered, but over the past few years, confused by her grandmother's gradual change from doting on her to criticising her every action, and expecting her to earn praise where once it had been given freely, she had become suspicious of all adults. She loved her father more than anyone, other than Duncan, but she resented the fact that when her grandmother's attitude had hardened towards her, her father had been too involved in business to defend or protect her.

'I just thought . . .' he persisted now, painfully ' . . . that learning how to dance might be a good thing. You're growing fast, Lydia, and you need to meet more young folk of your own age.'

Glancing up from beneath her thick dark lashes, Lydia caught him looking past her to the mantelshelf, and the clock upon it. In his mind, he was already slipping away from her, beginning to plan the day ahead – plans which did not include her. If she made things too difficult for him, she might miss the opportunity he was offering her.

'I wouldn't mind trying,' she admitted, adding swiftly, 'but if I don't like it, I'll not go back.'

Relief flooded over Alexander Geddes. He had not expected her to agree so easily. 'That's fair enough. I'll not hold you to anything you don't want to do. I'll ask

Eppie to find out when you can start.' He smiled across the table at her, and she smiled back, tentatively. Then her smile wavered and disappeared as he went on, 'I visited your grandmother yesterday. She's settled in well, and is looking forward to seeing you. She says you've not visited her as yet.'

An all-too-familiar, mulish expression settled on her pretty face. 'If she wants to see me, then let her visit me here.'

'She's your grandmother, Lydia, and it's your place to call on her.'

'But she doesn't like me!' Lydia's voice took on the childish whine he had begun to dread. 'She's happier without me – and I'm happier without her!'

'That's nonsense. She likes you very much – you're her only grand-daughter.'

'And you both think that I should love her just because of that? It's not fair!' Her lower lip began to protrude. 'Why do we have to like folk just because we're related to them?'

'Because we're flesh and blood kin, and because it's your duty.' He began to get angry. 'You should be grateful that you have a grandmother who cares about you and wants to see you.'

'But she doesn't care, Father! She thinks that I should earn her love and yet she doesn't think that she should earn mine, just because she's old and I'm still a child.' The girl pushed her plate away and clenched both hands on the table. Her face was flushed and her eyes sparkled with unshed tears of anger; a glance at her told Alexander that he was in danger of moving into the sort of unpleasant scene he had witnessed between his daughter and his mother the day he found them, and Eppie, in Lydia's bedroom.

He took a deep breath and tried to subdue his own growing exasperation. The last thing he wanted was to alienate her. His mother had done that, and had lost her. 'Lydia, we all have to do our duty towards others, particularly towards older people. Your grandmother may not seem to care for you, but she does, in her own way. She misses you. The trouble is that she has forgotten what it's like to be your age. You must try to understand that, and learn to forgive her for it. If you punish her by staying away, you'll only hurt her, and since she's my mother, you'll hurt me as well. And one day when you're her age you might remember this, and wish that you had been kinder to her. If that happens you'll feel the same hurt, only it will be too late to make it up to her.'

There was a long silence, during which the grandfather clock in the hall chimed the hour. Alexander resisted the urge to look at his watch; he was expected at the quarry shortly, but he could not afford to leave this discussion with his daughter unfinished. The men awaiting him would just have to wait, even though it would hold up the work in progress.

'Do you remember what it was like to be my age?' she asked at last.

'I do indeed.' He would never forget his lonely childhood; school had been the only place where he felt free to be himself, among his friends. He recalled how hard it had been, and how painful, having to spend day in and day out earning his mother's approval and her cold idea of affection. Lydia, he realised, didn't even have school friends, and he himself had not defended and protected her as he should have done. He had let her down, and in doing so, he had also let down his beloved Celia, who had given her own life in order to give him his daughter.

Recalling his decision to use the dance classes as a

bribe to make her visit his mother, he felt bitterly ashamed. If Eppie was right – if Lydia loved to dance – then she would go to the classes and have the chance to meet other young people while she was indulging in something she cared for. And he would no longer insist on her being a dutiful grand-daughter. He felt that having let her down when she most needed his protection, he had no right to bargain with her.

He opened his mouth to say so and then closed it again as, to his astonishment, Lydia said, 'If it's what you want, Father, I'll visit Grandmother tomorrow afternoon – if Eppie can come with me.'

'Of course she can. And now you can go downstairs and tell her to find out when the next dance class is held.' In his relief, and his shame at being so close to blackmailing this child that he loved more than anyone else in the world, he rose and went round the table to take her flushed face in his hands and kiss her forehead.

The gesture was so unexpected that they were both embarrassed, and both relieved when Alexander stepped back.

'You'd best be off, Father,' Lydia said primly, 'you must be late, surely.'

'I am,' he said, and then paused at the door. 'Eppie tells me that you are helping to plan the meals and do the shopping now.'

'I must be the mistress of the house now that Grandmother's no longer here.' She tilted her chin at him, as though defying him to object.

With every year that passed, he thought with a sudden ache in his heart, she looked more like her mother.

'Of course you must,' he said, and went out, the memory of her soft face imprinted on his lips.

When she was alone, Lydia got up from the table and

skipped around the room, twirling and swooping to the music in her mind. Then she sped downstairs to tell Eppie the good news, and to insist that the two of them went into the town at once, to find out when she could start her dancing lessons.

Halfway down the kitchen stairs, she stopped so suddenly that she almost tipped forwards. Her father had kissed her – for the first time in her life, he had kissed her. She closed her eyes for a moment, hugging herself with both arms as she recalled the moment. Then, smiling, she ran on down the steps and burst into the kitchen.

13

Helen Geddes's new home looked down over Portsoy's jumbled roofs to the Moray Firth beyond. As Eppie and Lydia neared it the girl's steps began to slow, and by the time they had reached the gate she was clinging to Eppie.

'You'll come in with me, won't you? And stay with me?'

'Of course I will. The time'll pass quickly, you'll see. Just think of the pleasure you're giving to your grandmother. She's very fond of you, Lydia, and it's only natural that she wants to see you,' Eppie coaxed. She freed her arm from Lydia's grip and took hold of the doorknocker, her own heart fluttering nervously.

A maidservant, neat in her white apron and with a small starched cap on her head, escorted them upstairs to the parlour, where Helen waited in the narrow, tall-backed chair she had brought with her from Shorehead.

'Lydia – you've decided to visit me at last.' She waited, then frowned as Lydia stayed close to Eppie's side. Eppie gave her a nudge and whispered, 'Kiss your grandma,' and the girl went forwards slowly.

Helen tipped her chin up and inclined her head slightly

to one side to receive the kiss, then said, 'Sit in that chair, child, near me.' Then, to Eppie, 'You may go.'

Lydia, about to sit down, looked panic-stricken. 'But Eppie said she'd stay . . .'

'I'm not in the habit of entertaining servants in my parlour, Lydia. Sit down,' Helen ordered. 'You may return in one and a half hours' time to take my grand-daughter home.' She told Eppie coldly. She picked up a small brass bell from the table by her chair and rang it, adding, 'Not a minute before and not a minute after. Maisie, you may show this person out – by the back door, of course.'

'Eppie—'

'I'll be back, don't fret.' Eppie said, then she was back in the hall, being led away from the front door and towards the kitchen. 'Come an' have a cup o' tea while you're waitin',' Maisie said once the kitchen door was closed behind them and there was no chance of her mistress overhearing. 'You dinnae mind, do ye, Annie?'

The cook, rolling dough at the kitchen table, glanced up and nodded at Eppie. 'O' course no'. Sit down, lass.'

'Mrs Geddes might not like it.'

'Mrs Geddes doesnae like anythin',' the woman said, adding with heartfelt sincerity, 'She's an auld bitch, that one. Have ye ever worked for her?'

'For five years.'

'Five years!' Maisie almost screeched. 'I doubt if I'll last near as long as that. Five weeks, mebbe. And Annie's lookin' for another place already.'

'I am that.' Annie set her work aside while Maisie poured three mugs of tea.

'She'll ring the bell for her own tea in half an hour,' she said, nodding at the tray, set and covered with a muslin cloth. 'We'll no' be bothered till then.'

'Aye, we're safe till then,' Annie said, her face bright

with anticipation of a good gossip. 'Was that auld yin up there always so difficult tae please?'

One and a half hours and two cups of strong black tea later, Eppie was led back into the hall. 'Ye'd best wait here,' Maisie advised before she took Lydia's coat and hat up to the parlour. The girl herself came hurrying down the stairs almost at once, marching past Eppie without a glance and hauling the front door open before Maisie could reach it.

'It looks tae me like that one's as bad as her gran,' the maid murmured out of the side of her mouth as Lydia stalked down the path. She was stepping along the road so fast that her skirts tangled around her legs, and Eppie had to run to catch up with her.

'Will you slow down? We're not running a race!'

'You promised to stay with me!' The girl rounded on her, tears of sheer fury in her eyes. 'You said you'd stay and then you went away and left me!'

'How could I stay when I wasn't wanted?'

'But you promised!'

'Lydia!' Eppie caught hold of the child's wrist, dragging her to a standstill. 'You're behaving like a spoiled wee bairn instead of a lassie who's almost grown. D'you know what the maidservant said to me when you walked out the door without as much as looking at her? She said that you were just like your grandmother.'

Sheer shock dried Lydia's tears in an instant. 'I am not like her! I'll never be like her!'

'You will if you don't learn to stop this nonsense. Now listen to me – Mrs Geddes is alone now, apart from her servants, and you've got me and your father – and the bees. And as far as I'm concerned you can dance all over the house, in and out of all the rooms and up and down the stairs from now on, and there won't be a word of complaint – as long as you spend just a wee while every week bein' a dutiful grand-daughter.'

'All over the house?'

'On the roof, if you want,' Eppie said. 'D'you know what I hated most at school? Latin. I never could get my mind round it, so when we were being taught Latin, I used to sit and say my favourite nursery rhymes in my head all the time, to keep from showing how much I hated it. If visiting your grandmother gets to be difficult, you could always dance in your head.'

'In my head?'

'You can do anything in your head and nob'dy knows about it – as long as you keep a pleasant smile on your face,' Eppie said, and to her relief, Lydia's temper was gone, replaced by a huge and delighted grin.

Mr Forbes, the dance teacher, had turned the top floor of his house in the High Street into a studio with a sturdy wooden floor and seats around the walls for the adults – most, like Eppie, were maidservants accompanying his young students.

The class on Lydia's first afternoon was for beginners, a group that ranged from five-year-olds to several girls and two lads around Lydia's age. It took some coaxing to get Lydia on to the dance floor, where the other beginners were already huddled together, looking for all the world like a herd of cows seeking shelter and comfort on a wet day. But once the teacher's daughter had seated herself at the old piano in the corner and began to play something made up of rippling notes that seemed to Eppie to flow like the Soy Burn hurrying to the sea, the girl's tense body noticeably relaxed. It was almost, Eppie marvelled, as though the music took Lydia over. When the class was urged by the teacher to move about the floor in time to the music, she was one of the first to step to the rhythm. While most of the others were still walking about self-consciously, her shoulders and arms and hands began to move easily. She even tried a tentative, graceful swirl that lifted her skirts about her ankles, and then, encouraged by the teacher's, 'That's grand, lassie, you've got the idea. Just think about enjoyin' yourself . . .' she began to move faster, with an easy, assured grace. Eppie watched, astonished, reminded of the way the fishing boats, once they had been nursed between the harbour walls and out into open waters, unfurled their big, dark-red sails to the wind and began to dance through the waves, dipping gracefully from one wave to the next.

They went on to learn some simple basic steps, and in every case, Lydia was the first to grasp what the teacher wanted them to do. When the lesson ended the others scurried from the floor at once, in a hurry to retrieve their coats and hats and get out into the fresh air, while Lydia stood alone in the middle of the floor for a moment, her face dazed, as though she were still listening to some inner music. When Eppie touched her arm she blinked, awakening from her trance to look around, surprised to find herself alone.

'You did well – the best in the class,' Eppie said proudly as they walked home. Lydia, still in a daze, said nothing, but as soon as they returned to the house she went straight to her room, and Eppie, passing the door on her way to put the laundry away, heard her singing to herself, and knew that she was dancing, lost once more in a world of her own.

Lydia had awakened from her trance by the time her father came home, and throughout the entire meal that evening she described every moment of the lesson to her father. 'It was as if I've always known what to do, but this was the first time anybody had ever told me to do it,' she tried to explain to him.

He listened intently, smiling, asking questions, and watching them Eppie thought that she had never seen them so close.

'D'ye ken that there's things bein' said in the town about you?' Maisie asked on the following week. Again, Eppie was being given tea in the kitchen.

'What sort of things would anyone find tae say about me?'

'Ach, it's just daft nonsense about you and Mr Geddes bein' alone together in that big house now that the old one's moved out.'

'We're not alone at all – Lydia's there, and her governess is in every mornin' but Sundays.'

'Aye, but the only other one in the hoose at nights is the lassie, and she's no' what ye'd call a – what is it?' Maisie sought for the word and finally found it. 'A chaperone.'

'But they cannae be gossipin' about me and Mr Geddes bein' – surely not!' Eppie said, horrified. 'Who would start nasty gossip like that?'

'You've said more than ye should, Maisie,' the cook broke in. 'D'ye want tae lose yer place here?'

Maisie shrugged. 'I'm not that bothered. In fact, it would be a blessin'.'

'Wait until ye've got somewhere else tae go afore ye take chances.'

Maisie said nothing more, but as her eyes met Eppie's over the rim of her cup they widened, then rolled in the direction of the door.

'Mrs Geddes?' Eppie said.

'Maisie, I'll no' have ye sayin' another word about the mistress in my kitchen!' the cook snapped, quite unaware that she had answered the question herself.

'No' anither word,' the maidservant agreed meekly, winking and nodding at Eppie. 'Except that, wherever the slander comes from, it's runnin' a' round the place.'

'But it's nonsense!' Eppie said angrily.

'Ye know what folk are like when they get their teeth intae a bit o' gossip – they go after it like a dog after a rat, and they dinnae let go until another good piece o' scandal comes along tae take its place,' Maisie said, then subsided as Annie snapped, 'Maisie – one mair word an' I'm goin' tae tell the mistress aboot you makin' eyes at the gardener!'

Eppie tried to dismiss the maid's idle gossip, but as she and Lydia returned to Shorehead she found herself looking with suspicion at the women she passed in the street, and fancying that one or two of them looked back at her in a strange way and then murmured something to their companions behind her back.

She was trying to tell herself that it was her imagination when Lydia, skipping along by her side, relieved that the ordeal of visiting her grandmother was over for another week, said, 'Why is it wrong for you to eat your dinner with us?'

'It's not wrong at all.'

'That's what I thought, but Grandmother had on one of her grumpy faces when she asked me if it was true.'

'It was your father's idea, so that I can teach you how to behave at the table.'

'I knew that it was Father's idea – I said that to Grandmother. But I didn't know why,' the girl said casually.

Over the next few days Eppie tried hard to tell herself that she was imagining the sudden interest being shown towards her when she went about the town, but there was no denying that conversation faltered every time she went into shops, then picked up again as she left. This, she knew, had never happened before.

As it happened, Lydia's next visit to her grandmother fell on the cook's day off, which meant that Eppie could ask Maisie outright about the gossip in the town.

The girl spread her work-reddened hands on her knees and leaned forwards, her eyes alight with the pleasure that only a good gossip could bring. 'It's the mistress that's behind it all right – her an' her friends that visit tae take tea wi' her. They like nothin' better than tae pull folk's reputations tae shreds – it doesnae matter who, rich or poor. They've been talkin' about you gettin' Mr Geddes tae put his mither out of his hoose so's the two o' you can be together in peace.'

'That's not true!'

Maisie shrugged. 'They're no' bothered about whether it's true or no'. That doesnae stop them sayin' it. And I know for certain that the auld bitch up there . . .' she jerked her head towards the upper floor, '. . . is still ragin' at her son for makin' her move intae this place. She wants tae blame someone, and it's you.'

'How do you know this?'

'Because they talk aboot it openly in front o' me when I'm servin' their tea. Ye know what the gentry are like,' Maisie said contemptuously, 'they seem tae think that servants are born deaf tae anythin' but orders. Though I sometimes think there's a deliberate way to it as well – they talk gossip in front of the likes o' you an' me so's we can repeat it tae folk they'd no' lower themselves tae gossip wi'. Whatever the way o' it, I can promise ye that it's a' roond Portsoy that you and Mr Geddes have a fondness for each other.'

'If Mr Geddes gets tae hear this, he'll—'

'I doubt if he will, for men dinnae enjoy gossip the way women dae. It's you she's out tae hurt, an' if ye take my advice,' Maisie reached for the teapot and replenished their cups, 'ye'll pay no heed. Somethin' else'll come along soon enough tae take up their attention.'

Eppie tried to do as the girl suggested, but it was impossible. When folk smiled at her in the street and wished her a good day, or when a shopkeeper thanked her for her custom, she was convinced that there was an element of malice or amusement behind every word and look.

She said nothing to her family when she visited Fordyce. For one thing, although she knew that she and her employer were innocent of any wrongdoing, the very fact that they were being talked about made her feel ashamed and embarrassed, and for another, she knew that this was something she had to resolve for herself. Finally, unable to bear the situation any longer, she made her decision, waiting until Lydia had gone to her room for the night before making her way upstairs to tap on the door of the library.

Alexander Geddes's normally neat desk was strewn with papers and he was scribbling busily when she went in. 'I'll not be a minute, Eppie,' he said without lifting his head from his work. 'Sit yourself down.'

She stayed on her feet, looking up at the two portraits on the fireplace wall, going hot with shame at the thought of what those two gentlefolk who had been wed to her employer would think of his name being linked with that of his housekeeper.

When he looked up a few moments later and saw that

she was still standing on the other side of the desk, her hands gripping each other tightly, his eyed darkened and his shoulders tensed. 'It's not something Lydia's done, is it? I thought that she was much happier with her life now.'

'It's not Lydia, Mr Geddes. I've come to tell you that I must leave your employment.'

'What?' He looked stunned. 'Leave us? But why?'

'I've been here for five years now and it's time to move on. I'll not leave you until I've found a suitable replacement, you've no need to worry about that.'

'Is it the wage I pay you? When did I last increase it?' He ran a hand through his greying hair. 'I'll pay you more, of course I will. You deserve it. Or do you need more help about the house?'

'It's nothing to do with the money, or more help – you've always been a generous employer and Sarah and Chrissie aren't afraid of hard work. I just feel that it's time to go elsewhere.'

'Someone's offered you more money, or more time off.' He got to his feet and began to come round the desk. 'Eppie, I thought that you were content here, and I know that Lydia's happier now, and she likes you. It was your idea to send her to those dance lessons, and there's such a difference in her since she started. She feels safe with you . . .' He broke off, glancing back at the cluttered desk. 'I can't be doing with this sort of upheaval just now,' he said. 'I have enough to worry about without more domestic problems. Whatever you've been offered, I can better it. You only need to tell me what I can do to keep you with us.'

'There's nothing you can do – I just need to go!' She had not realised that it would be so difficult. 'I'll find you another housekeeper, and then I must leave.'

She took a step towards the door, then another, but

before she could take a third Alexander Geddes caught her by the shoulders, whisked her about, and sat her down in a chair. Then he propped himself on the edge of the desk and said in a steely voice he kept for the men who worked for him in the marble quarry and his other businesses, 'I will not accept this, Eppie. You're lying to me and you will not leave this room until I have the truth out of you.' Then, as she gaped up at him, fear in her eyes, he modified his tone a little as he added, 'If I can do anything about whatever troubles you, then I will. If not, then I must accept your decision. But surely we've known each other for long enough – there should always be truth between us, even if it means you criticising me or even my daughter.'

'It's nothing to do with Lydia, sir, or with you.'

'I'm glad to hear that, at least.'

'It's . . .' She gulped nervously, then said in a rush, 'It's the folk in Portsoy.'

'All of them?' He looked startled. 'I doubt if even I can make a difference to every soul that lives in this town, but if you would explain just why they are troubling you, I'll try . . .'

'It's the gossip, sir. The gossip about me and . . .' the final word stuck in her throat like a fish bone, but as he said nothing, waiting for her to find the courage, she finally did '. . . me and you.'

'What?' He shot upright, coming off the edge of the desk to stand over her, staring down at her in disbelief. 'What have we done to cause gossip?'

'Nothing, sir – we've done nothing at all, but that doesn't stop folk's tongues wagging and I can't be doing with it, so I must go.'

'Wait!' He held up a hand. 'Let me get the sense of this. What is it that folk are saying about you and me?'

'That I persuaded you to send your mother away so that we could be . . . because I want to become mistress of this house.' Just saying the final words shamed her so much that she could only mumble, staring down at her lap.

There was a pause, then, 'Dear God!' Alexander Geddes said. 'What is it that makes folk so eager to malign their neighbours? To think that we sit shoulder to shoulder with them every Sunday morning in the kirk, and shake hands with them afterwards and we all wish each other well – and then they return to their homes and their malicious tattle.' His voice began to deepen with anger, and he started to pace the floor. Glancing up timidly, Eppie saw that he was scowling and that his fists had begun to clench.

'It's just the way folk are, sir. The best thing is usually to ignore their nonsense, but this time I can't do it, so I've decided tae go back to Fordyce.'

'You're letting them drive you away?'

'Mebbe it's time I went back to my own folk. I've not had the raising of my own daughter – she'll soon be full-grown and I'd like fine to spend time with her before it's too late.'

'Who would spread such scandal?' Geddes asked. 'I've never heard a whisper of it, but if I had I would have put a stop to it at once – you must know that. Not that it would trouble me as much as it's troubling you. But who would want to drive you out of the town like—' He stopped suddenly and swung round to face her.

'I don't know, sir,' Eppie said swiftly. 'Gossip can just start from a chance remark in a shop or on the street . . .' But she knew, by the stunned anger in his face, that he had already realised the truth.

'Whoever it was,' she hurried on, rising from the chair,

'that doesn't matter now. Now that you understand why I must go, I'll start looking round for a suitable housekeeper tomorrow. I'm sure I'll find one soon. Mr Geddes?' she ended timidly as he stared past her, lost in his own thoughts.

He blinked, and looked at her. 'Lydia is well settled with you, and so am I. If I put a stop to this nonsense – and I promise you that I *will* put a stop to it – then you'll stay with us?'

'No, sir. Once an idea's put into folks' heads they hold on to it, and I can't bear that. And as I said, I want to spend more time with my own bairn before it's too late. Goodnight, Mr Geddes,' she said, and hurried from the room before he could stop her.

14

Alexander's first reaction was to face his mother, make her admit to her malicious trouble-making, and demand that she end it at once. But on the following morning he realised that he would only be playing into her hands.

He was still a child when he first realised that Helen Geddes had an amazing ability to erase wrongdoing from her mind as soon as it was uncovered. She would only deny her involvement in this latest business, then go on to discuss it in the guise of concerned mother and grandmother. She would advise him, in a sweet and reasonable voice, that should such gossip be allowed to spread through the town, it would damage his reputation and upset his daughter.

And she would then suggest that the only way to put a stop to it was for him to dismiss Eppie Watt and find a more suitable housekeeper – someone older and beyond reproach. She would, of course, offer to undertake the task of appointing a new housekeeper – someone who would be answerable to her and who would keep her informed of all that went on in his household. He had no illusions as to the lengths she could go to.

He groaned as he recalled the number of times that her gentle, reasonable voice and those sincere blue eyes had turned him in a direction he had not intended to take. And the number of times he had come to regret listening to her.

No, there must be some other way to retain the harmony that had only recently come to bless his home, while at the same time putting paid to his mother's mischief-making. A way that he must find for himself.

And find it he did, after three days of searching. He examined it carefully from all angles, and decided that it was sound and acceptable.

Lydia had taken her new duties as mistress of the establishment very seriously. Instead of spending most of her time in her room when she was not with her governess, she had taken to flitting about the house and garden during her free time, planning meals in the kitchen with Eppie, overseeing the housework, or tending to her beloved bees, now beginning to stir from their winter sloth. Every time her father entered the house she was there, waiting to greet him and to make sure of his comfort.

This new and quite delightful Lydia pleased him, but at the same time it made it difficult for him to speak to Eppie in private. The only time he could be certain of being on his own with the housekeeper was when Lydia was asleep.

Three evenings after Eppie had handed in her notice, he pulled the little-used bell rope that hung by the library fireplace. When Eppie arrived he nodded to her to sit down, then began to pace the floor, his hands tucked behind his back.

'I want to talk to you about your decision to leave my employment.'

'Yes, sir. I've heard of a woman who lives in Fochabers

– a widow with her family all up and married. She has very good references and she expects to leave her present employment in three or four weeks' time.'

'I don't believe that that will be necessary. Lydia is well settled now, and I feel that bringing in a new housekeeper at this time would not be good for her.'

'I'm willing to stay on for a week or two, to see the woman settled in and make certain that you and Lydia are content with her.'

'Even so – you've encouraged my daughter to take an interest in the running of this house, which pleases me as it's time she began to learn these skills. And she's enjoying her dance classes more than I thought she would. They give her the chance to meet young folk – a chance that I now realise has been denied her,' he added guiltily. 'She needs more young company, and since one of your reasons for leaving us is that you want to be with your own daughter, it seemed to me that we could solve the problem by inviting her to come, as a friend and companion to Lydia.'

'Bring Charlotte to Portsoy?' Eppie blinked at him, startled.

'Why not? I can assure you that she will lack for nothing. I would provide for her as I provide for Lydia. She could share Lydia's governess, or if you prefer it, she can attend the girls' school. I believe that it is very good; I am considering sending Lydia there after the summer.'

Eppie was trying to collect her scattered thoughts. Her first reaction to the suggestion that she could have Charlotte close by was delight, but it would not, she realised, solve the problem. When Alexander finished speaking and pacing, and turned to look at her, his eyebrows raised, she shook her head.

'It's very kind of you, Mr Geddes, and generous too.

But it wouldn't stop the gossips. We'd still be the only adults in the house, and my Charlotte coming to bide here would only make them all the more certain that you and I are . . .' she stopped, her face burning, then said in a low voice '. . . living in sin. I can't do that to my daughter, or to yours.'

He heaved a long sigh, and began to pace again. Eventually he came to another stop before her and said, 'Then we must resolve the problem in another way. Face the gossips – let them think that they were right, if it pleases them – and stop them in their tracks once and for all.'

'But how do you propose to do that?'

'A simple solution,' said Alexander Geddes. 'You and I will be wed.'

Looking back on the scene, Eppie was shamed by the fact that sheer astonishment brought on a choking fit. She had no option but to snatch up her apron and bury her crimson face in it while she coughed and coughed again, each breath she struggled for resulting in yet another bout.

When she finally got herself under control again, her eyes streaming and her heart thumping, her employer was standing before her, offering a glass of water.

'I put a little brandy in it,' she heard him say above her own whooping and gasping. 'Try to drink it.'

Mercifully, the brandy was not strong enough to make the water unpalatable, or to send her into another paroxysm of coughing. She sipped cautiously and let the cool liquid trickle down her raw throat. While she drank, Alexander Geddes returned to his own side of the desk and sat down, his dark eyes fixed on her face.

'My apologies, Eppie – I had no idea that my proposal would alarm you so much.'

'It was the suddenness of it,' she finally managed to say.

'I suppose I could have put it better. I'm more used to business than to – other things. Would you like some time to consider my suggestion?' he asked.

'No, Mr Geddes, I would not, for there's no way I could agree to it.'

'Oh,' he said, then, 'am I such a bad catch?'

'It's got nothing tae do with that, Mr Geddes. When I wed Murdo Watt it was because I loved the man, and I still do. I'm not saying that I'd never marry again, but if I do, it'll be for love, not for convenience.'

'Not even for your daughter's sake?'

'She's happy enough where she is. I've no need to wed for her benefit.'

'But you're still apart – marriage to me would have allowed you to bring her here, and to still the gossips' tongues. In fact,' Geddes said, 'I would still be happy for you to bring your daughter to this house. It would be of benefit to Lydia to have a close friend.'

'It's kind of you, sir, but it would be no help to the situation I find myself in. The gossiping would probably get worse if I brought Charlotte here.' Eppie got to her feet. 'Will there be anything else, Mr Geddes?'

'No, there won't,' he said.

By the time he went to his own room for the night Alexander was beginning to see the humour of the situation. If his mother only knew that the housekeeper she had treated with such disdain had turned down his offer of marriage! He startled himself by laughing aloud at the thought, and then slapped a palm against the bedpost.

'By God!' he said. 'I'll do it. I'll see her expression for myself. It's the least she deserves for her meddling!'

* * *

On the following morning he was on his way to his mother's house astride his sturdy gelding when he recalled that in his haste, he had forgotten to take papers needed for a meeting that afternoon in the town of Elgin, several miles away. He muttered a curse under his breath; he would not have time to return for them after leaving his mother's. There was nothing for it but to turn the horse about, and hurry home.

When he let himself in at the front door the house was silent apart from the murmur of voices from the small parlour, where Lydia was at her lessons with Miss Hastie. Hurriedly, Geddes collected his papers and was on his way out when he heard the governess's voice say, 'You are a very stupid girl!'

He stopped in his tracks, unable for a moment to believe that he had heard correctly. Then the voice came again. 'I've a good mind to make you sit in the corner with a dunce's cap on your head.'

'I'm not stupid – I'm not!' Lydia shouted. 'You're a liar!'

'How dare you speak to me in that fashion! Your father will hear about this, madam, make no mistake about it. He'll punish you for your impertinence!'

Two strides took Alexander Geddes to the door of the small parlour. He threw it open to see Lydia, her face crimson with rage and mortification, glaring up at the governess, who was looming over her. The two of them swung round as the door opened.

'Ah, there you are, Mr Geddes. I'm afraid that Lydia has just been very rude to me!'

'I heard her, Miss Hastie. I heard you both. Lydia, go downstairs and ask Eppie to give you some milk and a biscuit. I have something to discuss with Miss Hastie.' Alexander stood aside and as his daughter passed him and he saw the way her teeth were clamped into her lower lip to stop its trembling, he felt such a wave of love go through him that it left him shaking.

'I scarcely think,' the governess said sharply as he closed the door, 'that your daughter should be rewarded. Bad behaviour should always be punished.'

'Miss Hastie, my daughter is not stupid, and I will not allow anyone to tell her that she is.'

The woman had the grace to look slightly ashamed, but only for a moment. 'No, she is not stupid, I agree with you there. But she has an unfortunate attitude towards authority. She resents being told what to do, and she refuses to accept chastisement, even when it is well deserved. If you ask me, Mr Geddes, she is a perfect example of the old adage. Spare the rod, Mr Geddes, and you will certainly spoil the child.'

'When I first interviewed you for the post of governess to my daughter, did I not explain to you that she had been unsettled by recent changes in the household? I had hoped that you would understand my meaning, and treat her gently.'

The woman's sparse eyebrows rose. 'Gently? Did you not tell me, Mr Geddes, that you wanted the child's education to be brought up to an acceptable standard for admission to the girls' school?'

'I did, but telling her that she is stupid does not seem to me to be the right way to achieve that standard.'

'If you will forgive me for saying so, sir, I am a trained schoolteacher. I know how to get the best out of children.'

'By treating them harshly?'

'By instilling discipline. It was the way I was raised, and I am grateful to those adults who taught me to listen and to obey without argument.'

'I have a feeling, Miss Hastie, that you must have been a most unhappy child,' Alexander said. 'But I will not have my daughter treated as, clearly, you were. I think it best that I find another governess for her – one who can follow my instructions.'

The woman's pale face suddenly flooded with hot blood. 'You're dismissing me?'

'Sadly, I must, for my daughter's sake. You may leave now, and I will make sure that you are paid until the end of the month. Goodbye, Miss Hastie,' Alexander said, and went down to the kitchen, where Eppie and Lydia sat close together at the table. As soon as he went in the two of them stood up; Lydia's mouth was set in familiar, mutinous lines that were at odds with the tears glistening on her cheeks, while Eppie had an arm about the child, so that they were both confronting Alexander. It looked, for all the world, he thought, half-amused, half-exasperated, as though he were the enemy, rather than that unpleasant bully of a woman he had just dismissed.

'She's leaving the house,' he said abruptly, 'and she will not be back.'

'Miss Hastie?' Suddenly Lydia's face was radiant. 'Oh, Father!'

To his astonishment she broke away from Eppie and ran round the table to throw her arms about his waist. He looked down at the dark head against his chest, and was shaken by a second wave of fierce, protective love. Awkwardly, he patted her soft shining hair. 'There there,' he said, and then, over her head to Eppie, 'And now I must find another governess.'

Another governess – and another housekeeper, he thought a few minutes later, on his way to his mother's house once more. Would he never be free of the problems that beset him?

Arriving at the house, he paid a lad to take charge of his mount before rapping on the front door with such determination that he could hear the maid running through the hall in her haste to answer the summons.

'Your mistress is in?' he asked abruptly as soon as the door opened.

'Aye, sir. She's in the parlour. Will I take yer hat an'—'

'There's no need for that,' Alexander said crisply. 'I'll not be staying.' And then, tossing the words over his shoulder as he marched across the hall and began to mount the stairs, 'I'll announce myself.'

Helen Geddes was reading her newspaper, sitting with her back to the window to catch the light, and holding the paper at arm's length. Her fine blue eyes had been dimming slightly over the past year, but she was so proud of their beauty that she was doing her best to delay the day when she would have to hide them behind spectacles. Now, she looked up with a start as the door was thrown open and her son strode in, whipping off his hat as he entered.

'Alexander – I didn't expect you this morning.' Her eyes swept over him. 'You might have left your coat in the hall, my dear. I'll tell Maisie to bring tea—'

'I don't need tea, Mother, for I'll not be staying for long. I'm on my way to Elgin, but first, I have a matter of business to discuss with you, if you have a moment?'

'Yes, of course.' She folded her newspaper and put it aside, motioning him to a chair. He glanced at it, but did not sit down, choosing instead to force her to look up at him.

'I have a problem, Mother, so I have come to talk it over with you.'

'Naturally.' Helen was delighted – she had known that sooner or later her son would have to turn to her for advice instead of dealing with everything on his own. 'Is it to do with Lydia?'

'Not at all. As a matter of fact, her sulkiness has much improved now that she's going to these dance classes. She enjoys them greatly and I'm told that she's a fine dancer. I should have sent her years ago.'

A frown creased the soft fine skin on her forehead. 'Are you sure that you're right in encouraging this fancy of hers, Alexander? Is it wise? You don't know who she's mixing with, or what diseases she might pick up. She's always been a delicate child—'

'She seems sturdy enough to me, and if learning to dance makes her happy then I'm contented with it. No, Mother, I'm here on another matter entirely. A daft thing, but annoying all the same. I've been told that some foolish tales are sweeping through the town; tales concerning me and my housekeeper.'

'Really?' Now Helen's eyebrows arched carefully. 'What sort of gossip?'

'You don't know, Mother?'

'I make it a rule never to listen to tittle-tattle,' she said primly.

'Of course not. That would be beneath you, would it not? Well, then, I must tell you, unsavoury though it is for me to tell and for you to hear. It seems that some vindictive woman – it must surely be a woman,' he added scathingly, 'since men have more to do with their time than meddle in matters that don't concern them – some vindictive woman is busy telling folk that Eppie Watt and I are living in sin.'

'My goodness! That's terrible, Alexander. Has Lydia heard this?'

'Not as far as I know, and I intend to make sure that it never reaches her ears.'

'This must have come about since I left your house. The gossips, whoever they are, must have assumed that I was removed in order to leave the way clear for the housekeeper to make a good marriage.'

'That,' Alexander said, 'is exactly what I heard. Strange that it should come into your mind word for word, when you say you've not heard it for yourself.'

Colour flooded his mother's face, and she fanned her flushed cheeks with one hand. 'The very thought of it has upset me. Would you open that window, please? I need some air.' Then, as he did as asked, she hurried on, 'I can see why you need my advice. Alexander, you have no choice but to dismiss Eppie Watt. You and I are well known in this area, and well respected; we cannot afford to be tainted by scandal. What your father would say if he were still with us I do not know. I will find a good elderly woman to take her place.'

'But Lydia likes Eppie, Mother, and she trusts her. Changing housekeepers now will only upset her.'

'And discovering – almost certainly from one of the children she meets at this dance class of hers,' Helen said pointedly, 'that her father is the subject of gossip will do her no good either!'

'Exactly. That is why I have decided,' Alexander said, relishing every word, 'that the best way out of this unpleasant business and at the same time beat the scandal-mongers at their own game, is for me to marry Eppie.'

15

Alexander Geddes had not meant to upset Eppie with his proposal of marriage on the previous evening, and he had been quite concerned by her reaction. Now, though, he watched with secret pleasure as his mother, with a shrill scream of 'What?' shot out of her chair and then almost immediately collapsed back into it as though her knees refused to bear her weight. The telltale flush ebbed swiftly from her cheeks, leaving them ashen.

'You cannot be serious!' Her voice was little more than a whisper, and one hand went up to clutch at her throat as though she were defending herself against a physical attack.

'I am perfectly serious. My main concern is for Lydia – as, I am sure, is yours. She needs a mother, and she has come to trust Eppie. Eppie has a daughter of the same age, which means that Lydia would have a sister. And by making Eppie my wife,' Alexander finished cheerfully, 'I would silence the malicious gossips once and for all. As you can see, my decision would deal with several problems at one stroke.'

'I won't allow it!'

'I'm a grown man, Mother, and I have already buried two wives. I don't see that you can have any say in whether or not I should take a third.'

'But she's a servant! And a fisher lassie before you took her into your kitchen. Alexander, do you not realise that if you marry this woman you will make me a laughing stock? My friends will refuse to speak to me – they will whisper and point behind my back. You cannot marry that woman!'

Helen Geddes seemed to have aged a good ten years in the past few minutes. She sat huddled in the chair she had filled comfortably when he first entered her parlour, her white face shrunken and her eyes huge. And filled with genuine pain, he suddenly noticed. It was time to relent and end the farce before he frightened her into a fit of apoplexy.

'No, Mother, I cannot marry her.' He sat on the edge of a chair close to hers. 'I already know that because last night I asked her to be my wife, and she turned me down.'

'She refused you?'

'Sadly, she did. Eppie Watt is a woman of greater integrity than I realised. She would rather be widow to her dead husband than mistress of my home. The loss,' Alexander said, 'is mine.' And then, as the clock in the hall chimed the half hour, 'I must go.'

He got to his feet and looked down at his mother, who was still struggling to come to terms with what she had just heard.

'But I intend to retain Eppie as my housekeeper – in fact, I am determined on it. As I said, she is a woman of great integrity; this vicious and uncalled for scandal-mongering has upset her so deeply that she is talking of leaving my employment. But I'm just as determined that she shall stay where she is. So, Mother, I would appreciate it if you could put a stop to any further gossip – should it happen to reach your ears. If it doesn't end very soon, I will be forced to make it known – through the pages of the *Banffshire Advertiser* if needs be,' he added, stooping to pick up the newspaper from the floor, where it had fallen when Helen leaped from her chair, 'that I offered to make Eppie my wife, and she refused me. That, if all else fails, should stop the chattering. Or at least turn it on me, and not on my blameless housekeeper. Good day, Mother.'

On his way out he took time to look in at the kitchen door. 'I believe that your mistress would like a hot cup of tea,' he told the servant, 'and perhaps some smelling salts.'

Claiming his horse, which was cropping grass by the roadside, he tossed an additional coin to the lad who had been tending it and then leaped up into the saddle. As he went on his way to the distant town of Elgin, he began to whistle a cheerful tune.

It was a pleasant day, though with a stiff wind that chased the clouds across the sky before they had time to think of releasing rain on to the ground below, and whipped the tops of the high waves on the firth into white lace. Alexander's thick coat and the scarf about his throat kept him snug. He always enjoyed this journey to Elgin; the road he had to travel took him past the turn-off to Fordyce on the left, then Sandend on the right, and through farming country for a few miles before reaching Cullen, home of the wealthy Seafield family, feudal lords of Portsoy.

The wide main street fell away before him steeply, so that it seemed as if he and his horse were going to ride straight into the sea, which was framed in a stone archway, part of the great viaduct that ran above the town. On the other side of the arch the road swung to the left; following it, he looked down on his right to the roofs of the fisher cottages squeezed between the road and the shore, then he was riding uphill again, back to the green fields.

One of the reasons why he preferred to travel on horseback rather than by coach was that Alexander Geddes was a man who felt more comfortable in his own company than in the company of others. He enjoyed looking about him at the fields where sheep and cattle grazed, or up at the birds wheeling and calling overhead, or out to the Moray Firth which, whatever the weather, was one of the bonniest sights he knew.

But today, once the euphoria of besting his mother had eased, his mind was claimed by more sombre thoughts. Freeing himself and his household of Helen Geddes's domination had come at a cost. At the time, he had thought to buy her a small but pleasant house in its own little garden, with one live-in servant and extra help for the heavy work brought in on a part-time basis. His plans had included a part-time gardener as well. He could afford to run both households, but even so, the large house his mother had chosen had cost him dear. He had assumed that she would take the furniture from her bedroom and her private parlour with her, but with maddening perverseness she had decided that she would leave most of that furniture behind, and furnish her new home afresh throughout. This meant that he had been forced to spend a lot of money on the expensive pieces she selected, not to mention the wages for more servants than he had first expected, and a full-time gardener, with a boy to help him.

He may have won his freedom, but his mother had made sure that he paid a heavy price.

And then there was the loss of the *Grace-Ellen*. A date had not as yet been set for the Board of Trade investigation into the tragedy, but when it did take place Alexander was determined to get as much compensation for the families of the crew as he could – the widows, the young children, and the elderly parents who had lost the sons they relied on to help them through the enforced poverty of helpless old age. In the meantime, he was paying each family a small monthly pension from his own purse, which seemed to emptying before his very eyes.

A century ago Portsoy had been a major trading port, but tariffs imposed on wines, silks and other imports during the Napoleonic Wars in the early part of nineteenth century had caused a decline in trading. Alexander did well enough, and the two cargo ships he owned took fish, grain, serpentine from the marble quarry and soapstone to Europe, bringing back coal, bones, flax and anything else that could be sold at a profit. In the early part of the year one of them had been badly damaged in a storm, only just managing to limp into Calais and was then forced to remain there for some time while costly repairs were carried out. Then there was the marble quarry. A week earlier he had received a letter from Edward Ramsay, the principal share-holder, informing him that with the advent of modern machinery it was felt that the time had come to consider making changes to the small Portsoy quarry. Someone would be travelling north within the next few months to assess the quarry and discuss future business projects with him. Alexander groaned, so preoccupied in his thoughts that the turn-offs to the fishing villages of Portknockie, Findochty, Portessie and the town of Buckie fell away behind him unnoticed.

Riding down the narrow main street of Fochabers and crossing the bridge over the waters of the River Spey, Alexander wished that Ramsay would either leave him in peace to continue as things were at present, or take responsibility for the quarry off his hands altogether.

Then, riding out along the final stretch to Elgin, he fell to thinking of Lydia. She had benefited from her dancing classes, though from what he gathered from the things she did not say rather than what she did say, she was not finding it easy to make friends among the other young people who attended the class. This, he felt, was because she had had a lonely childhood, with only his mother and the governess for company. Perhaps he should find a girl's school that took in boarders – if the fees were reasonable, he could manage them. But he was not certain that her education to date had equipped her well. It would be madness to send her to a school where she was unable to compete academically with her fellow pupils.

It was almost a relief when he realised that he was riding into the handsome and elegant cathedral town of Elgin, and was finally free to concentrate his mind on the day's business, instead of fretting over domestic problems.

The fresh air had whetted his appetite and there was time, before his meeting, to eat in one of the town's inns. Handing his mount over to the stable boy, he stretched his limbs before going indoors to wash the road's dust from his hands and face.

One of the men he was to meet with later was already seated at a table, so Alexander joined him, relieved for once to have someone else to talk to instead of having to deal with the thoughts that were still chasing round in his brain – Lydia's future, Eppie's imminent departure and the business of trying to get accustomed to a new housekeeper, not to mention his mother and her expensive lifestyle and vinegar tongue.

'Did ye ride in?' his companion asked when they had ordered their food. And then, when Alexander nodded, 'So did I, since it's a pleasant enough day. I've no' long arrived – I must have come down the road frae Fordyce as you were leavin' Portsoy. A few minutes either way and we could have ridden in together.'

'You live in Fordyce?'

'Born and bred, and weel content tae die there when my time comes. It's a bonny wee place. Have ye ever visited it?'

'No, but my housekeeper comes from there. Eppie Watt – that's her married name; she's the widow of a Portsoy fisherman. I've no knowledge of her own name.'

His companion frowned over the name for a moment, then said, 'I think ye'll find that she was born a McNaught. Her faither's a schoolmaster.'

'I believe I've heard that.'

'A good one, tae. I could have sworn that my lad was beyond learnin', for he'd never sit on his rump long enough tae let anythin' stick tae his shoes, let alone stick in his noddle, but Peter McNaught has the patience o' a saint an' the ability tae hold a youngster's interest. I don't ken how he did it, but by the time my son came out of the Academy he was able tae add and subtract and make a good fist at writin' too. And he knew his geography. He's in Leith now – he owns a ships' chandlery and does well out o' it. Aye, the McNaughts are well thought of in Fordyce,' the man went on as the waiter arrived with two platefuls of food. He tucked a large handkerchief into his shirt collar and then picked up his knife and fork and began to saw busily at the large chop set before him. 'He's got two lassies of his own. I think your hoosekeeper's the younger. The other one's as clever as her father – she teaches in the infant school and I've heard good reports of her too.'

The conversation turned to talk of the forthcoming meeting, but on the way home later that afternoon Alexander returned to fretting over what to do about Lydia, and how to find a way of retaining his housekeeper. And then, as he passed the end of the Fordyce road, the answer came to him.

He wasted no time when he got back home, entering the house by the side door that took him straight to the kitchen.

Eppie, rolling out dough on the big kitchen table, her sleeves tucked up above her elbows to keep them clean, was startled when he walked in, still in his outdoor clothes. 'I didn't hear you come in, Mr Geddes . . .' she began to dust flour from her hands and roll her sleeves down.

'Where's Lydia?'

'At her dancing. I'm off in another five minutes tae fetch her home.' Now that Lydia had settled into the dance class Eppie only needed to take her and then bring her home again. 'Can I get you some food before I go?'

'Nothing at all. Go on with your work.' Alexander pulled a chair out from the table and sat down. 'I've been thinking that mebbe I should send Lydia to the girls' school after the summer. She needs to meet folk of her own age. What d'you say?'

'I think it would be the right thing, Mr Geddes.'

'What school does your own daughter attend?'

'She did well in the infant school, but now that she's getting older, she's in the girl's school. My sister's tutoring her at home too.'

'Is she clever – your daughter?'

'So they say,' Eppie admitted, unable to prevent a note of pride creeping into her voice. 'Marion – my sister – says she takes in knowledge like a cloth soaking up water.'

'I don't believe that any of Lydia's governesses have made a good job of teaching her. It was all very well when she was small, but she should know more than sums and lettering and reading by now.' Alexander settled his spine more comfortably against the chair's wooden back and stretched his booted legs across the flagstones. It was pleasant to be sitting in this warm, fragrant kitchen, watching Eppie's rounded arms send the roller across the dough with smooth, easy sweeps. Every few seconds she put the roller down and turned the dough, shaping it with quick, deft pats of her floured hands before picking up the roller again.

'I was thinking,' he said, 'that she could do with special tuition over the summer to prepare her for the school. Would your sister be willing to take on the position?'

'Marion? I don't know, sir. Mebbe she would.'

'You'll ask her for me, then, next time you go to Fordyce?'

'If you're sure. But it would mean Marion coming here every day, or Lydia going to Fordyce. There's surely someone nearer here than Fordyce.'

'I need a good governess. If your sister's willing, she could spend the summer here. We've got plenty of room, and if your own daughter would like to come as well I'd be willing to pay your sister to tutor both of them. Your girl would be company for Lydia, and,' he played his trump card with the carefully casual expression of a gambler displaying his winning hand, 'with your own sister here to keep watch over the two of us, the gossips will surely be silenced once and for all.'

* * *

To Eppie's surprise, Marion did not turn down the offer of employment as soon as she heard it. She narrowed her pale blue eyes and pursed her neat firm mouth in deliberation, then said, 'And Charlotte and I would both live as guests of Mr Geddes's?'

'Bed and board would be included, of course, but you'd be paid a wage for your work as governess to his daughter – and to Charlotte.'

'Please, Aunt Marion,' Charlotte beseeched, hopping up and down. She had never tired of asking Eppie all about Lydia during her visits home, and the thought of actually meeting the girl, and seeing her fine home, thrilled her. 'Please say yes!'

'I'll think about it,' Marion decided, 'and tell you before you go back tomorrow.'

'Just think,' Charlotte whispered in the dark of the night, when she and her mother were in bed together. 'We're going to spend the whole summer together, you and me!'

'Only if your Aunt Marion decides to accept Mr Geddes's invitation,' Eppie warned, terrified in case the girl built her hopes up too high and had to cope with disappointment.

'She will! I'm sure she's as eager as I am to see the fine big house where you work. Anyway, I told the bees about it this afternoon, and I explained to them that it is very important for you and me to be together,' Charlotte said. 'And I told the good Lord too, when I said my prayers. Aunt Marion will say yes, I know she will!'

A few days after the school term ended Marion McNaught and her niece travelled to Portsoy in a hired carriage sent by Alexander Geddes to convey them and their luggage. The heaviest item was a large box containing the textbooks that Marion deemed necessary for the task that lay before her.

They arrived, as arranged, at the front door, and stood in the hall, gazing in awe at the handsome panelling and the large paintings, while the driver, with the aid of a man hired by Alexander Geddes, carried their luggage to the upper bedroom the two were to share.

Lydia, as excited as Charlotte at the prospect of a meeting, had been watching out of the parlour window for the new arrivals for over an hour. When the carriage drew to a standstill below, she rushed along the hall and down the back stairs shrieking, 'They're here, Eppie – they're here!' and then, suddenly struck by an attack of shyness when Eppie opened the front door, she hovered at the rear of the hall.

'Lydia . . .' Eppie, suddenly remembering the girl, turned and held a hand out to her '. . . come and meet your new governess, Miss McNaught, and Charlotte, your fellow student.'

The girl came forwards slowly, and then at a firm nod from Eppie, she dropped a curtsey to Marion before holding out a hand to Charlotte. 'How do you do?' she said in a stilted little voice. Charlotte, overcome with a sudden shyness of her own, shrank back against Marion – choosing her aunt, and not her mother as a refuge, Eppie noted with a pang – and then, urged forwards by Marion, she put her hand into Lydia's.

'How do you do?' Her voice was little more than a whisper.

'Lydia, show Charlotte the room that she and Miss McNaught will share, and then I'm sure she would like to see your dolls. I will take Miss McNaught to the schoolroom.'

'This was used by Mrs Geddes as her private parlour,' she explained to Marion as they went into the room, 'but it was also used by Lydia and her governess. Mr Geddes has decided that for the summer, at least, it is to be known as the schoolroom, and at other times you will use it as your own parlour.'

'That's very civil of him.' Marion, trying hard to behave as though she were used to visiting grand houses, looked around the small, well-furnished room with approval. 'When do I meet my new employer?'

'This evening. He'll be back in time for dinner. I do hope that you're going to be happy here, Marion.' Eppie knew that if her sister decided to return to Fordyce, Charlotte would have to go with her.

Marion gazed with rapture at the pretty little writing bureau where Helen Geddes had whiled away many hours penning notes to her friends. She imagined herself sitting there, planning out the next day's schoolwork. It would be such a delight to live like a lady for the next three months.

Aloud, she said casually, 'I'm sure that it will be a pleasant diversion, and in any case, it's only for the summer.'

16

In the bedroom that Charlotte was to share with her aunt, she and Lydia eyed each other in a wary silence.

'It's a nice room,' Charlotte ventured at last. And then, as Lydia pursed her mouth into a rosebud but said nothing, 'May I see your dolls now?'

Lydia considered the question for a moment before leaving the room. Charlotte followed her across the hallway, her eyes widening as she walked into an Aladdin's cave of toys. They were piled along the bottom of the bed, with its pretty rose-sprigged white counterpane and its pile of pillows, and lined up on a shelf running the length of the room. There were delicate Eastern dolls with perfect, slant-eyed porcelain faces, wooden dolls with painted smiles, rag dolls and dolls with wax faces and real hair. There were baby dolls in long robes, girl dolls and boy dolls, and elegant lady dolls dressed in silks and lace.

A handsome snow-white rocking horse decked out with an elaborate leather saddle and a deep-scarlet harness was mounted on a wooden frame that allowed him to move back and forth. When Lydia saw Charlotte's face soften with desire at sight of it she immediately climbed into the saddle and set the horse in motion, the tiny silver bells attached to the reins tinkling with each movement. The animal had flared nostrils and large dark eyes, and Charlotte could see that the thick tail, as well as the mane on its proudly arched neck, was made of real horsehair.

A puppet theatre was set out on a table by the window, and another shelf held a long row of books. Charlotte's fingers itched to take them down and open them to see what wonders they held within their stiff covers, but she resisted the urge, aware that it was too early for her to presume.

The front of the large doll's house lay open, and its interior was far beyond anything that Charlotte had ever seen, or even dreamed of. Again, her fingers yearned to touch, so she tucked her hands behind her back to keep them well away from temptation while her eyes feasted on every detail.

The ground floor held a large kitchen with an adjacent pantry, both complete with everything that would be found in real kitchen premises. Above was a parlour with paintings and tiny vases of flowers and miniature plants on long-legged occasional tables. There was a marble fireplace and velvet curtains, and plush chairs and sofas where the master and mistress of the house reclined. The dining room table was set for a meal, with elegant glasses and dishes, a delicate candelabra in the middle, and even cutlery laid out at each place.

The floor above held a nursery with its own doll's house, rocking horse and tiny toys, as well as a baby in its lace-bedecked cradle and a small child playing on the rug, supervised by a uniformed nursery maid in a rocking chair by the fire. There were two bedrooms on that floor, one with a four-poster bed, and the very top floor held a servant's dormitory.

The rocking horse's silver bells tinkled faster and faster as Lydia threw her body back and forth, urging her mount to greater speeds. Finally, she let it slow down, then slid from its back.

'You have lovely toys,' Charlotte ventured, and Lydia tossed her head in acknowledgement of the compliment.

'My father gave them to me, and my grandmother too. Some of them came from other countries in my father's ships,' she said, taking a delicate little Japanese lady, in full traditional costume, from the shelf. 'This one,' she said, and then, putting the doll back and lifting a little Dutch doll, 'and this one. They're all mine. I have bees too, in the garden.'

'I know. They came from my grandfather's garden. He has bees.'

'The ones in our garden are mine,' Lydia said swiftly. And then, with a sidelong glance. 'Are you clever?'

'I don't know. Are you?'

'My father asked Miss McNaught to be my governess over the summer because he thinks I've outgrown Miss Hastie. I'm glad, because she wasn't a nice person.'

'My Aunt Marion is a very good teacher,' Charlotte said quickly. Unfortunately, her attempt to defend her aunt was construed by Lydia as a strong hint that, having already had the benefit of Marion's teaching, she was cleverer than Lydia.

'I,' she said coolly, 'am the mistress of this house. Eppie says so. I plan out the meals with her every evening before I go to bed.'

'You're very fortunate to live in such a beautiful house. And very pretty,' Charlotte added with genuine admiration. Lydia's green eyes widened slightly, and her delicate oval face flushed with pleasure at the unexpected compliment.

'Do you think so?'

'Oh yes, indeed. I wish I had black hair like yours.' Charlotte caught up a handful of her own brown curly hair and gave it a good tug. 'Mine is so ordinary.'

'My father says that I look like my mother.' Lydia opened a beautifully enamelled box on one of the nursery shelves and brought out a little silver-framed portrait. She brought it to Charlotte and the two girls studied it, their heads close together.

'She's beautiful too,' Charlotte said. 'And you do look very like her.'

'She died on the day I was born, so every birthday I have is sad for my father because it's also the day she died,' Lydia explained. 'I wish she were still here.'

'I wish my father were still here. He drowned when I was little and I don't remember him.'

'We're both orphans then.'

'Half-orphans,' Charlotte corrected. 'You still have a father and I still have a mother.' She had always been a generous child, and for a moment she was tempted to suggest that perhaps they could share each other's living parents, then she realised that it was too early in their new and somewhat fragile acquaintanceship to suggest such a thing.

'Half-orphans,' Lydia agreed. And then, fetching her least favourite doll from the shelf, 'You can hold her if you want.'

After investigating her sleeping quarters and unpacking her things, Marion descended the kitchen stairs and settled herself at the table to watch her sister prepare the evening meal.

'Don't you think that it will be difficult for the two of us – me upstairs as the governess and a guest in the house while you're the housekeeper, living below stairs?'

'Not at all.' Eppie herself had been worrying over the situation, but she was determined that spending the summer with Charlotte was worth any embarrassment. She chopped carrots briskly. 'I'm not in the least troubled, and neither is Mr Geddes. It will do Lydia the world of good to have a companion of her own age. Her grandmother spoiled her and discouraged her from playing with other children. I'm fond of her, but I warn you, Marion, you may find her a bit of a handful at first.'

'Hardly – you forget that I'm used to dealing with children.'

'Be careful with her, Marion,' Eppie said anxiously, 'I doubt she's of the same standard as Charlotte.'

'I doubt it very much, since Charlotte's had the benefit of my teaching since before she was old enough to start formal schooling.' Marion's voice was smug, and Eppie had to bite her lip and take her frustration out on the carrots instead. It hurt her to think that due to her circumstances Marion had had more to do with her beloved daughter than she had herself for so many years.

'I believe that Charlotte herself has more natural academic ability than poor Lydia ever had,' she pointed out, unable to keep a slight edge from her voice.

But Marion was not to be bested. 'Of course,' she agreed. 'After all, she comes from an academic family.' And then, mercifully changing the subject. 'This is a very handsome house. And very comfortable too. I looked into the dining room before coming downstairs and I see that the table is set for five. Is there to be a guest this evening?'

'No, it's for the household – Mr Geddes and Lydia,

who is allowed to dine downstairs in the evenings now – and you, me and Charlotte.'

'You dine at the same table as your employer?'

'Only for the evening meal, and only since his mother moved into her own house. Mrs Geddes would never have allowed it when she was mistress of this place, but Mr Geddes felt that it was better for Lydia to have the two of us with her at the dinner table.'

'I see. Going by what I hear of him, he seems to be quite a modern employer.'

'I suppose he is,' Eppie agreed blandly, adding the carrots to the casserole she was making.

'When will be he home?'

'At around seven, I believe. We will eat at eight, and Lydia and Charlotte will go to bed immediately afterwards. I will come back downstairs, and you will be able to use the small parlour. I'm sure that you have a lot of preparation for your first lesson tomorrow.'

Alexander Geddes returned home at two minutes after seven. As he mounted the stairs to his room, Lydia came rushing from her nursery.

'They're here!' she mouthed elaborately, and would have tugged him into her room if he had not held back.

'Come in here, you can talk to me while I shave.'

His shaving things had been laid out, and a jug of hot water had been placed in the room only minutes before his arrival. While he shaved, Lydia perched on the edge of a chair, telling him all about the newcomers.

'She – Charlotte – says that I'm very pretty!'

'Indeed? She's quite right.'

'Do you think so?'

'I've always thought so.'

'But you never said,' she pouted.

'Only because I don't want you to become too proud.' He cast a sidelong glance at her, and was amused by her scowl. 'So – I hope you made Charlotte feel at home?'

'Yes, of course. Father,' she lowered her voice to a confidential murmur, 'I believe that she's very clever.'

'Did she say so?'

'No, but she seemed interested in my books. And she looks clever.'

'Is she as pretty as you?'

'I don't think so, and she doesn't think so.'

'Then she can envy your looks, and you can envy her brain. And just think – if you work hard at your lessons over the summer, you can become just as clever as she is. But she might not be able to become as pretty as you are.'

'Oh yes!' Lydia was clearly charmed by the thought.

'And what of your new governess – Miss McNaught?'

'She seems quite nice.'

'Good.' Alexander patted his face dry. 'I'm sure that we are all going to get along very well. And now you can return to your own room, for I must change into fresh clothes before dinner. You don't want me to disgrace you before your new companion and your new governess, do you?'

Twenty minutes before dinner was due to be served, he went to his library and rang the bell. When Eppie arrived he said, 'I hope that your sister and daughter have settled in?'

'Oh yes, thank you, sir. They're very pleased with their room, and Marion is delighted with the classroom.'

'Do you think that Miss McNaught would be willing to take a glass of sherry with me before dinner, Eppie? I would like to discuss Lydia's lessons with her.'

'She's in the small parlour, Mr Geddes. I'll fetch her.' Eppie whisked off and returned in under a minute to usher her sister into the room. She introduced the two of them swiftly before excusing herself and hurrying back to her pots and pans.

'Welcome to my home, Miss McNaught. I hope that you enjoy your stay with us. Will you have a glass of sherry?'

'Thank you, Mr Geddes.' Marion, suddenly and most unexpectedly shy, kept her gaze lowered.

He motioned her to a chair by the fire, and after bringing the wine to her – in a very handsome crystal glass, she noted with pleasure – he seated himself in the chair opposite. 'I understand that your niece, Charlotte, does well at her lessons.'

'She's a clever child,' Marion acknowledged, 'with a quick, enquiring mind. But then, she's had the benefit of being raised in a household that can boast two teachers.'

'While Lydia seems to have had little success with her governesses – unless, of course, she is simply not very academic. That is what I need to find out. Unfortunately I am a busy man, and so a great deal of her upbringing has been left to my mother, who lived with us until recently. No doubt,' he added, giving her a level look, 'Eppie has told you something of our family life.'

'A little – but nothing of a private nature.' For the first time Marion met his glance fully, and was surprised to realise that her heart had begun to skip like a lamb in the spring sunshine, and her face was beginning to feel quite warm. As soon as she could, she glanced away and took a steadying sip of wine.

'I am quite sure of that. I have always found your sister to be discreet. But I must speak openly to you about Lydia if you are to be of any help to her. Her own mother died when she was born, and my mother spoiled and indulged her more than I realised at the time. She would never allow Lydia to mix with other children and had little interest in the child's formal education. When Lydia reached the age where she developed a mind of her own, her grandmother saw that natural development as bad behaviour. When she was chastised, the child became rebellious. Finally, more for Lydia's sake than hers, I admit, I realised that my mother would be happier in a house of her own. I feel quite ashamed of all those years when I put business affairs before my own child,' he admitted.

'But you had a duty to provide for her.' Marion found herself rushing to defend him. 'You had little choice but to make sure that your business prospered, and it was natural to believe that your daughter was safe in the hands of her grandmother and a governess.'

'That may be so, but as a result of her upbringing I fear that you will find quite a difference between Lydia and Charlotte in academic terms. And you may also find that my daughter can be quite rebellious.'

'From what you've told me, I would say that she's been confused by her grandmother's move from indulging her to criticising her. She needs to feel secure again, and to settle into a proper routine. I can promise you that I will do all I can to build up her confidence. And as for her academic skills – I will assess her carefully, without her knowing it, and if it is necessary I will work out a way of bringing her up to the standard of others in her age group. As for Charlotte – she is a pleasant, agreeable child and I think that she will make a good companion for Lydia. Do I have your permission to take your daughter out and about, Mr Geddes?'

'Indeed you do – I plan to send her to the girls' school in town when you judge her to be ready for it, and I want her to learn how to mix with other children. Thanks to Eppie, she's now taking dance classes and enjoying them more than I had believed possible. It seems that she has a natural talent for dance – something that I had to learn from your sister since I did not realise it myself,' he added ruefully.

'Perhaps Charlotte should also be enrolled in that class.'

'I will be happy to pay her fees. Does she also have a natural talent for dancing?'

'Not at all.' A smile turned up the corners of Marion's mouth, and twinkled in her eyes. 'Although she has a quick mind, in the physical sense she can be quite clumsy at times. But I believe that it will be good for Lydia to see that while Charlotte may outdo her in one way, she can outdo Charlotte in another.'

As he watched the new governess leave the room Alexander Geddes felt that at last, he had done the right thing by his daughter. He had already formed a good opinion of Marion McNaught, with her calm, forthright manner and her neat appearance. Her hair was a darker brown than Eppie's, and drawn tightly back from an oval face. During the few occasions when her gaze had met his for an instant he had noted that her eyes were blue and her features more classic than her sister's. He felt more cheerful than he had for some time, and confident that this latest governess would be an excellent mentor for his daughter.

For her part, Marion had hurried upstairs from the study to the room she was sharing with Charlotte. It was empty, so there was nobody to see her pour cold water from the pretty jug into the matching china basin and then proceed to splash her hot face again and again, until it began to cool down.

Drying herself, she looked over the top of the towel,

meeting her own wide, somewhat dismayed blue eyes in the mirror. She was going to find it hard to sit meekly at the dinner table with her normal serenity, because for the first time in her well ordered, controlled and eminently sensible life, Marion McNaught had fallen, suddenly and entirely unexpectedly, in love.

17

'The way Mrs Geddes sees it, Lydia will eventually marry a man with money, and the only things she needs to know is how to run a house and how to behave in social circles – not that the poor wee thing's had much practice in that way either,' Eppie had explained to her sister when she first spoke about Marion and Charlotte spending the summer in the Geddes household. Even so, Marion was shocked when she realised just how little the child knew.

'She's scarcely been taught more than her letters and the very beginnings of numbering,' she told Eppie. 'Charlotte's away ahead of her!'

'You'll not let Charlotte get a swelled head over it, will you?' Eppie asked anxiously. She knew, although Charlotte had not said a word to her, that there was awkwardness between the two girls, mainly due to Lydia's insecurity and nervousness with other children. The last thing she wanted was for the poor girl to feel inadequate in the schoolroom.

'Of course not – and she's got more sense than to crow in any case. But at the same time, we can't allow her own education to be harmed. I must find a way of encouraging Lydia and opening up her mind, while continuing to work with Charlotte at her level. It won't be easy,' Marion said, and then, enthusiasm beginning to sparkle in her eyes and put steel into her voice, 'but I shall do it!'

At first her attempts met with little success; it was as though Lydia had erected a stone wall around herself and was daring her new governess to try to break it down. But Marion, with a patience that Eppie had never suspected her sister possessed, chipped away at it day by day, making the most of every flicker of interest she saw in her new pupil's eyes. While Charlotte worked diligently at her own lessons Marion set herself to find different ways of attracting Lydia's attention and interest.

Sometimes, she suddenly called a halt to the schoolwork and announced that it was too nice a day to waste time indoors. Instead, they went out into the garden to play games or watch the bees in their busy comings and goings, or went into the town, or down to the shore. Without Lydia noticing it, each of these outings turned into a lesson and each step forward the girl took was rewarded with a warm smile and a quiet, almost casual word of praise.

Marion professed an innocent ignorance in the few subjects that Lydia felt comfortable with, finding ways of allowing the girl to turn the tables and teach her teacher. Within two weeks of Marion's arrival Lydia had begun to lose her nervous aggression, and to learn to approach lessons with, as Marion had intended, an open mind instead of a fear that she would fail and be judged ignorant.

Once she had begun to break through the girl's defences, Marion found some time to consider her own situation. There were moments, in those first few weeks after she and Charlotte had arrived in Portsoy, when she wished that she had never accepted the post of governess to Lydia Geddes. Ever since childhood she had thirsted for knowledge; before she was old enough to attend the infant school her father had taught her the alphabet and basic arithmetic. While other little girls dressed their dolls and wheeled them out in their perambulators Marion gathered hers into a class, with herself as the teacher.

She had always known that she would follow in her father's footsteps, and had been impatient with Eppie when her younger sister, well able to teach had she wished to, chose marriage instead. Proudly independent, Marion had never even considered matrimony for herself – until the day she looked into Alexander Geddes's face, and put her hand in his.

Since then, she had scarcely been able to stop thinking of him. At the breakfast table when Marion, at his suggestion, sat opposite him, the urge to drink in the sight of his heavy-lidded dark eyes, his firm mouth that rarely smiled – but when it did, revealed a smile of intense charm – and his thick dark hair with its fine shading of grey over the temples was almost more than she could bear. She longed to smooth his hair back, to ease the melancholy look that came into his eyes when in repose, to coax his mouth into the smile that made her knees feel too weak to bear her weight.

In the small hours of the morning, lying awake with Charlotte sleeping soundly by her side, she was keenly aware that he was only a matter of yards away, in his own room across the square hall.

She knew from what Eppie had told her, that Helen Geddes was determined to make sure that her son would not marry for a third time. It seemed to Marion that Mrs

Geddes must be won over if there was to be any chance for her. When she accompanied Lydia to her grandmother's house shortly after her arrival in Portsoy, Marion dressed carefully in her best clothes – a full skirt of dove grey silk and wool with a matching high-necked, short-sleeved jacket. Skirt and jacket were trimmed with dark brown braid, and pretty brown tortoiseshell buttons ran down the front of the bodice. Her bonnet was of the same grey, with a pale blue lining and ribbons.

'I should go in to see your grandmother with you,' she said as they waited at the door.

'She'll not let you stay,' Lydia said mournfully.

'Even so, I think it only right that she should meet your new governess, if only for a moment,' Marion said, and once they were inside the house she followed Lydia upstairs to the parlour, ignoring the maid's doubtful, 'Mrs Geddes'll want tae see Miss Lydia on her own . . .'

'Who's this?' Helen Geddes looked Marion up and down. 'I don't recall inviting anyone except my granddaughter to visit me.'

'I am Lydia's new governess, Mrs Geddes. How do you do?'

'Indeed? You may come back for Lydia in one and a half hours,' the woman said coldly. 'No sooner and no later.'

'Yes, ma'am,' Marion said meekly, and left without protest. As she wandered about the town she felt that she had made progress, even though it was very little. At least Helen Geddes had seen her.

She had made more progress than she first thought. When Lydia came down from the parlour later she said, 'Grandmother wants to see you. I have to wait here.'

Marion allowed herself a small triumphant smile as she went upstairs and tapped on the door; by the time she had entered and half-curtseyed to Mrs Geddes it had been replaced by an eyes-lowered meekness.

She was not invited to sit down, so had to stand, hands clasped primly at her waist, while she was interrogated as to where she came from, her family background, her qualifications – and her intentions as to Lydia's education.

'Mr Geddes wishes Lydia to be educated to the standard of other girls her age who attend the local girls' school, but of course, I will also see to it that she learns social skills,' she told the older woman sweetly. 'I have an excellent book on etiquette for young ladies in my possession, and I intend to make good use of it.'

'I understand from my grand-daughter that you are sister to my son's housekeeper.'

'That is true, Mrs Geddes.'

'And that the woman's daughter is also staying in Portsoy for the summer.' There was no mistaking the contemptuous note in Helen Geddes's voice. Marion drew in a deep, slow breath before saying calmly, 'Charlotte is an exceptionally clever child, and would be of considerable assistance to Lydia.'

'I cannot hide from you, Miss McNaught, my concern over this situation. In fact, I cannot think why my son is doing this. Your niece may well be a perfectly respectable girl, but you must admit that she is not the type of child that my grand-daughter should be mixing with.'

Eppie was quite right when she said that Helen Geddes only thought of herself. It must be terrible, Marion thought, to be so self-centred, and so stupid. Aloud, she said, 'I believe that Charlotte will be of benefit to Lydia – and they will only be together for the summer.'

'Hmmm.' Helen Geddes surveyed the new governess in silence for a long moment. The young woman was neatly dressed and well spoken; she knew her place, seemed sensible enough, and also seemed to be aware of the great responsibility Alexander had entrusted her with. He could, his mother thought grudgingly, have found worse.

'My son is a busy man, and not always aware of what is going on within his own household,' she said at last. 'I trust that should there be anything I ought to know, you will inform me?'

'Of course,' Marion agreed meekly. 'Men have so much on their minds, and at times they do not understand the responsibility of raising sensitive young ladies such as your grand-daughter. I'm grateful, Mrs Geddes, to know that if in need, I can turn to you for advice.'

As she and Lydia walked home, she exulted inwardly. She had met the woman she already regarded as the one person, apart from Alexander Geddes himself, who was most likely to stand in the way of her hopes for a future life with him. She had met the enemy and it was an enemy she was determined to best.

It was obvious within ten minutes of Charlotte's first visit to the dance studio that she had no sense of rhythm at all. Watching her daughter's determined attempts to obey the teacher's entreaties to 'Just follow the music, lass – let it carry you along with it . . .' Eppie's heart ached for her.

In another corner of the studio, Lydia was floating across the floor, scarcely seeming to touch the wooden boards, her face lit up with the pleasure of the moment. She had no problem in following the music and letting it carry her along; every now and again, when the old piano produced a sudden rippling flurry of notes, Lydia twirled and spun as though attached to the music by an invisible, silken thread.

When Marion touched her arm and suggested in a

whisper that they go out for some fresh air Eppie agreed at once, glad to be free of the pain of watching Charlotte's failed attempts to dance.

'We have half an hour before we need to collect the girls,' Marion said as they emerged into the daylight.

'I'm going to call on Barbary. The bairn's due any time now and I like to keep an eye on her. It's at times like this that I wish I still lived next door.' Eppie had thought that as time passed, her friend would have picked up the threads of her life again, but Barbary had become more withdrawn. She roused herself only to attend to her children, but other than that she seemed to have lost her former zest for life.

'My poor Charlotte . . .' she went on as they set off for the row of cottages where Barbary lived '. . . perhaps I should withdraw her from the class, for it's clear that she'll never be a dancer.'

'Nonsense, of course she must keep going to the class. It will be good for her, and good for Lydia. She struggles in the schoolroom while Charlotte's way ahead of her. Lydia needs to realise that while she may be behind Charlotte academically, she is ahead when it comes to something else – even if it is only the ability to dance. It will encourage her and develop her confidence.'

Eppie stopped short and glared at her sister. 'Did you know that Charlotte couldn't dance to save her life when you suggested that she join the class?'

'Of course not – well, perhaps I had an inkling of an idea,' Marion admitted airily. 'The school had that little concert last year, as you know.'

'The one where Charlotte did a reading.'

'Exactly – she was given something that she could do well.'

'Because she wasn't good enough for the little dance

troupe. Marion, you knew! How could you let her be humiliated like this?'

'Don't be so . . .' for once, Marion had to fumble for the right word and could only think of '. . . maternal. Charlotte will benefit from the dance classes too,' she said in her most firm, schoolteacher voice. 'Knowing one's shortcomings is character-building.'

'Sometimes I wonder if you're putting Lydia before your own niece.'

'Charlotte has had the benefit of my teaching, and Father's, all her life. Lydia has not. She has a lot of catching up to do. And Mr Geddes is paying me handsomely to raise his daughter's education to the necessary standard for her age,' Marion was saying haughtily as they reached Barbary's cottage.

Nearing the cottage, they could hear wee Thomas crying, a monotonous sobbing as though he had been crying for some time. Without stopping to announce her arrival by rapping lightly on the door, Eppie went straight in.

She saw the two older children first, huddled together and staring across the small kitchen. Following their gaze, Eppie saw Barbary sitting on a low nursing chair, her arms wrapped about her swollen belly. Uncombed black hair straggled about her face, which was red and gleaming with sweat.

'Barbary?'

A guttural, animal-like groan was the woman's only answer. One of the children whimpered, and then came another whimper, this time from Marion.

Eppie was at her friend's side in an instant. She put an arm about the woman's shoulders, and Barbary reached up to catch her free hand in a hot, tight grip.

'It's all right,' Eppie said as much to Barbary as to the

frightened children. 'Your mam's all right – it's just time for the new wee bairn tae come tae live with you. Marion, take them to the hoosie across the road – and the wee one as well – and ask Agnes tae come over quick. Tell her the bairn's on its way.' And then, as Marion just stood and stared at Barbary, one hand at her mouth, she said sharply, 'Marion!'

Her sister stood as though rooted to the ground. A faint moan could be heard from behind the clenched fist held to her lips.

'I'll take them over myself,' Eppie said. 'You help Barbary on to the bed and I'll be back right away.'

'No! I'll take them.' Marion was suddenly galvanised into action. She scooped the baby from his crib and took wee Martha's hand. 'Come on now. Then I'll have to go and fetch the girls,' she said as she manoeuvred herself and the children out of the door.

'There's plenty of time before then, and plenty to be done, so come straight back with Agnes.' Eppie turned her attention to Barbary. 'Let's get you tae your bed, you'll be more comfortable there.'

'It's dead,' Barbary said flatly, making no move. 'My bairn's dead.'

'Of course it's not dead!'

'Aye, it is. Tolly told me.' Barbary gasped as a bout of pain struck her. Her entire body clenched and her fingers tightened so cruelly on Eppie's hand that she had to bite her lip to hold back her own cry of pain.

'He's that lonely without us, Eppie,' Barbary panted when the paroxysm had eased. 'He needs the bairn for company.'

A chill ran down Eppie's spine but she managed to keep her voice even as she said, 'And all your bairn needs right now is tae be birthed. Can ye stand up?'

'Tolly'll look after it until I can go to them,' Barbary assured her, making no effort to move. Just then, to Eppie's relief, the door opened. But Marion was on her own, her eyes large with fear in an ashen face.

'Agnes is with a friend. Her grandson's been sent to fetch her. I have to go to the girls . . .'

'Not until you've helped me to get Barbary on to the bed, and fetched a basin of hot water and a clean cloth.' As she spoke, Eppie worked at releasing her aching hand from her friend's grip. 'Come here, Marion,' she ordered as her sister began to back out of the door. 'If you dare tae run away and leave me I promise ye I'll pull out every hair from your head when this is over!'

The childhood threat they used to use on each other worked, and at last Marion did as she was bid. Together, they managed to settle Barbary on the bed, where she sprawled like a beached whale, her skirt twisted about her white thighs.

'Pull her skirt down and help her tae look decent,' Eppie ordered, unwilling to trust Marion with the kettleful of steaming hot water. She was filling the basin when Marion gave a sudden cry and backed away from the bed, both hands now clapped to her mouth.

'Blood,' her muffled voice wailed. 'She's – she's . . .' Then she ran to the back door, wrenched it open, and stumbled outside.

As Eppie heard her start to retch out in the yard, the street door opened and, to her relief, Agnes came bustling in.

On her way to fetch Charlotte and Lydia, Marion forced herself to take slow, deep breaths, filling her lungs to their full capacity each time. Just before she reached the dance studio it started to rain, and she paused at the door and looked up at the grey sky, then halted again in the passageway in order to dry herself with a handkerchief. By the time she reached the girls she had regained some of her composure.

'Where's my mother?' Charlotte wanted to know.

'She's with Barbary. She'll come home later.'

'Is Barbary having her bairn?'

'What bairn?' Lydia wanted to know.

'Have you not noticed?' Charlotte asked in amazement.

'Noticed what?'

Marion broke into a light sweat. This was no time for Lydia to start learning about the facts of life. 'Come along,' she said firmly, hustling the two of them along the passageway and out of the door. 'It's started to rain and we'll have to get home before it gets worse, for I forgot to bring my umbrella.'

As the three of them hurried to Shorehead she kept the conversation fixed on the dance lesson. To her relief, Charlotte was happy to turn her own efforts to dance into an amusing story, and Lydia more than ready to listen.

'If Barbary's having her baby,' Charlotte said as they went into the house, 'that means that Mother could be out all night. She won't be here to make dinner.'

'Why will she be out all night?' Lydia asked.

'I'm capable of making the supper,' Marion said swiftly.

'I'll help you,' Charlotte volunteered. 'We both will.'

Eppie had still not arrived back by the time the rest of the household sat down to supper. As they ate, Lydia proudly told her father all about her own part in cooking it. 'Charlotte helped,' she conceded, 'and Miss McNaught told us both what to do.'

'And an excellent business you all made of it.' His smile

swept across all three of them. When the meal was over and the two girls had helped Marion to clear the table before going to bed, he invited her to take tea with him in the library.

'Lydia seems more settled now, and more at ease than I have ever seen her,' he said as she poured out the tea, concentrating hard on the task in an effort to prevent her hands from trembling. 'I am most grateful to you, Miss McNaught.'

'She's a pleasant child, and intelligent. It's just a case of finding ways to stimulate her interest. Children can't be made to do things against their wills – that is,' Marion corrected herself, 'they can, but they will never give their best if there is no enthusiasm or willingness to succeed.'

'Lydia can be difficult sometimes. I blame myself – I should have found more time for her instead of leaving her in her grandmother's company so much.'

'It's not easy for a man to be mother as well as father to a child,' Marion ventured. 'Especially to a daughter.'

'It's kind of you to try to reassure me, but . . .' He broke off, then said after a pause, 'I thought that I had done a better job of raising my son, but it seems that I failed him as well as Lydia.'

Marion's fingers itched to smooth away the lines on his forehead and about his mouth, but she could do nothing other than say, feebly, 'I wonder when Eppie will be back.'

'Bairns make their own decisions as to when they will enter the world. It's only natural that Eppie will want to stay with her friend after what the poor woman has been through recently,' he said easily, then, 'Talking of Eppie, that's another reason for me to feel grateful to you. If you had not agreed to come to Portsoy for the summer

Eppie would have left us, and I would have been hard put to find someone to take her place.'

'Eppie was going to leave your employment? Why would she do such a thing?'

He looked over at her, surprised. 'I thought she would have told you about my proposal of marriage.'

Marion had just lifted her cup from its saucer; she jumped so violently that the saucer almost went flying one way and the cup the other. Hurriedly, she managed to reunite them and set them back down on the desk.

'I see that she did not. I should have known – Eppie has always been the soul of discretion.'

'You proposed marriage to my sister? And she turned you down?' Marion heard a strange, far-away ringing noise in her ears. She could scarcely believe that her own sister had been offered the very thing that she herself longed for and, even worse, had rejected the offer.

'She rapped my knuckles severely, and she was quite right. I proposed to her in a fit of despair, thinking that it was the only way to stop the malicious gossips who had realised that once my mother moved to her own house, Eppie and I were alone together here, apart from Lydia. She was determined to silence them by leaving, while I was bent on trying to find a way of stopping her. You see, Miss McNaught, what foolish creatures men can be?' He smiled, inviting her to share his amusement, but she could only stare at him.

'In any case,' he went on, 'things have turned out even better than I could ever have hoped. Now you are here, and Eppie is staying – and she has her daughter close by, while my own daughter is receiving the best education she has known to date.'

The clock chimed the hour and Marion suddenly realised that her mouth was gaping open in shock. She shut it so firmly that she heard her teeth click together and a stab of pain ran along her jawline. 'If you will forgive me, I must go to bed now,' she said, getting to her feet and then, as he rose from his own chair and she turned towards the door, her skirt brushed against a pile of papers balanced on top of his desk, sending them fluttering to the ground.

'How clumsy – forgive me!' she almost sobbed as they both knelt to gather up the mess.

'The fault is mine – please don't feel upset, Miss McNaught,' he said, misunderstanding the cause of her agitation. 'The Board of Trade is to meet soon to look into the loss of the fishing vessel that widowed Eppie's friend and made the bairn being born tonight fatherless. And I've been so busy with other matters that I haven't yet found the time to sort out the paperwork and find a way to present my own contribution to the inquiry.'

'I could help you, if you wish,' Marion said without thinking. 'I could put the papers in order and make note of the particular points you should know.'

'You would do that?' the smile broke out again. 'My dear Miss McNaught, I would be eternally grateful!'

She smiled back, still slightly shaky, but beginning, now that the subject had moved on to business matters, to regain her natural confidence. 'Why don't I make a fresh pot of tea?' she suggested, 'and we can make a start tonight.'

18

Eppie returned to the house in the early hours of the morning – so early that the streets were empty and she walked through them and past darkened house windows without meeting a soul. A dog crossed her path, nose to the ground as it eagerly snuffled up an intriguing story of scents from the cobbles and flagstones. Now and again a cat slid by soundlessly, one of them stopping to look back at her, its knowing golden eyes the only spots of colour in the gloom.

Before going into the house she walked further, to the edge of the inner harbour. Most of the boats were out at the fishing and even the farlins, normally busy with fisher lassies gutting and packing herring, were silent and empty. It was a still night and the few boats left in the harbour rocked almost imperceptibly, the tops of their masts swaying against the star-scattered sky. She could hear the muted sound of the sea beyond the outer harbour walls, hurling itself against the black rocks thrusting up above the surface.

She drew in a deep breath of salt-laden air and stretched her arms high above her head. It had been a long night, and a hard one for poor Barbary. But now the delivery was over and when Eppie finally left the cottage her friend was in a deep, healing sleep, her long black hair spread over the pillow, with her new little son, also asleep, nestled in the crook of one arm and Agnes watching over them both.

'Poor souls,' she had murmured just before Eppie left. 'Mebbe the wee one'll help tae ease her loss.'

Eppie knew from her own bitter experience that nothing could fill the aching gap left by the premature death of an adored husband. Standing on the harbour wall, looking out to where the unseen sea kept trying and failing to bury the sharp, hungry rocks, she suddenly felt closer to Murdo than she had in many a year. She lingered for a while, talking to him with the silent voice in her head, until the early morning chill began to burrow through her flesh to her bones. Finally, she turned to make her way back to the Geddes house.

She was halfway there when a sudden scuttering sound made her jump. She halted, then gasped and stepped back as a large rat ran across the ground in front of her, its body almost brushing against her shoes. It paused and eyed her, crouching low, with its belly pushed against the stone. It opened its mouth to hiss at her, and the moonlight gleamed white on sharp teeth. She stamped her foot hard on the ground and it melted into the darkness, dragging its long reptilian tail after it.

Suddenly, the silent harbour did not seem to be such a pleasant place to linger; Eppie hurried the rest of the way home and in another minute she was in her small bedroom by the kitchen.

When she lit the lamp and began to undress she realised that there were spots of blood from the birth on her blouse. She changed into fresh clothes and took the soiled ones to the kitchen, where she put them into a basin of cold water to soak. With the energetic use of a poker she roused the range fire from its glowing slumber and made herself a cup of tea.

Then, deciding that there was little point in going to bed now, she fetched flour, eggs and lard from the larder and set to work on the day's baking.

Two floors above her, Alexander Geddes slept soundly, a slight smile on his face. He had finally bested his mother, had retained his housekeeper – and at last he had acquired the right governess for Lydia; an intelligent, sensible young woman who was even willing to help him with the mountain of paperwork required for the Board of Trade inquiry. At last, his home had become a pleasant place to return to at the end of a busy day.

In her pretty bedroom, Lydia, too, smiled in her sleep. She was dancing better than she had ever danced before – swirling and swooping, so light and so fast that she skimmed above the ground, covering mile after mile of space, her body and her mind free of all worries and duties.

Charlotte was not even dreaming. She slept deeply, unaware that beside her, her aunt stretched her toes luxuriously to the very foot of the bed and hugged herself in glee. She had found a way to be of help to Alexander Geddes, a way that would allow her to work alongside him.

Even the shock of hearing about his proposal to Eppie, and the greater shock of hearing that her sister had actually turned him down, could not dampen her happiness. She should be grateful to Eppie, she reasoned as the clock in the hall below struck four, since her sister's refusal meant that he was still free.

'How is your friend?' Alexander Geddes asked as Eppie laid a neat bundle of letters, just delivered, by his plate at breakfast.

'She had a wee lad last night. They're both fine.' She fetched the silver letter knife from a sideboard drawer and put it close to his hand.

'Can I see him?' Charlotte asked at once, and Lydia chimed in with 'I want to see him too!'

'Next week, perhaps,' Marion told them both firmly. 'You must wait until he and his mother are rested and able to receive visitors. In the meantime,' she glanced at the clock on the wall, 'you have five minutes to finish your breakfast, and another ten minutes to prepare for your lessons. I will expect to see both of you in the schoolroom at nine o'clock exactly.'

'Poor woman, Geddes said as he slit open the first letter, 'left on her own with another mouth to feed. If there's anything she and her family needs, let me know. If you want to give them any food, no need to ask, just take it.'

'Thank you, Mr Geddes, that's very generous of you.'

'There's no generosity in sharing something you've plenty of – mind that, Lydia,' he added to his daughter. 'Remember it when you're a grown woman.' Then, as his eyes ran over the page he had taken from the envelope he gave a sudden exasperated grunt.

'Is there something amiss?' Lydia asked at once.

'The Glasgow man who owns the bulk of the marble quarry is sending someone to Portsoy within the next two weeks to "discuss improvements to the site".' He quoted the last few words in a mocking, angry voice. 'I've already been warned that it would happen, but I had hoped that it would not be for months yet. It's the last thing I need just now, when I'm trying to get justice for the families of the men on the *Grace-Ellen*. Eppie, you'd best get a room ready since we don't know when he might descend on us.'

'The back bedroom, Mr Geddes?'

Lydia had been eating her porridge, seemingly uninterested in the conversation, but now her head came up suddenly and her spoon clattered into the bowl, sending a few drops of milk bouncing on to the tablecloth. 'That's Duncan's room!'

'It used to be your brother's room, but now it must be made available for anyone who needs it,' her father told her sharply.

'But you can't let anyone else sleep in Duncan's room!'

'Lydia, how many years has it been since your brother last used it? Five, by my reckoning. 'Five years, and not a word from him. I doubt if giving this man from Glasgow the use of it over the next week or so is going to inconvenience Duncan.'

'He'll come back – I know that he'll come back!' Her face was red and she was close to tears.

'That's enough, Lydia.' Her father pushed his chair back and got to his feet. 'I am quire sure that this conversation is making our guests and Eppie feel uncomfortable. Eppie, you may prepare the back bedroom for our visitor, if you please.'

When he had gone, Marion reached out to touch Lydia's shoulder. 'My dear, from what your father says, it's unlikely that your brother will come home soon . . .'

'But he will come back one day,' the girl insisted, her voice wobbling and a tear beginning to tremble on her lashes, 'and it could be any day at all. He hasn't forgotten me – I know he hasn't!'

'Of course he hasn't,' Marion began, while Eppie

moved towards the child, her arms opening to hold her. But before she got to the table Charlotte was on her feet and taking Lydia's hand in hers.

'Come on, Lydia,' she said, 'let's tell the bees. It's the best thing to do.'

Left alone in the room, the sisters looked at each other in silence for a moment before Marion asked, 'Do you think he'll come back?'

'I thought he'd have done it by now.' Eppie began to stack used dishes on the tray she had brought in with her. 'He thought the world of Lydia and I'm surprised he's left her on her own for so long. I'm sure his father's longing to see him too, only he's too proud to say so. Poor wee Lydia thinks that she's the only one who misses the lad.'

'Men are hopeless at dealing with emotions,' Marion said, as though she knew all about it. She gathered up the letters. 'I'll take these in to Mr Geddes – some of them will probably be about the inquiry into the loss of the fishing boat.'

'Are you sure it's right to go into the library? He might want to be on his own.'

'I'm quite sure.' Marion pulled her shoulders back and shot a triumphant smile at her sister. 'As a matter of fact, he asked me last night if I would help him with his preparations for the Board of Trade inquiry. I thought you should know, since there should be no secrets between sisters. At least,' she added, 'as far as I am concerned.'

'When have I ever kept a secret from you?' Eppie asked, stung by the cool note in Marion's voice and the accusation in her gaze.

Her sister gave a little toss of her head. 'You never told me that Mr Geddes had asked you to be his wife. He told me about it last night,' she added, as Eppie felt hot colour flood her throat and face. And then, unable to resist, she burst out with, 'And you refused the man, without even discussing it with me! Why did you turn him down when you and Charlotte could have been settled comfortably for life?'

'Because I'd never marry for such a reason – surely you know that. And I didn't tell you because I knew that if I did, you'd try to talk me into accepting him just to make my life more comfortable.' Eppie's hands flew about busily, gathering the last of the plates and cutlery. 'And that wouldn't have been fair on him *or* me.'

'What about Charlotte – and Lydia? They'd both have had a mother and a father.'

'They're well looked after, and loved. In any case, even if I had said yes to the man his mother would have found a way to put a stop to any such idea. You know what she's like – she'd move heaven and earth to prevent him marrying again, especially someone from our class,' Eppie retorted, before picking up the laden tray and escaping to her kitchen.

Left on her own, Marion picked up the neat bundle of letters and made her way thoughtfully to the library. Having met Helen Geddes, she fully agreed with what Eppie had said.

But there were ways and means. And if it came to a battle of wills, as in the end it must, then Marion McNaught intended to be the winner.

Over the next two weeks, Alexander Geddes and Marion spent most of their spare time in the library, preparing for the investigation into the sinking of the *Grace-Ellen*. Although Eppie noticed a sparkle in her sister's eye and a new spring in her step, she assumed that the change was brought about by Marion's pleasure in discovering that her quick mind was of good use outside the schoolroom as well as within it.

Eppie herself was fully occupied with her household duties and caring for Barbary, who was now up and about after the birth of her baby. She ate little and her clothes hung loose on a body that had once been strong and agile. For the first few days of his life, Jeemsie, her new little son, had wailed pathetically, beating his tiny fists in frustration against his mother's empty breast.

'The bairn's goin' tae waste away for want o' milk,' Eppie fretted while Barbary rocked to and fro, the screaming child cradled against her. 'You must eat more, Barbary!'

'The weans need the food more than I do,' her friend said, fixing her with empty eyes. 'I've enough tae dae me.'

'But not tae dae wee Jeemsie,' Agnes said, and went out, to return ten minutes later. 'Eppie, Myra Beaton two doors up's got a new bairn no' much older than Jeemsie, and she says she's got more than enough milk tae satisfy the both o' them. Take the wee one up tae her house.'

In another ten minutes Jeemsie was suckling greedily, almost choking himself in his efforts to take in as much desperately needed nourishment as he could before being deprived again. Eventually he fell asleep, his little belly as tight as a drum and a thin trickle of milk glistening at the corner of his rosebud mouth.

From then on, either Eppie or Agnes took him to Myra's cottage every few hours, since Barbary could not be relied on to remember her duties, even when she heard the child crying with hunger.

One problem solved, Eppie thought with relief as she tucked him into his little crib, but what of Barbary herself? Nothing, not even Jeemsie's birth, seemed to shake her free of her grieving for Tolly. As she straightened up from the crib, Eppie's eye was caught by a photographic likeness on the wall facing her; Barbary, strong and handsome, sitting in a chair with newborn Thomas in her arms, while George and Martha crowded at her knee, the two of them staring with wide, bewildered eyes at the camera. Tolly, his likeness caught for all eternity, stood behind his wife, one hand on her shoulder, beaming and proud of his lusty, good-looking family.

He had died only months after the photograph had been taken by a travelling photographer who moved from village to village seeking, and always finding, work. Eppie had a very similar photograph among her possessions; herself, with small Charlotte in her arms, standing beside Murdo, who was holding the baby's hand and, like Tolly, grinning proudly into the lens.

So many of the cottages in this village, and no doubt in every other village along the coast, had similar portraits hung on their walls, or standing on mantelshelves or chests of drawers. So many men, Eppie thought, captured for ever in sepia shades on card – so many men claimed by the sea, never to grow old; caught in a moment of time that had passed on, leaving them behind.

When the date of the inquiry arrived, Alexander asked Marion if she would be willing to attend it with him. 'I realise that you will have to take time from your duties towards the two girls, but I would appreciate your company.'

'Of course,' she said demurely, while her heart leaped for joy. 'If that is your wish, Mr Geddes.'

'The hearing may last for longer than one day, so I will book two rooms at a hotel just in case.'

'Very good, Mr Geddes,' she said, and then, startled by a sudden and unexpected warmth spreading from her throat to her cheeks, she picked up a letter and took it over to the window on the pretence that it had to be read in a better light. She had never blushed in her life before and she found the experience profoundly disturbing.

She spent some time going through her meagre wardrobe in search of an outfit that was businesslike, but at the same time, flattering. Finally she settled for her dove-grey skirt and jacket to travel in and to wear in court, and for the evening, just in case they were required to stay overnight – her pulse quickened at the very thought – a green and yellow silk dress in large black-edged checks with sloping shoulders, a wide skirt and long cream muslin sleeves beneath short pagoda over-sleeves.

She carried the clothes down to the kitchen, where she spread them out on the table, after carefully covering it with a clean sheet, and examined them inch by inch to make certain that there were no stains or marks. Then she started working with the flat irons that had been heating on the range.

'Do you think they'll do?' she asked her sister, who had been watching, first with surprise and then with carefully hidden amusement.

Eppie stroked a fingertip over the silk gown. 'I think you could safely be introduced to Queen Victoria herself. It's only an inquiry you're going to, not a banquet.'

'But if the inquiry lasts more than the one day we'll have to spend the night in a hotel. I need something to change into for the evening.' Much to her own vexation, Marion flushed. 'I don't want to let Mr Geddes down.'

It was only when she saw the rush of colour come to her sister's cheekbones that the truth dawned on Eppie. 'You'd never let him down,' she said earnestly, her amusement gone. 'You always look respectable – and grand too.

Mr Geddes would never have asked you to accompany him to Aberdeen if he didn't care for the thought of being seen in public with you.'

Marion's smile was radiant. 'You think so?'

'Of course I do,' Eppie told her firmly, and then, as Marion carefully gathered up the newly ironed clothes, she added, 'Marion . . .'

'Yes?' Marion asked just as Eppie realised that what she was about to say could so easily be misunderstood.

'Nothing,' she said. 'I can't remember what was in my mind.' And Marion tutted at her, before bearing her clothes back upstairs.

Eppie had always looked up to Marion, the older sister, the clever one, the calm, self-possessed woman who had dedicated her entire life to the education of other women's children. Had anyone asked her, before Marion came to Portsoy, as to the right man for her sister, she would have said at once that any man in the kingdom would be proud to take Marion as his wife.

But 'any man in the kingdom' did not include her employer. Eppie was convinced that Alexander Geddes had no wish to marry again. When he had asked her to be his wife, it had only been said in a desperate attempt to retain the housekeeper he and his daughter were both used to, and comfortable with. Even if Marion did manage to find her way into his heart, his mother would make certain that nothing came of it.

Although they had grown up together, Eppie had never really got to know Marion well. While Eppie played with her friends, Marion had stayed at home; reading, writing, studying and learning, but in the few weeks since she and Charlotte had come to Portsoy Eppie had come to know her better. She was proud of Marion's obvious devotion to her work and to her young pupils, and her calm, yet confident manner had brought a new serenity to a household that until recently had been dominated by Helen Geddes's sharp-tongued, self-centred intolerance. Eppie had come to love Marion where before she had merely admired and respected her, and she did not want to see her sister dealt a hurt that could well cripple her emotionally for the rest of her life.

But the damage was done – she could tell that Marion was truly and deeply in love, and if Alexander Geddes did not return her feelings, then she was doomed to suffer – and there was nothing that Eppie could do about it.

19

Alexander Geddes and Marion left early on the morning of the investigation, taking with them in the coach that he had hired for her comfort a large box filled with papers.

Lydia and Charlotte, delighted to have a free day from the schoolroom, started to make plans even before the coach was out of sight.

'Can we go out on our own, for once?' Lydia begged Eppie. 'We're not bairns to be taken all over the place.'

'Your father . . .'

'My father's in Aberdeen for the day, and if you let us go out on our own we promise not to tell him, don't we, Charlotte?'

Charlotte nodded agreement. 'You know that I can go all around Fordyce on my own, Mam – and Lydia's right, we're not bairns.'

They were certainly not bairns, Eppie thought, looking at the two of them as they stood before her in the kitchen. In fact, she realised with sudden shock, Charlotte's eyes were on a level with her own and Lydia was only half a head smaller than Charlotte.

'I'll think about it,' she said and then, as both pairs of eyes lit up, 'but if I say yes you'll have to look out for each other, and keep in mind that if you do anything daft it'll be sure to get to Mr Geddes's ears, and then I'll be dismissed from my post.'

'We won't be daft, we promise!' Lydia said at once, horrified by the prospect of losing both Eppie and Charlotte, while Charlotte chimed in with, 'I'll look after her, Mam!'

'I can look after myself – and you into the bargain,' Lydia said huffily.

'You'll look out for each other,' Eppie cut in before they could start arguing. 'But before you go out, Charlotte, you can help me to put the hoose to rights.'

'I'll help as well.' Lydia was not going to be left out of anything.

'Then the two of you can start by making Lydia's bed and tidying her room. After that you can see to your bedroom, Charlotte.'

She furnished the two of them with dusters and brushes and when they had scampered upstairs she started work in the library. Since all the papers that Alexander Geddes had been working on had gone to Aberdeen with him, she was finally able to give his big desk a good polish, something she had been longing to do for weeks.

Upstairs, Charlotte taught Lydia to make a bed properly and then the two of them put all the toys and books in order and dusted the deep window sill and every other surface they could find. Then they moved into the room shared by Charlotte and her aunt, where Lydia got the chance to show off her new bed-making skills.

'You learn fast,' Charlotte said approvingly, and Lydia only just managed to hide her pleasure at the compliment by snatching up a duster and whisking it briskly over the top of the chest of drawers.

Since Marion was a very neat person and Charlotte had been well taught by her aunt, there was little to do once the beds were made. When everything had been put to rights the two girls hovered by the door, making sure that nothing had been overlooked.

'It's a very small room, isn't it?' Lydia said thoughtfully. 'Not nearly as big as mine, and yet there's two of you sleeping in here.'

'You should see my room at Fordyce, it's more like a cupboard. But I don't mind,' Charlotte added swiftly. 'I like it because the window looks out on the back garden, and the bee skeps. In the summer evenings when I'm supposed to be in bed I can sit there and watch the bees coming and going.'

'I'd like to see your room. I've never been to Fordyce.'

'Have you not? It's very pretty.'

'Prettier than Portsoy?'

'Different,' Charlotte said diplomatically. 'My gran and granda live in a cottage that's much smaller than this house, but it's got a pretty garden. And there's the castle not far from our house.'

'A real castle?'

'It's quite wee,' Charlotte admitted, 'but it's still a real castle.'

'Does a princess live in it?'

'No, but one of the four ladies who looked after Mary, Queen of Scots lived there once . . .'

Lydia's eyes rounded. 'Did Queen Mary visit her there?'

'She was dead by then, poor woman.'

'I'd like to see your castle. We could go there today,' Lydia suggested. 'You'd like to see your grandparents, wouldn't you?' Then, making for the door, 'Let's go and tell Eppie that that's where we want to go.'

'I'm not sure,' Eppie said when the two girls ran her to ground in the schoolroom. 'Your father might not like it, Lydia.'

'I don't see why not – and we don't even need to tell him. He won't be back until late, and we'll be home long before then. And it means that you'll be with us all day,' Lydia pointed out slyly, 'so you wouldn't have to worry about us getting up to mischief on our own.'

'Please, Mam,' Charlotte begged. 'I'd like to see Gran and Granda, and so would you.'

'Well, if you're sure, go and get ready,' Eppie conceded and the two girls fled upstairs, shrieking with pleasure.

It was a pleasant day for a walk, and they had time to dawdle along, which was just as well since Lydia, unused to walking distances, had to pause several times to catch her breath. When they finally entered the outskirts of the village the girl was charmed by the narrow, quiet streets and the neat cottages, each with its colourful, well-tended garden.

She insisted on a slight detour to see the castle, a small, neat structure cheek-by-jowl with the surrounding houses but taller than they were, with its crow-stepped gables and a corner tower proudly proclaiming its superior status.

At last they turned their backs on Fordyce Castle and crossed the road to enter the lane where the McNaught house stood. As always, Eppie felt her steps quicken and her spirits begin to rise as she neared the house where she had spent her happy childhood, and where she still felt safe and contented even when life was at its hardest.

As they neared it, Lydia paused and stared, entranced. 'It's like a picture hanging on a wall!' she said, and both Eppie and Charlotte glowed with pride. The front garden was small, but thanks to Annie McNaught's love of colour and fragrance and her husband's fondness for balancing his sedentary job as a teacher with an enthusiasm for manual work and fresh air, every inch of earth was rich with colour. Hazy blue drifts of fragrant lavender blended with white and red and pink daisies, clumps of scarlet poppies, morning glory, marigolds, red hot pokers, and lupins in white, creamy yellow, deep red, sky blue and purple. Hollyhocks were staked out along part of the low grey stone wall separating the garden from the lane, and a stand of huge yellow sunflowers stood at one corner of the house, their brilliant petals almost brushing the slate roof. A rainbow of red, white, pink, peach and orange was thrown over the soft grey stone walls by climbing roses massing around the windows and the blue-painted front door. The air was fragrant with mingled scents, and the contented humming of bees collecting pollen from the flowers was soft on the ear.

As they stood at the gate, allowing Lydia time to drink in the riot of living colour before her, the door opened and Annie McNaught hurried down the short path. 'Eppie? Charlotte? I didnae ken ye were comin' today. And ye've brought us a visitor too. Come in, m'quine, intae the shade and rest yourself. It's a hot day for a long walk.'

Lydia, suddenly shy, would have hung back and taken refuge by Eppie's side, but before she could do so she found herself being bustled along the short flagged path to the door. Sprays of Solomon's Seal, curving down on to the path, seemed to her confused mind to fall back before her feet like the waves of the Red Sea, allowing access to the door and then through it, surrounded by the perfume of dozens of roses that brushed against her hair and her shoulders as she went into the cool, shady interior.

As though by magic, glasses of lemonade and a plate of shortbread appeared on the kitchen table. Charlotte plunged out of the back door and returned almost at once with Peter McNaught, who had been working in the back garden. He washed his hands at the sink before shaking hands with Lydia and bidding her welcome, in his gentle, almost musical voice, to his home.

Suddenly, her nerves melted away and she felt as though she had been a member of the McNaught family for her entire life. They looked on, smiling indulgently, as Charlotte showed her friend her tiny bedroom and took her out into the back garden to introduce her to the bees. Annie handed a bowl to each of them as they went out, and after visiting the skeps they picked plump gooseberries for the meal that Eppie and Annie McNaught were preparing.

When the bowls were filled Charlotte picked another gooseberry and bit into it. 'Try one, they're good.'

'Will your grandfather not be angry?'

'Only if we eat too many and spoil our appetites. Once when I was a little girl I ate a whole lot of them before they were ripe and got a bellyache. But they're ready for eating now. Go on,' Charlotte urged, and Lydia pulled a large berry, pale green and almost as translucent as marble, from the bush and bit into it. It was one of the most delicious things she had ever tasted – pleasantly sweet, and fresh as a summer drink.

As the two of them settled down on a bench at the back door to top and tail the gooseberries Lydia thought of her own grandmother, with her straight back and thin mouth and hard blue eyes. And she envied Charlotte with all her heart.

Dinner consisted of fish that Eppie had brought from Portsoy, served with potatoes, carrots and peas fresh from the back garden. They finished the meal off with a gooseberry crumble and cream. Afterwards, Lydia would have liked to return to the back garden and lie on the soft grass, listening to the bees as they gathered honey from the bushes close by their hives, but to her disappointment Eppie decided that it was time to return to Portsoy.

'We've got a long walk ahead of us, and I want these two in their beds before Mr Geddes comes back.'

'Aye, best be on your way, lass,' her father agreed. 'There's bad weather comin' in across the water.'

Lydia, her skin glowing from a day spent in the sun, found it hard to believe him, but just as they entered Portsoy, Eppie carrying a basket of fresh picked fruit and vegetables from the McNaught garden and Lydia's ears ringing with Mrs McNaught's final, 'Now that ye've found yer way here, m'quine, haste ye back,' ringing in her ears, the sky ahead of them began to darken and a stiff breeze played around their skirts.

By the time they reached the house they could hear the sea booming against the harbour walls and they were scarcely indoors before rain began to pepper the windows.

The lamps had to be lit earlier than usual, as the girls went to bed, both too full to eat anything else, rain streamed down the window panes and Eppie, snug in her kitchen, could hear the wind howling around the house walls as though trying to find its way in.

She doubted that Alexander Geddes and Marion would be back tonight, but just in case, she set the makings of a fire in the dining room fireplace, ready to crackle into life should the travellers return. Then she set the table for two before making sure that a hot meal could be prepared at short notice. Her work done, she settled herself by the kitchen range with her knitting wires flickering in her hands and the ball of wool in her lap shrinking fast.

The storm, by the sound of it, was getting worse; as the clock ticked the minutes away Eppie yawned, laid her knitting aside, and had just decided that her employer and her sister must be snugly ensconced in an Aberdeen hotel and that it would be safe for her to go to bed when someone began to wield the front door knocker vigorously.

She hurried up the stairs, tutting in exasperation as the knocker continued to bang hard against its metal plate. She could well understand her employer's anxiety to get indoors and out of the storm, but surely, she thought to herself as she ran along the hall, Mr Geddes knew that she would get there as quickly as she could – and he also knew that the two girls would be in bed and asleep at that hour of the night. The racket he was making would waken them.

As she fumbled with the big key it suddenly occurred to her that he might be in a temper because the inquiry had resulted in bad news. Please God, let that not be true, for women like Barbary, left on their own with children to feed, were dependent on receiving some compensation for the loss of their menfolk.

She had no sooner unlocked the door and put a hand to the latch than it shot up from beneath her fingers and the door flew open, almost knocking her down. She skipped back just in time as a man surged into the hall on a gust of wind and a shower of icy rain.

'Are ye deaf, wumman?' he growled from behind the

thick scarf that muffled the lower half of his face. 'This is no night for a man tae have tae staun' ootside!'

Eppie's heart missed a beat, and almost leaped into her mouth. This was not Mr Geddes. The voice was deep and rough, with an accent alien to the Moray Firth; a wide brimmed hat had been jammed down over his head and the eyes glaring down at her, all she could see between scarf and hat brim, were much lighter than her employer's. This man was not as tall as Alexander Geddes, but considerably broader in the shoulder.

'Who are you?'

'A veesitor, that's who I am, come a long way in this foul weather an' expectin' a ceevil greetin' an' a good hot meal. God save us, whaur's the boy got tae noo?'

He swung the door open, letting in more of the gale and another handful of rain, and went back out on to the top step to lean over the rail and shout into the turbulent darkness. One or two of the paintings on the walls shifted uneasily in the blast of wind whistling along the hall, and Eppie could see rain darkening the rug by the door. She looked around for a weapon with which to defend herself and her two charges if necessary, but all she could see was the brass gong that Helen Geddes had insisted on being used to summon the family to their meals. Eppie snatched up the stick, which was padded but better than nothing at all, and seeing that the man was clear of the door, she threw herself against it in the hope of being able to shut and lock it before he realised what she was up to. That done, she would run back downstairs and out through the kitchen door to seek help.

But luck was against her. He turned just as the door began to swing shut, and reached out a long arm. Once again, she was tossed back, this time against the wall.

'Mam?' Charlotte's voice quavered from above, and

Eppie, the breath almost knocked out of her, looked up to see two small faces smudged against the darkness of the stair head.

'Go to your rooms and close the doors,' she shouted, just as another man, not nearly as burly as the first, surged in from the wild night. The house was being invaded, she thought, terror beginning to overcome her.

The man with the rough, frightening voice followed his companion in and slammed the door shut, then as both men removed their hats and began to unwind the scarves from their faces there came a piercing scream from above.

'Duncan!' Lydia Geddes flew down the stairs, her bare feet scarcely touching them, her long nightdress flying out behind her, her face radiant. 'Duncan – you've come home!'

And while Eppie, the stranger and Charlotte, clinging to the banisters at the top of the stairs, watched in bewilderment, the girl launched herself into her brother's arms, heedless of the rain saturating his coat and dripping steadily on to the floor.

20

Marion was torn between excitement and compassion as she listened intently to the evidence given at the Board of Trade inquiry into the sinking of the Portsoy fishing vessel, the *Grace-Ellen*. Excitement because she had never been at an inquiry before and found the solemnity and formality of it absorbing, and compassion because, as she had to keep reminding herself, she was listening to the story of how a well-built and well-maintained fishing vessel had ended up on the seabed, no longer a boat, but a coffin for eight strong, brave men, every one of them someone's son, brother, husband, or father.

The list of names alone, with its occasional repetition of surnames, was enough to make her heart twist and set her eyes prickling with sudden tears, for among the crew were two brothers from one family, two cousins from another and a lad on his first voyage.

Alexander Geddes sat so close to her that their sleeves brushed together; she could tell, by the way his breath caught in his throat as the names of the dead were read out, slowly and clearly, that he too, was suffering. Unlike her, he had known every single one of those men, and in all probability he knew their bereaved mothers and wives or sweethearts as well.

His name was called first, as the major shareholder of the *Grace-Ellen*, and representative of the two minor shareholders, who were not present. One of them, she knew, was related to the dead skipper, and had taken to his bed when the sinking was confirmed. It was believed by all who knew him that he would never recover from the blow.

As his name was called, Marion saw that his hand tensed on the papers he held, and heard him take a long, deep breath before he rose to take his place on the witness stand, where he waited, seemingly calm and composed, stacking his papers neatly on the shelf before him and then bowing slightly to the officers of the court.

He produced a copy of the fishing boat's registration and then, his voice calm and unemotional, gave details of her build and her exemplary past history. He described the fishing gear on board and the lights she would have been showing when the accident occurred, and assured the lawyer representing the owners of the other ship that the *Grace-Ellen*'s skipper was a competent, experienced man who would have made certain on the fatal night that everything was in order and nothing overlooked.

'Apart from being one of the most respected skippers on the Moray Firth, and a man I would trust with my very life, sir,' he said clearly, 'I can vouch with confidence that he would not have shirked his duties by one inch on that last voyage, since the crew in his care included his own cousin and that cousin's son, a lad of only fifteen years, aboard the vessel for the first time. If I may give more details of the crew . . . ?'

He glanced at the sheriff, and then, on receiving a nod, proceeded to read out the list that Marion had helped to make up. This time, each name was followed by details of the dead man's dependents – wives, children, and parents. In some cases, the man had been the breadwinner for three generations of his family.

Although his voice was steady and lacking in any form of emotion, there was something in the sombre way he spoke that brought the human tragedy home to Marion. When he had finished, the court was silent for several seconds. The sheriff, Admiralty officers, lawyers and Geddes himself stood with heads bowed in silent homage, while the only sound that Marion heard from the rows of seats behind her was a woman's muffled, hurriedly suppressed sob, and then a very faint ripple of sorrow that seemed to pass through the listeners like a summer breeze drifting across a cornfield. She herself had to swallow hard and blink her eyes several times to hold back the tears that threatened to spill down her cheeks.

Geddes was asked a few questions and then allowed to step down. As he settled himself by her side she could tell that he was trembling slightly and she yearned, but did not dare, to reach out a hand and place it on his.

As soon as he left the stand the sense of mourning for the dead that the reading of the list had created was swept aside by the brisk way in which the next witness, the master of the ship that had run the *Grace-Ellen* down, was called to give his own evidence. Marion felt a wave of indignation at the sudden change of tone, but as the inquiry proceeded and witness after witness was called, she came to realise that to the sheriff who presided over the hearing, the Admiralty's three nautical assessors who sat with him and the advocates hired to represent the owners of the two vessels involved in the night-time collision, the details were little more than hard facts to be discussed, questioned and considered.

It was almost as though, to them, the incident was a story, a thing of fiction and imagination, she thought, then she realised that this inquiry was by no means their first, or their last. It was their task to ascertain facts and to apportion blame, should there be any, fairly and justly. They could not afford to dwell on the tragic, human side of every case they were asked to consider.

The master of the other vessel, a larger boat than the *Grace-Ellen*, told the sheriff that at one point, although he had seen nothing, he had the feeling that another boat had passed close to his own, moving swiftly through the darkness. Not long after that his own vessel shivered slightly, as though it had brushed against something. He thought then that he saw a light on the sea and heard a voice call out, but nobody else on board his ship saw or heard anything. The storm was coming up fast and the wind had been too strong for him to risk ordering the ship's boat out, lest it be blown into the night and lost; in any case, there seemed little sense in such an action since they had no reason to suspect that there had been a collision of any importance at that time.

Other members of the crew told of feeling 'a shock' and a momentary halt in the movement of their vessel while those on deck ordered more lights to be brought in order to scan the sea around them. But by then the waves were mounting and their ship being tossed about; there was nothing to be seen other than the waves rushing at them out of the dark, each one higher than the last, and nothing to be heard other than the roar of the storm.

Men from some of the other vessels that had been fishing in the vicinity reported seeing the *Grace-Ellen* bring her nets in as the storm began to make itself felt, then leaving the fishing grounds. They themselves were too busy, hauling in their own nets and battening down the hatches before running for home, to notice anything else.

The skipper of the *Homefaring* was the final witness; he told of fishing near to the *Grace-Ellen* and seeing the other boat haul in her nets before turning home, her lamps lit and in good order. He had returned to harbour, fully expecting to see the other vessel already berthed there, and had then taken his own boat back out into the storm in search of her, thinking that she might have lost her mast and be in need of help. But there had been no sighting of her, and since his own boat and its exhausted crew were sailing into danger, they had no choice but to turn back to Portsoy.

It was a long and tiring day and although she had done little more than sit and listen, apart from the short break allowed for lunch, Marion was exhausted by the time the Board of Inquiry gave its verdict. The master of the Aberdeen vessel was chastised for not ensuring that a better watch system had been in place and for deciding against putting the ship's boat out, when lives might have been saved. His certificate was suspended for nine months, and a claim for damages was made on behalf of the dependents of the crew of the *Grace-Ellen*.

Marion had been so involved in the rising drama being acted out in the meeting room that she had not heard the wind beginning to moan around the building and rain beating against the windows. But it seemed fitting, when she, Alexander Geddes and his lawyer finally stepped outside, to find that although it was only late afternoon on a July day darkness was already falling. The sky above was black with heavy storm clouds and she gasped as the wind plucked at her skirts and hurled raindrops in her face.

Geddes had made arrangements for the three of them to dine at the nearby hotel where he had booked rooms in case the inquiry ran for longer than a day. The food was good, but Marion, who had been looking forward to dining in a hotel for the first time in her life, discovered that she had lost her appetite.

She picked at her food while Alexander Geddes and the lawyer mulled over the evidence they had heard that day, and agreed that the court's decision had been just.

'At least the dependants will get some money,' Geddes said, 'though that's little consolation for the terrible loss they've suffered.'

'It's the way it goes for folk who make their living from the sea,' the lawyer opined, then flinched visibly when Geddes turned on him and snapped, 'Mebbe so, but that doesn't make it any easier for the poor souls, or for the women and children and parents they leave behind!'

Then Geddes glanced at the two shocked faces before him and lifted his shoulders in a tired shrug. 'I beg your pardon; it was unfair of me to lose my temper like that. But I knew those men – they worked for me. I can't just dismiss them.'

'Of course not,' the lawyer said uncomfortably. 'Your sensitivity does you credit.'

'Sensitivity,' Geddes pointed out drily, 'costs nothing, especially not lives.'

The conversation round the table became somewhat strained after that, and it was no surprise to Marion when the lawyer excused himself as soon as the meal was over, pleading the need to get home before the storm became any worse. He left the small, comfortable dining room, only to return almost at once.

'The weather is much worse – I would advise you not

to set out for Portsoy tonight. You said that you had reserved rooms? I think you should make use of them.'

Alexander Geddes accompanied him to the door and came back brushing raindrops from his coat sleeves. 'It's not a night to venture out, as he says. I've told the hotelier that we'll stay here for the night. He will take our luggage to our rooms and arrange accommodation for the coachman. I regret the inconvenience, Miss McNaught, but I'd rather stay here than expect you to undertake a very uncomfortable journey home in this weather.'

'It's not in the least inconvenient,' Marion said primly, while at the same time she exulted secretly over the adventure she was having. And then, seeing the shadows beneath his eyes and the slight slump of his usually straight shoulders, 'I think I will go to my room now.'

'No, stay,' he said at once, and then, as though embarrassed by his own words, 'I mean – there's a fire burning in the parlour and I thought we might have a cup of coffee before retiring.'

'Of course.' She rose swiftly to her feet, glad to know that the adventure was to be prolonged. 'I would like that – after all that has happened today I'm sure that my mind is too active to let me sleep.'

The parlour was quiet and the log fire comforting. They settled down close to it and Geddes ordered coffee and two small brandies.

'I believe we both need the brandy,' he said almost apologetically as the waiter bustled off. 'It has not been an easy day.'

'It must have been very difficult, having to give evidence.'

'And just as difficult spending an entire day listening to such a harrowing story.'

'At least there will be some financial compensation for

you and the other owners of the boat – as well as the families of the crew,' she ventured.

'All the money in the world can't make up for the loss of one life before its natural God-given span is over,' he said, the shadows returning to his features. 'My share of the compensation will be added to the money paid out to the dependents. That lad on his first voyage – he was younger than my own son by almost five years. I know from my own experience that it's hard to lose contact with a child, but as least I have the certainty of knowing that my son is safe and well.'

The coffee arrived and Marion poured it out. 'It must be very hard for you, even so.'

'I wonder, every time I think of him, where I went wrong, that he should have decided to go as he did.' He sipped at his drink and then went on, 'But that's dishonest – I know very well where I went wrong. I tried to force him into a future that he didn't want, just because it was his mother's wish. Perhaps I should have given more thought to the living rather than the dead. I should have remembered what it was like to be led along a path that is not of one's own making.'

'It happened to you?'

'In a way. My father died when I was young and it seemed only natural that I should take up the reins of his business interests when I was old enough. Did that not happen to you, Miss McNaught? I understand that your father is a schoolteacher.'

'He is, but it was what I wanted – what I have always wanted. My parents never sought to influence me, or Eppie.' Even as she said the words Marion realised that although her parents had left their daughters to choose their own destinies, she herself had tried to guide Eppie along the same path she had taken.

She took a small mouthful of brandy, her very first taste of the fiery spirit, and after managing to suppress a desire to cough she allowed its spreading warmth to ease the guilt. At least Eppie had gone her own way and had dealt bravely with the results of her own decision.

'My mother, unfortunately, has never been one to let other folk find their own way in life,' Alexander Geddes was saying. 'I am well aware that she chose my first wife, Duncan's mother, for me – not that I fault her for that, for we were contented enough throughout the eight years we had together. But it was when I met Lydia's mother . . .' his face suddenly softened and he smiled across at her; a smile that brimmed over with good memories, and gave her a heart-stopping glimpse of a younger, happy Alexander Geddes '. . . that I knew what true joy feels like. My mother was displeased, but we had a very happy marriage. I wish Celia could have lived – a girl needs her mother as she grows older. Don't you agree, Miss McNaught?'

'Yes, I do. But I'm sure that you have done your best to make it up to Lydia for her loss.'

'Your sister has been a good influence on the girl, and I see an improvement in her since you and Charlotte came to the house.'

'I like Lydia; she has a clever and enquiring mind, and she can be very charming and lovable when she wants to be.'

'When she wants to be,' he agreed with a wry twist of his mouth.

'Young folk of her age can only learn about the world by stretching their boundaries. They look to us to tell them when they are going too far, even though they resent us for it. I know how to handle Lydia, you have no need to worry about that, Mr Geddes.'

'I can assure you that I have no worries as far as you and your sister are concerned, Miss McNaught. I have every faith in both of you and consider myself fortunate to have met you.'

Marion hugged the words in her mind as she lay in bed later that night. The thought of leaving his house in September and returning to the life that she had considered to be complete until she met him, was quite unbearable. She must do something before it was too late.

While her sister was sipping brandy in the Aberdeen hotel, Eppie was saying in Portsoy, 'You might have sent word ahead that you were coming.'

'Mr Ramsay had already sent word that I'd be here sometime soon. I didnae think that I needed tae let Geddes know the time tae the very minute.' The man's voice was once again muffled, but with food this time, not the heavy scarves that he had used to protect his face from the wind and rain on his journey to Portsoy. 'Anyway, I believe in surprisin' folk. That way ye see matters as they are, wi' no chance tae hide the truth.'

He was at the kitchen table, demolishing a heaped plateful of food. The girls had been ordered back to bed, but Lydia, clinging to her brother like a limpet to a rock, had refused to leave him. Finally, Duncan had taken her upstairs while his companion, divesting himself of his coat and hat, made himself comfortable in the kitchen, ignoring Eppie's suggestion that he would be better upstairs.

'She's gone to sleep, at last.' Duncan came into the kitchen. 'Eppie, I'm starving!'

'You always were, as I mind,' she said drily as she opened the oven and withdrew the food she had been keeping hot for him.

'I'm still a growing lad,' he teased, and then, a more serious note coming into his voice as he dug his fork into the food, 'Eppie, I'm pleased to see that you're still here. Has Lydia not grown into a beautiful young lady? I've missed her such a lot!'

'And she's missed you, every day. You should have kept in contact with her, Duncan.'

'I wanted to, but my father was so angry with me for ending my studies and going off to Glasgow that I thought it better for Lydia if I just stayed silent. How is he, Eppie?'

'He's well. You know that your grandmother's got a house of her own now?'

'And your sister is Lydia's new governess and your daughter's staying here as well. Yes, Lydia told me all of it. D'you think that he'll welcome me, or throw me out by the scruff of my neck?'

'Jist let him try – he'll have me tae reckon wi',' the older man growled.

'This is between me and my father, Foy,' Duncan told him. 'I'll deal with it. Well, Eppie?'

She recalled the angry exchange she had overheard between her employer and his mother, shortly after Duncan ran away. Helen Geddes had said that her son should follow the boy and march him home. But Alexander Geddes had said, 'He's made his mind up . . . if he wants to come back to beg my forgiveness he will have it, but the move must come from him.'

Now Duncan was back, and soon he and his father would come face to face.

'I think he's missed you. I think he'll be pleased tae see you back.'

'I hope so,' he said, and returned to his food. Eppie, with nothing else to do, picked up her knitting and sat down by the range, studying the boy with quick sidelong glances.

When he left Portsoy he had been fifteen years of age, with a childish chubbiness still covering his bones, but in the five years that had passed since then, he had become startlingly like his father in many ways – and yet unlike him in others.

He had Alexander Geddes's lean build, heavy-lidded eyes and longish nose. His hair was the same dark shade although tonight, still damp with rain, it erupted over his head in a mass of curls. But his eyes were lighter than his father's – a warm brown, sparkling with life and quick to smile. And when he glanced up, caught her eye and grinned at her from his seat at the table, his mouth lifted easily at the corners, as though smiles came easily to him. In that respect, he was not like his father at all.

'Why have you come back now, with no warning?'

'By God, Eppie, I'd forgotten what a grand cook ye are.' Five years of working as a quarryman had altered his speech. 'There was warning,' he went on thickly through a mouthful of food, 'a letter sent tae say that folk were coming from Glasgow tae have a look at the marble quarry. But me and Foy here didnae know just when we'd be free tae travel and it was all arranged at the last minute. Lydia said Father's in Aberdeen.'

'Aye, he and my sister are at a hearing to find out the truth behind the loss of the *Grace-Ellen*.'

'The *Grace-Ellen*'s gone?' Duncan's head came up swiftly and he stared at her with horror in his eyes. 'I mind her well – I've been out on her. What happened?'

She told him as briefly as possible, then said, 'There's more tea in the pot if you want it. I'd best go and get your bed ready.'

She left him with his silent companion to get over the

shock of her news and when she returned to the kitchen both men were sitting by the range, smoking pipes.

'Duncan's bed's too narrow for two folk,' she said to the man who had come with him, 'but there's a truckle bed in the attic we can fetch down . . .'

'No need, I'll sleep here.' He patted the arms of the chair he sat in.

'It's no' very comfortable, Mr . . .' she recalled the name Duncan had given him ' . . . Mr Foy.'

'I've slept in far worse places, I can tell ye. A pillow an' a blanket'll do me fine. An' it's no' "Mister Foy", just "Foy",' the man said.

Duncan knocked out his pipe and yawned, stretching his arms high above his head. 'Nobody calls him Mister, Eppie. It's just Foy, as he says. I think I'll away to my bed, if it's ready.'

When he had gone, Eppie fetched a pillow and some blankets; when she brought them back to the kitchen Foy took them from her when she would have made up a bed for him in the chair.

'I can manage. I'm used tae seein' tae mysel'. Off ye go tae yer ain bed,' he said, and shooed her from the kitchen as though she were a hen being chased back to the her house.

In her own room, she opened the small window for a moment. The storm was at its height; wind gusted in, bringing with it a handful of icy rain, and she could hear the sea booming against the harbour walls. It sounded like a huge chorus of voices, every one clamouring to be allowed into the light and warmth of the houses on the shore.

She shivered, closing the window and latching it securely against the night, and the voices, before going to bed. She lay awake for a while, listening to the muffled sounds of the storm and thinking of Duncan, who had left as a boy and returned as a man, bringing with him a stranger, a man with only one name who spoke in a harsh, ugly West of Scotland dialect totally alien to the soft, musical tongue of the people he had come amongst.

And she wondered, before sleep finally claimed her, how Alexander Geddes would react to his son's return.

21

The storm blew itself out in the early hours of the morning, and Eppie awoke to a blessedly silent morning.

She dressed swiftly and went out of her small bedroom, only to reel back, hand to her throat in sudden panic, at the sound of an animal-like grunt from the kitchen. Then she remembered that Foy, the stranger who had arrived the previous evening with Duncan, was sleeping there.

He was still sprawled over her armchair by the range, his head tipped right back and his mouth gaping open, with loud snores ripping at regular intervals through the air. One knobbly bare foot was propped on the kitchen chair he had pulled over to face the armchair, while the other lolled on the floor. He looked uncomfortable, but even so, his sleep was deep.

Averting her eyes, Eppie let herself out of the back door and walked down to the edge of the harbour to breathe in the fresh, salt-laden air.

The boats had come in early the night before, fleeing before the oncoming bad weather, still high in the water, their holds not more than half filled. Since fish could not be left unattended for long, the fisher lassies would have had to work into the stormy night, those at the farlins gutting and packing beneath makeshift tarpaulin shelters, and those in the smokehouse splitting the fish open and stringing them on poles before hanging them over the fires.

At rest now within the safety of the harbour, the boats shifted gently, brushing against each other now and again like a herd of animals crowding together for comfort. Beyond the outer harbour she could hear the sea, calm now, whispering around the sharp-toothed rocks where, last night, it had foamed and crashed and whirled in a thousand impatient eddies.

The first sparkle of sunlight was already tossing bright lights over the water on the horizon, and although the sky above was still a soft pearl grey, as yet untouched by the rising sun, far out to sea it had already begun to turn blue – like a swathe of material scrubbed clean by the storm's violence and then rinsed by the final rain, but still holding a small drift of white cloud, like soapsuds, here and there. Peace had returned to the coast and the fishermen who relied on the dangerous waters for their livelihood were safe again – until the next time.

Eppie closed her eyes and sent up a brief prayer that the next time would not come too soon, and then as she turned to walk back to the house she was sharply reminded of the drama waiting to unfold within its sturdy grey stone walls. What sort of welcome would Duncan get from his father, after their years apart, and what would Mr Geddes make of the strange man who had come to Portsoy with his son?

Foy was still snoring, but when she began to rattle the poker between the bars to clear the ashes and rouse the fire in readiness for the day's work the snores stopped suddenly and he seemed to jump from sleep to waking, bounding out of the chair and stretching his hands far above his head.

'Good mornin' tae ye.' He yawned mightily and then clawed his hands busily through his tousled hair, for all the world as though he were trawling the thick tangle in search of head lice. 'Where can I get a wash?'

'You can wash here, at the sink, if you'll just give me five minutes tae start the breakfast.'

'D'ye no' have a tap outside?'

'There's the wash house . . .'

'That'll do. Out the back, is it?'

She nodded to the door in a corner of the kitchen. 'Through there. Not that one!' she said hurriedly as he snatched up the cloth she used for drying the dishes. 'Here . . .'

He waited with ill-concealed impatience while she looked out a clean towel and then said scornfully as she handed it to him, 'Ye're awful pernickety.'

She bit back the sharp retort that sprang to her lips and said instead, 'You'll want hot water.'

'I'm no' that fussy. Cold water never hurt nob'dy.' He swung through the door, throwing it open and then letting it bang shut behind him.

When he returned some fifteen minutes later, fresh and vigorous and ready for the day, his clothes, which had been crushed and creased after a night's sleep, were miraculously straightened and tidied, and his hair, still wet, was tamed down into a dark-chestnut helmet fitting snugly over his skull.

'When d'ye expect Geddes back?' He slung the damp towel over the back of a chair.

'When I see him.' Eppie rescued the towel and spread it over the metal rail in front of the range. 'The inquiry might still be going on, or mebbe it only lasted the one day but they decided to wait out the storm before travelling back.'

'They?'

'My sister Marion's with him. She's governess to the two girls for the summer,' Eppie explained as he raised shaggy eyebrows. 'And she's been helping him with the papers for the inquiry.'

'Is that a fact?' He sniffed the air, then came over to the range to eye the pots and pans simmering there. 'When'll the food be ready?'

'Whenever you are. I've set the table upstairs. No doubt you'll find Duncan there.'

'Nae need tae eat upstairs, here'll be fine.' He began to draw one of the chairs out from beneath the table.

'In this house,' Eppie said shortly, 'we eat in the dining room. If you want food, that's where ye'll have tae go for it.'

He surveyed her for a long, thoughtful moment before saying, almost admiringly, 'There's no' much o' ye, wumman, but what there is, is awfu' nebby.'

Eppie gasped at the sheer effrontery of the man. 'D'ye want your food on the table upstairs, or thrown about yer ears?' she asked, and this time his craggy face cracked into a grin.

'Since ye put it that way, it'll have tae be upstairs.' He crossed to the table and picked up the loaded tray waiting there.

'I can see tae that.'

'If I must eat upstairs I might as well take it for ye,' he said, and left the kitchen.

During breakfast Lydia, who had seated herself opposite her brother, bombarded him with so many questions that on several occasions Eppie had to order her to get on with her meal and leave Duncan to do likewise. During one of the enforced silences she noticed that Foy, seemingly concentrating on shovelling food into his mouth for all the world as though he hadn't eaten for days, was watching the girl from beneath his shaggy eyebrows. When he had emptied his plate and wiped it clean with a hunk of bread he sat upright, gave a satisfied sigh, then said to Lydia, 'Lassie, ye're the spit o' yer mother.'

Charlotte had remained silent through breakfast, lifting her gaze from her plate only to throw an occasional nervous look at Foy, but Lydia did not seem to find the man in the least frightening. 'Did you know her?' she asked eagerly.

He pushed his empty teacup towards Eppie, who filled it for the third time. 'Aye, I kenned her well when she wasnae much older than you are now. Jist as bonny as yersel', and jist as lively.'

'You never told me that you'd known my stepmother,' Duncan said, and Foy grinned at him. 'It's never wise tae tell folk everythin',' he said enigmatically and commenced to spoon sugar generously into his tea.

'Tell me about her,' Lydia commanded.

'Mebbe I will – another time.'

The scowl that had once been part of Lydia's everyday expression but was now rare twisted her pretty face. 'I want to hear all about her now!'

'Ye'll have tae want,' Foy said calmly.

'There'll be plenty of time later for talk,' Duncan cut in. 'We're going to be here for a wee while and I've got a lot to tell you myself – and to ask. D'you still have the bees?'

'Of course, and Charlotte and I talk to them every day. That's why you're here,' Lydia said. 'I asked them every day to tell you to come back home. But you're not here to stay, are you?'

'No. I've got work to do in Glasgow. But I'll be here for a while,' he repeated reassuringly.

'How do I know that you'll not go away again without telling me?' Lydia argued.

'I give you my word that I'll never do that again.' He reached out to cover her hand with his own.

When he had eaten and drunk his fill Foy went down to the harbour with his pipe while the girls were sent upstairs to tidy their rooms and make their beds. Duncan helped Eppie clear the table and carry the used dishes down to the kitchen.

'Mind you,' he said, leaning against the table to watch her at her work, 'the length of time I stay here depends on my father.'

'You mean that you'd be willing to settle here again if he wanted you to?'

'Not that – at least, not right now, for I'm well contented in Glasgow and I like the work I'm doing there. But Foy and me are expecting to be here for a week at least, probably longer. We've got grand plans for the marble quarry, Eppie.' His voice suddenly filled with enthusiasm and when she glanced up she saw that his brown eyes sparkled. 'Foy's been in the Americas studying the way they quarry marble and we're going to use their system here, in Portsoy. We'll erect a shed on the land above the quarry, and install a crane to raise the blocks when they're cut, and a steam engine to shape them . . .'

'You've not changed, have you? Still full of ideas – and you ken fine that I don't understand the half of it!'

He laughed. 'You see and hear and understand more than you let on, Eppie Watt,' he teased, and then, suddenly serious, 'I was so glad to see that you're still here. You've done wonders with Lydia – she's growing up to be a fine young lady.'

'That's none of my doing. And I like working here. Your father's a good man to work for.'

He dug a hand into his pocket. 'There's another reason why I'm pleased you're still here,' he said.

Eppie stared at the hand he held out to her. 'What's this?'

'The money you loaned me when I last saw you.'

She shook her head. 'I wasn't looking for it back. It was a gift.'

'It was a loan, and it was given in kindness and friendship. I've never forgotten how good you were to me. Take it, Eppie,' he insisted, and then, as she reluctantly did as she was bid, 'What happened to make my grandmother leave the house?'

'It's just that your father thought she'd be more comfortable in a place of her own. And a bonny house it is too. You'll see it when you visit with her.'

'You're not telling me that she left here without a murmur?'

'It's not my place to tell you anything about your family.'

'Mebbe not, but tell me this, Eppie, for the sake of the friendship we always had between us – d'you think my father'll put me out when he finds me here?'

She turned from the sink to look straight at him, and saw that his young face was troubled. 'I doubt it. He's missed you, Duncan.'

'I missed him, and Lydia, and you, but I had to do what I did. Just think, if I hadn't run away I'd be a physician now, as miserable as sin and probably killing off my poor innocent patients in error. I'm glad that he didn't try to force me back to my studies.'

'Your grandmother wanted him to – and if you tell a

living soul that I told you this I'll deny every word, for I wasn't supposed to overhear. But your father said that you were the one who had to decide to come back. And you have. I'm glad of that, lad, for Lydia's sake more than anyone else's.'

'I'm not home to stay, mind, just on business to do with the quarry.'

'Even so, it'll bring the family back together,' she said as Foy stamped in.

'Ready, lad? It's time we went tae have a look at this wee quarry. We'll be back at noon for some food.' He tossed the final sentence at Eppie as casually as if he were tossing a chewed and discarded bone to a stray dog.

'I'm more than ready,' Duncan said, and a moment later Eppie, seething at the man's impertinence, was alone. She went upstairs just as Lydia came hurrying down from her bedroom with Charlotte on her heels.

'Where's Duncan?'

'Gone to the quarry with Foy – and you're not to go there,' Eppie said sharply. 'They've work to do and you'll only get under their feet and mebbe end up getting hurt. Quarries are dangerous places.'

'Duncan will look after me.'

'Your brother's got more on his mind than looking out for you. The two of you can take a basket and a list and go round the shops for me. I'm too busy to do it myself. I'll write the list.' The truth was that she was anxious to be in the house should Alexander Geddes and Marion return so that she could break the news of his son's arrival as gently as possible.

The prospect of being entrusted to do the day's shopping had its appeal, and ten minutes later the two girls had gone into the village, leaving Eppie alone in the house.

While awaiting her employer, she had to resolve the problem of where Foy should sleep that night – certainly not in her kitchen. As far as she was concerned he could sleep on the harbour wall, but when all was said and done he was her employer's guest, and had to be treated as such. She looked into Duncan's small bedroom and saw that if his bed was moved over against the wall there was just enough room for another narrow cot. Access to the loft was by a narrow flight of steep wooden stairs tucked into a corner of the upper hall; she fetched a lit candle and with some difficulty managed to get the stiff door to open.

The space below the roof was dark and stuffy, and the exposed rafters meant that she had to stoop all the time. Once or twice she thought she heard a scuttering noise in a corner, and stamped her feet loudly to deter whatever made the noise from showing itself.

The few items stored in the loft were stacked neatly and it did not take long to find a wooden cot that might not be very comfortable, but would surely be better than the chair in the kitchen.

Duncan and Foy could fetch it down later, she decided, and climbed back down the stairs after latching the loft door firmly, just in case there were any unwelcome residents that, once disturbed, might take it into their sharp-teethed, furry heads to find their way down into the living quarters.

She looked out blankets and sheets and a pillow, then got to work on her usual morning duties. When the girls arrived back, they helped her to unpack the basket and put everything away, and then she sent them into the garden. Duncan and Foy arrived back sooner than she had expected, but disappeared at once into Alexander Geddes's library, only emerging when summoned for their midday meal.

'You've had a good morning?' Eppie hazarded as she ladled stew on to their plates.

'A grand morning,' Duncan said enthusiastically. 'It was good to see the quarry again. It's doing well.'

'But it could do better.' Foy dug a serving spoon deep into the big bowl of potatoes Eppie had set on the table. 'And it will.'

'I'd a look in the loft this morning – there's a bed up there that'll do you, and space for it in Duncan's room, if the two of you could bring it down after you've eaten.'

'No need,' Foy said easily, tearing a hunk of bread from the loaf she had put out, and dipping it into his gravy. 'I've arranged tae lodge at the quarry foreman's house while I'm in Portsoy.'

Eppie, catching the bright-eyed way the two girls watched him biting off a mouthful of dripping bread, gave a slight cough to catch their attention, then delivered an intense stare. She had no wish to see them copying the man's uncouth eating habits. 'Oh, but Mr Geddes would want you to lodge here, surely,' she said, when Lydia and Charlotte had both lowered their eyes hurriedly to their own plates.

'I doubt that, and I'd be more comfortable elsewhere.'

'More comfortable? This is the most comfortable house in Portsoy!'

'There's comfort,' Foy said enigmatically, 'and there's comfort.' And then he devoted all his attention to his food.

As soon as the meal was over he and Duncan returned to the library while the girls were sent off to their dance class, delighted to be unaccompanied for once.

Eppie took a tray of used dishes to the kitchen and was returning for another load when her sister swept in through the front door, which she had left on the latch.

'There you are, Eppie!' There was high colour in her face, and her eyes were bright. 'We're back, and it's been such an adventure . . . !'

'Where's Mr Geddes?' Eppie interrupted. There was no time to waste in idle chatter.

'I'm here,' he said from the open doorway. 'What's the matter?' And then, his voice sharp with anxiety, 'Is it Lydia?'

'She's fine, Mr Geddes, but—'

Eppie stopped in mid-sentence as his gaze suddenly swept past her, fixing on the library door. She turned and saw Foy standing there, feet apart and thumbs hooked into his waistcoat pocket, looking as much at home as though he, and not the new arrival, owned the place.

'So ye're back, Geddes?' he said amiably.

There was nothing amiable about Alexander Geddes. Even before he spoke Eppie was aware of tension and antagonism filling the hallway. She heard her employer draw his breath in with an audible hissing sound, then he said coldly, 'Foy. What the devil are you doing in my house?'

'Sent frae Glasgow on business. Did ye no' get word that I was comin' north tae discuss the future o' the quarry with ye?' Foy's rough voice was still relaxed, with perhaps just a slight undercurrent of amusement at the other man's reaction.

'I got word, but if they'd told me that you were the one they were thinking of sending I'd have made sure they changed their minds.'

'Mebbe that's why they didnae mention me. Surely ye know that I'm the best quarryman they've got – always was, an' always will be. I've no' come empty-handed, though,' Foy went on when Geddes would have spoken. 'I brought a wee gift, tae sweeten yer mood.'

He stepped aside to reveal Duncan, who had come to stand in the doorway at his back.

'Hello, Father.' His voice was quiet, with just a slight catch in the throat. 'I hope you're pleased to see me, after all these years.'

22

'Duncan.' For a long moment it seemed that that was all Alexander Geddes had to say; then, clearing his throat, he added, 'So you've come home again – at last.'

'Better late than never – eh, Geddes?' Foy said.

To her astonishment, Eppie saw her employer throw a look of sheer hatred at the man. Then, almost at once, it was gone as he turned back to Duncan and held out his hand. 'Welcome home.'

Duncan's face cleared and he bounded forwards to shake the proffered hand enthusiastically. 'I'm glad to be back, sir, even though it's only for a week or so.'

'A week or so?' Geddes asked, but Foy's voice was louder than his as the man said, 'Are ye no' goin' tae introduce me tae yer lady friend, Geddes?'

Again, contempt swept over Geddes's face; for a moment Eppie thought that he was going to offer a sharp reproof, but his voice was calm when he said, 'Miss McNaught, I would like you to meet my son, Duncan Geddes, and this . . .' he waved a hand at the other man, almost as though dismissing him '. . . is Foy. Miss McNaught is my daughter's governess.'

Foy looked Marion over with open approval. 'So ye're a governess, Miss McNaught?'

'A teacher, Mr Foy, from Fordyce.' Marion offered her hand. Her colour had been high when she first hurried into the house, but now Eppie saw, by its deepening from pink to rose, that far from disturbing the fastidious Marion, the open admiration in Foy's eyes and in his voice pleased and excited her.

'It's no' Mr, it's just Foy.'

'Really?' Marion said, intrigued and apparently oblivious to the fact that he still held her gloved hand in his.

'Eppie, we've not eaten since we broke our fast early this morning,' Alexander Geddes cut into what looked like becoming a conversation. 'I'm sure that Miss McNaught must be as hungry as I am.' And then, glancing towards the stairs, 'Where are the lassies?'

'At their dancing class, Mr Geddes. I've got food waiting, for I thought you'd be back any minute. I can have it on the table in ten minutes.'

'I'll help you, Eppie,' Marion said, and followed her sister through the door at the back of the hall, leaving the three men on their own. 'Who is that strange man?' she asked as soon as they were safe from being overheard. 'And what sort of a name is that – Foy?'

'You know as much as I do. He arrived last night with Duncan – they're here to see what can be done with the quarry. Duncan's been staying in Glasgow with his stepmother's family, the Ramsays, these past five years. He seems to to be awful fond of that Foy, for all that Mr Geddes doesn't care for the man at all,' Eppie said uneasily. Her employer's antagonism towards Foy had been tangible enough to thicken the air in the hallway.

'He's – I don't know – different, somehow. He has a way of looking at folk . . .' Marion's voice trailed away and Eppie looked up to see a flush on her sister's face, and a gleam in her normally serious eyes.

'Aye, he does – and not in a way that I like,' she said briskly. 'To my mind, a man like that could be dangerous.'

'Sometimes,' Marion said, 'danger can be exciting.'

'And more often it can just be dangerous,' Effie said drily. 'There's something worrying about the way Mr Geddes looked and sounded when he found Foy here. Did you not notice it yourself?'

'I can't say that I did.'

'Never mind him – what about the inquiry? Did the families of the men from the *Grace-Ellen* get justice?'

'As much as they could, seeing they'll never get their menfolk back. The master of the other vessel was blamed for not having enough men on watch and for not putting out his ship's boat to see if he could find survivors. And he's lost his certificate for nine months. Mr Geddes and the other owners have made a claim for damages in the name of the crew's dependents.'

'So Barbary'll get some money to help feed and clothe the bairns. That's something, at least. Mebbe,' Eppie said without much hope, 'it'll help her to put her grief behind her, and look to the future.'

'It was such an adventure, Eppie. We would have been back late last night, but the storm was so severe that Mr Geddes decided it was safer to stay in the hotel.'

'What was it like?' Eppie had never before known anyone who had stayed in a hotel.

'Like a big house – very grand, and my room was nearly the size of our cottage. We dined in a very large room with a lot of tables, and waiters – that's what it must be like for folk that live in grand houses, with footmen serving their food to them. Mr Geddes's lawyer dined with us. I would have gone to bed after he left, but Mr Geddes asked me to take a cup of coffee with him in the parlour. And I took a glass of brandy with it as well.'

'Marion McNaught!' The family were not against drink as such, but they rarely had the opportunity to taste anything other than the elderflower wine that Annie McNaught made each year.

'It was only a very small glass.'

'What did it taste like?'

'It had a real sting to it. I had trouble in keeping a cough back, and tears came to my eyes with the first sip. But then I had a lovely warm feeling all down here . . .' Marion put the flat of her hand against her bosom '. . . and down into my stomach. The next sip was easier, and the next again. And we talked until I could scarce keep my eyes open.'

'What about?' Eppie could not imagine her employer, a man who never spoke for the pleasure of hearing his own voice, talking far into the night with her own sister, of all people.

'Oh – this and that,' Marion said vaguely. For some reason, she wanted to keep the memory of the previous evening as her own secret, to be taken out when she was alone and played over and over, word for word. 'Lydia's schooling, and what was said at the inquiry.'

She was unaware that the splash of vivid colour over her cheekbones, the sparkle in her eyes and the quickened lilt in her voice was giving her innermost thoughts away.

'Marion,' Eppie said hesitantly, 'Mr Geddes has buried two wives. He's never going to seek a third.'

'I don't know what you're talking ab . . .' her sister began hotly, and then, as Eppie said nothing, but eyed her steadily, she gave a flounce, rather than a shrug, of her shoulders. 'Mebbe a third wife's what the man needs – someone with no intention of going to an early grave. Someone who's determined to stay by his side for the rest of his life. D'you not think the man deserves happiness?'

'Of course I do.'

'Well, I can tell you that he's not happy with the life he has now. There are too many cares on his shoulders, and Lydia's one of them. It's hard for a man to raise a lassie on his own. If I can find a way to help him, I'll do it. I just want to make him happy, Eppie,' she suddenly pleaded as her sister continued to look at her levelly. 'You surely know that I care for the man and I'd never want to do anything to hurt him.'

'I know that. It's you I'm fretting for. Mr Geddes isn't what you'd call free tae make up his own mind, Marion. There's his mother to deal with first.'

'She approves of me – I've made sure of that.' Marion gave her sister a conspiratorial smile. 'I've never lost a battle yet, once I've set my mind to winning it.'

Then she picked up one of the two trays Eppie had been loading and marched from the kitchen, her head held high.

The two girls hurried home after their dancing class ended, for Lydia could not wait to return to Duncan. When she burst into the house, Charlotte at her back, Eppie was clearing the empty dishes from the dining room table and the three men – Alexander Geddes, Duncan and Foy – were in the hall.

'Father, you're home – wasn't it a surprise to find Duncan here?' Eppie heard Lydia say, so excited that she almost sang the words.

'Indeed it was,' her father agreed just as Eppie took

the full tray from the dining room. She saw with relief that he was smiling down at his daughter, clearly as pleased to see Duncan home as Lydia was.

'We've so much to talk about – where are you going?' the girl asked, suddenly noticing that the men were in their outdoor clothes.

'To the quarry.'

'Now? But I've just got home! And I have so many questions to ask Duncan!'

'You'll have plenty of time to ask them later.'

The little group was blocking the way to the kitchen, so Eppie had no option but to wait, balancing the tray against her hip. Charlotte and Foy, she noted, were both in the background, unnoticed and forgotten. Her daughter was watching the Geddes family with a shy half-smile on her lips, while Foy seemed unable to take his eyes from Lydia's pretty, animated face. He stood by the library's open door, and every now and again, Eppie noticed, he glanced into the room and then looked back at Lydia.

'Can I come with you?'

'Of course not. We have business to discuss and the quarry is a dangerous place for young ladies.'

Lydia's lower lip began to push forwards. 'But I haven't seen Duncan for years!'

'And you heard your father say that you would have plenty of time to speak to him later,' Marion's voice cut in from the schoolroom door. 'Since you have both missed lessons for two days, I think that we should spend the rest of the afternoon with our books.'

Charlotte looked relieved, and so did Alexander.

'Miss McNaught is quite right,' he told his daughter firmly. 'Upstairs now, and change to your indoor clothes, then come back down to the schoolroom.' Then, as

Lydia, shoulders drooping, did as she was told, with Charlotte at her heels as always, Alexander suddenly noticed Eppie.

'Eppie, about accommodation for – for our guest . . .'

'No need, Geddes,' Foy said easily. 'I've arranged tae lodge with ye foreman an' his family while I'm here.'

It seemed to Eppie that her employer's relief at the news was as obvious as his strange dislike of the man from Glasgow.

Later, when the men had gone out and Marion and the two girls were shut in the schoolroom, she glanced in through the open library door, as she had seen Foy do, when she happened to pass it on her way upstairs.

He had been staring at the portrait of Celia Geddes, and comparing her to Lydia, who looked so like her mother.

Foy marched into the kitchen by the back door some thirty minutes later, demanding tea. 'My throat's dry,' he announced and Eppie, busy packing a basket of food for Barbary and her young family, nodded at the tea kettle, puffing steam on the range.

'It's there if you want it.' She was determined not to run after this man who had, for some unknown reason, upset Mr Geddes, even though he had brought Duncan home. To her surprise he nodded, as though he had expected to be told to wait on himself.

She watched as he took two cups from the dresser and poured tea into them both, then sought out, and found, milk and sugar.

'For a man, ye've a good idea of the way a kitchen's run,' she said, curiosity overcoming her. 'D'ye have a wife and family of your own in Glasgow?'

He gave her a sidelong glance from eyes more of a

deep golden shade than ordinary hazel. 'I'm no' the marryin' sort, but I've been around a few kitchens in my time.'

He slid the second cup across the table to her and as she took it she saw that his broad hands were covered with the silvery gashes left by long-healed scars, and that the knuckles were unusually large and very knobbly.

'Every quarryman's got scars like these,' he said easily, following the direction of her glance. 'And there was a time,' he ran the tip of a finger along the knuckles of the other hand, 'when I'd tae earn my keep by bare-knuckle boxin'.'

'That's a heathenish thing tae do!'

'It put food in my belly and taught me that the world's a hard place an' we a' need tae learn tae look out for ourselves.'

'So Duncan's hands'll get cut like yours?' She thought of the boy's hands, graceful and long-fingered like his father's.

'Mebbe they will, but it'll dae him no harm.'

'His father wanted him tae become a physician and use his hands tae heal, not tae tear rock open. It was what his mother wanted too.'

'But not what the boy wanted. He's goin' tae be a grand quarryman, and he's got brains, tae. And what harm will it do if he picks up some scars along the way? Our hands are the best tools we have, and it's only natural that folks' hands tell their own story.'

With a sudden movement Foy caught hold of one of Eppie's hands in a warm, rough grasp. Startled, she tried to pull away but he held on, turning her hand over and running a fingertip over her palm. 'Ye've got some scars yersel', lassie.'

'That's from workin' with the herrin'.'

'Ye see?' He released her hand and picked up his mug. 'The only folk wi' smooth white hands are the employers and the nobility. We all come intae the world wi' soft hands, but maist o' us end up takin' the scars o' our labours tae the grave. They're our medals – an' damn the credit we get for carryin' them.' Then, eyeing the basket she was packing, 'What are ye doin'?'

'Taking some food tae a friend who's got bairns tae feed and a man lost at sea some months back. I've got Mr Geddes's permission,' she added swiftly. 'I'd no' do this without it.'

'I'll carry it for ye.'

'Should you no' be at the quarry?'

'Duncan's there wi' his faither and I'm leavin' it tae him tae tell Geddes aboot the plans we have for the place. The lad's learnin' well and it's time he took on some authority. I'll go with you tae yer friend's house,' he finished, picking up the basket and marching out of the back door, leaving her with no option but to follow, which she did with poor grace.

'Have ye known Duncan since he ran – since he left Portsoy?' she asked as they walked to Barbary's cottage.

'It was me that found him sleepin' in the stables at the back o' the house one mornin'.' He gave a bark of laughter at the memory. 'I couldnae unnerstaun' it, for the laddie was well enough dressed an' no' like the usual beggars ye come across on the Glasgow streets. So I nudges him awake with my foot an' he opens his eyes and looks up at me an' he says for all the world as if he's come tae the front door and I was the butler that had opened it, "Tell Mr Ramsay that Duncan Geddes has come to call on him."' He mimicked Duncan's educated accent. 'An' him wi' straw stickin' oot his hair and a smudge o' horse shit on the shoulder o' his fine jacket.'

'Why was he sleeping in the stables?'

'He'd arrived in Glasgow in the middle o' the night and didnae like tae waken any'b'dy. So I made him tidy himsel' up an' took him tae the hoose. An' after a good long talk wi' the lad, Mr Ramsay took him in and handed him over tae me. "The lad thinks he can make a good quarryman, so let's see what you think of it," he says. "If he's right we can make good use of him."'

A stout woman with a basket looped over her arm came towards them, taking up the full width of the footpath. They both had to step into the roadway to let her pass, and as they returned to the pavement Foy resumed his story. 'I worked him hard, for there was nae sense in molly-coddlin' him, an' lettin' him think that he was somethin' he could never be. But he stuck at it wi' never a word o' complaint, and one day he's goin' tae be as good as me.'

'Modest, you mean?' Eppie asked.

'There ye go again wi' that sharp tongue. It's fortunate that I like my women tae have minds o' their ain,' he said, and then, before she could retaliate, 'Quarry work's what the lad always wanted, and it's what he does best. The boy's got a good brain in his noddle and laddies like him dinnae take kindly tae bein' told what tae dae wi' their ain lives. He'd never have made a decent physician – his heart wouldnae have been in it. His father was wrong tae try tae force him tae go against his own wishes. But that's Alexander Geddes for ye – he aye thought that money could buy anythin' – and more often than not,' he added, his voice suddenly grim, 'he was proved right. But no' with Duncan, thank God.'

'You speak as if you've had dealings with Mr Geddes before,' she said, and then glanced up at him, conscious of his swift sidelong glance. But he had already returned to looking at the road ahead.

'Aye, mebbe,' he said, 'but that's for me tae know an' you tae wonder aboot.'

'Does Mr Ramsay not work in the quarry himself – or is he too grand?'

'He did. He was a braw worker, and no' afraid tae pull his weight along wi' the rest o' us. Him an' me learned the trade thegither, but ten year ago he got caught in a bad rock fall an' lost the use o' his legs. When his faither died no' long efter that, Mr Ramsay set me up as his quarrymaster.'

'Does he have any family?'

'He and his wife had three bairns, but they were all lassies, and none o' them lived tae make auld bones. They've been an unlucky fam'ly a'thegither, an' they deserved better, for they're the best folk that ever walked the earth.'

'It would be Mr Ramsay's sister, then, who married Mr Geddes? You're right about their bad luck, for she died young herself.'

'Aye.' The word fell to the ground at their feet as though it were a piece of slate and Foy seemed to close himself down; it was just as though he had slammed and bolted a door, shutting himself in and leaving her alone on the outside.

23

Barbary was in her usual rocking chair by the range, with the baby asleep on her lap. The back door was open and the other three children were in the backyard, contentedly making mud pies with earth from the neglected vegetable bed, and water from the kettle, which sat on the flagged path beside them.

Barbary scarcely seemed to notice Eppie, who set the basket on the table and hurried out to rescue the dented kettle. Five-year-old George beamed up at her.

'We're makin' biscuits for our mammy's tea,' he announced proudly, slapping a fistful of mud between his hands to flatten it. He was wearing an old short-sleeved smock; dirty water oozed down his bare little arms and the front of the smock was soaked and filthy. Martha was in an even worse state, with mud tangled in her dark hair and smeared over her round face. Wee Thomas was sitting on the path, making swirling patterns in the soft mud with wide sweeps of his hands.

'Are ye hungry?' Eppie asked them, and when they all nodded vigorously, 'I've brought better things for ye tae eat than these pies. Come on inside and wash yer hands, then I'll put the dinner on the table.'

In the kitchen, Foy was crouched by Barbary's chair, talking quietly. She was smiling at him, but all her attention seemed to be focused on a large pink shell that she held to one ear. Tolly had brought it back from the previous autumn's fishing at Lowestoft, having bought it from a man who had travelled the world.

Deftly, Eppie washed the three children and put them into clean clothes, then she sat George and Martha at the table and put plates of food before them while she took Thomas on her knee. As she spooned food into his willing little mouth, she told Barbary about the Board of Trade's decision, finishing with, 'And so you and the bairns'll have some money comin' soon. That'll make a difference, will it no'?'

Barbary nodded and smiled, but Eppie was not sure that she had taken in a word of what had been said to her. She turned to glance at Foy, but he had gone. Then she saw him out in the backyard, shovelling the mud from the path and sweeping the dirty water into the vegetable bed.

Thomas fell asleep almost as soon as he was fed, and Eppie laid him down in his cot before taking the baby, now wakening, from his mother's arms.

'Go and eat your dinner, Barbary, while I take wee Jeemsie along the road,' she urged, and the young woman obedient as a child, laid the shell down on the table by her place before spooning food into her mouth, her eyes fixed on the opposite wall as though watching something that nobody else could see.

Now that he had a wet nurse to feed him, the baby was thriving. Eppie changed his napkin and then handed him over to his foster mother. When she returned to the cottage, Foy had found an old hoe and was working on the vegetable bed. After settling George and Martha down on the floor with their few toys she tidied the place and put the provisions she had brought into the larder. Barbary had eaten most of her food and was listening to the shell again, a slight smile on her face.

Eppie touched her friend's arm; although Barbary ate everything put before her, her once-round arm was so thin that Eppie could feel the skin loose on the bone. 'Barbary, did ye hear what I said, about Mr Geddes gettin' the court tae send money tae help you and the bairns and the other folk that lost their men?'

'Aye, I heard.'

'It means that you'll no' have tae worry about money, no' for a good whiley anyway.'

'Aye. He's a good man, Mr Geddes,' Barbary said, and then held the shell out. 'Listen tae that, Eppie . . .'

Eppie took the pretty thing and put its pink and white whorled opening to her ear to listen to the soft continuous roar of the sea. Barbary had loved the shell from the moment Tolly had put it into her hands, and she had often encouraged the children to play with it, laughing at the wonder on their little faces when they heard the shell's murmuring.

'D'ye hear it?' Barbary was saying now, her eyes, sunk into their sockets, holding Eppie's gaze.

'Aye, I hear it. I hear the sea.' Eppie had always marvelled at the way the shell, on dry land and far from the warm tropical seas that had given birth to it, could still carry the sound of the ocean.

'But can ye hear *them?*' Barbary said. 'Can ye, Eppie?'

'Them?'

'Them,' Barbary insisted. 'Can ye no' hear the voices, callin' tae ye?'

'Just the sea, Barbary. There's no voices – there's just the sea.'

'Of course there's voices.' Barbary snatched the shell back and clamped it to her ear, her face knotted with anxiety. Then it smoothed into a contented smile. 'It's all right, they're still there. Still talkin' in the shell.'

All at once Eppie remembered the previous night, when she had opened the window of her small room before going to bed, and had then shut it hurriedly because she fancied that within the crash of the waves being hurled across the firth she could hear the multitude of men the sea had taken in its time, asking, pleading, demanding to be allowed back to the dry, warm lamplit homes they had been forced to desert against their wills.

She drew back, then jumped and only just suppressed a squeal of fright as the street door opened and Jeemsie's wet nurse carried him in, fed and contented.

The woman stayed to chat for a moment, and not long after she had left, Foy came in from the backyard, dusting earth from his hands.

'She's in a pitiful way, yer friend,' he said as they made their way back to the Geddes house. 'She's taken the loss o' her man badly.'

'She'll be all right, once Mr Geddes gets the claim for payment settled,' Eppie assured him. 'She'll be able tae look tae the future then.'

But deep down, she did not believe her own words. It seemed to her that Barbary was slipping away from her, out of her grasp, and unless something could be done to help her, she would one day slip out of reach entirely.

Duncan Geddes hesitated before the house where his grandmother now lived, conscious of a sudden dryness in his throat. He had turned down his father's offer to accompany him, for he was a man now and this was something that he had to do on his own. It was his duty, he told himself sternly, setting one hand on the latch of the gate. And any man worth his salt had to do his duty, especially where elderly female relatives were concerned.

In any case, his grandmother already knew that he was back in Portsoy, so there was no chance of completing the business he and Foy had come on and then creeping back to Glasgow without seeing her.

His thoughts carried him through the gate and up the flagged garden path to the front door. Almost as soon as he had used the polished brass door knocker he heard a faint scurrying sound from within – the sound, he thought wryly, either of rodents behind the wainscoting of a room, or of a maidservant who had been trained to within an inch of her life, and lived in terror of her employer's anger – and then the door opened to reveal the servant herself, neat as a new pin in her snowy cap and apron, and trying hard to conceal her breathlessness.

'Aye, sir?'

'Duncan Geddes, come to call on my grandmother.'

The maid looked at him with sudden interest, mixed with curiosity. It was a look he had come to know well since returning to his birthplace. In fact, he had been stopped several times on his way to his grandmother's by folk anxious to greet him and to find out what he had been up to during the five years of his absence.

'If ye'll come away in, sir, I'll see if the mistress is at home.' The woman reversed with practised skill, drawing the door with her in order to widen his access. When she had closed the door she took his hat. 'If ye'll just bide here for a wee minute,' she said, and hurried upstairs.

Duncan waited in the large entrance hall, looking about

him with interest. The hall was furnished like an anteroom, with a large rug covering most of the polished floor, flock paper on the walls, brocade curtains at the windows on either side of the front door and chairs with tapestry seats and backs grouped about a small table. The house was very comfortably furnished – no doubt at his father's expense. He guessed that his grandmother had struck a hard bargain before agreeing to move here.

The maid came scurrying back down. 'This way, sir,' she said, and set off on a second trip upstairs. By the time Duncan joined her in the upper hall she was tapping on one of the doors.

His stomach clenched as a familiar voice snapped something from inside the room. For a moment, he was a little boy again, summoned to his grandmother's parlour to answer for some real or imagined wrongdoing.

The maid opened the door. 'Mr Duncan Geddes, ma'am,' she said, and Duncan resisted an urge to smooth his hands over his hair and check that his shoes were polished before following her into the parlour where Helen Geddes awaited him sitting in a high-backed chair by the window, her wrinkled hands gripping the carved wooden armrests.

'Well, Duncan,' her voice was as strong and as harsh as ever, 'so you've decided to come back to Portsoy at last? You may kiss me,' she added as he hesitated in the middle of the room, unsure as to what to do next.

As he approached obediently she tilted her head to one side, graciously, offering her cheek to his lips. Her skin was very soft and wrinkled, making him feel that if he was not careful to keep the kiss light, his mouth could easily sink right into her face. She smelled of lavender water, and he saw, as he straightened up, that although she had aged a great deal in the past five years, her pure white hair was still thick and her eyes of the vivid blue he remembered. Looking at her with a man's eyes rather than a boy's, he realised with a shock that his grandmother must have been a very beautiful woman in her youth.

'You may sit there.' She indicated a chair opposite her own, where the light from the window would fall on his face. He sat, and waited as her sharp eyes studied his features, then his clothing.

'You're a man now.'

'Twenty years of age, Grandmother.'

'You did a terrible thing, running off the way you did without a word of explanation, then staying away for all those years.'

Nothing had changed, Duncan thought wryly. Here he was, being chastised for his behaviour. But at least this time, he was a man, and well able to speak up for himself.

'I had to leave, Grandmother, because I was being forced into a profession that wasn't right for me.'

'That's nonsense! Laddies don't know anything about the world; it was the responsibility of me and your father to make sure that you got the best education and the best chance in life. You could have been a physician or a banker or you could have gone into your father's business so that you could take over from him, but instead you chose to be a common workman!'

'A quarryman, Grandmother. It's an honourable calling, and a family business. I work for my Uncle Ramsay.'

'The Ramsays are no kin to you!'

'No,' Duncan admitted, 'but as far as Uncle Ramsay's concerned, close enough, since Lydia is his niece, and my half-sister. He has no sons of his own.'

'So he's making you his heir?'

'I don't know about that. As you say, we're not blood kin. But he's a fair man and I think I can always be sure of a position in one of his quarries when he's gone.'

'You're daft to be so trusting,' Helen Geddes snapped, and then, 'Let me see your hands.'

Almost of their own volition, his hands shot forwards for inspection, turning over when she raised an eyebrow in mute command. He found himself glancing down at his own fingernails and was relieved to note that they were neatly cut, and scrubbed clean.

'They're not the hands of a gentleman. A common workman,' she repeated, settling back against the high, rigid backboard of her chair.

'An honourable calling,' Duncan said again, obstinately, 'and one that I chose for myself. I'm here to use my knowledge to help my father. Foy and I have great plans for the Portsoy quarry, and my father will profit by our ideas.'

'Who did you say?'

'Foy's my uncle's quarrymaster. He's taught me everything I know about quarrying,' Duncan said with pride.

'Is it Mr Foy you mean, or is that the man's Christian name? I've never heard the like.'

'Just Foy. It's what he prefers to be called.'

'It's a heathenish name – no doubt for a heathenish man.'

'I can assure you, Grandmother, that Foy is not a heathen. He's travelled the world to learn his trade. And my education wasn't neglected just because I left Aberdeen for Glasgow. Uncle Ramsay sent me to college to learn the history and theory of quarrying, as well as geology and something of architecture and lapidary. I've got all sort of plans for the quarry here in Portsoy . . .'

He was so caught up in his explanation about introducing a steam engine and a crane to lift the larger blocks of marble to the new workshop which he and Foy intended to build on the high ground above the quarry that he didn't notice Helen's eyes glazing over. She suffered his enthusiasm for a few minutes, and was just about to cut him short with a sharp remark when Maisie brought in the tea tray.

'So, how are you, Grandmother?' Duncan enquired politely, nibbling at the corner of a sandwich so small and thin that he could have eaten it in one gulp and scarcely noticed.

'Older. Frail and alone.'

'You're not alone – you have servants, and friends, and Lydia tells me that she visits every week.'

'Lydia! What d'you think of your sister, Duncan?'

'I think that she is growing fast, and soon she will be a very beautiful young woman, the image of her mother.'

'She's spoiled. Your father indulges her too much – he and that housekeeper of his! She's got her own companion now – the housekeeper's daughter, of all people. The moment he managed to push me out of his home – and mine for all those years – and into this place,' Helen Geddes looked around the elegant, beautifully furnished parlour as though it were nothing more than a hovel, 'your father took the housekeeper's daughter into his house – of all people!'

'She seems a pleasant, well-raised lassie.'

'Hmmm! Just you wait – one day Lydia will inherit your father's share of the quarry, and money from his estate besides, and that's when the "pleasant lassie" from Fordyce will show her true colours. She'll make herself indispensable to my grand-daughter – your sister, Duncan – and not be content until she's fattened herself on poor Lydia's wealth.'

Duncan was beginning to find it hard to remain civil in the face of such vindictiveness. 'I doubt that very much. Eppie's a kind, honest woman and I'm sure that she would never raise her daughter to be avaricious.'

'You're like your father – far too trusting.'

'And the governess, Miss McNaught, seems to be making a good fist of Lydia's education.'

'Alexander will find the entire family running riot over his home if he is not careful. You must speak to him about it, since he seems determined to ignore anything I have to say.'

'As I understand it, my father was anxious to find a good governess for Lydia, and from the way she speaks of Miss McNaught and Charlotte, Lydia is enjoying their company.'

It would seem, Helen Geddes thought, that she was not going to find the ally she had hoped for in Duncan. 'The governess seems to be a sensible young woman, I'll grant you that,' she conceded with poor grace. 'She's taken to visiting me regularly to report on Lydia's progress and very respectful and well-spoken she is. That's because of her education, of course.'

She leaned forwards in her chair, her blue eyes fixed on her grandson's face. 'You see how important a good education is, Duncan? Two sisters raised in the same cottage in Fordyce and both, presumably, given the same education. Yet what a difference between them. One makes full use of it and comes as near as anyone with her background can to being a lady, while the other spurns the chances offered to her and marries a fisherman. Now she's a mere servant.'

The scone Duncan was eating was still warm from the oven, and as light as a feather, but all at once it seemed to lie in his mouth like a lead ball, and he had to take several sips of tea before he could swallow it.

He could scarcely bear to wait for the next ten minutes to pass, and when they did, and he was free to make his farewells and leave the house, he drew in great gasping lungfuls of salt air, blowing it out hard several times in order to flush out the poisons and prejudices he had been subject to while in Helen Geddes's presence.

How his father could have borne to have that woman in his house for all those years he could not understand. As he strode down into the village, swinging his arms vigorously as he went, he was furious with Alexander for having exposed his children to her vindictive, snobbish narrow-mindedness; then, as the good sea air did its work, cleansing mind and body of the atmosphere in his grandmother's house, he found himself admiring his father for having finally found the courage to regain his own home, and for introducing Eppie and her sister into it. They would surely be the saving of Lydia!

He was still walking quickly and as he passed a baker's shop he almost bumped into a girl as she stepped out from its doorway.

'I beg your pardon.' He put one hand to her elbow to steady her while the other went up to tip his hat. 'My fault entirely, I wasn't looking where I was going.' And then, as she glanced up at him, 'Miss Charlotte – I am doubly sorry. Please excuse my clumsiness.'

She clutched her large basket against her body as though using it to prevent him from getting too close. 'It's perfectly all right, Mr Geddes, I got a wee fright, that's all.'

'You've been sent out to do the shopping?' And then, when she nodded, 'Have you much more to do?'

'It's all done.'

'Then we can walk back to the house together,' Duncan felt himself in need of some pleasant company. 'I'll carry your basket.'

Charlotte looked up at him with such horror that he laughed out loud, then had to hurry to assure her that he was not laughing at her. 'Well, not entirely. For a moment you looked as though you thought I might bite you. But I have just had tea with my grandmother and I am so full that I couldn't even manage a nibble.'

He had already decided that she was a very quiet, serious girl, but the unexpectedness of his comment brought a fleeting smile, which she hurried to bring under control.

'I can carry the basket easily, it's not heavy. And I'm sure that you have other places to go – the quarry, perhaps? Please don't feel that you have to walk to the house with me.'

'I would enjoy your company,' he said firmly, taking the basket. And then, as they set out, 'That pendant you always wear, with the Portsoy marble – I remember helping Eppie to choose it, not long before I left Portsoy. It was for your birthday, I believe.'

A hand flew to her throat. 'It's my favourite possession,' she said, flattered that he had noticed it and delighted to hear that he had had a hand in the choosing of it.

'I'm glad to hear that you are so pleased with it.'

A passer-by stopped Duncan before they had gone far to welcome him back to Portsoy, and to ask about his future plans. Charlotte hesitated and her hand moved towards the basket he carried, as though to take it and walk on alone, but he gave her such a pleading look that her hand fell back to her side and she waited until he was free again.

'They must have all told each other that I'm back home, and what my plans are, over and over again, for I've told so many people,' he said, 'and yet they all seem to want to hear it from my own lips. I'm tired of repeating myself.'

'They're just pleased to see you after all this time,' she said reasonably.

'I suppose so. Do you have to go back to the house right away?'

'Not at once.'

'Come out to the headland with me for a wee while. I've been cooped up in my grandmother's house for the past hour and I need to look at the sea and breathe in its salt air and talk to someone sensible.'

24

Charlotte had done her best to let Lydia have Duncan all to herself since his visit was to be short. Now the prospect of being on her own with him, and even worse, of being expected to talk sensibly about goodness knows what, alarmed her.

'You don't have to listen,' Duncan was saying now, almost as though he could read her thoughts. 'A nod now and again would do.'

He grinned down at her, and she found herself smiling back at him, and following him as he turned away from the harbour.

It was a fresh day with a strong breeze. They found a grassy spot not far from the quarry, and Duncan insisted on putting his coat down for Charlotte to sit on. She need not have concerned herself about having to make conversation because he immediately launched into a description of the plans that he and Foy had for the quarry, and although she scarcely understood a word of it she found herself caught up in his enthusiasm.

She watched his brown eyes come alive and his long arms and work-roughened hands sweep and circle through the air as he spoke. Occasionally, one hand paused in its outlining of some piece of machinery or the shape of a building to sweep a tumble of wind-blown dark hair from his eyes.

The words poured from him and filled the air around Charlotte, and she found herself being affected by his sheer exuberance. One day, she told herself as she listened, she wanted to care as much about something as he did about quarrying. One day, she wanted to have her own dream to follow.

Then a church bell sounded the hour and the spell was broken. 'My mother will be wondering where I am – I must go.'

He helped her to her feet, shook his jacket out and put it on, and then picked up the basket. 'I apologise for talking so much, but I must persuade my father to agree to our plans, and I believe that I was using you for practice. It was unfair of me.'

'I found it all very interesting, though I didn't understand much of it.'

'When I next come back to Portsoy I'll take you to the quarry, if you like, and explain things to you properly.'

'I'd like that very much.'

'Then we'll make a point of it. And now,' he said as they began to walk back to the harbour, 'tell me something about yourself. Are you enjoying your stay in Portsoy?'

'Oh yes, it's exciting to live in such a large house when I've always been used to a cottage.'

'How do you get on with my sister? She can be overbearing at times.'

'It was difficult at first,' Charlotte acknowledged, 'but I think that it was just as hard for Lydia to share things with me when she's not been used to it before.'

'You wouldn't have been used to it before either, but I suspect that you managed it better than Lydia.'

'It was harder for her,' Charlotte said in a matter-of-fact tone. 'She has so much more than I have, which means that she had much more to share.'

'Ah.' Duncan estimated that the serene and sensible girl hurrying along by his side was probably Lydia's age – some twelve years old. But she seemed so much older and wiser.

'She dances beautifully,' Charlotte was saying. 'We both go to classes, but Lydia's so much more graceful than me. It's as though she's being lifted up and carried along by the music. I feel so clumsy beside her.'

'I can't dance either. I went to a ball once, and I made a complete fool of myself. My partner and I were hand in hand and she had to sink into a curtsey, then I had to draw her to her feet. Unfortunately all I managed to do was to pull off a pretty ring she was wearing, and the poor girl was sent tumbling back to the floor.'

'How dreadful!' They had reached the kitchen door of the house and Charlotte looked up at him, her eyes wide. 'What did you do?'

'I laughed and the young lady never spoke to me again,' he said cheerfully, then, 'Have you tried ice-skating?'

'No.'

'It's easier to be graceful on the ice. I must come to Portsoy in the winter, and teach you to skate on Loch Soy when it's frozen,' he announced.

They both went indoors smiling, Duncan because thanks to his young companion he had been cleansed of the memory of his grandmother's vindictive nature, and Charlotte wallowing in the glow of her first taste of hero-worship. The pendant, with its chip of red marble, had become even more precious to her than before.

★ ★ ★

Although he was lodging with a family in Seafield Terrace, Foy spent most of his time in the Geddes house. He ate some of his meals in the dining room with the family, though more often he preferred to eat on his own in the kitchen.

He spent most of what spare time he had in the kitchen, watching Eppie at her work. Sometimes he was silent, and to her surprise she found that it was a comfortable silence with no awkwardness to it. When he was in a talkative mood he wanted to know about Portsoy and the folk who lived in it, and something of her own life. She answered his questions easily, for there was nothing about her past that required being kept secret.

But she soon discovered that her attempts to find out more about his background were met with evasion and skilful changes of subject. He was willing to talk only about Glasgow, his work and his employer and friend, Edward Ramsay, Lydia's uncle and Duncan's patron.

'He dotes on that lad. The man had no kin tae speak of until Duncan came intae his life, and ye can be sure that the boy's been well cared for and well educated – his father should be pleased about that, since it seems to be the only thing he wanted for the boy.'

As always, she was quick to defend her employer. 'It's natural for Mr Geddes to want the best for his children. That's a father's duty.'

'Faither's duty!' he snarled, and spat through the cast iron bars and into the hot fire. The gob of saliva did not entirely pass through the gap between the bars, and some sizzled on the hot metal. Eppie, who had done her best to stop him from the disgusting habit, tutted loudly and glared at Foy, who avoided her eye as he went on, 'Mebbe faithers should mind that it's human bein's they're raisin', no' possessions. There's more decent folk crippled for life by ambitious faithers than I've had hot dinners.'

'You sound as if you know a lot about it. Are you a father yourself?'

'Me?' He gave an abrupt laugh. 'I made up my mind years back that I'd no' let mysel' be guilty o' ruinin' some poor bairn's life. Anyway, I dinnae believe in merriage.'

'I'm sure that the womenfolk of Glasgow would be pleased tae know that.'

'Oh, there's plenty weemen can appreciate a man withoot tryin' tae turn him intae a husband,' he said slyly, giving her a sidelong glance. But if he had hoped to shock her, he was disappointed, for she kept on with her darning, and only said, 'We'll have a cup of tea in a minute, before you go off tae your lodgings.'

Since doors were rarely locked and barred at night in Portsoy, she sometimes found him sitting at the kitchen table early in the morning, eating food foraged from the pantry. On those days, the range had been cleared of the night's ashes and was burning brightly, ready for the day's work. When he arrived early on the next washing day she went into the washhouse to find that the boiler was hot and the fire she had lit below it the night before to give herself a good start in the morning had been replenished.

He returned to the house later that day, more restless than usual. He walked about the kitchen, peering out of the window then going to the range to fidget with the pots and pans before strolling to the table, where Eppie was trying to make pastry, to pick at a piece of dough.

'Put that down – what's amiss with ye?' she asked, exasperated. 'If ye cannae settle, go outside and let me get on with my work.'

'Duncan's upstairs wi' Geddes, showin' him the plans

we have for the quarry. I'm feart that the man'll give him a difficult time.'

'Why should he? He's happy to have the lad back home; I can see it in his face every minute of the day. He'll want to please Duncan.'

'It's no' Duncan that's the problem, it's me.'

'What d'you mean?'

'Nothin'. Just get on with yer work an' stop naggin' at me,' he said roughly. Colour flooded into her face and she had just opened her mouth to order him out of her kitchen when the inner door was thrown open and Duncan stormed in, his own face flushed and his eyes bright.

'He'll have none of it!' He glared at Eppie, and then at Foy. 'He says the quarry's fine as it is and he'd not listen to a word I said!' He threw a fistful of papers on to the table, heedless of the baking preparations. A cloud of flour billowed up, some of it going over his brown jacket. He ignored it.

'Mebbe ye didnae explain it right,' Foy said, and the young man rounded on him.

'I explained it fine! It's him – he's as thrawn as ever he was. No wonder I left home when I did. I should never have come back!' His voice broke and he made for the back door, dashing an arm across his eyes as he went.

'Duncan—' Foy put a restraining hand on his arm and was thrown off so violently that he fell back against the table. By the time he had steadied himself Duncan had gone, slamming the door hard behind him.

'Go after him!'

'No,' Foy said. 'Leave him tae calm down. He'll no' want an audience at the moment.'

'But he might do something daft!' Eppie had visions

of Duncan walking blindly into the harbour, or even throwing himself in.

'He's got more sense than that. He just needs tae be left tae his own company for a while.' Foy glanced up at the ceiling, his face darkening. 'That man has tae learn how tae deal with his own blood kin,' he said savagely, and made for the inner door.

'Wait – wait until you've all had time to draw breath . . .' But the door closed on the final word, and Eppie was alone.

She caught her apron up, twisting the material around both hands as she always did in times of stress or uncertainty, looking first at the back door, and then at the inner door. Then, unsure of what to do, she rescued the pages that Duncan had flung down and brushed flour from them.

They were covered with detailed sketches of machinery and buildings, with notes and measurements written neatly alongside. Even after five years she recognised Duncan's tidy hand. Foy was probably right – angry as he was, Duncan was too sensible to do anything rash. But Foy was another matter . . .

Eppie put the papers down on the dresser, out of harm's way, and hurried upstairs. As she gained the upper hall she heard the men's voices behind the library door; they were both talking quickly and angrily, but at least they were talking and not fighting. Not as yet. For some reason she could not understand there was bad feeling between the two of them, and who knew where an argument might lead?

Once or twice Eppie had overheard things not meant for her ears, but each time it had been by accident. Never before had she deliberately eavesdropped, but now she pressed her ear against the door, determined that if the talking gave way to violence, she would do all she could to stop it, even if it meant running out into the street to fetch help.

'. . . what's best for this quarry,' Alexander Geddes was saying. 'It's small and it works well as it is.'

'It could be extended,' Foy replied. 'This area's rich wi' the stuff. There's serpentine below ground right back tae the Hill o' Fordyce, an' south nearly tae Knock Hill. How can ye ever hope tae bring out the most o' it without the help o' steam engines an' cranes?'

'I'll not see the countryside plundered and ravaged just to make Edward Ramsay wealthy.'

'Ye'd become wealthy yersel',' Foy pointed out. 'An' if *we* dinnae dae it, someone else will.'

'Let them, when their time comes. For now, I'll not agree to your proposals.'

'They're more than proposals, Geddes. Mr Ramsay holds a greater share in the quarry than you dae, and I've a wee share an' a'. Ye could be outvoted.'

'I'll put up a fight if it comes to that. As things stand at the moment, I'm the man who's in charge of mining this quarry, and for that reason alone, if no other, I've got the right to be heard.'

There was a brief pause, then Foy said slowly, 'Duncan's fair upset by yer stubbornness. The lad's worked hard on these plans and he's done a grand job. It's hit him hard, his own faither turnin' doon his ideas without even givin' him the courtesy o' considerin' them first.'

'Duncan's a man now – he has to learn to accept disappointment. God knows,' Geddes said bitterly, 'that we all have to live with it.'

'You an' me ken that mair than most, Alexander. If ye ask me, ye're treatin' the boy hard because ye're angry wi' him for runnin' off tae Glasgow and meetin' up wi' Edward Ramsay. The lad doesnae ken it yet, but Ramsay's plannin' tae leave what he has tae Duncan. Your son's goin' tae dae well for himsel', Geddes, but what does that matter tae you? Ye're angry wi' Duncan and eaten up with envy at me an' Ramsay, because we like the lad, and he likes the baith o' us. Ye've no' got the common sense tae know that nob'dy'll take your place in the boy's life. Duncan's loyal, an' ye're no' man enough tae see that.'

This time the silence lasted so long that Eppie began to grow uneasy. Then, at last, Alexander Geddes said levelly, 'Why would I punish Duncan for the past by refusing a plan that would benefit the quarry? I've no quarrel with him.'

'But ye have wi' me.'

'If I have, it's because you've managed to draw my son under your influence, and you've done it deliberately, to punish me for taking Celia from you.'

'Well now!' Foy's voice was triumphant, 'Ye've faced up tae the truth o' the matter at last, Geddes. Though I cannae see why you should have any grievance against me, since you're the one who got her.'

'She made the choice. I didn't influence her.'

'Ye didnae need tae. If you'd no' set eyes on her, she might have chosen me – oh aye, Geddes, there was a time when her an' me were as close as that. But then you had tae come intae her life, and why would a lassie like Celia Ramsay choose tae marry wi' a quarryman when she could have a fine gentleman like yoursel', Geddes, wi' yer big hoose an' yer genteel ways?'

'Why indeed? But even though you knew that she wanted me you did your damnedest to come between us. D'you think I didn't know about your pathetic attempts to turn her and her father against me?'

'Mebbe if I'd had your fine education, *Mister* Geddes, I could have done better.'

'Whoever she chose, it's all in the past,' Geddes said sharply. 'Neither of us has her now.'

'But you've got yer memories, an' yer bonny wee daughter that's the image o' her mother. It fair stopped my heart when I first caught sight of Lydia. It was like seein' Celia brought back tae life.'

'Don't speak my daughter's name, Foy!'

'Ye've got the lassie – surely ye cannae deny me sayin' her name now and again?' Foy's voice was suddenly taunting. 'If things had been different Celia might have ended up with me And mebbe she'd be alive today if I'd had the right tae look after her as she—'

There was a sudden exclamation and Foy's words ended in a strange gurgling sound. Something crashed over inside the room and Eppie, throwing caution to the winds, turned the door handle and burst into the room to see Foy on the floor, and her employer kneeling over him, his hands at the other man's throat.

'Mr Geddes!'

He looked up, startled by the intrusion, and for a moment she didn't recognise his face, distorted as it was by sheer naked hatred. His normally pale skin was dark red and his heavy-lidded eyes wide and glaring. Hair flopped over his forehead and his lips were drawn back to reveal clenched teeth.

'Mr Geddes!' she said again, this time in little more than an appalled whisper. Her hands flew to her mouth and for a split second she felt more frightened than she had ever been in her life. Then the primal rage ebbed from his eyes as Foy's arms came up and then swung apart, breaking the other man's hold.

'Eppie? Is there something wrong?' Marion called nervously from the hall. 'Mr Geddes?'

'Get her out o' the way,' Foy hissed, pushing Alexander

Geddes aside and scrambling to his feet. 'Go on now, we're fine!'

Eppie backed out and closed the door before turning to where Marion stood in the open doorway of the schoolroom, Lydia and Charlotte peering round her shoulders.

'Is Mr Geddes ill? I thought I heard someone fall to the floor.'

'It's nothing – Foy's in the library with him, and he fell over a chair. I was dusting out here,' said Eppie, hoping that her sister wouldn't notice that her hands were empty, 'and I thought the same as you. But it's nothing.'

'That man's so clumsy,' Marion tutted, then whisked round on her pupils. 'And who gave you two permission to stop your work? Back to the table, if you please.' She shooed them into the room and closed the door while Eppie, shaken by what she had heard and then witnessed, hovered in the hall for a moment, uncertain as to what to do next.

There was silence from the other side of the library door, then someone spoke, low-voiced. It seemed to Eppie that the speaker was moving towards the door, so she hurried to the rear of the hall and had only just closed the door at the top of the kitchen stairs when she heard the library door open.

She rushed back to the kitchen and got there just in time to be busy with the range when Foy came in. To her surprise he was grinning broadly.

'How can you look so pleased with yourself after what I've just seen?' she asked, outraged.

He winked at her. 'I never thought tae see the day I'd get Alexander Geddes tae behave like a man instead of a mammy's boy!' he crowed, and then, suddenly suspicious, 'Here – were you listenin' outside that door? Did you hear what we were sayin'?'

'If I had been listenin', I know it would just have been about the quarry – what else would you two ever want tae talk about?' she said tartly, banging a pot down on the cast-iron range. 'Of course I wasn't listenin' – I'd just come up to speak to Marion when I heard the stramash from the library. I told her you'd fallen over a chair.'

'An' so I did, though it was him that knocked me against it. I'll away an' see if I can find Duncan,' he said, and went out, whistling to himself.

Eppie went to the sink to splash cold water on her face and wrists, shocked at the sins she had committed in the past hour. She had deliberately listened at the library door and then lied to Marion – and to Foy. The wonder of it was that they had both believed her. She was not entirely surprised about Marion, but she would not have expected to get away with lying to Foy. She must be good at it, she thought, concerned. It wasn't as if she had ever had the chance or the inclination to practice.

She had no sooner dried her face and hands than Alexander Geddes came down to the kitchen.

'Eppie—'

'Marion and the girls heard a noise from the library,' she cut in swiftly. 'I told them that Foy had fallen over a chair. I was on my way to speak to her about something,' another lie! 'when I heard the noise as I was passing the library door. I'm sorry I didn't stop to knock, but I thought you might have hurt yourself.'

'Oh.' He hesitated, then said, 'I must apologise for losing my temper as I did, Eppie. I can assure you that it will never happen again.'

'I know that, Mr Geddes.'

'D'you know where Duncan is?'

'He went out a while ago. He was – a bit upset. Foy's gone to look for him.'

'I see. Thank you, Eppie,' he said, and went back upstairs while Eppie, her mind whirling with what she had heard at the library door, got on with her work.

At last she knew why there was such enmity between Foy and her employer, and the reason why Alexander Geddes, normally the most self-controlled of men, had behaved so badly, attacking a guest under his own roof.

A shiver ran down her spine as she thought of what might have happened had she not burst in when she did. Her fear was not for Foy, but for her employer. If Foy had chosen to retaliate – or had been given time to retaliate – he might have injured Alexander Geddes seriously, or even killed him. The man's burly body and big, scarred hands singled him out as someone well used to facing up to foes.

She recalled him at her kitchen table, telling her that he had once earned his keep as a bare-knuckle fighter. A man who could thrive in such a barbaric world would be able to kill the likes of Alexander Geddes without even meaning to.

25

Neither Duncan nor Foy returned to the house for supper. Since Helen Geddes had moved to a home of her own, meals had become a time for conversation and the members of the household were encouraged to take turns to say grace. Foy viewed the custom with some amusement and when he was first invited to contribute he had said smoothly, 'Ach, I wouldnae know how tae start. The way I see it, I work hard for my ain food, so I'm no' minded tae thank anyone else for providin' it for me.' But this evening, though it was Marion's turn, Alexander Geddes asked briefly for a blessing before picking up his soup spoon.

'But Duncan's not here yet,' Lydia pointed out. 'And Foy usually eats with us too.'

'I see no reason why the rest of us should go hungry because of them,' her father said curtly. 'If they choose to come late to the table they'll still be fed.'

The rest of the meal was eaten in silence. Lydia and Charlotte, subdued and clearly aware that something was wrong, glanced at each other occasionally, but at nobody else. Geddes, at the head of the table, concentrated on his food and scarcely lifted his eyes beyond his plate, while Marion, as always, watched her two charges in order to catch and quash any lapses of etiquette.

When supper was finished Marion sent the girls out into the back garden to play before bedtime while she helped Eppie to clear the table and take the dishes back to the kitchen.

'What was going on earlier?' she asked as soon as they got there.

'What d'ye mean?'

'You know very well what I mean. In the library, when I was in the schoolroom with the girls.'

'I told you – Foy fell over a chair, clumsy creature that he is and took it and himself to the floor. I got a fright myself at the noise of it.'

'Eppie Watt, I could tell by the look on your face when you came out of the library that there was more to it than that.'

'I've told you all I know myself,' Eppie fibbed desperately. It was not her place to talk about her employer's private life.

'I still say there's more to it than that. Those two men can't bear the sight of each other and we don't know why. D'you think it's all to do with Duncan?' Marion wondered aloud. 'He's awful fond of Foy, and I could understand his father feeling as if his own nose is being put out of joint.'

'I thought you disapproved of gossiping,' Eppie reminded her, and it was Marion's turn to flush.

'I wasn't – I just wondered,' she said, and then, with a toss of her head, 'I'd best get back to the schoolroom. I've not set tomorrow's lessons yet.'

The kitchen was blessedly peaceful, though Eppie kept expecting Foy to come barging in through the back door as he so often did. She even hoped that he would – as long, she told herself, as he brought Duncan with him. There was enough food keeping warm on the range for both of them.

She looked around for the soup tureen, then realised that she must have left it on the sideboard in the dining room. She went back upstairs to fetch it and was passing the library door, which was ajar, when Alexander Geddes called from within, 'Is that you, Eppie?'

'Aye, Mr Geddes.'

He was sitting at his desk, papers spread before him and a half-filled glass and an empty decanter by his elbow. 'Would you bring another bottle of port up from the cellar?'

'Aye, sir.' Another journey, Eppie thought as she carried the tureen downstairs, then went to fetch the port. It was little wonder that once age began to creep up on her Jean Gilbert had had to give up her work. In Jean's time Helen Geddes had been living in the house, and her continuous demands for attention must have kept poor Jean running up and down stairs all day.

Still intent on the papers before him, her employer waved a hand vaguely towards a corner of the desk when she took the port into the library. Putting the bottle down carefully to make sure that it did not cover any of the papers, she noticed that they looked very like the sketches that Duncan had thrown down as he stormed out of the kitchen. Geddes was making swift notes on a clean sheet of paper.

'Is Duncan back yet?'

'No, sir.'

He grunted, then said, 'Thank you, Eppie, that will be all.'

As she turned to go her eyes went to the portrait hanging

over the fireplace. Celia Geddes's green eyes seemed to be filled with life, and the slight but unmistakeable curve of her full mouth hinted, as it always did to Eppie, of a smile about to illuminate her beautiful face.

It was no wonder that both Alexander Geddes and Foy had fallen in love with the woman, Eppie thought as she went back downstairs. The wonder, to her mind, was that Celia Ramsay, as she had been then, would ever have considered marrying an uncouth man like Foy.

But at the same time, she had to admit that there was something about the man that caught her own interest. He was nothing like Murdo, and yet . . . She cleared the silly thoughts from her mind by making herself check the pantry shelves to find out if anything needed replenishing.

When the girls were in bed and the next day's lessons prepared, Marion came to the kitchen and took a cup of tea with Eppie before announcing that she was off to her bed. She was on her way towards the door when it opened and Alexander Geddes came in, dressed in his outdoor clothes.

'Miss McNaught.' He smiled down at her. 'I take it from the silence upstairs that the girls are both in their beds.'

'Yes, Mr Geddes. They've done well today and we've caught up with the lessons missed while I was in Aberdeen. I'm just off to my own bed.'

'Is Duncan not back yet, Eppie?'

'Not yet, sir, but I'm sure he won't be long.'

'I'm going out for some fresh air. No need for you to wait up.'

'I wonder if he might want a companion on his walk?' Marion said when he had gone. 'I should have asked him.'

'He might want to be on his own, and anyway, you told him that you were just off to your bed.'

'So I did. I wonder why I said that?' Marion said, vexed. 'Now I'll have to do it – and I quite fancied a wee breath of fresh air myself.'

Rain was falling when Alexander Geddes stepped out of the house; a soft but persistent summer drizzle that seemed, from the state of the streets and pavements, to have been falling for some time. He turned up the collar of his coat and decided that Duncan was probably up at the quarry.

The sky was heavy with clouds and there was no starlight or moonlight to illuminate his way. Not that he needed any light, for he knew this place so well that he could even have found his way in dense fog – and had done so, on occasion. Duncan knew it well too, he recalled, staring out across the darkness that was the Moray Firth. The fishing fleet had set out some time earlier, and now they were well over the horizon, with not even a speck of light from the masthead lanterns of the few stragglers to be seen.

Duncan loved this place, and the quarry. He cared enough about the quarry to spend hours working on the well-drawn plans he had brought to the library that afternoon – and what had his father done? Dismissed them out of hand, and all because – Alexander found it hard to admit the truth to himself – of his intense dislike of Foy.

As he struggled up the hill he also admitted to himself that he should have seen Duncan's plans as an opportunity for father and son to work together – instead, he had only seen the plans as Foy's way of taking over the quarry that Alexander had come to look on as his sole property. One day, he now knew from what Foy had told him, it would be part of Duncan's inheritance, which was exactly what Alexander would have wanted for him. And surely, as the future major shareholder, the lad had the right to think of the quarry's well-being?

He had arrived on the headland and was standing on the area that Duncan – and Foy, a small voice in his head added, before he ordered it to be silent – had earmarked for a workshop where the men could shape the blocks of marble under cover and with no worry about the tides that regularly covered most of the beach they worked on.

The great blocks of marble would be lifted from the quarry, not by manpower as happened now, but by a steam-driven crane which would also power the machinery used to work on the marble blocks. A shed to house the steam engine would also be built up here.

It all made sense, Alexander admitted, and despised himself for having crushed Duncan's enthusiasm without stopping to think of his feelings. It was, he realised bitterly, the sort of thing his mother would have done.

'I thought I might find ye here. Ye shouldnae be staunin' sae near tae the edge.'

The harsh, flat voice left him in no doubt as to who was behind him. Geddes turned slowly, taking his time, moving his feet carefully but confidently on the wet grass only inches from the drop to the quarry below. Night had come on since he had left the house and now Foy was almost lost against a background of wasteland and lowering sky.

'Why should that worry you? D'you find the temptation to push me over the edge too much to bear?'

'Dinnae be daft, man, what wid I want tae dae a thing like that for? Anyway, I'm no' thinkin' o' you, but o' the folk that'd miss ye. Duncan for one, an' that bonny wee daughter o' yours, and the wee school teacher that can scarce take her eyes from ye.'

For a moment Alexander's attention was diverted. 'Miss McNaught? You don't know what you're talking about!' he snapped.

'It seems that I ken more than you dae,' Foy's rusty chuckle rang out. 'Yer blind, man, tae the folk round ye – even yer ain son!'

'I doubt if Duncan would miss me much,' Alexander's bitterness returned. 'He managed to get through five years without me – but then, he had you instead.'

'Dinnae tell me yer still frettin' aboot that? You didnae see him, or hear him. There was scarce a day that you an' Lydia didnae get a mention from him, an' Duncan's no man enough yet tae be able tae veil his eyes. Oh, he missed ye – every bit as much, I'd say, as you missed him – but he left here because he wanted tae prove tae ye that he was his own man an' he could make his own way in the world. And what did ye dae when the time was ripe and he came back wi' the proof? Ye turned him doon without even givin' him the chance tae talk his ideas ower wi' ye.'

'*His* ideas?' Alexander deliberately put emphasis on the first word. 'No, Foy – you used him to get me to do what you want for this quarry.'

'For God's sake!' There was such a flare of sudden anger in the Glaswegian's voice that Alexander braced his body and clenched his fists, preparing for an attack. 'D'ye really think that those drawin's are mine? I'm a labourer, no' a planner. I dae the manual work, and mebbe I'm far travelled and I ken mair about quarries an' how tae get the best out o' them and out o' the men that work them than you'll ever pack intae that arrogant noddle o' yours, but how could I come up wi' the ideas that Duncan has?

That takes scholarly learnin' and I never got any' o' that. But you did, an' mebbe it's time ye started tae make yer heid work for ye.'

'You're telling me that these plans are all Duncan's work?'

'One day he'll be able tae come up wi' ideas that are just as good as these, mebbe even better, but the lad's ower young yet for that. It was him and Edward Ramsay that worked it oot atween them, then wi' Edward's guidance, Duncan drew up the plans.'

'I thought . . .'

'Ye didnae think, ye jumped tae conclusions. You decided that I had Duncan in my pocket, did ye no'?' Foy said with disgust. 'You think I'm some sort o' puppet master that just pulls on the strings and makes the boy dance tae my tune. D'ye know somethin', Geddes? I'm staunin' here, in the rain and the dark, wonderin' why the hell this Lord God ye worship sae religiously every Sunday mornin', an' thank for every bite o' food ye put intae yer mooth, ever saw fit tae bless ye wi' a son like Duncan. Can ye no' unnerstaun' that he's his own man now, like you and me are? He doesnae belong tae me, or tae you for all that he's yer blood kin. He doesnae belong tae anyone. He's his own person, and if you cannae grasp that, an' grasp it soon, he'll be off again an' this time, ye'll no' see him back.'

His voice stopped and he turned his head to the side and spat his anger and exasperation out on to the grass. For a moment there was silence apart from the soft hiss of rain falling steadily, and the sound, far below, of the incoming tide rattling on the stony beach, each wave clutching at the stones with white foaming fingers as the sea dragged it back, then giving way to the next wave, which gained a little more ground before being pulled, in its turn, back to the firth's maternal bosom.

Then Foy said, 'Onywey, I just came lookin' for ye tae tell ye that the lad's back at yer hoose. He had his supper wi' me at the hoose where I'm bidin'.'

'He's come home?'

'Aye. It's where he belongs, is it no'? It aye the place he'll come back tae, if ye can find the sense tae speak tae him man tae man tomorrow aboot those plans o' his – and Edward Ramsay's. I'm no' sayin' ye should agree tae them just because o' what I've telt ye, but ye should at least hear the lad out, an' think o' what's best for the quarry. Guid night tae ye,' said Foy, and began to walk down towards the town.

'Wait . . .' Geddes called after him. He started forwards and one foot landed awkwardly on a clump of wet grass and skidded back, throwing him off balance. He tried to swing his weight to the other foot, only to realise, too late, that it was nearer the edge than he had thought. Despite strenuous efforts, he lost his balance entirely, and cartwheeled clumsily over the edge.

Foy, hurrying downhill, heard a faint cry followed by another, the second more prolonged. He stopped short.

'Geddes?'

There was no reply. He hurried back to the spot, as closely as he could estimate in the darkening night, where he had left Alexander Geddes, calling the man's name. There was silence at first, and then his ears caught a faint sound that might have been the call of some nocturnal bird, or perhaps the scream of a rabbit startled by the sudden agonising snap of a fox's jaws.

He threw himself down on the grass and started squirming his body towards the edge of the cliff, fingers clawing at tussocks of grass and using them to drag himself along. Then there were no more tussocks, only space. He eased himself forwards slowly until his head was clear of the ground and surrounded by nothing but air. He drew in a deep breath and bellowed, 'Geddes!'

He thought, again, that he could hear a faint cry in answer. It could have come from the void that he knew, but could not see, below, or from somewhere out on the water.

'I'm comin'!' he bawled, and began to ease himself back over the solid ground. When he judged himself to be safe, he scrambled to his feet and ran, cursing as he went, towards the town.

Eppie was damping down the range for the night when the street door flew open and Foy lunged into the kitchen as though all the fiends of hell were after him. His clothes, face and hands were muddy, and he was labouring to draw breath into his lungs.

'Dear heavens, what's happened? Did ye get yersel' intae a fight? Sit down at the table, man, and let me have a look at ye.' She took his arm, the sleeve soaking wet, and tried to draw him towards the table, but he fought her off, still whooping and wheezing as he tried to get his breath. For a moment they wrestled in the middle of the kitchen before Foy found his voice.

'It's no' me that needs – help, it's Geddes . . .'

Her hands flew to her mouth and she stared at him over her fingers. 'What have ye done tae him?'

'He went – over the cliff at the – quarry. Where's Duncan?'

'Gone tae his bed.'

'Tell him what's – happened and fetch – him doon. I havenae got the breath yet – for those stairs!'

When Eppie burst in with the news Duncan, who had been reading, shot from the bed with one movement and was reaching for his clothes before she had finished talking.

'Tell Foy to wait in the kitchen for me. You rouse some of the quarrymen,' he ordered, and she fled, bumping into Marion who was standing in the hallway, a robe clutched about her shoulders.

Her face drained of colour when Eppie told her what had happened. 'I'm going with Duncan!'

'You're needed here,' Eppie said as Charlotte's frightened face peeped round Marion's arm and Lydia's bedroom door opened. 'Foy's in the kitchen waiting for Duncan. You don't know where any of the quarrymen live so I'll have to rouse them. Put a hot brick in Mr Geddes's bed and make sure there's plenty of hot water, for he'll be cold when we get him home. And see to the lassies,' she added as both girls began to babble questions.

Duncan overtook her when she was halfway down the stairs and arrived in the kitchen before her. When she got there he was questioning Foy, who had recovered his breath.

'You're certain you heard him?'

'I think so, though it could have been anythin'. I don't know my way down tae the quarry in the dark, but you do, lad.'

'So do the men who work there. Eppie, rouse as many as you can and tell them we'll need lanterns and ropes and mebbe canvas in case he's hurt himself and can't climb up. Foy and me are going to the harbour to find a boat.'

'A boat?' Foy yelped.

'Aye, a boat. The tide'll be comin' in now, and if he's hurt and he's gone all the way down . . .' Duncan said, his young face suddenly ageing as fear drew the skin taut over the bones beneath it '. . . then he could drown before anyone manages to get down to him.'

'I don't know how tae work a boat!'

'But I do.' Duncan hauled the door open and hustled the other two out into the rain. 'Run, Eppie,' he ordered, and set off at a fast pace towards the harbour himself, hauling Foy along with him.

Eppie raced round the streets, heedless of the shawl slipping from her head and the rain soaking her hair so that it came loose and hung round her face in dripping strands. The first quarryman she roused said as soon as she had gasped her message, 'You go along that way, m'quine, an' I'll go the other way. Tell them tae bring ropes an' make for the top o' the quarry as quick as they can.' Already, he was hopping about as he struggled into the trousers he had brought to the door with him. In a fishing community a sudden violent knocking at the door in the night could mean only one thing – someone was in danger, usually on the seas, and so the menfolk kept their clothes near to hand when they retired.

When she had roused two more men one of them woke his two sons and sent them out to continue raising the alarm. 'You go on home, m'quine, and get yoursel' warm. We'll get him, never fear,' he said. 'We'll have him home afore ye know it.'

Home – but dead or alive? Eppie didn't voice the words, for nobody could tell her the answer as yet. She hurried off obediently, but instead of returning to the Geddes house she made for the headland. She might be needed at the quarry, she told herself as she ran, and in any case she couldn't face returning to the house, and to Marion's anxious questioning. If her employer were injured, she could at least tear up her petticoats and use the material as bandaging.

How could he not be injured? The quarry, small though

it was, had had its share of injury and death over the years. She had seen it in daylight, with its terraces of jagged rocks that had been split open and made to give up the beautiful marble they had nursed over the eons, like infants in their wombs. No human could fall from the top of the quarry and hope to miss those sharp outcrops, as hard as iron and as merciless as the black heart of the devil himself.

She thought of Lydia and Duncan and Marion – how would Marion bear it if anything happened to the first man she had ever cared for? – and began to murmur prayers as she ran.

A group of men had already gathered on the headland; someone held Eppie back as she tried to thrust her way to the forefront. 'Na, m'quine, you stay back. There's one over the edge already,' he said, 'an' we dinnae want you tae go as weel.'

'Have they found him yet?'

'No' yet. Roddy Finlay's taken a lantern an' gone doon on the end o' a rope, looking for him. Roddy's all right,' the man told her, 'he's got a good head on his shoulders, and no fear o' heights. I've seen him dancin' his way along the cliff here tae amuse the rest o' us, and never once has the man slipped.'

'What about the doctor?' Eppie suddenly remembered. 'I never went tae his hoose . . .'

'He's been told. One o' the boats seemingly had tae come back in wi' a crewman who got hurt. The doctor's seein' tae him, and comin' here as quick as he . . .'

He stopped as a faint shout was heard from below. He, and the men in front of Eppie, pressed forwards, all falling silent to allow one of their number to be heard as he shouted through cupped hands to the man on the end of the rope. Eppie only just heard a second faint call, and then the group gave a collective groan that made her blood run cold.

'They've found him? Is he . . . ?' She couldn't bring herself to say the word.

'Roddy's seen him, but the man's tumbled a' the way doon to the beach and the tide's comin' in. We'll have tae find a way tae get doon there quickly – an' that's no' easy.'

Rain ran into Eppie's eyes as she tilted her head back to look up into her companion's face, dimly lit by the lantern he held. Although she could not make out his expression she could tell by the tone of his voice that he, and no doubt the others, held out little hope for Alexander Geddes. 'They're sendin' down more ropes, and another two men,' he went on, passing the information to her as he received it, 'and they're makin' a canvas sling, but . . .'

'Duncan and Foy went to look for a boat. Duncan knew about the tide.'

'They might be our best chance,' the man said. And then, looking out towards the sea, 'Though God help them, for it'll no' be an easy task.'

26

Duncan had expected to have to do the rowing himself, but the skipper of the fishing boat that had been forced to return to harbour with an injured crewman was still on board. As soon as he grasped what was happening the man said, 'We'll take our wee boat and you and me, m'loon, can take an oar each.'

When they cleared the outer harbour the sea was suddenly choppy, and Duncan, who had not rowed a boat in years, was grateful for the help of the man who was with him. Foy crouched in the bows with a lantern and a coil of rope from the fishing boat.

'We'll have tae row out tae sea first,' the fisherman said, 'then we'll bear roond tae the quarry once we're clear o' the worst o' the rocks.'

His advice was sound; although it seemed to Duncan, desperate to find his father, that they wasted too much time rowing away from Portsoy. When the boat began to curve round towards land they had clear water, though as they neared the shore they began to meet submerged rocks. Occasionally, if the rock was below the surface and Foy didn't notice it, they brushed against it and then, as the fisherman coaxed the boat on, it gave out a grating sound that set Duncan's teeth on edge and convinced him that they were going to founder before reaching the quarry. He could hear Foy cursing non-stop, and agreed heartily with everything the man was saying.

His arms began to ache, and it was a relief when Foy shouted that they were almost at the quarry. 'Look – there's lights up on the headland! They've brought lanterns.'

Duncan blinked the rain from his eyes and stared into the darkness, eventually making out tiny glimmers, like a collection of fireflies dancing up in the sky.

They took the boat in, bumping against more rocks and sliding away from them noisily, until they could make out the sound of waves rattling through pebbles on the beach. Under orders from the fisherman they eased the boat between two rocks looming from the water and wedged the oars against them in a bid to keep the boat as still as possible.

The skipper had brought a loudhailer with him, and although the men on the headland only had the use of their cupped hands, the sea was quiet enough in the sheltered little bay for those below to make out the gist of their shouts, and to gather that Alexander Geddes had fallen all the way down to the beach and was lying motionless across a rock, half-in and half-out of the water. It was almost impossible for the men on land to get down to him, though they were doing their best.

'And the tide's still coming in – we've got to get him out before he drowns, or gets washed out to sea!' Duncan said urgently.

'An' we'll dae just that, m'loon,' the fisherman assured him calmly. Then, to Foy, 'Haud the lantern high, man, so's we can see – there he is, see? Lyin' across that rock.'

Duncan's heart, which had been racing after the strenuous row from the harbour, almost stopped as he spotted the limp figure sprawled over a large rock and looking like a rag doll tossed away by a bad-tempered giant child. The incoming waves were washing over it.

'Can ye no' get ony closer?' Foy roared from the bows.

'No' unless ye want tae join him,' the fisherman responded. 'We'll rip the bottom from this boat if we try it.'

'Then I'll jist have tae go in an' get him. Take a haud o' that.' The Glaswegian handed the lantern to the fisherman before picking up the coil of rope. Swiftly, he found the end and knotted it securely around his waist, then located the other end and tied it to the thwart, tugging on it with all his might to make sure that it would hold.

'I'm coming with you.' Duncan began to rise, but even as Foy barked 'No!' the fisherman put a hand on his arm and pushed him back to his seat.

'We're both needed tae keep her steady. If we slip out frae between these rocks there's little chance o' gettin' the man on board.'

'Foy!'

'Do as yer told, lad. I'm stronger than you are an' I can manage on my lone,' Foy said, and then, to the fisherman, 'Mind an' keep the boat steady till we get back.'

'We'll do our best.'

'Ye'll have tae dae better than that,' Foy said, and then he was overboard and waist deep in water. The incoming waves helped him to move forwards, though once or twice Duncan caught his breath as he saw the man being thrown against the rocks scattered between him and the motionless figure several yards away. When the waves that had helped him to move forwards hurried back to the sea they tried to draw him along with them, which meant that he was thrown against the same rocks for a second time.

'He'll never make it!'

'If he doesnae,' his companion said grimly, 'nob'dy else can.'

The rope Foy had tied to the thwart tightened as it ran out, pulling the boat further in between the rocks. Wood grated uneasily against pitiless stone as a wave larger than the others came rushing by, lashing the rocks and dashing cold spray over the two men.

Duncan peered ahead, afraid that the rope had not been long enough, then saw that Foy had reached his father.

With a strength that borrowed something from the desperation of the situation, the Glaswegian lifted Alexander Geddes clear of the rock and gripped him close, as though in a loving embrace.

'I'll try tae hold us steady,' the fisherman shouted above the noise of the waves. 'You take the rope and pull with a' yer might, m'loon. He'll never make it withoot help.'

He wedged his booted feet against Duncan's oar in an attempt to keep it steady against the rock as Duncan scrambled forwards, wrapped the rope around his arm and began to pull. Foy, he saw, was keeping his back to them in an attempt to protect his burden from the worst of the waves and the rocks.

Once the slack had come in and the rope was taut between the boat and the two men in the water Duncan felt as though he were trying to drag the headland itself towards the boat. It seemed as if he was doing no good at all, but when he was forced to pause for a second to catch his breath he saw that Foy was nearer than he had been before.

Hours, months and even years seemed to have passed before the man's hand reached out and gripped the boat. 'Now,' the fisherman shouted, hauling his oar in and lunging forwards, 'pull – it's the only way!'

Freed from the brake formed by the oars, the boat bucked, then dipped ominously at the bows as Duncan and the fisherman both went forwards. Water poured in, but Foy, with a final superhuman effort, took advantage of the dip to turn and half-lift, half-throw the man in his arms up and over the gunwale. Duncan tumbled backwards into the well of the boat as the dead weight that was his father landed on top of him; the bows dipped even further as the fisherman leaned precariously over the side and thrust an arm towards Foy. His own arm came up out of the water and the two men connected, hands grasping elbows.

The fisherman pulled with all the skill and strength developed from hauling in nets loaded with fish, and Foy's boots grazed Duncan's shins as he landed in the boat. For a moment the four of them were caught up in a wet tangle while the boat, taking advantage of a sea-going wave, backed away from the rocks where it had been wedged. It started to swing around, out of control, then the fisherman was grabbing at one of the oars and yelling at Duncan, 'Get tae yer oar, man! We need tae control the boat afore the rocks take us!'

Somehow, Duncan managed to struggle back to his seat and grasp the other oar. Between them the two men got the boat under control and turned towards the open sea while Foy, coughing and spitting seawater, pulled himself up into the bows, clutching Alexander Geddes around the waist to keep the unconscious man's head clear of the water swilling round in the bottom of the boat.

* * *

While the doctor tended Alexander Geddes upstairs, Eppie saw to Foy, now wrapped in blankets while his wet clothes steamed on the dryer before the kitchen range.

'It's no' ointments an' tea I need, wumman, it's whisky,' he grated at her through clenched teeth. He was shivering so hard that the chair he sat on rattled faintly against the stone floor.

'Try tae hold still, Foy – and what sort of daft name's that?' she snapped, a reaction to the events of the evening bringing on a sudden bout of irritation. 'Ye must have a Christian name – why don't ye use it like other folks do?'

'Mebbe I have, an' mebbe I havenae,' he shot back at her. 'If I dinnae choose tae use it, then that's my business.' Then, pushing her hands away as she tried to wash out a gash in his shoulder, 'For God's sake will ye fetch me a *drink*?' And then, 'Aboot time!' as Duncan came in with a bottle in one hand and a filled glass in the other.

Scorning the proffered glass, Foy seized the bottle and tipped it up to drink greedily.

'For goodness' sake!' Eppie said, scandalised, then as he gulped whisky down as though it were water, 'Duncan . . . !'

He grinned down at the quarryman. 'Leave him be, Eppie, he deserves the whole bottle – the whole cellarful – for what he did tonight. I'll have this.' And he drank deeply from the glass.

When Foy finally set the bottle down it was just over half full, but his eyes, which had been dull with exhaustion, were brighter and his voice, when he said, 'By God, I needed that!' was stronger. 'Any word o' the man upstairs, lad?'

'Not yet. But at least he's alive, thanks to you.'

'Ach, dinnae be daft,' Foy said, and took another swig from the bottle.

'What about the girls?' Eppie asked. Lydia had gone into hysterics when she saw her father's limp body being carried into the house, and Charlotte had been hard put not to join her, while tears had poured down Marion's ashen cheeks.

'In Lydia's room. She's calmed down and I said that Charlotte could stay with her tonight. She needs the company.'

'I'll go to them later – once I've seen tae you,' Eppie added to Foy.

'I'm fine!'

'Look at you . . .' she pulled at the blanket covering his upper body to reveal a muscular torso well decorated with dark bruises and abrasions. When he yelped and tried to gather the blanket back, she handed it to Duncan and went on scathingly, 'For goodness' sake, ye daft loon, d'ye think I've never seen a man before?'

'Ye've never seen this yin.'

'I doubt if you're any different from the rest. Sit still now.' The sea had washed any blood away, and she was glad to see that his injuries were all superficial. She dipped clean rags in a mixture of water and vinegar and ran them across the torn skin; he didn't say a word, or even draw in a sharp breath, but she could tell by the very slight tensing of muscles beneath her fingers that the treatment stung. His skin, surprisingly smooth to the touch, was still cold.

'There,' she said at last, taking the blanket back from Duncan and putting it gently about the man's shoulders. 'That'll dae ye, though you're goin' tae be stiff tomorrow, an' black an' blue for a whiley.'

'It'll no' be the first time, or the last,' he grunted, taking another deep drink from the bottle.

'And I don't know why we're botherin' tae dry your

clothes,' she said, looking at the rags steaming on the wooden clothes horse, 'because they've been ripped tae shreds.'

'Nothin' that a good seamstress couldnae put right, surely.'

'If ye're thinkin' that I'll mend these for you, you're wrong. They're no' worth the trouble.'

'I cannae afford tae throw good clothin' away just like that!'

'I'll go to your lodgings and fetch dry clothes for you,' Duncan decided. 'And I'm sure my father'll be happy to buy all the new clothes you need to show his gratitude for what you did tonight.'

Foy screwed his face into a scowl. 'God save me from gratitude – I've no time for it.'

'Aye ye have, if it takes the form of some good new clothes,' Eppie said, and then stepped back, wafting one hand before her face. 'The smell of whisky from your breath's makin' me feel light-headed.'

'Me an' all, an' it's just what I need,' Foy told her with the first grin she had seen on his face since Duncan had helped him into the kitchen, staggering with fatigue, and with seawater pouring off him. 'On ye go, Duncan, an' fetch those dry clothes so's I can get back tae my lodgin's.'

'He'll go later, for you're staying here tonight,' Eppie said firmly. 'For one thing, you're needing a good sleep, and for another, you're so full of whisky that you'd probably fall into the harbour if you tried tae find your way home tonight. Ye don't want another wettin', dae ye?'

To her surprise, he didn't argue. 'I could do with some food in my belly,' he said. 'A' that sea water's left me famished!'

'Duncan, mebbe you could look in on the lassies again while I get food ready for the two of you.'

'I might get word of my father too,' Duncan was saying when the doctor came into the kitchen.

'He's gashed his head and sprained an ankle, and he's going to be bruised and sore for a few days,' he announced cheerfully, 'but the man's lucky, it could be a lot worse.'

'Can I see him?' Duncan asked at once.

'He's sleeping, but there's no reason why you shouldnae go up. Miss – McNaught, is it? – is sitting with him. Give him a bowl of soup when he wakens, and bland foods for the next twenty-four hours,' the doctor said to Eppie. 'What he needs more than anything else is to rest and be warm. We want to avoid a chill if we can. Now then . . .'

He advanced on Foy, who scowled at the man as he submitted to an examination of his cuts and bruises.

'Aye, you've been well looked after,' the doctor said, and then, glancing at the whisky bottle, which was almost empty, 'in every way.'

'Would you like a cup of tea?' Eppie asked. He shook his white head.

'Don't trouble yourself, m'dear. But if you'd be so kind as to fetch another tumbler I'll have something from that bottle before I go off to my bed.'

An hour later the household finally began to settle down for the night. Duncan fetched a set of clothing for Foy and then retired to his room, and Eppie saw Foy settled in her room before putting the kitchen to rights and going upstairs. When she opened the door of Lydia's room she saw that the two girls were fast asleep, Charlotte's golden brown curls and Lydia's black curls mingling on the pillow.

Alexander Geddes had roused and taken the soup recommended by the doctor, then immediately fallen asleep again. A lamp burned in the room, shaded from the bed, but giving enough light to illuminate his face, and Marion, a blanket over her knees and a shawl about her shoulders, was sitting in a chair by his bedside.

'I'll have tae share your room tonight,' Eppie whispered. 'Foy's in mine, and I've let Charlotte sleep in Lydia's room tonight, for company.'

Marion nodded briefly without raising her eyes from the face on the pillow. 'On you go then. I'll stay here.'

'All night? Marion, you need your sleep, and the doctor says he's going to be fine.'

'Even so, I'll not leave him on his lone.' Marion glanced up briefly, and the lamplight made the tears in her eyes sparkle like precious gems. 'Just think, Eppie – he could have been killed!'

'But he wasn't killed. He's all right.'

'No thanks to that Foy!'

'Foy saved him! Duncan says that he might have drowned or been carried out to sea if the man hadn't gone into the water after him.'

'Mebbe so, but who put him there in the first place?' Marion's voice was hard and cold. 'From what I've heard there was nobody else but Foy there when Mr Geddes fell down into the quarry. And you know as well as I do that they detest each other. They must have been quarrelling, Eppie, and Foy pushed the poor man over!'

'That's nonsense,' Eppie began, her voice rising, and then, remembering that her employer might well hear them although he seemed to be asleep, she lowered her voice to a whisper. 'Foy wouldn't do that – and if he had, would he have risked his own life tae save the man?'

'He might, to cover up what he had done.'

'You're havering!'

'We'll see – when Mr Geddes wakens tomorrow. Oh,

Eppie,' Marion's voice broke, 'look at the man – he's so pale.'

'He'll be grand after a good night's sleep. Come to bed, Marion – we can leave the door open so you'll hear him if he calls out in the night.'

But her sister settled more firmly into the chair, gathering her warm shawl more closely about her shoulders. 'I'm not leaving him,' she insisted, and Eppie, bone-weary after all that had gone on, left her to her vigil.

She woke at her usual time in the morning to find that she was still alone. There wasn't a sound from the other bedrooms, and when she silently opened the door of Alexander Geddes's room and peered in, she saw that patient and nurse were both sound asleep.

Foy was sitting at the kitchen table, eating a sandwich made up of two thick slices of bread stuck together by what looked like a good half inch of butter topped with honey, and drinking a mug of strong black tea.

'About time,' he said, spraying crumbs. 'My stomach thinks my throat's been cut.'

'Since you're so good at helping yourself,' she said drily, looking at the massive sandwich clutched in his hands, 'you should just have gone on and fried half a dozen eggs and a side of bacon.'

'You're better at that than I am.' He got up to fetch another mug, moving stiffly. 'Ye'll have a cup o' tea while ye're workin'?'

'Aye, I will. How d'you feel this morning?'

'Ach, I'm fine.' He winced slightly as he turned from the dresser, mug in hand, then added as he caught her eye, 'It'll ease off once I get tae the quarry.'

'You're going to the quarry this morning?'

'Of course. The man upstairs isnae goin' tae be able to

for a week or mebbe more, so Duncan an' me'll have tae see tae things for him – as far as the quarry's concerned, at any rate.'

'Foy,' Eppie said carefully as she stirred the oatmeal she had left soaking overnight, and added a generous handful of salt before putting it on the range, 'what happened last night?'

'Ye ken whit happened. Geddes lost his footin', an' fell frae the top o' the quarry intae the sea.'

'Before that – how did you know he'd gone over the edge? Were you there?'

'O' course I was, how else would I have known he'd fallen? I went up tae have a look at the place, and Geddes was a'ready there, so I telt him that Duncan was back home. I'd jist started back tae the village when I heard him call oot, an' when I turned, he was gone. Lucky I was there, else he'd have lain there until—'

He stopped suddenly, staring at her. 'Are you thinkin' that I might have pushed the man?'

'No, I just – there's no' much love between the two of you. Last night I came into the library and saw you . . .'

'Don't be daft, wumman,' he said. 'It was him that went for me then, no' the other way around.'

'He might have tried again, later.'

'Well he didnae, so ye can just put that sort o' nonsense out o' yer heid,' he said as Duncan came in, yawning and stretching, and ready for his breakfast.

27

Helen Geddes swept past Eppie as soon as the door was opened, demanding to see her son at once. 'Where is he?' Her tone was heavy with accusation, as though she suspected Eppie of hiding him from her.

'In his bedroom, and he's mebbe asleep. The doctor said to let him rest,' Eppie went on, hurrying up the stairs behind the woman, 'but he's had a good breakfast and he's not hurt bad.'

'I'll be the judge of that,' Helen snapped over her shoulder, then threw open the door of her son's bedroom. 'Alexander?'

If he had been asleep, he certainly would not be now, Eppie thought. But when she reached the door she saw that her employer was awake and propped up on several pillows. Marion, who had been standing by the bed, gave a slight bob of her head when Helen came in.

'Miss McNaught. What are you doing here?'

'Being of assistance to me. Good morning, Mother.' Geddes said as Marion stepped back, out of the woman's line of sight.

'Alexander, are you all right? What on earth has been

going on?' Helen sat down by the bed and studied him closely. 'What a thing to have to hear from the servants! Why did you not send word to me at once?'

'I'd other things on my mind,' he told her drily. 'Eppie, could you bring some tea for Mrs Geddes?'

'Aye, sir, at once.' She closed the door thankfully and went back to her kitchen, shooing the girls in front of her as they appeared from the schoolroom. 'Away out to the garden and play.'

'Was that my grandmother I heard?'

'Aye, Lydia, she's come to see how your father is.'

'Are we not supposed to have lessons?' Charlotte asked. 'We've been waiting for Aunt Marion.'

'I think she's too busy looking after Mr Geddes to see to your lessons today. Out you go, now. I've got tea to make for Mrs Geddes.'

The girls fled, delighted at being allowed to miss a morning's work.

In the bedroom, Helen Geddes was saying, 'And what were you doing out on the headland at that time of night? Alone with that grim-faced Glasgow man too. I've seen him going about the town and I'd not trust him anywhere near my house. There's some folk saying that he attacked you.'

'That's nonsense!' He was still pale and drawn, but his voice was strong when he said angrily, 'It was entirely my own fault – I slipped on the wet grass and went over the edge. It's fortunate for me that Foy was there, for he raised the alarm and then went out in a boat with Duncan to get me.'

'What were the two of you doing there at that time of night?'

'Talking over Duncan's plans for the quarry – and if you hear any more nonsense about an attack, or a fight,

I'd be grateful if you would put a stop to it at once.'

'It would never have happened if I'd still been living here. Perhaps I should move back in, at least until you're recovered. You look as though you have a slight fever.'

'The doctor has assured me that I have no fever, and there's no need for you to move in.'

'But you're my only son. I should be looking after you.'

'Eppie looks after Lydia and me very well. In any case, the house is full with Duncan back home. You'd not be comfortable.'

'I'm sure that Miss McNaught and her niece would be willing to return to Fordyce, given the circumstances.' She seemed to have forgotten that Marion was standing quietly in a corner.

'But I don't wish to see Miss McNaught and Charlotte return to Fordyce until they have to. Lydia needs her tuition if she is to go to school in September, and Miss McNaught has also been assisting me with my work.'

'Indeed?' Helen was saying as Eppie came in with a tray.

Helen stayed for some time, and when the bedroom door closed behind her back Alexander gave a long, weary sigh and felt his body relax into the mattress.

'Would you like some beef tea?' Marion came over to tidy the bedclothes. Her hand brushed against his for a moment; it felt deliciously cool.

He smiled at her gratefully. Throughout his mother's fussing he had been aware of the neat, still figure in the corner. 'Later, perhaps.'

She nodded. 'I think you should sleep now. You look tired.'

'My mother tends to have that effect on me. But there's more work that I should see to – letters . . .'

'After you've rested. There's plenty of time and I can help, later.' She settled his pillows into a more comfortable position and then drew the curtains against the morning sunlight. 'There, that's better.' And then, on her way to the door, 'Mr Geddes, Charlotte and I could return to Fordyce if you felt that you would like to have your mother near until you've regained your strength. Lydia's done very well this summer, and I'm quite sure that she's ready for school.'

'But Miss McNaught, I want you to stay,' he said, and she turned and gave him a dazzling smile that gave her normally serious face such unexpected beauty that it almost took his breath away.

For some time after she had left the room Alexander Geddes lay in his bed, his eyes closed and that radiant smile glowing on the inside of his lids. Earlier, when he told his mother that he did not wish Marion McNaught and her niece to leave his house until the agreed time, the words had been spoken automatically, but he now recalled Foy saying, as they faced each other on the headland above the quarry, 'the wee school teacher that can scarce take her eyes from ye,' and his own instant denial. He ran the words over again in his mind. After a difficult start, Lydia enjoyed Charlotte's company and he enjoyed Marion's. He liked to see her sitting at his table, neat and composed, keeping a watchful eye on the two girls, or working in his library, her smooth forehead taking on a puzzled little frown as she sought to grasp the sense of the paper she was studying – and then the sudden flash of satisfaction as the solution came to her. He liked to wake in the mornings and know that she was in the house.

He puzzled over this new and strange realisation for a few minutes and then, deciding that his mother could be right when she said that he had a slight fever, he put the matter from his mind and let sleep creep over him.

His last thought was that before the day was out, he would summon Duncan to his room, and ask the lad to talk him through the plans he had drawn up for the quarry.

Marion leaned back against the bedroom door for a moment after she had closed it quietly behind her, the smile still lighting up her face. He wanted her to stay – he didn't want her to go!

Humming to herself, she almost danced down the stairs to the lower floor.

Alexander Geddes made a swift recovery but his ankle, badly twisted, kept him confined to his room for a few days. Marion ran between the library and his bedroom, fetching papers and books as he needed them and writing letters at his dictation while Charlotte and Lydia rejoiced in their new-found freedom and made full use of it.

Eppie was kept busy providing tea for the visitors who came and went – the doctor, business friends, and Helen Geddes, who visited her son daily.

The invalid found his limitations frustrating, and despite Marion's concern and his mother's protests, he was soon out and about with the aid of two strong walking sticks. He had made use of his enforced idleness to spend time with Duncan, and by the time his son was due to leave for Glasgow the two of them had come to know and understand each other, not as father and son, but as adults. Alexander had gone through the plans carefully, and with Marion's help had worked out the financial costs and possible benefits. Although he had not committed himself to an agreement, he was at least prepared to give the proposals long and serious thought.

* * *

Once Alexander Geddes was up and about again, Marion returned to her duties in the schoolroom and life for the household went back to normal. To Eppie's relief, Barbary seemed to be in better spirits and she began to take more of an interest in her appearance, and in her children and the cottage.

She was still fascinated by the pretty pink shell that her husband had given to her, and as often as not Eppie would find her friend sitting in her fireside chair or on the bench in the backyard, watching the children at play and rocking wee Jeemsie's cradle with one foot, with the shell on her lap or held to her ear while she listened intently, a slight smile on her lips.

'I've fairly let the hoosie go,' she said on one of Eppie's visits. 'Tolly would be angered at me if he could see it. Will ye help me tae set it tae rights properly for him?'

'If you want, though it looks fine tae me.'

'My Tolly's aye been particular.' Barbary bent to the cradle to chuck the baby under the chin. 'And I've sat around the place long enough. I want tae give it a good turnin' out.'

Charlotte volunteered her help, and so, to Eppie's surprise, did Lydia. The three of them advanced on the cottage one sunny morning and soon the place had been put to rights; the range was black leaded, the steps at the front and back of the cottage scrubbed and whitened, curtains and bedding washed, the rugs beaten, pots and pans hung up in order of size and the few pieces of furniture polished with beeswax from the Geddes bees.

The pretty gold-edged plates that Tolly McGeoch had brought back for his wife from his annual fishing trips to Lowestoft and Yarmouth were all washed and put back into the corner cupboard, and when Foy found out what was afoot he offered to paint the front and back doors and the window frames.

When it had all been done, Barbary looked around her home with a sigh of satisfaction. 'That's better! He's a nice man, that one with the strange way o' speakin'.'

'Foy? He's no' frightened o' hard work,' Eppie acknowledged.

Foy, for his part, was pleased to see Barbary start to take an interest in herself and her surroundings again.

'She's a bonny lass, an' too young tae mourn for the rest o' her life. She needs a man tae help her raise they bairns o' hers. Women wi' wee ones tae raise need menfolk aboot the place.'

'We don't always have a choice, and if we lose our menfolk we just have tae manage. Most of us do,' she said drily.

'Mebbe, but it's no' natural,' said Foy. Then, cocking his head to one side and surveying her thoughtfully, 'Would ye never conseeder a second marriage yersel'?'

'Mebbe – if the right man came along.'

'An' what sort o' man would that be?'

'For a start,' Eppie said, enjoying the slight flirtation, 'I'd have tae know his full name. I've no time for men with only the one name.'

'Weemen are the nosiest creatures on this earth, apart from cats.'

'Everyone's got a first name, even you.'

'I've heard tell,' Foy said, 'o' a tribe o' heathens that live in the jungles o' Africa. Awfu' superstitious they are, an' they believe that anyone who gets a hold o' their names gets a hold o' their minds, and if that happens, they cannae be independent any more. I've aye thought that they have the right way o' it.'

'Mebbe they've just got somethin' tae hide – like you.'

'Wumman, ye're like yer own rock cakes,' Foy said. 'Soft and tasty on the inside but awfu' crusty on the outside.'

Because of Alexander Geddes's accident Duncan and Foy had remained in Portsoy longer than originally planned. When the day of their departure finally arrived Lydia wept and clung to her brother, begging him to stay.

'I must go back to my duties,' he told her gently. 'But we'll write to each other, and I'll be back in the spring.'

'You didn't write to me last time, and you didn't come back for years and years!'

'It's different now. I promise,' he said, his eyes meeting Charlotte's over his sister's shoulder. He smiled and she smiled back, hoping that when he did return to Portsoy she would see him. The new school term was coming closer and soon, all too soon, she and her aunt would be going home to Fordyce. Although she was close to her grandparents, Charlotte had loved being able to see her mother whenever she wanted, and now looked upon Lydia as her best friend. She would miss them both dreadfully.

In the library, Alexander Geddes said to Foy, 'Duncan's to come back to Portsoy in the spring, to reach a decision about the machinery, and the sheds – you'll be returning with him?'

'If Mr Ramsay hasnae got some other work for me. But yer lad's learnin' fast and I've no doubt that he could deal wi' things on his lone.'

'You'll always be welcome in this house, Foy,' Geddes held a hand out to the other man. 'I'll not forget that you saved my life.'

'Och, that? I didnae dae it for you; ye could hae drowned for all that I cared,' Foy said gruffly, taking the proffered hand. 'I did it for Celia. Mebbe I still feel that she chose the wrong man, but I have tae admit that she cared for ye, and I know that ye made her happy. That's why I had tae get ye off that rock afore the tide got ye.'

'I never thought it was just for me,' Alexander Geddes told him, straight-faced.

'I'll mebbe see ye next year,' Foy said in the kitchen, ten minutes later.

'I'll see that the pantry's well stocked then, since ye've eaten poor Mr Geddes out o' hoose an' home while ye were here.'

'If ye werenae such a good cook I might no' have eaten so much.' He picked up the canvas bag that held all his possessions and slung it over his shoulder. 'That's me away then.'

When he had gone and she got her kitchen back to herself again, it took a while to get used to the silence, and the peace.

And, at times, the sense of loneliness.

A few days after Duncan and Foy returned to Glasgow, Alexander Geddes called Eppie and Marion into the library to hear his offer to pay Charlotte's fees if Eppie agreed to let the girl stay on in Portsoy and accompany his daughter to the girls' school in Durn Street when the new term started.

'I know from what Marion says that she's an exceptionally clever lass, and if you agree, Eppie, it'll mean that she'll be near to you.'

At first Eppie was uncomfortable with the idea of her employer paying Charlotte's school fees, but to her surprise Marion was in favour of the idea.

'Charlotte's already getting a good education in Fordyce,'

Eppie pointed out when the sisters had retired to the kitchen to discuss the offer.

'I know that, but she'll do just as well in this new school. And she'll be with you all the time,' said Marion, who was glowing inwardly. He had called her by her first name, and although neither he nor Eppie seemed to have noticed it, it was all that Marion could think of. Another reason for leaving Charlotte in Portsoy was that she would have more reason to visit the house once the new term started and she had to go back to Fordyce.

'What would mother and father say?'

'I think they'd want what Charlotte wants. We'll ask them – but first,' Marion advised, 'we should speak to Charlotte herself.'

Charlotte – and Lydia – were delighted, and as Annie and Peter McNaught had no objections, the matter was settled.

On the day Marion took both girls to Elgin to buy their school uniforms Alexander Geddes, restless and unable for some unknown reason to concentrate on anything, returned home in the middle of the morning. He was standing in the hall, wondering what to do next, when Eppie appeared in the library doorway, a duster in one hand.

'It's yourself, Mr Geddes. Have you forgotten something? It's not your ankle bothering you again, is it?'

'No, it's fine.' His ankle was almost completely healed now, though he still walked with a slight limp. 'I just thought I'd get some paperwork done while the place is quiet,' he said vaguely.

'I'll be out of here in just a minute or two.'

'There's no hurry,' Alexander said, and wandered into the schoolroom. He looked around the place, at the books neatly stacked on the bookshelf, and at a tidy pile of papers on the desk that Marion McNaught used. A book lay on top of them; he picked it up and saw that it was a books on French grammar. When he opened it he was surrounded by the delicate scent of the eau de cologne she wore. It was almost as though she were standing beside him, the top of her head, with the dark brown hair drawn neatly into a small bun at the nape of her neck, reaching halfway between his elbow and shoulder.

'That's the library done now,' Eppie said from the doorway, and Geddes closed the book and put it down hurriedly, strangely guilty at being seen with it in his hands.

'Did your sister say when she and the lassies are expected back?'

'Some time in the afternoon, I think. Will you be wanting something to eat at midday?'

'No – maybe – I'm not sure,' he said, and went to the library.

Eppie looked after him, puzzled. He was missing Duncan, she thought as she started to put the schoolroom to rights. It was understandable, given the long years the lad had been away from home. But this time was different, for Duncan would come back, again and again.

And perhaps Foy would come with him.

28

Eppie, on her way to Barbary's cottage, could sense a hint of autumn in the air already – a slight mellowness, as though Mother Nature were slowly, reluctantly drawing summer to a close. In two weeks' time Charlotte and Lydia would be at school, and Marion back in her usual classroom in Fordyce.

Once autumn had taken hold the local fishing boats would be scrubbed, overhauled, painted and made ready to follow the herring shoals on the long journey down the coast to Scarborough, Yarmouth and Lowestoft. The gutting crews would travel south by train and the few fishermen left in the town would put away their nets and turn to line fishing for haddock and codling.

'Nessie Jamieson came by yesterday tae ask me if I'd go on her crew for the Yarm'th fishin',' Barbary said when Eppie mentioned the coming English season.

'Are ye thinkin' o' it?'

Barbary smiled the slow, placid smile she had recently adopted. It was nothing like her former joyous smiles, but it was an improvement. At last, she was beginning to adapt to life without Tolly. 'Agnes said she'd move in here wi' the bairns while I was gone, but I dinnae think so. I've things tae do here.' Her hand strayed to the pink shell, always close by her.

'Mebbe next year, when wee Jeemsie's older.'

'Aye, mebbe next year. Things'll be more settled next year,' Barbary agreed. She held the shell to her ear, her eyes half-closed as she listened to its voice murmuring to her. The baby was tucked into the crook of her free arm, and after a moment she put the shell to his tiny ear. 'D'ye hear, my bonny wee loon?'

Jeemsie, half-asleep, opened the dark blue eyes that were just like his father's, and gazed into Barbary's face. Then he smiled up at her.

'He can hear it,' she said, satisfied, and put the shell back down on the hearth.

There was something about the shell, and Barbary's fascination with it, that made Eppie uneasy, but it seemed to bring comfort to her friend, and so she said nothing, other than to Marion.

'If it gives her comfort, then I see no harm in it,' her sister said.

'It does, but it's almost as if she can't do without it. It's never far from her hand, and she keeps getting the bairns tae listen tae it.'

'Children like that sort of thing. Stop fussing about the woman, Eppie,' Marion said irritably. 'She's old enough to do as she pleases, surely.'

Marion had more important things on her mind than whether or not Barbary McGeoch was putting her ear to shells too frequently. It was almost time for her to return to Fordyce, and the thought of having to leave Alexander Geddes was almost more than she could bear.

She had tried reasoning with herself and she had tried speaking to herself sharply, but it was no use. Common sense, her greatest ally and comfort since childhood, had deserted her at first sight of the man, and there was little she could do about it other than feel utter misery at the prospect of having to return to the home and the career that, until he came into her life, had been all that she wanted.

Dripping silent tears into her pillow at night, terrified in case she wakened Charlotte, she began to realise why Eppie had turned down the idea of becoming a teacher in order to marry the man she loved.

Over the summer Marion had worked hard to win Helen Geddes's approval, and she had succeeded – but what was the point of that, she asked herself miserably, if she could not find some way of making Helen's son fall in love with her? Eppie was probably right when she said that the man was still enraptured by Lydia's mother, and that for him, there would never be another woman.

Once or twice since their conversation in the Aberdeen hotel, Marion had fancied that he looked at her with a new interest; once or twice she believed that she'd detected a warmth in his voice and in his eyes – but she knew that it was all in her over-active imagination. He saw her as nothing more than his daughter's governess and, from time to time, a useful assistant in his own work. Soon she would leave his house and he would forget all about her.

These thoughts were running through her head while she sat at the desk in the library, writing a report as he dictated it to her. He paused to consult a document and as she waited, Marion found her gaze lifting, as it always did, against her own will, to the portrait above the fireplace. Celia Geddes smiled down on her kindly, graciously, secure in the knowledge that a Plain Jane such as Marion McNaught could never take her place in Alexander's heart.

Working with him in the library had at first been a joy and, she thought, a step forward; but because of that portrait it had turned into a torment. A lump came into Marion's throat and when she swallowed hard to dislodge it, it immediately turned into tears pressing against the backs of her eyes. Before she could blink them away they were trembling on the edge of her lower lids. She was so busy trying to banish them that when Alexander Geddes started dictating again she didn't hear him.

He was pacing the room as he spoke, and it wasn't until he had delivered another two sentences that he reached the window, turned to pace back towards the desk, and noticed that she was not writing.

'Miss McNaught? Miss McNaught,' he said again as she paid no heed. 'Is something wrong? Do you feel unwell?'

She raised her head and the light from the window caught her tears, still poised to fall, and made them sparkle.

'Miss McNaught?' he said again, alarmed. She made no reply, but simply stared at him, her neat little mouth trembling. One tear slowly spilled from each blue eye to course down her pale cheeks, and as he watched, something inside Alexander Geddes seemed to break open, releasing a surge of emotions that he had not known for a long time – not for all the years of his daughter's life.

'Miss McNaught . . .' he said yet again, and then, since it seemed much more natural and right, 'Marion . . .'

How it had happened, Alexander Geddes was uncertain; all he knew was that it had, and he was very happy about it. He had never thought, in the long lonely years after his beloved Celia's death, that he would ever find another woman to take her place, and yet here he was, on his way to his mother's house to announce his forthcoming marriage.

As he walked up the path towards the front door a sudden, familiar sense of panic began to cloud his vision. He swallowed hard – and then a gloved hand brushed against his palm, and as his own fingers automatically curled around it, he knew that he *could* face his mother; could face anyone and anything, with her by his side – Miss McNaught, now Marion, and soon, as soon as possible, the third, and final, Mrs Alexander Geddes.

He smiled down at her as they reached the doorstep, and seized the doorknocker, banging it hard against its polished plate. 'Good morning, Maisie,' he said cheerfully to the maid, 'I trust that my mother is at home?'

'Yes, sir, but she's expectin' some of her friends to call in half an hour's time.'

'Our business won't take as long as that,' Alexander assured her. 'We'll announce ourselves – and don't bother with tea.'

Helen Geddes was at her usual early-morning task of checking every surface in her parlour for dust and shifting ornaments very slightly to prove to herself that the maid had not put them back where they should be.

'Alexander, this is unexpected.' Her eyes went from him to Marion by his side. 'Maisie should have announced you.'

'I'm your son – I . . .' he had been going to say 'I paid for this house,' then amended the sentence to '. . . Surely I don't need to be announced.'

'Perhaps not – but on the other hand, you haven't come alone.' She tipped her head, bird-like, to receive his dutiful kiss. Once it had been delivered she went on, 'I take it that as Miss McNaught is with you, you've called on a matter concerning Lydia.'

'It has nothing to do with Lydia. She's in the best of health and looking forward to starting school next week. Sit down, Mother, I have news for you.'

'I can't think of any news that requires the presence of Lydia's governess,' Helen said, and then, as her son said nothing, but stood smiling at her, she moved to her usual chair and folded her hands in her lap. 'Very well, give me your news. I am expecting friends to call.'

'So Maisie told us.' Alexander ushered Marion to the sofa and seated himself beside her. 'We won't keep you long. I just wanted you to know that I am soon to be married – to Marion.' He took Marion's hand in his.

Helen sat absolutely still, her face suddenly as hard and as cold as marble hewed from the quarry.

'Married?' she said at last, in a harsh croak. 'To Miss McNaught?' And then, beginning to recover her voice, 'Don't be ridiculous, Alexander, you can't possibly marry this woman.'

'I can, Mother, and I will.'

'But you'll be the laughing stock of the village!'

'I doubt it, but if they want to laugh, let them, I say.' Alexander Geddes had not known such a sense of freedom, well-being and sheer joy in years. His entire body tingled with vitality; he felt intoxicated although he had not had a drop to drink.

'Think what the shame will do to your children!'

'Lydia and Duncan both like Marion very much. I believe that they will both be delighted to accept her as their new stepmother.'

Helen stared at her son, at a loss for words. He had changed, and in a way that made her uneasy. He was more confident than ever before, and younger, and – she sought for the word – defiant. It was almost as though he cared nothing for her opinion.

'I forbid it,' she said at last, and even to her own ears, the words sounded feeble. 'Alexander, I will not allow this marriage to go ahead!'

To her horror, he laughed. 'My dear Mother, I'm far too old to be forbidden to do anything I choose to do. Marion's father is a schoolteacher, highly regarded in Fordyce, as is Marion herself. Her brain,' he turned to smile fondly at her, 'is as sharp and as fine as any man's, and I intend to make her my wife as soon as it can be arranged. We wanted to tell you before we tell anyone else, including Lydia, but we are not looking for your blessing.'

'Although,' Marion spoke for the first time, 'we would like to have it. I would like to have it. Mrs Geddes,' she rose from the sofa and moved to a chair close to Helen's, 'I think highly of you, and I have enjoyed our talks together in the past. I would dearly like to know that our decision to marry will have your blessing. It would,' she went on smoothly, her pale blue eyes holding Helen's sapphire glare without flinching, 'be so much easier for all of us if we were to face the world as a united family instead of allowing the people of Portsoy to see us at loggerheads. I know that you dislike malicious gossip as much as I do. We are alike in that – and in caring deeply for Alexander. We both want him to be happy, do we not?'

She had lain awake the night before, rehearsing her speech. While her mouth formed the words, her gaze delivered its own message, from one woman to another.

All at once Helen Geddes realised that she had finally met her match. Alexander's first wife had been her personal choice, and hers to mould in her own image; his second wife, aware that she would not have been Helen's choice of daughter-in-law, had been anxious to placate and please. But this one had somehow, without Helen noticing what was happening, taken over Alexander's heart and she obviously fully intended to keep it. This one would not be denied, and any attempt to fight her would alert the village gossips, many of them Helen's own friends. Alexander and his future wife might not care about being laughing stocks, but Helen did, and Marion McNaught knew it.

'We would indeed like your blessing, Mother, if you could find it in your heart to be pleased for us,' Alexander added, rising to put a hand – a possessive, husbandly hand – on Marion's shoulder. She turned slightly to smile up at him, and then turned back to Helen. Again, their eyes locked, while Alexander, totally unaware of the brief, silent war that had just been waged in front of him, waited without great concern for his mother's answer.

Helen suddenly felt old and feeble. She had finally met her match and the time had come to hand over the reins to a younger and much more able woman. She had no option but to force her lips into a semblance of a smile and give her blessing.

'But you can't marry Mr Geddes!' Eppie said, horrified.

'What's to stop us? I'm a spinster and he's a widower.'

'But he's my employer! And yours!'

'Mine only for another week until the school year starts. As for your position,' Marion said, 'there's no reason why that can't continue, at least for the time being. If you're unhappy about it then I shall find someone else, for I don't know much about running a house. In any case, I'll be assisting Alexander with his business interests. I've discovered that I enjoy that sort of thing.'

'Mrs Geddes won't allow it,' Eppie insisted, and Marion gave her a sweet smile.

'On the contrary, we've just come back from visiting her, and she's given us her blessing. It'll be all over the place in no time, since she was preparing to entertain some of her gossipy old friends. We're about to tell Lydia, and then we're off to Fordyce to tell Mother and Father.'

'You're really going to marry him?'

'I'm really, truly, going to marry Alexander Geddes and oh, Eppie, I'm so happy!' Marion's voice started to shake as tears sprang to her eyes. 'I had never once considered marriage, and yet the moment I set eyes on him I knew that without him my life could not be complete. I can't thank you enough – if it hadn't been for you we might never have met each other.'

She swooped across the kitchen and caught Eppie up in a tight hug. 'I promise you that I intend to live until I reach a hundred, at least, and I mean to make him happy, every single day that we spend together!'

Lydia greeted the news with shrieks of joy and immediately demanded a new dress for the wedding. 'Just think,' she said to Charlotte as the two of them got ready to travel to Fordyce with her father and her future stepmother to break the news, 'this means that we'll be sisters.'

'Sort of sisters, since I'm Aunt Marion's niece. And now,' Charlotte said, awed by the thought, 'your father will become my Uncle Alexander!'

'Sisters,' Lydia insisted firmly. 'We both need a sister. Have we got time to go and tell the bees before the carriage arrives?'

29

Winter was settling in. The sea, cold and grey, raged against the harbour wall, while the chilly, damp air kept most of the townsfolk indoors, only venturing out when they had to.

With most of the boats down in England, the harbour was almost completely empty. The entire town felt lonely, Eppie thought as she hurried to Barbary's house, a filled basket over her arm. It would not waken until the day when the first sighting of a cluster of red sails on the horizon hailed the return of the Portsoy fleet. On that day, and on every day thereafter until all the boats and their crews were home, the town would suddenly come alive, whatever the weather. Doors would be thrown open and men, women and children would flock down to the harbour to welcome the fishermen home. Every seaman's kist – the wooden trunk that held all their possessions – and every fisher lassie's box would be crammed with gifts brought from the south, some to be given out on arrival, some to be kept for the New Year celebrations.

The entire town would be in festive mood; even those, like Eppie, whose men would never return, joined in the pleasure of those fortunate families who were complete again now that their menfolk – and the women who had gone with them to gut and pack the herring – were home again, where they belonged.

But for Barbary, still in the first year of widowhood, it would be a difficult time. Eppie recalled her own secret pain, carefully hidden behind bright smiles, the first time she had watched her neighbours greet their men when the boats came home. But with each year that passed, as Barbary would have to find out for herself, the pain eased, little by little. Nearing the cottage, Eppie resolved to make a point of spending as much time as possible with her friend when the fishing fleet started to return.

She could afford to give Barbary more of her time now that Charlotte and Lydia were both at school. Charlotte, used to being in a classroom, loved her new school and was doing well, but it had been difficult for Lydia at first; moving from a small schoolroom within her own home to a classroom shared with more than twenty other girls.

She had reacted by retreating to her old ways and becoming irritable and arrogant, but forewarned by Marion, Eppie had managed to coax her out of her black moods and there was no doubt at all that having Charlotte in the classroom with her, the only person she knew and trusted, had helped the girl settle in, albeit reluctantly. With time, Marion assured Alexander and Eppie, Lydia would even begin to like school.

Marion herself, busy with her own work and with preparations for her wedding in the spring, visited Portsoy as often as she could – in order to keep an eye on Charlotte, she said, although Eppie was convinced that Alexander Geddes was the real reason. The two of them were like a pair of young lovers, glowing at the very sight of each other.

Once she came to accept the fact that it was impossible to stop the marriage Helen Geddes decided to behave as though she had been the one to choose Marion as her third daughter-in-law. Marion and Alexander, caught up in the wonder of finding each other, were happy to let her have her pretences. A truce of sorts had been established.

On reaching Barbary's cottage Eppie bustled through the door, glad to get out of the cutting wind, and into the warmth. The fire burned brightly in the range, and the place was spotless. George, Martha and Thomas, playing contentedly on the rug before the fire, looked up and beamed at Eppie.

'Where's your mammy?'

'Gone out. I'm lookin' after the bairns,' said George importantly. He already considered himself as the man of his family.

'Gone tae the shops?' It wasn't like Barbary to leave her children on their own, but perhaps she was only going to be away for a few minutes. Martha had recently recovered from a bad chest cold, and Barbary had probably decided against taking the child out on a cold day.

'Not tae the shops,' George said. He beamed at Eppie, a wide, delighted grin. 'She's gone tae fetch my daddy.'

'What?' Eppie wasn't sure that she had heard right.

'Gone tae get my daddy. That's what she said. If we're very good and don't touch anythin' while she's away, daddy'll come home with her.'

'Daddy,' Martha confirmed, her smile as wide and as happy as George's, while Thomas, scrambling to his feet and toddling over to Eppie, his fat little arms held up to her, echoed, 'Dadda!'

She put down her basket and lifted the toddler, using his solid, warm little body as an anchor. A chill began to steal over her. She suddenly noticed that the three children, like the room itself, were spotlessly clean, and that they were all dressed in their best clothes, instead of the smocks they usually wore.

'How did she know that your daddy was coming home?' She tried to speak naturally, though to her own ears her voice sounded far away and as though it belonged to someone else.

'He telt her,' George explained, 'in the shell. He spoke tae her and he telt her he wanted back hame. So she's gone tae fetch him.'

'She's pretty,' Martha added. 'A pretty dress, and a pretty shawl, and red flowers in her hair.'

Eppie's gaze flew to the window where Barbary always kept a bunch of bright-red paper poppies. Barbary loved the big splashy flowers and sometimes, to amuse herself and the children, she would wind them through her thick black hair. Tolly, Eppie recalled with mounting horror, loved to see his wife wearing poppies in her hair. Now, the jug was empty of flowers.

'He told her in the shell,' George had said. The pink shell too, was gone from its usual place on the hearth. Then Eppie realised that the shell and the flowers were not the only things missing. The crib was empty, the blankets pulled back carelessly, the pillow still bearing the imprint of a small round head.

'Jeemsie – where's wee Jeemsie?'

'He was cryin', so Mammy took him with her,' George said placidly, intent on the wooden train he was running over the rug.

The children were confused, Eppie tried to convince herself. They had got mixed up. Barbary had had to go to the shops, and because the baby was crying she had taken him with her. They would be back at any minute.

But she knew that Barbary would not have put on her best clothes and woven red poppies through her hair just to go to the shops. Something terrible had happened, or was going to happen, to her and her baby.

Swallowing back the terror that threatened to engulf her, she put Thomas back down on the rug.

'You two look after Thomas while I go to fetch Mammy and Jeemsie,' she said.

'An' Daddy,' Martha said, smiling her father's sweet smile.

'I'll not be a minute,' Eppie assured them, and almost fled from the house. She didn't know what to do or where to go; she only knew that she needed to fetch help. Remembering that Alexander Geddes had been going to the salmon bothy that afternoon she was on the point of turning towards the harbour when her name was called.

Spinning round, praying that the call had come from Barbary hurrying home with a parcel in one hand and wee Jeemsie snugly wrapped in her shawl, she saw Jeemsie's wet nurse coming along the footpath. To Eppie's relief, Jeemsie himself was in the woman's arms.

'Barbary handed the bairn in tae me a while back,' the woman said, puzzled, when they met. 'He was girnin' and she said he was hungry, but he's scarce taken a suck. He jist wanted a wee bit o' a cuddle – did ye no', my wee loon?' she added to the baby, who was busy chewing at his fingers.

'Did Barbary say where she was going?'

'No' a word, but she was a' dressed up and lookin' excited, as if she was expectin' visitors.'

'D'ye think ye could stay with the bairns for a wee whiley?' Eppie begged. 'I have tae find her.'

'Aye, I can stay for a bit. Ye dinnae think somethin's wrong, dae ye?'

'I dinnae ken, but I don't want the bairns tae worry. I'll try tae find her,' Eppie said, and ran.

The salmon bothy was a three-storey building on the opposite side of the harbour from the marble quarry, in the old part of Portsoy known as Seatown. Portsoy salmon were caught by means of large open-mouthed nets set on poles to catch the fish as the incoming tides brought them to the shore. Once caught, they were washed, then weighed and packed in ice at the bothy before being taken to Aberdeen, and from there to be sold in Edinburgh and London. Salmon fishing was one of the local businesses that Alexander Geddes was involved in.

As Eppie turned into the harbour she caught sight of a splash of colour on the grey, rain-washed stones. She knew what it was before she reached it – a scarlet poppy made from paper.

Alexander Geddes was standing outside the bothy talking to another man when she got there. As soon as they caught sight of her, running, and with her shawl blown half off one shoulder, both men immediately came to meet her. 'What's amiss?'

'It's my friend Barbary, Mr Geddes.' Eppie paused to suck air into her labouring lungs. 'She's left her bairns alone, dressed in their best, and she told them that she's gone to fetch Tolly – her man that went down with the *Grace-Ellen*,' she explained urgently. 'She says he told her that he's coming back home from the sea. She gone to meet him.'

It sounded far-fetched, but both men had lived by the sea all their lives, and they knew all about the terrible things that loss and grief could do to folk.

'Is there somewhere she used to go to watch for his boat coming in?' Geddes asked swiftly.

'Up there . . .' Eppie pointed across the harbour to the

headland opposite. 'At The Breeks – there's a path down tae a ledge where ye can see the boats comin' over the horizon.' She pulled her shawl off and tied it about her head and shoulders, knotting the ends to make sure they could not come loose.

'I'll go there now – you gather some of the men together and send them after us,' Geddes told his companion. 'Send some of them along the shore.' He glanced out to sea. 'The tide's ebbing, so they should be able to get along below the headland. You go back to the children, Eppie.'

'Someone's with them. I'll come wi' you – Barbary knows me.'

He didn't waste time arguing with her, but set off, with Eppie, having had a moment to gain her breath, puffing after him.

As they climbed to the top of the headland they became more exposed to the wind, which seized on its new playthings with delight, buffeting them with increasing violence. Eppie gripped her shawl but the wind made several bids for Geddes's tall hat. He pulled it down over his ears as firmly as he could, but it was lifted up and carriyed away.

He caught her arm and dragged her along with him, his support helping her to stay upright when her feet stumbled over loose stones or clumps of grass. At last they were above The Breeks, a double-pinnacled rock formation that looked like a pair of trousers, upside down and sticking out of the water.

'There's the path,' Eppie gasped, 'the one that leads down to the ledge. And look . . .' she pulled away from him and went towards the edge of the headland.

'Eppie!' he thundered at her as she stooped and turned to him, holding out a limp, sodden paper poppy. He caught hold her wrist again, pulling her back towards safety.

'I thought you were going over there!'

'It's one of the poppies the bairns said she put in her hair before she went out. She's down there, watchin' for Tolly, or mebbe she's hurt an' needin' help!'

'If she's there at all the men going along the shore will see her. If we try to go down in this wind we'll be plucked off and sent down on to the rocks. We'd be no help to her if that happened.'

The wind whipped his dark hair around his face as he turned and looked down the way they had come; following his gaze, Eppie saw two men below, on their way up.

'Wait here and don't move.' Cautiously, Geddes moved towards the edge. As he neared it, he knelt down and then lay almost flat on the wet grass before starting to worm his way towards the edge. She watched, her heart in her mouth, as he looked down, then he began to wriggle backwards to safety.

The men who had been on their way up arrived in time to help him to his feet. 'I can see the men coming along the shore, they're almost below us now,' he said, the wind snatching the words from his mouth and hurling them out to sea. 'There's nobody on the ledge, but I think I saw something – a wee splash of scarlet. A neckerchief, mebbe.'

'A poppy,' Eppie said dully. 'A paper poppy.'

And as she said the last word they heard a hoarse cry from the men down below . . .

It was said, among the fishermen, that what the sea wanted, it took, and what it took should not be claimed back. Many of them, should they happen to find a body among the thrashing, glittering herring their nets brought up, returned it to the deep with a swift prayer rather than anger the sea by taking it ashore.

The sea had not wanted Barbary McGeoch, and so as the tide went out it abandoned her after first tucking her body behind a small rocky outcrop where a dip in the shingle formed a natural open-ended pool. When the men on the shore found her she was floating placidly and easily just below the surface of the salt water. It was the bright glow of the few poppies still entangled in her long black hair that led them to her.

Alexander Geddes paid for the funeral, and when Barbary had been laid to rest, old Agnes McBrayne and her daughter, with help from Eppie and wee Jeemsie's wet nurse, took it in turns to look after the bewildered children.

Although most folk in the community had large families, Barbary had been the only child of parents in their early forties when she was born, while none of Tolly's four siblings had survived beyond their first few years. Both sets of parents were dead, and the only living relative who could be found was an elderly aunt of Tolly's who lived on her own in Buckhaven, further along the firth.

Alexander wrote to her, and received a scrawled reply informing him that Mrs Macready would visit Portsoy on the following Wednesday afternoon to see the children.

Eppie and Agnes were both there when the woman arrived. She was grey-haired, grey-faced and angular, and she inspected the children, all dressed in their best, closely, as she sipped at her cup of tea.

'I'm a widow woman,' she said in a voice that sounded rusty and in need of oiling, 'and I didnae even ken Bartholomew, for his faither an' me never got on, even as bairns. I havenae set eyes on the loon since he was a bairn,' she continued as Eppie and Agnes, after a puzzled glance at each other, came to realise at the same time that by 'Bartholomew' she meant Tolly. 'I live in two rooms and I'm no' wealthy.'

'There's the compensation money in the bank,' Eppie offered. 'Mr Geddes saw to it that the families of all the crew members on Tolly's – Bartholomew's – boat got compensation after the accident.'

'That wid help,' the woman conceded and then, when she had finished her tea and taken a second cup, she said, 'I'll take the two eldest, for they're of an age tae be useful about the house. But I cannae be doin' wi' the wee ones. I dinnae like children and I thank the good Lord that me an' my man were never burdened wi' any.'

Eppie looked at the children. Jeemsie, rosy from sleep, was propped on cushions in his cot, chewing at a mutton bone to ease the teething pains in his gums, while the other three, unusually subdued, were watching the adults' faces closely. Young though they were, they seemed to sense that their futures were under discussion, and they were trying hard to follow the conversation passing to and fro above their innocent little heads. She glanced across the room at Agnes and saw her own horror mirrored in the older woman's face.

'They're a family,' she said. 'They've lost their father, and now their mother, and they've only got each other. They have tae stay together.'

'The only thing they need,' said the woman, 'is tae be fed an' housed an' clothed, an' I can dae that for the two eldest. I'll dae my Christian duty by them, ye need have no worries aboot that. The other two are comely enough – mebbe local folk'll be willin' tae take them in. Or there's an orphanage in Aberdeen. Now . . .' she dusted down her skirt and rose to her feet '. . . I have tae be on my way. If ye'll gather up the older ones' clothes I'll take them wi' me. As for the money set aside for them, mebbe Mr Geddes that wrote tae me about Bartholomew and his wife'll send it on tae me.'

George took one step back, and then another, bringing him up against Eppie's thigh. He grabbed a handful of her skirt and twisted it tightly in his fist, looking up at her with his brow wrinkled and his dark eyes apprehensive. She smiled down at him and he immediately beamed back at her, the wonder and unease replaced by utter trust.

'No,' she said. 'No. The children are going to stay together. Mr Geddes owns this cottage and he has already said that it can continue to be their home. We thought that you might like to come and live here, with them.'

'Me? Live in Portsoy?' The woman looked almost affronted. 'I'm Buckhaven born and bred. I'd no' be content anywhere else.'

'The bairns are Portsoy born and bred,' Agnes pointed out in her gentle voice. 'They've got friends here and Geordie's doin' well at the school. They dinnae ken anywhere else.'

'Bairns can get used tae anywhere,' Mrs Macready said scathingly. 'Their brains arenae right grown yet – they havenae got the sense tae ken where they are and they're too young as yet tae get attached tae any place.'

'They're staying here,' Eppie said firmly.

'An' who's tae look after them? I'm the only blood kin they've got an' I'm no' goin' tae bide here, money or no money.'

'They don't need blood kin, just folk that care for them,' Agnes told her, and Eppie added, 'We'll manage. We'll think of something.'

'And now,' Agnes said when the woman had gone and the children, aware that they were freed from some threat but not knowing just what it had been, were playing happily, 'we'll have tae think o' somethin'. They're grand wee bairns, Eppie, but my rheumatism's no' gettin' any better and wi' the winter comin' on it'll be all I can manage tae help my own daughter wi' her wee ones.'

'I know that. Don't fret yourself, Agnes,' Eppie said, her mind already made up. 'I'm going tae move in here as soon as Mr Geddes finds another housekeeper. I'm goin' tae take Barbary's place.'

30

'Are you sure about this?' Alexander Geddes asked.

'I'm certain. It'll be a lot easier to find a new housekeeper for you than someone to look after those bairns. And after missing out on years of my own daughter's growing, I'll enjoy being with Barbary's bairns.'

'I'll find another housekeeper, Alexander, since it's my responsibility now,' Marion said. It was the day after George and Martha had been saved from an unhappy life in Buckhaven with Mrs Macready. 'You'll want to move into the cottage as soon as you can, Eppie?'

Eppie smiled gratefully at her sister. 'I do.'

'Then I'll start looking for a suitable woman at once. Since Eppie wants to move as soon as she can, Alexander, and I must be here to settle the new housekeeper in, would it not be advantageous for us to marry sooner than we had planned? Next month, say, instead of in the spring?'

His face lit up. 'An excellent idea – if you think that you can make arrangements in such a short time.'

'I shall speak to the school tomorrow; I'm sure that they will agree to let me leave earlier, given the circumstances. And as we're both agreed on a quiet wedding there's little to arrange. You'll help me, won't you, Eppie? And,' she added sweetly to her intended, 'I shall visit your mother later today to explain our new plans, and ask for her help as well. I'm sure that she will be happy to do all she can for us.'

It was strange, but delightful, Marion thought, how fate worked out at times. Now that she had finally won Alexander she could not wait to become his wife, and spring had seemed so far away.

Although it was only mid-March there were already days, scattered in among the winter's final blustering attempts at intimidation, when spring seemed to be just around the corner, and this was one of them.

Eppie had spent the morning washing the curtains and beating months of dust from the rugs, with some hindering help from the children. She had been in the cottage for almost three months, following Marion and Alexander Geddes's wedding on Hogmanay, the last day of 1870. By then, the new housekeeper, a cheerful, capable woman, had been installed in what used to be Eppie's kitchen.

It wasn't until she moved into the cottage, with its small cosy rooms and the knowledge that neighbours were just through the wall on either side, that she realised how much she had missed it. Marion was in her element as mistress of the Geddes house with its large, lofty rooms, but places like that were not for Eppie.

At first, she had thought to augment the money that had been banked for the children by returning to her former work at the farlins, but Alexander Geddes had taken it upon himself to act as unofficial guardian to the orphaned family and insisted on paying a regular amount of money into the bank account that had been set up for Tolly's compensation money, enough to support Eppie and the children without the need for her to work.

As the cottage was small and also noisy because of the four children, it had been agreed that Charlotte could best continue her studying if she remained at Shorehead. As she and Eppie could still see each other every day the arrangement suited them both well enough.

Eppie's new little family was thriving, and she was even beginning to think of returning to the farlins, if not that year then the next, if she could find someone to keep an eye on the children while she was at work. She appreciated her new brother-in-law's determination to make life as easy for her as possible, but she was independent, and liked to feel that she was earning her own keep.

There was just one thing missing in her life now, and at the moment she could not quite put a finger on the cause of the restlessness she felt when the children were in bed and she sat alone by the fire at nights.

The feeling was strong that day, and after putting the beaten rugs back on the floor and making sure that the curtains were pegged securely on the line and unlikely to be pulled down by the wind, she gave the children their midday meal and then started putting them into their outdoor clothes.

'We'll go for a walk along the shore,' she announced. A long walk and a good blow would tire them out, and perhaps settle her.

The children jiggled around excitedly, and it took some time to push arms into sleeves and feet into boots. But at last they were ready, and she picked Jeemise up and ordered the other three to stay close to her until they were past the harbour.

Then she opened the door, just in time to see a familiar figure come striding along the footpath. He turned in at the gate and then halted at sight of Eppie in the open doorway, the baby in her arms and the other three children clustered about her skirts.

They looked at each other, and as Eppie's stomach tangled itself into a knot she knew what had caused the restlessness, and what was missing from her life. At the same time she felt a slight sinking of her spirits. Did she really want another bout of sparring and arguing, to be followed by another parting?

Foy had swung his canvas bag from his shoulder, and as she looked at him, pleasure and dread chasing each other around in her head, he let the bag fall to the ground and then raised both arms in the air before dropping them to his sides in a submissive gesture.

'My name,' he said, 'is Ludovic.'

Bibliography

Old Cullen and Portsoy by Alan Cooper. Published 2001 by Stenlake Publishing, 54–58 Mill Square, Catrine, Ayrshire.

Mither o' the Meal Kist, a Pictorial History of Fordyce by Christine Urquhart. Printed by W Peters & Son, Ltd., 16 High Street, Turiff.

Portsoy, Onwards From My Youth by Mrs M. A. (Bunty) Williams. Produced 2001 with assistance from the Banff Partnership Ltd.

Portsoy Manuscript of 1843. Produced 1993 by Portsoy Old Harbour Tertencentenary Committee (with thanks to Texaco Oil Company for their assistance)

Staying On

To my husband Jim

who never knows where he will have to go next,
or what he will be expected to research next,
but copes so well with the constant uncertainty.

Acknowledgements

I am indebted to the following people, who assisted with background information for this book:

Robbie Sloss, James and Anne McAlister, Marion Ritchie and Elizabeth Currie for their time and patience in teaching me about farming on the beautiful Island of Bute. Any technical errors in this book are mine, not theirs.

Former Women's Land Army member Sheila Inglis, for her invaluable assistance.

Robin Taylor, who answered all my questions about the boat-hiring business.

Margaret Currie, who was evacuated to Bute during the Second World War and still lives there. As well as describing her war experiences in detail, Margaret kindly allowed me to use some of them.

Betty Greig and Ian 'Scotia' Scott, for their general assistance in connection with background information.

How could any writer possibly survive without libraries and the people who run them? My everlasting gratitude goes to the staff at Rothesay

Library; to librarian Eddie Monaghan and library assistants Patricia Pollock and Patricia McArthur; and to the librarians and staff of Ardrossan, Paisley and Johnstone Libraries for their assistance with research on Bute, farming, the Second World War and the Land Army. You are all wonderful – and rest assured that I will return to pester you again.

1

Albert McCabe leaned on the rail as the paddle steamer *Duchess of Fife* sailed across Rothesay Bay and began to pass a stretch of graceful waterside houses built in the nineteenth century by wealthy industrialists. He glowered down at the water, seeing no beauty in the way the bow-wave foamed creamy lace along the steamer's flanks, or in the approaching town, neat and clean beneath the June sun.

As far as the Glasgow docker was concerned, water was meant for cargo ships to sail on and towns were places for folk to live, and there was no beauty in either. His idea of a grand sight was a foaming beer mug at the end of a hard day.

He stood immobile at the rails, a great solid slab of a man, and his fellow-passengers, crowding excitedly to look at the splendid houses and their colourful gardens, the ruins of Rothesay Castle rising from a whirlpool of neat tenements, the long curving shoreline and the cool green slopes of the hills beyond the town took care not to jostle him. There was something about Albert McCabe that sent out a warning to anyone in his vicinity.

In any case, none of them wanted trouble, for they were all on board the steamer with a single shared intention: to enjoy a day, a week, even mebbe, for the fortunate, an entire fortnight on this beautiful island in the Firth of Clyde. They had struggled through to the end of the second worldwide war suffered by the century and they had survived.

War had touched the Island of Bute too. Its mark could be seen in Rothesay Bay itself, where sleek submarines nestled against a depot ship and another vast salvage ship lay at anchor. It could be seen in the Army vehicles parked along the embankment opposite the shops, and in the rolls of barbed wire that had only recently been drawn back from the beach. Even so there was something about the town and the island that held out the promise to war-weary travellers of peace and a welcome, and the chance to move on from the hardships and sufferings of the past six years.

Now it was time to celebrate before returning to their normal lives. They were all in the mood for celebration and the small accordion band on board – now playing, inevitably, 'Sweet Rothesay Bay' – had done well when the collection box went round. Even those who looked as though they scarcely had two pennies to rub together had contributed.

Fools, Albert had thought, waving the box away with a scowl. Why celebrate the ending of a war when peace made little difference to working folk like them? Ahead of them lay the same hard graft as before, day in and day out, and probably the same old worry about whether they'd be working come next week.

For him the war's end had only one benefit – getting his wife and weans back home in Glasgow where they belonged. He should never have allowed Nesta to go with the weans when they were bombed out of their own home, but she had begged to be allowed to stay with Sam, the youngest, who suffered badly from asthma. And once she got to Bute she had turned a deaf ear to his demands that she leave the children there and return to take up her duties as his wife.

She'd had a grand war, Albert thought viciously, enjoying herself on a Clyde island while he managed as best he could in Glasgow, working in the docks and sleeping on a rickety sofa bed in his parents' tiny flat. Well, she was about to get her comeuppance, that was for sure.

A city man to his fingertips, he hated being out of the city. He had hated every minute of his journey, first by train and then by steamer. The minute he got his hands on Nesta and the weans, he'd have the lot of them off this lump of earth and back home.

As the steamer slid gracefully alongside Rothesay Pier, where men waited onshore to catch the mooring ropes, McCabe strode to where the queue was forming; parents and children and elderly relatives all coping as best they could with bags, cases and boxes carrying all they might need for their stay away from home. Impatient to find his family and get off the island as soon as possible, he jostled his way to the head of the queue, ignoring those who protested at being pushed aside or, if they were particularly vocal, turned to stare coldly until their eyes slid away from his. He was in no mood for niceties.

As soon as the gangplank was in place he was down it, striding along the length of the pier until he reached the road.

'Westervoe Farm,' he barked at a lad idling on the pier. 'Name of Scott. Where is it?'

'Westervoe? It's round near Stravanan Bay. You'll want that bus over there.'

'I'll walk.'

'Suit yourself,' the boy shrugged. 'It's miles.'

Albert hesitated and then stamped over to the bus stop. More money wasted . . . Nesta was going to regret giving him all this bother once he got her back home, he promised himself.

The bus, like the streets, was busy. After ordering the driver to let him know when he had reached his destination, Albert squeezed his bulk into a back seat and scowled at the floor as the vehicle jolted its way out of the main island town and into the countryside.

When he finally reached his destination he alighted, staring distrustfully about as the bus rattled on its way. Then, following the direction indicated by the bus driver with a jerk of the thumb, McCabe started down a rutted lane leading to a huddle of buildings, walking with long strides, impatient to collect his wife and children and be on his way home.

The lane opened into a central courtyard with buildings on all four sides. The place was shabby and run-down; even city-bred Albert could see that; some of the outhouses had an empty, neglected look and weeds grew in their guttering. At the far end of the yard two long trestle tables had been set out near an open door, with wooden seats and benches beside them. A plume of smoke rose into the blue sky from the chimney, indicating that that was the farmhouse. Hens clucking and scratching about the uneven paving stones scattered away from McCabe's large hobnailed boots. It looked, he thought as he bore down on the place, as though the folk who lived there were preparing for a party. Well, he'd party them, he promised himself, pleasure stirring in the depths of his mind at the prospect of meting out some hefty, well-deserved punishment. They'd learn, Nesta and the youngsters, what he thought of being made to come all this way! And it would be their own fault; if they had only heeded the letter he'd sent, ordering them back home, there would not have been any need for unpleasantness.

His huge calloused hands began to curl into fists in pleasant anticipation and then he halted as a familiar figure appeared in the doorway, bearing a tray so large that she had to turn slightly sideways to get through the door. The woman saw him, and was just narrowing her eyes against the sun to look more closely when McCabe roared, 'Nesta! Come here!'

She gave a high-pitched squeal, like a rabbit being nipped by a ferret, and dropped the tray with a crash. Then, instead of doing as she was told, she disappeared into the house, leaving broken plates and cups rolling about on the ground.

Almost at once a girl popped out of the door, shading her eyes with both hands as she stared over at him. 'Dad? Daddy!' She came rushing towards him, her face split by a huge grin. 'Dad, it's me, Senga. Have ye come tae take us home?'

'Where's your mother?'

'In the kitchen.' His daughter nodded with her chin towards the open door. 'That's the farmhouse. We bide over there, see, in that wee cottage.'

'Get yer things,' Albert grunted, shouldering her out of the way and making for the door.

It led straight into a low-beamed kitchen where most of the space was taken up by a huge table covered with dishes bearing bread and butter, scones, pancakes and oatcakes. A party right enough, he thought, and it was well seen that the folk who lived here knew nothing about the miseries of food rationing. A big man who worked hard and enjoyed his food as well as his drink, Albert McCabe had had a hungry war, even though his parents had gone without in a vain attempt to satisfy his appetite.

He snatched up a scone and crammed it into his mouth, blinking to adjust his eyes to the darkness of the kitchen after being out in the June sun. It took a moment for him to discover his wife, backed against a big range by the far wall.

'There ye are, Nesta!'

'Albert?' she quavered in reply.

'Oh, so ye know me now, do ye? And don't pretend ye didnae see me out there. What the hell d'ye mean by runnin' away when I called ye?' He grabbed the lapels of his jacket and jerked on them, a favourite gesture when he was working himself into a rage. 'I've come tae take the lot of yez back where yez belong. Why did ye no' come when I wrote for ye?'

Nesta McCabe's locked hands writhed nervously against each other. 'Did you not get my letter, Albert? I wrote back to say that our Sam was doin' awful well in the school and I didnae want to take him out till he was finished, with this bein' his last year. His chest's much better since he came here, Alb . . .'

'Oh aye, I got your letter.' He dragged it from his pocket and started tearing it into small pieces. 'Here's yer bloody letter,' he said through his teeth as he ripped at the paper. 'And here's what I think of yer damned cheek!'

The letter was nothing but confetti now; he threw the pieces across the table at her and she flinched as they fluttered down onto the food. 'Never mind our Sam's schoolin', he's near old enough to go out and work anyway. I'll not be defied, Nesta; I'm yer husband and ye have got no right tae go against my wishes. Have ye learned nothin' in all the years we've been married, woman?' His voice began to rise. 'Workin' all those years in the docks,' he raved at her, 'and havin' tae bide alone because my wife was away enjoyin' hersel' . . .'

'Your m-mother was there to look after you . . .'

'A mother's no' the same as a wife, ye daft bitch! I got married tae get away from my mother, and if I'd wanted tae go back tae her I'd have done it long since. Now fetch the weans, for I've found us somewhere else tae live. You're all going back where you belong, and the sooner the . . .'

He broke off as a child wailed. Peering across the room, McCabe suddenly saw that there was a little boy clinging to Nesta's skirt.

'What's this?' he asked. Then, his voice suddenly heavy with suspicion, 'Have you been . . . ?'

'Of course not! How could you think such a thing!' Shock gave strength to Nesta's voice as she bent and picked the little boy up. 'He's Jennet's wee lad . . . Jennet that lives here on the farm. Hush now, Jamie, it's all right. And I cannae just come back with you like that, Albert,' she added, facing up to him, 'for there's folk comin' in hungry from the potato howkin' at any minute, wantin' their dinners.'

'Well, they can just see tae their own bloody dinners. Get your things together . . . now!'

Nesta's mouth and chin quivered in the way that had irritated him right from the first days of their marriage. It always made the palms of his big hands itch and the only way to soothe them was to give her a good hard slap. 'Wh-why don't you sit down and have your dinner with us, Albert?' she suggested. 'I'm sure Mrs Scott wouldnae mind. Then you can meet her, and Jennet and her brother Angus. And afterwards we can talk about going home.'

'There's nothin' tae talk about, ye stupid bitch!' McCabe's temper suddenly snapped. 'You're comin' with me now, and the weans an' all! An' if you don't shut that brat up, I'll do it for ye!' he added as the little boy began to scream with fear, clutching Nesta's neck and burying his face in her hair.

'Albert . . . !'

'Right, that's it. You're needin' tae learn yer manners!' He began to make his way round the table towards his disobedient wife and then stopped as a man's voice asked from the yard door, 'What's going on here?'

Not so much a man, McCabe saw, as he swung round. More of a lad, and a cripple at that, with a crutch jammed beneath one armpit. He looped his thumbs into his belt and gave the newcomer a cold smile.

'What's goin' on is that I'm here tae take my wife and my family back tae Glasgow with me, and the sooner we can get out of this place, the better pleased I'll be. So ye can just step aside and let me tend tae my own business.'

'Is that right, Nesta? Is this your husband?'

'Of course I'm her man. D'ye think I'd want a poor-lookin' creature like that if I had my choice?'

'Nesta?'

Her head, already shaking with fear, managed a deeper bob. 'It's my Albert, come from Glasgow,' she said, her voice a mere thread floating through the room.

'D'you want to go with him?'

The effrontery of the question stunned Albert. 'It's got nothin' tae do with want! She belongs back in her own house with her own man, and that's all there is tae it!'

The younger man limped further into the room. 'Your wife's not a parcel, Mr McCabe, she's a person with a mind of her own. D'you want to go, Nesta?' he asked again.

By now she was too frightened to give a coherent answer. 'I . . . Albert . . .' she stuttered, and McCabe gave a jeering laugh.

'Are ye quite sure that she's no' a parcel? She's always seemed like one tae me,' he sneered. Then, his voice hardening, 'Of course she wants tae go home, it's where she belongs!'

'It's where we all belong!' Senga said from the door. She burst into the kitchen, lugging a cheap little card-board suitcase. 'C'mon, Daddy, we'll get the next boat and the rest of them can come when . . .'

'Shut up, you,' her father said without taking his eyes from his wife. 'Nesta, get yer things together or leave them behind – it's your choice. Either way, ye're comin' home . . . today!'

'You don't need to bully her.' The younger man had

managed to ease himself round the table to take up his position in front of Nesta, without Albert realising what he was about.

'Bully her?' McCabe stared. 'How can a man bully his own wife! It's her duty tae do as she's told. Now get out of my way.'

'Angus, best do as he says,' Nesta said anxiously, but the newcomer dug the end of his crutch into the floor and stayed where he was.

'Not until I know what Nesta wants.'

Albert's docker's fists curled into two tight knots. 'Tae hell with what she wants, it's what I want that matters. Now . . .' He took a step forward, his head thrust forward, 'get out of my way, sonny boy, afore I make ye sorry ye were ever born!'

2

'Would you look at this place? They've not even set the tables yet.' Celia Scott's voice was sharp with irritation as the three women plodded into the yard.

'They'll be doing their best. Mollie and me can help get things right before the rest of them come in for their dinner,' Jennet said swiftly. After a morning spent lifting potatoes by hand beneath the sun's heat she was stiff and sore and certainly did not need one of her grandmother's outbursts.

'Of course we can, it'll not take a minute,' Mollie McCabe chimed in, massaging her back.

Celia strode forward, as erect as ever although she was in her seventies and she, too, had been working in the potato field all morning. 'Where's Nesta, and that lassie Senga? The folk'll be right behind us looking for their dinner and not a thing ready,' she raged. Then, as she rounded the nearest table and saw hens and cats busily scavenging the contents of a fallen tray outside the open farm door, her voice rose. 'Would you look at that mess? All that waste!'

'Out of my way,' a man's deep voice shouted from inside the house just then, 'afore I make ye sorry ye were ever born!'

Mollie's freckled face turned ashen beneath its grime as Gumrie, the farm dog, shot past Celia and made for the door, barking. 'That's my dad's voice. Oh, Mrs Scott, my dad's here! Where's Mam? Mam . . . !' She broke into a run, almost falling over Gumrie, and disappeared into the house.

'Quiet!' Celia ordered the dog. 'For pity's sake, Jennet, shut him into the byre while I go and see what's going on.' And she plunged after Mollie, the long mackintosh coat that she always wore for farm work billowing out behind her scrawny figure.

Jennet grabbed Gumrie, named by her brother Angus after Field Marshal Montgomery, and almost threw him into the empty byre in her haste to reach the kitchen. There she found her grandmother confronting a large and burly man who looked, with his head lowered and thrust forward belligerently between broad shoulders, and his small eyes gleaming with malice, for all the world like one of the island's bulls.

Nesta McCabe was backed as far as she could get into a corner by the range, Jamie in her arms, while Angus, supported by his single crutch, stood between her and the newcomer. Mollie's younger sister Senga watched from another corner, her eyes flickering between the adults while one hand, as usual, twisted at a lock of the auburn hair she had carefully been cultivating into a Veronica Lake dip over one eye. Steam curled from the big pots on the range and the room was fragrant with the smell of the stew Nesta had prepared for the folk coming in from the fields.

'I asked, what's going on here?' Celia was saying as Jennet arrived.

'And who are you when ye're at home?'

'I,' Celia said frostily, 'am Mrs Scott, and I *am* at home. Who are you?'

'I'm her man, that's who I am.' McCabe flung an arm out to indicate the cowering Nesta.

'Are you indeed? You'll forgive me for not recognising you,' Celia reverted to the ladylike voice she normally reserved for the Women's Rural Institute meetings, 'since in all the years your family have been billeted on this farm, you've not once visited them.'

'I've been too busy workin' tae come pussy-footin' down here! There's been a war on, missus.'

'There has indeed, and it is still going on in the Far East. And we have all been playing our part in the war effort, Mr McCabe, but even so most of us were able to find the time to do the right thing by our blood kin.' The words fell from Celia Scott's thin lips like icicles from the eaves of a house.

'Are you sayin' that I should have spent my hard-earned money comin' all the way tae this godforsaken place just tae see them enjoyin' themselves?' McCabe indicated the laden table with a sweep of one massive paw. 'I'd enough tae do, but now I've got us a new place tae bide and I've come tae take my family back where they belong!'

'Not at this moment, for we're picking the early potatoes and I need all the workers I can get,' Celia told him, her voice brisk and matter-of-fact. 'You are very welcome to come and collect your family in a week's time, provided you do so in a more civilised manner. Until then they're busy helping to feed the country.'

The man's eyes bulged in a face scarlet with temper. 'A week, is it? A week? Listen you to me, missus, they're comin' with me right now, whether you like it or not. Oh, I know about your kind usin' evacuees like my wife and bairns for cheap labour. My lassie here wrote tae me about the way ye've forced them tae work tae suit yer own ends.' He jerked his chin towards Senga, who thrust her artificially reddened lower lip out and stared at a point just behind Celia Scott's right shoulder.

'Albert, Mrs Scott never . . .' Nesta began timidly.

'Shut yer mouth, you!' her husband ordered without bothering to turn in her direction. She did as she was told, trying at the same time to cringe her way through the wall at her back.

'Cheap labour?' Celia's voice shot up half an octave. 'I've been housing and feeding your wife and your children for years, man. Of course they've worked to earn their keep – everyone works on a farm. Where d'you think I was when you arrived? Out in the fields, that's where, and me an old woman too! As for that precious daughter of yours . . .' she delivered a withering scowl at Senga, 'I'm surprised to hear that she could find enough words for a whole letter, let alone spell them. Her teachers at the school were always complaining about her lack of attention, and now that she's working in one of the Rothesay shops I've had nothing but complaints from them too, about her laziness and her time-keeping.'

'Daddy, are you going to let her talk about me like that?' Senga bleated, taking a step forward and then retreating when her father snapped, 'Hold yer tongue, you. Ye'll work all right when I get ye back tae Glasgow, for there's plenty needin' done there. The new house is like a midden. Ye're all goin' tae work hard when I get yez back home.' He rounded on the woman cowering behind Angus, pointing a huge forefinger at her. 'For the last time of tellin', get yer things together!'

'Albert . . .' Nesta was white to the lips and shaking like a leaf. 'Did ye not see in my last letter that our Bert's got a good job with Mr Blaikie on the next farm? He likes it here, Albert, and he wants to stay . . .'

'Well, he can't. I've got him a place on the docks alongside me.'

'Just a wee while longer, just till Sam finishes the school? Please, Albert?'

'He doesnae need schoolin', he needs tae get work. That'll knock this asthma nonsense out of him once and for all. Now keep yer tongue still and get yer things. That's the last time of tellin', Nesta,' he added threateningly.

Nesta flinched again – like an ill-treated dog, Jennet thought, appalled by the sight. Mollie's mother was a good, kind, hard-working woman and it was terrible to see her so cowed and terrified.

'Just a minute,' Celia squawked, but the big man hunched his shoulders against her voice.

'Where's our Bert? And Sam?'

'They're both out working.' Mollie spoke up for the first time, edging carefully round her father in an attempt to reach Nesta. Her face gleamed white in the dim room and Jennet realised that her bullying father cowed even Mollie, who was never afraid of anything. For the first time she glimpsed something of the life Mollie and the rest of her family had known before coming to the farm as evacuees.

'I thought you said the lad was still at the school?' McCabe snarled at his wife. 'And now I'm told he's out workin'? What are ye tellin' lies for, eh?' He took a slight step forward and Mollie moved swiftly into his line of vision, using the chance to step between her parents.

'They've closed the schools, Dad, because the farmers need all the help they can get with liftin' the potatoes. They do the same at harvest time.'

'Oh, they do, do they? So much for all this precious schoolin', then. And would ye just look at yersel'?' her father said contemptuously. 'Ye're as filthy as a tink. Away and wash yer face and get some decent clothes on. I'd be ashamed tae be seen with ye in that state.'

'It's good clean earth,' Celia informed him. 'The lassie's been lifting potatoes along with the rest of us.'

'Well, she's goin' back tae a proper decent place where potatoes are bought in the shops, no' howked out o' the dirt. Senga, away and fetch yer brothers. Tell them we're all on the next steamer out of this place.'

'But Sam's out in the far field and I don't know where Bert is,' Senga whined.

'Then they'll just have tae follow along on the next boat. And if they don't,' McCabe added menacingly, 'they'll be in trouble. Now then, sonny.' He doubled his fists again and eyed Angus up and down. 'I'm takin' my wife and my lassies back where they belong, so ye can just get out my way afore ye get hurt.'

'You've heard Nesta . . . She wants to stay here on Bute for another week.'

'An' you've heard me, unless ye're deaf as well as lame.' McCabe leaned forward, bawling the next words into Angus's set face. 'My fam'ly belongs in Glasgow, no' on a wee scrap of an island in the Clyde. And they're comin' back home tae Glasgow, with me, right now!' A blunt, thick finger prodding at the air between them punctuated the final six words.

'Come on, Mam, Glasgow's a lot better than this dump,' Senga said eagerly, emboldened by her father's presence.

'I want to stay here an' all, Daddy.' Mollie reached

behind her for her mother's free hand, and clutched it tightly. 'You can't make us go back.'

'Oh, I can't, can I no'? I'm the head of this family,' he roared at her, setting Jamie off on another bout of tears. 'I'm Albert McCabe and I can make all of yez do anythin' I want yez tae do, as you well know, my lassie. And I'll no' stand for my own flesh and blood defyin' me! Now . . .' Again, the big finger swung towards Nesta, 'get movin', ye daft bitch!'

'Here, here . . .' Celia, outraged, poked the man's back with her own forefinger, shorter and thinner than his, but hard and sharp, as Jennet knew to her cost. 'I'll not tolerate such language in my house!'

'Will ye no', missus? In that case the sooner me and mine get out of yer house, the better pleased we'll both be. Come on!' McCabe swung back to his wife, 'Move!'

'Albert . . . !'

'Right, that's it!' He took a step forward, seizing Mollie by the shoulder and spinning her out of his way. With the other hand he reached for Nesta.

'That's enough!' Angus clamped his free hand on the man's arm and, to Jennet's horror, McCabe swung round on her brother, pushing him back so that he lost his fragile balance and reeled against the table.

'Don't you dare touch my grandson,' Celia screamed at the man. 'Can you not see that he's a cripple?'

'I'm no' goin' tae hurt him, ye daft old woman. I just . . .' McCabe began, turning his head to look at her and then he yelped as Angus, steadying himself against the table, lashed out with his crutch. The sturdy wooden support cracked down on McCabe's wrist and, instinctively, he drew back his other fist as he spun round on the younger man. With a screech that would have done credit to a witch, Celia snatched up the long-handled floor brush from where it stood against the wall by the door and swung it back over her shoulder. Jennet saw it coming just in time and ducked as it cut through the air above her head, then whistled round in a wide swing that ended with the bristles scraping across Albert McCabe's ear. He yelped and clapped a hand to his head.

'Old, am I?' This time Celia drew her elbow back and lunged forward with the brush instead of swinging it in the kitchen's confined space. It landed on the back of the man's neck. 'Daft, am I?'

As McCabe turned to face her, bellowing and more bull-like than ever, the wooden part of the brush head landed with a crack on the bridge of his nose.

'Don't you dare speak to me like that in my own house!' Celia shouted, dancing round the man until she was behind him and driving him out through the open door with more swift blows on his ears, his shoulders, the back of his head, his thighs. A lifetime of doing a man's work on the farm had given Celia Scott brawn, as well as the brains she had been born with. 'Get out of here . . . out, I'm telling you! Get back to Glasgow and don't ever set foot on my property again!'

'You'll be sorry!' McCabe yelped, his arms thrown

up to protect his head and the studs in his boots sparking off the flags.

'Not as sorry as you'll be, if you don't get off my land. The men'll be coming in from the fields any minute now for their dinner. If they find you still here they'll teach you to bully women and cripples. I'll set the dogs on you!' Celia threatened while Gumrie, the sole representative of his kind on the Scott farm, yapped frantically from behind the byre door.

'I'm comin' with you, Daddy.' Senga pushed past Celia and ran into the yard, clutching her case in her arms. 'Wait for me!'

'Senga, no! Stay here with the rest of us!'

The girl scowled at her mother from the safety of McCabe's side. 'Stay in this dump? Youse lot can do what you want, but I'm for home with my daddy!'

'And ye'd better not stop her, or I'll have the polis on ye for keepin' her against her will,' her father added threateningly to Celia, who lowered the brush and gave a contemptuous laugh.

'You think I'd want to keep that shiftless lassie a minute longer than I have to? You're welcome to her. Go on, the pair of you!'

She lifted the brush again and Albert McCabe spat on the flagstones, then turned and stalked towards the road with his daughter, weighed down by her bag, wobbling after him on her high heels. Celia followed, the brush held at the ready like a lance.

'Jennet,' she said over her shoulder. 'Make yourself useful. See to your brother.'

In the kitchen Mollie had lifted the fallen crutch and returned it to Angus.

'Are you all right?' Jennet asked.

'Of course I'm all right!'

He scowled at her, then at Mollie when the girl said, 'He was great, wasn't he?'

'I wasn't as great as my old grandmother.'

'You were wonderful,' Mollie insisted. 'You refused to let him get near me and Ma, and I've seen him beat a man so hard you couldnae tell who it was for the blood all down his face . . .'

'Stop fussing!' Angus snapped at her, while Jennet gathered two-year-old Jamie into her arms, holding him tightly.

'He's all right,' Nesta assured her nervously. 'Just frightened by the noise.'

'Right, that's them away. Come on, now, the folk'll be here any minute looking for their dinners!' Celia bustled back into the kitchen, the fallen tray in one hand and the brush in the other. 'Nesta, more bread to make up for what you dropped. Angus, you can mash the tea. Jennet, fetch the lemonade from the larder. These folks have been working hard in the field since early morning and they've got a long afternoon in front of them, too. They've every right to expect to see their dinner on the table when they get here.'

'They will, Mrs Scott,' Mollie panted, staggering out under the weight of a huge pot of steaming potatoes.

'It wasn't Nesta's fault, Gran,' Jennet protested, and earned herself a cold glare.

'Was it not? Who else is married to that . . . that animal?'

'Mrs Scott . . .' Nesta began, and was waved to silence.

'We'll discuss the matter later. They're here,' Celia said as the first of the potato howkers, worn out from their back-breaking toil, came slowly round the corner of the old stable and into the yard.

'These,' Mollie murmured to Jennet, 'will be the men your grandmother threatened my dad with?'

Jennet looked at the people filling the small yard and hoped that her sudden broad grin looked to them like a welcoming smile. 'It's as well he didn't stay long enough to see them,' she agreed as the motley band, mainly women of all ages and schoolchildren eager to earn some extra pocket money, sank gratefully onto the benches.

Westervoe was a small farm and during the war years, while her brother Martin was in the Army, Jennet and her grandmother and Angus had run it on their own with help from Jem, a man in his late seventies, and from the McCabes.

They had only planted one field of potatoes, and as those with larger farms on the Island of Bute had commandeered most of the able-bodied islanders, as well as all the Irish potato pickers, or howkers as they were known in that part of Scotland, who had come specially to harvest the early potatoes, the Scotts had had to make do with what they could get. Now some of the people sitting at the trestle tables looked exhausted.

Celia, who never seemed to tire, bustled about organising everyone. 'You go and fetch the teapot, Jennet. Mollie, you can hand the plates out when I've filled them. Mrs McCabe, have you not started pouring the lemonade yet? These folk are parched.'

It was strange, Jennet thought as she went back into the house for the teapot, that in all the five years the McCabes had been billeted on Westervoe as homeless evacuees, the two older women had never reached first-name terms. But then, her grandmother was not the sort of woman to invite such liberties. She had been furious when Jennet fell into the way of calling Mollie's mother Aunt Nesta, warning her that familiarity could only lead to trouble.

In the kitchen thirteen-year-old Sam McCabe, too thirsty to wait for the lemonade jugs, was downing a cup of water from the tap. 'I'll carry that for you,' he offered.

'You should be sitting out there getting your dinner. You've earned it.'

'I'm just goin' and I might as well take the teapot with me.' His face was glistening with sweat and filthy from all the times he had wiped a hand over it.

'It's hard work, isn't it?' Jennet asked sympathetically, and he grinned.

'Aye, but it's grand!' he said. Then, the grin fading, 'Is everything all right?'

'Why shouldn't it be?' Best to let his mother and

sister tell him in their own words what had happened.

'My mam looks a bit . . . different. And where's our Senga? Have they had another row?'

'No, I don't think so. Go on now and get your dinner,' Jennet told him.

Outside, the potato howkers were all eating as though they had not seen food for weeks. Everyone was there . . . except Angus, Jennet noticed. Deciding that she would not be missed for a few minutes, she slipped into the kitchen and then through the inner door at the back. This led to a short corridor with stairs going to the upper floor, a door to the rear of the house and two other doors, one to the parlour and the other to a room that had been the best parlour, but was now her brother's bedroom.

There was no reply when she tapped on the door, but when she opened it cautiously she saw him sitting on the edge of his bed, staring out at the small garden where Celia and Jennet grew fruit and vegetables for the family's use.

'You'd best come for your dinner before it's all eaten.'

'I'm not hungry.'

'Don't let that man bother you, Angus, he won't come back.'

'You think I'd let the likes of him trouble me?' he asked. Then, his voice suddenly flat, 'Did you hear what she said, Jen? "Women and cripples." That's all she sees when she looks at me now . . . a cripple.' He banged a fist on his right leg, which had been badly crushed in a railway accident in 1939.

'She didn't mean it the way it came out. She spoke in the heat of the moment, without thinking.'

'When folk speak without thinking they say what's really on their minds. You know the thing that sticks most in my craw, Jen? I brought this on myself. If I'd got hurt or killed because of a tractor accident, like the one that killed poor Drew Blaikie at Gleniffer, there might have been some sense to it. But this happened because of my own stupidity!'

'How could you have known that the train was going to run off the rails?'

'I should never have been on that train, Jen. I should have been here when the accident happened, working on the farm. But, oh no . . . I was so desperate for a bit of adventure, so keen to get away from here for a wee while.' He groaned, burying his face in his hands. 'And look at me now, a cripple like Gran says, of no use to anyone.'

'You're not useless! Look at the way you defended Aunt Nesta and then gave the man a right good crack on the arm with your . . .' She stopped suddenly, shying away from the word, and settled on, '. . . when he tried to pull her out of the house.'

'And he would have beaten me to death for my cheek, if Grandmother hadnae gone after him with that floor brush. God, Jen, I wish I'd had a proper ending to it. I wish I'd died in that crash.'

'No!' Sick with horror at the very thought of a world without Angus, she dropped to crouch in front of him, grabbing his shoulders and shaking him.

'Don't you ever say that to me again, d'you hear? Never! If anything had happened to you, I'd not be able to bear it!'

'You'd have got over it in time, the way folk always get over these things.'

'I wouldn't,' Jennet said fiercely. She did not remember their mother, who had died when she was a baby, and she only dimly recalled their father as a kindly adult who had carried her about the farm, talking to her about the animals. As she grew older, Angus had become the most important person in her life.

She straightened and looked down at him, trying to find the words that might bring him out of his depression. Once, he had been full of laughter and mischief, always looking for new challenges. When war broke out and Angus decided to enlist, though as a farmer he would have been exempt from call-up, he had persuaded his brother Martin and Struan Blaikie, the son of a neighbouring farmer, to do the same.

Knowing that Celia Scott and Struan's parents would have put a stop to their plan if they knew of it, the three of them invented a story about being invited to play in a football match on the mainland. After they had enlisted Struan and Martin came straight back to the island from Glasgow, while Angus, keen to make the most of his day away from Westervoe, travelled on to Saltcoats to visit a girl he was courting. Just outside Saltcoats station the train was derailed. Two people were killed and several injured, including Angus, who was trapped in the wreckage.

Jennet, a schoolgirl at the time, still had nightmares about that first sight of him in a hospital bed, his face cut and bruised, both eyes blackened, one arm broken and a great mound under the blankets where they had placed a protective cradle over the crushed tangle of bone and flesh, nerve and sinew, which had been a strong, healthy limb only hours before. She had thought that he was dying.

'Jennet!' her grandmother shouted from the kitchen just then. 'Where are you? We're near ready to get back out to the field!'

'Just coming!' Jennet called back and then, to her brother, 'Come outside with me and get some dinner.'

He shook his head. 'You go. You earned your food, and you've still got a hard afternoon's work ahead of you. I can eat any time.' His voice was heavy with self-loathing.

3

Potato picking by hand was one of the worst jobs Jennet knew of. The howkers spent most of their time bent double, shuffling along each row, their boots sinking into mud in wet weather, at the mercy of rain, sleet, sun and wind. Today the weather was fine, but even so it was one of those jobs that never seemed to have an end.

Nervous in case Albert McCabe returned, Jennet had opted – against her grandmother's wishes – to bring Jamie out to the field with her. Now he toddled along the furrows, squatting to pick out a potato here and there and offer it to the nearest howker with a sweet smile.

'I wish I was his size,' Mollie said longingly from beside her. 'Then I'd not need to bend my back like a hairpin to get down to the ground.' Then, after a pause, 'I could kill my father, humiliatin' my ma like that.'

'It was brave of her to refuse to go back with him.

I couldn't have done that.' The memory of Albert McCabe with his big tough body and his bullying voice, storming and threatening in the farm kitchen, made Jennet shiver.

'If you knew him, you'd understand her tryin' tae say no tae him. One of the first things I can remember is him hittin' her. I mind when I went tae the school at first, I was surprised because the teacher didnae have a bruise on her face or her arms. It was the same for the rest of us; he just lashes out when he's got a drink in him.'

'If she did go back, would you go with her?'

'And leave you? Of course not. We're blood sisters, aren't we? Well, skin sisters,' Mollie said. 'It still makes us special, even if we didnae have the courage tae keep goin' with the blunt knife.'

They had known that they were special when they discovered, the day after Mollie and her family had come to Westervoe, that they had been born on the same day. Gashing their wrists and mingling their blood had been Mollie's suggestion; Jennet could still see her, trying in vain to tuck wisps of fiery red hair behind her ears, explaining that as blood sisters they would be pledged to befriend each other till death and beyond, a pledge that could never be broken. To Jennet, who had never had a real friend in her life, it sounded wonderful.

Unfortunately, the penknife Mollie produced – specially stolen for the occasion from her brother Bert and carefully sterilised beforehand in a fire made from bits of dry stick – was blunt, and Jennet had been unable to make the cut on her wrist deep enough. Mollie had jeered, but when her turn came she fared no better. Instead, they bound their wrists together with grasses and pronounced themselves skin sisters. 'One for both and both for one,' Jennet had proclaimed while Mollie, not to be outdone, added grimly, 'Let no man put us under.'

Now, popping another potato into the sack tied about her waist, Mollie declared just as grimly, 'You needn't think you're going to be rid of me that easy, Jennet Scott. I'm stayin' on here, and so's my ma and the rest of them. Senga's a right fool – we're better shot of her. Right, that's another load in.'

'Me too.' They straightened, holding onto each other for support.

'I feel as if my leg muscles have been cut in two with a rusty saw,' Mollie moaned as they hobbled, weighed down by the sacks of potatoes, to the end of the row, where they emptied them into a large box. When the box was full it would be heaved onto the horse-drawn cart and taken to the farmyard. Westervoe had its own tractor, but it was old and temperamental, and the Scotts much preferred to stick to the traditional methods and use Nero, the horse, whenever possible.

'The terrible thing is,' Mollie moaned on as they returned to the row and coaxed their aching backs to bend again, 'I know that I'll feel twice as bad tomorrow mornin' when I try tae get out of my bed.'

'But you know it'll get better eventually,' Jennet consoled her.

'Thank you, Pollyanna,' Mollie growled.

Although they had their own living accommodation in the cottage adjacent to the farmhouse, the McCabe family ate in the farm kitchen, which was only fair since Nesta did most of the cooking.

Jennet had thought that her grandmother might mention Albert McCabe's visit during the evening meal, but Celia remained silent, her eyes fixed on her plate.

'If she's got something to say I wish she'd come out with it,' Mollie said that evening as the two girls shut the hens into the small portable hen coops known as arks.

'They'll need to be moved to the other end of the field soon.' Jennet closed an ark door and straightened her painful back, glancing about the field where the hens spent their days pecking and scratching for delicacies not provided in their daily food ration. The arks were on long carrying poles, so that they could be moved around to give the hens fresh ground. 'What can Grandmother say? What happened today's over and done with and we'll just have to hope that your father doesn't come back.'

Mollie shook her head. 'There's something about this silence of hers that minds me of a teacher I had back in Glasgow. She could say more with her mouth shut than most tongue-waggers could say in a month.'

'No, in there, you daft creature!' Jennet managed

to stop a hen that, halfway up the ramp leading into its ark, had suddenly decided to make a dash for freedom. Most arks had netting runs attached, but some runs, like the arks themselves, had fallen into disrepair and so the hens roamed free, which made things difficult at night. 'D'you want the foxes to get you?' she scolded, scooping the bird up and easing it in through the door. 'I don't know which is worse in the summer, getting Jamie to go to his bed or getting the hens to go to theirs.'

'I wish we could turn things round.' Mollie shut the door of the ark and straightened slowly and carefully before moving on. 'Wouldn't it be grand if the hens had to put us to bed? I'd go like a shot.'

'Me too, though I'd not want to be milked by the cows in the morning,' Jennet said, and they both shrieked with laughter.

Darkness was falling by the time all the hens had been shut in safely and the girls were free to make their way back to the farmhouse arm in arm . . . holding each other up, as Mollie put it.

'Imagine living in a city tenement when you could be here instead.' She lifted her freckled face to the sky, where the first stars were beginning to come through. 'Even if Ma did give in, I'd want to stay on this island. Our da can't make me and Bert go back – we're too old for that – and Sam will be fourteen come the summer.' Then, scratching with her free hand at her scalp, 'The midges are out. Come on quick, before they eat us alive.'

They separated in the yard, Mollie going to join her family in the cottage while Jennet went to the farmhouse. Sometimes she spent the evening in the cottage, but she knew that tonight, when Aunt Nesta would have to tell Bert and Sam about their father's arrival, the McCabe family were best left on their own.

Celia Scott was reading the weekly newspaper with the aid of a large old magnifying glass that had belonged to her mother. She had been using the glass for months now, but she refused to admit that there was anything wrong with her eyes, claiming that the newsprint was to blame. 'It's this war . . . nothing's right any more,' she kept saying. Now she looked up at her granddaughter. 'You're sure all the hens are in?'

'Every last one of them.' Jennet sank into a chair, wearied to the bone. 'Some of the arks are in a terrible state.'

'We'll mend them in the autumn after the harvest, when we've got more time.'

'There's a good half-dozen past mending. I don't know how they'll be moved again without falling apart.'

'We'll just have to mend them,' Celia retorted sharply. 'I'm not made of money; I can't afford to buy new all the time. Make a cup of tea.'

Jennet, who had been thinking of going to her bed, struggled to her feet to obey. When the tea was poured she put a cup in front of her grandmother, who said, 'I've told Mrs McCabe that she and her family will have to go.'

'Gran!'

'I'll not put up with another scene like this morning's. We've more than done our Christian duty by them, and nobody can fault us on that score. We took them in when they had nowhere else to go and now we can do no more.'

'What's the sense in taking them as evacuees, then putting them out?'

'Don't be cheeky, Jennet Scott,' Celia said, as she had said all Jennet's life, every time she tried to argue. 'When they came here their home had been bombed, but now the war's over and you heard that dreadful man say he'd found somewhere else for them to stay . . . and so it's time for them to go back to Glasgow.'

'You can't send Aunt Nesta back to that man. He hits her, Mollie told me. He hits them all! You saw what he was like, Gran. What happened wasn't their fault!'

'Mind your own business, young woman . . . and your tongue as well. I took them in because I'd no other choice. Just the same way I took you back when you came running home with a fatherless bairn in your belly,' Celia reminded her coldly. 'I've got a duty towards you, since you're my own blood kin, but not to them. Your brother Martin'll be coming home any day now to take over the place and he'll not want strangers here. When he marries and has a family of his own, you, me and Angus'll have to find somewhere else to live too.'

'Angus's the oldest,' Jennet said sharply. 'He shouldn't have to leave the farm if he doesn't want to.'

'And how could he run the place, the way he is?'

'He could manage, with help. Mebbe Martin will be willing to work for him.'

'Play second fiddle when he's the one who'll be doing most of the work? No, no, we're relying on Martin to take over the place now. If he chooses to let Angus stay, then that's his concern.'

'Aunt Nesta and Mollie aren't strangers – you can't treat them as if they are.' Jennet dragged the conversation back on course. Her grandmother frowned.

'Did I not say when you started addressing that woman as Aunt that it would cause trouble? It was just the same when you put names to the pigs and made pets of them. Then when they were slaughtered you broke your heart, year after year, over and over again. And now you're encouraging that bairn of yours to do the same.' She reached up to her straggly grey hair and pushed a hairpin back where it belonged. 'You're far too kind-hearted, I keep telling you so. Thanks to you, the McCabes probably think they've got a claim on us, but the sooner they're gone, the better pleased I'll be.'

'And how are we to keep the farm running without their help?'

'We'll manage till Martin comes back. I've told

Mrs McCabe that they can stay for a few more weeks; that should give them ample time to make other arrangements if they're so determined not to go back to Glasgow,' Celia swept on, folding her newspaper neatly. 'Time for us to get to our beds, so drink that tea and rinse the cups out.'

'I knew that we couldnae stay here for ever,' Nesta McCabe was saying in the adjoining cottage, 'but even so, I kept thinkin' . . . hopin' . . .'

'I wish I'd been here when Da came and spoiled everything.' Bert, just turned seventeen, doubled his fists on the table. 'I'd have had a thing or two to say to him.'

'He'd just have taken his belt to you, son.'

'It's been a while since he last belted me and I've been putting in some hard work since then. I'd be a match for him now.' It was not an idle boast. Bert was not tall, but he was broad-shouldered and muscular and not afraid of manual labour. Andra Blaikie, the farmer who had taken him on as a full-time labourer when he left school, had been heard to say that even though Bert was city-born, he put in as good a day's work as any of his other employees.

'I'm glad you were out of the way, for it would just have caused more trouble if the two of you had started fighting. But I'm worried about our Senga,' Nesta said, 'back in Glasgow with her daddy, and me not there to stand between them if he takes too much to drink.' Her roughened hands fretted with the handkerchief she held and she sniffed constantly to hold back the tears.

'Senga can look after herself. Listen, Mam, if you don't want to go back to Glasgow and the life he made you lead there, you don't have to.'

'What else is there for us to do? Where would we live? How would we eat?' Nesta cast an irritated look at the budgie, bouncing about his small cage by the window and chirping happily. 'Sam, will you cover that bird up? I'm not in the mood for his noise tonight.'

'I'll do it.' Mollie talked softly to the little bird before covering him, and he sidled along his perch to listen, his head cocked to one side. When he first arrived on Bute, huddled morosely in a battered cage, Cheepy had looked sad and moth-eaten, having lost most of his feathers in the explosion that destroyed the McCabes' Glasgow tenement home. Now, in a smart cage that Sam had found in a pawnshop in Rothesay, his feathers all restored, he was a handsome and happy bird.

As Mollie draped a bit of old curtain over the cage, a light tap was heard at the door. 'Come on in, Jennet,' she called.

'Are you sure?' Jennet ventured in, eyeing them nervously. 'My grandmother's just told me. I thought you might not want to see me tonight.'

'Don't be daft.' Mollie bundled her friend into the kitchen.

'I'm truly sorry,' Jennet said miserably as Sam

offered her his stool. 'I've tried to get Grandmother to change her mind, but she won't.'

'Ach, we'll be all right. It's not your fault,' Mollie told her robustly. Raised on the Glasgow streets, where she had learned at an early age that shy and retiring kids went to the wall, she had worked hard to instil some of her own confidence and bounce into Jennet when they first met. It angered her to see how easily Mrs Scott could crush and humble the girl. There were some folk, she reckoned, who could use their tongues instead of their fists and deliver bruises unseen by human eyes, but just as sore as any physical evidence.

Mam was right; lessons learned early in life stuck like glue. Her own home life had been far from perfect, thanks to her father's temper and his drinking binges, but she reckoned that even that was better than being raised by Jennet's old witch of a granny.

'It's all right, lassie.' Nesta's tears were banished and she spoke with quiet dignity. 'Your granny's right, we should have found somewhere else to stay before now and I'm grateful for all she's done for us since we first came here.'

'I'm staying on, no matter what,' Bert said defiantly. 'Mr Blaikie'll likely let me sleep in one of the bothies the Irish potato howkers use when they're on the island, and I'll be well fed as long as I work for him. But what about you and Mollie and young Sam here?'

'I can work alongside you when I leave the school,'

Sam piped up hopefully, and his brother reached out to tug gently on his snub nose.

'You're the cleverest of us all and you might be able to make something of yourself. There'll be no farmwork for you, if we can find something else that uses your brain instead of your muscles.'

'There's mebbe work to be found in one of the boarding houses in Rothesay,' Jennet suggested; then, brightening, 'My aunt and uncle might be needing more help this summer with their boarding house. Now that the war's over there'll be hundreds of trippers coming here in the summer.'

'That's right!' Mollie sat upright. 'Me and Mam could clean and cook and help with the holiday folk.'

'And I can clean boots and run messages,' Sam piped up, determined to do his bit.

'And help Uncle George with the boat-hiring,' Jennet suggested.

'I could do that no bother,' he said eagerly. Then, glaring at Bert, 'That surely takes brains, stopping folk from getting drowned.'

'D'ye think they'd want a whole family landed on them?' Nesta was doubtful.

'There would only be the three of you. The best way to find out is to ask. I'll go and see them tomorrow. You'd not mind sharing a room if you had to?'

Mollie beamed at her friend. 'We'd not mind sharing a bed, if it meant us being able to stay on the island. I knew you'd come up with the answer, Jennet

Scott. Have I not always said that you'd more brains than me?'

'And more beauty too,' Bert said, and got a clip on the ear from his sister for his cheek.

'Don't get too excited,' Jennet warned with the wisdom of one who had never been able to take anything for granted. 'My aunt and uncle might not be able to help you.'

'Ach, they will,' Mollie said confidently. 'You'll talk them into it, I know.' Then she yawned and stretched, wincing. 'I don't know about the rest of you, but I'm ready for my bed. I'm goin' to sleep like a log tonight.'

Jennet was so worried about the McCabes' future that she went to bed convinced that she would be unable to sleep a wink that night, but no sooner had she turned out the lamp and put her head on the pillow than she was roused by Jamie bouncing about in his cot and talking to his toys.

'Mummy!' he said gleefully when she lifted her head and blinked at him in the dawn light.

'Wha . . . ?' She reached for the old clock by the bed, then as she heard her grandmother's booted feet on the stairs she pushed it away and leaped onto the cold linoleum, gritting her teeth against the waves of pain radiating from her back muscles.

By the time she had splashed water from the jug she had filled the night before into a bowl, stripped off her night-gown and washed the remains of sleep away with cold water and harsh soap, her back had loosened up slightly. She ran the flannel over the little boy, who squealed and squirmed as the chill water came in contact with his sleep-warmed skin, then towelled him briskly to warm him up, before dressing him and combing his silky hair.

When she had been forced to return pregnant and disgraced from Glasgow, where she had gone to take up a nursing career, her grandmother had done everything possible to force her to reveal the name of Jamie's father, but Jennet had held her tongue, even when the words spilling from her grandmother's vicious tongue sent her running from the house to weep her heart out in one of the barns, huddled against a bale of hay. Gumrie, she remembered, had followed her in and lain beside her, his cold nose pressed comfortingly against her neck.

Angus had found her there and said, 'Listen, Jennet, you're the only one who knows who the lad is and nobody else needs to know, not even Grandmother. But I'm certain sure that this bairn you're carrying'll bring its own joy to you. And whatever happens, I'm here to look out for the two of you.'

Angus had been right . . . Jamie was a cheerful, lovable and loving little boy who had brought a new and much-needed pleasure into their grey lives. Celia was over-harsh with him, but at the same time Jennet feared that her grandmother was trying to take control of him, as she had done of his mother and uncles. Hers was a tyranny that had overshadowed their childhood and sent Angus on the desperate break for freedom that had ended in a smashed railway carriage. Sometimes it seemed to Jennet that every day was a continuation of the silent struggle between herself and her grandmother over Jamie.

Now she took a moment to cuddle him as she carried him from the room, revelling in the fresh clean baby smell of him, the softness of his hair and skin against her face. Jamie, who had had his second birthday three months earlier, was now old enough to rebel against being fussed over.

'Not kiss face,' he reproved her, then, 'Down!'

He had been going up and down the steep narrow staircase for months now, at first on hands and knees and then on his feet, step by step. Even so, Jennet was nervous about it, so she slowly backed down ahead of him, ready to catch him if he should lose his footing. But he clung to the banister above his brown curly head, his round face a mask of concentration as he clambered down, until he reached the bottom and toddled into the outer kitchen, where he submitted impatiently to having his outdoor clothes pulled on.

Celia and Mollie, with Gumrie's help, were already bringing the small herd of cows along from their field when Jennet and Jamie arrived. The toddler skipped fearlessly among the huge animals, slapping a leg here, pulling at a tail there, roaring 'Ho!' and 'Get up will ye!' in imitation of the adults. The cows, as used to him as he was to them, paid him no heed as they ambled along the lane and into the yard, a familiar route that they took twice a day.

In the yard they milled about for a moment, forming their usual line before going on into the byre. Each cow knew her regular stall and objected if another animal tried to take it. They always entered in the right order, eager for the handfuls of hay that Angus and Sam were putting into their individual racks.

By the time the milking was done, the herd returned to the field and the milk cooled, Jem, the old farm-hand who had come out of retirement to help after Angus's accident, had arrived, just in time to help the women and Sam manhandle the milk churns out to the head of the lane, where they would be collected by lorry and taken to the ferry. Then the byre had to be cleaned and made ready for the afternoon's milking before they were free to get their breakfast.

4

Andra Blaikie, tenant at Gleniffer, the neighbouring farm, arrived while they were still breaking their fast. A tall, burly man, he filled the doorway, blocking out the light and darkening the kitchen.

'Young Bert tells me you'd some trouble last night, Celia.'

'Just some vermin,' Celia said calmly from the stove. Nesta, who was working beside her, flinched slightly. 'I sent him packing with a flea in his ear.'

'You should have fetched me. I'd have given him somethin' tae think about.'

'You're a good neighbour, Andra, but I can fight my own battles. You'll have a cup of tea now you're here?'

'I might as well.' He stepped over the threshold, nodding to the room's other occupants, and settled himself at the table.

'And you'd best put some good food in your belly while you're about it.' Celia heaped a plate with rashers of bacon, link-sausages and two fried eggs and put it down before him. Although rationing was in force the farming community, who raised livestock and grew potatoes and turnips, leeks, cabbages and grain in their fields and used a form of barter among themselvcs, ate better than most. And as Celia kept pointing out, they deserved to, since they had to work hard to keep the country fed.

'Has there been any word from your Martin?' Andra wanted to know as he picked up his fork.

'The occasional letter, but no word yet of him being let home. Why they had to send him to Germany when I've got sore need of him here, I don't know. What about your Struan?'

'We'd word the other day, he'll not be long in getting back.' Blaikie pushed a forkful of food into his mouth, then swilled it down with half a mug of hot tea. 'Martin might well be with him, since they were both sent tae Germany.'

'Please God.' Now that everyone had been served, Celia and Nesta brought their own plates to the table. Jennet tied Jamie into the wooden high chair that she and her brothers had used as babies, then sat down beside him and started to feed him from her own plate.

'Jennet, Mr Blaikie's mug's empty,' her grandmother said almost at once.

'You're lookin' fit the morn, Jennet,' the farmer said as she went to the range to fetch the teapot. 'I swear that the lassie that first owned those trousers never filled them as well as you do.'

'They're just right for farm work,' she agreed, embarrassed by the way the man was studying her, as though she was one of the Clydesdales that he, like many other Bute farmers, bred. It was Andra himself who had given her the sturdy corduroy jodhpurs left behind by one of the Land Army girls who had worked on his farm, which was much larger than Westervoe. Buttoned up the calves, and with a fullness at the thighs to make movement easy, the jodhpurs were ideally designed for heavy farm work and Jennet wore them most of the time.

'By God,' Blaikie went on with an unexpected burst of enthusiasm, 'it's been a while since I've had my arm about a nice wee waist like yours.'

'I'd not advise it.' Angus spoke for the first time. 'Not while my sister's got that big heavy teapot in her two fists.'

The farmer barked out a laugh. 'Ye're mebbe right there,' he said, while Jennet poured his tea.

'He'll be away home to eat another breakfast,' Angus said when Andra left.

'He's entitled to his meat,' Celia told him sharply. 'He works for it.'

'And if that's not a hint I don't know what is.' He levered himself to his feet, reaching for the crutch and tucking it into his armpit. 'Come on, Jamie son, you and me'll go and feed the hens, eh?'

'It's time we were going too,' Mollie told her brother. She had a job in a shop in Rothesay, the island's only town, where Sam went to school.

Because of the sudden rise in the population caused by evacuees coming to the island, his classroom was a converted shop in the town.

When the two of them had gone, Mollie riding on Jennet's old bicycle and Sam on Angus's, Jennet said casually, 'I thought I'd go to see Aunt Ann and Uncle George tomorrow afternoon.' Then she added, as Celia's lips pursed as they always did when her late daughter-in-law's family was mentioned, 'It's been six weeks or more since I was last there. I've scarcely been off the farm in all that time.'

'Very well, if you must. I suppose you'd better take some eggs and a few rashers of bacon from the pantry,' her grandmother said somewhat ungraciously.

'I will. And some butter too,' Jennet said, and winked at Nesta.

It was a struggle to get herself and Jamie, and the bags she had packed for her uncle and aunt, onto the small bus and into a seat, but Jennet managed it. As the vehicle trundled placidly along the few miles between the farm and Rothesay town, her sense of freedom grew with every turn of the wheels.

'Look . . . look . . .' Jamie perched on her knee, his hands sawing the air as he tried to point out everything that caught his fancy He stared wide-eyed when they reached the town's outskirts, with its houses and shops instead of the fields he was used to seeing, not to mention the busy pavements. When they alighted he clutched at her hand, nervous among so many strangers, then he let out a squeal of excitement as he caught sight of the superstructure and funnels of a steamer lying at the pier.

'Let's go and have a look.' Jennet took a moment to organise her bags before leading him across the gardens, once a handsome stretch of smooth lawns and bright flowerbeds separating the street from the waterside, but sadly neglected now, since during the war the area had been used to park Army tanks and lorries. As she led her son onto the pier she relished the cool breeze about her legs, and the sensation of her skirt drifting about her knees. It made her feel feminine again, and it was so different from the heavy dungarees and the jodhpurs she wore on the farm. She didn't possess a pair of silk stockings, but she had put on leg make-up, and early that morning Mollie had found time before going to work to draw a 'seam' down the backs of her legs with an eyebrow pencil.

The steamer had almost finished loading by the time they reached her. Passengers hung over the rails, taking a last look at the town with its impressive glass-domed Winter Gardens and the curved splendour of the Pavilion Theatre further along the coast road.

'Horsie!' Jamie jiggled with excitement as a great Clydesdale was led along the pier towards the steamer. The horse jibbed at the gangplank and the farm lad leading it took off his jacket and tied it about the animal's head so that it could not see the boat. Then he managed to urge it step by step up the gangplank and onto the deck, where it was led aft.

The ropes were cast off and a bell clanged deep within the boat. Slowly she moved away from the pier, her bows swinging out and her paddles beginning to churn. Jennet led Jamie as close to the edge as she dared, so that he could watch the paddles turning within their box, slowly at first and then faster and faster until they could only be seen as a blur. Then the steamer turned away and headed out into the huge bay.

''Bye, horsie, 'bye!' Jamie waved so energetically that if she had not been clutching his hand he might have worked his way off the pier and into the green and white water foaming below. As the steamer beat her way across the great bay towards the mainland, leaving behind a train of sparkling white foam, Jennet was struck, as always, by the way the paddle boxes on each side gave the otherwise graceful boat the look, from directly astern, of a pregnant cow.

'Is that not a picture?' Ann Logan asked as she and Jennet stood at her parlour window watching the elderly man and the tiny boy walk along the pavement. 'George is that tall and your Jamie's that wee – the one has to bend sideways and the other has to reach away up, just so's they can link hands.'

'It's good of Uncle George to take the time to keep Jamie amused.'

'I think it's you that's doing him the favour, lending the wee one. He loved taking our Geordie down to the river when he was that size, and explaining everything to him.' Ann lifted a photograph from the small table in the curve of the window and looked down at the likeness of a young man in the uniform of an Able Seaman, his arms formally folded but his round face split by a huge grin.

'Enjoy every minute of your wee one, Jennet, for they don't take long to grow up,' Ann said. Then, putting the portrait back, she went on briskly, 'We'll just have a fresh pot of tea, will we? In the kitchen, for it's cheerier there. It's daft to feel like a visitor in my own parlour, but in the summer months this room belongs to the boarders, not to us.'

She whisked out of the room while Jennet returned to the window to catch a last glimpse of her son and her uncle, two men together, turn the corner and disappear from sight. Then she paused on her way to the kitchen to study her cousin's picture.

Geordie, who had spent most of his short life in and around the water, helping in the family boat-hiring business almost as soon as he could walk, had enlisted in the Navy when war broke out and had gone down with his ship in 1942. It was strange, and terrible, to realise that she would never again see him skipping deftly from dinghy to dinghy, or charming the lassies with his laughing eyes as he handed them into the motor boat, ready for a sail round the bay.

Jennet blinked several times, then picked up another framed photograph, this time of two attractive young girls not much older than she herself was.

Although Ann Logan was now grey-haired and

middle-aged, she still had the clear, sparkling eyes and wide smile of the girl on the left. Her sister Rose, the mother who had died when Jennet was less than a year old, was slimmer but she, too, brimmed with life and happiness. While Ann's hair had been plaited into long braids and wound about her head, Rose's hair, a mass of curls, was held back by a ribbon. Jennet had inherited her mother's hair, and although at times it got in the way of her work, she had steadfastly refused to give in to Celia, who referred to it on occasions as a burst mattress, and have it cut.

Celia had never spoken to her grandchildren about their mother's death, or her son's disappearance shortly afterwards. Jennet would never forget the day, in her first year at school, when an older girl had shouted to her in the playground, 'Your daddy ran away because he didnae want tae live with you!' Everyone had looked at her, and she had cried, but when she asked her grandmother about it, Celia had merely tightened her lips and then said, posting the words through the remaining slit, that gossips should never be listened to.

As ever, it had fallen to Angus to explain to his bewildered little sister that their father had just walked away one day, not long after their mother's death. He had looked at her, a long level look, and said, 'I don't know why he went, but it wasn't because of us, it was because our mother died. But that's all right, because you and me and Martin have each other, and we don't need anyone else . . . not even Grandmother, and not *him*, wherever he may be. We can manage fine without him! And if anyone else says that to you, don't let it hurt you, right? Just tell me and I'll bash them for you.'

Later, when Jennet came to know Aunt Ann and Uncle George and her cousins Geordie and Alice, Ann had explained as carefully as she could that James Scott had felt so alone when his wife died that he had not been able to stay at Westervoe.

'But he had us, and Grandmother,' Jennet had argued, puzzled. 'She's his own mother. Why didn't he want to stay with her?'

'Nobody knows but him, dear,' Ann had said helplessly. But as she grew up under Celia's thumb and became old enough to realise that there was nothing of her mother's in the farmhouse, and that her grandmother never mentioned either of her parents, Jennet began to understand more. But not all. 'Why,' she asked now as she joined her aunt in the kitchen, 'did my grandmother have such a down on my mother?'

Ann gave her a sidelong look. 'Because our Rose wasn't her choice as a daughter-in-law. Because the poor lass died young and your gran had to take over the three of you, just when she'd thought her life was getting easier, with your father running the farm and all.'

'Angus says you'd think our poor mother had died on purpose, just to be difficult.

A smile flickered across Ann's face. 'I doubt that, for I've never known anyone who loved life more than our Rose. Oh, you should have seen her and James together, Jennet, it would have warmed your heart. They were just right for each other. Like bookends, George said, and it was true enough, for poor James was never the same after Rose died.'

'He certainly didn't stop to think about what was to happen to us,' Jennet said with sudden resentment.

'Now, don't go blaming him. The man was grieving so much that he didn't know what he was doing,' Ann Logan said swiftly. 'I think he just had to get away from everything that reminded him of her. He was mebbe too gentle for his own good, James was. More interested in drawing pictures than in working the farm, and that didn't suit his mother at all.'

'Were the pictures good?'

'They were very good. He had a right talent, and I just wish he'd left some with us, so's I could show them to you. George and me offered to take the three of you and raise you along with our own two, and we'd have been happy to do it, but your gran would have none of it. She's got it into her head that we'd encouraged him, since James and my George had got so friendly when they were courting Rose and me. We used to go out in a foursome. Then, after we all married, James would come to Rothesay now and again to help George and his father with the boats; he enjoyed that. It was a sad business, right enough. Your gran's not had it easy, losing her husband just years after they wed, then seeing her only child go from her as well.'

If her father had been raised in the same disciplined, unloving way she and her brothers had known, Jennet thought, it might explain why he could not bear to go back to his mother's domination when he became a widower. But she would never really forgive him for leaving her and her brothers at the mercy of the same upbringing.

'I can tell you one thing,' Ann was saying. 'Both Rose and James would be right proud of all of you if they could see the way you've turned out.'

'Even me, after what I've done?'

'If you're talking about Jamie, he's a fine wee lad and you're making a good job of raising him,' her aunt said firmly. 'You're a loving mother and if there was one thing that could be said for both your parents, it's that they were loving folk. They'd be proud of you, and of him, you mark my words. No word about Martin coming home yet?'

'Not yet.'

'It surely won't be long now.' Ann took the boiling kettle off the gas ring and poured some water into the teapot to heat it.

'How's Alice?'

'Och, she's fine. Doing all right at the school, but she's pining for the holidays as usual. It'll be good to see all the trippers back and the place humming like a bee's nest, the way it used to be.' She poured the kettle's contents into the teapot.

'Are you going to take in holidaymakers again this year?'

'All my rooms have been booked already.' George Logan's mother had let out rooms in the three-storey house, and when he and his wife inherited it they had carried on the tradition.

'You'd not have a wee attic room to spare, would you?'

'D'you know, Jennet, we've been thinking along just the same lines. With Martin coming back home to take over the farm, and probably finding himself a wife soon and starting a family, we'd been talking about asking if you and the wee one would like to come here. You'd both be very welcome,' Ann rushed on before Jennet could say anything. 'It would be grand to have a bairn about the place, and I could do with some help when the trippers arrive. And you've still got most of your life in front of you, lassie. You could go back to nursing or whatever you might want to do, and we'd look after the wee one for you while you were studying.'

Jennet drew a deep breath. 'It's not me that I'm asking for, Aunt Ann, it's the McCabes.' She gave her aunt a brief account of Albert McCabe's unexpected arrival and the way her grandmother had sent him packing, then of Nesta's determination to stay away from the life she had suffered with her domineering husband.

'Poor woman . . . I cannae understand how these men get away with it myself, for it'd take a brave man to take his tongue to me, let alone his fist,' Ann said while her hands, big-knuckled and roughened with work, their only decoration the gold band on the third finger of her left hand, clenched slightly on the table before her.

'I thought he was going to hurt Angus. . .' Jennet shivered at the memory, 'and he might have done, if Gran hadn't seen to him.' Then the shiver gave way to a sudden giggle. 'I wish you could have seen him scrambling out of the door and into the yard with her after him and his arms all over the place, trying to protect himself from the floor brush!'

'Bullies usually have cowards sharing their skins. But your gran's being a wee bit hard on the poor woman and her bairns, ordering them out of the farm like that.' Ann poured more tea into both their cups. 'So you want us to take them in?'

'Just Aunt Nesta and Mollie and Sam. Bert's well settled at the Blaikie farm; he says he doesn't mind sleeping in their bothy if there's nowhere else for him. And Senga went back to Glasgow with her father. It's not just charity, for Aunt Nesta and Mollie are hard workers; they'd be a real help to you. To be honest, I don't know how we're going to manage without them till Martin's home. And Sam's a willing lad, he'd help about the house and run messages, and he could work with the boats now that Geordie's . . .'

She stopped abruptly, ducking her head to stare down at her tea.

'As a matter of fact, George has been thinking of taking on a lad out of the school to help when the season starts,' her aunt said. 'There's no shortage of laddies here for their holidays and desperate to help with the boats, but someone who'll be here all through the season would be a good idea. And there's two wee rooms at the top of the house that could be cleared out.'

'So you'd be willing to take them?'

'I'll need to speak to your uncle, of course,' Ann said primly, then got to her feet. 'Come and see the rooms and tell me what you think.'

During the summer months Ann and George Logan and their daughter Alice lived on the ground floor of the house, Ann and George sleeping in the wall-bed in the kitchen and Alice in a tiny adjoining room. They used the outside privy and bathed in a tin bath in the wash-house at the back of the property. The four rooms on the first floor were given over to holidaymakers, who shared the large bathroom on the landing and had the use of the front parlour. The top floor, with its slanted ceilings under the eaves, consisted of a loft where George kept some of the paraphernalia needed for his boat-hiring business and two small rooms used as storage space for unwanted pieces of furniture.

'I could give them a good clean out and there's extra chairs and beds and chests of drawers here that they could make use of.' Ann pushed open the skylight in one room to let in the fresh warm air. 'It's not very fancy.'

'It would do fine, I'm sure.'

'Anything else can be put away in the garden shed or mebbe the workshop. They'll only be sleeping here anyway, for there's enough work in the summer to keep us all busy during the day. D'you think the McCabes could manage up here?'

'I'm sure of it. They'd be so grateful, Aunt Ann.'

'Then you can tell them when you get back that I'll be expecting them whenever they're ready to move in.'

'Are you certain that Uncle George'll be in favour?'

'Why not? For all that he's the head of the family, he's gone along with everything I've decided since the day we got wed, God bless him. And he's never had cause to regret it, so there's no reason to believe he'll not go along with this. I've just met the McCabe lassie a time or two when you brought her here, but she seems decent enough, and if they're hard-working they should fit in with us. But not a word to your uncle when he comes back . . . let me have a chat when we're on our own, just to give him his rightful place as head of the household. Is that them back already?' Ann added as the front door opened. 'We'd best get down and make a fresh pot. Your Uncle George could drink the stuff all day, and Alice should be coming in soon.'

5

A big wooden box carrying all that was left of their possessions after the blitz that destroyed their home had preceded the McCabes' arrival at Westervoe Farm early in 1940. Celia, grim-faced with disapproval at having to take on evacuees, had ordered the carter to leave the box in the cottage that she had cleaned out for the newcomers.

'As if we have nothing else to do with our time,' she had sniffed as she and Jennet scrubbed floors, cleaned windows and arranged the few pieces of furniture they could spare from the farmhouse, together with some items that the Red Cross had given them. 'And no doubt they'll have it looking like a midden before the week's out. Tenement folk know nothing about cleanliness.'

That was ironic, Jennet thought a few days later, watching the lodgers arrive and noting their shocked reaction as they passed the manure pit, where the used bedding from the cow byre and the dirt from the hen houses was piled up to mature before being scattered on the fields as fertiliser. Dirt came in many forms.

City-pale and anxious, carrying shabby suitcases bound with string, hung about with various bags and parcels, the Glaswegian family had edged into the yard, huddled together for safety, bewildered by the hens and the trees and the prospect of being marooned on an island, away from the streets and tenements and trams and cinemas they knew.

Nesta, clutching an ancient cage inhabited by a mangy-looking bird, was ashen with strain and exhaustion, while Sam was already wheezing and coughing with one of the asthma attacks that, in those days, had been brought on very easily by anxiety. Senga was sullen and Bert's attempt to be the man of the family disintegrated into panic when the farm dogs, Gumrie and his elderly mother Bess, so old then that she could scarcely walk, came to investigate the newcomers.

Then fourteen-year-old Mollie stepped out of the group, skinny as a rake, her tired white face blotchy with freckles and with straggly red hair that made her look, Celia said later, like a match that had just been struck. She said, 'Call your dogs off before I give them a good kicking, missus, and tell us where my ma can sit down before she falls down. She could do with a cup of tea, too. We've had a right bugger of a day.'

And even as the air whooshed out of her grandmother's lungs in a mighty gasp of shock, Jennet knew that at last she had found a proper friend.

The two girls went to school together, discovered the joys of the local dance halls and picture houses together when they were a little older, and fell in love with the same film stars. To Jennet, it seemed as though Mollie's flaming red head lit up the farm, sparking it into new life.

It was Mollie who, on discovering that Jennet nurtured a secret ambition to study nursing in the hope of being of practical use to Angus, egged her on to fulfil her dream.

'Of course I'll miss you,' she had said, 'but you need to do something with your life, and you'll be helping the war effort, too.'

'I don't know if I could live in Glasgow all by myself,' Jennet quavered. 'I've never been away from home before.'

'You'll not be all by yourself. Glasgow's hoachin' with folk. You can't cross a street without bumping into a dozen of them crossin' the other way. You'll like it,' Mollie had insisted. 'Mebbe it'll be a wee bit frightening at first, but you'll make friends.'

'I've got a friend. I've got you.'

'I know, but you need to meet folk, Jennet. You're like a wee mouse sometimes. It would do you good to go to a bigger place.'

'What if I don't like it, or I can't do the studying? What if I fail?'

'You'll only fail if you don't try,' Mollie argued. 'If it doesnae suit, then you can come back home and tell everyone you tried it but you didnae like it. Nob'dy can call you a failure for tryin'. I'll not let them.'

It was Mollie who, when Jennet returned home only a few months later, pregnant and disgraced, had crept into the house every night for weeks, buying Gumrie's silence with saved scraps of meat, crawling up the stairs and into Jennet's bed where she held her weeping friend, not once asking anything about Jamie's father; unlike Celia, who had badgered and hectored until Angus had finally told her that, if she didn't stop it, he and his sister would both leave Westervoe. After that, Celia manufactured some story about a young serviceman tragically killed just as he and Jennet were about to marry.

Five years on, the McCabes had changed beyond recognition. They had all put on weight and the pale city look had long since given way to a country glow. The anxious lines had been largely smoothed from Nesta's face, and Sam, taller and broader, no longer suffered from chest troubles. Mollie was still as thin as a whip despite her excellent appetite, and her red hair and cocky grin were still in evidence, as were the freckles, but now her skin was creamy rather than ashen and her hair glossy.

As she put her case down by the roadside and hugged Jennet, her face was wet with tears. 'It was easier tae leave Glasgow than tae leave this farm,' she said tremulously. 'It's daft . . . I was born in Glasgow!'

'You're not going all that far away. We'll see each other often enough.'

'Mind all the good times we've had, Jen?'

'How could I ever forget them?' Together they had yearned over Clark Gable and envied Myrna Loy, and had walked all the way home from the pictures on a Saturday night arm in arm, planning wonderful futures in which they would wear satin dresses and white furs, and smoke Russian cigarettes through ivory holders, and be wooed by handsome men driving beautiful motor-cars.

'Mind the Winter Gardens, and buying two tickets for the dancing?'

'Then running upstairs and out onto the balcony to throw them down to the rest of the crowd so that the next two could use them to get in . . .'

The dances had been wonderful, because there had been plenty of partners, Polish and French as well as British. During the war commandos had trained on Bute, and as well as the submarine base in Rothesay Bay itself, there had been a repair depot ship off Port Bannatyne, dealing with damaged ships that had managed to limp as far as the Clyde.

'Mind how disgusted our Senga was when we first came and she discovered that milk came out of cows and eggs from hens' backsides?' Mollie's face almost split in two with amusement.

'And when she found out that the sausages she was enjoying came from one of our own pigs,' Jennet said, and they were just embarking on a great rush of memories when the bus came into view and there was a scramble to get everything collected up.

Nesta's hug was brief, but warm. 'Thanks for

getting your auntie to take us in, pet. You'll not regret it, I promise you that. Take care of yourself, and that wee laddie of yours.'

Sam, fast approaching his fourteenth birthday, too old for hugging and too young for shaking hands, concentrated on making his most fulsome goodbyes to Gumrie, who had accompanied them along the farm lane. Now he gave the dog a final pat, snatched up a mass of bags and parcels, settled for a gruff ''Bye then' to Jennet and rushed so quickly onto the bus when it stopped that his parcels got caught up round the pole.

While the grinning bus driver and the conductor helped the lad to sort himself out and then ushered him and his mother onto the bus, Mollie spun round, pecked Jennet swiftly on the cheek and whispered, 'Don't let your gran turn Angus back into an invalid.'

Then the bus was trundling along the road and out of sight, leaving Jennet behind. The war was over and the McCabes were gone from Westervoe.

Gumrie, sitting patiently at her side, gave a little whine as though he, too, felt as if something safe and familiar had come to an end. 'Come on, then,' she told him and turned back to the farm.

Celia's father and then her husband had bred Clydesdales, the beautiful big workhorses that for centuries had been invaluable to farming communities. As a young widow, struggling to keep the farm going, she had had to give up the Clydesdales, and now Nero was the only horse at Westervoe. Angus was grooming him in the stable when Jennet trailed back after seeing the McCabes off.

As she appeared in the doorway he broke off the soft tuneless whistle he always adopted when working with the stock to say, 'They got away all right, then?'

'You should have come with us.'

'It was only to the end of the road, and they're just going to Rothesay.'

'I'll miss them. And so will you.'

'Things change,' Angus said tersely. 'Folk move on.'

'You'll miss Mollie.'

'Aye . . . the way I miss the midges in the winter,' he said sarcastically.

'After all she did for you? You're ungrateful, d'you know that?'

'And you're sentimental and that's worse,' he shot back at her. 'Folk come and go, there's no sense in trying to pretend that anything good stays for ever!' He threw the brush down, then as Nero, sensing the tension in the air, shifted uneasily, Angus stooped clumsily to pick up the brush, clutching at the horse's foreleg for support. Then he turned his back on his sister and began to whistle again as he resumed work. Jennet, furious with him, marched off across the yard.

Twisting round as best she could to see her friend as the bus started to gather speed, Mollie was struck by how lonely Jennet looked, standing on the grass verge.

For a moment she wanted to stop the bus and jump off, then her mother said anxiously, 'D'you think the Logans'll like us? D'you think we'll suit?' All at once Mollie knew where her own duties lay.

Life hadn't been good to her mum . . . an unhappy childhood with parents who had been in their forties when their only, and unwanted, child was born, then marriage to a man who had turned out to be violent. Despite Celia Scott's coldness, Westervoe had been the most secure home Nesta had ever known, and now she was being pitch-forked into yet another unknown future.

Mollie wanted to put her arms round her mother, birdcage and all, and tell her that everything would be all right, always. Instead she said briskly, 'Of course. I've met the Logans before, with Jennet. They're nice. We'll be happy there. And we'll be settled, at last.'

'I'm sorry about the stairs,' Ann Logan said as she led the way upstairs, 'but you'll see for yourself by next week that we need all the rooms on the middle floor for the holiday folk.'

'We're used to stairs,' Mollie assured her, suitcase in one hand and birdcage in the other. 'We used to live three floors up.'

'You were bombed out, weren't you? It must have been terrible.'

'We managed,' Nesta said tersely. Then, as they reached the attic floor, she gasped as Ann opened one of the two doors on the tiny landing and sunlight flooded out to meet them. The room was adequate, though small and sparsely furnished; but light poured in through a large skylight, making the fresh flowers that had been arranged in a vase glow.

'There's a double bed behind here . . .' Ann drew back a curtain in the corner. 'I thought mebbe you and Mollie could share that, Mrs McCabe. And the wee room that opens from this one is for your boy.'

She opened the door and Sam shot inside, then reappeared, grinning. 'Ma, come and see this!'

The room was little more than a long cupboard holding a single bed and a chair, but once again it was well lit by a skylight.

'There's a row of hooks there for your clothes, and that wee cupboard by the bed to hold some things. And there's room for things under the bed, too.'

'And I can see the sea, Ma,' Sam carolled, his head and shoulders almost out of the open skylight.

'You'll do more than see it.' Alice Logan, who had followed them upstairs, spoke for the first time. 'My dad's expecting you to help out with the boat-hiring.'

'He'll let me work with the boats? Can I learn to row?'

'You'll have to. I'll teach you if you like,' Alice offered, then blushed scarlet.

'We'll leave you to get settled in. Come downstairs when you're ready,' Ann said, 'and I'll make a cup of tea.'

'I can make it,' Nesta said swiftly. 'We don't want

to be a nuisance. We can see to this stuff later.'

Please, Mollie prayed silently, removing the cover from the bird's cage, please let her make the tea, Mrs Logan. Don't make Ma feel like a burden.

And as though in answer to her prayer she heard Ann Logan say, 'Why not? That's the best way to find out where everything is.'

His cover removed, Cheepy blinked, stretched one leg and then the other, fluffed his feathers and began to chirp.

Everything was going to be all right.

'They're looking sonsy. You'll not be short of a good cut of bacon this winter.'

Jennet, taking a moment as she passed the low stone wall to lean over and have a word with the two pigs within the sty, jumped and whirled round. 'Struan Blaikie!'

'Ye didnae think it was one of them speakin', did ye?' Struan nodded at the animals, grinning. 'D'you often have conversations with them?'

'I wasn't talking, I was just . . . Where did you spring from? Nobody told us you were home.'

'I got through all the business of being demobbed quicker than I'd expected, so I got the first train I could, then the first ferry. I telephoned the house when I got to Rothesay and they sent someone to fetch me.' The Blaikies were one of the few families on the island to own a telephone.

'When did you get back?'

'An hour ago, just.' He hadn't even taken time to change; he was still dressed formally in his ill-fitting demob suit. It, and his short bristly Army haircut, made him look like a stranger. 'Here, I'll take that.' He took the pail she had been carrying, holding it awkwardly away from his formal clothing as he walked ahead of her, glancing about at the trees.

'Is all this greenery not grand? I've seen nothing but stone and dust and bombed buildings for months now. It's good to be back,' he said and then, as they turned into the yard, 'and this place is as bonny as ever.'

Jennet surveyed the small, solid farmhouse and the flagged courtyard, trying to see it through his eyes, but failing. She was keenly aware that the yard's flag-stones were cracked and that the walls of the outbuild-ings had not been whitewashed for years. Sprigs of grass stuck out above the guttering and the paintwork on all the doors and window frames was sadly in need of attention.

'D'you think so?'

'Oh, aye. It's just grand to be back where the River Clyde's all about you, holding you safe on the one wee lump of green land.'

She blinked, surprised. Struan Blaikie had never been so expressive before the war. 'Your mother must be pleased to see you.'

'Aye, she is,' he said and then blushed scarlet. 'She cried, Jennet. I'd never seen my mother in tears. It was hard tae take.'

Jennet, too, found it hard to imagine Lizbeth Blaikie, deeply religious and ramrod-straight in character as well as in deportment, weeping, yet now that she was a mother herself she could sympathise with the woman. 'You can't blame her,' she said gently. 'After all the worry about you and Allan away fighting, and what happened to Drew.'

'That was a bad thing for them both. For all of us. You'd be upset yourself,' Struan said, a slight upward inflection in his voice, a question in the eyes suddenly fixed intently on her face. 'After all, you were the reason he stayed on.'

'Drew stayed because he felt that someone should go on working the farm with your father,' Jennet said sharply.

'Jennet, he was sweet on you from the time you went into your teens, we all knew that. And you did walk out with him once you left the school . . . for a wee while.'

'Yes, but there were never any promises made, Struan. I was as sorry as anyone else when he was killed, but we weren't sweethearts.'

Though Drew would have liked them to be sweethearts. In that way going off to Glasgow had been a relief, for Jennet had begun to find his interest in her more than she could cope with, especially as both his mother and Celia Scott had made it clear that they were in favour of a match between the two families.

Drew had died just before she returned to Bute, pregnant with Jamie, and ever since then Lizbeth Blaikie had avoided her whenever possible, and had been cold towards her on the few occasions when they were in each other's company. Whether this was because she blamed Jennet for her son's death, or for the shame she had brought to Lizbeth's crony Celia, or even a mixture of both, Jennet had no way of knowing.

'Aye, well, what's done's done,' Struan said now. 'We cannae bring the past back.' Then, lowering his voice slightly, 'What about Angus? How's he doing?'

'Fit as a fiddle, Struan,' Angus said from behind him. 'Never better. But then, I've not been as busy as you over the last few years.'

Struan spun round, startled. 'Man, where did you spring from?'

'I've been sweeping out the byre.' Angus leaned one shoulder against the byre doorframe, taking time to adjust his crutch for balance. 'I'm useful for that sort of thing, if nothing else.'

'It's grand to see you again!' Struan's voice was over-hearty. He began to hold his hand out.

Angus cast a glance down at his right leg, twisted so that his toes only just touched the ground. 'Funny, I never think of saying that when I catch sight of myself in a mirror,' he said, and Struan's hand, ignored, fell back to his side. 'Who'd have thought six years ago that the casualties were going to be Drew and me, the two who stayed behind? And you, Martin and Allan got through the war safe and sound. It makes you laugh, doesn't it?'

'No.'

'It makes me laugh, anyway,' Angus said, with not the shadow of a smile. 'But then, I get so little to laugh about these days.'

Although the air was warm enough, Jennet hugged herself against a sudden chill. 'Have you had any word of our Martin, Struan? We've been expecting him back home any day now.'

'The conquering hero home to claim his inheritance,' Angus agreed. 'At least, that's how Gran sees him. Is he still waiting to be demobbed? We thought he'd mebbe just turn up without warning, the way he usually did when he got leave.'

'Aye, I did see him just a few weeks ago.' Struan licked his lips, glancing nervously from brother to sister, then said in a rush of words, 'That's why I came over here right away, to get the matter settled.'

'What's happened?' Jennet asked sharply. 'He's . . . he can't be wounded, surely? Not now that it's all over and done with!'

'He's fine. It's just that . . . he's not coming back to Bute. To the farm. To . . .' Struan stopped, and it was left to Angus to say, 'To us. That's what you've come to say, isn't it? He's turned his back on us.'

'He might come home later, you never know.' Struan struggled to find the right words. 'The war's unsettled a lot of the lads. Some of them were desperate to get back to normal, like me, but others . . . Life's changed too much for them to be the way they were.'

Jennet and Angus stared at each other; this was the last thing they had expected. 'What'll Grandmother say?' Jennet voiced the thought in both their minds. 'Who's going to tell her?'

'Look, I have to go. I just dropped my kitbag off at home and told them that I needed to come here before . . .' Struan stopped as Celia Scott called from the farmhouse door.

'Struan Blaikie, is that you? Come in here at once. My, you look smart.' She came striding towards the three of them. 'Did Jennet not even offer you a cup of tea and a homemade scone? What are you thinking of, lassie, keeping the man standing in the yard and him just back from fighting for his country?'

'I was just going, Mrs Scott . . . I've just arrived . . .' Struan bleated, taking a couple of steps back.

Even though she was in shock at the news he had brought, Jennet was amused by his panic. Celia no longer used the cane that had once hung on the kitchen wall and was still kept in her bedroom, but her tongue lashed and stung and her eyes poked and prodded as her forefinger had once done. Full-grown though they now were, those who had been afraid of her when they were children still felt uneasy in her presence.

When she said, 'Nonsense, you're not setting foot off this farm without some hospitality inside you,' then headed back towards the house without a backward glance, Struan could only look helplessly at Jennet and Angus before plodding across the courtyard, his shoulders slumped and his feet suddenly dragging.

Following him, with the familiar shuffle and thump of Angus's progress at her back, Jennet wondered how they were going to tell Grandmother that Martin – the apple of her eye, the saviour she had been waiting for all those long weary war years – was not after all going to come home to the farm that she had been struggling to maintain for him.

6

'You'll have a drop of whisky to celebrate your homecoming.'

'No, no, Mrs Scott, I cannae do that.' Struan, more or less forced into the most comfortable armchair in the kitchen, looked anything but relaxed. 'My mother wouldn't like it and I'm just on my way back home.'

Celia looked at him with genuine warmth in her eyes. She had always liked the three Blaikie lads. 'Would you just listen to yourself, man . . . You've been fighting for your country all over the world and now here you are, fretting about your mother smelling drink on your breath.' Then, as Struan blushed and floundered, she added, 'But that's nothing to be shamed of. You'll just have the whisky in your tea, then.' And before he could do more than squeak a protest, she had tipped the bottle up and poured a generous measure into his cup, saying over her shoulder, 'Jennet, butter some scones while Struan tells us all about his travels.'

'I'd not call them that, Mrs Scott.' Struan took a mouthful of tea and blinked at the strength of its alcoholic content. 'We . . .' he cleared his throat, then went on, 'we just went where we were taken. Half the time we'd no notion where we were. And there was little to see but mud and bits of houses.'

'Your mother said you were in Germany at the end, same as our Martin.'

'Aye, that's right.'

'That's why neither of you got home as soon as the fighting was over. Though Martin should have been, with the farm to see to and all.' Celia's voice was heavy with resentment 'Not that he should have gone at all, being a farmer.'

'He wanted to do his bit for his country,' Angus said harshly from the corner, where he leaned against the wall. 'Same as the rest of us.'

'And a fine headache that idea caused me one way and another,' his grandmother snapped. 'It's been nothing but heartbreak for me these past five or six years!'

Jennet, embarrassed, tried to smile at Struan as she handed him a buttered scone on a plate. But his gaze was on the inner door.

'Hello,' he said and, turning, Jennet saw Jamie hesitating in the doorway, still drowsy from his afternoon sleep, his light brown hair, soft and curly like her own, tousled from the pillow.

'How did he get out of his cot?' Celia asked. Then, to Jennet, 'You must have left the side down. Have I not told you time and time again that it's dangerous?'

'It was up, but he's learning to climb over it when the mood takes him.'

'Hello, my name's Struan.' The young man held out his big calloused hand. 'What's yours?'

'Speak when you're spoken to, Jamie, and shake hands with Mr Blaikie,' Celia ordered. After glancing at his mother and getting a slight nod of encouragement, Jamie crept forward and put his own small fingers into the waiting palm.

'I didnae catch your name. Are you going to tell me what it is?'

'Jamie Scott.'

'I'm pleased to meet you, Jamie Scott. You're a fine strong laddie, are you no'? Mebbe you'll come over to Gleniffer some time and help me with the farm work.'

'Aye,' Jamie agreed eagerly, and Struan laughed.

'I'll mind that promise when we next need an extra farmhand.'

'Off you go now and play outside,' Celia commanded. Jennet, catching the little boy's wistful glance at the tray of freshly baked scones, split and buttered one for him.

'There you are, that'll keep you going until dinnertime.'

'And ruin his appetite,' Celia said as the child went out into the yard. 'You spoil that bairn, Jennet.'

'He's a nice lad,' Struan volunteered.

'We've done our best by him, given the circumstances,' Celia said, and Jennet felt the colour rise to her face. Struan gave her a swift glance, then crammed the last of the scone into his mouth and washed it down with a big gulp of tea.

'So what are your plans now you're back with us?' Celia wanted to know.

'I'll be content enough to work the farm with my dad, and take over when it suits him.'

'I thought mebbe Allan would see it as his duty to come back to the island, seeing as he's the eldest now.'

'He's got no wish to go back to the farming. He's well settled at Uncle Frank's shop and he likes the butcher business well enough. And from what I've heard . . .' Struan's grin flashed out, 'he's got friendly with a Glasgow lassie.'

'Oh?' Curiosity sharpened Celia's voice. 'Lizbeth never mentioned that to me.'

'She doesnae know. Allan says she'd start going on at him to bring the lass here to meet us and name a wedding date. If anything comes of it, he'll tell her in his own good time.'

'Did you see Martin at all when the two of you were in Germany?' Celia asked.

'It's a big place, Gran,' Angus put in. 'That's like asking you if you live next door to someone in Scotland.'

She shot him an irritated look and was opening her mouth to deliver one of her stinging retorts when Struan blurted out, 'Aye, Mrs Scott, I did see him just before I left, as it happens.'

Celia's face lit up with joy; it was on these rare

occasions, Jennet thought, that she caught a glimpse of the beautiful young woman her grandmother had once been. 'Is he well? Did he say when he'll be demobbed?'

A mixture of expressions rushed across Struan's face and the tip of his tongue shot out to moisten his lips. 'As a matter of fact . . .'

'As a matter of fact, Gran, our Martin's not coming home at all,' Angus said from his corner.

Celia wheeled round on him. 'What? Don't be daft, you don't know what you're talking about,' she snapped.

'I know what Struan told me and Jennet out in the yard.' Angus eased himself from the wall and limped over to take hold of the back of the other fireside chair. 'Martin's decided that he prefers life off this island.'

'Angus!' Jennet didn't even realise that she had spoken until the word hung in the air. Her brother looked across at her, one side of his mouth curving up in a strange little smile that had only appeared since his accident. For some reason that escaped Jennet, he enjoyed riling their grandmother, and each time it happened he smirked as though he had scored a mark for himself in some secret game between the two of them.

'Of course he's coming home,' Celia said. 'He has to come home!'

'He doesn't seem to think so. He's found the big wide world, Gran, and he's going to stay in it. Who wouldn't, given the choice?'

'Leave it, Angus,' Struan Blaikie said quietly.

'But . . . he has to come home.' Celia sounded bewildered and confused. She put one hand out behind her and it found and clutched at the table for support, while the other hand flew to her mouth. 'He has to,' she said from behind it in a strange, fluttery voice. Jennet was shocked to see that her grandmother had aged ten years in a few seconds.

'Mrs Scott . . .' Struan was out of his chair in an instant, passing Jennet and taking the older woman's arm in both hands. 'Sit down for a minute.'

He guided her into the chair he had just left, while Jennet, suddenly coming to her senses, flew to refill her grandmother's cup. 'Here, Gran . . .'

'Whisky might be better,' Struan suggested over Celia's bent grey head. It lifted so suddenly that both he and Jennet took a startled step back.

'Whisky? Are you daft? Me that signed the pledge when I was six years old and had to be lifted onto a chair to do it? Whisky's for visitors, and the day one drop of the filthy stuff touches my lips is the day my soul's damned for eternity!' Celia seized the cup from Jennet, drank the hot liquid down, then slammed the cup back onto the saucer with a crash and fixed her piercing grey gaze on Struan.

'Tell me. Tell me every word that he said to you!'

'Well . . .' he swallowed hard. 'As I mind it, he just said that he wanted to see a bit of the world.'

'Has he not been doing that for the past five years, while I've been working my fingers to the bone . . .'

Celia, ignoring any contribution Jennet and Angus had made to the farmwork, thrust her swollen hands, the skin red and cracked, out towards Struan, 'trying to keep his heritage intact for him? Have I not been counting the days till I could hand it all over to him and take a well-earned rest?' Then, suddenly, 'Is it a woman? Is that it?'

'What?' He gaped at her, taken aback.

'Is that what's kept Martin from his duties here? Has he found some woman that wants to keep him from us? One of those women in the services, or mebbe someone in Germany. Is that it? Has he met up with a foreigner who wants him to turn his back on his own blood kin and stay with her in her country?'

'Not as far as I know.'

'Are you sure? We might live on a wee island,' Celia sniffed, 'but we've heard things about our soldiers and the women that chase after them with no thought to the harm they might be doing. Did he not even give you a letter for me?'

'Oh . . . aye,' he suddenly remembered, fishing in one pocket and then changing his mind and going into another. Finally he brought out an envelope, glancing at the name on the front before holding it out. 'This is for you,' he said and then, as it was snatched from his hand, 'my father says to tell you that him and me'll do all we can to help. He says he'll be over later to see you.'

'Your father's been very good to us, Struan, but he

shouldn't have to go on helping out. Martin has to come home!'

'He's a man, not a child, Gran,' Angus pointed out. 'He's been fighting for his country for the past five years. He'll do as he wants.'

'He'll do his duty!'

'I'm sure Martin will come back . . . eventually.' Struan stood before her like a naughty child hauled from the safety of his desk to explain himself to the teacher. 'Once he gets over all that's happened to him in the past few years.'

'All that's happened to *him*?' Celia emphasised the final word and then skirled a high-pitched derisive laugh. 'He survived, didn't he? What more does he want from life? Well, mebbe when his lordship decides he wants to come back, he'll find that he's not wanted any more. Two can play at that game!'

'Mrs Scott, you'd surely not . . .'

'It was good of you to visit and we're all pleased to see you back, Struan,' Celia said dismissively. 'But don't let us keep you from your parents any longer.'

Jennet followed Struan into the yard. 'I'm sorry about . . .' She gestured towards the house.

'D'you think she means it about not letting Martin come home?'

'I don't think she knows what she means right now. She's upset. We'll have to give her time to calm down.'

He pulled his cap on. 'I wish I hadnae had tae be the one tae tell her,' he said, then glanced at the kitchen window, lowering his voice even though they had moved too far away from the house to be heard. 'Martin asked me to give these to you and Angus.' He slid a hand into the pocket he had first reached into and drew out two envelopes identical to the one he had given Celia.

Jennet, too, glanced guiltily at the window before slipping the envelopes deep into the pocket of her big apron. Struan began to turn away, then paused, his eyes on Jamie, who was running about the yard pulling his cart behind him.

'That's a fine wee laddie you've got there. My mother said his father was killed in the fighting.' It was half statement, half question.

'Yes.' Jennet had learned, over the past two and a half years, that the only way to deal with inquisitive questions was to speak in a flat monotone and meet the gaze of the questioner full on. That way she made sure that people were too embarrassed to pry any further.

'It's a shame he didnae live to see his son. You're going to raise him on your own?'

'I am.'

He hesitated and then at last he went, striding over the cracked flagstones with the square-shouldered, cocky walk he had inherited from his father.

Andra and Lizbeth Blaikie both came round that night.

'How are you, Celia?' Mrs Blaikie asked sympathetically.

'As well as can be expected, given the news your Struan brought us today.'

'Aye, he told us. It's a bad do this, Celia,' the farmer said, dropping heavily into a chair by the table.

'A bad do? It's more than that . . . it's downright ingratitude,' his wife snapped. 'What possessed him? Is it a woman, d'you think?'

'Either that or the war's done something to his brain. Jennet, make some tea and bring out that fruit-cake, will you? I don't know what I've done to deserve it all,' Celia said plaintively. 'He's turned out to be just like his father, a weak reed.'

'He wants time to himself after what he's been through,' Angus butted in.

'That's no excuse,' Mrs Blaikie told him. 'Your Martin should know where his duty lies, and it's right here, at Westervoe. Your poor grandmother can't go on for ever, and who's to run the place if he doesn't come home soon?'

'The main thing is what's to be done about the situation he's put you in, Celia,' Andra broke in. 'I'm sure you'll manage, with our help. Now Struan's back, we'll be able to help you with the harvesting and threshing and with anything else that's needed.'

'It's very kind of you, Andra, and I know you mean it, but that's not the right way to run a farm, is it?'

'Ach, don't be daft, woman! I know that you and yours would do the same for me.'

'Aye, if we were able.' Celia cast a contemptuous look at her grandchildren and added, 'But the way we are just now, I doubt if we'd be much use to a jumble sale!'

'So what did he have to say to you?' Angus, collecting eggs with Jamie's help, intercepted Jennet the following day as she returned from a small field where she had been cutting back an unruly hedge.

The ribbon that kept her hair out of her face had slipped; she pulled it off, then began to retie it. 'What did who say?'

'Our dear distant brother, of course,' Angus said impatiently.

'Not much.' Just a few scrawled lines that, in their lack of feeling, had said a lot about Martin's determination to break away from his former life and the people in it. 'That he couldn't face coming back here, that he wants to make his own way in the world.'

'Bad hen!' Jamie's muffled voice scolded from inside one of the wooden arks. There was a flurry and a squawk and then a hen rushed out of the small arched door and fled to join her sisters. Jamie, bent double, followed her out and handed a warm egg to his mother when he had straightened up. 'Here.'

'Thank you.'

'All done,' Jamie announced to his uncle and ran ahead of them as they turned towards the farmhouse.

'I wonder what Martin wrote to Grandmother?' Angus said thoughtfully.

'I doubt if she'll tell us.'

'Did he say anything about our father in your letter?'

Jennet bit her lip. She hadn't wanted to mention that part of Martin's brief letter. His pen had suddenly cut deep into the cheap paper as he wrote, 'I can understand now why our father walked out after our mother died. She must have seemed like his only escape from his sterile upbringing . . . and any life without some sort of love in it is sterile, Jen. He couldn't face going back to his past and I can't face it, either. I want to live, and the only way I can do that is by staying away until I feel strong enough to dominate Gran instead of letting her dominate me. If that day should ever come.'

'Yes,' she said. 'Yes, he did mention him.'

'Damn him!' Angus's voice was suddenly vehement. 'Damn him to hell! Does he think he's the only one who wants to escape from this place?'

'You both make it sound like a prison.'

He gave a derisive laugh. 'Aye, complete with jailer.'

'Gran's old-fashioned, just. She loves us in her own way.'

'Sometimes folk mix up love with possessiveness. I'd have been away with Martin, if it hadn't been for my accident, and you tried to get away too, as soon as you were old enough. You shouldn't have come back.'

Jennet stared at the egg cooling in the curve of her palm. Its shell was pale brown, and downy feather scraps clung to it. Seventeen years old, she had been, pregnant and terrified and alone in a big city.

'I couldn't think of anything but coming home.' She placed the egg carefully into her brother's basket.

Angus dug the end of his crutch into the ground as he swung along by her side. 'More fool you. She made you suffer as much as if you'd committed a crime, and she's been making you suffer ever since. What was there to come home to?'

You, she wanted to say, but dared not for fear of angering him even further. She had been unable to think of anything other than running back to Angus and to Mollie. The two of them had been her safety net at that terrible time.

'You were a fool,' he went on when she said nothing. 'If you'd only written to me first, I'd have told you to stay where . . .'

'That tractor's acting up again,' Jem McKenzie came to meet them as they turned into the yard.

Angus sighed. 'What's wrong with it?'

'How should I know? I'm a farm worker, no' a bloody engineer.'

Jem had worked for the Scott family for more than fifty years, and in a lifetime of knowing him Jennet had never seen the man smile. Old age and resentment at having to go on working, when he should have been enjoying a well-earned retirement, had not sweetened his disposition at all.

'If you really want tae know what I think, I'd say that it feels the way I dae,' he went on. 'It's done its bit for Britain and it's old and just wants tae be left in peace. But it never . . .'

There was a shout of pleasure from Jamie and a mad scramble of paws as Gumrie came dashing into the yard and made straight for the little boy, licking his face while Jamie hugged him.

'Stop that, ye daft animal!' Celia came round the corner, brandishing her sturdy stick at the dog. 'Jamie, how many times have I told ye not tae let him do that?'

'Likes me,' Jamie said. 'My friend.'

'He's a working dog!' his great-grandmother said, exasperated. She had done all she could to make Gumrie behave like a proper farm dog, aloof and dignified, but even though he was well trained and obedient, he still loved people. In Celia Scott's eyes that was a fatal weakness.

'Get out of it,' Jem roared as Gumrie headed towards him. The dog suddenly checked its rush, swinging round and trotting off to bully the two cats sunbathing in a corner, with a casual air that said that was what he had intended to do all along.

'It's not as if the wee soul has any other friends to play with,' Angus pointed out to his grandmother.

'You're surely not suggesting that his mother should have more bairns just to keep him company?' Celia glared at the three of them. 'So all the work's done, then, that you've got nothing else to do but stand there and gossip?'

'I'm just here tae say that the tractor's b-broke down again,' said Jem.

'Can you not fix it?'

'He's a farm worker, no' an engineer,' Angus informed his grandmother, straight-faced.

'It's a pity that wee Sam McCabe's no' here any more. He'd a way wi' gadgets,' Jem said, and Celia's mouth tightened.

'Wc can manage without him and his family. We'd best have a look at it.'

'No' me.' Jem tugged his cap more firmly down on his head. 'I'm away home tae my tea.'

'Already?'

'It's my usual time, and Bessie gets agitated if I'm not back at the right time. It's a long day for her on her lone. She's missin' havin' me about the place tae help with the things she cannae do any more,' Jem added meaningfully. His wife suffered badly from arthritis.

'Oh, very well, if you must. On your way past Gleniffer Farm,' Celia called after the old man as he headed for the lane and freedom, 'you can go in and ask if Andra or Struan could come and have a look at the tractor tomorrow morning.'

Jem turned and gave her what Ann Logan would have called an old-fashioned look. It was understandable, for the lane that led down to the Blaikie farm was long, and the old man's walk home would be doubled in length by the time the message was delivered.

Then he turned back a second time, his gloom lightening a little now that he had remembered more bad news. 'That dry-stane dyke down by the shore field's beginnin' tae crumble. Best see tae it afore one of the cows gets out and manages tae drown itself,' he advised and then disappeared round the corner as Celia gave a huff of exasperation.

'Angus, you'd better candle these eggs and clean them while we look at the wall.'

'I'll go with you, and Jennet can see to the eggs. She looks as if she could do with a rest.'

'We could all do with a rest, but by the time you get down there the whole wall could have crumbled. Your sister and me can manage between us,' Celia said scathingly and marched off without a backward glance.

7

Jennet, not daring to look at her brother's face, scurried in her grandmother's wake, fury boiling up inside her. She waited until they were out of the yard and into the narrow lane leading down past the two fields that lay between the farm and the Firth of Clyde before she said, 'There was no need to speak to Angus like that.'

'Like what? I said nothing but the truth and if he's not man enough to take it, that's his concern. You're too soft, Jennet. We all know that he cannae do a man's work any more.'

'He does all he can.'

'Mebbe, but it's not enough, so I'm not minded to give him a medal for it.' Celia stopped for a moment and swung round to face her granddaughter. 'We're farming folk, lassie, no' the landed gentry. And on a farm there's no room for sentiment. If an animal cannae earn its keep, it has to go.'

'So you're suggesting that we should send Angus to the slaughterhouse?'

'You're not too old to get a clout round the ear when you've earned it, madam!' Celia dealt the grass by the side of the lane a hefty swish with the stick she always carried. 'I'm saying that now that your brother's lame, he has tae accept that there's things he cannae do any more. If we waited for him to hop and shuffle around the place with that crutch of his, nothing would get done. Now stop talking and keep walking, for we've not got all day.'

There were indeed the beginnings of a break in the dry-stane wall between the lower field and the narrow strip of shore, where two or three of the top level of boulders had tumbled. Jennet clambered over the wall and the two women worked silently, one on each side, heaving the boulders back into place, then wedging them there with smaller stones until, at last, Celia was satisfied.

Before leaving she walked the length of the wall, searching for any other weak points, while Jennet followed, her own eyes straying to the view she had loved all her life, in all weathers. The Scott farm was on the west of the island, looking across the pearly waters of the Sound of Bute, a narrow section of the Firth of Clyde, to the island of Arran, its mountain range known, because of its distinctive outline, as the Sleeping Warrior.

When she turned away from the river, the inland view of fields and trees was just as beautiful. The road ran along a low hillside, and from it Westervoe, tucked into a dip in the fields, was scarcely seen. She glimpsed several cyclists at a bend in the road before they were hidden by trees, though the musical ting of a bell and the faint sound of voices and laughter rang through the air as they passed. The island was already bursting with holidaymakers, and she had heard that every steamer that arrived from the mainland carried a full complement of passengers.

Jennet loved every part of the island, but Angus was right when he said that, to them, Westervoe was more of a prison than a home. Perhaps that was how it felt to her grandmother, too. Like Jennet, Celia Scott had been born and raised there; her husband had moved there after their marriage; and when he died tragically young, Celia had worked hard to keep the place going for the sake of her son James, who had not been much older than Jamie was now.

When James grew up and married and began to raise his own family, Celia must have felt as though a load had lifted from her shoulders. But his wife's death and then his own desertion had left her with three grandchildren to tend, as well as the farm. No wonder, Jennet thought, her grandmother had become bitter. And no wonder Martin's decision not to come home had been the final straw.

'Jennet! Stop dreaming and get a move on.' Celia was already halfway up the lane, the hem of her long mackintosh swinging around the top of her wellington boots. She had two coats for farm work: the mackintosh for summer and a thick tweedy coat for the colder weather. Both were very old, but durable. A man's hat was jammed on her head throughout all the seasons.

Would it have been better if Celia had given up and let the farm go, or accepted the Logans' offer to raise her grandchildren? In some ways Jennet wished that that had happened, but in another . . .

She glanced back at the Sound of Bute and knew why her grandmother had held on through the long, hard years. She would do the same, if it were for Jamie's sake.

As the Scott family dwindled in size, so did Westervoe Farm; now it was so small that it could support only a thousand hens, the two pigs bought in each year for fattening and about fifteen cows, each of them named and with her own personality.

Today a young animal, new to milking following the birth of her first calf, got into the wrong stall by accident, and her panic when she realised her error, together with the chaos she caused among the others, reminded Jennet of a group of elderly, respectable women who had wandered into a public house in error, mistaking it for a cake shop.

'Here, Gloria, in here!' Most of the cows were named after flowers, but Mollie had insisted on calling the new cow after Gloria Swanson, the American film actress. With help from Angus, Jennet shooed her into the proper stall and untangled the others.

While his mother and uncle resolved the problem, washed the cow's udders and then settled to the milking, Jamie bustled happily up and down the line, issuing a pat here and a reprimand there.

Hand-milking had become one of Jennet's favourite pastimes. In the winter the byre was warm compared to outside, and in summer, when the farming day stretched from dawn until dusk, it gave her a chance to sit still for a while, listening to the cows chewing contentedly at the chopped turnips in their feeding troughs, and leaning against their warm flanks as she worked. Sometimes it was even possible to drowse off while her hands automatically squirted the milk into the bucket. On more than one occasion the cow had wakened her with a gentle nudge when the bucket was full, although with one of the more temperamental animals Jennet might well be roused by a sudden shifting of her support, which almost sent her crashing from the stool, or the bucket would be tipped over by a carefully aimed back hoof.

Today Gloria managed to surprise Jennet by suddenly swishing her tail, sending its tip into the creaming milk.

'Oh, Gloria, look what you've done!'

The cow, surprised at the sudden fuss, looked round at Jennet with large, naïve eyes that bore no trace of her namesake's sultry gaze, while Jamie came scurrying up to inspect the damage. 'Naughty cow, no sweeties this week!' he scolded. And Jennet, milk dripping from her dungarees, only just managed to rescue the pail before it tipped over entirely.

'It'll do for her calf,' Angus advised, rising stiffly

from his seat in the next stall. 'D'you want me to finish her? The rest are done anyway.'

'She is finished . . . She waited until the last minute.' Jennet stooped to pick up the pail. 'I'll get changed, then take this in to the calf while you and Jem take the animals back out.'

Struan Blaikie had arrived to look at the tractor, looking more like himself now that he had replaced his demob suit with heavy corduroy trousers and an open-necked shirt, though the ugly Army haircut, bristly and cropped close to the skull, still set him apart from the Struan she remembered, with his unruly tumble of blue-black hair. He grinned when Jennet emerged from the byre opposite, milk dripping from her clothes, and called across the yard, 'Throwin' yourself intae the work, eh?'

'Something like that,' she agreed, going into the house with Jamie trotting by her side. When they emerged, the cows, well able to find their way back to their field without assistance, were heading out of the yard, with Jem, Angus and Gumrie ambling along behind them.

Normally Jamie would have run to join them, but he had made a particular pet of Gloria's calf, so today he was happy to follow his mother into the calf shed. Watching him struggle to hold the pail steady while the little creature thrust her woolly head into it and sucked noisily at the milk, Jennet dreaded the day she would be taken to market. The Scotts, like most of the farming folk, had formerly sold only the bullocks and raised the heifers for their own milk herd, but a few years back Celia had decided that the calves were too time-consuming that it would be easier to sell them all on and buy in heifers when needed.

'He's going to make a fine farmer when his time comes.' Struan, rubbing oil from his hands with a rag, came to lean on the lower half of the double door to watch Jamie with the calf.

'He might not get the chance, the way things are going.'

'Is your gran still angry with Martin?'

'She'll not have his name mentioned.'

'She'll come round,' he said unconvincingly and then opened the lower part of the door and came into the shed, lowering his voice. 'I was wondering if you fancied a visit to the pictures on Friday?'

'Me?' She stared at him, taken aback. 'I don't know, Struan. I've got Jamie to see to, and I doubt if my grandmother . . .'

'I'd really like it if you'd come,' he urged. 'There's a Western picture on at the Ritz; with that Roy Rogers in it. And a scary picture with Boris Karloff at the Palace. You could choose.'

She hesitated. She hadn't been to the cinema or a dance – or even a party – since Jamie's birth. Somehow she had fallen into the habit of thinking that she had forfeited the right to pleasure or frivolity.

'There's surely plenty of girls you know that would be pleased to go with you.'

'I'd as soon go with you, and I'm sure you deserve

a wee night out every bit as much as I . . .'

He spun round guiltily as Celia said from just behind him, 'There you are, Struan. How's the tractor?'

He snapped to attention. 'I've not quite finished with it, Mrs Scott. It'll only take another five minutes.'

'Then don't let us keep you back. I hope Jennet's invited you in for a cup of tea?'

'I was going to,' Jennet said, 'but . . .'

'I was just asking if she'd like to go to the pictures with me, Mrs Scott,' Struan butted in, his face flushing. 'Friday, I thought. Would that be all right?'

'The pictures?' Celia looked from one to the other. 'Well, mebbe it's time you had a night out, Jennet. I'll see to the child for you.'

'Are you sure?'

'Just tell the man yes, before I change my mind,' her grandmother said. 'I'll make the tea.'

'So it's all right then?' Struan asked Jennet as Celia went into the house.

'I don't . . .'

'Your gran says it is.'

'Then why don't you take her?' Jennet asked, suddenly exasperated. 'What did you want to go and tell her about it for?'

'I just wanted to be sure that it was all right.'

'I'm a grown woman, Struan Blaikie. I can decide these things for myself.'

'Does that mean yes?'

She opened her mouth to argue and then decided

that it was not worth the effort. 'I suppose so,' she said ungraciously. 'Why not?'

Struan beamed. 'I'll call for you at half past six then.'

'I'll meet you at the bus stop. And Struan?'

'Aye?'

'We'll go to the Western,' Jennet said.

To Celia's annoyance, the tractor was not going to be repaired easily. It required a new part, and these days spare parts were not easy to come by.

'I might be able to find one,' Struan offered while he was having his tea. 'We've got an old machine that's not used any more and if I can't get what you need from it, I could try round the other farms. Some of them got more modern machines during the war, so they could have older tractors, like yours, sitting in their sheds. If I can't find anything, I'll have to order the part, but with shortages still making everything difficult I don't know when it'll get here. It's getting a wee bit old, too, and that might make it more difficult to get the part.'

'Well, do your best, for I'd like it to see our time out. It's not worth putting the money out on a new machine, even if we had that sort of money to throw about.'

'I'll do what I can, Mrs Scott.'

'You're a good lad,' Celia said fondly. 'Have another oatcake.'

* * *

The following day Celia surprised her grandchildren by arriving downstairs dressed in the black costume and ivory silk blouse that she wore for weddings, funerals and Women's Rural Institute activities and announcing that she had decided to pay a visit to her sister Rachel in Largs, a coastal town on the mainland.

'I've not been to see her for a good long while and, after all, she is my only sister.'

'Since the mountain won't come to Mahomet . . .' Angus murmured as Jennet handed his plate to him. She turned a giggle into a cough. Celia's younger sister, plumper but just as strong-willed, rarely visited Bute, for she disliked crossing the water and she loathed animals. She had been more than happy, while still in her teens, to marry an office worker and exchange her island farm home for the mainland.

'What's that you said, Angus?' Celia asked from the stove, where she was cooking, having covered her 'good' clothes with a large apron to prevent splashes.

'I was just clearing my throat. We'll manage fine, Gran.'

'I doubt that, but there's not much to do today that can go wrong, and Jem will be coming.'

She departed immediately after breakfast, and as her back view disappeared down the lane leading to the road and the bus stop, the atmosphere seemed to undergo a change. Even Gumrie's shining eyes took on an added sparkle and Angus went about his work with energy and enthusiasm, deftly utilising his crutch so that it became a natural part of his body, instead of a clumsy man-made contraption of wood, leather and padding.

If only he could be left alone to get on with things in his own way all the time, Jennet thought, watching him. Ever since the accident Celia had treated him like a helpless child, refusing to allow him to do anything that might hurt or upset him. Meanwhile, Jennet looked on helplessly, certain that Angus was being damaged both mentally and emotionally, as well as physically, but unsure what to do about it.

Then the McCabes had arrived and Mollie, heedless of Celia's silent fury, had taken it upon herself to get Angus back onto his feet. The Glasgow girl had teased, nagged and coaxed him day after day, blithely indifferent to his sullen resentment. At first he had taken refuge in silence, but once she had managed to goad him into shouting back at her, Mollie began to dare him to take control of his own life and get back on his feet. She had been like a terrier baiting a bull, dancing in close enough to sting and then darting off, deflecting all his anger and his insults with her wide grin until, finally, he had given in.

It had taken a whole year, and all the time Celia had simmered like a kettle on a low heat, saying nothing openly to Mollie but undermining her efforts as much as she could. Then came the day when Angus stumped into the kitchen on his two crutches and tossed one into a corner, then he did a lap round the big table with only the other crutch for support.

'And that one I keep,' he told Mollie, 'so that I've got something to hit you with when you get too cheeky.'

She stuck out her tongue at him. 'You'd have to catch me first.'

'Oh, I'll do that all right,' he said and flourished his free arm, like a magician who had just performed a particularly difficult trick and was inviting the audience's applause. 'What d'you think, Gran?'.

Celia had turned from the range, surveyed him and then said dourly, 'You'd best sit in. Your dinner's ready.'

The day passed all too quickly. Jem worked with a will when Celia was not there to boss him around, and even the animals cooperated. When Celia arrived back early in the evening the work had been completed and Jamie was being bathed in the old tin tub in front of the kitchen range. For once the three of them had turned bath-time into a game and when Celia marched in the little boy, over-excited, screeched, 'G'eat g'an!' and waved a wet soapy arm joyfully in the air.

'Look at that . . . water all over my good rug! Sit still and behave yourself,' she admonished him.

'He's just pleased to see you,' Angus told her.

'He doesnae need to soak the place to prove it.' Celia drew three large hatpins from her hat, then removed it without ruffling one iron-grey hair. 'Make a cup of tea, Jennet, while I get changed. The steamer home was packed with folk, and their boxes and bags and cases were all over the deck. A body could scarcely move! And Rothesay's no better – bairns running about everywhere when they should be home and in their beds.'

'They're on holiday, Gran.'

'That's no excuse to let their standards go, Angus. Badly behaved bairns grow up to be badly behaved adults.'

'How was Great-Aunt Rachel?' Jennet made a fresh pot of tea while keeping an anxious eye on Jamie, praying that he wouldn't slop water over the side of the bath.

'Very well. She sends her regards to you both. I'll be back down in a minute.'

When Celia had gone, Jennet whipped a protesting Jamie out of his bath and hurried him into his pyjamas, then left Angus to give him his supper of bread and milk while she emptied and dried the bath, put it away and mopped the floor.

While Celia, back in her usual work clothes, drank her tea, Jennet put Jamie to bed and then went downstairs to dish out the supper. All through the meal Celia harangued them about idle, slatternly holidaymakers who didn't know what it was like to have to work all year round and never have time for luxuries like holidays. Afterwards she insisted on shutting up the hens herself, in order, Angus pointed out, to have the chance to check that everything had been done to her satisfaction.

'I don't care,' Jennet said from the sink where she

was washing the dishes. 'She can inspect all she wants, it's just nice not to have to do the hens for once.'

By the time Celia arrived back the kitchen was cleared and tidy for the night. Jennet took the opportunity to go out and weed the garden, leaving the other two talking about the haymaking, which was soon to start. The garden was an added chore, but she enjoyed working in it; out there she could be on her own for once, and was able to let her mind range free while her hands worked.

Haymaking should be good this year, she thought as she teased weeds from between the rows of carrots. The weather was fine and if the rain stayed away, then the hay, which had to be left lying in the field once it was cut so that it could be turned and turned and thoroughly dried, should do well.

When the midges became too much to bear she poured several scoops of water from the butt over the growing plants, then eyed the well-tended beds with satisfaction. It had been a good day all round, and now she was ready for her bed.

She had reached the living room when she heard raised voices from beyond the door leading to the kitchen. All at once the peace and tranquillity of the day ebbed away.

8

'You can't just wipe him off the map like that . . . He's your own grandson,' Angus was saying. 'You raised him!'

'Aye, I did, and if I'd known what a worthless, thankless young man he was going to become, I'd have thrashed it out of him while I still had him in my charge!'

'Mebbe you thrashed it into him,' Angus suggested as Jennet came into the kitchen.

Celia drew in her breath with an outraged hiss. 'You dare to say that to me? The belt's the only thing bairns understand, and if they grow up wrong it's because of a lack of it, not too much. As far as I'm concerned, your brother's no longer part of this family.'

Jennet, fearful that the raised voices might disturb Jamie, closed the door behind her. 'You can't pretend Martin doesn't exist, Gran. What if he needs us, or wants to come home?'

'Then want must be his master.' Celia's voice, hard

as flint, dredged up a favourite saying of hers, one that had been dinned into her three growing grand-children. 'I want him here right now, but he's not here, is he? As to whether I can put him out of our lives, I can do whatever I wish and you'd both be wise to remember that.'

'You can do what you must, but I'll not shut my own brother out of my life,' Angus told her.

'Then you're a fool. He's let you down as well, leaving all of us to go off to the war when he should have stayed here where he belonged, working this farm. But, oh no, not Martin. All he could think of was having a fine adventure, and never mind his duty.'

'That was more my fault than his. I was the one who came up with the idea of us going to enlist along with Geordie Logan.'

'And look at us now . . . you dependent on a crutch, your cousin dead and your brother refusing to come back home.'

Angus winced, but persisted. 'He's still our own flesh and blood.'

'So am I, and when does anyone consider my feel-ings?' Celia's voice rose. 'Not one of you ever thinks about the struggle I've had to keep the place together so that Martin could inherit it and work it.'

'Angus's the oldest,' Jennet said, and Celia stared at her.

'What?'

'It's not Martin who should take over the farm anyway. Angus is the oldest.'

'Don't be daft!'

'Angus knows about farming. He won the ploughing competition two years in a row, and . . .'

'Leave it, Jen,' her brother said gruffly.

'Aye, stay out of things that don't concern you!' Celia stood with both hands clamped over the back of a kitchen chair, glaring at the two of them and breathing hard through her nose. Jennet was reminded of a carthorse she had once seen at the cattle show in Rothesay, a great fearsome creature with the same fierce stare and the same way of blowing air through its flaring nostrils.

'I'm an old woman and mebbe it's time you both minded that. I'd already decided to go and stay with my sister Rachel in Largs once your brother came back to take over the farm, and I see no reason why I should change my plans. She's been on at me to go over there for years now, so I've decided that come Martinmas I'm giving the factor six months' notice to find a new tenant.'

Now it was Jennet's turn to say 'What?' She looked at her brother and, when he just looked back at her stony-faced, continued, 'Angus, d'you hear that?'

'I've already heard it. Why else d'you think we were arguing when you came in?'

'After all these years you surely can't just walk away from this place?' Jennet asked her grandmother in disbelief.

'Everything has to come to an end. I should have moved out years ago, when your father got married, but since he saw fit to marry a lassie who knew nothing about farming, I'd to stay on to teach her the way of it. Not that she ever showed much ability for it,' Celia said. 'And the next thing I knew, they were both gone and I was left with the three of you on my hands. But now the time's come for me to let it all go to someone else.'

'We can surely manage,' Jennet protested. 'There's men coming back to the island from the war, needing work. We can hire the folk we need.'

'And what do we pay them with? This place hasnae made much money for a good while now. It's only the bigger farmers, like Andra Blaikie, that can afford to hire workers. I've been hard put to it to find the rent these past few years . . . But you'd not know anything about that, would you? It's left to me, as usual.'

'We'd have been more than willing to be involved, Grandmother, if you'd only given us the chance,' Jennet protested. Then, as Celia's nostrils flared again, she went on hurriedly, 'There must be things we can do to make more money.'

'Indeed? Mebbe you'd tell me about them, milady, since you're so smart!'

The contempt in her words whipped heat into Jennet's face, but she forged on. 'We could take in holidaymakers. There's the cottage the McCabes used.'

Celia gave a screech of contemptuous laughter. 'Trippers? Folk from Glasgow and the like? We'd just be makin' more work for ourselves.'

'We could use part of the money they'd bring in to pay a woman to do the cooking and cleaning, then you and me would be free to work outside with Angus and Jem. And there might be enough left to hire a young lad willing to learn farmwork. Quite a lot of the farms let out their spare rooms – the estate allows it.' Bute was owned by the Marquess of Bute, who lived in Mount Stuart, a splendid estate on the island. The Scotts, like almost all the other farmers on the island, were tenants.

'I'll not have strangers making free of this house!' Celia thundered.

'That'll happen anyway, if you let Westervoe go to new tenants.'

'And where do you suggest we should live when you've handed the farm over?' Angus asked swiftly as Celia rounded on Jennet. She contented herself with a narrow-eyed glare, then turned back to him.

'That's what Rachel and me were talking about today. She's got a ground-floor room you can have, Angus, and Jennet can go back to learn nursing in Glasgow.'

'I couldn't manage to take Jamie with me.'

'Of course not. He'll stay with Rachel and me while you're training.'

'But I . . .'

'Beggars can't be choosers, Jennet. He's well behaved for a child, and he can live with you once you've finished your training and you're able to support him. I hope you realise that it's very good of my sister to offer to take the three of us in.'

'So it's all been settled already, without consulting us,' Angus said.

'I'm discussing it with you now, and you can't deny that I've still got your welfare at heart. The welfare of all three of you,' Celia added.

'And Angus is expected to leave his home and the island, just like that?'

'He's not got much of a choice, have you, son? How could you manage without me to look after you?'

Angus bit his lip while Jennet watched him anxiously, willing him to tell Celia that he would have nothing to do with her plans. Instead, he lurched to his feet. 'I'm going to my bed.'

'Gran . . .' Jennet began when he had gone.

'Don't give me any more trouble than you already have, Jennet. Everything's decided and it's time we were all in our beds.' Celia got up, pausing on her way out of the room to give her granddaughter a long, level look. 'You know that your brother can't run this place on his lone, so the three of us must settle for what's best, like it or not.'

It was Celia Scott's proud boast that once her head hit the pillow she was asleep. And it was a known fact that once she fell asleep nothing roused her, until her eyes flew open on the stroke of five-thirty in the morning.

She was ignorant of the summer nights when her grandsons had gone out, first to play and later to court local girls, or when Jennet had slipped out to sit and giggle with Mollie McCabe in the warmth of the cowshed, or had tiptoed down to Angus's room, as she did that night, to talk to him.

He was still awake, reading by the light of the paraffin lamp on his bedside table.

'What are we going to do?' Jennet asked, settling on the side of the bed.

He turned a page. 'You're going back to your bed and I'm going to get on with my reading.'

'You're not. You're going to help me decide what we're going to do about Grandmother's plans.'

'The way I see it, things are already decided. The estate will find another tenant farmer. On the other hand, I don't know what's going to happen at the end of this book, so if you'll just go back to your own room and leave me in peace, I can find out before . . . Hey!' he finished indignantly as she whipped the book from his hands.

'The butler did it – so now you don't have to go all the way to the end of the book to find out.' She closed it and put it on the chest of drawers, out of his reach. 'Angus, we can't just stand by and let Grandmother give Westervoe to new tenants. It's yours by right, not hers to throw away as if it was an old coat.'

'For pity's sake, Jen, she's quite right. How can I run a farm?'

'You can manage to do a fair bit yourself, and you could get someone in . . . Bert McCabe might come back to work for you, and there's plenty of lads just out of the school and willing to learn . . .'

'And where would I find the money to pay all those workers?'

'We could find ways. We have to do something,' she challenged. Then, as he leaned back and glared at her, 'D'you really want to go and live in Great-Aunt Rachel's house?'

A shadow crossed his face, but he only said, 'Jen, when that train went off the rails at Saltcoats, I lost the right to make my own decisions. We're not strong enough to stop Grandmother once she's made up her mind. Anyway, she's done her best by us and she deserves a rest. We forget how old she is.'

'Mebbe *she* deserves to stop working so hard, but *you've* still got most of your life in front of you! I couldn't bear to see you shut away in that house in Largs,' she said passionately. 'It would drive you mad, and you know it!'

'Never mind about what's going to happen to me; just you get back to your nursing and make a living for you and Jamie. That's the important thing.'

'I'll not leave Jamie with Grandmother.' A sudden, violent shiver shook Jennet's body. 'I couldn't do that to him. I might not even get him back, Angus!'

'Of course you will. D'you think she'd want the trouble of raising another generation of this family? Think about it,' he urged, leaning towards her. 'It'll only be for a few years at most.'

'A few years? He'll have started school by then and I'll not be there to see him through that. You know what he's like, Angus, he changes and grows every day and I'll have missed all of that!'

'You can't manage to look after him and study as well. I'll be with him in Largs; I'll keep an eye on him and see to it that he knows why you're not there, and why he has to wait a wee while before you can fetch him and make a home for the two of you. I'll make sure you never lose him.'

She looked at him in despair. Angus had always been the one to see that things were all right for her. It was Angus who had stood up for her when Martin and the Blaikie lads got tired of her tagging after them and tried to keep her out of their games; Angus who had helped with her homework and taught her how to play conkers, and lifted her up to ride in front of him on the big Clydesdale horses; Angus who had carried her over the deepest streams and rubbed her nettle-stung legs with dock leaves, and scooped water from a puddle once, to cool a nasty swelling bump on her forehead after a fall.

But this time he was wrong. This time she had to do the thinking for both of them. She ground the heels of her hands into her tired eyes and forced herself to review their options carefully. And an answer came almost at once.

'If you promise to think about taking over the farm I'll ask Aunt Ann to look after Jamie for me. It would leave me free to help you take over the tenancy.'

'There's no point in even discussing it, for it's out of the question.' He started to haul pillows from behind his head, dropping them on the floor. 'It's getting late and, since I'm to be denied my book, I might as well go to sleep.' Only one pillow remained now; he settled his head on it and drew the bedclothes up to his ears, turning his back on her. 'Goodnight, Jen,' he said, his voice muffled in the pillow. 'Put the lamp out before you go, will you?'

In Jennet's mind, Struan Blaikie was still a childhood friend – more than that, another brother – and it seemed daft to be going out with him, she thought on Friday evening as she slipped on her only decent summer dress. And if Struan hoped that there might be more to their evening out than just a jaunt to the pictures, she would nip that in the bud right away.

After a hunt she found the lipstick she had carefully hoarded in those carefree days when she and Mollie had gone together to the pictures and dancing in Rothesay, and ran it over her mouth. A small bottle of Evening in Paris lay beside it in the drawer; she sniffed at it, then dabbed it behind her ears, her knees and on her wrists. Not enough to drive Struan wild with desire, but possibly enough to mask any farmyard smells that might be lingering about her person.

Then she gave her hair a good hard brushing in an attempt to tame it, and went downstairs to the kitchen.

'Ooohh!' Jamie said, awed by the sight of his mother dressed for once as a woman. Angus came out from behind his newspaper and eyed her up and down, then grinned.

'Very nice. You should dress like that more often.'

'I would like to, but I daren't – it would probably drive the hens wild and put them off the lay.'

'Have you not got some powder to take the shine off your nose?' Celia, always the faultfinder, wanted to know. 'I think I might have a powder puff somewhere.'

'There's no point, Gran; my face is so weather-beaten the powder would probably fall off. I've given my shoes a good rub and that should be enough.'

'You'll do, I suppose. Now then, Jamie, come here; you'll just crush your mother's nice skirt,' Celia said, and hauled at the little boy, who was clutching Jennet's knees and demanding to be lifted. As she crossed the yard Jennet heard him calling after her. How could she possibly go off to Glasgow and leave him behind for weeks, mebbe months at a time, she asked herself? It would break her heart, and goodness knows what it might do to Jamie.

Struan was waiting at the bus stop, dressed in his demob suit, with a clean white shirt and tie. His face shone, as though he had taken a scrubbing brush to it, and his hair had been well slicked down Jennet's heart sank when she saw that he had put more effort into this evening than she had.

To her embarrassment he insisted on paying her fare on the bus and on paying her into the Ritz Picture House, which was busy. If he tried to put his arm about her, Jennet thought as the lights began to dim, she would die! Fortunately he kept his hands to himself, and after the first half hour she began to relax, although she wasn't sure that she had chosen well, for the Western, with its wide-open plains and its cattle and horses, reminded her too strongly of the farm and the problems facing them all. Even Roy Rogers' bravery and his pleasant singing voice failed to lull her away from her own worries for more than five minutes at a time. She wondered, briefly, if she should have opted for the Palace Picture House and its Boris Karloff offering, but its title, *The Old Dark House*, sounded too like Westervoe as it was at the moment, with an atmosphere of gloom hanging over it.

When they left the cinema, blinking as they made the transition from dark to dusk, Struan suggested a visit to a café for a drink before catching the bus back home.

'You look different,' he said across the table.

'I'm wearing a skirt instead of britches.'

'No, it's not that. Something's bothering you. Is it to do with Martin? Have you heard from him?'

'No, and even if we did, Grandmother's decided to disown him.'

'She'd never do that!'

'Would she not? She says she's going to tell the factor next rent day to find another tenant for the place.' Rent days came twice a year, in May and November. Any farmer wishing to end his tenancy had to wait until the next rent day, then put in six months' notice of his intentions.

'But what'll you do? Where'll you go?'

'She's got it worked out that she's taking Angus and Jamie to her sister's in Largs and I'm to go back to my nursing training in Glasgow.'

Struan frowned, then asked, 'Is that what you want?'

'Of course not. For one thing, I don't want Angus to lose the farm. He loves it and all his life he's looked forward to becoming the tenant. But now Gran says he's not able.'

'I'm sure he could manage with some help. It wasnae his head that got hurt, just one leg.'

'That's what I said.' She looked at him with gratitude. 'I wish you'd speak to him, Struan. He's all set to do whatever Gran wants, and I know that it'll just make him miserable for the rest of his life if he lets her give Westervoe up.'

'I'll have a word with him,' Struan promised. 'We'd best hurry if we're to get the next bus.'

After the town, with its street and house lights, the countryside seemed very dark when they left the bus. It took a minute or two to adjust to the change, and when they did they discovered that the sky, so dark a moment before, was filled with stars.

Struan sniffed the air and gave a sigh of pleasure. 'A grand night. We might be able to start cutting the hay soon if this weather holds.'

'Mebbe. Well, goodnight, Struan, mind and talk to Angus soon, will you?'

'I'll walk you home.'

'Don't be daft, I just live down the lane.'

'Even so,' he said, putting a hand beneath her elbow.

They walked the length of the lane in silence; Jennet was happy to be left in peace to listen to the murmur of the night breeze in the trees, the muted scuffling of small animals in the long grass and the occasional mournful call of an owl, out hunting for food. Then the stables blanked out a square wedge of starlit sky, marking the entrance to the yard.

'Here we are, safe and sound.' Jennet turned and looked up at Struan, a faceless figure against the starry night. 'Thank you for this evening, Struan, I enjoyed it. I'll not ask you in, for they'll be in their beds by now.'

'Aye, it'll be the same at home.'

'Goodnight, then.'

'I was thinking, Jennet,' he said.

'Thinking about what?' If he was about to ask her to go out again, she would say no. Pleasant though the evening had been, she had neither the desire nor the time to let it become a regular event.

But it was not another outing to the pictures that Struan had in mind. 'I was thinking,' he said, 'that it would make sense for us to get wed. To each other, I mean.'

For a moment Jennet was too taken aback to say anything. When she found her voice she said the first thing that came into her mind. 'It would be a lot of nonsense, you mean!'

'You're against it, then?'

'Of course I'm against it. What on earth made you come up with the idea in the first place?'

'I've been thinking of it ever since I came home, and when you said about Mrs Scott wanting to leave Westervoe, it made even better sense for us to wed each other.' Although she couldn't see his face clearly, Jennet could tell by his voice that he was blushing. 'You want Angus to stay on here and work the farm, and she says he's not able to do it all on his own, but if we wed and I came to live at Westervoe, Angus and me could farm it between us. That way the problem would be solved.'

'But Struan, you're going to take over Gleniffer when your father decides he's had enough. He needs you there.'

'He's got plenty of farmhands, and if you married me we could work the two farms between us, and take over Gleniffer as well as Westervoe when the time came. D'ye not see what a help it would be to you and Angus?'

He was right . . . It was the answer to Angus's situation, but at the same time it only created more problems for her. 'Folk don't get married just to help their neighbours out,' she argued feebly.

'It would be more than that. I like you, Jennet; I've always liked you. I want to marry you. I'd look after you well, and Angus too, and your gran if she wanted to stay on. And Jamie too – he's a grand wee chap, and we'd be giving him brothers and sisters in a year or so.'

'Struan, your mother would never allow it.'

'That's the good thing about it,' he said. 'She's taken our Drew's death really hard. She doesnae say much, but she's got this wee cupboard in her bedroom and it's full of pictures of Drew, and things he owned, even some old receipts he signed. It's like one of those places folk have for saints: what-d'ye-call-ems . . .'

'Shrines.'

'Aye, that's the word.'

Jennet was stunned; she would never have imagined such a thing of Lizbeth Blaikie. 'How do you know about it? She surely didn't tell you?'

'No, Helen did, the lassie that sees to the house and helps my mother with the hens and the calves and that. So I had a look for myself when she was at the church with my father, and it's all there right enough.'

'What has that got to do with us getting . . . with you and me?'

'The thing is,' Struan said, 'if we wed, it would bring your Jamie into our family, and that would be a great comfort to her.'

'A comfort? Struan, your mother's scarcely spoken to me since I came back from Glasgow. She cannae even bear to look at me when we're in the same room. As far as she's concerned, I'm a fallen woman with a child that can't name his father.'

'But don't you see, once we were wed Jamie would have a father . . . me. And he'd have the Blaikie name intae the bargain. It would be like giving Drew back to her!'

A suspicion began to dawn in Jennet's confused mind. 'You think that Drew fathered Jamie?'

'Of course he did. Oh, I know the word is that you met a man in Glasgow, but you werenae away all that long, were you? And ever since I came home and saw him, the wee chap's reminded me of our Drew. If my mother only knew the truth she'd welcome the two of you with open arms.'

'Struan, you're wrong. Drew isn't Jamie's father.'

'He must be!'

'He's not!

There was a pause and then he said, 'Are you sure?'

'Of course I'm sure! D'you think I've been sleeping with every man I meet?'

'No, of course not! It's just . . . I was so certain.' Disappointment weighed his voice down. 'The way he turns his head sometimes, the way he smiles . . . And I thought that was why you came back here when you knew he was on the way – to tell Drew, only he was dead by the time you got home.'

'I came back because I didn't know what else to do, where else to go.'

Struan was silent for a long moment, then he rallied. 'I still want to marry you.'

'And it's very nice of you to ask, but as I said before, it would break your mother's heart if you made me your wife.'

'Then she's a fool, for all that she's my own mother,' Struan said, his voice hard with anger. 'You're the same fine lassie you always were, and whether he's got Blaikie blood in his veins or not, that bairn of yours needs a proper father. And there's Angus to think of as well. We could make a right go of this place, the three of us, and it would be here for Jamie if he wanted to take over the tenancy when he grew up. Don't give me an answer now, just think about it.'

'I'll think about it,' she agreed, and he gave a sigh of relief and then ducked his head to deliver a hurried, clumsy kiss on the corner of her mouth.

'That's fair enough,' he said. 'But make it soon, will you? Goodnight to you, Jennet.'

9

'He did what?' Mollie yelped two days later.

'Shush, folk'll hear you!' Jennet skipped aside to avoid a small boy charging along the pavement towards them, pursued by his anxious young parents. They were walking along the Esplanade at Rothesay, battling against a sea of holidaymakers going the other way. 'These are far too big,' she went on, frowning at the loaded ice-cream cone Mollie had just bought for her.

'Ach, stop fussing, I can afford it,' Mollie said blithely. 'Anyway, you're a growing lassie, you need the nourishment, specially with the romantic life you're leading all of a sudden. Here was me, asking about your date with Struan Blaikie and expecting to hear about a goodnight kiss, not a proposal of marriage. What did you say? Did you accept him? Can I be a bridesmaid?'

'I said I'd think about it. I don't love him, Mollie.'

'Even so, it must be nice to know that someone

loves you with a hopeless, secret passion. Did you know he loved you?'

'I'm not sure that he does . . . and if he does, it sounded more hopeless than passionate. He said that if we wed, the two of us and Angus could run Westervoe and take over Gleniffer later. Mollie, I'd just go from one lot of worries to another. Can you see Mrs Blaikie welcoming Jamie and me into her family? It's been hard enough living with Gran's disappointment and disapproval. I don't want to have to take the same thing from Struan's mother.'

'I suppose not. Are you going to tell Angus?'

'I don't know. You see, there's another problem,' Jennet began, but just then Mollie interrupted her.

'There's our Sam.'

The boat-hirers were strung out all along the front, each one with a queue of people waiting their turn. Sam McCabe, a peaked cap pushed to the back of his head, was dealing with the queue for the Logan boats, book and pencil in hand. Down by the water's edge Alice, who was helping a young couple into a boat, waved a tanned arm at her cousin and Mollie.

'Number five'll be in soon,' Sam was saying as they arrived. 'See, that's them coming now, the boat called *Tern*.' He pointed at the incoming rowing boat and nodded to the small family at the head of the queue. 'You can go down to the slip now.'

'Hello, Mr Boatman, any chance of a row?' Mollie asked.

'You don't know how to row a boat.'

'But you do. You could take us out.'

Sam frowned importantly. 'Can you not see I'm busy?'

'A motor-boat, then?'

'You'll have to take your turn, and there's a lot of folk waiting for them already.'

Mollie tutted. 'Och, you'd think that with me having a brother running the show we'd we able to get a wee shot whenever we wanted it.'

'Well, you can't.' Sam squiggled in the book, then stepped aside and nodded the next set of people to where Alice, having pushed one small boat off, was reaching out to help the next to dock.

'If you wait five minutes, Joe'll be bringing the launch back from its trip round the bay. I'm sure he'd be *delighted* to take you.'

He smirked and then dodged as Mollie lifted her hand to slap him.

'Don't you be so cheeky!'

'Who's Joe?'

'Just a lad who works the boats with Mr Logan,' Mollie told her airily.

'Joe Wilson, and he's sweet on our Mollie,' Sam offered, keeping out of his sister's reach.

Alice came up the beach, rosy from the sun and as placid and unruffled as ever, and took the book and pencil from Sam. 'I'm worn out hauling these boats in and shoving them out again. Time for you to use your muscles.'

'How's he doing?' Mollie asked as her brother scampered off.

'Fine. You'd think he'd been born to it. Where's the wee lad?'

'At home. I just came to bring some eggs to your mother,' Jennet said. Then, as Alice turned to the people who waited patiently in line, they left her to it.

'Our Sam's learning to row, and this morning he went out early to bring the boats round from the inner harbour. I think I'd like to learn to row, too,' Mollie confided as they went, sidestepping and dodging other pedestrians from time to time. It was the second week in July; the Greenock Fair holidays were coming to an end and the town was packed with holidaymakers.

'D'you think there's anyone left on the mainland?' Jennet asked as they paused to lean on the railings. The great sweep of Rothesay Bay was dotted with rowing boats, skiffs, small motor-boats and round-the-bay launches, while two steamers disgorged their passengers at the pier.

'Lots of 'em, and every one wishing they were here,' Mollie said through a mouthful of ice cream. 'Folk who have to live in tenements and work in shops, factories and shipyards can't wait to get to the seaside in the summer, and there's the end of the war to celebrate as well. Every room in your auntie's house is taken, right to the end of the summer, and she could have let the rooms over again. Even the Skeoch Woods are so busy there's scarce room for the trees.'

The Skeoch Woods edged the great sweep of Rothesay town at one side, and it was common for holidaymakers who could not find accommodation in one of the boarding houses to set up camp there. In summer the woods were known to the locals as the Skeoch Hotel.

'And the weather's been good, too.' Mollie finished her ice cream and began to nibble delicately round the edge of the cone. 'The boarders are out from morning to night.'

'Aunt Nesta and Aunt Ann seem to be getting on well together.'

'They are. Moving to your auntie's house has done Mam the world of good. Though we miss you all, of course,' she added hurriedly. 'You and wee Jamie and Angus. And your gran.' After all, that old crow Mrs Scott was Jennet's granny and she shouldn't be missed out.

'You don't need to be polite,' Jennet told her. 'It's much better for your mother to be here, where she's appreciated. But we miss all of you an awful lot.'

'You, mebbe. I don't know so much about your granny and Angus. Has he said anything about me?' Mollie asked casually.

'He's got a lot on his mind just now.' Jennet squinted at the blue sky, hoping that the weather would hold for the haymaking.

'If you don't hurry up with that ice cream, it'll start dripping onto those folk down below us on the beach. Are you not enjoying it?'

'I am, but there's a lot of it. The little ones would have done us fine and cost you less.'

'Ach, toffs is careless and I can afford the occasional ice cream now. Sometimes folk even leave a wee tip when they go home. Mrs Logan lets me keep the tips for myself.'

'Why not, since you've earned them.'

'There's plenty of employers would claim the lot, but not your auntie. She's awful nice, and your uncle too . . . and Alice. Would you look at that big woman paddling!' Mollie gave a trill of laughter. 'I swear the steamers at the pier lifted a good half-inch in the water when she went in.'

'Let's go down and sit on that bit of beach for a minute,' Jennet suggested. 'I'll need to get back to the farm and I've something to tell you.'

'Something bad?' Mollie asked apprehensively.

'Something worse than that,' said Jennet.

'You can't let her do that to you and Angus,' Mollie said decisively five minutes later, 'specially Angus. You might want to go back to nursing, but Westervoe's his home and it's wicked of her tae drag him away from it.'

'I can understand in a way; she's getting old and she's tired, and now Martin's let her down the same way my father did.'

Mollie tossed her long red hair back over her shoulder with an impatient whisk of the head. 'That's your trouble, Jennet Scott, you're too quick to put yourself into other folks' shoes. It's a pity some of them don't bother to wonder how it is for you.'

She had been the first to see Jennet on her unexpected return from Glasgow. The girl had walked into the yard, white-faced and red-eyed, just as Mollie stepped out of the byre. While she gaped at the apparition, wondering how Jennet could possibly be in Glasgow studying and at the same time back home on Bute, her friend had dropped her suitcase and rushed at her, clutching her and almost knocking her down, sobbing, 'Oh, Mollie!'

Nesta had come running from the farmhouse kitchen just then, white-faced and calling out, 'Jennet? What's wrong, pet?'

And Celia Scott had looked over the stable's half door and said in her harsh voice, 'What's usually happened when a lassie who was brought up to know right from wrong comes home with guilt pouring off her face? She's brought shame on me and her brothers, that's what's wrong! Am I right or am I wrong, madam?'

From that day on Mollie had had to watch helplessly as her friend was made to pay over and over again for her pregnancy out of wedlock. She had never said a word about Jamie's father, and Mollie had never asked. There were times when secrets had to be kept, even from the closest of friends.

'It's Angus I'm worried about,' Jennet was saying now, staring at the glittering bay without seeing it. 'It's as if he doesn't care any more.'

'He has tae care! It's a terrible thing tae lose the place your family's lived in for all those years, and he has tae find that out now, while there's still time, instead of later on when he's suffocating in some wee house, bein' fussed over by two old women. I'll never forget us being bombed out the first night Clydebank got blitzed,' Mollie said soberly. 'We were all in the basement with the other folk from the tenement, and afterwards my mam was determined to go back and get her insurance policies. The stairs were still there, so the ARP man said she could try to get into the flat if she was careful. I went with her.'

This was her secret, something she had never mentioned before to her friend, because for years it had been like a raw wound inside her, liable to break open and bleed if disturbed. It was dark, and with the stairs covered with rubble and the air thick with dust, it didn't feel in the least like the tenement she had known all her life. The two of them had had to feel ahead with each foot as they went, Mam first and Mollie close behind, their hands linked so tightly that afterwards Mollie's fingers ached.

'Did you get into the flat?'

'The door was still there and it was still locked. Mam had to use her key to get in. The funny thing is,' Mollie said, not feeling at all funny, 'when we got in, the house was gone.'

'What d'you mean, gone?'

'There were just a few floorboards on the other side of the door, then a big hole. The roof was gone and at least that meant that we could see better, because of the stars and the anti-aircraft searchlights slashing across the sky, but we couldn't have walked to the far wall because there was no floor to walk on. Even if there had been a floor, there was no wall – just a gap and the shape of some of the other tenements against the sky. But the wall where the mantelshelf stood was still there, and the shelf had the box on it with the insurance policies, our birth certificates and Mam and Da's marriage papers. And Cheepy was still in his cage with half his feathers gone, chirping away as if nothing had happened. It was lucky we kept his cage on the mantel. So we were able tae fetch him as well as the box.'

'I don't think I could have walked over that floor, with half of it missing.' Jennet shuddered.

'It was still our home.' It was as simple as that; although most of it, walls and furniture, had disappeared, the familiar mantelpiece and the sound of Cheepy singing meant that what was left was still home. And home – even a part of home – felt safe. Looking back, Mollie realised why some city dwellers insisted on living in the ruins of their bombed flats when possible. Where else would they want to go?

'On the way out,' she remembered, 'Mam saw her good coat still hanging on the back of the door. It was filthy with white dust and all shredded by the blast, but she took it off the hook anyway and brought it away with her. She said it had cost a lot of good money and she'd not see it left there. She'd to throw it away the next day because it could never be mended.'

A child nearby called out to his mother and the shrillness of the cry brought Mollie back to the present. 'It was only a room and kitchen, and it had dampness and it was bitter cold in the winter because the windows didn't fit, but it was still ours, and it hurts to lose the place where you grew up. I don't want that to happen to Angus and you and wee Jamie.'

'Knowing that your home had gone, seeing it like that . . . It must have been terrible for you.'

'Aye, it was.'

'I didn't realise that it had been so bad. You've never said a word about it before.' Jennet's voice was hushed, as though she was speaking in a church.

'It's not the sort of thing you want to talk about afterwards. You just want to put it away and get on with your life.'

There was more, but that wound went deeper and was still raw. Mollie might never be able to tell anyone about glancing up into the night sky during the trek to the school where they were to be given food and shelter for the night, and seeing a human leg tangled among the telegraph wires. Or the woman who, when they sheltered in her doorway for protection against the raid, opened the door and ordered them to be on their way as though they were common tinks.

She blinked, shivered in the warm sunlight, then forced her mind to dismiss her own memories as she heard Jennet say, 'So you see, Struan's proposal could make all the difference to us. If I married him it would solve all our problems.'

'Are ye mad? It would only make them worse!'

'With Struan to help him, Angus would be able to take over the tenancy of the farm, and Grandmother could move to Largs and . . .'

'And you'd be stuck with a husband you don't love. Or are you going to tell me you've been crazy about him for years, and the sight of him walking back into your life made you go all weak at the knees?'

'This is real life, Mollie, not a film!'

'Even in real life I'd not consider tying myself to a man for ever unless he made my knees go all funny every time I thought about him. Tell me the truth, mind . . . Do you love Struan Blaikie to bits?'

'He's a good man and a nice man, and a dependable one.' Jennet was sitting on the beach with her knees drawn up and her arms linked about them. Now Mollie put a hand on one of them.

'Not a quiver. That means you don't love him, so don't marry him. That's my advice and you'd be a fool to ignore it.'

'Be sensible, Mollie. It would be the right thing to do as far as Angus's concerned.'

'No!' Mollie said the word so violently that a couple walking by hand in hand looked at her in surprise as they passed. She turned so that she was squatting back on her heels, facing Jennet. 'It would be the worst thing you could do for Angus, d'you not see that? You'd only be looking after him and protecting him, and that's not what Angus needs. He's had more than enough of that from your granny. If Struan Blaikie went to live on Westervoe, Angus'd just go on doing the easy jobs while Struan sees to the harder ones. He's a grown man, Jennet, he has tae learn tae make his own decisions and abide by them. If he's going to defy Mrs Scott and stay on at Westervoe, then he must do it himself, d'you not see that?' The words had flooded out in a passionate tirade and when they ended Mollie was breathless.

'I've tried to make him see that, but he won't, though I know he loves the place more than Martin ever did. If Angus had been able to go to the war, he'd have come back as soon as he was able, the way Struan has. He was a grand ploughman before his accident,' Jennet said proudly. Then, her face clouding over, 'But now it's as if he thinks he's got no right to tell Gran what he wants. He just agrees to everything she says.'

'Then make him change! Keep on at him, the way I did when your gran wanted him to spend the rest of his life in his bed or in a chair, being babied. It worked then and it could work again.'

'You're different. I don't have your cheek.'

'God almighty,' Mollie raised her eyes and her shoulders, 'now you're beginning to sound just like him. "I can't . . . I daren't",' she mimicked. 'Yes, you can, Jennet Scott, and you'd better dare before it's too late for all of you, including poor wee Jamie. How long have you got?'

'Grandmother can't give the factor six months' notice until Martinmas rent day in November.'

'November? And you're wasting valuable time sitting here on the beach blethering, when you should be at home nagging that obstinate brother of yours? Go home and start at once!'

'I need to get home anyway,' Jennet suddenly realised, scrambling to her feet. 'If I'm not back soon, I'll have Angus and Grandmother both out looking for my blood.'

'And don't forget – nag him until he can't take it any more. That's when he'll start doing what you want, just for the sake of peace,' Mollie panted as they raced along towards the bus stop.

There was indeed blood-letting when Jennet got home, but it wasn't hers. Old Jem was pacing around at the top of the lane when she stepped off the bus.

'Here ye are at last!' he greeted her, relief sweeping over his face, which was well lined and tanned like leather by a lifetime of working outdoors in all weathers. Jennet's heart seemed to stop in her chest.

'Has something happened to Jamie? Or is it Angus?' Pictures of Jamie finding his way down to the shore and drowning, or of Angus deciding that suicide was better than spending the rest of his life in Largs with Grandmother and Great-Aunt Rachel, flooded into her mind.

'No, no, it's the old yin.'

'Gran?'

'Are you comin' or are you no'?' the bus driver wanted to know, leaning across the gap between his seat and the open door.

'What are ye talkin' about, man? I'm no' wantin' tae go on yer bus. I'm just here tae fetch the lassie,' Jem barked at him, and the driver, grumbling, started up the engine.

'Come on to the house, quick!' Jem seized her arm and bustled her along the lane.

'What's happened to Gran?'

'The daft old b . . . old woman would have it that her and me should shift some of they chicken houses to another bit of the field. I told her to wait until you came, but no, she had tae have it done right away. And what happened?' Jem demanded.

'How should I know, I wasn't there!' Jennet was torn between running ahead to the farmhouse and keeping to his pace to find out what had been going on in her absence.

'She put her foot in a hole or tripped over a tussock, or somethin'. Anyway, she couped over, and the ark we were liftin' went over with her. She nearly had me over an' all. One of the carryin' poles under the ark ploughed a furrow in her leg. I'd the devil's own job tae get her tae the house,' Jem wheezed. 'We've bandaged her up, me and Angus, but I'm no good at that sort of thing and she was squawkin' and fussin' all the time, just like one of the hens. I mind when Jocky Turner lost his leg thon time when we were scythin' . . .'

They were in the yard now; Jennet took to her heels and left him behind.

Celia lay on the couch in the little-used living room, her legs covered by a blanket and a cup of strong tea on a small table by her side. Angus hovered around her uncertainly, while Jamie was wedged into a corner of the room with his thumb jammed into his mouth. As soon as he saw his mother he rushed to latch onto her skirt.

'There you are at last,' Celia greeted her granddaughter. 'I thought you'd never come home!'

'Have you sent for the doctor?'

'She wouldn't let us.' Angus was pale with shock and worry.

'I don't need a doctor, it's just a waste of money. I'm a good healer.'

'Angus, take Jamie outside and let me see to Gran,' Jennet instructed. It took a few minutes to persuade Jamie to release his grip on her, but he was finally bribed with a lollipop that Jennet had brought from Rothesay for him.

'You spoil that bairn,' Celia said sourly as the door closed behind uncle and nephew.

'I don't have time to give him the attention he deserves, let alone spoil him,' Jennet snapped back at her, too worried to care about causing offence. She lifted the blanket out of the way. 'Let me have a look.'

The wound was fairly shallow, but long and ragged. Blood still seeped from it.

'We should get the doctor out for this.'

'Don't you dare!'

'At least let me send Jem over to fetch Mrs Blaikie.' Jennet felt round the ankle with gentle fingers. 'This needs a cold compress.'

'I went over on my foot, just, and Lizbeth Blaikie has enough to do without running round here every five minutes. Put some disinfectant on the cut and bandage my whole leg properly and it'll do. I told you, I heal quickly.'

'Why didn't you tell Angus to disinfect it right away? And this bandage is too loose.'

'I just wanted him to do something to stop the blood getting onto my good sofa. Anyway, I'd no wish to have every male in the place staring at my naked leg. It was bad enough having to take my stocking off.' Celia indicated the surprisingly white, well-muscled leg stretched out on the sofa. 'I'm just grateful I've never sunk to wearing trousers, like you. A fine pickle I'd have been in then.'

There was no arguing with her. Jennet fetched from the kitchen the battered tin box that held the family's supply of bandages, sticking plasters and medication, then went back for a basin of hot water and clean cloths and towels. Celia winced and caught her lower lip between her teeth as the wound was cleansed and disinfected, but rallied in time to direct the bandaging process.

'That's better,' she finally decided and began to get to her feet.

'Stay where you are, Gran.'

'I've got work to do.'

Jennet pushed her back down. 'You've got a badly cut leg and a twisted ankle that needs a cold compress on it. If you try to get up and go out, you'll only start the bleeding again.'

'Aye, mebbe you're right.' Celia let herself be eased against the arm of the sofa. 'My ankle could do with a bit of a rest, but just till tomorrow.'

'I'll soak a towel in cold water, then make you a fresh cup of tea,' Jennet said.

10

After the three of them, with Jamie's help, did the afternoon milking, Angus undertook tasks near the house, so that he could look after Jamie and keep an eye on his grandmother, while Jennet and Jem finished shifting the arks to another part of the field. When the job was done Jennet straightened her back and wiped a hand over her perspiring face. 'I'd like to see some of them in a deep-litter house.'

'They'd be easier to look after,' Jem agreed. 'But you'd never get her to let ye do that, lassie. She doesnae like change.'

That night Celia insisted on going up to her own room, scowling at Angus when he tried to suggest that it would make more sense for her to sleep in the living room where she could more easily be looked after during the working day.

'I'll be back on my feet tomorrow,' she snapped, 'and for tonight I'd like the comfort of my own bed.'

'You'll not be back on that foot tomorrow, Gran,'

Jennet protested. 'Your ankle's still swollen.'

'A night's rest'll put it right, and I can strap it up and use one of the walking sticks, if I must. If Angus can manage, so can I. Go and turn the bed down for me, Jennet.'

'But . . .'

'Leave it, Jen,' Angus advised from the doorway. Then, when she joined him in the kitchen, he went on, 'Let her have her own way. Why shouldn't she find out for herself how hard it can be to get about with just one sound leg?'

Jennet had a struggle to get her grandmother to her bedroom. Although the woman was wiry, with not a pick of fat on her, she was difficult to manoeuvre on the narrow staircase and once or twice Jennet, her heart in her mouth, thought that the two of them were going to lose their footing and tumble back downstairs to where Angus stood at the bottom, watching and worrying. At last they managed to get along the upper corridor and into the bedroom, where Celia collapsed gratefully into the big lumpy bed she had shared with her sister and then with her husband for a few short years.

'I'll help you into your nightgown.' Jennet felt as exhausted as she had earlier when she and Jem were struggling with the arks in the field.

'You will not, I've not reached that stage yet! You can put some fresh water into that basin and bring it here, then leave me in peace so's I can wash myself.'

When Jennet took the jug of water upstairs, Celia

was still on the bed, her face drawn in the light from the lamp, but her voice was as sharp as ever as she said, 'Now, off you go and let me get to my bed. Wait . . .' she added, then as Jennet turned in the doorway 'you can mebbe bring me a cup of hot tea in ten minutes, and two aspirin to help the pain in my ankle.'

For once Celia wasn't first in the kitchen the following morning, and when Jennet went back upstairs with some tea she found her grandmother sleeping in the middle of an uncomfortable tangle of bedclothes. The older woman awoke with a start as the mug was placed on her bedside table.

'What time is it?' Her voice was unusually weak and she blinked about the room as though she didn't quite recognise it.

'Never mind the time . . . How do you feel?'

'I didnae sleep very well,' Celia admitted, 'but I'll be better once I'm up and on my feet.'

'You're not getting up till I see how your leg is.' Jennet drew the bedclothes aside and then eased Celia's nightgown just high enough to reveal the bandaged part of her leg. To her dismay she saw that the skin from bandage to ankle was a dark, shiny red. She touched it gently with her fingertips and Celia caught her breath sharply, then said, 'No need to be so rough, girl!'

'I'm going to fetch the doctor.'

'You will not.'

'Gran, that gash is badly inflamed. I'm fetching the doctor no matter what you say.'

'You could at least help me to get tidied up first,' Celia said peevishly. 'And before you do that, you can bring a drink of water, for my throat's parched. Then you can fetch the chamber pot out from below the bed.'

She drank thirstily before allowing Jennet to wash her face and hands, brush her hair and fasten it into a neat bun at the nape of her neck, then tidy the crumpled bed. It was clear that every movement caused her pain, but she set her lips and said nothing.

When everything was done Jennet woke Jamie and carried him and his clothes downstairs. 'She's settled for the meantime, but I'll have to cycle over to the Blaikies' and ask them to telephone for the doctor.'

Angus got up from his seat at the table. 'Have your breakfast first.'

'There's no time if I want to catch the man before he goes out on his rounds. Could you see to Jamie and then let the hens out before you bring the cows in for milking? Jem should be here soon to help you.' Jennet took her jacket from its hook on the back of the outer door. 'Gran's dozing off again, so I think she'll stay that way till I get back. She must have been awake most of the night with the pain in her leg.'

Struan was coming out of house when she got to Gleniffer Farm. At the sight of her his face lit up and he came to meet her.

'Jennet? Have ye come tae . . .'

There was no time for chat. 'My grandmother's hurt herself,' she cut in, 'and I need to telephone for the doctor right away.'

'Come on in.' He led her into the kitchen, where Andra Blaikie and his wife were finishing breakfast. As soon as she heard the story Lizbeth hurried to the telephone in the big square hall while her husband said, 'I'll send young Bert to help out as soon as I can spare him.'

'I'll go,' Struan offered.

'You've got the rest of the hay to cut,' his father reminded him. Then to Jennet, 'We're nearly by with that. I was going to come over to Westervoe today to tell Celia that we'd be free tae help her with the haymakin' next week.'

'The doctor'll be over within the hour,' Lizbeth announced, bustling back into the room, followed by the maid, 'and I'll be over too, just as soon as I've got things sorted out here.'

'There's no need, Mrs Blaikie.'

'And what sort of a neighbour would I be if I didnae help poor Celia?' the woman asked impatiently, adding, 'Anyway, you and your brother could never manage on your own.'

'I'm sending young Bert over.'

'Quite right, Andra. Helen, I can trust you tae see tae the men's dinners, can't I?'

'Aye, Mrs Blaikie.' The live-in maid flushed with pleasure at being put in charge of the kitchen.

'If you're goin' to Westervoe,' Andra told his wife, 'you might as well use the wee cart and take Bert with you.'

It wasn't until she was on her way home that Jennet remembered the light in Struan's eyes when she arrived, and realised that he must have thought she was rushing over to accept his proposal of marriage.

Angus and Jem were milking the cows when Jennet got back to Westervoe.

'The hens are fed and I've put your porridge to keep warm by the range,' Angus reported. 'I thought I heard Gran calling for you, but when I sent Jem up to see what was wrong, she just pulled the sheet up to her chin and shouted at him to get out.'

Jem's wheezy chuckle floated from the next stall. 'She glared as me as if I was there tae give her a fate worse than death. Even a bull wouldnae be that brave . . . or that desperate.'

'You're making altogether too much fuss,' Celia complained when Jennet climbed the stairs. 'The doctor coming . . . and Lizbeth too, for a wee scratch.'

'A scratch that should have been looked at properly when it first happened. And I didn't ask Mrs Blaikie to come over; she insisted on calling as a friend.'

'They're good neighbours, the Blaikies. I don't know how I could have managed all these years without Andra's help.'

'Angus and me can manage between us until you're back on your feet,' Jennet argued, and her grandmother looked at her with stinging contempt.

'You two? Manage to run this farm without me?' she said. 'I doubt it.'

The leg was badly infected and at first the doctor wanted to send his patient to hospital. Jennet, banished from the room by her grandmother and listening outside the door, prayed that Celia would agree, for as well as making life easier for her and Angus, it would give her the chance to talk to him about the future. But the old woman would have none of it, and after a heated argument the doctor gave in.

'She's a very stubborn woman, your grandmother,' he said when he found Jennet in the kitchen, where she had fled on realising that he was coming out of the bedroom. 'As I mind it, she always was. Not that we've had many dealings with each other, for she's as fit as a fiddle otherwise. I've seen to the leg and put on a fresh bandage, and I'll arrange for the district nurse to come in every morning to dress it until the infection clears up.'

'How long will that take?'

'It depends on whether or not she does as she's told. A week at least, I'd say. Give her these for the pain when she needs them . . .'

He began to put the small bottle on the table, then stopped, eyeing Jamie, who had come in from the yard to take a comforting fistful of his mother's britches. The doctor put the bottle on the high wooden mantelshelf instead.

'You've got a healthy-looking wee fellow there.'

'He's never ill.'

'Well fed and well loved,' the middle-aged doctor said unexpectedly. 'And lots of fresh air. That's the way. Let me know if she gets any worse . . . the leg, I mean,' he added with a sudden, almost mischievous smile, and went on his way.

Lizbeth Blaikie and Bert McCabe arrived shortly afterwards in the smart little trap that Andra always referred to as 'the wee cart'. The Blaikies had a motor-car, but since the beginning of the war, and the introduction of rationing, the agricultural petrol doled out to farmers had been treated with red dye to ensure that it was only used for farm work. Some local farmers managed to fit in the occasional jaunt by car, but if they were caught using agricultural petrol for their own purposes they were hauled into court and fined. So the Blaikies, stalwart churchgoers and pillars of the community, had brought the small carriage out of retirement and rarely used the car.

Mrs Blaikie showed alarming signs, when she came downstairs from visiting Celia, of wanting to take over until her friend was fully recovered.

'Helen's been well trained, for I've had her with me since the day after she left the school, and she can see to things at home. I can come first thing every morning and . . .'

'It's not necessary, Mrs Blaikie, we can manage.'

Since the doctor's visit, Jennet had rushed about the kitchen like a madwoman, tidying and dusting, polishing and cooking. Now the room was filled with tempting aromas from the meat pie in the oven and the big pot of soup simmering on top of the range. Pots of potatoes and turnips were also cooking and Jennet had even managed to start on a batch of scones.

Lizbeth Blaikie looked round the room but could find nothing to criticise. 'Westervoe's just a wee place, I know,' she said, 'but even so you'll never manage without Celia. She's held this place together since the day her man died, and if you ask me . . .' she settled her ample, well-corseted frame on one of the upright chairs at the table, 'she's worn out more than anything else. She's had a hard life, and just when she was expecting to let go of the reins and see to her own comfort for once, she was landed with your Angus an invalid and the shame of . . .'

She glanced at Jamie, playing on the hearthrug with a domesticated farm cat, and let the rest of the sentence hang in the air in letters of red fire.

Jennet's hands tightened on the rolling pin. Although Andra Blaikie was always affable, Lizbeth had found ways of making it clear that as a high-principled, strongly religious woman, she thoroughly disapproved of Jamie's presence in the world, let alone on Bute.

For two pins Jennet would have bounced the rolling pin on the woman's head; instead, with a great effort, she moved it slowly and evenly over the dough on the table and said with icy politeness, 'It's kind of you to offer, Mrs Blaikie, but I can see to my grandmother, and to the house.'

It did not seem possible that Mrs Blaikie, already whalebone-rigid, could stiffen any further, but she managed it. 'Are you saying that you've no need of my help? Is that what you're saying?'

'I'm saying that I've got my own way of doing things in my own house, just as you must have in yours, and I'm best left alone to see to them,' Jennet replied, the effort of trying not to shout putting an edge of steel into her voice.

'Well . . .' The woman glanced again at Jamie. 'We all know you've got your own ways, and they're certainly not mine, or poor Celia's.'

Jennet set the rolling pin down on the table amid a cloud of flour. 'You'll always be welcome here if you want to visit my grandmother, Mrs Blaikie,' she said, amazed at her own daring, 'but I'll see to the house myself.'

The woman gave an outraged sniff, and left.

Watching her drive out of the yard, ramrod-straight in the trap, Jennet knew that even if the sight or the thought of Struan had made her knees go funny, as Mollie put it, she could never become his mother's daughter-in-law. There had to be some other way to keep Westervoe.

'I've offended Mrs Blaikie,' she said when Angus, Jem and Bert came in for their dinner.

'Easy done.' Her brother picked up his knife and fork. 'How did you manage it?'

'I refused to let her take over this house while Grandmother was in her bed.'

'Quite right,' Jem boomed, while Bert winked at Jennet. 'She'd have the lot of us runnin' round like school bairns and I cannae be doin' with that. Your gran's as difficult a woman as I want tae deal with.'

'Mebbe you were a bit hasty, Jen.' Angus's forehead creased with worry. 'How can you do your farm work and help with Gran's as well, and look after her and the house and the wee fellow, too?'

'Mr Blaikie says I can help out every day now the hay's nearly done,' Bert offered.

'And mebbe Mrs Blaikie's over there right now complaining about the way she was treated and getting him to change his mind about being such a good neighbour,' Angus fretted.

'He'd not do that. She doesnae rule that roost as much as she thinks she does.' Bert winked again.

'As to how I'm going to manage, I've made my own plans,' Jennet broke in. 'If you can do without me for an hour this afternoon, Angus, I'm going into Rothesay to ask if Aunt Ann could spare Mollie for a few days.'

'Gran won't like that.'

'But I would, and that's all that matters to me.' Jennet brandished the ladle at them. 'Anyone for more pie?'

* * *

When Jennet reached her aunt's gate Ann Logan was at her open front door talking to a man with the distinctive ill-fitting suit and cropped haircut of a former soldier. Behind him stood two boys of school age and a woman with a little girl in her arms.

"There's been such a rush of folk,' Jennet heard her aunt say, 'that I've not even got an empty cupboard to offer. Have you tried that house across the road?'

'Aye, and every other house in Rothesay.'

'I wish I could help, but I can't think of anyone who's got a room left to let.'

'Thanks anyway, I'm sure we'll manage. We'll just have to try somewhere outside of the town.' The man nodded, picked up the heavy case by his side and turned away, muttering an apology as he realised that Jennet was waiting to get to the door.

'I hate turning folk away,' her aunt said as they watched the little family trail along the pavement, 'specially when they've got bairns.' Then, with pleasure, 'Come in, come in, this is a nice surprise . . . two visits from you in two days?'

'I can't stop, I have to get back. Gran's had an accident and she's had to take to her bed and . . .'

'Oh, my dear! How bad is it? Come in and have a cup of tea, at least. Mollie and her mother are in the kitchen, we were having a wee rest.' Ann drew her into the house, talking all the while. 'How are you going to manage? It's Jennet again,' she added, throwing open the kitchen door. 'Mrs Scott's taken poorly.'

'She gashed her leg and it's got infected, so she'll have to stay in her bed for a week at least, the doctor says,' Jennet explained as she was ushered to a seat at the table. 'That's why I have to get back as quickly as I can. Mr Blaikie's sent Bert over to help Angus, but there's nobody in the house to see to Gran and Jamie.'

Ann clucked sympathetically. 'Is there anything I can do to help?'

'You could let me borrow Mollie for a few days, if she's willing,' Jennet said hopefully.

'Of course I'm willing!' Mollie's face lit up. 'If it's all right with you, Mrs Logan.'

'We can manage fine. With this nice weather the boarders are out most of the time, and Nesta here's been working like I don't know what, Jennet. I can't get her to slow down.'

Nesta McCabe's face glowed. 'I'm enjoyin' it,' she said, and Ann put an arm about her shoulders.

'And George says that Sam's worth his weight in gold as well, so no need to worry about us. You just see to your gran and the farm, and Mollie can stay for as long as you want. You'll have a cup of tea while you wait for her,' she added as Mollie whisked out of the kitchen.

'I've just minded,' she said to her mother when she came back downstairs, bag in hand, 'that I said I'd go to the pictures with Joe tomorrow night. Get our Sam to tell him what's happened, will you? Come on then, Jennet, we'd best go if you want to catch the next bus.'

'Mind now . . . if there's anything we can do, just send word,' Ann called after them as they set off.

'She's awful kind,' Mollie said. 'I've never seen Mam so contented, and Sam can't wait to get up and get out in the mornings. He fair loves these boats!'

'Talking about boats, is it the Joe that works with the boats that was taking you to the pictures?'

'Aye, but it's just a friendly thing.'

'It seems a shame to be leaving him in the lurch like that.'

'Ach, I'm sure he'll find someone else,' Mollie said airily. 'The lads workin' the boats are always meetin' lassies. And lassies on their holidays are always keen tae be asked out. Even by our Sam.'

'He's surely too young to think about that sort of thing.'

'That's what Mam says, but he's come back more than once with stars in his eyes. And he's started shavin'.' Mollie giggled. 'He's got as much hair on his face as I have. Listen, does your gran know I'm coming back to the farm?'

'Not yet.'

'She'll not be pleased,' Mollie predicted as they rounded the corner and caught up with the family who had been looking for accommodation. The father had put down his big suitcase and taken the little girl from her mother. The woman was hefting the case up when Jennet stopped and said on an impulse, 'Excuse me . . . I believe you were asking my aunt back there if she had any rooms to let?'

'Aye.' The man smiled at her. 'We should mebbe have thought tae write ahead and book somewhere. We'd no idea the place would be so busy, but I've just been demobbed and since the wee one . . .' he indicated the toddler hiding her face shyly in his shoulder, 'has had a bad time with the croup, we thought it would be a good idea tae give her some sea air and have a bit of a holiday intae the bargain. Someone said Port Bannatyne would be worth tryin'; it's just along the coast – is that right?'

'Would you fancy a working holiday?' Jennet asked, then as they looked at her warily, 'On a farm, I mean.'

'A farm? That would be great, Dad!' the older boy piped up. He, like his younger brother, wore his straight hair cut in a pudding-bowl style.

'I don't know about that,' the man said, exchanging doubtful looks with his wife. 'What sort of work d'ye mean?'

'We've a small farm near Stravanan Bay. The thing is, it's coming up for haymaking time and my grandmother's ill in bed and there's a lot to do round the farm, so you and your sons could help with bringing in the hay,' Jennet gabbled, wondering at her own cheek in accosting this group of strangers. 'You'd not be expected to work all the time of course, just at the haymaking. There's nice walks around the place and we're near the shore, so the children could go down to the water. We've a cottage you could have: it's not smart but it's furnished.'

'The cottage is nice,' Mollie chipped in. 'Me and my family used tae live in it.'

'A cottage? We were thinkin' of a room, just. What sort of rent would you be askin' for a whole cottage?' the man asked cautiously.

'Hardly anything . . . nothing at all if you'd be willing to help Mollie here out with the housework and the cooking,' Jennet said to the woman. 'Folk get very hungry during haymaking. And I've a wee boy round about your daughter's age. They'd be company for each other.'

'Is there horses?' the older boy asked, wide-eyed.

'And sheeps?' his brother clamoured.

'We don't have sheep, but we've got a horse and two pigs and there's cows and hens and cats and a dog.'

'Can we go, Mammy . . . Daddy?' the boys chorused while their father turned to his wife.

'What d'ye think, Mary?' he asked, then when she nodded uncertainly he beamed at Jennet. 'When can we go?'

'Now, with us.' Mollie handed her bag to Jennet and grabbed the case. 'We're just off tae catch the bus.'

On board the bus ten minutes later she murmured to Jennet under cover of the engine's rattle, 'Your gran's goin' tae kill you!'

'I have to do what I think's best for the farm, and for her. Anyway, she'll have to catch me first, and the way her leg is just now she's not got a chance of doing that,' Jennet rapped back at her, then settled in her seat.

Part of her was scared of what her grandmother would say, of what Angus would say and of whether the unknown lodgers were going to be more of a hindrance than a help.

And part of her wanted to dance up and down the bus's narrow aisle, for at last, for the first time in her life, she was taking control of things.

11

'I will not have it!' Celia Scott stormed. 'I do not want trippers on my farm!'

'The Dicksons are a nice respectable family from Glasgow, Gran. Mr Dickson's just been demobbed and he just wants to have a wee holiday with his family. They're willing to help with the haymaking and Mrs Dickson doesn't mind giving Mollie a hand in the . . .'

'There's another one,' Celia fumed, fussing at the bedclothes. 'I thought we'd seen the last of the McCabes and now you're bringing them back again.'

'Only Mollie, and only until the haymaking's over and you're better. I can't possibly manage to look after you and see to all the outside work as well, can I?'

'Since you've finally admitted that, then why don't you ask Andra and Lizbeth Blaikie for help? They're our own sort.'

'If by "our own sort" you mean they're farming

folk, they've got enough to do on their own farm without having to help to work ours, too. By the time the haymaking's done you'll be on your feet again.'

'And then there'll be the oats to harvest.'

'We'll worry about that when the time comes.'

'You're going to ruin this place, d'you know that? Inviting God knows what sort of folk onto my farm . . .'

'It's not just your farm, Gran, it's Angus's and mine as well and we're doing our best to keep it going, given the circumstances.'

Celia glared, then said, 'Fetch Angus here at once, I want to see him.'

'He's out in the fields somewhere and anyway, he can't manage up the stairs.' Jennet made for the door. 'I've got things to do. Is there anything you want just now?'

'I want some tea, and this bed needs freshening up. And . . .'

'I'll ask Mollie to see to the tea, and she can tidy the bed when she brings it up.'

'Jennet, I will not have . . .' Celia was beginning as Jennet went out and closed the door gently behind her.

'I'm not surprised Gran was angry,' Angus said when his sister told him what she had done. 'I don't know that I'm very pleased myself.'

'Emergencies need quick action, and you're surely not angry with me for getting more folk to help with the haymaking. The Dicksons' wee girl's been bad with croup, and they need a holiday by the sea now that Mr Dickson's home at last.'

'Never mind the long sad story,' Angus snapped and went ahead of her across the yard, banging the point of his crutch onto the cobbles and ignoring the two Dickson boys, who were standing at the cottage door, staring wide-eyed at the farm yard. As Angus went into the farmhouse, Gumrie, who had been trotting at his heels, peeled away and went to investigate the strangers. The smallest boy immediately slid behind his brother, who paled but faced the dog with clenched fists and a fearsome scowl, reminding Jennet of Mollie the day she and her family first arrived at Westervoe.

'It's all right,' she called out. 'He just wants to say hello to you. Hold out your hand and let him have a sniff at it. That's how dogs decide if they like folk.'

'Mebbe he'll no' like us, but,' the lad objected, a tremor in his voice.

'Why would he not like you?' Jennet squatted down by the dog. 'His name's Gumrie. What's yours?'

'Walter. And that's Colin.'

A small face peered out from behind Walter, watching as the older boy finally stuck out his hand, holding it as far away from his body as possible, at the end of a thin, rigid arm. Gumrie sniffed the grimy fingers, then wagged his tail and licked them. Walter laughed, a surprisingly deep chuckle.

'He's got a tickly tongue. Can I clap him?'

'To tell the truth, you should never pet farm dogs because they're workers, not pets, but our Gumrie likes it, don't you, softie?' Jennet rubbed the dog's coat and he wriggled with pleasure, then wriggled again as Walter patted him. Colin emerged slowly, willing to be coaxed into introducing himself to the dog.

'Can we clap the chooky hens an' all?' he wanted to know.

Jennet shook her head. There was something very likeable about the two stolid little boys with their Glasgow speech, their masculine little faces and vulnerable, wide-eyed wonder. 'Hens don't like to be touched, and they don't like folk to rush around, either. It frightens them.'

'Who's the limpy man?' Walter asked.

'That's my brother Angus.'

'Was he hurtit in the war? Was he a sojer like my dad?'

'No, he got hurt when a train he was in ran off the rails and crashed.'

The brothers looked at her, then at each other, horrified. Then Colin said in a gruff voice very like his brother's, 'We came from Glasgow in a train, then in a boat.'

'Most trains don't run off the rails,' Jennet said reassuringly, then left them with Gumrie and tapped at the open door of the cottage. 'Is everything all right?'

'More than all right, Mrs . . . eh,' Mr Dickson

beamed at her. 'Come in, come in! Was that your husband you were with? I'll have to thank him for his hospitality.'

'My name's Jennet and that was my brother Angus you saw. I'm not married. We live here with our grandmother and my wee boy Jamie.'

'Oh.' Mrs Dickson's eyes flew to Jennet's ringless left hand. There was an awkward pause, then her husband said, 'I'm Eric, and this is Mary. And this is wee Marion here.' He nodded at the little girl clinging to her mother's skirt. 'When would you like us to start work?'

'It's just at the haymaking we'll need a hand, sometime over the next day or so. Until then you can just please yourself and do whatever you want. Has Mollie told you that we can sell you milk and eggs?'

'She'd a right face on her when I took her tea up,' Mollie reported when Jennet went into the kitchen. 'She's not pleased tae see me back here.'

'She's not in a good mood with anyone just now, poor woman. She must be suffering with that bad leg of hers.'

'I don't think Angus is pleased to see me, either.' Mollie's voice was bleak and her shoulders, as she turned back to her work at the range, were slumped. Jennet put an arm about her.

'It's me he's annoyed with, for bringing the Dicksons to stay in the cottage. But we need their help and Angus knows it. Where's Jamie?'

'Out in the back garden with a drink of milk and a crust to dip in it.'

'It'll be good for him to have other children around.'

Mollie raised her eyes to the ceiling to indicate the upper floor. '*She* wants her notepad and a pen and I don't know where they are.'

'I'll get them for her,' Jennet said wearily, and went upstairs.

'Fetch my notepad, my inkwell and my pen. I'm writing to Rachel,' Celia announced as soon as her granddaughter arrived, 'to ask if she'd come to look after me properly.'

'Gran, you're being looked after properly as it is, and Great-Aunt Rachel hates being on the farm. It wouldn't be fair to drag her over here!'

'The top drawer of that chest over there,' Celia directed. 'And the inkwell, pen and blotter's on top of the chest.'

'She'll not come, and in any case Mollie's staying, Grandmother, for Jamie knows her, and she can help with things like feeding the hens, too.'

Searching for the notepad, locating it and the pen and ink, then settling them all on a tray so that Celia could write her letter, Jennet marvelled at her own bravado in answering her grandmother back. But it was the only way, she realised, to keep things together. At the moment Angus was an unknown quantity; she had no way of knowing whether he was going to fight for the farm or let their grandmother decide his future for him.

'I'll leave you in peace to write your letter. But there's no point in inviting Great-Aunt Rachel here,' she added from the bedroom door. 'Even if she agreed – and she won't – I've got enough on my hands with the haymaking without having to look after her as well. Anyway, there's nowhere for her to stay. With the cottage occupied, Mollie'll have to sleep in my room, since I've not got time to turn out the room Martin and Angus used to use.'

It was like the old days, when she and Mollie used to sneak out late at night while everyone slept, to wander along the lane to the seashore, or sit in the byre or in the stable with Nero if the nights were cold, talking and giggling and making wild plans for the future.

'But this is even better,' Mollie whispered into the darkness, 'because we don't even have to get out of bed to meet up with each other.' She wriggled into a more comfortable position. 'This bed's lumpy.'

'It always was. I've slept on this mattress all my life. It's been in the family for generations.'

'Back as far as the crusades, if you ask me.' Mollie wriggled again, then settled, yawning. 'I think one of your ancestors must have left a bit of his armour in it. I thought farming folk had nice mattresses stuffed with straw or hay?'

'Only the rich ones. We need all our straw and hay for the animals.'

'At least the bed's big enough for the two of us.'

Mollie was silent for a long moment and then said sleepily, 'Does Jamie always sound like that?'

'Like what?' Jennet, alarmed, sat bolt upright in the bed, straining her eyes through the darkness of the room to see the cot in the corner of the room. 'What's wrong with the way he sounds?'

'I didn't say there was anything wrong. Does he always breathe with these wee puffy sounds?'

'Yes, it's the way children breathe.'

'It sounds nice,' Molly said, and Jennet, her alarm over, fell back against her pillow.

'What about Joe, then?'

'He's just a nice lad, that's all. I'm not going to marry him.'

'How do you know?'

'He's not the right one.'

'Does that mean you've found the right one?'

There was a pause, then Mollie said, 'Mebbe.'

'Who is it?' Jennet was wide awake again.

'That's for me to know and you to find out.'

'Tell me!'

Mollie yawned again. 'Clark Gable. Now shut up and go to sleep,' she said.

Jennet lay staring at the grey patch of window beneath the house eaves. She had thought, once, that she had found the right one. But she had been wrong.

'Mollie . . . ?' she said tentatively after a long silence and was answered by a soft snore.

* * *

Struan had managed to find the part he needed for the old tractor, and as soon as the Gleniffer hay was gathered in he brought it over to Westervoe, where he spent half a day in the tractor shed before emerging to announce triumphantly that the machine was once more in working order.

'Since Jem's not here, I'll take it out to let you see for yourselves,' he offered, then gaped when Jennet said, 'No, I'll do it.'

'But you don't know how to drive a tractor!'

'You're old-fashioned, Struan Blaikie. Have you never heard of the Women's Land Army? Two of them worked on your father's farm.'

'But you were never in the Land Army.'

'As good as.' Celia, reluctant to have strangers on her land, had decreed that she and Jennet could manage the farm during the war with help from Angus, Jem and the McCabes. Bert, who took to farming like a duck to water, had been a great help and Jennet, determined to play her own part, had persuaded Jem to teach her to use the tractor. Now she marched towards it with Struan saying as he followed nervously, 'I'll start it for you.'

'Don't be daft,' she snapped at him. 'What's the use of being able to drive the thing if I can't start it myself?'

'It's got a terrible kick,' he warned as she seized the starting handle.

'I know. Why don't you go into the house and teach my grandmother to suck eggs, Struan?' she suggested rudely, and swung the handle. It took three tries, but when it did roar into life she was ready for the kick-back and managed to get away with only a mild jolt from wrist to shoulder. She eased the arm surreptitiously as she marched round to the side of the tractor and clambered aboard.

'Stand out the way.' She had not driven the thing for a while and deep down she was nervous, particularly as the roar and clatter of the old tractor brought Angus, Mollie, Jamie and the entire Dickson family out to see what was going on.

Blinking as she moved from the shed's darkness to the sun-bright yard, Jennet turned the unwieldy vehicle towards the lane. The Dicksons and Mollie were cheering and clapping and Gumrie was barking; she knew that because she could see their mouths opening and Gumrie bouncing about, the way he always did when he barked. Struan was shouting something and flapping his hands at her, but she couldn't hear a thing for the noise. Angus stood back, leaning against the byre wall, his face expressionless.

Jennet had forgotten how much the tractor jolted and shook. She settled her hips firmly into the shallow curved seat and concentrated on steering a straight course up the lane to the place where it bulged out on both sides. There, she managed to turn it and then drove it back, the onlookers who had followed her from the yard scattering to right and left to let her pass and then regrouping to run after her into the yard, where she did a lap of triumph before cutting the engine outside the tractor-shed door.

'There,' she said, climbing down to applause. 'Once you learn how to drive you don't forget.'

Struan's face was a mixture of expressions; on the one hand, she knew, he resented seeing a mere woman do something that had traditionally been done only by men. On the other, he admired her.

'Not bad,' he said.

'That's what I thought.' Her body still throbbed from the tractor's vibration but at least her voice was steady. She looked past Struan to where Angus stood watching and called across to him, 'Your turn now.'

'Jennet, for pity's sake, you know the man can't do that any more,' Struan hissed at her.

'I know nothing of the kind. Come on, Angus, I'll start it for you if you like.'

He shook his head. 'I think I'll leave it to you, since you do it so well,' he said, and turned to go back into the byre. Suddenly the Dicksons were shuffling about uncomfortably. Walter, the oldest boy, began to say something and was shushed by his father. Jennet hesitated, wondering if she had gone too far, then saw Mollie, her eyes clearly signalling 'Go on!'

It had worked with the crutches; it should surely work with the tractor, Jennet thought, putting her fists on her hips. 'Angus Scott, come here and try out this thing. You were always the best driver on the farm. You're surely not going to let me beat you?'

He had turned back to the yard; now he glared as he limped towards her. 'If it'll keep you happy,' he said, then as he reached her his voice dropped, 'but I'll probably make a right fool of myself.'

'You'll be more of a fool if you don't try,' she murmured.

He brushed past her, shook his head when Struan stepped forward to help, and propped his crutch on the tractor, making sure that it was out of the starter handle's way. After starting the vehicle up with the first swing of the handle, he used the crutch to get round to the side and then propped it up again and hauled himself up and into the seat, leaning down to lift the crutch and wedge it securely by his side. Then he swung the tractor round in a wide arc before taking it out into the lane with everyone following.

At the widest part of the lane, where Jennet had used the space to turn the machine in a circle, Angus operated the controls deftly to swing the tractor round, then reverse it so that he could turn it back towards the yard, where he reversed it into its shed before sliding to the ground.

When he emerged, crutch snugly tucked beneath his arm, there was an excited scatter of applause. Mollie, Jennet noticed, had put Jamie down in order to clap wildly, her freckled face beaming from ear to ear.

Angus acknowledged the cheers with a faint ducking of the head. 'All right?' he asked his sister. 'Can I get on with my work now?'

'You've been practising, haven't you?' she asked, her voice too low for anyone else to hear.

'You don't think I'd have touched the thing in front

of all those folk if I'd not been sure of myself, do you?'

'You . . . !' She punched him lightly on the arm. 'Why haven't you been driving it in the fields instead of leaving it all to Jem?'

'I couldnae bear the thought of Gran making a fuss and fretting in case I managed to turn the thing over with me underneath. Mebbe I would have, too; mebbe I've lost the right way of working it.'

'I doubt that,' Jennet said, and if it hadn't been for the onlookers she would have hugged him, even though their grandmother disapproved of unseemly demonstrations.

When she went into the kitchen Celia's walking stick was beating a steady tattoo on the bedroom floor above.

'Where have you been, and what in the name's going on out there?' she burst out as soon as her granddaughter appeared. She was sitting up in bed, her hair in stiff spikes around her head. 'It sounds as if the world's gone mad!'

'Struan's fixed the tractor, that's all, and I took it up the lane to try it out.'

'It sounded like more than that,' her grandmother said suspiciously. 'Who was doing all the clapping and cheering?'

'Just Mollie and the folk renting the cottage.'

'I knew they'd be a mistake. How's a body to get any rest with rabble like that carousing about the place day and night?'

Jennet began to smooth the blankets and shake out the pillows. 'They're not going to be carousing about the place at all,' she said. Then, realising that she might as well tell the truth now, rather than be caught out later, she continued, 'They just clapped when Angus took a shot as well.'

'Angus?' the old lady squawked. 'You let your brother drive the tractor? D'you want to kill him altogether?'

'He's perfectly able, Gran.'

'Of course he's not able, you stupid lassie, he's only got the use of one good leg. And how did he get into the seat? If Struan helped him up, I'll have something to say to that young man.'

'He climbed up himself, and he took the tractor into the lane, then brought it back and put it in the shed and climbed down again. He's as good with it as ever he was, Gran.'

'How can he be? Look at what happened to poor Drew Blaikie. What were you thinking of?'

'I was thinking that it's good for Angus to do more about this place. He's got the sense to know what he can and can't do.'

'Neither of you,' Celia said darkly, 'has the sense you were born with. Sometimes I think Rachel's right when she says I should wash my hands of you both, and Martin, too!'

The tirade flowed on, while Jennet tidied the bed and combed Celia's hair and wished, silently, that she would follow Great-Aunt Rachel's advice. There was nothing Jennet would like more than to be washed off her grandmother's hands.

With Mollie and Mary Dickson running the kitchen and looking after the two children and Celia, who was still confined to her bed, Jennet was free to work out in the field with the menfolk.

Angus and Jem had scythed the hay and, as tradition dictated, it had been left lying in the field for three weeks, 'hearing the church bells ring three times' and being turned regularly to ensure that it was thoroughly dried. Had there been much rain during the drying process, it would have had to be gone through again, but this year Nature had been kind.

It was a long tiring job, working from early morning until well into the evening, gathering up the dried hay and tying it by hand into bales that were then taken by cart to the hayloft. Eric Dickson proved to be an asset, cheerfully following orders without question or complaint, while his sons, brown as berries now, played in a corner of the field, out of the way but within calling distance so that they could be summoned to help where and when they were needed.

When their father sent them off to the farm to tell their mother that the workers were ready for some food, the two of them scampered off at once, to reappear half an hour later, each hauling on a shaft of the old red wooden dog cart that had once been harnessed to a pony and used to transport the Scott women and children.

Jamie was perched on the cart, giggling as it jolted from rut to hummock, while little Marion Dickson sat beside him, smiling nervously and clinging to the raised sides. Baskets filled with food and drink were packed around them, and Mollie and Mary Dickson walked on each side of the cart, keeping an eye on the children.

They were cheered into the field and almost knocked off their feet by the workers, hot and parched and starving. 'You don't mind, do you?' Mollie asked Jennet as she lifted Jamie down from the dog cart, then began unpacking the food. 'I remembered seeing this when we lived in the cottage, and it saved us havin' tae carry the wee ones as well as all the food.'

'It's nice to see it out and about again. Is Gran . . .'

'She's been fed and the nurse has dressed her leg. She thinks it's looking much better today. In fact, she thinks your gran could come downstairs for a wee while in a day or so, but she wants tae arrange for the doctor to visit first,' Mollie said while Jamie and Marion, who had become firm friends, scampered off across the field hand in hand, returning later to claim their share of the picnic.

Jennet sank down thankfully on the field's grassy fringe and mopped her face with a corner of her sacking apron. Across the Sound of Bute, glittering in the sunshine, Arran was mistily tranquil beneath a blue sky. Passenger steamers on the Tighnabruaich run churned along the Firth now and again, and the white sails of yachts slid past.

'It's grand, isn't it?' Struan came to sit by her side, nodding at the field, the shore beyond, the water and the hills that seemed, with the heat haze about them, to float on the water. 'I keep wondering if I'm going to wake up and discover that I've just been dreaming and I'm still far away from home.'

'D'you want me to pinch you just to make sure?' she asked, and he grinned.

'It would be better than a nip from a louse. That's what usually woke me when I was away.'

'You never had lice!'

'Of course I did, and so would you if you'd been days and nights without even the chance to take your uniform off or have a wash.'

'That's the sort of thing we didn't even think about, back here where things were much the same as usual.'

'Best not to think about them. And don't ever mention them to my mother, she'd not like the idea at all,' he said. Then, 'You've got bits of hay in your hair. Sit still a minute.'

His breath touched her cheek as his hands gently teased the dried grasses from the mane of hair she had tied back with a scarf. 'That's better,' he said, and then, his voice suddenly husky, 'Jennet, I swore tae myself that I'd not pester ye for an answer, but ye look that bonny today with the sun in your hair that I cannae wait any longer. Have ye thought about what I asked?'

Her heart sank. She looked round for Mollie in the hope that she could signal her friend to come to the rescue, but she, and the others, were watching the children playing among the hayricks. 'Struan,' she began carefully, 'I still don't think it would be the right thing for us to marry.'

'If it's my mother you're thinkin' on . . .'

'It's not . . . well, not just her. It's me, I don't want to get married to anyone.'

'Is it because ye're still pinin' after the wee lad's father?'

Surprised, she turned to look into his sun-warmed face. 'Of course not, that's all in the past.'

'Then I suppose I'll have tae accept what ye say.' He got to his feet, then stood for a moment, looking down at her. 'But I'll ask ye again, because you're the one I want, Jennet.'

12

As Struan went off to play with the children, Jennet, unable to face the others just then, began to pile loose hay on the dog cart to make a soft bed for the children's return journey. As she finished she saw that Angus, sitting with Andra Blaikie, Eric Dickson, Jem and Bert McCabe, was watching Struan and the children, his mouth tight and his fingers shredding a grass stem.

For a moment she thought that he disapproved of the way his friend was gambolling about like a child himself, then she realised that he was envious of Struan's ability to tumble about with the youngsters when he himself could not.

He met her gaze and grabbed his crutch, using it to lever himself up from the ground. 'Back to work,' he bellowed, brushing away Eric's attempt to help him to his feet. Mollie and Mary, who like the rest of her family had blossomed in the few days they had been staying in the farm cottage, scooped up the exhausted toddlers and sat them in their nest of hay, then they each took a shaft and began to haul the cart back to Westervoe while the others returned to their back-breaking work. Jennet and Struan were using long-handled pitchforks to pass hay up to Andra and Eric, who stood on the bed of the cart.

By mid-afternoon the Dickson boys had begun to weary of the field. Their father lifted them onto the back of the loaded cart, where they were able to swing their legs over the tail.

'I just hope they don't get any ideas when we go back home,' he said as his sons went off, grinning. 'Cadgin' a ride in the country's one thing, but it's not the same in a city street.'

'Did you never run after a cart and jump onto the back of it for a wee hurl, man?' Angus challenged, and the man laughed.

'Of course I did, but my father and mother never liked it any more than I do now it's my own bairns.'

It was a relief when milking time came. Jennet rested the butt of her fork on the ground so that she could straighten her stiff back gradually, and pushed back her hair, damp with sweat, with a swipe of her hand. Eric jumped down from the cart to take over from her, nudged on by Andra's 'Come on, man, the hay'll no' float up here on its own!'

She and Angus hobbled rather than walked to the field where the cows, waiting patiently by the gate to be taken to the byre, blinked at them in gentle-eyed surprise.

'They think we've aged years since the last milking,' Jennet said as she swung the gate open.

'And they're right,' Angus answered as the two of them trailed after the animals like tired children tagging along after their parents. At one point Jennet dozed off in the byre, slumped against a round warm flank, not realising that she was asleep until Mollie said from above her head, 'Are you really going to dive into that pail of milk, or would you settle for a cup of tea instead?'

Jennet sat hurriedly upright. 'I wasn't sleeping . . .'

'Only thinking; I know, your brother's tried that one on me already. Here,' Mollie thrust the steaming mug at her. 'Get that down your throat before you go back. And you can take this with you.' She indicated the bottle-filled basket at her feet. 'They must be parched out in that field.'

Some farmers made use of a wooden-toothed, horse-drawn hay gatherer known as a 'Tumblin' Tam', which left the hay in piles to be built into haystacks out in the yard, but at Westervoe the hay was carted from the field to the hayloft.

'And a good thing too, since we'd have to hire someone to thatch it properly,' Jennet explained to Eric Dickson as they perched on the tailgate of the cart, swinging their legs. 'It takes a master craftsman to do that job well enough to leave the hay weatherproof.'

'It's good to see the field cleared and know the job's been done right.' He indicated the cleared area as the cart jolted out of the gate. Dusk was falling and the midges had begun to bite; he leaned forward, holding on with one hand and using the other to scratch at the calf of his leg. 'It's amazin' how much there is to know about the country. I've learned more in the past few days than I learned in a year before.'

'And you've had to work hard. This is supposed to be your holiday.'

'It's been the best ever, for all of us,' he assured her.

The light spilling from the kitchen's open windows was welcoming, but Andra scorned Jennet's offer of supper before going home.

'We'll have the supper, but we've got the last load of hay to stow away before then.'

'But it's nearly eleven o'clock!' groaned Jem.

'If a job's worth doing, it's worth doing well. You go in and help with the food, Jennet . . . Angus, you can tend tae your horse. The rest of you . . . get on with it.'

'They're working on and Jem's not best pleased,' Jennet reported when she went into the kitchen, blinking and putting a hand up to shade her face. Soft though the lamplight was, it seemed over-bright after the darkness outside. 'I doubt we'll see him at the early milking tomorrow.'

'He'll look happier when he's got a good supper in his belly,' Mollie predicted confidently from the range, where she and Mary Dickson were hard at work.

'We'll all feel happier.' The smell of cooking made Jennet's mouth water. 'How's . . .'

'She's fed and watered and the same goes for the pigs,' Mollie said blandly, but with a gleam in her eyes. 'And all three of them are comfortable. The hens have been shut up and the cats fed, and I'm just about to put Gumrie's dinner out for him. And the byre's ready for the morning.'

'Mollie, you're an angel.'

'I know I am, but it's thanks to Mary here that I was able to get out and get the work done. I nearly fed the calf, before I remembered that the wee thing's not here any more.'

'We'd a bad time with Jamie when she was taken away. He looked high and low for her for days. I don't know what he'll be like when the pigs have to go in the autumn. Did he go to his bed all right?'

'He's not exactly in his bed,' Mollie said. 'He's in yours. They were all asleep on their feet, even the big lads, so we tucked the lot of them into the same bed. It was the best way, since Mary's working here with me.'

'I hope you don't mind,' Mary added anxiously. She and her pretty little daughter had never quite lost their shyness, though their menfolk had made themselves at home in and around the farm within the first twenty-four hours.

'Of course not, it's a good idea. I'll just look in on Grandmother.'

'Not until you've stopped being a scarecrow.'

Mollie nodded at the grasses that had drifted to the floor around Jennet's feet. Hurriedly she retreated to the yard, where she took off her big apron and her headscarf and shook them hard to get rid of most of the hay caught in their folds. Then she brushed herself down and ran her fingers through her hair before tying it back again. The men were still bustling round the cart in the last of the day's light, hefting bales of hay between it and the shed that housed the hay-loft.

'How's the hay doing?' Celia said as soon as Jennet put her head round the door.

'I thought you'd be asleep by now.'

'How can I sleep when it's haymaking? What's happening?'

'The field's cleared and the men are just putting the last of it into the loft.'

'Mind and give them a good supper. They deserve it and Westervoe's always been known for its hospitality.'

'Mollie and Mary are setting out a banquet fit for a king. Would you like me to bring something up for you?'

'I've got no appetite, stuck here day after day,' Celia grumbled. 'But since you're here at last, you could fetch the bedpan. I could fairly do with it.'

'You should have got someone up before this.'

'I don't care to be beholden to strangers,' Celia said stiffly.

'Mollie's not a stranger . . . and Mary's a very nice

woman. She'd be pleased to do anything she could for you. Hold onto my arm and I'll ease you up.'

'You smell like a hayfield,' her grandmother said as she was settled on the chamber pot. 'It's a good smell.' The longing in her voice was so strong that Jennet wished she could lift the old woman up in her arms and carry her downstairs and out into the fresh air, away from the claustrophobic room, which must be like a prison cell to someone so used to being out and about all the time.

But she had to settle for saying, 'It's a good crop. We'll be all right for the winter feeding.'

'Someone else will, you mean,' Celia said harshly. 'I've decided that we'll move out as soon as the factor finds a new tenant. No sense in waiting until the spring if we can go before winter. Don't just stand there, lassie. How can I do my business with you staring at me? Come back in a minute or two.'

Jennet moved on to her own room. In the dim light from the window the four children sleeping in her bed were just a smudgy row of heads on the pillows. The air was filled with the sound of breathing, some of it snuffly, some of it light and even. Jennet tiptoed out again and waited in the dark corridor, leaning against the wall, until the muffled sound of Celia's bladder being emptied ended, and it was safe to go into the room and help her back to bed.

Despite the exhaustion of a long, hard day's work, elation at knowing that yet another task had been successfully completed turned the late supper into a party. The mountain of food prepared by Mollie and Mary vanished with surprising speed and the big teapot was refilled again and again.

Finally Andra pushed back his chair, slapping both hands on his generous belly. 'By jings, that was good! I'm that set up I could go out and do another day's work.'

'You'll have to in just a few hours,' Angus reminded him wryly.

'Ach, well, we can catch up on our sleep during the long winter nights. That's the way it is in farming. Come on then,' Andra ordered his son and Bert McCabe, 'time we werenae here.'

Even the business of removing the Dickson children from the bed had not roused Jamie fully. He murmured irritably when Jennet eased him into her arms, swatting at her with a limp hand; then, as she shushed him, he fell back into sleep, his soft breath stirring against her neck.

For a long and precious moment she stood by the window, holding him close and looking out at the night. She would have remained like that for much longer if Mollie hadn't come in with a lamp, yawning and knuckling her sleepy eyes.

'What a day! It's a lot easier looking after lodgers.'

'I'm sure it is.' Reluctantly Jennet laid Jamie down in his own little cot and drew the blanket over him. Behind her Mollie busied herself with the bed, plumping up the two pillows and smoothing the lower sheet.

'At least none of them have peed in it. I wondered when Mary suggested putting them all in here together if it would be all right, but I didnae like to say anything.' She began to undress.

'Struan asked me again, today.'

'When did he manage to find the time?'

'When you were all watching the children playing. I turned him down, Mollie.'

'Quite right, and better to do it now than keep the poor man waiting and hoping. Was he all right about it?'

'He says he'll ask me again, later.'

'How is it,' Mollie asked, irritated, 'that men cannae just take no for an answer when they never seem to have any trouble with "yes"?' She buttoned her pyjama jacket and picked up her hairbrush. 'He must be really sweet on you.'

'I wish he wasn't. Now I know I've got it all to go through again.'

'Best leave what happens next till it happens,' Mollie said philosophically, her hair crackling and glowing like flames in the lamplight as she brushed it.

A bicycle spun into the yard the following evening, its rider ringing the tinny little bell on the handlebars to announce his arrival and setting the hens squawking, and Gumrie barking, while the cats arched their backs and spat.

Mollie, giving Jamie his bath while Jennet made his supper, jumped up and looked out of the window. 'It's that Joe Wilson!'

'The lad that works with Uncle George?' Jennet joined her at the window. 'So it is. He's come to call on you, Mollie.'

'The cheek of him, just turning up without as much as a by your leave!'

'Since when did folk have to make an appointment to see your ladyship?' Angus asked from the table, where he had taken the chance to have a quick look at the newspaper.

'Well, I mean . . . He's got no right to come chasing after me like that!' Mollie, flustered and pink-cheeked, made for the door. 'I'll find out what he wants and send him off home.'

'You will not, you'll ask him in, since he's cycled all this way just to see you,' Jennet called after her. Then to Jamie, who had taken advantage of the sudden inattention to lift a soapy arm high above his head and was preparing to smack the flat of his hand down hard on the water, thus creating a tidal wave, 'No you don't, young man. I've got enough to do without mopping up the floor after you.'

She snatched up a towel and scooped him out of the bath, then carried him to the big wingback chair that was usually her grandmother's property. Secretly she was glad of the chance to dry her son's wriggling little body and tuck him into his pyjamas. She loved the weight of him in her lap and the freshly bathed smell of him, and the way his damp, fairish brown hair stuck up in little spikes about his neat skull. Since Mollie had come back to Westervoe to help out, Jennet had missed her time with Jamie.

Mollie came stamping back into the kitchen followed by Joe, a young man no taller than she was, his fair hair rumpled from his bike ride. He shook hands shyly with Angus and Jennet, chucked Jamie under the chin and refused the offer of some tea.

'You'll take it,' Mollie snapped. 'It's not polite to refuse.'

'Mebbe you'd prefer a glass of lemonade,' Jennet suggested. 'It's a warm evening.'

'Aye, that would go down well,' he agreed, and allowed Mollie to push him down into a chair by the table. Angus, who before his accident had been the most social member of the Scott family, folded the newspaper, cleared his throat and announced that he was going to start putting the hens in for the night.

While Mollie fetched the lemonade, Jennet began to supervise Jamie's supper, a bowl of bread and milk. 'You'll be keeping busy with the holidaymakers?' she asked their visitor, wiping a dribble of milk from Jamie's chin.

'It never stops. As fast as a boat comes in it's out again.'

'You'd think with all the hirers round the bay, and at Port Bannatyne too, that there might not be enough customers to go round.'

Joe grinned, more relaxed now that he was on a

subject he knew. 'Not a bit of it. Ye can see the folk dashin' off the steamers as soon as they come in tae get tae the wee boats. It's like watchin' ants round an anthill, so it is. Some of them come to the island every year, and they have their favourite hirer and their favourite boat. They get right irritated if someone else's got it out when they come lookin' for it.'

'You'll be glad of Sam's help then.'

'He's a nice lad and he fairly likes workin' with the boats. I'm teachin' him to row,' Joe said proudly. 'He's comin' along well.' Then, his grin widening, 'The other day . . .'

'Now don't you start on any of your boring stories, Joe Wilson,' Mollie broke in. 'Jennet's got more to do than sit and listen to you goin' on about these blessed boats of yours.'

'I do want to hear about them, and I'm not doing anything else, because it'll take Jamie a while to work his way through this bowlful.' Jennet frowned at her friend, who frowned back. 'What were you saying about Sam?'

Joe had just taken a mouthful of lemonade. He choked slightly, then managed to swallow it down despite the way Mollie thumped his back. 'He came with me the other mornin' tae fetch the boats round from the inner harbour. They're all linked together, see, with a motor-boat at the front so's they can be towed round to the bay fast before the holiday folk get down there. They have to be washed out first, see, and I'd done my lot and got back into the motor-boat and started the engine ready to go. Sam was climbin' intae the punt at the back tae wash it, only he slipped and fell, didn't he?'

'Into the water? Can he swim?'

'After a fashion – we all have to be able tae do that, the number of times we go in. Anyway, he managed to catch hold of the side of the punt, so I knew he was all right. I'd started up and I could see one of the other hirers on his way to fetch his boats, so I just kept going, out of the harbour and round in front of the pier to our berth, with Sam bein' pulled along behind me.' He gurgled with laughter, slapping his knee. Jamie, who had been following the story closely without understanding it, burst out laughing too, spraying the table with bread and milk.

'And when did he get out of the water?' Jennet asked, mopping the table and Joe's arm, both speckled with her son's supper.

'That was the laugh; by the time I got round, folk were already beginnin' tae queue, so I was too busy tae do anythin' about Sam. One lady says tae me, "Boatman, d'you know there's someone out there in the water, holding on to one of your boats?" and I says, "It's all right, ma'am, that's just our Sam, he'll keep."'

'Was he all right?' Despite her irritation, Mollie had been following the story closely.

'Right as rain. Looked a bit like a wet day by the time I got round to haulin' him out, though,' Joe added. 'He'd to go sloppin' off tae the house tae get changed.'

Though Jamie wanted to stay with their visitor, Jennet took him up to his bed as soon as he had finished his supper. 'Who's that downstairs?' her grandmother called out to her as she passed her bedroom door.

'Just a friend of Mollie's.'

'A friend? A man by the sound of it.'

'A very nice young man. Be still for a minute,' Jennet told her son, who was wriggling about in her arms.

'We've got more to do than entertain her callers!'

'He'll not be staying long. Mollie didn't know he was coming here and she's not pleased about it. I'm just putting Jamie to bed,' Jennet said, and escaped to her room.

When she returned to the kitchen, tiptoeing along the corridor so that her grandmother would not hear her and summon her to an interrogation, Joe got to his feet. 'I'd best be gettin' back.'

'You don't need to rush away,' Jennet assured him. 'Stay as long as you like.'

'I was wonderin' if Mollie would like to come out for a wee run with me, seein' as it's such a nice night.'

'A good idea, she's been working too hard and she needs some fresh air, don't you, Mollie?' Jennet smiled into the other girl's angry eyes. 'Just give me some time to help my brother with the hens, then you can be off.'

'He seems nice enough, Mollie's young man,' Jennet said as she joined Angus at the hen houses.

He grunted, shooing in the last hen, which had stopped for a final peck at the ground, then slamming the door down behind it.

'Gran wasn't pleased. She seems to think that Mollie's got no right to have followers.'

'If she had her way, the world would come to an end because nobody'd be allowed to have followers,' he said over his shoulder as he made for the next ark.

'It depends who they are,' Jennet said. 'Gran and Mrs Blaikie did all they could to push Drew and me together. And we weren't even all that bothered about each other.'

'It was always Allan Blaikie you were keen on, wasn't it?'

Jennet, about to close an ark door, stopped and straightened, staring at him. 'What makes you think that?'

'Oh, wee things. Like the way you always made sure your hair-ribbons were neatly tied when you knew he was coming over.' A teasing note crept into his voice. 'And your sudden interest in baking when you discovered how fond he was of gingerbread. Martin and me weren't, but we'd to eat it anyway. And the way you went all pink whenever Allan walked into the kitchen. Just as Mollie did when her friend Joe arrived a wee while ago.'

'I was only a schoolgirl then,' Jennet told him sharply. 'Schoolgirls always need to have a crush on someone. And you don't know as much about women as you think, Angus Scott, for Mollie was flushed because she was angry with Joe for arriving out of the blue, not because she fancies him.'

'Aye, that'll be right,' he said sarcastically, and swung himself towards the next row of arks.

13

'Joe had no right to embarrass me in front of you and Angus,' Mollie said that night when Angus had gone to bed.

'How did he embarrass you? He's a nice lad, there was nothing wrong with him calling on you.'

'It's not my house, though. What did Angus say? Was he angry about Joe?'

'No, why should he be angry?'

'The way he went out not long after Joe arrived . .'

'You know Angus, he's not good with strangers since his accident. And he'd have gone out anyway because the hens had to be shut in for the night.'

'And I don't know what got into you, making me go out with Joe.'

'You needed some time off; he's a nice lad and he'd come all that way just to see you.'

'He's asked me to go to the dancing with him tomorrow night, at the Winter Gardens.'

'I hope you said you would. You love dancing.'

'So do you. Why don't you come, too?'

'Have you never heard that two's company and three's a crowd?'

'I'm serious, Jennet. You need time off more than I do. I'm sure Joe could find someone for you.'

'No, thanks.'

'Och, go on! It could be like the old days.'

'I couldn't leave Angus on his own with Jamie and Gran to see to.'

'I'm sure Mary Dickson would help out. She's a nice woman, when you get past her shyness, and she's good with Jamie. He's loving it, having wee Marion to play with.'

'The Dicksons are going home the next day and it wouldn't be right to expect Mary to help out on her last night here. Anyway, I don't really want to go dancing any more,' Jennet said stubbornly, and nothing Mollie said could change her mind.

Dancing belonged to another time, another Jennet. The past could never be brought back.

'You're squiggling it, I can feel you squiggling it!'

'I am not,' Jennet retorted, 'it's your legs, they're all bandy.'

'Cheeky b . . .' Mollie, standing on a chair in the kitchen, remembered just in time that Jamie was an interested observer, and changed it to 'Cheeky thing. I've got lovely legs, haven't I, Jamie?'

'Got tea on them,' he said, giggling.

'Only because your Auntie Mollie can't afford to buy stockings. And she's too respectable to get them from a Yank.'

'There aren't any American soldiers on Bute, you mean.' Jennet paused to lick the stubby eyebrow pencil that Mollie had managed to keep all through the war years, then returned to the task of drawing a straight line down the calf of her friend's left leg, to simulate the seam of a stocking. Mollie had already rubbed strong tea into both legs to create an instant tan.

'Now if I was our Senga, I could have all the silk stockings I wanted, on the black market,' Mollie said. 'Did I tell you her boyfriend's one of those spivs that can get you anything you want?'

'For a price.'

'From what I know of our Senga, she'll be payin' in kind.' Mollie's voice was heavy with disapproval. 'I don't know what Da's thinking of, letting her behave like a . . .' Again Mollie paused, remembering Jamie, then she went on, 'like that. Too busy with his own fancy woman, I suppose.'

'Stop chattering, you're putting me off. Can you go over there for a minute, pet?' Jennet added to Jamie, who was watching her work so closely that his head was pressed against hers. His tongue, like hers, was sticking out; now he drew it in to say, 'I'm helping!' and then it appeared again and his eyes, close to Mollie's tea-stained legs, concentrated so hard that they went into a squint. Jennet had to swallow down her amusement in order to focus all her attention on getting the line straight.

She had reached Mollie's heel when Angus walked in from the yard. Mollie immediately shot off the chair, pushing down the skirt she had been holding up round her thighs. The chair rocked back on two legs and Jennet had to catch and steady it as Mollie hurriedly put her shoes on.

Angus looked in surprise at the three startled faces. 'What's amiss?'

'Drawing on Mollie's legs,' Jamie explained helpfully, and the girl swooped on him, tickling him until he was helpless.

'See you, you've got a big mouth, Jamie Scott.'

'So have you. It's red,' he said between shrieks of laughter. 'And you smell.'

'That's perfume! Say you like it . . . say it or I'll tickle you to bits!'

'I like it, I like it!' Jamie shrieked.

'Joe's taking Mollie dancing tonight,' Jennet explained to her brother. 'Doesn't she look lovely? Let him have a look at you, Mollie.'

The girl released Jamie and stood awkwardly before Angus, looking for all the world, Jennet thought, as though she were a naughty child who had been sent to the headmaster for punishment.

Mollie's eyes were bright with embarrassment under Angus's scrutiny and her hair curled round her flushed face. She was wearing a floral-patterned skirt and a short-sleeved peasant-style blouse that she had embroidered herself with poppies and cornflowers along the low elasticised neckline. It had slipped at one side, revealing the curve of a shoulder, and now she pushed it back into place, her flush deepening.

'Very nice,' Angus said, his voice flat, and went over to the sink. 'The byre's swept out and ready for the morning.'

'Is that all you can s—'

'I'd best go,' Mollie cut in, snatching up her jacket and her bag. 'I said I'd meet Joe at seven, to make sure we got in all right.'

'Mind now, you don't have to hurry back tomorrow morning. We can see to things,' Jennet instructed as she and Jamie followed the girl out into the yard, where Jennet's battered bicycle was propped against the wall. 'It'll be nice for you to spend a night with your mother and Sam. Tell them all that we're asking after them. And have a lovely time.'

'I'll have a great time. It'll be good to be dancing again.' Mollie finished tying a scarf over her hair to keep it from being blown to bits, slung her bag into the basket and seized the handlebars. 'I'll tell you all about it when I get back,' she called as she pushed off. Then, with a cheerful trill on the bell, she headed across the courtyard and into the lane.

As she cycled along the road to Rothesay, where Joe was waiting for her, Mollie blinked hard to hold back the tears that threatened to ruin her carefully applied mascara.

'Very nice,' he had said, in that flat voice that he always used when he was angry, or bored. He hadn't even looked at her properly. He never did, because as far as he was concerned she was nothing more than a nuisance, an evacuee from Glasgow, a pest who had nagged him out of his chair and onto a crutch. He had been glad when she and her family left Westervoe, and dismayed when his sister brought her back to help out after Mrs Scott's accident. She knew it.

She sniffed hard and told herself that he didn't matter a jot. If that was the way Angus wanted it, it was all right with her. Mollie McCabe had her whole life in front of her; she was going places, and one day he might realise that there was more to her than just a Glasgow lassie who got in the way of his precious life. But his discovery would come too late, because by then, she vowed to herself, she would have found someone else who could make her knees go weak and her heart flutter by being in the same room.

She rang the bell for no reason at all, just as an exclamation mark to her decision. She was going dancing and it was going to be a great evening, and Joe was waiting for her. Joe liked her. It was good to have a lad who liked you.

She came to the top of a hill and stuck her feet out to the sides, freewheeling down, forging through the rush of air that sought to hold her back. 'Look out, world, Mollie McCabe's coming,' she shouted into the wind.

But deep inside she couldn't forget that flat voice

saying, 'Very nice', and the way he had immediately turned away and started talking about his precious byre.

'You might have been more enthusiastic,' Jennet said when she returned to the kitchen. 'Mollie looked lovely, and you know it.'

'I said she looked very nice, didn't I?'

'I've heard you compliment one of the cows with more enthusiasm. You disappointed her.'

'Don't be daft, she doesn't give a damn about my opinions.'

'Of course she does. You're a man, aren't you?'

'I doubt if that's the way Mollie McCabe sees me,' Angus said. He had washed and rinsed his hands; now he reached for the soap and started again. Anything to keep his back turned to Jennet and her nagging, he thought sourly.

He looked at the water gushing from the tap, and the soap bubbles foaming over the backs of his hands, and thought about the flush on Mollie's pretty face, the way her eyes had been sparkling with excitement at meeting her lad. He recalled the glimpse of the hollow between the tops of her soft full breasts as she stooped to put on her shoes, and the way her pretty blouse had slipped, revealing the smooth creamy curve of her shoulder.

Angus swallowed hard in an attempt to rid himself of such thoughts and seized the small stiff-bristled brush, scrubbing at his nails until the skin immediately below them stung. Then he rinsed again and again before straightening and reaching for the towel.

He dried each finger meticulously, then picked up the crutch that came between him and everything he wanted most in the world and made his way through the kitchen to his room.

Celia Scott managed to get downstairs the next morning with help from Jennet and the nurse, who warned as she settled her patient in the wingback chair, 'Mind now, no walking around. You'll only make the wound worse again.'

'I'm not a daft bairn, or a silly-headed lassie,' Celia snapped. 'I know how to look after myself!'

'If you knew that, then why did you hurt yourself so badly in the first place?' asked the nurse, who had known her for years and was in a position to take certain liberties.

Any rebellious plans the invalid might have had soon disappeared. Since Jennet and Angus were busy and Mollie was not yet back from Rothesay, Celia was left in charge of Jamie, who was under strict instructions to be a good boy, fetch anything Great-Gran needed and make sure that he didn't go too close to her bad leg. He followed every instruction to the letter, but even so Celia was exhausted and longing for her bed by the time Jennet came in to make a cup of tea in the middle of the morning.

She helped the older woman upstairs and came back down to find Jem sitting at the kitchen table eating biscuits while Angus made the tea. 'She's not nearly as able as she thought she was, and I had the devil's own job getting her upstairs on my own. I don't know when she'll be able to get back to working the farm, if ever.'

'She'll manage it,' Jem predicted. 'I know that woman. I came tae this farm as a lad, not long after she got wed. I was here when yer father was born, and I mind that she dropped him as easy as winkin' and got back tae her farm work within days. A wee cut on the leg won't hold her still for long.'

'It was more than a wee cut, Jem, it was a right bad gash and it went septic. She's not as young as she used to be, remember.'

'None of us are, lassie,' the old man said, his eyes suddenly bleak. 'None of us are.'

Just then there was a sudden flurry in the yard, and the brisk tinging of an old bicycle bell. Angus, slumped at the table with a mug of tea between his two hands, groaned. 'She's back again.'

'Just in time for her tea,' Jennet said as Jamie tumbled out through the door to welcome Mollie. She swept into the kitchen, beaming round at all and sundry, with the little boy clamouring at her heels, 'Present?'

'Jamie! Mind your manners.'

'Ach, leave him alone, Jen. Yes, I did bring you somethin', Mr Nosy, but you'll have tae wait till later, when I've had a nice cup of tea. I'm parched!'

'Did you enjoy the dancing?'

'It was grand,' Mollie said enthusiastically. 'We danced every dance and your auntie said to invite Joe back for his supper after, so we'd a nice time at the house as well.'

'Come on, Jem, time we were back at work.' Angus planted his hands flat on the table and heaved himself to his feet.

'I don't know what's wrong with Angus,' Jennet said as the men went out with Jamie trailing behind them. 'He's been out of sorts all day. Mebbe it's because Grandmother was downstairs earlier.'

'Ach, it's just his way,' Mollie said airily. 'Anyway, about the dancing . . .'

The Dicksons left the following morning, tanned and happy after their holiday.

'The best yet,' Eric said enthusiastically, pumping Jennet's hand, then Mollie's, vigorously.

'Eric's right, the bairns had a wonderful time, and so did we, didn't we, Eric?' Mary's face, wan and creased with worry when Jennet had first met her, was wreathed in smiles now.

'I'm goin' tae be a farmer when I grow up,' Walter announced, and his brother, not to be outdone, chimed in, 'An' I'm goin' tae be a tractor man an' all!'

'This is for you . . .' Mary handed an envelope over. 'It's the rent we agreed on.'

'But that was before you all put so much work into the haymaking,' Jennet protested. 'You earned the cottage.'

'Then call it a thank you for your kindness in taking us in,' Mary urged, while Eric chimed in with, 'We just want to show our appreciation.'

'Me and Mam and the rest of us were just the same as them, all peely-wally when we arrived, and fit and brown when we left,' Mollie mused as they waved goodbye to the Glasgow family. 'There's somethin' about this place that's good for folk.'

'Unless you grow up here,' Jennet said wryly, and then, opening the envelope, 'This is too much, I'll have to make them take it back!'

'Hold on . . .' Mollie put a hand on her arm as she was about to set off across the yard. 'Let's see.' She took the envelope and tipped its contents into her hand, skimming deftly through the notes and coins. 'No, it's fine. Less than your auntie charges, but she provides breakfast as well. And don't even think about giving it back, it'll be the money they put aside for this holiday, and decent working folk like them don't like to feel beholden.'

'If you're sure that it's what they want . . . It'll help to pay for the hire of the threshing mill in November,' Jennet said as Mollie nodded vigorously. 'Or it could pay for an extra farmhand to help out with the oat harvest.'

'When I was staying in Rothesay the other night after the dance,' Mollie mentioned casually, 'your auntie was saying that the place is still full to bursting. She wondered if you'd be willing to take in some more trippers.'

'Gran would never agree to it. She only let the Dicksons stay because they were here by the time she knew about them.'

'Jennet, you're a grown woman with a child of your own and a mind of your own, too. And Angus is older than you are. Is it not time the two of you stopped fretting about what your gran wants? Surely the farm belongs to you just as much as to her, now.'

'You're right, and if renting the cottage out brings in some money, it would be worth doing. And it's only until the holiday season's over. I'll speak to Angus,' Jennet said.

'It's not worth the fuss Gran would make,' Angus said decisively the next morning as he and Jennet went to bring the cows in.

'But we need the money, and surely this is our chance to show her that we can bring in extra money and run the place perfectly well between us. She's still determined to let it go back to the estate, come Martinmas. We don't have all that much time to take matters into our own hands.'

They had reached the gate; Angus unfastened it and gave it a push so that it swung wide. The cows began to amble out, supervised by Gumrie, and when they were all clear of the gate Jennet gave it a hefty push, then managed to slip through the narrowing opening before the big gate hit against its post.

'We're not bairns playing pretend games now,'

Angus said irritably as he latched the gate. 'This is real life.'

'And it's the only one we've got, so we should make the most of it. You surely don't want to leave this place?' She indicated the fields, the great blue arch of sky above, the familiar rutted lane and the cows themselves, their great backsides swinging rhythmically and their tails swishing at the occasional fly.

'I tried making the most of my life once, and look where it got me. Come on,' Angus added impatiently to a cow lagging behind the others. She gave him a surprised look from her large gentle eyes and then hastened her pace slightly. 'How could the two of us run this place?'

'Gran managed when we were growing up.'

'Only by making the three of us work here every minute we were out of school. D'you not remember having to get up at the crack of dawn and work till it was time to go to the classroom, then starting again when we came home, until it got dark? D'you really want that for Jamie?'

'It doesn't have to be like that for him. I'm sure that you and I could think of a better system. Anyway, we had good times, too,' Jennet argued.

'Not many, and there was no chance of us choosing what we wanted to do with our lives; Martin and me had it dinned into us from the time we could walk that we were going to be farmers, and the three of us were taken out of school as soon as we were old enough to work here full time. Not that we had much in the way of brains, but you could have stayed on in school, Jennet, if she'd let you. You could have made something of yourself.'

'I got to Glasgow, remember? And it wasn't Gran that spoiled my chances there – I did it myself. We could make a go of Westervoe between us, Angus, with help from Jem and Mollie.'

'Mollie's a city lassie,' Angus said scathingly. 'She can't run a farm any more than I can.'

His apparent determination to look on the black side began to anger Jennet. 'She can look after the house and the garden and Jamie, so's I can get on with the work. She can feed the hens, the pigs and any calves we might have. She can look after the holidaymakers who'd rent the cottage.'

'Jen . . . !' he began, then shrugged and let the matter drop as they turned in at the farmyard.

Jennet picked it up again later, once the cows were back in their field and the milk had been cooled and poured into large churns that Mollie, Jennet and Jem manhandled between them to the lane, to wait for the cart that would take them to the boat. Angus had been brushing out the byre; now Jennet joined him, picking up a wide shovel and hefting straw and dung into a barrow.

'You saw how much the Dicksons enjoyed helping out on the farm, Angus, and other folk would enjoy that sort of thing, too. They see it as something different. It's not like work to them; it's pleasure because they're only doing it for a week or mebbe two. And Aunt Ann says she can send folk to us.'

'You think Grandmother would agree to that?' Angus asked.

'You're the oldest and the farm's really yours now, specially since Martin's not coming back. It's you who should decide these things, not her.'

He stopped work and leaned on the brush. 'Do as she says, Jen, go back to Glasgow, get on with that training and think of your own future, and Jamie's.'

'And what about yours?'

'This,' said Angus, slapping his crippled leg with the flat of his hand, 'is the rest of my life. And whether I spend it in Largs or Outer Mongolia doesn't matter.'

'For God's sake, man, you've got a bad leg and that's all that's wrong with you! The rest of you works fine, so why shouldn't you be a farmer like you've always wanted?'

'Mebbe what I want now is peace from your naggin'. Mebbe all I want to do is get out of this . . . this prison and go and live in a place like Largs, where I might meet folk and enjoy myself!'

'All right then, you go and have a good time with Grandmother and Great-Aunt Rachel. I'm staying on here, Angus, and I'm keeping this farm going for me and Jamie, and if you won't help me I'll find some other way.'

'Supposing he grows up like his Uncle Martin and throws it all back in your face?'

'So that's what's been gnawing away at you?' Jennet picked up the handles of the loaded barrow, taking a moment to steady herself against the weight. 'You were counting on Martin coming back so that you could work the farm between you. And now you think you're going to lose it. But you don't need to. Martin might not be here, but I am,' she stormed, and when he turned his back on her and said nothing, she flounced out of the byre – or as close to flouncing as she could get, weighted down as she was by a barrowful of dung.

14

'I'm going to my sister Rachel's,' Celia Scott announced as the midday meal ended. 'She's willing to have me and there's a nice garden at the back where I can sit out and rest this daft leg of mine.'

She glared from face to face as though waiting for a comment, but both her grandchildren were so surprised by the unexpected news that it fell to Jem to say, as he pushed his chair back, 'Aye, well, that's the sensible thing tae do. Ye're of no use tae anyone here as ye are. I'm off back tae the end field tae have a look at the hedgin',' he added to Angus, and stumped out.

'He's right of course, I'm useless round here until my leg mends, so I might as well get out of the way. And it'll give me and Rachel the chance to sort out what's to happen once this place is off our hands.'

'When are you going?' Angus asked.

'Rachel's coming over today to help me with the travelling.'

'Great-Aunt Rachel's coming here? Today?' Jennet rose in a panic, looking round the kitchen. Great-Aunt Rachel, like Mrs Blaikie, disapproved of untidiness.

Celia glanced at the clock. 'She'll be on the boat now. She'll get the bus out here, and Andra Blaikie's kindly offered to take us back to the pier so's you can both get on with seeing to this place.'

'When did you arrange this? Why did you not tell me sooner, so that I could have got things ready for Great-Aunt Rachel?'

'You've been too wrapped up in your work to pay any attention to what a poor old body like me has to say,' Celia said spitefully.

'Gran, you know I'd have listened!'

'Well, it was only arranged yesterday. The nurse called in at Gleniffer to ask Lizbeth if she'd telephone Rachel, and as it turned out Rachel wasnae doing anything today, so she was willing to come and fetch me. Lizbeth brought word when she called in yesterday to see me.'

'There's your clothes to pack, arrangements to be made . . .'

'I'll only need clothes for a week or two. Mebbe it'll not be a bad thing for you two to be left to manage on your own for once, without me there to keep an eye on the place.'

'Of course we can manage,' Jennet said sharply. 'Angus's more than capable of running the place.'

'I doubt that,' Celia said, then added pointedly, looking at Mollie, who was working at the sink, 'but whatever the truth of it, I don't think that this is a matter to be discussed before outsiders.'

'Mollie is not an . . .'

'Come on, Jamie pet,' Mollie said, reaching for the towel. 'We'll go and give the pigs their breakfast, will we?'

'Mollie,' Jennet said quietly when she and Angus were alone with their grandmother, 'is not a stranger. She's part of this family.'

'She is not, and never will be, part of my family,' Celia rapped out, fisting her hands on the table and easing herself slowly and painfully to her feet. 'And I'll expect her to be back where she belongs by the time I come home. Now . . . help me upstairs so's I can be ready when Rachel arrives.'

As Jennet helped her grandmother to the door she looked at Angus over her shoulder, trying to signal with her eyes; but he stayed where he was at the table, staring down at his hands.

Celia's packing took up most of Jennet's morning. Since Celia wore work clothes most of the time and had only two sets of 'good' clothes – one for church and the Women's Rural Institute meetings, the other for more special occasions – there was little to be done as far as her clothes were concerned, but even so the suitcase kept having to be repacked to make room for items that Celia suddenly remembered . . . her Bible, a book of poetry she liked, the small jewellery box containing a few items that had been handed down from her mother, a little photograph album.

Then Jennet had to help her to dress and do her hair and choose a suitable pair of gloves . . . which led to more repacking, because they had both forgotten about gloves.

'I despair of you, Jennet, I really do,' Celia said at that point, completely ignoring the fact that she herself was equally guilty. 'You're turning into nothing more than a farmhand these days. You know that respectable women should always wear gloves!'

'As far as I'm concerned, they'd get in the way of milking and mucking out the byre,' Jennet retorted, almost at her wits' end. Although the flash of impertinence soothed her for a few seconds, it had to be paid for by putting up with a time-wasting lecture on manners to one's elders.

When she finally went downstairs Mollie and Jamie were in the kitchen; the table had been cleared and the dishes washed, and a pot of soup was simmering on the range. Jennet snatched her jacket from the nail behind the door. 'See to Grandmother if she calls, will you?'

'She'll not want me, she'll want you.'

'Then she'll just have to want, for I've never been as close to throwing her down the stairs,' Jennet said and fled to the comfort and security of the farmyard.

Mollie would have given all she had to run out after her friend, but she knew by the look on Jennet's face that she really was close to breaking point. Why did Mrs Scott have to be so difficult about everything, she wondered, as she washed Jamie's hands and face and combed his hair, much to his annoyance.

'Now you sit down there and play nicely,' she ordered, giving him his building bricks; then, deciding that they might look too untidy when Mrs Scott's sister arrived, she took them away from him and replaced them with a battered toy pony on wheels. Once he was settled she set to and cleaned the entire kitchen, rearranging the dishes on the dresser and even, when there was nothing else to do, brushing the toy pony's mane. Jamie, intrigued, insisted on taking over the task just as his great-grandmother called 'Jennet!' from upstairs.

Celia was sitting on the edge of her bed fully dressed, even to her hat and gloves. As soon as she saw Mollie, her face tightened in disapproval; as though, Mollie thought, she had been sucking one of those round green sweeties known to children throughout the west of Scotland as soor plooms.

'I called for my granddaughter,' she said haughtily.

Hoity-toity, Mollie thought, while aloud she said politely, 'Jennet's working outside, Mrs Scott. Are you wanting to be helped downstairs?' When the old woman hesitated, then gave a cool, reluctant nod, Mollie stepped forward. 'Take your stick in that hand and take my hand with the other,' she instructed, slipping her arm about Celia Scott and easing her up from the bed. 'And don't try to help yourself, just let me worry about that. I'll come back for your case after.'

Under her calm but precise directions they were in the kitchen in no time at all.

'Your sister won't be long now so I'll start the tea,' Mollie said as she settled the old woman into her wingback chair. She nodded to where the kettle gave out a plume of steam on the range. 'You'll be ready for a hot drink after the effort of getting yourself ready for the journey.'

'Where did you learn how to help folk like that?' Celia asked, impressed despite herself.

'There was an old lady in our tenement in Glasgow. She lived alone, but she was a right independent soul and she'd not move to a ground-floor flat,' Mollie explained as she set out the best cups and a plate of scones she had buttered earlier. 'She'd lived there for over fifty years and was determined that she was going to die there. And, poor old soul, she did, but luckily it was in her sleep just a week before the bomb hit the place, so that was a blessing. All the weans in the close called her Granny Adam.'

'I don't want any scones,' Celia said.

'Your sister'll be ready for something to eat when she arrives. Anyway, Granny Adam always needed help on the stairs and my mam showed me how to do it properly. She worked in a hospital before she got married to my da,' Mollie said proudly.

Nesta had been a ward maid, not a nurse, but by keeping her eyes and ears open she had learned a lot. The only thing she had not learned was how to judge a man. Mollie was convinced that if it had not been for her da, her mam would have done well for herself.

She finished laying the tea-things out and turned to the chair, a hopeful smile dying on her face as she encountered Celia Scott's scowl. Best not to put the milk out just yet, she thought, for that face'll just sour it before it's needed. Aloud she said, 'I'll just fetch your things down, then.'

'Andra Blaikie can do that when he comes over.'

'I'll save him the trouble,' Mollie said, and escaped through the inner door.

Estimating that the boat bringing Celia's sister over must have been in for a good half hour by now, she took refuge in the room she shared with Jennet and watched from the window. After five minutes a portly, smartly dressed woman walked gingerly into the yard, flapping her handbag at any hens who ventured too close.

Mollie bolted into Celia's room, snatched up the suitcase and the shabby little travelling bag beside it and arrived back in the kitchen just as Celia's sister reached the outer door.

The woman gave Mollie one swift glance, then swept past her into the room as though she did not exist. The gauzy scarf looped about her throat wafted along behind her like the wake of a large, perfumed ship. 'Celia, for goodness sake will you look at yourself!' she trumpeted. 'You're in sore need of some proper care and attention!'

Suddenly Celia Scott seemed to shrink and age.

She reached up to clutch her sister's hand. 'Rachel, it's so good to see you!'

'Where's Jennet? And Angus?'

'Working. Where else would they be?'

'They should be here with you!'

'I'll fetch them,' Mollie said, 'when I've poured the tea.'

'I'll see to that.' Rachel took control, almost barging Mollie out of the way. 'I can attend to my sister, thank you, while you fetch her grandchildren.'

Jamie, who had been ignored by both women, jumped up and scurried after Mollie, locking his hand in hers so that they left the house together.

'Don't you see that this is going to be our best chance?' Jennet said hotly to her brother. Then as Angus, leaning on the wall of the piggery and scratching the occupants' backs with a stick, remained silent, 'She'll be away for a good two weeks . . . a month mebbe. We have to do more than just keep the place going until she comes back. We have to prove that we can run it our way.'

'And just what is "our way"?'

'Bring in more lodgers so's we can earn a bit of money, and change anything we need to change. This farm's not moved on since we were born . . . since before we were born,' Jennet said passionately. 'There are probably easier ways of doing things.'

'Such as telling the estate in November that we're leaving.'

'And until then? We have to try, Angus!'

'If you want to try something new, then go ahead. I'll not stand in your way.'

'But we can't go behind Gran's back. I'll not have her coming home and changing things back to the way they were before. We have to tell her what we're going to do, and we have to tell her together . . . and mean it. Please, Angus!'

He heaved himself away from the wall and snatched up the crutch that had been propped by his side. 'If you're going to go on like this all the time Gran's away,' he said over his shoulder as he made for the yard, 'I think I'd rather go with her today and be done with it.'

'Will you stop feeling so sorry for yourself and start being the farmer you really are?' She followed him into the yard just as Mollie and Jamie emerged from the house.

'She's arrived and she's terrible, and I don't care if she is your blood kin,' Mollie said breathlessly. 'Your gran's ready to go and she's looking for the two of you.'

'We were just going in anyway. Come on, Angus.'

'Not me. I'll come and see her off when Mr Blaikie arrives.'

A loud rapping on the kitchen window brought their heads round to see that Rachel was signalling at them.

'We have to go in. Angus, we need to talk to Gran together!' Jennet said desperately, and he looked at her as if she were a stranger.

'You're the one with all the high ideas, so you can tell her yourself. I'll not get involved,' he said, and went into the stable. Jennet took a deep breath and rubbed her hands down the legs of her britches.

'All right, if I must, I must. Mollie, keep Jamie out here with you,' she said and marched into the house.

Mollie looked from her friend's retreating back to the open stable door. Then, drawing a breath every bit as deep as Jennet's, she went into the stable, with Jamie trailing along behind her. Angus, his back to her, was sorting through some of the tack.

'You might have gone in with her instead of leaving her to face them on her own.'

'Keep your nose out of our business, Mollie McCabe,' he said without turning round.

'Jennet is my business. She's my best friend, and you might think that I'm an ignorant Glasgow lassie and not worth bothering about, but I love this place and it's done a lot for me and my family. I can see why she cares about it. I just wish you did.'

'You don't know what you're talking about.'

'I didnae come down the Clyde in a banana boat, Angus Scott. I've got eyes, and I've got a brain between my ears and all. Jennet's right when she says this place should be yours. If it comes to that, it *is* yours.'

'If it was, the first thing I'd do is run you off it.'

'Mebbe you would, for you've never liked hearing the truth from the likes of me.' Mollie's temper boiled over. 'D'you know what you are, Angus Scott? You're a snob, just like your old witch of a grandmother. Mebbe you should do what you said – go with her today and rot in Largs with her and her snobby sister, for it seems to me that you all deserve each other. I feel sorry for Jennet, havin' you two as kin. She deserves . . .'

A small hand crept into hers. 'Where's the witch, Mollie?' Jamie enquired nervously, his eyes darting round the dark corners of the stable. She bent and swept him up into her arms.

'Not a real one, silly, there aren't any real witches. Angus and me are just playing a game. Come on, let's go for a nice wee walk, just the two of us.'

At the stable door she turned, the anger suddenly draining out of her. 'I'm sorry for what I said. Jennet's not the only reason I love this place,' she said, and then as he remained silent, 'You know that, don't you?'

'Go away.'

'Angus . . .' She took a few steps towards him.

'Just go away,' he said between gritted teeth, his back so rigid that much as she wanted to touch it, she was afraid in case she discovered that it was made of flint instead of flesh and skin and bone.

'I might as well,' she said, and carried Jamie out into the sunshine.

'You're all set, then?' Jennet was saying in the kitchen.

'Where's Angus?' Celia asked in reply. 'He should be here to greet his aunt and see me off.'

'He's on his way.'

'Janet, do you always come into the house with those big heavy boots on?' her Great-Aunt Rachel wanted to know, wafting a handkerchief before her nose. She always insisted on using the more refined version of Jennet's name and had never accepted the fact that her sister's granddaughter had been christened with the Scottish pronunciation.

Jennet glanced down at the offending boots. 'This is the working kitchen, Aunt Rachel. We don't wear our farm boots and shoes beyond that door, but if we took them off every time we came in and out of this room we'd never have time to catch up with all we have to do.'

'I'm sure it's unhygienic, bringing dirty clothing like that into the room where you cook and eat your food.'

'A peck of dirt never hurt anyone, Rachel,' Celia broke in. 'If you want another cup of tea take it now, for Andra'll be here any minute.'

'I'll wait until I get home before I have more tea,' her sister said in a voice that damned the Westervoe Farm version for ever.

'Gran, about me and Angus looking after the farm . . .'

'If there are any worries, just go to Andra for advice. He's promised to keep an eye on you.'

'Nobody needs to keep an eye on us,' Jennet said. 'We're grown adults and we know about farming. What I was going to say is, if we feel that changes need to be made while you're away, we'll go ahead and make them.'

'Changes?' Celia, who had been slumped back in her chair, looking like a stranger in her good black coat and hat, suddenly snapped upright. 'What sort of changes?'

'Anything that we think might make the work easier. Taking on another farmhand, for instance.'

'And where would you find the money to pay someone else?'

Jennet fisted her hands by her sides, digging her nails deep into her palms. 'I'm going to rent the cottage out again.'

'To trippers?' Celia asked, then as Jennet nodded, 'Over my dead body!'

'You'll not be here, Gran, dead or alive, so it'll not make any difference to you.'

'Don't be impertinent!' Great-Aunt Rachel said, outraged.

'I'm not, I'm just saying that since it's Angus's right to inherit this farm, it's his right to make whatever changes he thinks it needs.'

'And where is Angus?' Rachel demanded to know. 'I don't see him here, speaking out for himself. If you ask me, Celia, it's this little madam who's going to be making all the decisions behind your back.'

'I'm not going behind her back, I'm making things clear before she leaves. Not that it's any of your affair, Great-Aunt Rachel.'

'That's enough, young woman!' Celia rapped at her,

while her sister gasped. 'Have you not listened to what I've told you over and over again? We'll all be out of here by next April and you'll be doing your nurse training in Glasgow by September next, so there's no need for any changes. They'll be up to the new tenant at Westervoe.'

'But Angus needs to stay here and run his own life.'

'I'll look out for Angus.'

'By that, you mean that you'll turn him into an invalid between you.'

'He *is* an invalid, and closing your eyes to the truth won't change anything.'

'Plenty of folk manage fine with worse disabilities than Angus. What about Douglas Bader?'

'That's different!'

'How is it different?' Jennet persisted. Then, as her grandmother said nothing, 'Gran, I'm only asking for the chance to show you that me and Angus can take over Westervoe and run it together.'

'You're havering!'

'Give us a year . . . please. You've done more for us than any woman should have had to do and you deserve your rest. Stay with Great-Aunt Rachel, if that's what you want to do, and leave the farm to Angus.'

'What has Angus got to say about this daft notion of yours?' Celia asked. Then, when Jennet said nothing, she swept on triumphantly, 'I'll tell you what he said, Rachel . . . the same as me. That's why he's not in here standing by the girl. He knows he's not able.'

'He is able, and if he finds that he can't manage the place I'll take it on.'

'You? Don't be daft!'

'I've got Jamie's future to consider. Westervoe's his birthright too, and plenty of farms here on Bute have been run by women. You did it yourself.'

'I was looking out for my son and then for his bairns, every one of them born in wedlock,' Celia rasped. 'If you want to do the right thing by that lad ye birthed, ye'll let him get off this island to a place where nob'dy knows the shame he's brought on us.'

Each word was like a slap in the face, but Jennet rallied. She had too much at stake to let her grandmother's cruelty touch her.

'Let you have him, you mean? You'd never stop reminding him that he doesn't have a father. You'd hammer that shame into him with every breath he took.'

'I'd certainly teach him how to accept and overcome his bad start in life. As for keeping on Westervoe for his sake . . . he's got no right to it.'

'He's got every right. I'm a Scott and I'm his mother.'

'And who's the father, that's what I'd like to know.'

'The lassie mebbe doesn't know that herself, Celia,' Rachel said, her round, carefully made-up face pink with indignation and excitement. 'Since the war this country's fair littered with by-blows fathered by men from all over the world on lassies with no more sense than to let themselves be treated like . . . like . . .'

'Like common whores,' Celia ended the sentence coldly. Then her head whipped round as Angus said from the doorway, 'My sister is not a whore, Grandmother, and I won't have you miscalling her.'

'So she's told you who fathered the bairn, has she?'

'She has not and I've never asked, for it's her business, not mine. But I know Jennet, and you should know her too, since you raised her.'

Celia had the grace to drop her eyes from his gaze, but Rachel spoke up in her stead. 'Aye, she raised the pack of you and look how she's been repaid . . . Your brother running off, just like his father before him, and Janet bringing home a bastard to shame my sister in the eyes of all the folk on this island!'

'It seems to me,' Angus said coldly, moving further into the kitchen, 'that the rest of the island's not nearly as bothered about that as you two are. And since you don't even live here, Great-Aunt Rachel, I'll thank you to keep your neb out of this family discussion.'

'What? Are you going to allow him to speak to me like that?' Rachel rounded on her sister. 'And me opening my own house to him, too!'

'Just a minute, Rachel. About this nonsense Jennet's been talking, Angus . . .'

'I know what Jennet has in mind for this place.'

'And you've told her no, haven't you?'

'I did, more than once. I thought the same as you, Grandmother, but now that I've had time to think about it,' Angus said calmly, setting his crutch aside and leaning back against the wall, arms folded, 'I think some of her ideas might be worth trying.'

'What?'

'Why don't you just enjoy your wee holiday in Largs and let me and Jennet have a try at running the farm? Forget about handing in our notice at Martinmas and leave it until next May, when the Whitsun rent's due. That should give us time enough to test ourselves. After all, as Jennet keeps reminding me, it's my birthright.'

'But you're a cripple,' Rachel burst out, unable to hold her tongue any longer. 'You're not able!'

Angus's face had darkened at her use of the hated word. Now he looked her up and down before saying, 'There are different ways of being crippled. Mine's a bad leg, but some folk are worse off. They think they can see and hear, yet they cannae understand what they're seeing and hearing. Other folk are locked so tightly into their own minds that they cannae understand what they're being told. For myself, I'd as soon settle for havin' a bad leg.'

His grandmother gaped at him, her mouth opening and closing, but no words coming out. Even Rachel could not find any words. Then the silence gripping the kitchen was broken by the chug of an engine as Andra Blaikie's small saloon car turned in at the yard.

'Ready, Gran?' Angus said pleasantly. 'You'll have to go or you'll miss your boat.'

* * *

'God help us,' he said as they waved the car off, with Celia and her sister sitting erect in the back seat. 'What have you done to me, Jennet?'

'Did you mean what you said?'

'Scarcely a word of it, but they got me angry, the way the two of them were going on as if they were the only folk with the right idea of things. I think you've lost your reason, but even so you're my sister and I couldnae let the two of them speak to you like that.'

'Are they gone?' Mollie came round the end of the old stable, Jamie by her side. 'Have we missed them?'

'Aye. Lucky, aren't you?' Angus said. Then, turning back to Jennet, 'We're both going to regret this, you know.'

'At least we'll have tried.'

'I suppose so. But it's only until next May at the latest, mind.' Then when she nodded, 'So . . . where do we start?'

'By getting some lodgers in, and turning that old stable into a deep-litter house,' she said, feeling as if a load had been lifted from her shoulders. 'I'm sick of those old arks!'

15

In Rothesay local folk and holidaymakers flocked to the town's annual August Carnival, while at Westervoe Jennet and Mollie slaved to turn the old stables, once inhabited by the fine Clydesdales bred by Jennet's great-grandfather, into a deep-litter hen house.

'You're every bit as much of a slave driver as your gran,' Mollie complained, slapping whitewash on the stone walls. 'She's not been gone a fortnight and you've already got me working myself into a puddle of sweat.'

'If you want to go to Rothesay, then off you go.' Jennet, perched precariously on the top step of the old folding ladders, reached up as high as she could in order to get her brush into a difficult angle between wall and roof. 'You're not a prisoner.'

'No, just a fool. And watch what you're doing,' Molly squawked as whitewash from Jennet's brush dripped down on her. 'Anyway, how could I go and enjoy myself when I know you're half killing yourself in here?'

'We've got to get the hens out of the oldest arks and in here before winter comes. I can't face having to move all those arks about in the rain and cold, and some of them are just about ready to come apart in our hands. And it all has to be done before the harvesting starts.'

'And before your gran comes back, so's she can't put a stop to it.'

'How did you know?' Jennet peered down through the ladder's rungs at the top of her friend's red head.

'Because it's what I would do myself in your shoes.'

Since leaving for Largs, Celia had only written two short letters to her grandchildren, reporting on her own improving health and her sister's kindness and assistance, and asking about the farm work. She had not as yet mentioned her return. Although her letters were addressed to Angus alone, Jennet had replied with similarly brief and factual letters. She had made a point of mentioning the holidaymakers in the cottage and the progress of the deep-litter house, but Celia did not refer to them, or to the quarrel they had had just before she left Westervoe.

'D'you not think that Angus's looking a lot better these days?' Mollie's voice floated up from below.

'You're right.' Jennet had noticed that Angus seemed to be taller, easier in his movements and more relaxed these days, despite the hard work and the long hours.

'It's because *she's* not here,' Mollie said. 'The man never knew where he was with her – one minute she was telling him he shouldn't do this and that, then the next she was criticising him for not doing more. If you ask me, he's better off without her. You both are.'

'It's not as easy as that,' Jennet said glumly. 'She'll be back soon.'

A groan floated to her ears from ground level. 'Don't spoil a nice day,' Mollie implored her.

It had taken them a week of hard work to clear the stables of all the rubbish that had accumulated over the years and then shovel piles of dirt from the floor, before sluicing the place with water and disinfectant. Jamie had gone off to stay with the Logans in Rothesay so that his mother and Mollie could get on with the new hen house. To Jennet's relief and, at the same time, her distress, he had gone off eagerly on his new adventure without a backward glance.

'I wonder how Jamie's getting on?' she said now.

'He must be having a better time than we are. You're missing him, aren't you?'

'It's the first time he's been away from me. You don't think he'll be homesick? He doesn't know Aunt Ann and Uncle George all that well.'

'You'd be told if he was miserable. And he knows Mam well enough; she's looked after him loads of times when you were working. He'll be having a great time,' Mollie said robustly. 'Your auntie and my mam will be spoiling him, and your uncle and Sam will have him out in the boats all day.'

That only brought more worry for Jennet. 'What if he falls into the sea?'

'Don't be daft, they wouldn't let anything happen to him.'

The new cottage people, a young couple, stopped to exchange pleasantries on the weather as they left on one of their long walks. It would have been useful, Jennet thought, attacking a dark corner, if they had been as helpful as the Dicksons, but friendly though they were, the new lodgers had no interest in anything but each other. On their honeymoon, Jennet thought, but Mollie reckoned they hadn't got as far as the altar.

'Off walking . . . I told you, they're too keen to keep out of other folks' way,' she said now.

'That might just be shyness. And she's wearing a wedding ring.'

'For all you know, someone else might have put it on her finger.'

'You're terrible, Mollie, thinking the worst of them.'

'Folk arenae always the way they seem,' Mollie said darkly, then gave a sudden yelp and danced back, her brush thumping to the ground. Jennet jumped and had to clutch at the ladder to save herself from falling off.

'A spider!' Mollie whimpered from below.

'For goodness sake . . . you nearly had me off this ladder over a spider? The place is full of them; you should know that by now. Don't be such a baby!'

'But this one was the size of a dinner plate!' Mollie snatched up a spade and advanced cautiously, her eyes darting over the ground before her.

'Don't kill it, you might bring the rain,' Jennet

advised from above. 'We can't have that, not with the harvest due to start soon.'

'I'm certainly not going to invite it to stay for tea. And you're late in starting to fret about the harvest, for we must have killed hundreds of the creepy-crawly things since we started work in here. It's gone,' Mollie announced with relief, 'it must have run out.'

'Sensible creature.'

They worked in silence for another five minutes, then Mollie said, 'Did Mam tell you that our Sam's courting?'

'What? He's a child, just out of school!'

'Mebbe not courting exactly, but he's got pally with a wee lassie who was in his class at the school. Mr Logan told my ma that she's been down at the boats every day during the summer and Sam takes her out in one of the wee boats most evenings after they've closed down.' She coughed, spat and then asked, 'D'you not fancy a drink of water? My throat's full of dust.'

'I fancy a cup of tea. Hold the ladder steady while I come down.' Jennet descended cautiously and when she reached the ground she dragged the scarf she had been wearing turban-fashion from her head and shook it, releasing a shower of dust and grit. Bending from the waist, she ran her hands again and again through her long hair and then stood up, shaking it back over her shoulders. 'That's better; my scalp was beginning to feel all itchy. Think of the state Jamie could get into if he was trying to help us in here.'

She glanced around the big enclosure. Once the walls were painted they would put in laying boxes and cover the floor with a deep layer of straw. In winter the hens would stay indoors, snug and safe and easy to care for, and in summer they would be free to roam outside. 'It's beginning to look much better, don't you think?'

'Aye . . . as long as the hens aren't too particular.'

'It's a sight better than those old arks they've been living in. Come on, the men'll be coming in for a drink soon, so we might as well have ours first.'

'So that's Senga in Glasgow with a lad,' Jennet said as they crossed the yard, 'and Sam with a lass, and you with Joe . . . all of you courting. It must be the summer weather.'

'Joe and me aren't courting. I've told you time and again that he's just a friend.'

'The way I thought Struan was just a friend to me before he proposed out of the blue?'

'Joe's got more sense than to propose. He knows that he'd be sent off with a flea in his ear if he tried any nonsense like that.'

'I wish I'd been able to send Struan off with a flea in his ear,' Jennet said. The young farmer kept eyeing her wistfully when he was in her company and although he had not raised the question of marriage again, Jennet could not forget his declaration that he would ask her again 'later'.

'Joe likes you,' she said, pushing Struan from her

mind as they went into the kitchen, 'and he's a nice lad.' Joe had become a regular visitor to the farm.

'I like him too, but it would be a queer old world if we married folk just because we liked them.' Mollie threw a handful of tea leaves into the pot and filled it from the ever-ready kettle. 'And if he's good to me it's his own choice, for I'm not like our Senga, I'd never expect anything from a man.' She refilled the kettle at the sink, turning the tap on so hard that water sprayed everywhere.

'Stupid tap!' she roared, clashing the kettle down on the hob. Her face was filthy and splattered with whitewash, while rivulets of sweat had cut clean streaks down her cheeks. Poor Mollie, Jennet thought, running an arm over her own face, which she knew must look just as bad; if she hadn't been called back to help out at the farm she would be in Rothesay right now, enjoying the good weather instead of being stuck in the old stables.

'Jen, can I ask you somethin' very personal?'

'What is it?'

'Did you love Jamie's father?'

Jennet felt her insides shrink together, as though for protection. It was the first time anyone had asked such a personal question, other than her grandmother's angry demands to be told the truth at once. It had been easier, in the face of that cold, hard anger, to refuse to answer.

'Just say if I'm being cheeky and I'll shut up and never mention it again,' Mollie was stumbling on.

'No, you're not being cheeky at all.' Mollie was a friend, her dearest friend, and she deserved an answer. Besides, it was all in the past now. 'I really thought I did love him at the time.' Jennet sat down at the table. 'Of course I did, or I'd not have . . .' She bit her lower lip, then grimaced at the taste of dust and whitewash on her tongue. 'It was all so . . . He was on leave and he'd discovered that war wasn't the adventure he thought it was going to be. He was scared, and I suppose I wanted to make him feel that someone cared. And that was the only way I could . . .'

'Did he ever know about Jamie?'

'Yes, he did.' The bitterness that had ebbed away over the years came flooding back as Jennet recalled the way he had reacted; the colour draining from his young face, the panic in his voice. 'He didn't want to know,' she said, and Mollie reached across the table to put a hand on her arm.

'He sounds like a right sod, leavin' you in the lurch like that.'

'He couldn't take the extra worry. He thought the best thing would be for me to . . . you know.'

'Get rid of Jamie?' Mollie asked, horrified.

'He wasn't Jamie then, he was just . . . nothing, really. Just a problem that made me feel sick in the morning. Just something that wouldn't go away.'

'But you wouldnae do it.'

'I was going to . . . What else could I do? One of the girls I was training with got me the address of a woman who helped girls in my condition, but when it came down to it I couldn't.'

'I should think not! Imagine if wee Jamie had never been born!' Mollie said, shocked, while Jennet stared down at the scrubbed wooden table, remembering the side street with its high tenements, the children with runny noses playing on the pavement, the close with its smell of dirt and defeat, the scarred door behind which the illegal abortionist plied her trade. She had lifted a hand to knock on the panels and then lost her nerve completely and run back to the street.

'To tell the truth, Mollie, I was just like . . . like him.' She stopped herself just in time from saying his name. 'I was scared of being hurt and mebbe dying, so instead of going to the woman I came home to Angus. And to Gran.'

'And the man got away with it. D'you not hate him for the trouble he caused you?'

'Where's the sense in that? I've got Jamie, haven't I?'

'Aye, but you paid a hard price at the time. I'd still hate him if I was in your shoes. No matter how frightened he was with the war and all that, it wasn't fair to leave you to face things on your lone. You're too understanding at times, Jennet Scott. He was a bastard and it's time you came out and said it.'

'I've never said that about anyone in my life!'

'D'you still love him?'

'Of course not, but . . .'

'Then I dare you.' Mollie leaned across the table,

her eyes bright now with amusement. 'You've managed fine without him and you'll go on managing fine, but mebbe it's time you said what you really think. Letting yourself be angry's like vomitin', it gets rid of all the badness and makes you feel better.'

'How do you know about these things?'

'I've lived in a city,' Mollie said calmly. 'I've seen and heard all sorts. And my mam always said I'm like a sponge. I take everything in and forget nothing.'

'Are you sure she didn't mean the fluffy kind that's all jam in the middle?' Jennet was beginning as Angus, Jem and Norrie, the lad they had taken on and were paying with the last of the money earned from selling that year's early potato crop, came in from the fields looking tired, dusty and parched.

'You see to them,' Mollie jumped to her feet, snatching up her mug, 'and I'll take this with me and get back to the whitewashing.'

'You're supposed to put it on the walls, not your face,' Angus said as she passed him.

'This isnae whitewash, this is a very expensive mud pack, the sort that Claudette Colbert swears by,' she retorted, and went out.

Jennet opened her mouth to ask her brother, as he slumped down at the table, rubbing sweat and grime from his face, if he was all right, then she closed it again. Mollie was right when she said that his grandmother had smothered him, and Jennet was determined not to do the same.

She had forced them both to take a hard road, and

it wouldn't get any easier over the next few months, but they had to keep going until November was behind them and the twice-yearly rent paid. Then the farm would be theirs – hers and Angus's – for another six months at least. And during the winter – short days and long nights, the cows in the shed and most of the hens in the big new hen house – they would have time to take a rest and plan out the next year together.

'You look worn out,' Ann Logan said flatly when her niece arrived to claim her son back.

'It's been hard work, but we've finished the new deep-litter house, thanks to you looking after Jamie.'

'It's a pleasure to have him here. You've brought him up well, Jennet. Are you sure you don't want to leave him with us for a wee while longer, till you and Angus get on your feet?'

Kind though the offer was, it made Jennet feel uneasy. No matter how hard life at Westervoe became, she needed to have Jamie with her. He was her reason for living.

'No, you've got a full house as it is and I can manage fine, as long as you don't mind us keeping Mollie for a bit longer.'

'It's up to her. Nesta's a treasure and the two of us can manage well enough with some help from Alice. She's got Jamie down at the boats, but she'll be bringing him back in a wee while for his dinner.'

After a week, a wee while was too long to wait. 'I'll go down to the bay and walk back with them.

It'll give me a chance to see a bit of Rothesay for once.'

The town was still as busy as ever and Rothesay Bay still thronged with boats. Queues waited at every one of the boat-hirers, and Alice was on duty with the book while her father helped people in and out of the boats. There was no sign of Jamie.

'Come for the wee lad?' Alice greeted her cousin. 'Joe's taken him out on the launch.' She pointed a brown, freckled arm. 'See? They're coming back in now.'

As the boat came smoothly into the shallows, Jennet saw her son sitting aft beside Joe. The young man had given him his cap and Jamie had pulled it down until his small face was almost hidden by the long peak. When the trippers had left the launch Joe swung the little boy up into the air and across to George Logan, who jiggled him about, making him laugh, before setting him safely down on the shingle.

'Now then, me lad, who's this come to see you?'

He took the cap off and Jamie glanced at Jennet, looked away and then glanced back. For a heart-stopping moment she thought he had forgotten her, then a huge grin split his face in two, and with a screech of 'Mum!' he launched himself at her.

She scooped him up, holding tightly to the compact, wiry bundle of flesh and skin, bone and sinew. His hair and skin smelled of salt air and the indefinable scent that was – and always had been – Jamie's own. She had thought, before his birth, that only animals could recognise their young by smell alone, but she had been wrong.

'Did you have a good time? Did you miss me?'

'Mmm,' he said enigmatically. 'I was on the boats. I had ice cream and I digged a big hole in the sand and . . .'

He talked all the way back to the house, marching along between Alice and Jennet, holding both hands but occasionally releasing one or another to point something out.

'So he wasn't homesick?' Jennet asked her cousin over his head.

'Not a bit of it. He had a wee cot up in Sam's room and the two of them got on fine. It's done Dad and Mum the world of good, having him here,' Alice said warmly. 'I think it's helped them to get over losing Geordie. Jamie made such a fuss of Dad right from the start and he loves Sam and Joe. He scarcely bothered with the womenfolk. For all his age, I think he likes being one of the men. I suppose that's natural for wee laddies – they need their fa . . .'

Then, realising what she was saying, the girl stopped short, flushed bright red and changed the subject.

In mid-September Struan Blaikie and Bert McCabe helped bring in Westervoe's oat crop. Angus used the tractor to do the cutting, while the others – Jennet and some of the older youngsters from the local schools included – followed along behind, gathering up the oats, binding them into bundles by hand, then stacking them in stooks of six, three on one side, three on the other, carefully angled so that they leaned into each other.

'Just looking at these stooks makes the insides of my legs sting,' Angus said unexpectedly as he and Jennet walked out that evening to survey the stubbled field with its neat stooks.

'You mean the way we used to pretend they were horses and we were cowboys?' she asked, and he laughed.

'It was great, wasn't it?'

'We'd have got a right leathering if Grandmother had known what we were doing to the crop.'

'That was part of the pleasure,' Angus said. 'We didn't get much of a chance to be rebellious . . . but we paid a price in our own way.'

They had indeed. Every year the stiff stalks had taken their toll on the tender skin of their inner thighs and calves. After galloping to the end of the earth on their oat steeds, Jennet in her summer frocks and her brothers with their shorts on, they had all suffered agonies from hundreds of tiny scratches, especially in bed at night. But every year, until they got too old for such nonsense, they had gone back to play on the stooks.

'I mind once when you managed to sneak into Grandmother's bedroom while she was still downstairs,' Angus said, 'and you found some cold cream to ease the stinging.'

Jennet had forgotten, but now that he had triggered the memory she recalled skimming a lump of cream from the tin that Celia kept in a drawer by her bed and running like a scared rabbit back into the boys' bedroom, where the cream was doled out between them. 'It made the burning sting even more at first.'

'But it helped in the end. By God,' Angus said with a final backward glance at the field as they headed for home, and bed, 'if I caught any youngsters messing about with the stooks now, I'd tan their hides for them.' Then he said with a sudden change of subject, 'Is Struan not awful quiet, these days?'

'I never noticed,' she lied.

'You didn't fall out with him that night he took you out, did you?'

'It was just a night at the pictures, that was all.'

'Ach well, whatever's ailing him, he'll get over it,' Angus said and whistled to Gumrie, who was off investigating a rabbit hole. The dog came running, his plumed tail lashing from side to side, his long-muzzled face grinning.

'Daft animal,' Angus growled affectionately. 'Your mother must have been seeing a poodle without us knowing it. You've no idea how farm dogs are supposed to behave, have you?'

And Gumrie, who was an excellent farm dog when he wanted to be, widened his grin before falling sedately in at his master's heel.

16

The new deep-litter house looked quite magnificent. Snug and clean, with the walls whitewashed and the laying boxes, food troughs and water dishes installed and the floor covered with a thick layer of clean straw, it was, Mollie said, as good as Buckingham Palace, as far as hens were concerned.

Jem and Norrie had cut doorways and installed sliding doors so that in good weather the hens could be let out to forage in the yard and the small field adjacent to the old stables; in the winter, when they stayed inside, the daylight hours could be falsely extended by the use of lamps hung from the rafters.

They all gathered to see the chosen hens introduced to their new home, with Jem and Norrie staying on late for the occasion. Since hens were creatures of habit, they waited until dark before moving them, when most of the birds began to find their way to their own arks for the night.

One by one the arks that were being kept were

filled and closed, while the inhabitants of the old, rotting hen houses, on finding themselves shut out, huddled together miserably round the entrances, ready, Jennet hoped, to be gathered up and conveyed to their lovely, snug new palace.

But as always tended to happen with poultry, the sleepy birds roused themselves as soon as Jennet and Mollie attempted to carry them to their new home, squawking and panicking and fleeing in all directions. Those that went inside took one look at the huge interior, so different from the small crowded arks they were used to, and promptly rushed out again.

'If they'd just take a minute tae look at the place, they'd not want tae leave,' Mollie panted, heading for the deep-litter house with a hen tucked under each arm.

'Hens don't think like that. Hold them by the feet,' Jennet advised, 'you can carry more that way.'

'I cannae bring myself tae do that, but I'm gettin' tae the stage where I could wring their necks without lettin' it bother me,' Mollie added as one of the hens managed to flutter free and make a noisy escape, its wings and neck outstretched. 'Now I'll have tae catch it all over again!'

'I swear that I've carried the same hen in three times already,' Jennet said, resignedly. 'How many does that make now, Angus?'

'I don't know.' He dried his eyes, wet from laughter.

'What d'you mean, you don't know?' Mollie doubled her fists on her hips and glared at him.

'Every time I laugh I lose count again.'

'You're not supposed tae laugh, you're just supposed tae count. I thought you were clever?'

'You've got a feather on your chin and every time you speak it waggles,' Angus said, and began to laugh again.

'I suppose it's grand tae see him laughin' for a change,' Mollie said as she and Jennet plodded back to the arks to gather more hens. 'It suits him.'

'He used to do it a lot,' Jennet said, remembering. 'A long time ago.'

Celia Scott's weekly letter arrived the next morning, two days earlier than usual. Jennet, finding it on the kitchen table where Mollie had left it, stared down at the black, angular lettering on the envelope. There was something different about this one, she knew it. It must be the letter she had been expecting and dreading, the one that carried details of their grandmother's return. At least, she thought bleakly, the deep-litter house was completed and occupied; Grandmother couldn't put a stop to that new venture when she returned.

It was only when she picked the letter up to put it behind the clock for safe-keeping that she discovered another envelope, this one addressed to both Angus and herself. Letters were rare events at Westervoe Farm; usually only bills and reminders were delivered, and it was very unusual to receive two letters in a month, let alone two sharing the same post.

She turned the second letter, the one addressed to them both, over in her hands. The clumsy handwriting that sloped instead of keeping to neat lines was vaguely familiar; it took a full minute before she knew where she had seen it before – on the infrequent letters that Martin had sent home during the war.

Her first instinct was to rip it open; then, realising that she must wait until Angus was there, she settled for turning it over and over in her hands, feeling the weight of it. It was quite bulky, which meant that there must be more than one sheet of paper inside.

'Give them to me.' Jamie was clamouring about her, reaching up to the envelopes. He loved opening letters, and sometimes when Jennet or Mollie had time they wrote letters to him and posted them through the door. He cherished them, reading and rereading them and making up different interpretations of the scribbles on the page.

'They're for Angus.' Jennet put both envelopes behind the clock on the mantelshelf and tried to turn her mind to the day's work.

There was no opportunity to mention the letters to Angus, for they were both busy all day and when they met in the kitchen to eat, Mollie and Jem and Norrie were with them. The day seemed to drag by, and with every hour that passed Jennet felt as though the envelopes stuffed behind the clock were sending out urgent signals in her direction.

Angus, tired out after a hard day's work, went to his bed immediately after they ate that evening; Jennet made herself wait until Mollie went upstairs before taking the envelopes to his room, where he was reading in bed. No matter how tired he was, Angus always ended the day with a book.

'It's early,' he commented when she laid their grandmother's letter on the bed.

'Mebbe it's brought news,' she said, and saw her own apprehension mirrored in her brother's eyes for a second before he blinked it away.

'It was bound to happen sooner or later.'

'This came as well.' She laid the other letter beside the first.

'Martin!' He put his book aside after carefully marking his place, then picked the envelopes up, one in each hand, and raised his eyebrows at her. 'Which one first?'

'Martin's. No, Gran's. No,' she said swiftly, 'Martin's. I think we know what Gran's got to say.'

'Martin's it is.' He put the other letter aside, then opened the chosen envelope. 'D'you want to read it?' he asked. Then as she hesitated, 'I'll take it out and you read it aloud. I'd as soon hear it as see it.'

There were two sheets of paper, closely written. She glanced at the first few lines and blurted, 'He's out of . . .'

'Just read what he says, dammit!' Angus's eyes were like hot coals on her face, his hands tense on the quilt. Jennet licked her lips, shifted position slightly in order to bring the letter nearer to the lamp, then began to read.

Martin was out of the Army, and back in Britain. A mate from his platoon had found him a place where he himself worked, on a farm in the south of England.

'A farm, by God!' Angus interrupted. He barked a strangled, mirthless laugh. 'Here we are, struggling to keep this place going without him, and he's working on someone else's farm!' Then, as she glanced up, 'Go on!'

It was a big farm, Martin wrote, and he was working with the horses and lodging with his mate's family. 'I wrote to Struan Blaikie, and he told me that Grandmother's in Largs just now, so I knew it was safe to write to you without her getting the letter first. Don't be angry with Struan. I made him promise to keep quiet. I've been wanting to make things right with you two,' Jennet read on, then stopped when Angus snorted and made a sudden movement in the bed.

'Go on!' he snapped, and she returned to the letter.

'I'm not going back to Bute. I suppose I knew that the day I left to join the Army. I think it's what I had been waiting for all my life . . . getting the chance to leave Westervoe. I didn't know if I was going to make it through the war, but when it was over and I found myself still in one piece I knew that I would have to make a new life for myself somewhere else. Reg and me became pals because we were both farm lads, and that turned out to be lucky for me. I like working with the horses – I always liked animals and mebbe if things had been the way they used to be and

Clydesdales were still being bred at Westervoe, I'd have been okay about going back there.

'Or mebbe if our mother hadn't died and our father had stayed on I'd have been fonder of the place. I don't know, and there's no sense in wondering now about these things. Being brought up by Grandmother was like being locked in a dark cupboard, and I know war's a terrible thing, but for me it was like being set free into the fresh air and sunlight and being able to breathe for the first time in my life. Even if I had been killed or wounded, it would have been because of my choice, not hers. And that's why I could never go back into that wee dark cupboard.

'There's something else . . . someone else, I should say. I am courting Reg's sister Nancy, and if I am lucky she might agree to marry me when the time is right. She's a nice lassie; I hope that one day I will be able to take her to Bute to meet the two of you, but not while Grandmother's running the place. If it sounds as if I am afraid of her, then I suppose that is the truth.

'I just wish that you had been able to break free along with me, Angus, and I am sorry to have let the two of you down, for I know you must think that that is what I have done. I just wanted you to know that I am all right, and that I will not be back or looking for a share of Westervoe, or expecting anything from you.

'I am trusting you not to tell Grandmother where I am. If you think it best, you can give her my regards, but don't tell her too much. I hope you are both well and I hope, Jennet, that your wee boy is thriving. I would like to see him sometime. Reg and Nancy have a wee nephew and when I see him I think about your lad, who would be much the same age. I will write again sometime. Your affectionate brother, Martin.'

Angus uncurled his fingers, straightening them carefully, and leaned back, hands behind his head.

'So now we know that he's well, and that there's no sense in wondering if he's going to come back,' Jennet ventured after a long pause.

'Aye.' He stared up at the ceiling for a while and then said, 'I know what he means about the wee dark cupboard. Did you feel like that when you went to Glasgow? As if you'd been set free?'

Jennet had never thought of it in that way, but now she remembered the pleasure of meeting new people, walking Glasgow's streets in her spare time, wandering in and out of shops and deciding what she wanted to eat and when she wanted to eat it.

'Yes,' she said slowly. 'I suppose I did.'

'I wish I could feel like that,' Angus said wistfully. 'He always did like horses, our Martin. D'ye mind how he used to go across to Gleniffer whenever he got the chance to help with their horses?'

'Of course I remember. I was the one that was always being sent round on my bicycle to fetch him back. What are we going to tell Gran about this?' Jennet tapped the letter.

'Best to say nothing.'

'But surely she should know that he's not coming back. And that he's all right.'

'Fair enough, if she'd accept that and let it be. But you know her . . . She'll go on and on at us to tell her everything, the way she did with you when you . . .' Angus stopped, then said, 'when you came home from Glasgow. And she'll not be happy until she forces us to hand the letter over. D'you really want her to read what Martin says about her?'

'No!'

'Neither do I, though part of me says she deserves to see it. We'll leave things as they are for the time being,' Angus decided, then sat upright and leaned over to pick up the second letter. 'My turn to read it.'

He ripped the envelope open, scanned the single sheet of paper in one glance and then said, 'Good God.'

'What is it? Is her leg bad again?'

'She's fine,' Angus said slowly, rereading the letter. 'But she's mebbe not coming back.'

'Not coming home? But . . .'

'Read it for yourself.' He handed the page over and she was aware of him studying her face closely as she read.

Celia's letter was, as always, a single page, brusque and to the point. Rachel had looked after her well and, thanks to her sister, Celia had made a full recovery and was now well enough to return to Bute.

'However,' she continued – her writing, unlike Martin's, so spiky and black and so deeply scored into the paper that it almost spoke aloud – 'we are now approaching rent day and, as you know, I wish to hand Westervoe Farm back to the estate so that it can go to another tenant. I have settled well enough in Largs and I have fully made up my mind that when I return to Bute it will only be to arrange the farm's affairs and collect the rest of my personal belongings.

'Should you decide, or be persuaded against your better judgement, that it is in your own interests to continue trying to farm Westervoe, Angus, then you must do so without the benefit of my assistance and knowledge, for I have fully determined to spend the rest of my life here in comfort with my sister, my closest blood kin.

'You will still be made welcome, should you decide to join us here. Rachel is also prepared to take the child until such time as your sister completes her nursing studies and is in a position to care for him herself.

'Please let me know of your decision soon. Rachel sends her best wishes and her prayers that you will be guided to make the right choice. Your affectionate grandmother, Celia Scott.'

Jennet handed the page back and watched as Angus folded it neatly and tucked it back into its envelope.

'What are you going to do?' she asked at last, her voice husky.

'It's a big step, Jen, the two of us taking on this place.'

'We've been doing well enough since she left.'

'Aye, but that was different. I thought she was coming back and I was trying to keep the place for the three of us.'

'It's still the three of us, if you count Jamie.'

'That's another thing . . . You cannae go on trying to work the farm and look after the house and the bairn at the same time.'

'Plenty of women have done that.'

'Because they had to. Because they were widowed with growing families and nowhere else to go. If I was as able as I used to be . . . as able as our Martin,' he added with a return of the old bitterness, 'I'd say stay, and welcome, and I'll look out for the two of you. But I'll not feel beholden to you in that way.'

'This place is as much my right as yours and I'm sure that Mollie wouldn't mind staying on for as long as she's needed.'

'Mollie has her own life to think of,' Angus broke in sharply. 'We can't go on making use of her the way Grandmother made use of us. And Jem's not getting any younger. He's got his wife to look out for, the same as you've got Jamie, and I know that he doesn't want to go on working all his life. Norrie's willing enough, but he's still learning. Then there's your own future to think of.'

'Will you stop making excuses and finding reasons for us to do as Grandmother wants?' Jennet snapped, suddenly furious with him.

'I'm only being sensible. One of us has to be.'

'No, Angus, you're being difficult. Why don't you

stop finding reasons for leaving and start finding reasons for staying? This place could be the future for both of us!'

'Aye, if we're willing to work every minute of daylight that God sends. What if Jamie grows up to hate the place? Then you'll have sacrificed your lifc for nothing.'

'As long as it worked for you and me it wouldn't be for nothing. And Jamie won't have . . .' Jennet stopped and Angus finished the sentence for her.

'He won't have Grandmother to contend with? I suppose you're right. That woman's caused a lot of misery one way and another, Jen.'

'She meant it for the best.'

'Meaning things for the best can cause the most trouble,' Angus said drily.

'If it makes you feel any better I'll agree to stay for one year. If we can't make a go of the farm by rent day next November, I promise that I'll go back to nursing. Jamie'll be a bit older then, and mebbe you'll be managing so well that you won't need me.'

'I doubt that.'

'Will you try it?'

'I'll think about it.' He put both letters on the bedside cabinet. 'We've got weeks to go before Martinmas – no sense in rushing into decisions tonight.'

'Gran'll be waiting for an answer.'

'Let her wait,' Angus said.

* * *

The next day Jennet took an axe and set about the old arks, systematically reducing them to pieces one by one.

'You're goin' about these poor old things as if they were your mortal enemies,' Mollie said when she and Jamie came out to look for her.

'I never realised how satisfying chopping wood is.' Jennet, breathless, lowered the axe and pushed back the hair that had fallen about her hot face. 'It's a great way of working out your frustration. I should have gone into forestry work.'

'Here, we brought you something to drink.' Mollie held out a bottle of cold tea. 'What's bothering you this time?'

Jennet wiped her hands on her britches and unstoppered the bottle. After a good long drink she said, 'You might as well know . . . it's Gran again.' She ran through the letter's contents briefly, ending with, 'So now I've got to make him agree to take on the tenancy and make a go of this place.'

'For a start, you're never goin' tae make Angus Scott do anythin' he doesnae want tae do. You need to let him decide for himself . . . or let him think that he's decided for himself. And he's right, Jennet, it's a big decision and you both need to take time to think about it.'

'Whose side are you on? I thought you were keen on Angus and me staying here.'

'I am, but until now Angus has had his grandmother telling him what to do . . . and making him feel slow and useless most of the time,' Mollie added, scowling. 'The last thing he needs is for you to start taking her place. I know you'd not do that deliberately,' she added as Jennet gaped at her, 'but you have to stop pushing him to do what you want. He needs time.'

'We don't have much time left. Out of the way, Jamie.' Jennet picked up the axe and renewed her attack on a half-demolished ark. 'Whatever happens, Mollie, I'll not let him go to Largs. I'll not have him raised the way we were.'

'I'm sure your auntie would take him if it came to that, but it might not. Just be patient with Angus. Give him more time and when he comes to a decision, let it be his. Men need to feel as if they're in charge even when they're not.'

Jennet paused, the axe raised for a hefty blow. 'How do you know so much all of a sudden?'

'I've got a difficult father, and two brothers. I know about men.'

'I wasn't talking about men. I meant, how do you know so much about what works with Angus?'

'One man's much the same as another. And now I'm going to take Jamie out of your way,' Mollie said, 'so's you can pretend these old arks are your gran or me, or anyone else who's annoying you, and smash the life out of them.'

17

Time passed and still Angus said nothing about his plans for Westervoe, or his own future. In her next weekly letter Celia Scott made no mention of her ultimatum – seemingly she was prepared to wait for an answer, but Jennet found the waiting almost unbearable. Much as she hated it, she took Mollie's advice to bide her time and bite her tongue until her brother was ready to share his thoughts with her.

Every one of the old arks had been smashed to kindling wood and now she was getting some satisfaction from making sure that those being kept were wind-, snow- and water-tight for the winter. The cows would be brought in for the worst of the winter months, and the pigs, cosy enough in their stone-built pigsty with its high walled yard, would be taken away by the butcher early in November. However, the hens would have to stay out in the fields with the arks as their only shelter.

She was still waiting for an announcement from her brother when Bert McCabe called at Westervoe one night after work, tapping on the door and asking nervously if he might have a wee word with 'the master'.

'Of course you can, any time. Come in and sit yourself down, man.' Angus indicated a chair, but Bert shook his head.

'I'm fine as I am.' He stood in the middle of the kitchen, twisting his cap between his big, capable hands. 'In p-private would be best,' he went on awkwardly.

'You can't say what it is in front of Jennet and Mollie?' Angus asked, surprised, and the young man's face went beet-red.

'It's difficult.'

'For goodness sake, Bert, we surely know each other better than that by now,' Jennet snapped. Angus's silence was fraying her nerves as it was, and she didn't want any of Bert's nonsense. 'I'm not a delicate young lady with white hands and nothing but air between my ears!'

He took a step back, away from her anger. 'It's . . . it's personal, like.'

'Personal my foot,' Mollie broke in from the sink, where she was washing the dishes while Jennet dried them. 'Why don't you just spit it out and get it over with?' Then, as her brother glared at her and started stumbling over his words again, she went to stand beside him, drying her hands on her apron. 'The thing is, he's here because he's got himself into a right pickle, haven't you, you daft lump?'

'Will you just mind yer own business?' Bert appealed, crimson to the tips of his ears. 'D'ye have tae tell the whole world my business?'

'You're here tae tell them, aren't you? And it's not as if you've done anythin' terrible. It happens all the time,' she said flatly. Then, to the Scotts, 'This brother of mine's got the Blaikies' wee servant lassie intae trouble and Mrs Blaikie's livid about it. She wants the two of them off her farm and they've nowhere to go.'

'Mollie, for pity's sake!' Bert was so mortified that he was almost in tears.

'You were going tae take all night about it, and some of us would like tae go tae our beds. It's the cottage,' Mollie swept on, 'Bert and the lassie want tae get married, but they've nowhere tae live. And Mr Blaikie cannae let them have a cottage on his farm because Mrs Blaikie wouldn't allow that, the state she's in just now.'

'Is that right about you getting married?' Angus asked Bert, and when the younger man nodded, 'What does the girl's family say about it?'

'That's the thing, she doesnae have nob'dy but me. She's an orphan with nob'dy tae look out for her,' Bert blurted. 'And I was wonderin' . . . your wee cottage . . . Now the holidays are over . . .'

'Are you still working for Mr Blaikie?' Jennet asked.

'Till the end of the month just, because the missus is in such a takin' about havin' tae find another lassie and train her up that she says she doesnae want tae see sight nor sound of either of us. Mr Blaikie says that with the winter comin' in and Struan back home, he could let me go like she wants, but he'd mebbe find work for me in the spring once the missus has got over it.'

'That means that you could work for us instead,' Jennet realised aloud.

Bert's face lit up. 'That would be grand, if ye'd have me. And Helen's a fine wee worker, and good with the poultry, too. Mrs Blaikie trained her up well.'

Jennet opened her mouth to say something, caught the warning in Mollie's eye and left it to Angus.

He hesitated, pulling at his lower lip, then said finally, 'I'd not want to see you and the lassie homeless, Bert, and we could use a man like you around the place.'

'And if you both worked for us, you and the girl could have the cottage rent-free,' Jennet chimed in.

'Rent-free?' Angus asked when Mollie had escorted her brother outside, shutting the door on his gabbled thanks.

'If he's going to work for us and she's willing to help in the house, it seems only fair. We couldn't refuse, not with the way things are between them,' Jennet said. Then, with a sudden giggle, 'Imagine me with a lassie well trained by Mrs Blaikie, while she has to start all over again with someone else.'

'That'll be another black mark against you, as far as she's concerned.'

'At least we're being more Christian about the matter than she is. The thing is . . .' Jennet went on tentatively, 'if we leave the farm now, the new tenants might put Bert and his wife out of the cottage.'

'So we're stuck with this place, are we?' Angus asked. 'That's a pity.'

Something in his tone made Jennet suspicious. 'You were going to say yes all along, weren't you?'

'Mebbe I was and mebbe I wasn't.'

'Angus Scott, you're a right pig! Keeping me waiting and waiting, and worrying about what was going to happen to all of us, and all the time . . .' She picked up a cushion from the smaller fireside chair and shied it at him. He dodged sideways and it flew past him and into the sink, with Jennet in hot pursuit.

'It's gone into the washing-up water . . . It's all wet now!'

'You can explain it to Mollie,' Angus said, 'for I'll not. And I kept quiet about staying on to teach you not to nag at me in the future.'

'I'll never nag you again, and that's a promise. Oh, Angus!' The Scotts were not used to hugging and kissing, but even so she threw her arms about him and kissed him on the cheek.

'I'll write to Grandmother tonight before I go to sleep,' he said, disentangling himself from her arms. Then he added, with the ghost of a smile tugging at his wide mouth, 'She'll not be pleased.'

'Write to her tomorrow,' Jennet said on an impulse. 'Tonight we're going to have a bonfire.'

'A what?'

'A celebration bonfire, like the ones they had when the war ended.' Jennet suddenly felt as though her own war – hers and Angus's – had ended that night. 'And we can roast potatoes in the ashes.'

'And burn a guy?' Angus asked drily.

'I know we're too early for November the fifth, but we've got all that rotten wood from the old arks piled up and ready to light, and it's as dry as anything. I'm going to fetch Jamie out of his bed,' Jennet said. 'It's a family celebration and he needs to be with us.'

It was a splendid bonfire, and as it roared and crackled and tossed great handfuls of sparks up into the night sky, Jennet hugged Jamie, warmly wrapped in a blanket, and watched the awe and pleasure in his eyes.

'One day when you're a very old man,' she said, 'you'll tell your grandchildren about this and say it was the first night of the rest of your life!'

Later, snuggled into the bole of a tree, feeding him pieces of hot roasted potato, her fingers charred black from the burned skins, she murmured to Mollie, 'It was you that put your Bert up to it, wasn't it?'

'Me?' The other girl's eyes widened. 'How can you say such a thing? Him and that Helen did it all by themselves, with no help from me or anyone else!'

'I'm talking about the cottage, not the baby! You suggested it to him, didn't you?'

'Mebbe I did and mebbe I didn't. It's a good idea, though. Bert's just the man you need around this farm, and now everyone's well suited. Come on, you,' she scrambled up and plucked Jamie from his mother's arms, 'let's do what the Red Indians do and dance around the fire!'

Angus Scott watched from the shadows as she whirled in and out of the fire's glow, the laughing child in her arms, her red hair lifting about her face and the glow from the flames turning her green eyes to emeralds. He thought that he had never seen anything so beautiful, so desirable and so unattainable.

In Celia Scott's day the food-pig had always been slaughtered on the farm, making Martinmas an ordeal for Jennet, who had been put in charge of the pigsty and its occupants before her tenth birthday. Despite her grandmother's disapproval, she could not resist becoming attached to the pigs in her charge and she dreaded and hated the butcher's annual visit. She could still hear the shrill screams of her friends as they sensed their fate and could still see their lifeless bodies hung up in one of the sheds to be scalded and bled. She didn't want Jamie to go through that misery.

Like his mother, Jamie was fond of the pigs, and today, knowing the butcher was coming to have a preliminary look at the animals, Jennet had instructed Mollie to keep him well away from the yard until after the man had been and gone, just in case his sharp little ears picked up the wrong comment.

She herself had opted to start on one of her most hated jobs, cleaning out the arks. Ousted hens were clucking and scuffling and fussing outside, while Jennet, inside the confined and smelly space, chipped grimly at droppings that had accumulated on the floor and then been stamped into a solid mass by clawed feet.

It was a beautiful sunny early-autumn day, but within the ark, barely large enough for her to turn round in, it was dark and hot. She had pulled an old cap of Angus's over her head to protect her hair, and now she could feel sweat trickling from beneath it to run over her hot face, before dripping from the end of her nose onto the wooden floor. Every now and again she had to stop to wipe moisture from her eyes and forehead, and she was convinced that, if she really wanted to, she could wring out her eyebrows. Although she was only wearing light trousers and a blouse with the sleeves rolled up the heat made her body itch all over.

'Jennet!' Angus's voice was muffled by the wooden walls about her.

'What?' she yelled back irritably, her own voice echoing within the ark, and went back to attacking a particularly difficult section of dirt in a dark corner. At last it gave way beneath the onslaught from her scraper and she scooped it up and tossed it into the nearly full bucket by her side. That would do, she decided. A quick brush out, an armful of clean straw and one more ark would be done.

Carefully, lest some daft and vulnerable hen was behind her, she edged backwards through the small door of the ark, pulling the bucket after her, until with a sign of relief she was out in the fresh air and able to stand up.

'Jennet, did you not hear me?' Angus asked from the field gate.

'Yes, I heard you.' She stretched, easing her cramped limbs, 'but I wasn't going to crawl out just to find out what you . . .' She turned, then stopped short as she saw the man walking down the lane to the gate, head up and feet landing solidly and confidently on the ground, heel to toe. The Blaikie strut, Angus had always called it.

'Look who's come to see us!' Angus said triumphantly, as though he had pulled the newcomer from a magician's top hat.

'Hello, Jennet.'

'Allan Blaikie.' She approached the gate slowly, well aware of the fright she must look. 'What are you doing here?'

'He's come back to the island!'

Jennet's mouth went dry and a cold shiver ran from the top of her head to the soles of her feet. 'You've gone back to farming?'

'I'm staying at Gleniffer, but just until I get a place of my own,' Allan said, his clear blue eyes looking her up and down. 'My uncle's bought over Matt

McGuire's butcher's shop in Rothesay, and I've been sent to run it for him, since I know the island. Did my father not tell you?'

'Not a word.'

Allan opened the gate for her, then reached out to take the bucket from her hand. 'Mebbe he didnae see the news as important,' he said as the three of them began to walk back to the farm. 'You're looking well, Jennet.'

'How can you tell?' she asked tartly, well aware of the sight she must look, covered with muck and with her face red from the heat and no doubt streaked with dirt. When she hauled the cap off to let her hair fall free, it landed in a tangled mass against her neck, heavy and damp, and she had to fight the urge to give her scalp a good scratch.

'Angus's been telling me that the two of you have taken over the place.'

'That's right.'

'And you've got a couple of pigs you'll want rid of, come Martinmas. I thought I'd take a look at them while I was here.'

At the pigsty he opened the wooden door and went inside. Jack and Jill, rooting contentedly about their little yard, nosed at him in the hope that he might have brought some titbits. The sty had been cleaned only that morning and the pigs, Jennet thought, looked more respectable than she did at that moment. She leaned her folded arms on the wall and watched as Allan went into the sty.

The meat from one pig would keep them going over the winter, and the money they got from Allan for the other would go towards the farm rent and the cost of buying in winter feed for the cows to augment the hay and bruised oats they had grown during the summer. Renting the cottage to holiday visitors had helped a little, but as always the pigs were an important source of income.

'You've looked after them well,' Allan said.

'Oh, we still know how to farm,' Jennet told him sharply, 'even though my grandmother's not here to tell us what to do every minute of the day.'

As soon as the words were out she realised how childish and petty they sounded, but he merely raised an eyebrow and then said, 'Will ye want me to tend to your own animal here?'

'No!'

'Jennet wants them to be taken away this time,' Angus began to explain, 'because the wee . . .'

'Because I hate having them killed here,' Jennet interrupted. 'I never liked it and it's not going to happen here again.'

'I mind how much you hated it,' Allan said. 'Remember the day I found you hiding in the hayloft with your hands over your ears, saying prayers and multiplication tables and God knows what to keep the noise out?'

It was just as well, Jennet thought, that there was enough dirt on her face to hide the blush. 'I mind you laughing at me for being such a baby.'

'Did I? I was a right bully in those days, according to our Struan. When the time comes, I'll take your two over to Gleniffer and see to them along with my dad's pigs,' Allan assured her. 'Right, then, I'd best be getting back to the shop.'

To Jennet's horror her brother said, 'Come in and have something to drink first, man.'

Allan's eyes brightened and he opened his mouth to accept, then closed it again as Jennet said swiftly, 'Mollie's busy bottling brambles and redcurrants, so the kitchen's all upside down, and I'm not in a fit state to entertain you.'

'I'd best get back to the shop anyway.'

'Another time, though . . . What about Friday night?' Angus suggested. 'We could have a good talk then.'

'Would that be all right with you, Jennet?'

'Of course it is,' Angus said heartily. 'You're as eager to hear what he's been up to as I am, aren't you?' he asked his sister, who could have slapped the pleasure off his face. Instead she had to force a polite smile and say, 'Yes of course, Allan. Friday night.'

'Fine, we'll see you then,' Allan said, and he turned towards the van standing in the lane . . . then spun back to face the yard as a high, clear, unmistakably childish voice said sweetly, 'Come on, ye wee bugger . . .' And Jamie walked round the corner of the deep-litter house, trailing Gumrie behind him on a long string.

'Come on, ye wee bugger,' the little boy said again,

too intent on the dog at his heels to notice his mother until she said, 'Jamie, what d'you think you're doing?'

He beamed at her. 'Taking Gumrie for a walk 'cos he's . . .' He stopped short as he noticed the stranger.

For his part, Allan Blaikie stared at the little boy as though he had seen a ghost. He moistened his lips, then said, 'Is this . . . ?'

'Jennet's wee laddie,' Angus said. 'Your mother surely told you about him.'

'Aye.' Allan said as Jennet reached out to draw her son to her side. 'Aye, she did, but I never realised . . .' He stopped, then said, 'I thought he was a wee thing in a pram . . .'

'He was once, but that was a good year or two past. This is our Jamie,' Angus said proudly.

Jennet would have clung to Jamie, but he pulled free and marched forward, his hand held out as Celia had taught him from babyhood.

'Hello,' he said. It was a moment, Jennet knew, that she would never forget, a moment she had never wanted to see. Her son, her baby – and nobody else's, ever – walking away from her and towards the father he had never seen. The father who had denied him even before he was born.

She watched as Allan put his own hand out to take the child's small fingers, holding them carefully. 'How d'ye . . . how d'ye do, Jamie?'

'What's your name?' Jamie had to tilt his head right back to take in the height of the man towering over him.

'I'm Allan. I live at Gleniffer.'

'No you don't,' Jamie said flatly.

'I'm Mrs Blaikie's other wee boy, just the same as you're your mummy's wee boy, and I've been away. But now,' said Allan, 'I've come back home.'

The words sent a shiver down Jennct's spine, but Jamie gave a snort of laughter. 'Not a wee boy. Big old man!'

'Jamie Scott!'

'Leave him be, Jennet, mebbe he's got the right view of things, the way I feel sometimes.' Allan gave a wry smile that twisted one side of his mouth and raised one eyebrow in a way she had once found heart-stoppingly attractive.

'I like Struan,' Jamie said.

'And I hope you'll like me as well, once we get to know each other,' Allan replied.

'Here.' Jamie, still holding Allan's fingers, towed him back to the sty, where he picked up a stick leaning against the wall. 'Lift me up,' he commanded, and Allan did as he was told, setting the small booted feet on the rounded top of the wall and holding Jamie firmly about the waist.

'Mind now,' he cautioned as Jamie, putting all his trust in the hands supporting him, leaned his entire body forward to scratch the pigs' backs with his stick.

'Jack and Jill,' he said. 'My friends.'

'I mind someone else who had friends like that and they were called Jack and Jill, too.'

'Do they live near here?' Jamie waggled the stick

industriously. 'See, they like this' and he tickled them with the stick.

Jennet could not bear it any longer. 'Jamie, Mollie'll be wondering where you've got to. You know you were told to stay with her today.' She moved forward and took the child away from Allan, lifting him into her arms.

'Gumrie go for walk.'

'I'd best be going,' Allan said, his gaze still on Jamie. 'I'll see you on Friday.'

Jamie wanted to watch the van move off along the lane, but Jennet carried him back to the safety of the yard.

'You smell,' he remarked as they went.

'So would you if you'd been cleaning out the hen coops, you cheeky wee monkey.'

The house door flew open as they neared it, and Mollie erupted into the yard, coming to a halt as she saw them.

'There you are! I'm sorry, Jennet, I took him into the garden to get some kale for the dinner and the next thing I knew he'd gone.'

'It's fine. Everything's fine,' Jennet lied, while Jamie explained, 'Gumrie wanted walk.'

'He's a farm dog,' Jennet argued, lowering him to the ground, 'and farm dogs don't get taken for walks.'

'Gumrie does,' Jamie insisted. Then, to the dog, 'Come on, ye wee bugger.'

Mollie's hands flew to her mouth as boy and dog

trotted into the house. 'What did he say? And where did he learn it?'

'Probably from Jem.'

'I'm going to have a word with that old man. He should mind his tongue when the bairn's near!'

'You might as well order him not to open his mouth at all,' Jennet said.

18

Andra Blaikie walked into the kitchen when they were at their breakfast the next morning.

'Young McCabe tells me that ye've offered your wee cottage tae him and the lassie.'

'There's no reason not to, since it's lying empty,' Angus said shortly. Since Celia had gone, relations between him and the bluff farmer had become fragile, mainly because Angus mistrusted his neighbour, seeing Blaikie as his grandmother's ally.

'Ach well, if they've made up their minds tae wed I suppose they have tae find somewhere.' Andra drew out a chair and sat down without waiting for an invitation, which was as well since Angus did not seem disposed to issue one and Jennet was busy with Jamie. 'He says ye're willin' tae take him on over the winter, too.'

'Since he'll be right here on the farm anyway, and since you're letting him go, it makes sense.'

'He's a good worker, but I've got enough help with Struan back home, and there's not so much to do during the winter months. Thanks, lassie,' Andra said as Mollie put a plate of food before him. He forked a fried egg and a large lump of sausage into his mouth and said through it, 'I'd have kept him on, and mebbe found somewhere on Gleniffer for the two of them tae bide until they got themselves sorted out, but Lizbeth's taken a right scunner tae the lad.'

'That's my brother you're talking about, Mr Blaikie,' Mollie reminded him sharply, splashing some tea into a huge mug for him.

'Eh? Oh aye, so it is. But I don't mean anythin' against the laddie; you've just heard me say I was for keepin' him on. It's the wife; she took that lassie from an orphanage and trained her up to be a braw wee servant and good with the hens forbye. And with her bein' so keen on the church and its teachings, she's taken it hard that the girl's fallen just when she was doin' so well.'

He took a mouthful of tea and then changed the subject. 'Allan was sayin' he called in yesterday tae see the pigs. Ye'd be surprised tae see him back on the island.'

'We were.' Jennet kept a wary eye on Jamie, who was trying to stuff an entire egg into his mouth in imitation of their visitor.

'It seems that my brother's done so well for himself in Glasgow that he's bought over Matt McGuire's shop in Rothesay and set Allan up to run it. His mother's right pleased to see him back on the island. You and him were aye good friends when ye were growin' up, Angus.' Blaikie mopped his plate with a slice of bread. 'Any word from Celia?'

'We heard the other day. She's not coming back.'

'D'ye tell me?' Andra said in amazement, his jaw falling to reveal the last of his breakfast. 'How's that, then?'

'She wanted the farm to go to new tenants, but we've decided to keep it on.'

'Just the two of ye?' Blaikie looked from brother to sister and back again. 'Celia's not said a word about this in her letters tae Lizbeth.'

'I've no doubt she will; it's just been decided.'

'Ye think ye'll manage?'

'We'd not take it on if we thought otherwise, Mr Blaikie.' Jennet put a finger beneath Jamie's chin to close his mouth, which had also been hanging open.

'Well, ye've got big hearts; I'll say that for ye. And I'm just along the road when ye need help.'

'We'll try not to trouble you. After all,' Angus said, 'we'll have Bert McCabe here from Martinmas, and you've said yourself what a good farmhand he is.'

'Aye, he is. Well, good luck tae ye.' The farmer pushed his chair back and got to his feet, patting his stomach. 'That was a nice bit of food, lassie.'

'I'm glad you liked it.' Mollie, clearly still annoyed over the remarks about her brother and his future wife, sounded as stiff as Angus.

'You know that Mrs Blaikie'll be reporting on us

with every letter she writes to Gran?' Jennet said when Andra had gone.

'There's nothing we can do about that, except try to make sure that she can't say anything bad.'

'Jamie, don't you dare do that unless you're going to eat every bit of it,' Jennet said sharply to the little boy, who was gleefully wiping a slice of bread round his plate in imitation of their visitor. 'I'll not have you wasting food like that.'

'Talking of waste, you're very free with our food,' Angus told Mollie as he hoisted himself to his feet. 'You never heard me inviting him to sit at our table and eat with us, did you?'

'But your grandmother always made sure he was fed if he came in while we were at the table.'

'Mebbe so, but it's not my grandmother who's in charge now. I can't afford to throw good food away on a man who's on his way home right now for another breakfast!'

'What is the matter with this place this morning?' Mollie asked as the door closed behind Angus. 'He's beginning to sound just like old Mrs Scott . . . and you were in a right thrawn mood last night.'

'Of course I'm thrawn,' Jennet snapped, watching Jamie sauntering out to feed the hens with the unwanted slice of bread he had hidden up the front of his jumper. 'I always was. I'm a Scott of Westervoe, God help me!'

'For goodness sake, away you go and get on with some work and leave me to do mine in peace.'

'Mebbe this place is getting to be too much for us already,' Jennet said as she dragged on her jacket and tied a scarf about her hair. 'Mebbe Grandmother was right, and I should have gone back to Glasgow.'

'And left Jamie with her? Don't be daft. And when you come back for your dinner,' Mollie called after her as she left, 'see and have a smile on your face.'

That, Jennet thought, was highly unlikely. At that moment she felt as though she might never smile again. Not, at least, while Allan Blaikie remained on Bute.

Despite his protests Jamie was bathed and put to bed earlier than usual on Friday evening. When she had tucked him into his cot Jennet stayed with him for a while, reading story after story to him, partly as compensation for the earlier bedtime and partly as an excuse to be out of the way when Allan arrived.

Jamie was almost asleep when she heard Angus greeting their visitor, but even so his eyes flickered open.

'Who's that?' he mumbled round the thumb he had stuck into his mouth.

'The Sandman coming to take you to Beddy-byeland.'

'Can I go and see him?'

'Stay here and close your eyes. That's the best way to see the Sandman. I'll go on reading and we'll pretend we don't know he's here. That'll bring him upstairs as quick as a blink.'

She read on long after he had fallen asleep, but at last she had to close the book and go downstairs to where the men were talking at the kitchen table.

Allan, dressed in his good suit, got to his feet when she went into the kitchen and, to her surprise, shook her by the hand.

'D'you not want to take Allan in by, Angus?' she asked her brother.

'I'd as soon be here as in the parlour. I'm surely not a visitor in this house, Jennet.'

'I suppose not.' She fetched her mending bag and sat down on the smaller of the fireside chairs.

'Do we have any beer in?' Angus wanted to know.

'There's some in the press in the other room.' She began to get up again, but Angus waved her back into her chair.

'I'll get it.'

'When can I see you?' Allan asked low-voiced when they were alone.

'You're seeing me now.'

'Alone, I mean. I want to talk to you.'

'We did our talking, years ago, and there's nothing left to say. Nothing,' she added sharply as he opened his mouth again. For a long moment they locked eyes, then Allan Blaikie shrugged.

'Jennet, I only live a quarter of a mile away now. We're going to have to face each other sometime,' he said, then Angus was back in the room, fetching glasses and pouring beer.

* * *

'So how are things?' Allan wanted to know when Angus had settled down again.

'Not too bad, considering. Better now that we've got Westervoe to ourselves, eh, Jennet?'

Allan laughed. 'To hear my mother tell it, anyone would think the two of you had thrown the old woman off the farm and told her not to come back.'

'It was her own choice entirely, but she wasnae pleased when we said we'd try for running the place between us.'

'It is a shame Martin didn't come back.'

'That's up to him,' Jennet said levelly. 'We don't need him any more than we need Grandmother.'

'I'm sure you're right.' Allan's gaze slid from her to a spot by the leg of her chair. Glancing down, she saw a discarded ball on the floor. 'The wee fellow'll be in his bed by now?'

'Long since.' Jennet scooped up the ball and pushed it into her apron pocket while Angus asked, 'But what about you? Struan said something about a young woman a while back. Someone in Glasgow.'

'Oh, that.' Allan sounded uncomfortable. 'We parted a while since. She was wanting to settle down and I didnae see myself as her husband. What about you, Angus, and that lassie in Saltcoats?'

'It turned out that the thing she liked best about me was the way I could walk about on my own two legs,' Angus said harshly. 'Once I stopped doing that she lost interest.' Then, into the sudden awkward silence, 'So tell us what sort of war you had.'

'Much the same as Struan, and I suppose you'll have heard it all from him. We were both lucky to get through the fighting in one piece.'

'That must have come as a surprise to you,' Jennet put in. Then, when both men stared at her, 'Did you not say once that you were sure you'd be killed?'

For a moment he looked at her, his eyes blank, then he coloured as memory flooded back. 'Aye,' he said, the life suddenly gone from his voice. 'I mind that time. I mind it well.'

'I'm sure everyone caught up in a war must wonder if he's going to survive,' Angus said. 'Though I'd not have thought you'd have any doubts, Allan. You're not the sort to doubt.'

'Oh, I had them all right, a lot of them,' Allan said, still in the same flat voice. It took some coaxing from Angus, but finally he began to talk about his war. Jennet glanced at the clock; Allan would surely take himself off once he had had some supper, but it was still too early for that. She must endure another hour of his company first.

She kept her head bent over her work, trying to shut out his voice, then she found herself listening almost against her will, caught up in the vivid word pictures he painted of men who had been plunged by war into a half life, where they were no longer people in their own right, but single units forged into one war machine with no thoughts of the future because, for them, it might not last beyond the next day, or the next hour, or even the next minute.

A muffled cry from above brought them all back to the present, and when Jennet looked at the clock she was astonished to see that more than two hours had passed.

'Is that the time already? You'll be ready for your supper.' She jumped up, almost scattering her sewing over the rug, and picked up the kettle. 'I'll get this going, then I'll have to see to the wee one . . .'

'I'll do that, you tend to the bairn.' Allan got up from the table and took the kettle from her hand.

Normally Jamie, who rarely woke once he was down for the night, could be soothed back to sleep if anything roused him, but this time he must have had a bad dream. When Jennet got to him he was clawing his way out of the cot, his face red with panic and wet with tears. When she picked him up he clung to her, and squealed when she tried to put him back in the cot.

'Not tonight of all nights, Jamie!' she begged him, but it was no use. He was determined to be with her, and downstairs the two men were waiting, no doubt with growing impatience, for their food. She had no option but to wrap him in a blanket and carry him down to the kitchen, where Angus was setting the table while Allan, who had made tea, buttered some homemade scones.

'Angus showed me where they were. I hope it's all right to . . .' He stopped, his eyes on the child in her arms, then went on, 'to put them out.'

'Of course, they're meant for visitors.'

'There you go again. When has Allan ever been a

visitor in this house?' Angus wanted to know. 'There's new-made bramble jelly too, Allan, fetch it from that press.' He sat down and held his arms out to his nephew. 'Come on, wee man, come and tell your Uncle Angus what wakened you.'

Jennet would have preferred to keep Jamie on her lap, but to her annoyance he held his arms out to Angus and she had no alternative but to hand him over. Allan seated himself opposite.

'Remember me, Jamie?'

Jamie blinked sleep from his eyes. 'Mrs Blaikie's wee boy.'

'That's right.' Allan dipped a hand into his pocket. 'See what I've got?'

He drew a small mouth organ from his pocket and handed it over. The child turned it over in his hands, frowning.

'What's it for?'

'Give it back and I'll show you,' Allan offered, and when the instrument was returned he blew softly into it, producing a trill of notes.

Jamie squealed with excitement. 'Look, Mummy! Do it again!'

'So you've not forgotten how to play a good tune?' Angus asked, grinning.

'Try it for yourself.' Allan wiped the instrument on the heel of his hand and gave it to Jamie. 'It's been everywhere with me, and it's cheered up many a sorry night when we were all homesick. You blow into it, Jamie, like this . . .'

He pursed his mouth and blew gently, and Jamie did his best to copy him, but without success. 'You,' he demanded, handing the mouth organ back.

Allan cradled it in his two hands and lifted them to his lips. He took a breath, then filled the kitchen with the strains of 'Lili Marlene', swinging as soon as he had finished into 'Danny Boy'. Then he stopped and jumped to his feet as Mollie came in, her red hair tousled and her cheeks glowing from the cycle ride back to the farm after a night out with Joe.

After Mollie had fallen asleep that night Jennet slid out of bed and went to sit in the old nursing chair that stood by Jamie's cot. It was too dark to make out the details of the little boy's sleeping face, but her mind's eye knew every line of it, from the silky eyebrows down over the snub little nose to the mouth, now pursed in sleep, and the neat chin.

Once or twice during the first few days of Jamie's life she had detected something of his father in his tiny face, but now he was just Jamie, a person in his own right.

One of his hands lay outside the blanket, palm up and with the fingers curled like the petals of a half-opened flower. Jennet touched her own forefinger gently against his palm and he gripped at it, stirring and mumbling something before slipping back into slumber. She leaned forward, comforted by the contact, and laid her face against the bars of the cot, wishing that she could pick him up and hold him close for comfort and reassurance.

Home on leave before going overseas, Allan Blaikie had come to Westervoe to visit Angus, who was still experiencing pain in his crippled leg in the wake of his accident. As he was leaving, Allan had asked Jennet to walk down by the shore with him. It had been a mild autumn night, half dark and with the waves shushing gently a few feet from where they walked. Allan was off to rejoin his regiment the following day, and Jennet was leaving in two days' time for Glasgow.

'You'll be looking forward to it,' he said.

'I'm not sure. Glasgow's a big city and I've never been away from home before.'

'Och, it'll be grand. You'll meet new folk and you're learning a new trade. Anyway, it's time you were spreading your wings. If you stay here you'll marry into another farm and have a parcel of bairns, with no chance to see a bit of the world first.'

'That's what Martin said in his last letter.'

'He's right. Make the most of your youth while you can, Jennet. There's thousands of lads that'll not get that chance,' he said, a new, bleak note coming into his voice.

'I'll be coming back here often to see how Angus's getting on. Mebbe you could write to him while you're away, Allan, and tell him what's happening with you. He needs to keep in touch with other folk, and Martin's not much of a letter-writer.'

'Neither am I, but I'll try.' Allan paused to pick up a stone and throw it, with a powerful swing of his arm, far out to sea. It was too dark for them to see where it landed, but they heard the splash. He walked on quickly, making her hurry to keep up with him, then suddenly he said over his shoulder, 'I scarcely recognised him when I went into that room tonight. He's away to skin and bone and he looks so old, Jennet. He's not Angus any more!'

'Of course he is! He was in terrible pain at first, but it's getting better. And he's still the same laddie he always was.' It had been Jennet's fear, too, that the rail accident might have changed Angus in more ways than just physically.

'How can anyone get over what's happened to him?' Allan demanded.

'When I went to Glasgow for my interview I saw more than one man who'd lost limbs or eyes in the fighting, but they're learning to deal with it and get on with their lives. You must have seen folk like that yourself, for there are a lot of them about these days.'

'Aye, I've seen them, but I know that I could never be like them, or like Angus,' he said; then, low-voiced, 'Jennet, I couldnae bear it.'

'Of course you could, if you had to.'

'Allan Blaikie's able for anything and afraid of nothing,' Celia Scott used to say when Jennet and her brothers arrived home late and soaked through from damming a burn under Allan's supervision, or bruised and bloody and with their clothes torn because he had led them on some perilous expedition involving tree-climbing and rock-scaling. Although Drew was the older brother, it was always Allan who planned their games and set the dares. And it was usually Allan who triumphed, jeering at the others from the very top of the tallest tree or standing high above them on a sheer sheet of rock with scarcely a handhold to it. Allan, tall and strong, confident, sure of himself and fearless.

'When we were all growing up, you were the one who was never afraid of anything,' Jennet said now, remembering.

'That was when I was just a daft laddie,' he told her impatiently. 'All youngsters think they can handle whatever life throws at them. It's not till you get older and go out into the world, and see the sort of things folk can do to other folk, that ye realise what's real.'

'But even so . . .'

'Will ye listen tae what I'm sayin'?' Allan said, his voice suddenly rough and hard. 'If all I wanted was someone tae tell me nothing'll happen to me, I'd be home right now talkin' to my mother; and if I wanted someone tae tell me tae stop bein' a daft, imaginin' fool, I'd go tae my father. But right now I just need someone tae let me say what I think inside, and Angus's in no fit state for that, not with what's happened to him.'

He had begun to walk faster along the shoreline; now he stopped and turned to face her. 'We're not bairns any more, Jennet. Nob'dy's able tae put a bandage or a plaster on the bit that hurts and make it better, because it hurts here . . .' He slapped the heel of his hand against his head . . . 'and here.' He made a fist and punched himself hard in the chest. 'And it won't go away as long as I'm wearin' that damned uniform and carryin' a gun, and knowin' that somewhere over the hill there's a poor bastard like me, mebbe even a laddie from a German farm, with a uniform and a gun. And when the two of us meet, Jennet, one of us is goin' tae have tae kill the other. And d'you know what frightens me even more than that?'

'What?'

'Mebbe he'll be a bad shot,' he said thickly, 'and I'll end up a cripple for the rest of my life, like poor Angus back there!'

'Allan . . .' she began, then stopped because she didn't know what else to say. Words were an inadequate response to the anguish in his voice.

'D'you think I could say any of that tae my parents, or to your gran? They'd be shocked if they knew what a coward I am!'

'You're not a coward. All the other soldiers must be thinking the same as you.'

'If they are, then they're makin' a damned good job of not lettin' on. Some of them even seem tae be enjoyin' themselves, and all I can think of is whether I'm goin' to make a fool of myself when the time comes, and run away or pee myself, or . . .'

His voice broke and he turned away slightly, a hand

at his mouth. Jennet tentatively touched his shoulder and discovered that it was shaking. She gripped it, thinking that the contact might help, and then suddenly he turned and went into her arms, clutching at her, his face wet against her neck. 'Tell me, Jennet . . .' His voice was muffled, 'tell me it's goin' tae be all right. Make me believe it'll be all right!'

'It will.' She stroked his hair, which was free of grease and surprisingly soft, and when he straightened she wiped the tears from his cheek with the ball of her thumb. 'It'll be all right,' she told him fiercely. 'Nothing's going to happen to you. I'd not let anything bad happen to you, ever!'

He gave a choked laugh. 'How are you going to manage that, Jennet Scott?'

'Because I love you.' It was the first time she had admitted it to anyone other than herself. She had never dreamed that one day she would say it to the man himself. 'I love you,' she said again. 'I always have. And I'll never let anything happen to you!'

Looking back, she could not remember who kissed whom first, or when they moved to sit and then lie on a patch of grass beneath the dry-stane dyke that bordered one of Westervoe's fields. She only remembered their kisses, his hands and his skin and the smell of him, and the urgency of their lovemaking. She remembered the sudden pain as he entered her, dulled almost at once by the need to be close to him, to ease his misery and help him in whatever way she could.

They had scarcely said a word to each other later,

as they tidied themselves and walked back quickly to Westervoe, where Allan had said a hurried goodbye in the lane, then turned away in the direction of his own home.

'You shouldn't be out walking at night just now,' Celia had scolded her when she went indoors. 'The island's full of men we know nothing about these days, not to mention mines and all sorts. Still, as long as Allan was with you, I suppose you were all right.'

If only her grandmother had known, Jennet thought, with a wry twist of the lips as she eased her finger from Jamie's fist and crept back to bed. Because she had been in Glasgow for a full three months before it dawned on her that she was pregnant, and because she then waited another two months, not knowing what to do for the best, before returning home, everyone had assumed that Jamie's father was some unknown serviceman whom Jennet had met in the city. What would her grandmother think if she knew that Jamie had been fathered below one of her own dry-stane dykes by her best friend's son?

Mollie turned over as Jennet crept into bed beside her. 'What's the matter?' she mumbled.

'It's all right, I just thought I heard Jamie,' Jennet whispered, and almost at once Mollie was asleep again.

19

Nesta McCabe insisted on a proper wedding for her son and his intended bride.

'Just because there's a bairn on the way that's no excuse for the two of them to make a quick wee promise before the minister, then go on as if nothing's happened,' she said, and Ann Logan agreed with her.

'We'll have a party in our house after the church ceremony. Now the holidaymakers are gone, we can use the front room. And since the lassie has no family of her own it'll be nice for her to know that there's folk who care.'

She brought out her sewing machine, and between them she and Nesta made a dress and matching jacket for Helen, a shy, dark-haired girl who stayed close to Bert's side when he took her to meet his family and the Logans.

With Alice's help the two women cooked and baked for the occasion, using precious rations and bringing out hoarded tins, while at Westervoe Mollie and

Jennet, when she managed to find the time from her farm work, got the cottage ready.

To Mollie's dismay, her sister Senga accepted the wedding invitation sent by their mother.

'What made you tell our Senga about it?' she wanted to know.

'It's a family occasion, it's only right that she should be asked.'

'And did you send one tae my father an' all?'

'I did not. D'you think I want him spoiling things for Bert and mebbe bringing his woman friend to embarrass us all in front of the good friends we've made here? Oh, I know all about her,' Nesta added as Mollie gaped.

'How . . . ? Senga told you! That one couldnae keep her mouth shut tae save her own life!'

'I'd a right to be told. Oh, I know you kept quiet to spare my feelings . . .' Nesta put a hand on her daughter's arm. 'You're a good lassie, but it's as well for me to know the truth. Anyway, it's not bothered me one bit. To be honest with ye, Mollie, it's a relief to know he's got someone else tae keep him busy. That way, he'll leave us in peace.'

'Is Senga's boyfriend coming with her?'

'I don't think so. She never mentioned him. Mrs Logan says she can stay here . . . for nothing, she says, since she's my daughter.'

'Well, you can just tell her to charge Senga what she'd charge anyone else. From what she says in her letters she's not short of a shilling or two, and that boyfriend of hers seems to be very well off, thanks to the black market.'

'Now you don't know that for sure, Mollie. And even if he is,' Nesta added, 'I'd as soon not know anything about it. All I'm asking is that you and your sister get on well while she's here. This wedding's a family occasion and it means I'll have all my children round me again. I want to enjoy every minute of it.'

For her mother's sake Mollie bit her tongue and set out to be nice to her sister, who was wearing such high heels when she arrived that she had a terrible job getting down the gangway between steamer and pier. She tittuped towards the waiting reception party for all the world, Mollie thought, like a newborn calf staggering about a byre. A small hat, mostly flowers and veiling, was perched above one eyebrow and her costume clung to her plump body as tightly as she herself clung to the gangway railing.

'Has she got no luggage?' Mollie wondered, for her sister carried nothing but a shiny new-looking handbag. The question was answered when an elderly man, who had trotted off the boat behind Senga clutching a large suitcase, followed her over to where her mother, sister and brother waited, and put the case down with an audible sigh of relief.

'Thank you so much,' Senga crooned, fluttering her eyelashes – easy enough to flutter, Mollie realised, since they were artificial. 'You're so kind!'

He blushed, muttered something about it being a

pleasure, and tipped his hat to her and then to Nesta and Mollie, before disappearing back into the crowd.

'Who was that?' Nesta asked, and her daughter gave an elegant little shrug of the shoulders.

'I don't know. Just some old man that was on the boat.'

'It was kind of him to help you. D'you think we should have offered him a cup of tea?'

'What for?' Senga asked in amazement. 'He wanted tae carry my case, I didnae ask him to.'

'How long are you staying?' Mollie eyed the case.

Again, Senga twitched her shoulders elegantly. 'A few days, mebbe a week. It depends.'

'On what?' Sam, who had developed muscles as well as confidence after a few months of working with the boats, lifted the case as though it weighed no more than the bag.

On whoever she gets her claws into, Mollie thought, trailing after the others. All her life Senga had spoiled things for her. While working in a Rothesay shop after she left school, Mollie had gone out dancing once or twice with the shop's delivery lad. She had enjoyed his company, and he was a good dancer, but then came the wet, cold night when he had insisted on escorting her home on the bus. She had invited him in for a cup of tea, and by the time he left an hour later he was Senga's.

She had dropped him within a month, for he was not her type. With Senga, it was the chase that mattered, and the pleasure of taking someone else's property.

There were some things, Mollie thought, that you could never forget.

A gratifying number of guests crowded into the Logans' parlour after the church ceremony. Alice's young man was there, and the girl with whom Sam McCabe was walking out. Joe had been invited, and so had Jem and his wife. To his delight Jem, who had been friendly with Helen's uncle, had been asked to give her away at her wedding since she had no male relations of her own.

Dressed in his best clothes, without the filthy cap he always wore when he was working, and with his thick white hair and beard washed and trimmed, Jem was beaming with pride at being given a position of honour, scarcely recognisable as the gruff, irritable farm worker Jennet had known all her life. His wife, a shy little woman, could only walk with the aid of a stout stick, and it was touching to see how attentive Jem was to her.

The wedding presents had been set out in the parlour, with a large cut-glass bowl, Senga's gift, as the centrepiece. 'Goodness knows what use they'll have for it, but it's certainly bonny,' Mollie said low-voiced as she and Jennet surveyed the collection. 'You should have seen Helen's face when she took it out of its fancy box. She was like Cinderella bein' told that she could go to the ball, the wee soul. Trust our Senga!'

In a smart silky dress, the threads woven in such a

way that with every movement the colours seemed to shift and merge into each other, Senga moved about the Logans' front room like an exotic butterfly, her long-lashed eyes missing nothing, a slight smile curving her red lips as she watched and listened.

When Mollie went into the kitchen to make some more sandwiches, Senga followed, leaning against the dresser and taking a little enamelled compact out of her bag.

'She's a right wee mouse, that lassie our Bert's got into trouble,' she said, staring at herself in the compact's mirror, then licking the tip of a finger before smoothing a pencilled eyebrow carefully. 'You'd wonder how he managed it.'

'You should ask him if you're so interested. I wouldnae know anythin' about that sort of thing.' Mollie cut viciously into a loaf of bread.

'You mean you've never . . . ?'

'I leave these goings-on to you and our Bert.'

'You always were a prude, weren't you? So nothing happened between you and that Angus Scott?' Senga asked, and Mollie's knife plunged deep into the butter.

'What d'you mean?'

Senga prodded at a curl with a crimson-tipped fingernail, then slid the mirror into her bag and leaned back against the dresser, crossing slim nylon-clad legs. 'You used to have a right crush on him. Did you never do anything about it?'

'I never had a crush on him, I was just tryin' tae make him get out of that chair, because Jennet hated the way his gran kept wantin' tae turn him into an invalid.'

'A right wee Florence Nightingale you were,' Senga recalled. 'You mean to say he never thanked you properly for it?'

'You watch too many films. We're not all looking for romance.'

'Most of us are. Most of us like to enjoy ourselves while we're still young, though some of us are born middle-aged and dreary.' Senga's voice was spiteful. Then, as Mollie refused to rise to the bait, she lounged where she was, studying her sister closely. 'You sure there's nothing going on between the two of you? 'Cos he's different from the way he used to be,' she rambled on when Mollie said nothing. 'I mind being quite scared of him when we all lived at the farm, because he was so sour-faced and angry-looking all the time, as if he wanted to punch someone. But now he's quite good-looking really. Mebbe he's got himself a girlfriend. Well, has he? Cat got your tongue?'

'Sorry, I didn't realise you were waiting for an answer; I thought you were quite happy just babblin' away there and watchin' me workin'. No, Angus Scott's not got a girlfriend as far as I know. He's too busy workin' the farm tae think about that sort of thing.'

'Mmm. I've never had a boyfriend who's a cripple,' Senga said thoughtfully. She smoothed both hands down her skirt from waist to thigh, almost as though she was caressing her own rounded hips, and then said, her voice soft and creamy, 'I wonder what it's like tae make love tae a bloke with a gammy leg? I wonder if it's different?'

A chill flickered through Mollie. Not Angus, she thought, suddenly visualising him falling under Senga's spell, only to be thrown aside like all the others.

'I thought you already had a boyfriend in Glasgow. Or have you dumped him, the way you always do?' She tried to keep her tone casual.

'You don't dump Kenny.' The creaminess left Senga's voice; it took on a thin sound as she added, 'It's not somethin' he'd stand for.' Then, her confidence returning, 'But Kenny's not here, is he? And if Angus Scott doesnae have a girlfriend . . .'

'He might have, for all I know. The only man I'm interested in is my Joe,' Mollie said, her back to her sister. Even so, she could feel Senga's sudden change of mood so strongly that it was like a clap of thunder.

'He's quite a nice-looking chap.'

'I think so.'

'But you've not . . . gone all the way with him?'

'Not yet. I believe in taking my time.'

'You must be sure of him, then,' Senga said thoughtfully.

'Of course I am. He's not interested in anyone but me. Listen, they'll all be starvin' in the front room. Are you going tae stop behavin' like Cleopatra on her barge and help me with these sandwiches?'

Senga gave the practised twitch of the shoulders

that passed for a shrug and eased her backside away from the dresser.

'All right,' she said and, picking up the plate, half full of sandwiches, she sauntered back to the front room.

When Mollie took in a second plate five minutes later her sister was listening with wide-eyed fascination as Joe talked, his face alight.

'She's making a right fuss of your Joe,' Jennet hissed, taking the plate from Mollie. 'You'd better go over there and get him away from her!'

Mollie glanced across the room to where Angus was talking to George Logan, and twitched her shoulders in imitation of her sister's delicate shrug. 'Ach, she'll not be staying on the island for long,' she said. 'And anyway, I'm not bothered.'

Helen and Bert McCabe moved into the cottage on the night of their marriage, and the next morning, after Bert had gone to work, his bride presented herself at the kitchen door, waiting for her orders.

All the girl knew was work, and it seemed to be all she wanted to do. She scrubbed and polished, washed dishes and laundered clothes, baked and cooked, and scarcely said a word to anyone other than Jamie. On a few occasions when she believed she was alone with the little boy, Jennet heard them chattering to each other, but as soon as she or anyone else appeared Helen retreated into silence.

'I wish she'd just relax and be happy,' Jennet fretted to Mollie.

'She is happy, in her own way. Best to let her be. You'd not think any man would have a chance to get up to mischief with such a wee shy thing, would you?' Mollie echoed her sister's words on the day of the wedding.

'She reminds me of myself,' Jennet said drily, 'and look what happened there.'

Helen even made butter for the household, scrubbing and scalding the small hand-churn and slipping into the byre after milking time to skim cream from the top of the milk. In Jennet's childhood she had helped her grandmother to churn the farm's butter supply, but there had been no time for such luxuries once the war came. Jennet had forgotten how good the rich yellow stuff tasted on homemade bread, and Helen kept back the buttermilk from the process for herself and Jamie. 'It's good for both of us,' she said. Jamie loved the new drink and went about most mornings, until he was caught and wiped by one of the adults, sporting a creamy moustache.

Helen's hard work in the kitchen meant that Mollie was free to help Jennet clean out the big cowshed in readiness for the winter, when the cows would be brought in from the field. Angus, Jem and Norrie were busy ditching and checking the dry-stane walls and cutting back trees and hedges. The days were growing shorter and the evenings darker, and the smoky smell of bonfires made from dead tree branches and hedge cuttings hung in the air and lingered on Angus's clothing when he came into the kitchen.

Senga was right, Mollie thought, watching him; he had changed since he and Jennet had taken over the farm. His movements were more confident now and, although he was still quiet, the bitterness that had tightened his mouth and hooded his eyes had given way to determination and self-belief. She was grateful that Senga had left the island, for if her sister had had even the slightest suspicion of Mollie's true feelings for Angus Scott, she would have gone after him like a ferret after a rabbit.

She would have got him, too; Mollie had no doubt about that. Senga had never failed yet, and beneath the defence he had built up Angus was lonely. Senga would have got him and she would have broken his heart. And that might have spelled disaster for him and Jennet, as well as Mollie. She would rather spend the rest of her life without him than see that happen.

She was quite proud of herself for having tricked her streetwise sister into making a play for Joe instead. Once she left Bute he had come back to Mollie like a naughty dog begging for a second chance, but she wasn't at all minded to agree to that. Why should she take back her sister's leavings, she thought resentfully. But at the same time there was a certain amount of pleasure in letting Joe court her.

Angus even returned to ploughing, hoisting himself up onto the tractor seat with increasing dexterity.

'D'ye think it's safe?' Mollie asked anxiously as she and Jennet watched him drive off down the lane.

'What's got into you? You're the one that nagged him until he got back on his feet, and now you've started fussing over him driving the tractor.'

'I'm not fussing, it's just that these machines can be dangerous. I've heard all about Drew Blaikie's accident.'

'Drew was unfortunate. Angus's been driving a tractor since before he was ten, and if it's something he wants to do I'll not argue with him the way Gran did. She took the heart out of him and I'm going to put it back, even if it kills him.'

For all her brave words Jennet secretly worried herself sick that first time, and when she heard the tractor roaring and rattling back to the yard a few hours later it was all she could do to stroll – and not run – into the yard to see him arrive. Angus, exhausted but triumphant, slithered down to the ground and reached up for his crutch, which had been wedged in behind him.

'I've not lost the knack,' he told his sister, grinning.

'I never thought you had,' she retorted sharply. 'It's like being on a bicycle – you never forget.'

'That's elephants,' he said, and tugged on her long curly hair as he limped past her into the house.

Celia, who never missed a Sunday service unless it was unavoidable, always insisted on a proper family attendance at Harvest Thanksgiving. This year Mollie went with them, as did Jamie, wearing a little sailor suit that Jennet had bought for the occasion. With his face scrubbed until it shone like an apple, his shoes shined and his hair dampened with tap-water before being brushed into place, he perched on the hard wooden pew between his mother and Mollie, staring wide-eyed at the stained-glass windows. He tilted his head so far back to look up at the vaulted roof that it bumped against the high back of the pew, and then he asked in awe, 'Who lives here?'

'God,' Jennet whispered back.

'Is he playing the music?' Jamie tempered his own clear voice to a loud whisper.

'No, that's Mr McLennan that used tae teach our Sam at the school,' Mollie murmured.

Jamie craned his neck to see the pulpit, surrounded by piles of apples, turnips and cabbages, leeks and flowers and potatoes, all carefully arranged and backed by sheaves of golden oats and barley.

'Getting our dinner?'

'We'll be going to Aunt Ann's for our dinner afterwards. Just sit quiet and be a good boy,' Jennet urged.

She had arranged to sit by the aisle, ready to whisk him outside if he became restless or tried to talk too much, but Jamie sat quietly for most of the time, mesmerised by the splendour of the place and the sight of all the worshippers in their Sunday best. When the hymns were sung he accepted a book, opened it at random and stood on the pew, quietly singing his favourite songs and making things difficult for Mollie, who had to give up singing in order to stifle her giggles.

When the congregation filed outside afterwards several women eyed him with interest.

'They usually favour the man,' Jennet heard one sharp-faced woman murmur to her companion. 'I feel myself that that's the Lord's way of making sure that the men don't get off with it entirely.'

Her friend shushed her and then came to gush over Jamie, as if to make up for the unkind words. 'He's just a wee picture,' she enthused. 'And a credit to you. So well behaved, weren't you, little man?'

'We didn't get dinner,' Jamie informed her, 'Getting it at Aunt Ann's.' Then, spotting a friend, he suddenly let go of Jennet's hand and dashed over to the Blaikies. 'Struan!'

'Hello, wee man!' Struan picked him up, beaming, and Jennet had no option but to join them.

Lizbeth Blaikie's handsome face was rigid with disapproval as she watched her son toss Jamie up in the air. 'Jennet . . . Angus . . . er . . .' She nodded vaguely to Mollie. 'It's rare to see you at the church.'

'We always come to Harvest Thanksgiving,' Angus reminded her. 'The rest of the time we're usually too busy taking care of God's earth for him.'

Struan gave a muffled sound, which he turned into a cough. His mother glared at him.

'Allan's not with you today?'

'Not today, Angus, he had business in Glasgow.'

Angus nudged his sister and then, as she said nothing, he soldiered on. 'You'll be pleased to see him back on the island.'

'It's always good to see your own kin again. Speaking of kin,' Lizbeth said heavily, 'I'd a letter from your grandmother the other day.'

'So did we. She seems to be enjoying herself in Largs.'

'She deserves her rest. That woman,' Lizbeth said pointedly, 'has had a hard life, and I should know, being her friend for more years than either of us can remember. She's a saint. There's not many like her.'

'You're right there,' Angus said, and Struan had another coughing attack.

'She's worked her fingers to the bone for her family . . .' Lizbeth Blaikie was continuing when Jennet, making some excuse about keeping her aunt and uncle waiting, took Jamie from Struan and fled, with Angus at her heels.

'Why didn't you help me?' he hissed as they went. 'Standing there with your mouth shut and leaving me to do all the talking!'

'I can't bear to speak to that woman! She ignores my Jamie and she always does her best to make me feel like a criminal. But she's right, Gran did work her fingers to the bone for us.'

'And her poor leg, too,' Angus said, and the two of them, walking among the folk all dressed in their Sunday best, with their Sunday manners, began to giggle.

20

'If you ask me,' Mollie said, 'it looks evil.'

'I'd hate to be in it with all that water above my head,' Jennet said, and Mollie squealed, clapped her hands to her ears, and spun away from the edge of the pier, where the two girls were contemplating the British submarine on show as part of Bute Thanksgiving Week.

'Don't . . . it gives me the shivers just to think about it!'

The boat, long and narrow and dark, gave Jennet the same feeling, but young men had had to entomb themselves in it, deep below the sea's surface, in order to fight in the war. She marvelled at their courage and endurance.

'Joe wanted me tae go on board with him and see round it,' Mollie said from where she now stood a few feet away from the edge.

'Are you going?'

'I told him that if he wanted someone to hold his hand on board that thing he'd have to invite Senga.'

'You're being rotten to that lad!'

'That's what he says, but tae my mind he deserves it. I might allow him tae take me out again eventually, till someone better comes along. But even if I do, it'll be a while before I let him forget the way he mooned after that sister of mine. Come on, we'll go and have a look at the flower show. That's better than a submarine any day.'

'You're right.' Jennet reached down to take Jamie's hand and discovered that the little boy, who had been by her side a moment ago, was no longer there. 'Jamie?' She looked wildly round the crowds on the pier. 'D'you see him, Mollie?'

'He was here a minute ago. He can't have gone far.' Like the town's streets, the pier was crowded with folk, most of them local, but sprinkled with a few late holidaymakers and people who had taken the ferry over from the mainland for the day. A small boy, not much higher than the average adult knee, would easily be lost in that throng.

Jennet's blood ran cold. 'You don't think . . . he couldn't have fallen in the water, could he?' She edged forward to peer down at the narrow strip of black water between the pilings and the submarine.

'No, of course not, someone would have seen him, or heard him. He was here not a minute ago,' Mollie said urgently. 'He can't have gone far.'

'He's so little, and yet he can move so fast . . . You stay on the pier and I'll run up towards the street, just in . . .'

'Is this what you're looking for?' Allan Blaikie said just then, moving into Jennet's line of vision. Jamie, beaming, was perched on the man's shoulders with his chubby legs dangling and his hands gripped firmly in Allan's.

'Look at me, Mummy,' he crowed, 'I'm up high!'

'The king of the castle,' Allan agreed.

'You naughty boy, you know you're supposed to stay beside me or Mollie!'

Recognising her anger, Jamie's excited smile died and tears of surprise and shock began to fill his eyes.

'Don't be too hard on him,' Allan said swiftly, 'I'm sure he didn't mean to wander away. It's difficult for a wee bairn, in among all those legs . . .'

'Are you trying to say that I wasn't looking after him properly?'

'I just meant that he wasn't doing anything wrong.'

'Of course he was. He knows that he must never run away from me or speak to strangers.'

Allan's eyes narrowed. 'I'd hardly class myself as a stranger.'

'You are as far as Jamie's concerned.'

'There's no harm done, Jennet,' Mollie interceded. 'The laddie's safe and that's all that matters.'

'Give him to me!' Jennet reached for her son, but when Allan freed his hands, Jamie clutched at the man's hair.

'I want to stay up high!' His lower lip began to jut in a way that would have made Celia smack his legs.

'You'll do as you're told!' Jennet reached up and

began to untangle the small fingers, heedless of the pain she might be causing Allan.

'Another day, eh?' He lifted the little boy over his ducked head, then put him into Jennet's arms. 'Time to go back to your mummy, son.'

Once Jamie was in her grip, Jennet pushed her way past Allan and then along the pier, shoving through the crowds and not halting until Mollie caught at her arm.

'Slow down, Jennet, before you get yourself killed, and Jamie with you!'

Jennet stared at her uncomprehendingly and then looked around. She had reached the road, and if Mollie had not stopped her she might have plunged across it in front of a horse-driven cart.

'Where is he?'

'Allan Blaikie? Back on the pier, probably. You didn't need to be so harsh with him,' Mollie said, puzzled. 'He was trying to help us. If he hadn't found Jamie and brought him back, we'd have been in a right pickle. You nearly scalped the poor man, pulling Jamie away from him like that, and you've frightened the wee soul, too.'

It was only then that Jennet realised that her son was shaking, his face wet with tears.

'It's all right, pet, Mummy just got a fright when you went away.' She took the handkerchief Mollie offered and mopped his face and then her own.

'I'll take him for a wee while. We'll go and get a nice drink of juice, eh, Jamie?' Mollie suggested as she gathered him into her arms. 'And then we'll have a look at all the pretty flowers. And when we get back home mebbe you'll draw some flowers for me, eh?'

Jennet followed them along to the ice-cream parlour, her heart still thumping. At the sight of Allan and Jamie – laughing together, enjoying each other's company – all the pleasure had suddenly gone out of her day.

Although the days were getting shorter there was still plenty to do before winter arrived. The largest field had to be ploughed to allow the winter frosts to kill off any weeds before the spring planting, while other fields had to be manured to encourage the clover and grass that would eventually become hay. The dry-stane dykes had to be repaired and the dairy herd checked over. The older animals, their milk yield now low, had to be replaced by heifers, which then had to be put to the bull, for they would not give milk until they had calved.

Now that Helen McCabe was there to look after the house and Jamie, Mollie was free to help Jennet with some of the outdoor work. Together they cleaned out the cowshed, heaving bales of straw across the yard to be broken up and spread about the floor just before the animals came in.

'And they'll no sooner be in there, nice and dry and clean, than we'll have to clean it all out and pile it here,' Mollie mourned as she and Jennet turned to the next task, using big wooden forks to heft manure into the cart. 'All these years in Glasgow I never knew what went into growin' stuff tae eat. I think I liked it better that way . . . not knowin'.'

'Nothing's wasted on a farm,' Angus said from the bed of the cart, where he was levelling the manure.

'Ye're right there. I'm just glad you've got a proper lavatory instead of makin' us all use the dung-heap!'

'In the old days that's just what you would have had to do,' Jennet said. 'As Angus says, nothing gets wasted on a farm.'

'Only the folk.' Mollie paused to catch her breath and ease her shoulder muscles, looking down in dismay at her clothes, spattered with mud and dung. 'I'd do anythin' for a nice hot bath and half a bottle of Evening in Paris!'

Jennet knew just what she meant. It was at times like this that she wondered why she had been so determined to stay on the farm. But then again, she thought as she forked another load of manure and heaved it up onto the cart, then bent to lift another forkload, farm life had its compensations: bringing in the cows on misty early mornings when the sky admired its pearl-grey reflection in the placid surface of the Sound of Bute; the dew on the spiders' webs that made the hedges glitter gold and silver; and the birds stirring in their nests and just beginning to break into sleepy song. The memories kept the routine – stoop, dig in, stand, lift, empty the fork, stoop, on and on and on – bearable. And finally the cart was full.

'Last load for the day.' Angus picked up the reins.

'Thank God for that. Tell you what, Jennet, I'll race you when we get back to the field. The one that shovels the most sh . . . manure can get off doing the dishes after supper.'

'She always manages to stay cheerful,' Jennet marvelled to Angus that evening when Mollie had gone upstairs to luxuriate in the bath she had been craving all day.

'Too much, if you ask me.'

'She works hard, too.' For once she was taking time to leaf through the newspaper and now she tapped at the page as an item caught her eye. 'The Farmers' Dinner's being held on the nineteenth in St Blane's Hotel at Kilchattan Bay.'

'What about it?'

'You'll have to go.'

'Don't be daft.'

'Angus, you're the farmer here now. You should go to it.'

'You're the farmer, too.'

'I'd go in a minute, but it's always just the menfolk, so it has to be you.'

At first he was adamant in his refusal, but after a few days of arguing, as well as a visit from Andra Blaikie to suggest that Angus should go to the event with him and Struan in his car, he finally agreed. Jennet was pleased, for Martinmas rent day was approaching, and to her mind, Angus needed to do all he could to establish himself with the other farmers as the new tenant at Westervoe.

She and Mollie aired and brushed his one and only good suit and Jennet went into Rothesay and bought him a new shirt for the occasion.

'You look very smart. I'm proud of you,' she said when he came into the kitchen that evening.

'I feel daft.'

'You don't look it. I wish Mollie could see you.' Mollie was staying overnight with her mother and brother.

'I'm glad she can't. She'd probably say something sarcastic.'

'She wouldn't!' Then, as she caught the sound of a car in the lane, Jennet called out, 'Here they are!'

When Angus had gone off with the Blaikies, both scrubbed and dressed in their best, she settled down to relish an entire evening on her own. She found some pleasant music on the radio and was halfway through the first chapter of a book borrowed from the library in Rothesay when Gumrie began to bark out in the yard.

He wouldn't bark for Bert McCabe, who would be in his cottage with Helen at that time of night. Jennet put the book aside and opened the door to find Allan Blaikie outside.

'Angus's out,' she said at once, and began to close the door. He stopped her with a hand on the panels.

'At the Farmers' Dinner. That's why I knew it was safe to come over. Can I come in?'

She hesitated and then said reluctantly, 'For a minute, just.'

'Thanks. Your hospitality overwhelms me.'

'You're lucky I didn't slam the door in your face.' She stalked back into the room and he followed, closing the door.

'Will you scream for help if I take my coat off?'

'Go on,' she said grudgingly, and then when he had taken it off and hung it neatly over a chair, 'I suppose you'd better sit down.'

He glanced at her book, lying on the floor beside Celia's big chair, then sat down opposite. The last time they met, at Rothesay pier, he had been in flannels and a shirt under a sleeveless Fair Isle pullover, but tonight he was in the suit he had worn when he visited Westervoe shortly after his return to the island.

'I wanted to say I'm sorry if I upset you when we met in Rothesay, though I have to admit that I don't know what I did to deserve the way you treated me.'

She drew a deep breath and sat down, her hands folded primly in her lap. 'I don't want you to be around Jamie. I don't want you calling him "son".'

'But he is my son.'

'No, he's mine. You had your chance a long time ago, before he was born, but you didn't want him then.'

He stared down at his hands, then said, 'Jennet, what I did then was . . . it was a terrible thing. But I didn't realise it.'

'What you did when?' she asked coldly. 'When he was conceived here on the island, or when I told you in Glasgow that I was carrying him?'

'Both times. The first time, down by the water, I was so scared that I was near out of my mind. I'd just seen the state Angus was in, and between that and not seein' myself coming out of the war alive . . . And you,' memory suddenly softened his voice, 'so understandin' and carin'. You were the only person I knew who'd understand. And I . . . I lost my head.'

'And afterwards? If you had done the right thing by me when I told you about Ja . . . about the baby,' she said, her anger beginning to rise. 'If you'd married me, or even put a ring on my finger and told your parents and my grandmother and Angus that the bairn was yours . . . if you'd just done that, my life would have been a hell of a lot easier than it's been since then.'

'I know.' His voice was little more than a whisper. 'I let you down and I'll never forgive myself for it.'

They had met in a teashop in Sauchiehall Street on his next leave. On his way back to his regiment Allan had called in at the nurses' hostel, where at that very moment Jennet had been trying to write a letter telling him that she was pregnant. It had been such a relief to be able to tell him in person. Together, she had thought in her naïvety, they could work something out.

But instead his face had turned chalk-white and he had said, 'God, that's all I need!'

'All you need? What about me?'

'I'm due to report back tomorrow morning, Jennet. I could be thrown into prison if I don't turn up; shot mebbe. If it's marriage you're after, there's not enough time!'

The words 'you're after' had struck a chill deep within her, but she had struggled on, desperate to find an answer to the situation in which she now found herself.

'We could get engaged. Then at least I could tell Gran and your parents that we'll be married as soon as you get your next leave . . .'

His pallor had turned to a sickly grey. 'Tell my mother? I can't, Jennet, not right now, not so soon after . . .'

'After what?'

It was only then that she had found out that Drew had been crushed to death beneath his father's tractor while ploughing Gleniffer's top field.

'But . . . my grandmother never told me,' she whispered in disbelief.

'She didn't want to say it in a letter. She asked me to break it to you. That's why . . .' he stopped suddenly.

'That's why you came here.' Only for that reason; not to see her. For a moment Jennet had thought she was going to be sick.

'She thought it best,' she had heard Allan say as the wave of nausea ebbed away, 'since you and Drew had been walking out together . . .'

'But it's not Drew's child I'm carrying,' she had flared across the table at him. 'It's yours!'

'And that's why I cannae tell my mother the truth right now, what with her being broken-hearted over losing Drew. They all think of you as his sweetheart,' Allan had said wretchedly. 'They'd think we betrayed him.'

'Mebbe you'd prefer it if I just let them all think that it's Drew's child. That way your mother would have her grandchild and you'd be spared the bother of marrying me.'

The words had been heavy with sarcasm, but for a split second as he looked up at her she had seen hope flaring in his eyes at the suggestion. Then it died and he said, 'Don't be daft, I'd not . . .'

Jennet had pushed her untouched tea away, so angry that for two pins she would have thrown it over him, uniform and all. 'Go back to your regiment, Allan Blaikie,' she had told him as she got to her feet, 'and don't worry about me. I'll manage, somehow.'

And she had walked out of the teashop, ignoring his attempt to call her back, oblivious to the curious eyes of the other customers, and had taken to her heels, running and running until she was too worn out to run any more.

His letter had arrived a week later. She let it lie for a whole day, trying to summon up enough determination to destroy it unread. Finally she opened it. He had apologised, then suggested that an abortion might be the best solution for them both.

'I know that it is possible at a price,' he had written, 'because being with lads all the time, I hear about such things. They say that it is safe, if you go to the right place. I am enclosing all the money I can put together – I hope it will be enough. Let me know if it costs more.'

He had ended with a promise that he would not return to Bute or try to contact her, if that was what she wanted.

'I was going to have an abortion,' she said now, in the cosy warmth of the Westervoe kitchen. 'But then I couldn't go through with it.'

'Thank God for that.' When she looked up, surprised, there was horror in his eyes. 'Imagine wee Jamie not bein' alive. I never thought of it that way when I wrote the letter.'

'I spent the money.'

'What?'

'The money you sent. I could have returned it, but instead I took all the other nurses out to a nice hotel for their dinner the night before I came back here.'

The shadow of a smile brushed his mouth. 'I hope they enjoyed it.'

'They loved it. We never got enough to eat at the hostel or the hospital.'

'Jennet, let me make up for what I did.'

'It's too late for that. D'you know what folk call a woman who has a child with no man willing to give it his name?' The anger began to come back. 'D'you want to hear what my grandmother said about me when I came back here?'

He winced. 'I can imagine.'

'She thought – they all thought, your mother as well – that the father was some serviceman I'd met on a dark street one night. Mebbe not even British, my grandmother said. Mebbe I wouldn't tell her his name because I never knew it myself.'

'You can now. Marry me, Jennet.' He reached over and put his hand on hers. 'Let me give you and Jamie my name and look after you both.'

Although the kitchen was warm enough, his hand was cold. She withdrew her fingers from beneath it and then brushed it from her lap as though it was an unwanted piece of fluff.

'I needed to hear you say that three years ago. I don't need it now.'

'I wish to God I had said it three years ago! When you were tellin' me then . . . it was just words then, it wasnae real.'

'It was real enough to me, but then it's easier for men,' Jennet said bitterly. 'They can just walk away and get on with their lives. Women can't. But I survived, and Jamie was born. And now, just when we're managing fine, you turn up. Why couldn't you have let the two of us be?'

'I meant to, even when my uncle decided to send me back here. I thought we could live our separate lives and not get in each other's way, but then . . .' his voice faltered slightly, 'then I saw Jamie and he wasn't a word any more, Jennet, he was flesh and blood.'

'He's been flesh and blood since he was conceived.'

'Marry me, Jennet . . . please.'

At one time – on several occasions, if she was honest – Jennet's heart would have sung to hear those words from Allan Blaikie; now they just angered her further.

'Why should I do that?'

'To give Jamie a father, for one thing.'

'That's exactly what your brother said.'

'Struan?' Allan asked, astonished. 'Our Struan asked you to marry him?'

'Not long after he was demobbed. I told him the same as I'm telling you . . . I've no wish to marry anyone.'

'But I'm not Struan! Jamie's my own son and I . . .'

She was on her feet and raining open-handed blows down on his head and shoulders before she knew what was happening. 'Don't you ever call him that, d'you hear me?' she panted as she flailed at him. 'He's mine, and that's the way it's going to stay!'

He got up, but stood still, taking the blows. Then, as they showed no sign of abating, he tried to catch her wrists.

'Jennet . . .' he began, then yelped as one flailing hand caught the side of his face and the nail dragged a long scratch from his ear to the corner of his mouth. Jennet stopped, horrified by her own violence, and stepped away from him.

'You deserved that,' she said breathlessly.

He had taken a handkerchief from his pocket and now he dabbed at his cheek. When he took the handkerchief away she could see blood on it. 'That, and more,' he said.

'Go away, Allan.'

'You said, that night . . . you said you loved me.'

'That's more than you said to me,' she reminded him cruelly, and he winced.

'Do you still love me, Jennet?'

'You ask me that after all that's happened?'

'I want to know if it's still true.'

'No, it's not.'

'Are you certain of that?' he asked, and then when she said nothing, 'I've grown up a lot in the years since we last met. I want us to . . .'

Jennet walked to the door and opened it. 'We've nothing more to say to each other, Allan,' she said. And after a moment's hesitation he nodded and went past her and out into the night.

November arrived, bringing with it the farmers' rent day, and to Jennet's relief Angus went to the factor's office and officially put his name in as the new tenant of Westervoe.

'Yours, too,' he said when he got back to the farm. 'It was your idea and you should have a share of the place . . . warts and all.'

She had been fretting as the day approached, worrying in case he changed his mind at the last moment. Now that he had made the decision to move forward independently of their grandmother, that was all that mattered to her. It was not until the following morning, as the two of them, still half asleep, trudged down the lane to bring in the cows in a cold, wet dawn, that the reality of it struck her.

To one side a ploughed and manured field glistened beneath the rainwater; to the other the cows' hooves churned up mud around the gate as they gathered for milking. Raindrops dripped from the hedges, now stripped of their leaves, and the Sound of Bute was lost beneath a dreary grey mist that reached up from the water's surface to bond itself with the clouds above. Gumrie slunk alongside, wet and too miserable to run ahead as usual, and at each step that she and Angus took their feet sank into watery runnels in the lane's ruts and had to be hauled out in order to make the next step. It was as though the entire world was made of cold drops of water, falling from the sky and dripping from their noses and oozing slowly down their necks.

'It's ours,' she said, and Angus, reaching out to open the gate, gave her a sideways glance, blinking rain out of his eyes.

'What is?'

'All this.' She gestured to the cows and the mud and the river beyond the dim outline of the dry-stane dyke. 'Westervoe. It's our responsibility, our home. Ours.'

'Aye,' Angus said gloomily. 'Aye, we've gone and done it now.'

21

All other farm work, apart from milking and seeing to the livestock, came to a standstill when the threshing mill that travelled round the farms without a machine of their own reached Westervoe in mid-November. Threshing was a job that involved everyone on the farm, and in her younger days it had seemed to Jennet that the machine, with its belts and cogs and wheels, took over the farm like a dirty, noisy god feverishly worshipped and tended by the farmers and farmhands feeding bales of oats into its hungry mouth and gathering up the grain, chaff and stalks that it spat out at them.

In the week or so since the night of the Farmers' Dinner Allan Blaikie had not made any effort to contact Jennet. On the day he was due to collect the pigs she arranged to take Jamie to visit the Logans, being careful to stay away until the evening. She was just beginning to think that she was free of him when, to her consternation, he and Struan arrived from Gleniffer to help with the Scotts' threshing.

'I thought your father was coming,' she said to Struan when Allan was out of earshot.

'Ach, he'd other things to do, and Allan was keen. He misses the farming a bit.'

'Then he should have stayed in farming,' Jennet said sharply, and told Helen McCabe to keep the little boy by her side all day.

'I'll certainly do that,' the girl said earnestly. 'Threshing mills are no place for wee bairns.'

There was nothing more that Jennet could do, other than stay well away from Allan as they gathered round the mill to hear Angus's instructions. Mollie was set to clearing the chaff and cavings – short bits of straw – from under the machine as it worked.

'We could do that between us,' Jennet suggested.

'I need you on the rick, with Bert. Struan can cut the bales loose and Allan can feed the corn into the thresher. Norrie and me'll pass the bales up.'

'But clearing chaff and cavings at the same time is hard work for one person.'

'If it's too much for Mollie, she can help Helen with the wee fellow instead and Norrie can take over her job.'

'I'll manage fine,' Mollie said at once.

'Mind and wrap up well, for the chaff gets everywhere,' Jennet advised her before clambering up the ladder to where Norrie stood on the rick.

'Manage?' he asked cheerfully, reaching down to give her a hand.

'I know what I'm about.' She took hold of a bale, making sure that she was not standing on any part of it. Snapping at folk seemed to be the order of the day, she thought as she braced herself to lift the bale free. When she let go it landed in front of Angus, who had come up with the idea of propping his shorter right leg on a wooden box so that he could stand upright without having to use his crutch. He dug the prongs of his pitchfork into the bale and tossed it up to the thresher, where Jem deftly caught it and then swung it on up to Struan. He slashed the bonds and Allan then fed the loose corn into the drum where it was stripped of its grain.

Threshing was largely a matter of teamwork, made easier if they all cooperated with each other and with the chugging rhythm of the mill. They soon fell into the right pattern, and from then on the work was continuous, without time to talk or even rest for a moment. Once, when Jennet snatched a second to swipe an arm across her perspiring face, she caught Allan's eye. He looked away at once, but the momentary diversion must have thrown him off his rhythm for the machine's steady thrumming suddenly changed to a deeper, harsher note, indicating that too much corn had been fed into it.

'Mind what you're about, man!' Angus roared up at him as the mill tried to cope with the added load.

'Sorry,' Allan shouted back. It was clear who was in charge at Westervoe, Jennet thought with a rush of pleasure. She craned her neck precariously to see how

Mollie was getting on, but the other girl was hidden from sight by the machine's bulk.

Threshing was the nearest Mollie McCabe had ever been to hell. Chaff and bits of broken straw spewed out beneath the machine at a frightening rate and she had to work hard to pull them free before they gathered and clogged up the machinery. Above her head grain was pouring into a stretched tarpaulin, while the stripped straw was thrown out from another part of the mill to be used as animal bedding. But all Mollie could see was the area where she worked, raking and shovelling, throwing filled bags over her shoulder and hurrying them into one of the sheds before rushing back to start all over again. The chaff found its way everywhere – down her neck and inside her blouse, up her nose and down her throat and into her eyes. Fortunately she had had the sense to tie a headscarf turbanwise round her head and push all her hair beneath it, but even so she felt her scalp itching; whether because of chaff, or just in sympathy with the rest of her, she had no way of knowing. Her back, arm and leg muscles ached and, despite the cold wind, sweat poured from her.

On the way to the shed with yet another full bag of chaff she stumbled slightly and Angus, the muscles on his forearms standing out as he forked bales of corn up to the rick, shouted, 'Are you all right?'

'Yes.'

'D'you want Norrie to take a turn there? You've

done well,' he added as she stared at him from below lashes encrusted with chaff.

'I'll go on as I am,' she yelled back and stamped on into the shed, where she threw the bag down. He had deliberately given her the worst job of all in the hope of humiliating her in front of everyone and she was determined to stay at it for as long as she must. Her eyes watered with tears of tiredness and frustration, and then watered even more when, rubbing the tears away, she only succeeded in getting a piece of chaff in one of them.

'Damn it!' She blundered back into the yard, blinking, and got on with the job, leaving the fresh tears to pour down her hot face in the hope that they would also clear and soothe her eye.

It was still stinging when they stopped for the midday meal, trooping into the kitchen where Helen waited for them, each one trailing chaff and straw over the flagged floor.

'Here . . .' Allan stopped her, taking her face in his two hands. 'That eye's sore-looking; did you get chaff in it?'

'Aye, and in every other part of me that it could find! Bits I didnae even know I had myself,' she said, and he grinned.

'As to the rest of you, you'll have to see to that yourself, unless you're determined to make me do it,' he said, 'but I can help with the eye. Give me a bit of clean cloth, lassie,' he ordered Helen. Then to Mollie, 'Come back outside for a minute.'

In the yard he held her head steady with one hand and made her roll her eye up as far as she could. 'Now hold still,' he commanded, and she felt his breath light and warm on her cheek as he put his face close to hers, concentrating on probing her eyeball with the corner of the clean cloth.

'I can see it . . . No wonder your eye was sore, it must feel like a boulder.'

'Like Ben Nevis,' Mollie agreed.

'And rubbing it in didnae help, you should never do that. Be still for a minute . . . There!' he said triumphantly and stepped back. 'How does that feel?'

'Better. Much better,' she said gratefully, while fresh tears poured into her eye. He caught her wrist as she raised her hand to wipe them away.

'Don't start it up all over again! Let the tears clean it, then get the lassie to tip some castor oil into it from a spoon,' he ordered. 'That'll help it to heal. And now that's done, I'm ready for my dinner!'

'I thought,' Jennet said when the two of them re-entered the kitchen, 'that you'd given up farming for the butcher business, Allan Blaikie.'

'I have, but it's good to keep my hand in now and again.' He pulled up a chair by Angus's side and started on his dinner as though he had not eaten all week. 'By God, there's nothing like working out of doors to give you an appetite!'

'He's nice, that Allan Blaikie,' Mollie said that night. The long day's threshing was over, Jamie and Angus were in bed, and she and Jennet, having indulged themselves with deep, hot baths ('What your grandmother and the authorities don't know is perfectly legal,' Mollie had said firmly) and having washed the chaff and cavings from their hair, were lounging before the kitchen range in their pyjamas with mugs of cocoa.

'He's a charmer, like his father.'

'I've never thought of Mr Blaikie as charming,' Mollie said, surprised. 'Let's have some more cocoa. My mouth feels as if a wee furry animal's moved into it.'

'I'm fine as I am. It's the chaff; you'll be sneezing it and spitting it for the next two days.'

'I suppose Mr Blaikie's quite good-looking in an old man sort of way. But not charming.'

'I don't mean like Charles Boyer, I mean like . . .' Jennet searched for the right words. 'Just full of life, making folk think that they have some happiness secret that nobody else has. Grandmother always had a soft spot for Andra Blaikie.'

'Your gran never had a soft spot for anybody,' Mollie scoffed, returning to her chair with her refilled mug. 'So . . . did you have one for Allan Blaikie?'

'No.'

'A good-looking man like that living not half a mile away, and you were never sweethearts?'

'Allan preferred the more mature girls. Why are you so interested? D'you fancy him yourself?'

'He's not my type.' They had put the lamp out and

the room was lit by the glow from the range. Molly was lounging on the big wingback chair that had been Celia Scott's, one arm above her head, her legs stretched out before her and her bare feet on the cloth rug. 'This is the life,' she said contentedly. 'Where could I find a rich man, d'ye think? I fancy bein' able tae do this whenever I feel like it.'

'If I find a rich man I'll keep him to myself.'

'Some friend you are,' Mollie said, and they grinned at each other.

'I'm for my bed,' Jennet decided five minutes later, draining her mug and getting up to rinse it under the tap.

'I'll be up in a minute.' Mollie cradled her mug in both hands, reluctant to move. 'And don't you dare waken me in the morning, I'm going to sleep for weeks. I bet poor old Rip Van Winkle had been threshing before he dozed off for all those years.'

After Jennet had gone upstairs Mollie nodded by the fire, rousing herself when a coal rattled in the grate and telling herself that she must get to bed at once; then drowsing again to waken with a start, splashing cold cocoa over her wrist, when Angus said from the inner doorway, 'Jennet? Are you still up?'

'It's me.' She drew the lapels of her very respectable pyjamas together and pulled herself upright in the chair, muffling a yawn. 'Jennet's gone to bed.'

'What are you doing up at this time of night?'

'I was too tired to be bothered going to my bed,

so I was looking at the pictures in the flames. D'you want something?'

'A drink of water, just. That chaff's all down my throat.'

'Mine, too. Would you like some cocoa?' She began to get up, but he waved her back into the chair.

'Water's fine. I'll get it. D'you want anything else yourself?'

'No.' She gulped at the cold cocoa, making a face when the skin that had formed on the top clung to her upper lip. She wiped it away with the back of her hand. 'I should be getting to my bed.'

'You did well today,' Angus said from the sink. 'It's a miserable job, clearing the chaff from beneath the mill.'

'So I discovered.'

He brought his cup of water over and sat down opposite her. He too was in his pyjamas and bare-footed. 'I should have set someone else to help you.'

'Why didn't you?' she challenged, and then when he said nothing, 'Did ye want tae show me up as a city girl in front of all those farming folk?'

He started to deny it, then said, 'To tell the truth, I don't know. If I did, I was proved wrong.' Then, unexpectedly, 'What sort of pictures? In the fire, I mean,' he added as she hesitated, unsure of his meaning.

'Oh, them. Castles and dragons and fairies . . . the usual things.'

'Usual?'

'Did you never see pictures in the fire when you were wee?'

He gave her a grim smile. 'In this house, anyone caught staring into the fire was malingering and given something more useful to do.'

'Try it now,' she suggested. 'That's a castle over there, a tall thin one on a bit of a mountain. And that wee tongue of blue flame's a dragon in front of its cave. See? If we look hard enough we might see a maiden in distress and a handsome knight riding to rescue her.'

Angus leaned forward, then admitted after a minute or so, 'I can't see a thing.'

'Look harder, and closer.'

He leaned further down, so that their heads were almost touching as they both gazed into the red coals behind the range's black iron bars.

'Don't *try* tae see anythin', just keep your eyes on the fire and let the pictures come tae you.'

They sat silently, Angus staring into the fire while Mollie, her face turned towards the range, moved slightly in her chair so that she could flick occasional glances at him. She rarely got the chance to look at him properly. His face had rounded out slightly in the past few months, and the extra fullness suited him. The summer sun and long hours spent out in the fields had given him a tan, and the small flames danced in his grey eyes while the fire's ruddy glow outlined his features like an artist's pencil, highlighting and shading to show the strong slope of his nose, the permanent pain-lines etched on his forehead, the sweep of his cheekbones and his flat, strong cheeks. His hair, tousled from contact with his pillow, drew soft shadows about the harder lines of his face, and Mollie's fingers itched to smooth it back.

Instead she asked, 'What do you see?'

'Guns firing and buildings on fire.' His voice was sombre. He straightened, leaning back in the chair, his eyes closed.

'No dragons or knights? You're going tae have tae learn tae read the flames properly, Angus Scott!'

'Mebbe I'm too old for it.'

'You're not old at all. You've got all your life in front of you.'

'You think so?'

'I know so,' she said almost fiercely. Then, when he opened his eyes and looked at her, she added, flustered, 'Besides, it's never too late tae learn. I'll teach you.'

'I can just see Jennet doing all the farm work outside while you and me sit in here staring into the fire,' he mocked and raised the cup of water to his lips. His good foot, long and narrow, the toes straight and well tapered, stretched out on the rug, coming very close to her own. Mollie hastily withdrew both her feet, tucking one beneath her in the big chair and moving the other back so that it rested on the balls of her toes beneath the chair.

'The winter's comin' . . . long dark nights and plenty of fire. We can practise then. And once you learn, you can help wee Jamie to learn to see the pictures.'

He gave her a lazy smile. 'You make it sound sensible!'

'We all need some magic in our lives, no matter what age we are.'

His damaged leg was shorter than his good leg, but not much shorter, she noticed now. The lower part, protruding from his pyjama leg, was thin and the foot, twisted slightly, drooped like a flower in need of sustenance. She wondered if exercises might help to strengthen the wasted muscles.

'You'd not say that if you'd been raised by my grandmother.'

'Mebbe that's what's wrong with her,' Mollie said. 'Mebbe she needed some magic.'

'She needed something, that's for certain.' He lifted the cup again, draining it and then lowering it to say, 'On the other hand, mebbe she was right to be so practical.'

'There's nothing wrong with being practical,' Mollie said lightly, settling back in the chair. 'I keep meanin' tae try it myself some day. But it surely needs tae be tempered with a bit of fun.'

'Or a bit of magic?' The gleam in his eyes did not owe everything to the firelight. For once he was completely relaxed as he leaned back, his hands spread over the arms of his chair.

'Either . . . both.' Tired though she was, Mollie felt that she would be happy to stay there for ever, alone with Angus in the firelit room. 'But at least one of them.'

'I don't know, Mollie.' He was staring into the fire again, but she knew, by the set of his jawline and the deepening of the lines across his forehead, that his gaze had turned inward, to his mind. 'To tell the truth, I'm wondering already if I did the right thing, taking over this place.'

'Of course you did the right thing!'

'A farm takes an awful lot of work.'

'Are you doubting your own ability?'

'I'm doubting my own strength.' His wounded leg twitched slightly. 'I can't put too much on Jennet's shoulders.'

'They're strong, and so are yours. And you've got our Bert working for you now. You're talkin' as if your grandmother's the only person who can run this place.'

'She's more able than me.' He slapped at his damaged knee, a gesture that she had often seen before.

'For pity's sake,' Mollie said passionately, 'if she could do it at her age, surely you can do it at yours. Anyway, the rent's paid and the matter's decided. And Jennet's pleased, so you might as well just leave it at that.'

'And stop whining at you? I didn't mean to do that.'

'You're not whining, it's just . . . you've been raised to believe that you can't do anything without your gran's support, but you're a man now, Angus

Scott,' Mollie said. 'Is it not time you proved her wrong?'

As soon as the words were out of her mouth she wished them back. The last thing she wanted on this magic night was to anger him. But to her surprise his tension suddenly ebbed away and he grinned.

'You're right. I'll go ahead . . . but you'll have to answer to me if things go wrong.'

'They won't, I promise you.' Mollie yawned, as much from relief as from exhaustion, and reached for his cup. 'Give me that and I'll wash it along with my own.'

'No, I'll wash them while you get to your bed.' He hoisted himself to his feet. 'You deserve your rest.'

Thinking that the kitchen was empty, he had left his crutch in his room and now, carrying the two cups with a finger through their handles, he used his free hand for support as he moved around the table towards the sink. He moved fairly easily, but without the crutch the inch or two of difference in the length of his legs gave him a lurching gait.

'You know,' Mollie said thoughtfully, recalling the way he had worked that day with his bad foot propped on a wooden block, 'you might be able to have a special boot made, with a built-up sole and heel to it.'

She knew immediately, by the sudden chill in the air, that she had said too much. Angus paused before taking the final step towards the sink, where he dumped the two cups noisily on the draining board before turning, supporting himself against the edge of the sink with both hands.

'When are you going to learn to mind your own business?' He was too far away from the fire for her to see his face, but she could tell from the cold, hard voice and the rigid set of his shoulders against the dark grey of the window that it would be twisted with fury.

'I . . .' She moistened her lips. 'I just thought, after seeing how well you did at the threshing . . . I thought it might help.'

'Is it not enough that you pestered me like a wasp round a rotten apple until I got onto the one crutch? D'you know what an effort that was? And here you go again! Are you going to be buzzing round my ears for the rest of my life, wanting me to do this and do that?'

'Angus . . .'

'Why don't you look to your own life, Mollie McCabe, instead of trying to change mine? You're a grown woman, you shouldn't be hanging around this place as though you've as much right to be here as me and my sister.'

'D'ye want me to go?'

'There's little sense in you staying, is there? The fact is,' Angus said cruelly, 'it suited me very well when you took yourself off to Rothesay. It was Jennet who was so determined to get you back when our grandmother got hurt, not me.'

Mollie got to her feet. 'I'll go tomorrow,' she said through stiff lips, and walked out of the kitchen, her sudden fragile happiness just as suddenly smashed to pieces.

22

Jennet was dismayed by her friend's decision to return to Rothesay. 'But why now, when the holiday season's over and you're not needed at Aunt Ann's?'

Mollie flinched inwardly at 'not needed'. She was beginning to think that she wasn't needed anywhere. Aloud she said, 'The same could be said for this place. The work's slowing down now that winter's coming; the deep-litter house is doin' fine and the cowshed's ready for the beasts comin' in. And Helen's a trained farm servant, Jennet, she's of more use tae you than I am and she's desperate tae work in return for livin' in the cottage.'

'What are you going to do?'

'Your auntie and uncle are lettin' us stay on in their house, and Sam'll be working with Mr Logan, repairin' the boats, paintin' them and learnin' about how to build them, too. He's fair looking forward tae that. And Mam and your auntie need me tae help them tae get the house all done up for next summer. And

I want tae get a job too . . . in a shop, mebbe.' She babbled on. 'I'm missin' the dancing, too; I'm not from a farming family like you, remember.'

'Mebbe not, but you're as much family as anyone can be. Tell her, Angus,' Jennet appealed to her brother, who sat at the breakfast table, almost hidden by his newspaper. 'Tell her we want her to stay!'

'If the lassie feels the need to go,' he said from behind the paper, 'then you should leave it at that and not go on at her.'

'That's right.' Mollie busied herself with clearing the table, avoiding Angus's side of it. 'I'll only be in Rothesay, so you can come in on the bus and see me, and I can come . . .' She broke off, then said, 'Look at the time already. I'll see tae the hen mash today, and you do the dishes, Jennet. Come on, Jamie Scott, you can help me.'

'She never said a word about this last night when we stayed up together,' Jennet said when her friend had gone into the yard. 'D'you think something's upset her?'

'I think,' Angus said, folding his paper with swift, sharp movements, 'that she's a grown woman and well able to decide for herself where she wants to be and what she wants to do with her life. And I think you're making too much of a song and dance about it.'

He slapped his hands flat on the table, levered himself from his chair and snatched up his crutch. Outside, he could hear Jamie chattering in the little shed where the hen food was stored. Angus went on through the yard and out to the tractor shed. He would finish the ploughing while the weather was right for it; it was a job that would keep him busy all day, and the mood he was in, that suited him fine.

The morning was cold and it took a while to get the tractor engine going. Once it was chugging away Angus climbed into his seat, using the series of blocks that Jem had set up, under his direction, to assist him. The sight of them reminded Angus of Mollie's suggestion the previous night, and a sharp stab of anger went through him at the memory. He would be glad to see the back of her. It was high time she went back to her own family.

But she was in his mind all day, and even though she was gone by the time he returned to the house that night, he kept thinking that each time he glanced up he would see her sitting across the table, or helping wee Jamie with something, or turning from the sink or the range. And each time she wasn't there he felt empty inside.

When Jennet had gone to her bed that night he sat on in the kitchen opposite the big wing chair in which Mollie had been sitting less than twenty-four hours earlier. Narrowing his eyes, he could still see her there, leaning back, her legs stretched out and her bare feet on the cloth rug, her hair shimmering like polished bronze in the firelight. He could even smell her freshly washed hair, the way he had last night when, heads together, they had stared into the flames.

His eyelids began to ache, and when he relaxed them and opened his eyes fully she was gone. He wrenched his gaze from the chair and stared into the fire, but he could see no castles or dragons or knights in shining armour riding to rescue maidens.

There was no magic there at all – only the dying embers.

The floor of the big cowshed was liberally covered with clean straw and the feeding troughs filled before the cows left their field for the last time that year and came to winter indoors. The remaining arks were moved to a slight rise in their field, to lessen the danger of flooding in bad weather, and the farm's busy daily routine slowed as the days shortened.

With animals to tend every day there was still work to do, but less than in the other seasons, and now that Bert McCabe was working for Westervoe, Jennet had more time to devote to Jamie. From the first she had given him as much of her attention as possible, tying a shawl about her body to act as a sling in which she could carry him while she attended to her farm duties, then buying a second-hand pushchair as he got too heavy to carry.

Her grandmother had told her that she was spoiling the child, and it was character-strengthening to leave him to his own devices, but Jennet had insisted on doing things her own way, talking non-stop to her baby as she worked, even when he was asleep with his face almost hidden in the folds of the shawl; and taking time each evening, no matter how tired she was, to read stories to him. As a result, Jamie was chattering like a lintie by the time he reached his second birthday, and he had developed an interest in everything and everybody.

All too soon, she thought, watching him as he stood on a chair, helping her to bake scones, he would be going to school, and when that happened she would lose him to his teachers and his new friends. That was the way it should be, but until then he was hers, and she meant to make the most of every minute.

She had another reason for keeping him close; although he had not made another attempt to be alone with her, Allan Blaikie came about the farm occasionally and Jamie had taken a liking to him. Whenever they met, the little boy clamoured to hear the mouth organ, and for his part, Allan was clearly besotted with the child. It was impossible to keep them apart without telling Angus her secret, so Jennet had to settle for the occasional visit, making sure that she was always there at the time. To his credit, Allan had never attempted to see Jamie behind her back. On the few occasions when he had called at the farm and found Helen and Jamie alone at the house, Helen reported, he had gone away again.

'Ye'd make a good father,' Angus joked one day when Allan and Jamie were kneeling on the kitchen floor, making a toy farm out of cardboard boxes. 'I never thought I'd live to see Allan Blaikie playing with a wean.'

'Nor did I, but I suppose it comes to us all. See, Jamie, this one would do fine for your cows, would it not?' Allan picked up one of the boxes and handed it to the little boy, who considered it carefully, then said, 'No, for my friends that went away.'

'Your friends?' Allan looked at him blankly, then at Jennet, who mouthed, 'The pigs.'

'They runned away,' Jamie said. 'All lost.'

'Mebbe they're having a wee holiday,' Allan improvised.

'No, got lost,' Jamie said sadly; then, picking up one of his toy pigs, 'This one won't, 'cos I'll smack it if it does.'

'I was wonderin'. . .' Allan said casually to Angus over the child's bent head, 'have you never thought of raising beef here at Westervoe?'

'Why would we want to do that?'

'There's money in it, for one thing. Now that the war's by, the Government'll be easin' up on the need for crops, and this farm could do well with beef cattle.'

'The local butcher would do quite nicely out of the idea, too,' Jennet put in from the table, where she was kneading bread. His blue eyes met her grey stare unblinkingly.

'It's your interests I'm considering more than my own, though I'd not deny that it would be of benefit to me, as well as to Angus . . . and you.'

'We've always had the dairy herd, and we've always grown the crops to feed and bed them. That's the way Westervoe works.'

'I don't know, Jennet,' Angus put in thoughtfully. 'Allan might have a point.'

'The point is that we've just taken over this place. We have to run it as it is for a year at least before we start trying to change things.'

'What about the deep-litter house?' her brother asked mildly, but with an amused glint in his eye.

'That's different.'

'That's what women aye say,' Angus challenged, and she slammed the soft bread dough down on the table.

'It *is* different! Those old arks wouldn't have seen us through another winter and we didn't have the money to buy new ones. The stable wasn't being used and it made sense to get some of the hens into it.' She almost threw the dough into the loaf tin, saying over her shoulder as she put the tin into the oven, 'We stay as we are, for at least a year; that was our arrangement, Angus. I stay for a year till we get settled, and after that I go back to my training and you can do what you want with the place.'

Allan, who had been sprawled on the floor helping Jamie to move the herd of small wooden cows that had once belonged to Angus and Martin, sat upright on the floor. 'You're planning on going back to Glasgow?' he asked Jennet.

'Mebbe. If I want to.' She turned on the tap and began to wash her hands.

'It's the only way I'd agree to take this place on,' Angus explained. 'Jennet's got her own life to lead and I don't want to see her stuck on the farm the way our grandmother was.'

'And I've told you that perhaps that's what I want for myself and for Jamie. He likes farming.' Jennet nodded at her son, totally absorbed in laying out his little cardboard-box farm.

'You could come back here after you've finished your training, if you're so set on it. At least you'd have a trade to go to, if things didn't work out here.'

'They will.'

'You're as stubborn as the old woman,' Angus grumbled.

'Are you trying to get rid of me? Is that it?'

'I'm trying to look out for you. Tell her to finish her nursing, Allan, mebbe she'll listen to you.'

'I doubt if she'll mind a word I say,' Allan said. Then, getting up, 'I'd best be getting back to Gleniffer. My mother doesnae like it if any of us are late at the table.'

Jennet took advantage of the quieter working days to take Jamie to Rothesay as often as possible. She felt that it was good for the little boy to be with other folk, and it meant that she could spend time with Mollie, who seemed reluctant to visit Westervoe.

'I'd just be in the way there,' she said when Jennet wanted to know why.

'How could you ever be in the way? You're one of the family now, surely you know that?'

'I'm not certain that Angus would agree with you.'

'You know he has his moods. They don't mean anything.' Jennet had found Mollie painting one of the guest bedrooms, while her mother whirred away at the sewing machine in the kitchen, repairing some bedding, and Ann turned out another guest room. They could hear her now, shifting furniture about. Alice had taken Jamie off to the workshop where her father and Sam were getting the boats ready for the next holiday season. Joe, a summer employee, had found other work in town for the winter.

'Angus works hard and he deserves peace and quiet when he's in the house.'

'He can get it in his own room if he wants it. I think he's missing you,' Jennet said, and Mollie, applying cream paint to the frame of the door, paused and glanced over her shoulder.

'Has he said anything?'

'No, but I know Angus. He's awful quiet.'

'He always is.' Mollie returned to her work.

'Quieter than usual, I mean. Is there another brush?' Jennet wanted to know. 'I'm not used to doing nothing.'

'You can sandpaper that skirting if you like.' After a long pause in which she concentrated on smoothing the paint evenly while Jennet, on her knees, worked away at the skirting board, Mollie went on, 'I'm walking out with Joe again.'

'That's nice, I like Joe. You took your time forgiving the poor lad.'

'I'm not sure I have forgiven him. I don't really care one way or the other.'

'Why are you going out with him, then?'

'He kept asking, and he's a good dancer. And I don't like going to the pictures on my own,' said Mollie, who had found work in one of the Rothesay shops.

Jennet gave a startled exclamation as the little bit of sandpaper she was holding hit against a knot in the wood, catching her fingernail. She stuck it in her mouth and then said round it, 'That doesn't sound very romantic.'

'I've given up on romance,' Mollie said. 'And I suppose Joe's better than nothing.'

'Does he know that?'

'Of course not, you know how easily hurt men are.'

'You and Jamie go, and stay on if you like,' Angus said when Jennet announced after one of her trips to Rothesay that Ann Logan wanted to celebrate the first peacetime Christmas with a family party on Christmas Eve. 'I'll stay here and see to the place.'

'You're not going to miss Christmas, surely?'

'I'm not bothered; you know we never do much at Christmas anyway.'

'You mean Grandmother never did much.' Jennet rubbed tears from her eyes with the back of a gloved hand. She was helping him to repair one of the gates, which meant that they were right out in the open and in the path of a biting wind. 'We're on our own now and we have to make our own rules. And Jamie needs a proper family Christmas,' she argued.

Her brothers had never been as close to their aunt and uncle as she was, although they had helped out with the boats occasionally and they had been friendly with Geordie Logan and had enlisted alongside him when war broke out. As Jennet had said to Mollie, Angus seemed to be lonely these days, and she dearly wanted to draw him into the warmth of the Logan family circle.

'It'll be grand,' she pushed on. 'Bert and Helen will be there, and Alice and her young man, and Sam's girlfriend and . . .'

'And Aunt Ann and Uncle George and Mollie, and mebbe that fellow Joe that Mollie's sweet on.'

'I don't think she's sweet on him; she just goes out with him for company. If you ask me,' Jennet said thoughtfully, 'there's someone else on her mind.'

Angus's head, bent over his work, came up suddenly. 'Why? What did she say to you?'

'Nothing at all – that's what makes it so strange. Mebbe he's married already. I hope not,' Jennet fretted. 'It would be terrible for her.'

Angus went back to his work, driving a nail into the gate with hefty blows of his hammer. 'It sounds to me as if you're letting your imagination loose.'

'I wish she'd stayed on here, with us.'

'We'd no need of her here.'

'I had need of her.'

Angus gave the gate an experimental push. It swung

slowly into place and he latched it. 'That's that done. Come on, let's get out of this wind.'

'You'll come to Rothesay with me and Jamie on Christmas Eve?' Jennet nagged as they hurried back to the farmhouse.

'Mebbe. I'll see.'

'And we'll have a proper time of it here, too, for Bert and Helen as well, if they want to spend the day with us. I'm going to bring out the decorations we used to put up, and make a pudding and get some mincemeat for pies. Struan's offered to bring a wee tree over for Jamie.' Jennet put a gloved hand on her brother's arm. 'Imagine, Angus, this'll be his very first proper Christmas!'

If it hadn't been for his accident, Angus Scott might well have married the Saltcoats lassie he had been courting before the war. She had certainly been willing enough, and on his way to see her, immediately after enlisting in the Army, Angus had intended to ask her to be his wife. He liked the thought of knowing, while he was away fighting for King and country, that she was waiting for him at home, his ring on her finger.

But the train had never reached the station and on the girl's first, and last, visit to the hospital Angus had looked into her eyes and read his own future in them . . . a useless cripple, no good to any woman. Watching her walk swiftly from the ward and knowing, although she had not been able to bring herself to tell him to his face, that she would not be back, he had given up for ever on his dreams of one day having a wife and family of his own. Then Mollie McCabe had marched into the farmyard, clutching an untidy brown-paper parcel in her arms, limp red hair flopping about her pale face as she ordered his grandmother to call Gumrie off.

At first she and her family had simply been an unwelcome invasion, one of the necessary evils of war as far as Angus was concerned; then, as Mollie began to nag him into becoming mobile again, she had become a nuisance, a stone in his shoe or, he thought as he lay in bed that night, trying to read, the grain of sand that irritates the oyster.

Clearly imposed on the printed page before him he could still see her dazzling smile on the day he walked round the kitchen table using only one crutch. Then the picture changed, and kept on changing. Mollie lugging heavy pails of pig food out to the sty was swiftly followed by Mollie tossing Jamie up in the air, Mollie frowning with concentration, the tip of her tongue sticking out from the corner of her mouth, as she carefully fluted the edge of the pie she had just made.

He blinked hard and began to read his book, concentrating on the first line, the second and half of the third before she swam back onto the page, this time leaping from the kitchen chair in a swirl of long tea-tanned legs, cream petticoat and floral skirt on the day he had walked in to find Jennet drawing a mock seam up the back of her legs. Then came Mollie struggling out from beneath the threshing mill, exhausted and covered with chaff, but refusing to give in and give up. And Mollie later that night, her glowing freshly washed hair swinging round her face as she looked for pictures in the fire.

Angus laid down the book and rubbed at his face with both hands. The fanciful comparison between her and the oyster's grain of sand had been nearer the point than he first thought, for Mollie had, in time, become a pearl.

'Jennet's not the only reason I love this place,' she had said to him in Nero's stable as Jennet went to tell their grandmother that she wanted Angus to be allowed to run the farm. Startled, unable to believe that Mollie could possibly be trying to say that she cared for him in the way he cared for her, he had turned his back. And later, like a fool, he had sent her away from Westervoe.

He groaned aloud and threw his book across the room so vigorously that the back of his hand connected with the solid cupboard by his bed, sending a bolt of pain up his arm from the bruised knuckles.

He had shied away from the Logans' Christmas Eve invitation because he could not bear the thought of having to watch Mollie with her sweetheart; despite what Jennet had said earlier about her friend looking on Joe merely as good company, Angus was convinced that the young man was just the sort to suit someone as lively as Mollie McCabe. But now, rubbing his aching fist with the fingers of the other hand, he knew that he had to go, for not seeing her at all would be worse than seeing her with Joe.

His mind made up, Angus turned out the lamp and then wished he had kept it on, because all at once the darkness was filled with images of Mollie.

23

Sam McCabe opened the door to Jennet and Jamie on Christmas Eve, and immediately pulled them through the hall and into the Logans' front parlour.

'Look at this!' He scooped Jamie up into his arms. 'Look at the pretty things, Jamie!' he said, and the little boy's eyes rounded as he looked up at the ceiling, where homemade paper chains hung from corner to corner and looped across the top of each wall.

'They're in the kitchen too, and out in the hall. I helped tae make them,' Sam told Jennet proudly. 'Me and Alice, mostly. And look at this . . .' He led her to the bay window to show her the small tree, hung with silver balls. 'We've all been collectin' silver paper for ages. Isn't it bonny?'

'It is.' Jennet's eyes were on the tiny wooden Nativity scene . . . Mary and Joseph, the child in the manger, the shepherds and wise men and the animals. Her cousin Geordie had carved all the little figures several years ago, and they were brought out every year.

'Did you bring presents?' Sam asked anxiously, beaming when she assured him that she had. He helped her to take them out of her bag and lay them with the others beneath the tree, while Jamie looked on, stunned by the colour and the excitement; silcnt for once and sucking at one of his woollen mittens.

Mollie hurried into the room, then stopped short at the sight of them. 'Jennet! I didnae know you'd arrived.' She clapped a hand to her head, which was covered in rag curlers, her eyes searching the room, then said, 'Is Angus not with you?'

'He'll be along later with Bert and Helen, once the milking's done. What's this?' Jennet nodded at the curlers and her friend flushed crimson.

'I just fancied a change, that's all.'

'She's getting all prettied up for Joe,' Sam smirked, and Mollie glared at him.

'I'm nothing of the kind. And why didn't you tell us that Jennet and Jamie were here?'

'We were just comin' along tae the kitchen. I wanted tae show them the decorations and the tree first.' Sam took Jamie's hand. 'Come on up to my room with me, wee man, you can help me to make some more chains.'

'Don't get him all covered with glue,' his sister called after him, and then, to Jennet, 'He's not all that grown up, even if he does have a girlfriend. He's been as excited as a bairn all week. Right enough, we've never had a Christmas like this. It's goin' to be great!'

Nesta, Ann and Alice were in the kitchen, stirring

and mixing and rolling for all they were worth. The gas oven and all the gas rings were in use, and chilly though the day was, the door leading out to the long back garden with George Logan's workshop at the end of it lay open to let some air into the hot, stuffy room.

Jennet assured them that Helen was bringing the leg of pork and the baking that the two of them had prepared at Westervoe, then she took her coat off and set to work along with the others. By midday the preparations were almost complete, and after a quick snack to keep them going Mollie insisted on taking Jennet upstairs to help her with her hair.

'I should really take Jamie off Sam's hands,' Jennet said, 'for the poor lad's been looking after him for the past two hours.' Sam and Jamie had arrived downstairs in search of food, then gone into the parlour.

'Ach, he'll be enjoying himself now he's got someone of his own age to play with at last,' Sam's sister said callously; then, opening the parlour door, 'I hope you two aren't making a mess in here.'

'I'm teaching him tae play Snap,' Jennet heard Sam declare proudly. She looked over Mollie's shoulder to see both boys sitting cross-legged on the carpet, surrounded by playing cards.

'Aye, well, just remember that he's wee, so there's no gamblin' allowed,' his sister told him while Jamie yelled 'Snap!'

'That's no' fair, I wasnae lookin'!' Jennet heard Sam protest as Mollie closed the door.

Going upstairs she indicated the banisters, festooned with paper chains. 'Would you look at that? He's covered the whole place! Bless him, it's the first decent Christmas he's ever had and it'll take him months to get over it.'

Five minutes later, looking at her reflection in the small mirror, she wailed, 'Straight as a stair rod! I've been in agony all night with these curlers and I've not got a single curl tae show for it!'

'But your hair's lovely,' Jennet said truthfully. 'Look at the way it falls.'

'Aye, straight down from top tae bottom. I wish I'd been born with curly hair like yours. Even our Senga has a bit of a curl in her hair, but not me!'

Jennet tugged at a handful of her own hair, held back today by a blue ribbon that matched her skirt and the embroidery on her white blouse. 'I wish you'd this hair too,' she said ruefully. 'Yours is more . . . stylish.'

'Humph. It's not worth putting on my new dress now.'

'Of course it is. Let me see it,' Jennet commanded, then gasped when Mollie brought it out from behind the curtain that filled in as a wardrobe. 'Oh, Mollie, it's lovely!'

'D'ye like it?' Mollie held the dress out at arm's length. 'The material used up all my clothing coupons, and Mam helped me to make it. I just wanted tae have somethin' special for once.'

'Put it on,' Jennet ordered. Then as Mollie pulled

her jersey and skirt off and reached for the petticoat spread over the bed, 'You've lost weight.'

'Only a wee bit.' Mollie's rounded arms were definitely thinner, as was her waist; her face, Jennet suddenly realised, was thinner too, the cheekbones more prominent.

'Is there something wrong? Are you not eating properly?' Mollie had always had a good appetite.

'Like a horse, same as usual. And I'm fine.' Mollie slipped the petticoat on, then the dress. 'How do I look?'

'Wonderful,' Jennet said, and meant it. The dress, in a soft, woollen material that shaped itself to Mollie's body, was a pale oatmeal colour – a surprise in itself, since Mollie tended to like patterns. Trimmed with dark green velveteen at the hem, it had a V-shaped collar, cuffs on the short sleeves and wrapped around to button down one side to the hem, with large buttons a shade lighter than the trimming. A tie belt of green velveteen accentuated Mollie's trim waist and the straight skirt made her look tall and elegant.

Mollie twisted and turned, trying to see herself from all angles in the small mirror. 'D'you not think it would look better with curls?'

'Don't be daft, your hair looks just right with it.'

'If you're sure . . .' Mollie studied her reflection, chewed nervously at her lower lip and then, as though coming to a decision, began, 'Jennet . . .'

'What?'

'Is that the door knocker?' Mollie jumped to her feet. 'Mebbe it's Angus. Come on, let's go down.'

Joe, dressed in his best and with his hair oiled and smoothed back, caught up with Angus, Bert and Helen as they walked along to the Scotts' door. He and Bert greeted each other like old friends, and Angus's hope that the young man was bound for another house faded as Joe turned in at the gate with them.

Alice opened the door and as they all surged into the narrow hall, Joe, one step ahead of Angus, looked up and gave a long, admiring whistle. Following his glance, Angus stopped in the doorway at the sight of Mollie standing halfway up the stairs, the creamy shade of her dress complementing her red hair, which lay about her face like a cap of autumn leaves.

For a moment Angus's world stood still and then Joe, moving forward to lean on the banister, said, 'You look good enough tae eat!'

'I always thought that was a daft thing to say,' Mollie said tartly, continuing on her way down to the hall. 'Angus, are you goin' tae come in and close the door, before Sam's paper chains get blown down from the ceiling? The men are all out in the workshop at the back if ye want tae go through. We'll call you when the dinner's ready.'

Before the war, whenever they could slip away from the farm and from their grandmother's control, Angus and Martin had enjoyed helping their uncle and their cousin George with the boats; but so much had happened to change Angus's life since then that his teenage years had become more of a dream memory than reality. He had not visited his uncle's workshop for years, and he had forgotten how soothing the mingled smells of paint and varnish, sawdust and glue could be.

The boat George Logan was building with Sam's help took up most of the space in the centre of the shop. The men gathered around it while Jamie, who had found a pile of sawdust, pawed through it gleefully. After a few minutes Angus retreated to the bench alongside one wall, where he sat listening to his normally shy uncle talking animatedly about his boats.

Joe detached himself from the group and came to sit on the bench, offering his packet of Woodbine. Angus, who had not smoked for years because his grandmother disapproved of the waste of money, hesitated and then took one. The workshop was already filled with fragrant blue smoke from Bert's cigarette and George Logan's beloved pipe.

Joe struck a match and lit Angus's cigarette, then his own. 'Too strong for you?' he asked as Angus began to cough.

'It's fine, but I've not smoked for a while. There's never time for a cigarette on a farm.' Angus took a second drag, and this time the smoke went sweetly down into his lungs.

'Ye'll be glad Mollie's moved back here,' Joe said. Then, as Angus stared at him, puzzled, 'It means that now you don't have me callin' in and botherin' you.'

'Oh, it wasn't a bother,' Angus lied.

'She said it was. She was always gettin' on at me about it; she said you didnae like folk hangin' around the place. But I couldnae stay away. I missed her,' Joe confessed. He glanced at the others and then turned back to Angus, edging along the bench and lowering his voice. 'I made a bit of a fool of myself when her sister was over for Bert's wedding. Mollie was ragin' about it; she'd not talk tae me for weeks after. She mebbe told you about it?'

'We didn't talk all that much,' Angus said uncomfortably. 'She's my sister's friend.'

'I know.' Joe had been looking wretched during his confession, but now he summoned up a faint smile. 'She told me about the two of them bein' skin sisters. You'll know all about that,' he swept on while Angus struggled to make sense of the phrase, 'the two of them tryin' tae mix their blood when they were younger, and the knife bein' blunt and them not havin' the courage tae go through with it, so they just say they're skin sisters instead of blood sisters. Mollie thinks a lot of your Jennet, and she thinks a lot of you, too.'

'Does she?'

'Oh aye.' Joe moistened his lips with the tip of his tongue and glanced round again to make sure that he was not overheard. 'That's why I wondered if you knew what she thought about me, because I want tae ask her tae marry me and I'd not like tae set her off again by askin' at the wrong time. You've known her a lot longer than I have, so I wondered, what d'you think?' He finally ended the rush of words and peered hopefully into Angus's face.

'When . . .' Angus started, then coughed as the words caught in his throat, and tried again. 'When were you going to ask her?'

'My ma always says that the New Year's a good time for new beginnings, but I'm not certain.' Joe pulled a shred of tobacco from his lip. 'I was thinkin' of waitin' for a month or two more, for the thing is, Mollie can be right sharp when she's put out and I'd not want tae do the wrong thing. Has she ever said anythin' tae you about her feelin's for me?'

'Mebbe you should ask my sister about that,' Angus said, and Joe's eyes widened.

'I couldnae ask her, she'd only tell Mollie and then the two of them would get a right laugh. I know about lassies, I've got two sisters of my own and they're never off the gossip. I feel right sorry for the lads they go out with. I think I'll go ahead and ask her,' Joe said. 'I'm ready for settlin' down and I've been offered work at a garage in Rothesay, with enough pay tae cover the rent on a wee house. I'd work hard for Mollie, and I'd respect her and take care of her, ye neednae worry about that.'

'I'm sure you would,' Angus said. Five minutes earlier, at the sight of Mollie on the stairs, his world had stopped; now, in the smoky atmosphere of his uncle's workshop, he felt as though it was ending altogether. Best, perhaps, to get the misery over with.

Perhaps the knowledge that Mollie was lost to him for ever would help him to start looking forward instead of back.

'Mebbe the New Year would be the best time,' he said to the man who was dashing his hopes so cruelly. 'As your mother says, it's a time of new beginnings.'

'Ye think so?' Joe reached out and shook him warmly by the hand. 'Thanks, Mr Scott, for your advice. I appreciate it. It's grand tae be able tae talk tae an older man at a time like this,' he said.

Helen, considerably bulkier now than she had been at her marriage only weeks earlier, had insisted on helping in the kitchen despite Ann's attempts to get her to rest before the party began.

'This kitchen's awful hot for a lassie in your condition and there's a nice sofa in the parlour,' she coaxed, but Helen shook her head.

'I'm best to be workin', and anyway, Satan finds mischief for idle hands.'

'If that's an orphanage upbringing for you, I'm glad I didnae have one,' Mollie murmured to Jennet and Alice.

Ann, who had sharp ears, glared at her and then asked, 'Have you heard from your gran, Jennet?'

'A letter and a wee card, and some money to buy presents. We sent her a cardigan and a nice card.'

'She'd no thought of coming over for Christmas or the New Year, or mebbe having you over to Largs?'

'We couldn't leave the farm, and from what she says she's got no notion to come back to Bute,' Jennet said thankfully. That was one worry over . . . like Martin, her grandmother had clearly given up all claims to the farm and now all that she and Angus had to worry about was keeping the place viable.

When they finally got back to Westervoe Jennet carried Jamie upstairs and put him to bed, while Angus went out to make sure that the animals were comfortable. She went downstairs just as he returned to the kitchen.

'It was a grand party.'

'It was all right.'

'Did you not enjoy yourself?'

'I'm not one for parties, you know that.'

'Mebbe if you made more of an effort,' Jennet said, irritated by his scowl, 'you'd have enjoyed yourself better. If we'd all spent the evening sitting in corners the way you did, nobody would have had a good time.'

'You wanted me to go, and I went,' he snapped back at her. 'Just be grateful for that!'

'I am, but I wish that . . . D'you not want a cup of tea and a bit of cake?' Jennet asked as he made for the inner door.

'I'd prefer my bed and my own company.' The door slammed shut behind him on the last word, leaving her to wonder what could have happened to put him in such a bad temper.

Fortunately he was in a better mood in the morning,

though he looked as though he had not slept well and he stayed behind while Bert took the others to church, crowded together in the cart with Nero between the shafts.

After the service Struan and Allan both slipped parcels to Jennet when their mother's attention was elsewhere. Allan's, she discovered when she got home, held a small mouth organ for Jamie, and Struan's gift to the little boy was a wooden tractor. His parcel also contained a smart pair of ladies' gloves. She pushed them hurriedly into her apron pocket, then hid them later in a drawer in her bedroom and fretted about them for several days. Clearly, Struan had not given up his hopes of marrying her.

'Be kind tae him, you said. He's a decent lad, you said. And what thanks do I get for bein' kind?' Mollie wanted to know, then answered her own question. 'He turns round and asks me to marry him!'

'But surely it's nice to get a proposal of marriage?' Jennet had taken Jamie along to Rothesay to wish everyone a happy New Year and had scarcely had time to drink her aunt's homemade ginger cordial and savour a slice of Nesta's rich fruit cake before Mollie whisked her out for a walk, pleading a headache and the need for fresh air. Now the two of them marched briskly along the Esplanade in the teeth of a howling and icy gale.

'You didnae think it was nice when Struan Blaikie asked you to marry him, did you? Anyway, I'm still angry with Joe over the way he went running after Senga.'

'He should mebbe have waited for a few months longer.'

'Or until hell froze over,' Mollie snapped, walking even faster.

'I hope you didn't say that to him?'

'No, but I did say that I'd not fancy standing there in my wedding dress and veil watchin' my bridegroom makin' eyes at Senga.'

'Oh, Mollie! Hold on, I've got a stitch.' Jennet clutched the railing with one gloved hand and pressed the other deep into her side. 'Does your mother know?' she wheezed when she had caught her breath.

'No, of course not.'

'I won't tell.'

'Is that stitch not gone yet?'

Jennet took her fist from her side and walked a few steps. 'It's easier, but I'm turning back to the house now, for I'm frozen!'

'You mean she turned him down?' Angus asked, astonished, when she told him.

'She says he's not the right one for her. I think there's someone else she cares about, but I can't think . . .' Jennet began, then stopped as she saw that Angus had lost interest and had disappeared behind his newspaper again.

24

Struan Blaikie made his move towards the end of January, arriving at Westervoe on a miserably wet day. The hens, unable to get out to scratch about, sulked in their arks and in the deep-litter house, while Gumrie stuck like glue to the kitchen range, whining pitifully when Angus tried to make him go outside.

'Call yourself a working dog?' he had finally roared at the animal. 'It's time we got ourselves a proper dog for this place!'

'He's good at his work.' Jennet had tried to defend Gumrie, who crouched by the range with his ears back and his tail flopping gently in apology for his own weaknesses, 'And if you'd to fetch the cows in, he'd be there with you no matter the weather. You know that.'

'I know that we've put up with his nonsense for long enough. Another dog . . . then you'll not be needed any more!' her brother hissed at Gumrie before limping out into the downpour.

Jamie, anxious to play with the small second-hand tricycle they had bought him for Christmas, grizzled all afternoon and Jennet was almost at her wits' end with him when Struan arrived, shaking rainwater from his jacket and taking care to wipe the worst of the mud from his boots before stepping into the kitchen.

'Angus's gone off to see about buying in seed potatoes,' Jennet informed him.

'If this weather settles in it'll be a while before we can plant them.' Early potatoes were planted in the first two months of the year and lifted in June.

'There's time yet. We're nearly finished getting the field ready. Jamie, stop that,' she added to the little boy, who was following her around and tugging at her britches.

'Want to go out!'

Jennet glanced through the window and saw that the rain had eased to a light drizzle. 'All right, if you must, you must. Go and fetch your jacket and your boots.'

'Are you sure?' Struan asked doubtfully as the little boy, beaming, hurried to the short passage between the farm kitchen and the rest of the house. 'It's still raining out there – he could catch his death.'

'He'll not melt, and he'll be back in as soon as he starts to feel miserable. In the meantime, at least I'll have had a bit of peace.' Jennet knelt down to help her son as he came staggering back to the kitchen, the wrong arm through one sleeve of his jacket and his boots tucked precariously beneath the other arm.

'Stand still now, for the sooner you're ready, the sooner you'll get out.'

'The bike's in the wee outhouse, d'you think you could get it for him?' she asked Struan, and by the time she had dressed Jamie and clapped a cap on his head, ignoring his protests, Struan was wheeling the tricycle into the yard.

'He seems quite happy out there in the wet,' he said when he returned.

'He's of farming stock, he might as well get used to the weather.' She went on with her baking. 'Do you want to see Angus about something? He'll not be back for a while.'

'Nothing important.' He went to the window to peer out. 'Jamie's splashing through all the puddles,' he reported.

'I've no doubt of that.' Jennet put the scones into the oven and dusted some flour from her hands.

'He's fairly growing, Jennet.'

'Aye, and more of a handful with every day.' Jamie had become livelier since Celia Scott's departure. Now that there was no need for him to be seen but not heard, Jennet found herself having to put him in his place regularly.

Struan moved away from the sink to let her wash her hands and then asked, his voice carefully casual, 'Did the gloves fit all right?'

'The . . . ? Oh, yes, they're lovely.' She had almost forgotten about his gift. 'I'm sorry, I never got the chance to thank you for them.'

'That's all right, I just wondered because I'm not used to buying things for women,' he said. Then he rushed on, 'I got a letter from Martin the other day. He said he'd written to you as well.'

'That's right. He seems well settled.' Martin had written just before Christmas to tell them that he and the girl he fancied now had 'an understanding'.

'He says he's not coming back.'

'We knew that already.'

'That's a pity. Angus could mebbe do with his help.'

'Angus – and me – are managing fine without him.'

'But it puts a lot on your shoulders, Jennet.'

'Away you go; plenty of women on Bute have run their own farms.'

'But is that what you want?'

'For the moment, yes, it is.' Jennet took one of Angus's shirts from the clotheshorse, where it had been airing, and began to fold it. 'We've agreed that if I want to go back to nursing after that, Angus can manage on his own with Norrie and Bert and a bit of help from Jem, if needed.'

'You're thinkin' of leavin' the island again?'

'I don't know for sure.' She picked up a pair of Jamie's trousers, noted that they needed patching and put them aside instead of folding them. 'I'm giving this place a year before I make up my mind as to what to do next.'

'Have you thought any more about my offer?' Struan asked, and her heart sank.

'I've thought about it a lot and the answer's still

the same. I've no notion to marry anyone just now. Mebbe not ever.'

'I'm not just asking for myself,' he said. 'My mother wasnae too good at Ne'erday, she couldnae stop thinking about our Drew. I know it's been a few years now, but my father says it's preyed on her mind every Ne'erday since, and with me and Allan both back home, and Drew not with us, it was worse for her this year.'

'I'm sorry to hear that, but I doubt if you marrying me would make her feel any better.'

'Are you certain sure, Jennet,' he said, 'that that wee lad out there isnae our Drew's bairn?'

Jennet, about to put the clotheshorse away, banged it down again. 'I've told you he's not and if I have to, I'll swear to it on the Bible! And even if he was . . . which he's not,' she added swiftly, 'I don't think much of you wanting to marry me just so that you can give Jamie to your mother as a ready-made grandson!'

'It's not the only reason . . .'

'It seems to me to be a strong one, though. It makes you a good son, Struan, but a poor husband, so why can't . . .'

'I love you,' he said loudly. Then as she stopped, letting a silence wash over them both, he cleared his throat before saying it again, quietly this time. 'I . . . I love ye, Jennet. It's not an easy thing to say, but there it is.'

The shock of the declaration left her speechless.

'I should mebbe have said that when I asked ye before, but words like that don't come easy tae a man like me,' he blundered on while she was still trying to collect her thoughts.

'I know that, Struan, and I'm touched by what you say. But it doesn't make any difference to the way I feel.'

'So ye'll not have me.'

'I'm not the right one for you . . . I'm not,' she insisted as he opened his mouth to protest. 'If I was, I'd surely feel the same way about you. But I don't. I like you as the friend you always were, but that's all.'

'So. Well.' He shuffled his feet uncomfortably, then said, 'I suppose I'd best just get back to Gleniffer then.'

'Yes.' She followed him to the door, wishing she could find something else to say, but knowing that any attempt to comfort him would probably lead him to think that he might still have a chance of breaking down her resolve.

Instead of lessening, the drizzle had become a downpour again; rain teemed down from a low, grey sky, to bounce on the cobbles and splash into the puddles. The hens and cats that were usually scattered about the yard had found shelter and the only living creatures left in the place were Struan's dog, huddled against the house wall, and Jamie, careering round and round on his tricycle and screaming with pleasure every time the wheels ran through a puddle, throwing up a bow-wave of water. He showed no signs of becoming miserable. His cap, discarded, lay near the farm door and his light brown hair, normally as curly as his mother's, was darkened by water and plastered to his neat little skull, making him look entirely different.

'Look at me,' he shrieked when he spotted his audience, circling the bike round and away, laughing back over his shoulder at them, one eyebrow lifted and his grinning mouth, from that angle, seeming to tilt more at one corner than at the other.

Struan, pulling on his own cap, suddenly tensed. From where she stood close behind him and slightly to one side, Jennet could feel the muscles and bones of his back stiffen. He stood motionless, his hands by his head, until Jamie had rounded the top of his circle and was coming back towards them, grinning. Then Struan lowered his arms and turned to Jennet, his eyes boring down into hers.

'I'm such a fool,' he said. 'God, you must have been laughing at me all this time!'

'Why should I laugh at you?'

'Not Drew,' he said. 'You told me the truth when you said it wasnae our Drew. But I knew as soon as I looked at him that he was a Blaikie. He's Allan's bairn, isn't he?' Then, as she stared back at him, mute, 'Ye cannae deny me this time, can ye? I've been such a damned fool!'

'Struan, wait!' As he called his dog and strode away from her, splashing across the yard, Jennet ran after him into the rain, then had to give up as he passed Jamie without a glance and stormed into the lane.

'Look, Mummy,' Jamie clamoured, the bike wheels throwing water over Jennet. She didn't notice, but stood in the rain, staring after Struan.

Struan was halfway along the road that led to Rothesay when he remembered that it was early closing day, and his brother would probably be back at the farm. He swung round so abruptly that he almost fell over the dog trotting close to his heels.

'Out of my way,' he roared at it, and began the walk back to Gleniffer. By the time he reached the farm the persistent rain had soaked its way through his clothing and chilled his skin, but he ignored the discomfort as he threw the door back on its hinges and marched into the big kitchen where his mother, as usual, was working at the range. Allan sat at the table, paperwork from the shop spread out before him.

'Struan, would you look at the mess you've brought in with you,' Lizbeth Blaikie yelped, staring at the spreading pool of water about his feet. 'Get back outside to the wee porch and take your boots and your coat off this minute!' Then, taking in the water cascading unchecked from his hair to run over his face and down his neck, 'You're soaked through, man, where have you been?'

'Visitin',' he informed her, his eyes on his brother. After glancing up Allan had returned to his paper, but when Struan went on, 'Visitin' . . . with his bastard', Allan's head jerked up again.

'Don't you dare to use such language in this house!' Lizbeth said sharply. 'I'll have no blaspheming here.'

Struan turned his head to look at her, spraying her jersey with droplets. 'It's only blasphemy when it's a lie, Mother,' he informed her. Then, looking back to Allan, 'And this isnae a lie. I've been over at Westervoe . . .' a forefinger came up to stab towards Allan, 'visitin' his bastard and his whore!'

'Catherine,' Lizbeth rounded on the new maid, who stood at the inner door, her eyes wide in a shocked face, 'go upstairs at once and make the beds!'

'I made them hours ago, missus.'

'Then make them again. Go on when I tell you,' Lizbeth shrieked as the girl hesitated. Then when she had fled, 'What's going on here? Where's your father? He's never here when he's needed.'

'He's not needed now,' Struan tossed the words at her. 'I can handle this. Well, Allan, are ye going tae deny what I'm sayin'? Goin' tae call me a liar, are ye?'

Allan, on his feet now, glanced at his mother. 'Come outside, Struan. This is something best discussed between the two of us.'

'I think my mother should hear what you have to say.'

'So do I.' Lizbeth's normally ruddy face had turned as white as milk. 'What's he haverin' about, Allan?'

He ignored her, concentrating on his brother. 'What did Jennet tell you?'

'Don't fret, she didnae spill yer secret. She's been loyal tae ye, though God knows why. It was the bairn himself . . . I could see it in his face from the time I came back home, but I thought he was Drew's bairn. That's why I wanted tae marry her, tae give him his rightful name . . .'

'*You* want to marry Jennet?' Allan asked.

'What's wrong with that?'

'What's wrong with it?' his mother chimed in. 'You were going to bring that lassie and her . . . her . . .'

'The word's bastard, Mother,' Struan said clearly.

'. . . into my house? How could you?'

'Oh, don't fret; she turned me down, the first time I asked and again the second time. Mind you,' Struan said, his mouth smiling thinly at Allan though his eyes were murderous, 'who can blame her? It's one thing, our Drew not bein' able tae acknowledge his own bairn because he's dead, but it's another for you tae leave him without a name.'

'Hold your tongue!'

'That's just what I'll not do, now that I know. I looked at him today, Allan, and I saw your face lookin' back at me as clear as if you'd been standin' there. And Jennet couldnae deny it when I challenged her. So I'm not goin' tae hold my tongue at all. I'm goin' tae see that this whole island knows what ye've done, and how ye deserted her and the bairn.'

'It's not just me you'll shame, it's her and the wee one as well.'

'Jennet's been shamed since the day you fathered

the bairn on her. And he was shamed the day he was conceived,' Struan said. 'But you've got away with it until now. Not any more, Allan. I'm goin' to see that you're shamed the length and breadth of Bute. I'll see you hounded off this island and out of my . . .'

The words became a gurgle as Allan caught him by the throat, shaking him so hard that raindrops from his hair and clothing sprayed the kitchen.

'Stop it,' Lizbeth shrieked as Struan fisted his hands, then chopped them upwards from his side to break his brother's grip. He sucked in air and would have lunged at Allan there and then if his mother had not pushed her way between them.

'I won't have this in my house, between my two sons! For pity's sake, is it not enough that I've lost Drew without you two trying to kill each other?'

'Outside.' Allan, ignoring her, pushed his brother in the chest and as Struan staggered back he followed, pushing and nudging until Struan was through the open door and into the porch. Before Lizbeth could get through the door the two of them were in the yard and Struan was struggling with his jacket, hauling the sodden weight of it free, then throwing it down onto the ground. Allan stood back until the jacket was clear before launching himself at his brother, who met him halfway.

'Andra!' Lizbeth screamed at the top of her voice. 'Andra, for the love of God . . . !' Then, as her husband emerged from the stable, she flew over to him, dodging her sons as she went, and clutched his arm.

'What's goin' on here?'

'Struan came home with some nonsense about Jennet Scott and the wee . . . He called him a . . .' Lizbeth gabbled. 'And Allan tried tae choke him and now they're . . . Stop them, Andra, stop them before they kill each other!'

'You're gettin' soaked, woman, you'll catch the pneumonia. Come in here.' Andra pulled her into the shelter of the stable, a hard task since she resisted every step of the way.

'Never mind about me, put a stop to them . . . now, Andra!'

As Struan's bunched fist missed his brother's jaw and hit his shoulder, Allan twisted away, caught his heel on a raised flagstone and staggered back, arms windmilling, towards the stable. His father reached out and grabbed at the bottom half of the stable door, swinging it shut.

'Lizbeth,' he said, shooting the bolt home just as his son crashed against the door and then fell to the cobbles, 'I'm gettin' tae be an old man now and it's more than my life's worth tae try tae separate these two, now their blood's up. They're all muscle, the pair of them.'

'But they'll kill each other!' his wife wailed as Allan rolled away from Struan's determined rush and gained his feet, before launching himself back across the stones to grapple with his brother.

'Mebbe not, and even if they do, ye'd not want tae see me dead an' all, would ye?' Andra put an arm about her sturdy shoulders. 'Not after all these years we've spent together. Whatever's botherin' them, it's best tae let them work it out atween their two selves. Then, when the fires have damped down, you and me can chastise the both of them. That's what parents are for, is it no'?' he added soothingly.

As his sons rolled over and over on the wet ground, Allan trying to gouge Struan's eyes out while Struan attempted to bring his knee up into his brother's groin, and his wife had hysterics at his back, Andra Blaikie leaned his folded arms on the top half of the door and prepared to watch one of the bonniest fights he had seen in many a long year.

'Allan Blaikie?' Angus was saying incredulously in the Westervoe kitchen at that same moment. 'Allan Blaikie?'

'Aye, Allan Blaikie. You know who I mean, surely.' After keeping her secret so well for so long, Jennet had found it hard finally to admit the name. But she had no option . . . There was little hope of Struan keeping his mouth shut, and Angus had to hear it from her rather than from one of the Blaikies.

'I thought I knew him, but now I'm wonderin' if I really do.' Angus sank into a chair at the table, staring at her. 'And the same goes for you. I didnae even know that the two of you were . . .'

'We weren't. It was just the once, a daft mistake when he was upset about being a soldier and I was upset about . . . worried about Martin being away from home.' She couldn't admit to Angus that her worries at that time had been for him.

'Why didn't he marry you? Did you not tell him when you found out that . . . you know.'

'I told him, but the way things were we decided against marriage.'

'Both of you? I doubt that,' he said, an edge to his voice. 'You might as well tell me the truth, for if you don't I'll have to go over to Gleniffer and get it out of him.'

She bit her lip and then admitted, 'Allan was just about to be sent overseas when we . . . when I found out that Jamie was on the way. He thought he was going to be killed and he was scared of what his mother would think . . .'

'What his mother would think?' her brother asked in disbelief. 'You were carryin' his child, and you werenae married, and he was more worried about what his mother would think than about you and Jamie? What the hell sort of a man is he?'

'It wasn't as clear as that, not at the time.' She would never have believed, that terrible day in the Glasgow teashop, that she would end up defending Allan and seeing his point of view. 'Drew had recently been killed and you know that the Blaikie boys were nearly as scared of their mother as we were of Gran. He panicked.'

'So you came home on your lone. And you let Grandmother say all those terrible things about you and about the man that fathered Jamie, and you didnae say a word in your own defence?' Anger began to take over from shock. 'Why, in God's name? You should have told us, and the Blaikies. You should have told me, if nobody else, and let me deal with it. It was the least he deserved!'

'You weren't well and, anyway, I didn't want to talk about it! Can you not see that? I was ashamed, and there was no sense in causing more trouble than I already had. I might have set Gran and the Blaikies against each other and I didn't feel strong enough to cope with that sort of thing.'

'So you'd all the worry and Allan got off scot-free.'

'If he survived the war he was going back to work for his uncle in Glasgow. He'd not have been back here, and I thought it was better for me to have Jamie all to myself. D'you think I wanted Mrs Blaikie interfering all the time, criticising the way I was bringing her grandchild up? If Allan's uncle hadn't decided to buy a shop here on the island, and send him over to run it, nobody would ever have been any the wiser.' Her head was throbbing; she put her hands up to support it and felt her way into a chair.

'How did Struan find out?'

'He saw a family likeness in Jamie when he came back from the fighting.'

'I've never seen it myself.'

'When you look at him you just see Jamie, same as me. When he was just born,' Jennet admitted, 'I thought I saw Allan in him, but only in those first hours, and nobody else noticed it, not even Gran. But

Struan did, and it made him think that Drew had fathered Jamie. That's why he asked me to marry him.'

'Struan asked you to marry him?' Angus, gripping the edge of the sink, had been staring out at the darkening afternoon beyond the kitchen window; now he spun round to face her. 'You never told me that, either!'

'Why should I? I turned him down.'

'When was this?'

'Not long after he came home. He knew that Gran wanted to let the farm go and he thought that if I married him the two of you could run Westervoe together. And he wanted to give Jamie the Blaikie name, for Drew's sake.'

'It's Allan who should be offering you marriage, not Struan.'

'He did, when he came back to the island and saw Jamie.'

'He . . . ! Jennet,' Angus said, sitting opposite her, 'is there anything else you've been keeping from me? Because if there is I want to know it now.'

'There's nothing.'

'When Allan offered marriage . . . ?'

'I turned him down because I'm happy the way we are, Angus, with the two of us working the farm together. And Jamie's happy too – he's got you and me, and he's loved.'

'First thing tomorrow I'm going over to Gleniffer to tell Allan what I think of the way he's treated you.' His hands clenched on the table. 'I just wish I was able tae give him the thrashing he deserves.'

'Don't you dare! I just want things to go back to the way they were before.'

'I doubt if you'll get that wish,' Angus said as Jamie, who had been sent off to the parlour with some sheets of paper and some crayons, marched in, his towelled hair still damp, to show them his artwork.

25

Angus vanished the next morning, returning in time for the midday meal. It was late evening before Jennet was able to find out that he had indeed gone to Gleniffer to confront Allan.

'I asked you not to!'

'Nobody's going to treat my sister the way Allan Blaikie treated you, and get away with it. I had to catch him before he went to the shop. Not that he'll be going there today,' Angus added with a touch of satisfaction creeping into his voice, 'for he's a right mess and so is Struan.'

'They had a fight?'

'One of the best, according to Andra. Allan's covered with cuts and bruises and I gave him a right tongue-lashin' into the bargain. I can tell you, Jennet, that he's sorry he ever clapped eyes on you.'

'How is Mrs Blaikie?'

'She's never been as nice to me in her life. She's black affronted by the way Allan's treated you. She sent some of her home preserves over – pickles and jellies. I put them in the kitchen press.'

'So can we just let the whole thing blow over now?' Jennet asked hopefully.

'We can, but I expect the rest of the island's goin' tae have a grand time of it figuring out what happened to set the Blaikie lads against each other.'

The following morning Norrie hurried into the yard to report that on his way to work he had seen Struan, '. . . in a right old mess! His face was like one of those maps we used to have to study at the school, all red and black and blue,' Jennet heard him report gleefully as she came out of the kitchen with a steaming bucket of mash for the hens.

'I wonder what sort of trouble's come up between them two?' Jem said, puzzled.

'A woman, sure as day,' Norrie told him with all the authority of his sixteen years.

'Or money,' Bert hazarded as Angus led Nero from his stable.

'More likely a woman. Struan had a right swollen lip . . .' Norrie was elaborating when Angus intervened.

'And you'll have empty pay packets if you don't get on with your work. The potato field won't get itself ready, and there's silage to fetch and oats to bruise for the animal feed.'

'Wait a minute, Angus, they might as well know the truth of it.'

'Jen . . . !'

'The news will get round sooner or later and I'd as soon our own men heard the right story.' Jennet started to put the bucket down. Then, catching sight of two of the farm cats lurking nearby in hope, she hung it on a hook by the stable door before going to stand by Nero, stroking his strong warm neck for comfort. The horse's breath plumed from his nostrils into the cold morning air.

'Folk don't want the truth, Jen, they prefer to make up their own way of things.'

'I'm tired of keeping secrets. Struan and Allan were fighting because of me,' she told the three men confronting her, 'because Struan found out that Allan fathered wee Jamie.'

There was an uncomfortable silence during which all three farmhands stared at the flagstones as though they had discovered something interesting in the cracks. Then Bert cleared his throat before saying awkwardly, 'It's none of our business, is it?'

'No, it's not, but I thought you should know.'

'And now that you do,' Angus said, 'you can get on with your work.' As the men scattered, grateful for an excuse to be on their way, he asked his sister, 'Did you have to do that?'

'I'm fed up of secrets. The sooner this business is out in the open and gossiped over and then forgotten, the better.' Jennet collected the pail. 'Did you see their faces? They were so embarrassed they didn't know where to look. That means that if someone else mentions it to them, they'll feel embarrassed all over again, so they'll not want to talk about it.'

'I doubt if the Blaikies'll thank you for parading their business all over the place.'

'If I can face folk, then surely they can as well.'

'Somehow,' Angus said, 'I don't think Mrs Blaikie'll have your courage.'

'That's her worry. Now that I've told Bert,' Jennet suddenly realised, 'I'd better go and confess to Aunt Ann and Aunt Nesta and Mollie.'

'What about Grandmother? If you don't tell her, Mrs Blaikie will.'

Jennet sighed. 'I'll write a letter as soon as the hens are fed, and post it in Rothesay. Helen'll have to look after Jamie and see to the meals today, since I'll have my hands full.'

'Ye've had a bad time of it, pet,' Nesta McCabe said when Jennet had told the whole story to her and Ann Logan.

'And you've handled it well,' Ann agreed.

'I don't know about that.'

'You'll stay for your dinner? You might as well,' Ann said as her niece glanced at the clock. 'By the time you get back home it'll be the afternoon.'

'Yes, I'll stay. I'll walk down and meet Mollie on her way back from work.'

'I wish you'd told me before, Jennet,' Mollie said. 'You know I'd not have breathed a word to anyone.'

She gave her friend's shoulders a comforting squeeze, then asked, 'Is it terrible, knowing that everyone knows?'

'To tell you the truth, it feels grand. They'll talk about it for a week and then they'll get tired of it and I'll be free as a bird. No more secrets, no more worrying about someone guessing. Struan's done me a good turn,' Jennet said, and meant it.

'Jennet!' Angus called from the foot of the stairs that evening.

'In a minute.' She had just settled Jamie for the night, and she was helping him to say his prayers.

'Now would be better, Jennet! There's . . . there's somethin' needs seein' to in the yard!'

'What?' Jamie said at once, unfolding his hands as his mother reached the window in time to see Lizbeth and Andra Blaikie, both dressed in their Sunday clothes, crossing the yard.

'It's just a cat that's come to the wrong farm,' she improvised, trying to keep her voice steady. 'I'll go and shoo it away before our cats fight with it.'

'Me, too.' He began to struggle out from beneath the blankets and she hurried to tuck him back in.

'No, I can manage. Come on now . . .' She caught his hands and held them together within hers, 'Nearly finished. God bless Great-Grandmother and Great-Great-Aunt Rachel, Amen.'

He scrunched his eyes up and repeated the words in a meaningless gabble. 'Don't hurt the cat,' his voice followed her to the door.

'I won't. I think it's gone now anyway.' If only it was as easy as shooing a cat, Jennet thought as she paused before the parlour door, her heart hammering against her ribs.

Lizbeth Blaikie was perched on the edge of an armchair while her husband spilled his bulk over the shiny leather sofa. Angus hovered by the fireplace, his hands in his pockets.

'Jennet,' he said with relief, 'here's Andra and . . . and Mrs Blaikie come to see you.'

She smoothed her apron, wishing that she had thought to take it off, then sat down on a chair. 'You've come about me and Allan. I suppose he's told you all about it.'

'Not so much Allan as Struan,' Andra put in. 'The lad came tearin' in yesterday and tried tae kill Allan. He might have managed it, too, if they'd not been so well matched. In the end they just wore themselves out and once they were lying out on the flags in the rain, Lizbeth here went for Allan with the yard brush.'

'He was lucky I didnae get my hands on the pitchfork first,' his wife said bitterly.

'I'd tae haul her off.' Andra looked at her proudly. 'But she got in a good few wha . . .'

'That's enough, Andra. Our Allan deserved everything he got, Jennet, for he's done you a terrible wrong.'

'I think that's between me and Allan.'

'We got the whole story out of him eventually. He's that ashamed of himself for not marrying you right away and giving the bairn his proper name.'

'Jamie does have a proper name,' Angus put in, moving to stand behind Jennet. 'He's a Scott.'

'I never thought a lad of mine would have failed in his duty tae the lassie that carried his bairn. Look at me and Lizbeth here,' Andra went on earnestly. 'As soon as we knew she was . . .'

'It's not too late for him to put things right,' Lizbeth cut in sharply.

'Allan asked me to marry him not long after he came back to Bute, but I told him that I'm happy as I am, and so is my son.'

'Aye, he told us, but you can't let the wee one grow up as a . . . a . . .'

'I've never thought of him in that way, Mrs Blaikie. I left that to other folk,' Jennet said clearly, and the woman coloured.

'He's loved and cared for,' Angus put in, 'and he always will be.'

Lizbeth hesitated and then said, 'Could we . . . d'you think I could see him, Jennet?'

'He's asleep and I'd not want him disturbed.'

'It seems to me, Mrs Blaikie, that you've got a right nerve, asking a favour like that,' Angus said coldly. His hand landed on Jennet's shoulder, the fingers tightening. 'You've never looked in Jamie's direction because you thought his father was some unknown stranger. He doesn't look any different just because he's Allan's son. As we said, we'll manage. Nothing's changed at all.'

'So . . . we'd best leave it at that and not cause any more trouble,' Andra told his wife, rising to his feet.

'But . . .'

'Be told, Lizbeth. Ye've had yer say and Jennet's had hers, and that's an end of it.' He pulled his cap on over his grey hair. 'We'd best be gettin' home now.'

On the way out through the kitchen Lizbeth hesitated, staring at the tin bath, still waiting to be emptied, and at the toys scattered over the floor. Then she said to Angus, 'Thank you for hearin' us out at least.'

'We don't believe in bein' uncivil to neighbours,' Angus told her.

'I can't just let her go like that,' Jennet said suddenly as the two of them stood in the doorway and watched the older couple walk away. 'Look at her, Angus.' Mrs Blaikie's shoulders, normally as erect as a sergeant major's, were slumped and, as they watched, her husband put a supportive hand beneath her elbow. 'There were tears in her eyes when she saw the mess Jamie had left in the kitchen. When all's said and done, he's her grandchild!'

'And I'm your brother and if you call her back now I'll do a better job on you than Struan did on Allan.' Angus caught her arm and pulled her into the kitchen, shutting the door and leaning back against it. 'Are you mad, woman? She was one of the old witches who talked against you the most when you came home, even though Gran's her friend. And it's made my blood boil, the way she's looked at you every time you met since, and the way she ignored the wee one.'

'I think she's learned her mistakes the hard way.'

'Give the likes of her half a chance and she'd take all three of us over, and the farm intae the bargain.'

'No, she'd not. She couldn't, for we'd be the ones with the power. We have Jamie and we could always threaten to stop letting her see him if she started taking advantage.' Jennet began to gather up the toys.

'I don't know . . . Best to leave things as they are, if you ask me. At least sleep on it,' Angus suggested. 'You might feel different in the morning.'

Later, when she was ready for bed, Jennet drew the low nursing chair up to the cot and sat watching Jamie, fast asleep and blissfully unaware of the upheaval that his existence had caused. Lizbeth was right when she said that he had Blaikie blood in him. Perhaps it would be unfair to deny the people who, after all, were his grandparents the pleasure of seeing him now and again.

On the other hand, Angus was right when he said that Allan's mother had treated both Jennet and Jamie cruelly. Even so, Jennet recalled the sudden tears that had come to Lizbeth Blaikie's eyes as she looked at the tin bath with its cooling water, and the few wooden and rag toys on the carpet.

The really bad thing about having a child of your own, she decided as she got up and made her way to the big bed, was the way it made you realise that mothers – even mothers like Mrs Blaikie – could hurt badly where their own were concerned.

The following afternoon Lizbeth Blaikie opened her kitchen door to find Jennet and Jamie standing on the step.

'We were out for a wee walk and we thought we'd just come and say hello,' Jennet said brightly. She had almost turned back half a dozen times, and she had had to force herself to walk down the Gleniffer lane and then enter and cross the large, neat farmyard. But she had managed it, and now there was no turning back.

Lizbeth's eyes widened and even more colour than usual rushed into her cheeks. She gulped audibly before saying, 'Oh . . . that's nice. Come in.'

The kitchen was almost exactly as Jennet remembered it from her visits as a child; walls and shelves massed with bowls, pans, crockery for everyday use, jelly pans and jelly bags and moulds, and the pretty painted plates that she had yearned after. She had always promised herself plates like that when she grew up, but they had not yet materialised and she was beginning to doubt that they ever would.

The Women's Rural Institute that Lizbeth and Celia Scott had clung to all their lives was represented by the rag rugs on the floor and hand-knitted cushion covers on the fireside chairs and the small sofa below the window. But for all the items in the big square room, it was neat and spotlessly clean, as always, even down to the snowy runners on the backs of the chairs and across the chenille-covered table. A far cry from Westervoe's kitchen, Jennet thought ruefully as she followed Mrs Blaikie in, with Jamie clinging tightly to her hand.

'You'll have some tea?'

'I'd love a cup. Not that we're staying long,' Jennet warned.

'Even so, it's good to see you . . . both of you.' The woman beamed as she ushered Jennet to a chair. 'The kettle's just on the boil. D'you like buttermilk, wee man?' she added to Jamie.

'Aye,' he said in his gruffest voice.

'Yes, please,' Jennet reminded him.

'Yes, please,' he said, adding, 'Helen gives me buttermilk – it's good for me.'

'She's quite right. I'll get you some, and a wee bit of shortbread . . . if that's all right with your mother. How is Helen?' Lizbeth asked Jennet.

'She's fine.'

'She's a good lassie. I was vexed with her when I heard . . . but I'm glad you've taken her and Bert in. It was kind of you. Now then, my wee man, what about that buttermilk? And after you've finished it,' Lizbeth said tremulously, 'we'll go and see the new puppies, if your mother says it's all right.'

* * *

There was no sense in trying to keep the visit to Gleniffer a secret from Angus. Jamie was full of it, and he could not wait to pour out the story about the nice lady with the big farm and the puppies that the little boy had been allowed to play with.

Angus listened and smiled, commenting in the right places, but as soon as his nephew trotted into the yard to play with Gumrie he said to Jennet, 'I just hope you've not made a mistake, Jennet.'

'I did what I had to do.'

'You didnae have tae do it at all! Not after the way she behaved. And now that you've made friends with his mother, Allan'll probably think that the coast's clear for him.'

'He won't. I went to see her when I was sure that Allan and Struan wouldn't be around, and I made it clear to Mrs Blaikie that it would only be the occasional visit and that I'd not changed my mind where Allan was concerned. She's really mortified by what he did, Angus. I felt quite sorry for her,' Jennet admitted, and he groaned.

'That's just the beginning, you mark my words. She'll be getting the wee one to call her Granny next.'

'That's not going to happen, either . . . Not until he's old enough to understand and make up his own mind about it.'

'You think so? Once that woman and Grandmother get together they'll have nothing else in their minds but making a decent woman of you.'

'She's not even written to Grandmother yet.' Mrs

Blaikie had tentatively asked if Jennct had notified her grandmother, and when she replied that she had, the older woman had nodded.

'It's the right thing to do, lassie,' she had said. 'I write every week, but I was holding my own letter back to give you a chance to tell her your news. I'll write tonight and tell her about your visit, if I may.'

Celia Scott's letter arrived two days later. Angus had gone to Rothesay, so Jennet put it, unopened, behind the clock, where it managed to catch her eye every time she stepped into the kitchen. The day seemed to drag by, and it was a relief when she was finally alone with him, and able to hand it over.

'You read it first.' He slid it across the table to her when she put it down by his hand that night. 'It'll concern you more than me.'

'D'you want me to read it aloud?'

'No, just read it then pass it back.'

Surprisingly, the first half of the letter was just the same as usual; a dry report on the weather, Celia's health and her sister Rachel's health, and a mention of their daily outings to the shops. Then came the final paragraph: 'I was surprised to read of your sister's news; it is a great pity that she did not see fit to tell us sooner than this. It must have come as a great shock to you, Angus, and I am disappointed in Allan Blaikie. I had expected more of him, but at least you now have the satisfaction of knowing whose blood runs in the child's veins.'

Jennet read the entire letter, then handed it to her brother and began to gather up the used supper dishes. As she reached the sink a strangled grunt told her that he had scanned the page.

'At least she's been told,' she said, laying the dishes down by the side of the sink, 'and I can get on with my life in peace.'

'The old bitch!'

'Angus!' She whirled, a hand flying to her mouth. 'That's no way to speak of your grandmother!'

His face was crimson with anger. 'I could think of a lot worse words, but I'll not dirty my mouth with them.' He held the letter out, slapping the back of his free hand against it. 'Is that all she has to say about you and the wee fellow? She spent more words on the weather than she did on you! And she has the cheek to say that I've got the satisfaction of knowing Jamie's got Blaikie blood in him . . . as if I was bothered about his father. As far as I'm concerned, he's your bairn and my nephew. And that's all that matters!'

'You know what Grandmother's like . . .'

'I always thought I did, but I never realised she was such a wicked old . . . witch!' He got up and limped to the range, where he stuffed the letter between the bars of the fire. 'There,' he said with satisfaction as the sheet of paper flared up and then turned to ash, 'that's where it belongs!'

'Angus, I'll have to answer that letter and now you've burned it!'

'You don't have to answer it at all, and if you take my advice you won't. But if you must, just tell her about the weather. That's all she deserves,' Angus said. Catching the back of a chair for support, he bent and picked the poker up from the hearth, using it to push the remains of the letter deep into the glowing embers.

26

Because Helen McCabe's baby was due in a week or two Jennet thought it safer to arrange for her aunt to take Jamie when the time came for planting the early potatoes. Helen was not at all pleased, nor did she take it kindly when Bert and Jennet united to ban her from helping out in the field.

'All that bending and straightening for hours at a time . . . you'd never manage it,' Jennet said, while Bert chimed in with, 'Not in your condition, pet, you might harm the wee one.'

'What am I to do, then, with Jamie away?'

'There's the food to get ready for everyone – that's a full job in itself,' Jennet pointed out, and Helen finally had to give in, although she insisted on toiling out to the field regularly with a basket of food and bottles of cold tea.

Inching her way along a row, dibber in hand and with her booted feet sinking into the clinging, freshly ploughed earth, Jennet wished with all her heart that she, too, had the excuse of being heavily pregnant. The sackful of potatoes tied about her waist certainly helped her to feel as though she was.

It began to rain almost as soon as they started work, and each time she straightened to fetch more potatoes from the sack the cold sleety drops stung her in the face before running down her neck. Despite the sacking she had wrapped about her head and neck for protection, the rain found its way in to trickle down her back as she bent to make evenly spaced holes with the dibber, dropped the potatoes in and then straightened. Two sideways steps later she had to bend her aching back and start it all over again. There was some pleasure in reaching the end of a long row, but that was swiftly offset by the knowledge that she had to move forward and tackle the next.

When she finally rubbed the rain from her eyes and turned stiffly to monitor her progress it seemed as though she had scarcely gained more than a yard or so, though she felt as if she had been working for hours. Through the grey wet mist she could see other figures dotted about the field; some casual farm labourers had come along for the sake of a day's work, and Andra Blaikie had sent Struan and another of his farmhands to help.

When Struan first arrived, clearly unsure of his welcome, Angus had stuck his hand out and said bluntly, 'If I've got a quarrel it's with your brother. No reason why you and me should let what's happened get in our way.' Struan, his face flushing with relief, had almost wrung the proffered hand from Angus's wrist.

'I made a right fool of myself,' he said gruffly to Jennet as they sat in the cart on their way to the field. 'I've no regrets about tryin' tae batter the life out of our Allan, for he deserved it. I'm talkin' about askin ye . . .' He stopped, too embarrassed to say the words.

'Struan, it was a kind offer and I'm just sorry I'd to turn you down. But you deserve better than me.'

'I don't know about that. It still sticks in my craw that ye prefer Allan tae me.'

Dear God, Jennet thought, is this nonsense to go on for ever?

Allan had called in at the farm a week earlier and when she saw the butcher's van bumping along the lane, her first inclination had been to snatch Jamie up and run with him into the farmhouse and bolt the door. Instead she stood her ground, calling the little boy to her side.

'I'm not here to cause trouble, Jennet,' he said as soon as he was within earshot. 'And I'll be gone in a minute. I just wanted tae thank you for lettin' my mother see the wee one now and again. It means a lot to her.'

'It didn't seem right to deny her, considering she's . . .'

'It's a kindness anyway, and one that's appreciated.' His face was still patched with the yellow remains of bruises, and there was a fresh scar over one eyebrow. 'And I wanted you tae know . . .'

'Allan,' Jamie clamoured, ducking away from the hand Jennet had laid on his shoulder in order to tug at the man's trouser leg. 'I can play my . . .' He struggled for the right word, and Jennet said, 'Mouth organ.'

'Aye!'

Allan squatted down, his face close to the child's. 'Can ye? That's clever.'

'I'll show you.' Jamie turned and scuttled into the kitchen. Allan watched him – it was more like holding him with his eyes than just watching, Jennet thought later – until he had disappeared through the door.

'He likes it, then.'

'He does, but me and Angus are beginning to wish you'd thought of something else,' Jennet said wryly. 'He thinks it's music, but it's just a noise.'

When he laughed, he was the Allan she had known before the war. She even felt the sudden lift of the heart, the sudden catch in her throat that she had known in those carefree days when she had had a teenage crush on him. Then he said, 'I'd best go.'

'What was it you wanted me to know?' she asked as he turned away.

'Eh?' He swung back, frowning, then remembered. 'That I'll not bother you again,' he said. 'I've done you more than enough harm.' Then, his voice low and urgent, 'Jennet, I'd give anythin' to be able to turn the clock back. If I'd only kept my wits about me that time I saw you in Glasgow . . .'

'We'd all like to turn the clock back, but it can't be done,' Jennet said.

'Where's Allan?' Jamie asked a few minutes later when he found his mother alone in the yard.

'He had to go away,' she said, and Jamie's face fell.

'Wanted him to hear me. When's he coming back?'

'I don't know, son,' Jennet said.

It was only later that she recalled Allan's words: 'If I'd only kept my wits about me that time I saw you in Glasgow.'

At least he had not wished Jamie's life away.

'I'd keep an eye on that wee heifer if I was you,' Jem said before he left that night. 'She's shiftin' about an awful lot. I'm thinkin' that she's about ready tae drop her calf.'

'I'll move her into the wee shed and keep an eye on her during the night,' Angus said, and the old man nodded.

'Call Bert if ye need help. He's got good strong arms.'

Jennet offered to take her turn at looking in on the heifer during the night, but Angus would have none of it. 'No point in both of us having broken sleep and you'd the worst of the potato planting. I was on the cart, just. I'll call you if I need you.'

After her day in the potato field Jennet's back was aching and her blistered hands stung. She was glad to crawl, rather than tumble, into her bed, and as soon as her head touched the pillow she was asleep. It seemed only minutes before the harsh jangle of the alarm clock jerked her awake.

When she looked into Angus's room on her way to the kitchen she saw that it was empty, the bedclothes thrown back. In the kitchen the quilt from his bed had been tossed onto the big wingback chair, indicating that he had dozed there between visits to the cowshed. The fire had been kept going, and the kettle was steaming on the range.

Jennet, stiff from the previous day's work, started the porridge going, then took two mugs of hot strong tea to the shed, determined to take over and send her brother back to the warm kitchen for something to eat before the milking.

As she stepped into the shed she met Angus on his way out, his face strained and shadowed by lack of sleep. 'Jennet, go and fetch Bert.'

'Is the calf coming?'

'No . . . that's the trouble.' Behind him, she could hear the heifer's harsh, uneven breathing. She put the tea down on the window ledge.

'Can I not help?'

'Mebbe, but I need Bert too, so just go and get him!'

She was halfway to the cottage when the young farmhand burst out through the door, his shirt half buttoned and twisted about the shoulders as though it had been thrown on in a hurry.

'Jennet, thank God you're here. It's Helen, I think she's started . . .'

'So's one of the heifers. Angus needs you in the shed.'

'But Helen . . .' he began.

'You see to the heifer and I'll see to your wife. Go on now!' She grabbed him by the arm and almost threw him towards the shed before running to the cottage where Helen was stooped over the small sink, one hand clenched on the single cold-water tap and the other fisted and rammed into the small of her back. The tap had been turned on full force, soaking Helen and the surrounding area.

'I'll . . . be all. . . right . . .' she gasped when Jennet put an arm about her. 'Just leave . . . me be for a while and . . .'

'And you'll drown or die of pneumonia. Let go now.' After a struggle Jennet managed to prise the girl's fierce grip from the tap and turn it off. 'The front of your gown's sodden. You'll need a fresh dry one.'

'Upstairs.' The pain was beginning to ease and Helen transferred her grip to the edge of the sink. 'In the top drawer in the bedroom. I'll just sit here for a minute.'

'You'll not; you'll come upstairs with me if you don't want your bairn birthed on the floor or the table. Come on now . . .'

Step by step Jennet coaxed Bert's wife up the narrow staircase. A fresh bout of pain struck Helen when they were half a dozen steps from the top, and Jennet had a difficult time unclasping Helen's grip from her arm and guiding the girl's hands to the wooden rail screwed to the wall. Once that was done she herself was able to move down a step or two in the hope that, if Helen lost her balance and fell, she would be able to prevent her from tumbling all the way back to the kitchen.

Eventually she got the young woman to the bedroom and latched her clawed fingers to the iron bedstead while she scrabbled in the drawer, disturbing the neatly folded clothing, and found another nightdress. Then she eased the soaked gown away from the girl's body, which was so thin that it was child-like apart from the huge swollen belly, slipping it over her head and replacing it with the dry one.

'There, that's much better. Now, onto the bed with you.'

Helen resisted. 'The quilt . . . take the quilt off.'

'It's nice and soft, you can lie on top of it,' Jennet coaxed, but the girl shook her head.

'It was a wedding gift from the mistress.'

'Mrs Blaikie?'

'Aye. I'll not have it soiled.' She was so insistent that Jennet was forced to remove the quilt and place it, folded, in the small wardrobe. Only then would Helen consent to lie on the bed.

'Catch hold of the bedstead if you need to, I'll be back in a minute.' Jennet skimmed downstairs, her aching back and blistered hands forgotten, and out into the yard in time to see Norrie disappearing into the shed. She rushed in after him.

'I need Norrie.'

'Norrie?' Bert asked, shocked. 'Is Helen . . .'

'She's having the baby and I need Norrie to go for the nurse. You can use my bicycle,' she added to the lad. 'How's the heifer?'

'Not so good,' Angus threw the words over his shoulder. 'On your way to the nurse's house, Norrie, stop off and ask Jem to come in and lend us a hand.'

'Tell Jem on your way back,' Jennet put in. 'Attend to the nurse first. Then when you get back here you can start getting the cows ready for milking. I'll come and help you as soon as I can.'

Back at the cottage she filled the kettle and a pot and put them onto the small range, then stoked up the fire before splashing some water into a large baking bowl and snatching a clean dish towel from the clotheshorse. In the bedroom Helen lay writhing and moaning on the bed.

Thank goodness Jamie was in Rothesay, Jennet thought as she dampened the towel and wiped the girl's face and hands. Nesta was due to bring him back that morning; perhaps she could be persuaded to stay on for a day or two, since Helen would not be fit for work. She dried Helen's face, brushed out her long dark hair, tied it back loosely, and tried to make her comfortable on the two pillows. Then she found some clean towels and laid them beneath the girl's hips.

'There now, is that better?'

'Yes, thank you.' Helen's voice was weak and flat; now she lay on the bed like a rag doll and, when another wave of pain caught her, she jerked and twitched so severely that Jennet was hard put to keep her on the bed. Once it was over Helen went limp again and Jennet stood looking down at her, concerned. She had only a hazy recollection of Jamie's birth now . . . Nesta, who had helped to deliver him, had told her that it was Nature's way to wipe such memories from women's minds, because if they remembered every detail of childbirth they would probably refuse to go through it again. Even so Jennet was sure that she had had to struggle to push him into the world. Helen showed no sign of doing that.

She wished with all her heart that Nesta would come soon, or that the nurse would arrive, for she was beginning to feel that she badly needed help and advice. When brisk footsteps clattered up the wooden stairs she hurried to the door, almost in tears of relief. But it wasn't the nurse or even Nesta. It was Lizbeth Blaikie.

'The lad met Andra on the road, and Andra fetched me. We both came over. He's with Angus in the cowshed,' she said shortly. 'I thought you'd need help.'

'I do, Mrs Blaikie!' Jennet could have kissed the woman.

'Well now, Helen, yer time's come, has it?' Lizbeth moved past her to stand by the bed. 'How are ye?'

'I made her put the quilt aside, Mrs Blaikie,' Helen said feebly, and Lizbeth turned to raise an eyebrow at Jennet, who shrugged and shook her head helplessly.

'I think a wee cup of tea would be a good idea for

all three of us,' Lizbeth said. 'First bairns usually take their time. Would you mind making it, Jennet?'

While Jennet was dealing with the tea, Norrie arrived at the door, breathless, to announce that the nurse was off delivering someone else's baby, but word had been sent and she would be there as soon as she could.

'What about the heifer?'

'I think the master's right worried, and Mr Blaikie too,' the lad said, and Jennet's heart sank. She and Angus could ill afford to lose an animal from their herd, or the money that the calf would bring when it went to the auction rooms. She sent Norrie back to the shed with tea for the men and instructed him to tell Bert that his wife was doing fine.

By the time the tea was half drunk Helen's contractions had become stronger and more frequent. They had tied a sheet to the bedstead, and she was pulling at it so hard that the entire bed frame creaked.

'She should be further on than she is,' Lizbeth said to Jennet in a low voice when one of the bouts of pain had eased. 'She's not workin' hard enough. I'll be glad when . . .'

'Bert . . .' Helen moaned

Jennet bent over her. 'He's helping Angus. D'you want me to fetch him?'

'No!' Helen said fiercely. 'Don't let him come in. Don't let him see me like this, it'll frighten him.'

'It didnae frighten him tae get ye intae this pickle, did it?' Mrs Blaikie said grimly. 'I sometimes think men should see the results of their labours . . . Not that I'd ever want one of them at a birth, gettin' in the way.'

'Tell him I'm sorry to have been . . . a nuisance,' Helen said.

'Ye can tell him yourself, lassie, when your bairn's here,' her former mistress advised her.

'Will it be all right . . . the bairn?'

'Of course it will.'

'Then I'll not be here.' The other two women looked at each other, puzzled.

'Of course you will, Helen,' Jennet said gently, taking one of the girl's hands in hers.

'No, it doesnae work like that! My mother died givin' life tae me,' Helen whispered, 'and I always knew that I'd die givin' life tae my own bairn.'

'That's nonsense, lassie,' Lizbeth told her firmly.

'Beggin' your pardon, Mistress Blaikie, it's not. A life for a life. One comes and one goes.'

'If that was true, we'd all only have one bairn and they'd be motherless.'

'It's true for me. My mother . . .' Helen said, and closed her eyes.

Two contractions later she was exhausted, and the birth was no further on. Her helpers retired to the window to watch in vain for the nurse and to confer in low voices.

'It's as if she's made up her mind,' Lizbeth said. She had tried coaxing and hectoring, but neither had helped.

'Mebbe I should fetch Bert.'

'Only if we have tae. He'll just get intae a state and make things worse for us all. Anyway, he'll be covered with muck from the cowshed. Even if she changed her mind, he'd be carryin' enough dirt tae kill her and the bairn both. If she'd just work along with the pain,' Lizbeth said, 'instead of lyin' there like a useless lump, the bairn'd be here by . . .' She stopped and hurried back to the bed as Helen's sudden sharp cry signalled the onset of another contraction.

Ten minutes later, with the child no nearer being born and still no sign of the midwife, Jennet decided that it was time for a different approach.

'Helen,' she said clearly from the foot of the bed, 'you're having a baby and you're perfectly healthy. It's time you got on with it, because you're not going to die.'

'I am.' Helen's voice was just a whisper. 'I know it.'

'How d'you know it?'

Helen's fingers plucked at the sheet, now more like a rope than a stretch of linen. 'I told ye,' she said irritably. 'I'm just like my mother, and she died.'

'Who told you that?'

'My auntie that put me intae the orphanage.'

'Did she have any bairns?'

'No, she wouldn't take a man because she didnae want tae die in childbirth like my mother.'

Jennet and Lizbeth looked at each other, appalled at the stupidity of the woman who had terrorised the young Helen with her nonsense. Then Jennet said, 'Never mind your auntie, just listen to what I'm telling you. You're not going to die . . .'

'I . . .'

'No, you're not, because if you do die I'll put Bert out of this cottage. I will,' Jennet said steadily as the girl's eyes flew open. 'I'll put him and the bairn out the minute your funeral's over.'

Helen found the strength to raise herself on her elbows, her eyes frantic. 'Ye cannae . . .'

'I can, for it's my cottage. Bert's no use to us without a wife, and I'm far too busy to look after a newborn as well as my Jamie. They'll have to go, Helen, both of them. They can live in Skeoch Woods, for all I care. And it'll be your fault, not mine.'

'No!' Helen wailed, then as a fresh pain gripped her she fell back, the wail rising to a scream. Lizbeth moved forward.

'Come on now, lass, let's get this bairn out into the fresh air. A big push . . . now!' And as Helen bunched her fists and pushed until colour flooded her pinched white face, the older woman winked at Jennet. 'Well done,' she said to both of them. 'Now then . . .'

Five minutes later she spun round and handed a limp, blood-streaked little bundle to Jennet. 'Clear its mouth and get it breathin',' she said tersely before turning back to the bed. Panic-stricken lest she drop the little thing, Jennet scurried with it to the chest of drawers where she had laid out a folded sheet and a towel in readiness. Laying the baby down, she managed to get a finger into the tiny mouth and clear it of mucus, then she lifted its feet in one hand and smacked its buttocks once, twice, three times without success.

'Mrs Blaikie,' she whispered in a panic, 'it's not . . .' She smacked again, then a fifth time.

'Take it downstairs quickly. A basin of cold water and a basin of hot. Dip it . . . aahh!' Lizbeth said as a thin wail filled the room. 'D'ye hear that, Helen?' she asked her patient. 'That's yer wee . . . er . . .'

'Boy. It's a boy!' Jennet carolled joyfully.

'Yer wee laddie. Wrap him up warm and put him in the cradle, Jennet, then come and help me. There's an awful lot of blood,' the woman whispered when Jennet moved to the bed after settling the baby in the cradle she had loaned to Helen and Bert. 'I'm thinkin' that she left it too late tae start gettin' the wee one out.'

'No!' Jennet looked at Helen's face, waxy against the pillow beneath her head, her sunken eyes closed and her mouth a thin grey line. She looked more like a corpse than a living being. A chill ran down Jennet's spine. Mebbe the girl had been right after all. If she died, the last words she heard would have been Jennet's, threatening to throw Bert and their new motherless baby out of the home that Helen had so carefully prepared for them. And she would have to carry that memory with her for the rest of her life.

Tears were flooding her eyes as the door knocker rattled downstairs and a voice called, 'Yoo-hoo!' The nurse had finally arrived.

* * *

'In the nick of time,' Jennet said an hour later. 'I'll never be able to thank you!'

'Och, I don't know about that, lassie. You and Mrs Blaikie were managin' and I doubt if you'd have killed her, though she's had a bad time. It'll take a good week before she's on her feet again,' the nurse said. 'There's not much of her, and it's a fine big baby.'

'She can have as long as she likes.' Bert was upstairs with his family, having taken a minute to tell Jennet that the heifer had produced a bullock and they had both survived. Lizbeth had bustled along to the farm kitchen to feed the men.

By the time Helen was settled and the nurse was on her way, leaving Jennet free to return to her own kitchen, her knees felt so weak that she had to walk close to the wall for support. Everyone had eaten and left, and Angus was there on his own, washing the dishes.

'We kept some dinner for you,' he said over his shoulder.

'There's Bert and Helen, too.'

'I know, there's enough for them as well. The Blaikies had to get back to Gleniffer. It was a bit of a worry, but it all worked out. A nice wee bullock, Jennet.'

'A nice wee McCabe, too.' She lowered herself carefully onto a chair.

'It's a good thing we got the potatoes in yesterday. If we'd decided on today for it we'd have been in a right pickle.'

'Mum! Angus!' Jamie carolled from halfway across the yard.

'Is that the time already?' Jennet looked at the clock just as her son burst in through the door, hurling himself at her and immediately starting a long story about all the things he had seen and done in Rothesay. Over his head, Jennet saw Mollie standing in the doorway.

'I thought Aunt Nesta was bringing him back.'

'She wasnae feeling too well, so I said I'd do it.' Mollie hovered, as though unsure of her welcome. Her gaze moved from Jennet to Angus. 'I'll get the next bus back,' she said while Jamie left Jennet and ran to throw his arms about Angus's knees.

'No, wait. Can you stay for a day or two, mebbe a week? Helen's just had her bairn and she's not well, and it's so good to see you here, Mollie!' Jennet got up and put her arms about her best friend, her skin sister.

'Of course I'll stay,' Mollie said. Then, looking at Angus over Jennet's shoulder, 'If it's all right.'

He put a hand on Jamie's curly head, his eyes drinking in the sight of Mollie, her hair blown about and her cheeks and nose wind-reddened.

'Stay,' he said.

27

Although her baby thrived, Helen McCabe had lost a lot of blood, and it was indeed a week before she was strong enough to leave her bed. Mollie was indispensable and appeared to possess the ability to tend to Helen and her baby, Thomas, see to the cooking and cleaning, keep Jamie happy and care for the hens at one and the same time.

She was surprised to find that Lizbeth Blaikie had begun to come to the farm more regularly and was even prepared, when she visited, to roll up her sleeves and get on with some work.

'Who waved a magic wand over her?' Mollie wanted to know.

'Helen would have died if she hadn't been there when the baby came. And I've been taking Jamie over to Gleniffer now and again because, when all's said and done, the Blaikies are his grandparents. Not that he knows that, of course.'

'What about Allan and Struan?'

'We don't see much of them, thank goodness. And I don't let Mrs Blaikie take any liberties where Jamie's concerned,' Jennet added. 'He's my bairn and she has to be kept in mind of that.'

'Don't worry,' Mollie assured her. 'I'll keep her in mind all right.'

She had given up her job in order to help out at the farm, assuring Jennet and Angus that she would be able to find work again when she needed it. 'Specially once the holiday season comes in again.'

Angus's suggestion that she should be paid for her time at Westervoe was immediately turned down. 'I'd not think of taking a penny, so don't offend me by offering again. I'll be happy with my food and somewhere tae sleep. And mebbe a kind word now and again,' she added, giving Angus a sideways look.

He said nothing, much to Jennet's relief. She was anxious to keep Mollie at Westervoe for as long as she could, and she had been afraid that Angus would make it difficult; but he seemed content to get on with his own work and leave Mollie alone.

As the better weather came in there was plenty of outside work for Jennet to attend to. The second pregnant heifer dropped her calf early one morning, calmly and easily, needing no help, which meant that there were two new calves to care for. Arks had to be cleaned out and shifted to another field so that the hens had fresh grass to scratch on, and the pigsty prepared for its new occupants.

'Another Jack and Jill,' Jennet said as she, Mollie

and Angus finished work on the sty.

'Not again,' her brother protested. 'What about Hansel and Gretel for a change, or Buster and Keaton?'

'Or Rumpelstiltskin and Ermintrude,' Mollie said. 'It's only Jack and Jill because Jamie can say those names. It'll be nice to see the baby pigs settled in here.'

'In their own way they're every bit as lovely as wee Thomas McCabe, or the calves,' Jennet agreed. 'It's a shame to think that . . .'

'Don't,' Mollie turned from the sty, eyes closed and hands clapped to her ears. 'I can't bear to think about it.'

'It's what farming's all about,' Angus pointed out. 'We raise them, feed them, keep them happy, then they repay us. They might have short lives, but they're contented lives.'

'I suppose so. And it's a long time till Nov . . . Who's this?' Mollie said as they walked back towards the yard. A man was coming down the lane to the farm.

'A tink?' Jennet guessed. His clothes were odd; a long loose coat, trousers that flapped about his legs, a floppy hat clapped on top of his head. A sack, or possibly a bag, was slung over one shoulder. 'We've got soup to spare, haven't we?'

'And new-made bread and cheese and pickles,' Mollie agreed. No traveller was ever turned away without a parcel of food.

They met the man at the entrance to the yard. 'Afternoon.' He took his hat off and wiped an arm across his forehead. His grey hair was long enough to be unfashionable, and when he bent to put down his bag Jennet saw that there was a perfect ring of shiny hairless skin right in the centre of his skull, like a monk's tonsure. 'Mild, I thought when I was on the ferry, but when you've been walking for a while it's downright warm.'

'There's tea,' Mollie offered. 'Or lemonade if you'd prefer.'

Instead of answering, the man took a long moment to study her with interest. His skin was weather-beaten and his grey eyes were surrounded by a mass of fine wrinkles, as though he had spent a lot of his time screwing them up against a bright light.

'No,' he said at last, pointing a sturdy index finger at her, 'I can't place you. You're not . . .' Then, as his gaze moved to Jennet he gave a smile of pure pleasure. 'It's you, isn't it? You're Jennet.'

'Yes,' she said cautiously.

'I knew by the hair,' he said, then turned to Angus, his eyes widening as they took in the crutch and then moved up to Angus's face.

'You're . . .' He paused, one eye almost closing as he concentrated.

'I'm Angus,' Jennet heard her brother say, his voice suddenly cool. 'And you're my father. You're James Scott.'

* * *

It was an awkward reunion. Tactfully Mollie took herself off to the cottage where Helen was looking after Jamie, and Angus left almost immediately after that, pleading urgent farm work.

James pushed his plate away and got up from his seat at the table to watch Angus cross the yard. 'He's not pleased to see me back.'

'He'll be fine. He doesn't find it easy to talk to strangers.'

'Did he get hurt in the war?' James asked. Then, when Jennet gave a brief explanation, 'Worse for him than being wounded in the fighting, eh? And what of Martin?'

'He did go to war, and he survived; but afterwards he decided to go to England. He's working on a farm there, we hear from him now and again.'

'I must write to him, or mebbe visit before I go home. Mebbe,' James said, 'he'll understand why I left, since he's done the same thing himself and no doubt for the same reason.'

'You'll have to visit Grandmother, too,' she reminded him. On coming into the farmyard he had hesitated, surveying the house doubtfully, and had asked, 'My . . . your grandmother . . . ?' On being told that Celia had moved to Largs, the tension had suddenly left his thin shoulders. Now a shadow passed over his face.

'Has she changed?'

'You're still afraid of her, aren't you?'

'D'you blame me?' he asked and then when she

shook her head, 'What has she said about me?'

'She feels that you deserted her. So did your father, and Martin.'

'My father had the best excuse of the three of us, for he died young, poor soul. You, Angus and Martin must have grown up hating me for walking away from you the way I did.'

'Mebbe, at times; but we got over it. We've managed to build our own lives. Where's home?' she asked casually, pouring out more tea.

'France, in the Loire valley.'

'You've been there all this time?'

'Just for the past few years. I was everywhere before then, but I think I'm finally settled now.'

'In France, you mean?'

He smiled at her. 'Aye, in France. I've no intention of moving back here . . . For one thing, you and your brothers have made your own lives, and for another, I'd not have the right, after what I've done to you.'

So he wasn't back for good. Jennet felt relieved to hear it; having fought hard to give Angus his proper place, she would not have welcomed the idea of their father being the new tenant.

He had taken his tea back to the window. 'It's not changed at all, it's just as I mind it.'

'Shabbier, mebbe. We've not had the time or the manpower to look after it properly.'

'Who's that?'

Jennet joined him, and saw Jamie circling the yard on his tricycle. 'That's my son. You might as well be told now as find out later from one of the gossips,' Jennet went on steadily, 'that Allan Blaikie's his father, but I'm not married to him.'

'Allan Blaikie of Gleniffer? Andra's lad?'

'That's right.'

His eyes narrowed. "It's not like one of the Blaikies to let a lassie down like that. Is he married to someone else? Is that the way of it?'

'No, he's not. It's just the way things are, and there's no bad feeling between us.'

'So I don't have to go and knock young Allan's head off because he's betrayed my only daughter?'

'No, you don't.' Jennet crossed to the open door. 'Jamie, come here a minute.'

'Jamie . . . ?' her father said wonderingly. She turned to see that his grey eyes had suddenly taken on the pearly glow that the waters of the Sound reflected on a soft sunless day. It was as though they had been lit up from within. 'You named him for me? I don't deserve that,' he said when she nodded, 'but I thank you for it, lassie. And I'm doubly glad now that I came back to seek you out.'

Then Jamie was in the room, making straight for the protection of her legs when he realised there was a stranger there.

'Jamie, this is your grandfather, come to visit us. Say how d'you do.'

She nudged him forward and as he held out his hand obediently James took it in his brown clasp, very gently, as though afraid that his blunt fingers might crush the small hand. 'I'm very pleased to meet you at last, Jamie,' he said huskily.

'I suppose I'd best see the Blaikies,' he mused when Jamie had gone back to his tricycle. 'And are the Logans still in Rothesay?'

'They're still there and still hiring out boats. They lost Geordie, though. His ship was torpedoed.'

'I must visit George and Ann. They were good folk.'

'They still are.'

'Gold never tarnishes,' James said. Then, collecting his mug and the plate he had eaten from, he took them to the sink. 'I'm not here to make more work for you, and I'm sure you've got more important things to do. Don't let me hold you back from them.'

'Would you mind keeping an eye on Jamie for me? I'll not be far away if you need me.'

'Mebbe they'll want to put him into the cottage,' Helen said anxiously when Mollie told her about the newcomer.

'I doubt that. You and your Bert are worth more to them than a father they've not seen for years and years. Is it just Scotsmen that aren't always very good at being fathers?' Mollie wondered thoughtfully, hanging the last of Bert's shirts on the clotheshorse to air and putting the iron onto its rest to cool, 'or does it happen in other countries, too? There's your father that you never knew, and mine that me and Mam and the rest of us would have been better not knowin', and Jennet and Angus's father goin' away when they were little, and even wee Jamie's father denyin' him just when Jennet needed him most.'

'My Bert's not like that.' Helen looked down at the sleepy, milk-sated baby in her arms and stroked his cheek with the tip of a forefinger. 'Thomas has the best father in the world, haven't you, my wee bird?' she cooed to the baby.

'Which proves that some Scotsmen can be good fathers. The thing is,' Mollie said thoughtfully, 'you have to make sure you pick the right man. Give me a shot.' She took the warm little bundle from Helen and cradled him in one arm, gazing down at his tiny face. 'Isn't he perfect? Every wee fingernail and toenail and his wee nose and everythin'. It's a right miracle, isn't it?'

'Aye,' Helen agreed, smiling at her sister-in-law over the baby's head. 'It's the best thing that ever happened tae me, apart from meetin' Bert. It'll be your turn one day.'

'I doubt that,' Mollie said.

'It will. Why wouldn't it?'

'I'll put him in his crib, will I? Then I'll get out of the road so's you can have a wee lie down before he wakens up and starts yelling for more food.'

'I'm feeling much stronger.' Helen folded the blanket that had turned the table into an ironing board. 'I'll soon be able to start looking after the farmhouse and Jamie again.'

'Are you sure? You don't want tae tire yourself out too soon and make yourself ill again.'

'I'm fine. I took longer than most to get over his birth, but the nurse is pleased with both of us and I'm all right now.'

'Helen pet, listen . . . I'd count it as a favour,' Mollie said carefully, 'if you'd just take your time over gettin' back to work. There's no hurry at all and ye might as well enjoy bein' on your own with the wee one while ye can. I'm not in any hurry.'

She spaced the last four words out carefully, and Helen, who had been staring blankly, suddenly smiled. 'You mean you want to stay here longer,' she said, and just as Mollie started to nod, she added, 'near Angus Scott.'

'Angus? Why would I . . . how do you know?'

Helen gave her a long, slow, almost sensual smile. 'When ye love someone as much as I love your Bert,' she said without a trace of self-consciousness, 'ye see more than ye ever did before.'

'So he's not going to stay for ever, only for a month or two at the most,' Jennet reported to Angus that afternoon. 'He lives in France now and that's where he wants to be.'

'That's something, I suppose.'

'At least we'll get to know him properly while he's with us.'

'It's too late for that, Jen. We're adults now, not bairns; we don't need him any more.'

'I do. Now I'll be able to say that I know what my father looks like and where he is. And there's

Jamie . . . Now he has his own grandfather.'

'And what good will that do him? Fetch Mollie, will you?' Angus put an end to the conversation. 'It's time to put the cows back to pasture and we might as well do it now as tomorrow. We could do with her help.'

James Scott was sitting on the bench outside the kitchen door, sketching on a large pad balanced on his knees. The tricycle had been deserted and Jamie was leaning heavily against his new grandfather's shoulder, his curly brown head close to the man's tumbled grey hair and his tongue sticking out from between his teeth as he concentrated on following the swift crayon strokes.

'Go and fetch Mollie, Jamie. Tell her we're taking the cows out.'

'I'll help.' James put the sketchpad aside and got to his feet.

'You don't have to.'

'Lassie,' he said with a grin, 'this is a farm. Everyone helps.'

Acclimatised to being indoors, the herd emerged timidly from the cowshed at first, but as they smelled the fresh spring air the animals became excited, jostling each other in their hurry to get along the lane to their allotted field. Once the gate was opened they rushed through, galloping about the grass like teenagers instead of respectable matrons.

'It's all right for them,' Mollie said as Angus closed and latched the gate. 'They don't have to clean out the shed after a winter's occupation. Sometimes animals can be more trouble than the holiday folk at Mrs Logan's house.'

In the lane, James was drinking in the view over the river. 'The Sound of Bute,' he said softly. 'I've kept that picture in my mind for all these years and it's still true. The Clyde never changes. It's still one of the most perfect places on earth.'

'Yet you were happy enough to leave it,' Angus reminded him coldly.

'I'd not say that I was happy to go. I felt I had to leave because I lost your mother and everywhere I turned I was reminded of my loss. This is a beautiful island, but the thing about it is, it's small. Throw a stone on Bute and you're bound to hit someone,' James said, then turned to lean his folded arms on the gate and watch the excited animals.

'Freedom. There's nothing like it.'

'Some of us,' Angus continued relentlessly, 'never find out about that.'

'But you already have, lad. Mebbe you don't know it yet, but this is your freedom, here at Westervoe. You and your sister have done a grand job with the place so far, and you've all the time in the world. You'll do even better.'

Angus turned with a muffled snort of disbelief and started to limp back along the lane.

'Anger,' James said as he and Jennet followed along behind, 'is like pus in a wound. When it's finally drained out of him he'll be able to see the truth of what I'm saying. Then he'll know that everything he wants and needs is here, right under his nose.'

In the kitchen that night Jennet stared at the skilfully executed crayon sketch of Jamie, head down and face half hidden, cycling in the yard. Although the drawing was rough there was no mistaking the identity of the child, or the background details. The sweeping lines even managed to convey the movement of little boy's legs and the tricycle wheels.

'That's just like him!'

'I'd a good subject,' her father said, smiling.

Mollie reached for the pad, studying it in the lamp-light. 'You could make a living doing that.'

'I do . . . well, not much of a living,' James admitted. 'We manage though, between selling the occasional picture and growing vegetables, and keeping chickens and ducks and a pig and a goat. What we can't use ourselves is bartered for the other things we need.'

Angus had not taken any part in the conversation, but now he raised his head from his newspaper to ask, 'We?'

'I haven't told you yet about Anna, my wife.'

'You're married?' Surprise put a squeak into Jennet's voice.

'A year or two now. She's Yugoslavian. We met when I was there during the war.'

'Yugoslavia was occupied during the war,' Angus said, and his father nodded.

'And a lot of the people took to the countryside, living in the hills and in caves. Wonderful people!' he said warmly, taking the sketchpad back from Mollie and turning the pages until he found the one he was looking for. 'This is Anna.'

Mollie went to stand behind Jennet so that they could study the portrait together. Anna, sitting by an open door with a basin of potatoes in her ample lap and a knife in one hand, had dark hair tucked beneath a triangular kerchief. Her round face was calm but her eyes, looking directly out of the picture, danced with amusement and the corners of her full mouth seemed to tremble, as though she was just waiting for the crayon to be laid down before breaking into a full-bellied laugh. This time, the strong sweeping curves indicated warmth and serenity.

'She didn't come to Scotland with you?' Jennet carried the sketch over to Angus.

'Anna's had her full share of wandering. It was her decision that I should come back here to see what was happening to you all.'

'Her decision?' Angus pushed the pad back at his sister after giving it a swift glance. 'You're still taking orders from women, then?'

'Anna and I usually decide things between us, the way it should be between a man and a woman,' James said calmly. 'But yes, she was the one who persuaded me to come here. My own feeling was that it was too late.'

'That's my feeling, too,' Angus told him, and

Mollie, after a swift glance at his closed face, got up and moved towards the inner door.

'I'm off to my bed. You need tae be free tae speak about family business.'

'No, please stay,' James said. 'I'm sure that there's nothing any of us would want to keep from you. After all, you belong here.'

'I don't, I'm just here tae help Jennet . . .'

'Mebbe so, but it's clear to me at any rate that this is where you belong,' the older man said gently, and after a moment's hesitation Mollie sat down at the table.

'So you came to find out what had happened to us,' Angus said from the fireside chair. 'Well now, Father . . .' he said the word harshly, as if it were an insult, 'the story's easy told. Jennet had a fatherless bairn and you werenae here to make things right for her and see to it that the man responsible married her. I couldnae do it at the time for I was still a pitiful invalid after the train crash that chewed up my leg. You werenae here for that either, were you? Just as you werenae here to persuade our Martin to come home after the war . . .'

'Angus!'

'I don't see why we should make a big fuss of the man, Jennet. We might have killed the fatted calf if he'd come back sooner, when he was needed, but not now. As he said himself, it's too late!' Angus snatched up his crutch and made his way to the door.

'He's right,' James said when his son had stormed

out. 'And mebbe that's part of my reason for coming back. He needs to get rid of that anger and, since I caused most of it, it's best that he vents it on me and not on either of you.' He smiled at both girls. 'I think Anna was right after all. It was time for me to come back. But for now it's probably time you two were in your beds.'

'I'm afraid that you'll have to have Grandmother's old room,' Jennet said; then, seeing the sudden apprehension in his eyes, 'All her possessions have gone to Largs, and Mollie put the place to rights and made the bed up with fresh linen this afternoon.'

'At least there's no danger of her haunting the place since she's still alive,' James said, getting to his feet. 'I'll manage fine in that room.'

'It'll be better than a cave in Yugoslavia,' Mollie said, and he looked at her in surprise and then grinned.

'You're right there, lassie,' he replied.

28

'She . . . Anna isn't in the least like our mother,' Jennet said to James the next morning. He had slept late and Mollie had taken on her outside duties so that Jennet was free to talk to him when he finally came downstairs. She had asked him if she could look through the pad and he had brought it down to the kitchen, then got on with the food she put before him while she turned the pages one by one.

'No. There was only one Rose,' he said now, his face soft with sudden memories. 'D'you mind her at all? You were only wee when she . . . when we lost her.'

'Aunt Ann has a picture of the two of them in her front parlour. I look at it every time I visit. And I have a drawing of her,' Jennet said, 'a sketch, like these. You must have done it.'

'You've got one of my pictures?'

'There's a pad with several in it, in my bedroom. I'll fetch it.'

When she brought it downstairs he pushed the crockery to one side and laid it on the table, going over each page intently.

'Here's Rose.' With the tip of a finger he traced the young face, the mass of curly hair, so like Jennet's, the smiling mouth and slim neck. Jennet couldn't see his downbent face, but the love and longing in his touch were clear to see.

'I wanted to take this with me when I went away,' he said at last. He glanced up at her and she saw that his eyes were damp. 'But I couldn't find it. I thought my mother had burned it, the way she burned all the other drawings I made when I was growing up. She thought it was a terrible waste of time, farming folk drawing pictures.' He leafed through the pad with its sketches of the farm, and of children . . . Martin and Angus playing in the yard, a baby that Jennet took to be herself sitting at the table, held firmly in her chair by a long scarf looped crosswise about her chest and tied to the chair back. Then he turned back to the portrait of his dead wife and asked, 'Where did you find it?'

'In Gran's room when I was packing her things.'

Astonishment jerked his head up. 'She kept it?'

'I should have put it in with the other things being sent to Largs,' Jennet confessed. 'But I wanted to keep it here, where it belonged. I kept waiting for her to ask for it, but she didn't.'

'She couldn't, because she'd not want to admit she'd kept it,' her father agreed. 'I can't believe she did. Mebbe there's hope for her yet.'

'Take the pad with you when you go.'

'No, it's yours . . . but I'll do a copy, though,' he said. Just then Jem burst in, beaming for once, to shake James by the hand, and the two of them went off together.

The first people to descend on Westervoe when word got out about James Scott's return were Lizbeth and Andra Blaikie. Lizbeth swept into the kitchen in her usual way and was completely confused when James gave her a hug and a smacking kiss on each cheek.

'What d'ye think you're at?' she squeaked, freeing herself and trying in a flustered way to smooth her hair.

'It's the way we do things in France.'

'Aye, well, it's not the way we do things on Bute, is it, Andra?'

'It might be a good idea, at times,' her husband said, grinning. 'How have you been, man?'

'Not too bad. And yourself, Andra?'

'Much the same.' To Jennet, it was as though they had been meeting every day for the past twenty years.

'I hear, Lizbeth, that you and me are grandparents to the wee lad playing out there. Who'd have thought it, eh?'

Lizbeth's flush deepened. 'James, it was as much a surprise to us as it was to you. I cannae tell you how ashamed we are of our Allan – is that not right, Andra? He got a tongue-lashing, I can tell you, and if he'd been ten years younger I'd have taken the belt to him for what he did!'

'If he'd been ten years younger he'd not have done it, Lizbeth,' her husband pointed out, while James chimed in with, 'I didn't mean that. I meant, who'd have thought that we'd share a grandchild. I was sorry to hear about your Drew, it's a terrible thing to lose a bairn, even when they're grown.'

'Struan's a great comfort,' Lizbeth said.

'I'm sure he is. I'll need to come over to see him . . . and Allan, too. I suppose I'd best have a word with him.'

'I told you, it's all been sorted . . .'

'Whist now, Jennet,' James said amiably, 'I'm still your father for all that I've been away for a while. It's my duty to speak to the young man.'

'It is that, and I hope you give him a right flea in the ear,' Allan's mother said warmly. 'Speaking of family duty, when are you going to Largs to see your mother?'

James tugged at his ear and shuffled his feet. 'I've written to her and said I'd go over next week.'

'Not till next week?'

'To give her time to get used to the idea of seeing me,' James explained feebly.

But Celia Scott was not minded to wait for a full week before confronting her wayward son. Washing the dishes after the midday meal the following day, Jennet glanced out of the window to see her grandmother and her great-aunt advancing across the yard. She gave a horrified yelp and James, who had been working on one of his sketches, this time one of her and Mollie and Jamie, jumped to his feet and hurried over to join her.

'Is it the wee chap? He's not hu . . . Oh God, it's her! I'd best get myself tidied up,' he panicked, but he had only got as far as the inner doorway before his mother, showing no signs of her earlier injury, marched into the kitchen.

'So it's true, then. There you are, James,' she snapped. Then, acknowledging her granddaughter with a brief nod, 'Tea, Jennet, we're both parched after that long journey.'

'Would you not like some dinner, Gran? We've all eaten, but there's . . .'

'Just tea, and mebbe a scone or some shortbread. And we'll be off when I've had a word with your father.' Celia sat down at the table, drawing her gloves off. 'Andra kindly brought us from the boat, and he's comin' to take us back to the pier later.' She looked at the pad, then pushed it aside. 'I see you're still scribbling!'

'Aye, I am. Did you not get my letter?' James asked as Jennet hurried to make tea and butter some scones. 'I was going to visit next week . . . Good afternoon, Aunt Rachel.'

'You surely didn't think I was going to wait until next week? I've been waiting for more years than I can remember for an explanation of your conduct,

James Scott, and I was certainly not of a mind to wait another week. How's the farm coming on, Jennet?'

'We're managing fine.'

'I see you got that big hen house you were always on about.'

Jennet put a plate of shortbread down on the table. 'It's worked out well.'

'Are the new potatoes in?'

'Yes.'

'They've done a grand job,' James put in. 'I'm proud of them both.'

His mother fixed him with an eye as sharp and almost as painful as a well-honed dagger. 'That's very nice for you, James,' she said. 'I just wish I could say the same about you.'

'That's not . . .' Jennet began hotly, but James put a restraining hand on her arm.

'It's all right, pet, I can speak up for myself. And I can see to the tea as well, so you go and look to those hens of yours.'

'And tell Angus I'll want to see him before I go,' Celia called after her as Jennet made her escape.

'I don't want to see her,' Angus grumbled when Jennet delivered the summons. 'Nor her sister.'

'You can't let her come all the way here, then go all the way back without seeing you!'

He had been grooming Nero, one of his favourite tasks. Now he put the currycomb down. 'Look, Jen, I'm tired of being told what I should do on my own farm.'

'Our own farm!'

'All right, ours. Only it seems to me that it's not ours any longer, the way folk treat it. Thanks to you we've got Mrs Blaikie in and out of the place these days, and then there's this father of ours, and now Gran's back with Great-Aunt Rachel in tow.'

'Only for a few hours, to see Father.'

'You see? Not to visit us and ask how we're doing, but to see him. The sooner the pack of them get out and leave us in peace, the better,' Angus said savagely, snatching the currycomb up again.

'I'll come and get you when they've had their talk,' Jennet snapped back at him. 'You can surely be pleasant to them for five minutes!'

When she had gone he closed his eyes and leaned his head against Nero's solid, warm flank and then jumped when Mollie said from the doorway, 'I should be gone by the end of the week.'

'What?'

'I was tending to the calves . . .' Because the light was behind her he couldn't make out her face, but as she jerked her head to indicate the calf shed through the wall he could see flashes of dark red as fronds of her hair lifted and then settled. 'I could hear every word you said and you're quite right. How can you see to the farm properly with all of us about? Helen's much stronger now; she'll be able to get back to her own duties in a day or two.'

'I didn't mean . . .'

'It's all right, Angus, I know it's been difficult for you. I'll explain to Jennet that I've had the offer of a job in Rothesay.'

'Wait.' He ran a trembling hand along Nero's side for comfort and support. His last chance had come, and he knew it. 'That day you brought Jamie home, when I said to you to stay, I didnae just mean for Jennet's sake,' he said in a rush of words. 'I said it for me, too, and now I'm sayin' it again.'

'I could be all coy and confused,' Mollie said with a catch in her voice, 'but if I did that, you'd probably take fright and say you meant somethin' different. Then we'd be back where we were before and I couldnae bear that. So I might as well come out and say it. Are you askin' me to marry you?'

'I suppose I . . .' he began and then as Nero turned and looked at him, 'Yes. Yes, I am.'

'Then say it.' Mollie ventured a few steps into the stable. 'It's only going to happen once in my life, so I want to be able to tell my grandchildren and it needs to sound right.'

'It's not the first time, surely? Joe Wilson told me at Christmas that he was going to propose to you.'

She stiffened. 'He did, did he? And why should he say that to the likes of you?'

'He wanted my advice . . . as an older man.'

'He's got a right cheek on him, that Joe Wilson. What did you tell him?'

'To go ahead and ask you.'

'That was a daft thing tae do, considerin' you wanted me for yourself.'

'I thought he'd be the better man for you.'

'I know best about who's best for me. And you know fine and well that I'd already made my choice, though you've been too stubborn to admit it.'

'Until now,' Angus said. 'Now I'm admitting it and it's taking all the courage I have. So hurry up and tell me once and for all: will you marry me, Mollie McCabe?'

She moved closer and put one hand on Nero's burnished coat, close to his, then considered him with her head to one side.

'For God's sake say something!'

'I should ask for time to think, or something like that. It would be . . . proper. But if I did, you might take fright again,' she said. 'Of course I'll marry you, ye daft fool of a man!'

'Poor Joe,' Angus said when he finally got the chance to speak again.

'Ach, he'll find someone else easy.' Mollie's voice was muffled against his chest. 'I'd never have married him anyway, even though I'd almost given up on you when he proposed. I'd as soon have been an old maid as married to him, or anyone else.'

'You don't need to be one now.'

'I know,' she said happily. 'I'm so pleased, because I don't think I'd have been very good at it.'

'Mollie . . .'

'Mmm?'

'I've arranged to go to hospital next week to see if they can make a special shoe. If it works, I'll be a lot more mobile.'

She drew his face down to hers and kissed him long and hard. 'Who cares whether it works or not, Angus Scott?' she said when the kiss ended. 'You're perfect just as you are!'

'That caused quite a stramash,' James said thoughtfully as they all watched Celia and her sister drive away in Andra Blaikie's car two hours later. 'I just wish you two had made your announcement earlier, then I'd not have had to face my mother's interrogation at all.'

'We'd have announced it earlier if I'd had my way,' Mollie told him. 'A good six months earlier.' She giggled. 'Your gran's face was a picture, Jennet. And so was yours, come to think of it.'

'You might have told me! I thought we always told each other things like that.'

'This was different, Angus being your own brother. Come on, Jamie . . .' she pounced on the little boy, sweeping him up into the air, 'let's go and help Uncle Angus finish making Nero look all nice and smart.'

'How did you get on with Grandmother?' Jennet asked her father as they walked back to the farmhouse.

'Difficult at the start, but I held on to the thought of Anna and that kept my courage going. D'you know, Jennet, it's easier talking to her as an adult than as her son. We came to a better understanding than we'd ever had before,' James said. Then with a swift change of subject, 'That lassie's going to be the best thing that ever happened to Angus.'

'When the two of them walked in together, Grandmother looked as if she was sucking on something nasty.'

'She'll come round to the idea. In any case, it's none of her business.'

'You didn't seem to be surprised when Angus told us they were to be married.'

'I could tell it from my first day here, by the way they looked at each other. Even the careful way they didn't look at each other,' James said thoughtfully. 'Love was almost hanging over Westervoe like a mist.'

'You should be a poet.'

'No,' James said, 'I have trouble enough just being an artist.'

He spent a week in Rothesay with the Logans and then came back to Westervoe for one night before going to England to see Martin.

'I'll mebbe look in on my mother before I set off. That way she'll not be able to say I ignored her. And that reminds me, Angus, I hope I can tell her you'll be inviting her to the wedding.'

'It's just going to be a quiet wee occasion,' Angus protested. 'All we want to do's get wed and get on with our lives.'

'Even so, your grandmother enjoys a good wedding party. It gives her a chance to dress up a bit.'

'Gran . . . dressing up?'

'Oh, I mind the way she used to dress for special occasions. You never know . . .'

'Make sure Angus asks your grandmother to his wedding,' James reminded Jennet as she and Jamie walked with him to the bus stop at the end of the lane. He had refused to let her go as far as the ferry because, he said, he hated goodbyes.

'I think Mollie'll see to that. You'll be back some time?'

'I don't think so. I've done what I came to do, and Angus's still finding it hard to forgive me, which is his right. His anger's easier carried on my shoulders than on his. At least you've forgiven me . . . and no doubt you've forgiven young Blaikie for any harm he did you as well.' He touched her cheek swiftly and gently. 'You're your mother's daughter, Jennet; when life was cruel to her she could always put the hurt behind her and look to the future. I wish I could have done that when she died.'

Her heart sank as she heard a familiar sound from further along the road. 'Here's the bus coming.'

James bent and scooped his grandson up, hugging him and giving him a kiss on the cheek, despite Jamie's protests. 'Be a good laddie now, and take care of your mother for me,' he said.

There was still so much to say, so many questions to ask, but the bus had come into sight and the final minutes were swiftly melting away to seconds.

'A word of warning, Jennet,' James said as he put the little boy down and picked up his old canvas bag. 'Don't bury yourself here just because you think Angus needs you. He can manage fine on his own now, with Mollie to keep his spirits up.'

'But I love Westervoe!'

He squinted at her through half-closed eyes in the way that he had. 'Even so, you still have to make sure that living here is what you want forthe rest of your life. Not what's best for Angus or even for Jamie, but what you want for yourself.' He held up a hand to stop the bus. 'We've only got one life and it's wrong to give it over to someone else entirely.'

'D'you not think,' Jennet asked evenly, 'that you've left it a bit late to give me fatherly advice?'

The bus ground to a halt. The people on board stared through the windows as James Scott took his daughter into his arms and kissed her on one cheek, then on the other.

'I have indeed,' he said into her ear, 'and you're quite right to slap my knuckles. But think on.'

Then he climbed onto the bus, and went out of her life for the second time.

29

Angus and Mollie managed to fit in their wedding after haymaking and before it was time to bring in the harvest. Jennet was Mollie's Maid of Honour, and to Angus's surprise, his grandmother and Great-Aunt Rachel accepted their invitation and arrived 'dressed to the nines', as Lizbeth Blaikie put it.

'Celia always did know how to put on style when the occasion demanded it,' she told Jennet approvingly.

'I never knew that.' Jennet found it hard to believe that the elegant old woman in a dark blue costume with the small-brimmed, feathered hat over hair set in soft grey waves was the same Gran who had stamped about the farm in wellington boots, a long raincoat and a man's hat.

'You never gave her the chance, did you? If you'd had a wedding of your own . . .' Lizbeth began and then, realising her mistake, she flushed and changed the subject, nodding at Mollie and Angus. 'They seem to be right pleased with each other.'

'And so they should be, for they're perfect together.'

In the two months between his engagement and his wedding Angus had been back and forth to the mainland, and soon he was going to receive a specially made boot, which would help him to move about more easily. As it was, he and Mollie and his single crutch had done a good job of taking a turn or two round the church-hall floor when the dancing started.

He was going to be all right now, Jennet thought thankfully as she watched the two of them together. Everything had come right for him and she herself was free to consider her own needs . . . hers and Jamie's.

Her father's parting words – 'We've only got one life and it's wrong to give it over to someone else entirely' – had echoed in her ear every single day since they were spoken. 'Not what's best for Angus or even for Jamie,' he had said, 'but what you want for yourself.'

He had made his peace with Martin and had returned to his wife and his vegetables, his animals and his art. He wrote regularly, illustrating his letters with tiny sketches in the margins to amuse Jamie and to bring his everyday world to life for his son and daughter.

'So, Jennet,' Lizbeth broke into her thoughts just then with uncanny timing, 'what does the future hold for you now that Angus's settled?'

And without stopping to think Jennet replied, 'I'm going to complete my nursing training.'

* * *

It was so much easier now that Mollie was at Westervoe for good, and more than willing to look after Jamie while Jennet was in Glasgow. Once the decision had been made, everything seemed to fall into place, and at the end of August Jennet left Bute for Glasgow.

Angus was too busy to leave the farm and Ann Logan and Nesta McCabe were rushed off their feet since it was holiday time again, but Mollie and Jamie went with her to the ferry.

'The good old *Duchess of Fife,* bless her,' Mollie said as they watched the steamer coming in. 'That's the boat we came over in all those years ago. Who'd have thought that a German bomb could be the best thing that ever happened to me? Now, mind and write every week, and I'll write to you every week . . .'

'You'll be too busy being a farmer's wife.'

'I'll stay up all night if I have to,' Mollie said self-righteously. 'I have to let you know how Jamie's coming along. And you'll be sure to come home every chance you get?'

'Of course I will.'

'Good. Then I'll be able to make you help with cleaning out the deep-litter house and the byre, the way you always made me do them.'

'And I'll whine and complain all the time, the way you always did.'

'That,' said Mollie, 'was before I was a married woman. It's different now.' She moved her hand slightly, as she often did these days, to let the light catch the plain gold band that Angus had put on her finger.

Jennet knelt to hug Jamie. 'Be a good boy and I'll be back soon,' she said huskily, but he only had eyes for the great bulk of the steamer as she was skilfully brought alongside the pier.

'He'll be fine,' Mollie assured her. 'Angus and me'll see to that. And you'll be home before . . .'

Her voice trailed away and she stared at a point above and behind Jennet, who released Jamie and turned to see Allan Blaikie, dressed in his best suit, among the folk waiting on the pier to greet new arrivals or take the ferry back to the mainland.

'Allan!' Jamie rushed to greet him, then towed him back to Jennet and Mollie.

'I'm off to see a customer in Largs,' Allan said when he reached them. 'Are you taking this ferry too, Jennet? I didn't realise that it was today you were leaving. Well . . .' he held his hand out. 'Good luck with your training course.'

'Thank you,' she said feebly.

'They're starting to board, Jennet, you'd best go,' Mollie advised.

'Yes.' Now that the time had come, Jennet was not sure that she was doing the right thing. 'Mollie . . .'

'It'll be fine,' her sister-in-law hugged her hard. 'And if it's not, there's always Westervoe to come home to.'

'Let me take this on board for you.' Allan picked

up Jennet's case as she knelt to kiss Jamie for the last time.

'Be a good boy and do what Mollie tells you. I'll be back soon,' she said, then turned swiftly and headed towards the ferry.

'Noooo!' she heard Jamie wail as she walked away, and her heart sank. This was what she had feared ever since deciding to return to Glasgow. Although he had had his third birthday, Jamie was still little more than a baby, and they had never been apart in his short life, other than for his two brief sojourns with the Logans.

'Jamie . . .' she turned back, knowing that she could not bear his misery and prepared to stay if necessary; but as he struggled in Mollie's arms it was not his mother Jamie was pointing at, but the paddle steamer behind her.

'Boat,' he was yelling. 'Want to go on the boat!'

'Not today,' Jennet heard Mollie try to soothe him. 'We'll all go on the boat another day. Go on,' she mouthed at Jennet, who hesitated while people hurried past her to board the steamer.

'Why don't you let him go over to Wemyss Bay with you?' Allan suggested. 'We'll see you onto the Glasgow train, then catch the ferry back and I'll deliver him to Westervoe safe and sound. I promise I won't kidnap him,' he added as she hesitated.

'I don't . . .'

'It's a good idea, and very kind of you,' Mollie thrust the little boy into Jennet's arms. 'It'll give you a wee while longer with him, Jennet, and it'll be a treat for him. What do you say, Jamie? Would you like to go on the boat with Mummy and wave to her when she goes on the train?'

'Want to go on the boat!' Jamie locked his arms about his mother's neck.

'Mollie . . .'

Her friend, sister-in-law and skin sister gave her a smug little smile and went on to Jamie, 'You can go on the boat twice if you come back home with Allan, like a good boy.'

Jamie nodded his head, and the battle was lost as far as Jennet was concerned.

'What are you doing?' she hissed at Mollie as they followed Allan to the gangway.

'Keeping Jamie happy. And I like Allan Blaikie; even though he treated you badly, I think he deserves a chance to make it up to you.'

'I don't want him to make it up to me!'

'He wants to, badly. And you're just like Angus. He never knew what he wanted either, till it was almost too late. So think on . . . and enjoy Glasgow,' Mollie added, giving Jennet a push towards the gangway.

As they watched Bute slide away Jamie waved frantically at Mollie. Then, as Jennet put him down, he turned in a slow circle, looking at the deck, the seats, the railings, the people and the ever-present seagulls keeping pace with the steamer as she ploughed her way through the water. He heaved a great sigh of pure pleasure.

'Isn't he grand?' Allan said in awe. 'Can I take him down to see the engines? That was always my special treat.' Then, as an afterthought, 'Come too, if you want.'

Jennet shook her head and they went off hand in hand, leaving her free to lean on the railing and watch Bute become smaller before it finally slid aft of the steamer.

Wemyss Bay Pier, with its handsome Victorian glass-roofed railway station, was appearing on the horizon by the time the two of them returned, Jamie almost incoherent with excitement.

'We'll go and see the engines again on the way home, after we've settled your mother on the train,' Allan promised. Then, to Jennet, 'That should help him to see you off without wanting to go with you.'

'I suppose that's part of having a son,' she said ruefully. 'Only three years old and already he's more interested in engines than he is in me.'

'That's the way it is.'

'What about your customer?' she asked as they went to sit on one of the benches, with Jamie standing up between them so that he could see everything. 'Will Jamie not get in the way?'

'What customer?' Allan asked, and then, remembering, 'Oh, the one I have to see in Wemyss Bay?'

'You said you'd to see someone in Largs.'

'No, I said Wemyss Bay, and it'll not take me a minute. Jamie won't get in the way.'

'There isn't a customer at all, is there?'

'I'm sure I could find one . . . if I have to.'

'Allan, what are you doing on this boat?'

He looked at Jamie, then out across the water and then, finally, at her. 'Spending a wee bit of time with you before you go away. It was the only way I could think of,' he said. Then, as she opened her mouth to speak, 'I like your father.'

'You met him?'

'Oh, yes. Did he not tell you that he gave me a very hard time over the way I'd treated you?'

'He'd no right to do that! I told him that everything had been . . .'

'He'd every right, Jennet. I deserved it, and more. Since he didn't tell you about it, I don't suppose you know that when he'd finished with me I asked him for your hand in marriage.'

'You did what?' Astonishment made her voice over-loud, and some people standing by the railing turned and looked at them.

'I thought it was the right thing to do, and I wanted him to know that my intentions are honourable. Late, but honourable.'

'Very late.'

'He said that, and he also said that I'd not find a better wife if I travelled to Timbuktu and back,' Allan continued as bells rang and the paddles began to slow. 'He's right, of course. I'm staying put on Bute, and if you decide to come back to live there then at least I've got your father's permission to court you properly.'

'Allan . . .'

'I just wanted to tell you. I behaved badly all those years ago, Jennet,' he said, his face suddenly serious. 'I was a daft laddie then, but I've grown up now, and I've changed. When you feel like it, give me the chance to prove that to you. Have faith in me. I'll not let you down again.'

He got to his feet and lifted her suitcase. 'Come on, Jamie, let's you and me go and see them putting the gangway in place.'

She watched them go, hand in hand. 'Have faith,' he had said, while her father had advised, 'Decide what you want for yourself . . .' What Jennet wanted right now was to provide a good future for herself and for Jamie. But after that part of her life was settled . . .

Mollie had kept faith with Angus, even when it seemed that he would never reciprocate. Helen had kept faith with Bert, loving him and having his child, even though through all the long months of carrying wee Thomas she had had to live with her secret belief that the child's birth would mean her own death.

'Come on, Mummy!' Jamie yelled from the gangway, where he waited, one hand in Allan's, the other beckoning to her.

She looked at the two of them – one so tall and the other so small – and was struck by their resemblance to each other. Jamie's eyes were grey, but when he was happy, as he was now, there was a blue sparkle to them. His hair was lighter than Allan's, but darker than hers. And his mouth tended to lift more at one side than the other, just like Allan's. They looked right together . . . father and son.

Perhaps, when she had completed her training and returned to Bute, as she knew she would, it would then be time to put her faith in Allan. He had let her down once, but she knew that he would not let her down again.

Bibliography

All Muck, No Medals: Landgirls by Landgirls by Joan Mant. Published by The Book Guild, Lewes, 1994.

The Buteman and West Coast Chronicle. Printed by The Buteman Ltd, Castle Street, Rothesay, Bute, 1945. File now in Rothesay Library, Bute.

The Farmers of Bute: For Sixty Years and Beyond by William B. Martin. Printed by The Buteman Ltd, Castle Street, Rothesay, Bute, 1951.

Graips & Gumboots (Memories of the Women's Land Army) by 'Alex', WLA No. 906, and 'Bea', WLA No. 1223. Printed by Admin Systems, 1993; published by SMI and RSH, Dumbartonshire, 1993.

History of Bute by Dorothy N. Marshall, MBE, FSA, FSA Scot. Revised edition 1992 by Dorothy N. Marshall and Anne Speirs, BA, FSA Scot. With an account of Rothesay Harbour by Ian Maclagen, LLB,

FSA Scot. Published by Bute Print, 15 Watergate, Rothesay, Bute, 1992.

The Isle of Bute by Norman S. Newton, photographs by Derek Croucher. Published by The Pevensey Press, Newton Abbot, Devon, an imprint of David & Charles, 1999.

They Fought in the Fields – The Women's Land Army: The Story of a Forgotten Victory by Nicola Tyrer. Published by Sinclair-Stevenson, London, an imprint of Reed International Books Ltd, 1996.